NOSY IN
NEBRASKA

NOSY IN NEBRASKA

THREE ROMANCE MYSTERIES

MARY CONNEALY

BARBOUR
PUBLISHING

© 2008 *Of Mice. . .and Murder* by Mary Connealy
© 2009 *Pride and Pestilence* by Mary Connealy
© 2009 *The Mice Man Cometh* by Mary Connealy

ISBN 978-1-60260-418-6

Cover thumbnails: Design by Kirk DouPonce, DogEared Design
Illustration by Jody Williams

Published by Barbour Publishing, Inc., P.O. Box 719, Uhrichsville, OH 44683, www.barbourbooks.com

Our mission is to publish and distribute inspirational products offering exceptional value and biblical encouragement to the masses.

ecpa Member of the
Evangelical Christian
Publishers Association

Printed in the United States of America.

OF MICE. . .AND MURDER

Melnik, Nebraska—Population 972
Home of Maxie, the World's Largest Field Mouse

Being named in Great-Grandma's will was like hitting Bankrupt on *Wheel of Fortune*. The whole family held their breath while the wheel ticked around and around—or rather, while the lawyer opened the envelope. Then they all heaved a sigh of relief when the wheel stopped on Carrie's name.

Carrie the heiress. *Great.*

Clean up the house.

Clean up the yard.

Clean up Great-Grandma's rap sheet.

"I don't know why it has to be me," Carrie grumbled.

The empty kitchen—empty except for the garbage that Great-Grandma Bea had been amassing all her one hundred and three years—mocked her with its silence.

Silence except for the hammering on the porch, which stopped when Carrie started talking to herself.

Carrie froze, hoping the carpenter hadn't heard her. Spooky old house, spooky new resident.

The banging resumed. Now that her great-grandma wasn't around to drive off the hired help, the work would finally get done—except, of course, Carrie had no money. She'd have to break that to the carpenter pretty soon.

And while he pounded away, Carrie could break her back by cleaning up this old wreck. What a waste of a beautiful, brisk fall afternoon. She had to figure out how to get out of Melnik before she went nuts. But first she would—

A mouse dashed out of the kitchen pantry twenty feet away.

"Eeeek!" Carrie shrieked.

The mouse skittered toward her. Carrie ran the opposite direction and collided with the carpenter, who was dashing through the door clutching his hammer.

"What happened?"

The mouse skidded to a halt under the table and squeaked.

Carrie squeaked even louder and jumped toward the carpenter. He caught her against his chest, hooking one arm under her legs and the other behind her back.

NOSY IN NEBRASKA

It was nice of a stranger to come to the rescue. He was the kind of man who could do the whole "white knight" thing, with his lovely height and broad shoulders. The hammer he held—in the hand now under her knees—would make a fair lance, too.

"Forgive me." Carrie barely moved her lips.

"For what?" The carpenter's whisper pulled her attention away from the mouse.

Carrie noted the tidy logo of his company on the pocket of his shirt where a little polo player ought to be. OC with the word O'CONNOR arced above and CONSTRUCTION in a half circle below. Both of the placket buttons were neatly closed, and his hair was combed and gelled as if he were afraid it would break out and go its own way. His eyes glowed with humor and kindness, though.

"Oh, you weren't supposed to hear that. I was praying for forgiveness."

Their eyes locked. His were dark blue, a rich color that begged for a closer look. Hers were blue, too, but washed out like her white-blond hair, with the wimpy coloring of a pure Swede, not strong and clear like his.

After way too long, he smiled and whispered again, "For what?"

"Huh?" Her brain functioned slowly, somewhat like Jell-O.

"What do you want God to forgive you for? Jumping into my arms?" His smile faded as if that hurt his feelings.

"Oh no."

The smile returned. "Good."

"It's something I do when a mouse scares me."

"Why?"

"Because it's a sin to be afraid of a mouse."

A dimple appeared in each cheek as he smiled wider. "Is not. Where in the Bible does it say, 'Thou shalt not run and scream when you see a rodent'?"

Carrie switched from studying his eyes to studying his dimples. Really, a woman could keep busy forever watching him. "It should be. It's a sin to be this stupid about a tiny little creature obviously put on the earth by God to feed cats. Cats need to eat."

"Oh, well then, because cats need to eat, you've sinned for sure. And what does that have to do with you jumping into my arms?"

"There's a mouse." She glanced back at the floor.

The knight eased her back on her feet. "Mouse, huh?" He gave her an I'm-not-rolling-my-eyeballs-through-sheer-willpower look that tarnished his shining armor. "It's more afraid of you than—"

"Than I am of it. I know." And hadn't Carrie heard that a hundred thousand times before in her life? Hadn't helped then, didn't help now. Carrie saw the mouse turn and streak back under the closed pantry door. She grabbed a handful of the carpenter's shirtfront. He steadied her with a strong arm.

"Yeah, right, it's more afraid of me. Not even. Does that mouse lie awake nights fretting, 'What if a woman runs up my leg?' I don't think so."

"Uh, have you got a trap?"

Carrie turned back to the knight. "My hero." The words sounded reverent. "In that sack on the table. Thanks." She was just inches from him, and since she was there anyway, she let herself get lost in his eyes again. This close, she could smell his warm, clean scent.

"I'll see what I can do." He seemed even closer. "By the way, I'm Nick O'Connor. My hired man and I are repairing your porch."

"Hired man?"

"Wilkie Melnik."

Carrie gasped and backed off. *"You hired Wilkie Melnik?"*

The corners of Nick's mouth turned down, and the smile wrinkles at the corners of his eyes disappeared along with his dimples. Carrie regretted seeing them go, but it helped her mind work.

Nick smoothed the fist wrinkles she'd made in his shirt. "Yeah, he's not working out too well. He didn't show up yesterday or the day before, and he hasn't come today, either."

"That sounds like Wilkie. I'm Carrie Evans, and my great-grandma Bea died and left me this house. Thanks for the help. I heard that Grandpa tried to get you in earlier to fix things up for Great-Grandma Bea."

Nick rubbed his forehead absently. "Bea wasn't interested. So I'm doing it now."

A soft rustle of paper in the pantry made Carrie step closer to Nick.

"You know, clutter like this is mouse heaven. This house is probably infested."

Carrie shuddered.

"What you really need is a cat."

A loud *meow* turned Carrie's head toward the porch. The ugliest animal Carrie had ever seen crouched outside the back door.

"That isn't a cat." Carrie kept Nick between her and the grisly beast.

Nick turned and tilted his head. "Um. . .I think it is."

Carrie saw his hand tighten on the hammer.

With a couple of ruthless slashes, the cat shredded the already-tattered screen and slipped onto the porch.

Nick and Carrie stepped back, their motions in such perfect harmony that they could have been a pair of synchronized swimmers. The cat slunk across the porch on its belly, emitting a deep, humming yowl that sent a chill up Carrie's spine. It slithered into the kitchen, slipping under the table. He was mottled yellow, his fur matted to his body as if he'd been sleeping on it the wrong way for seventy-five years. He had one eye. The other was closed by a nasty scar. One ear stood up straight; its mate was slit and hung in tatters. Clumps of fur hung from under his belly. His tail had a nice upright S shape until the tip, where it took an alarming ninety-degree turn.

He was alley-cat thin and, from the look and sound of him, cougar-mean. It went against every instinct in Carrie's body to let him in the house. If she had a brain in her head, she'd be a thousand times more afraid of this cat than of a tiny mouse. And yet there was no eeeking and jumping.

A loud rustling noise came from the pantry. Carrie jumped sideways and shouldered Nick forward a step. Since she was hiding behind him, that shoved him closer to the cat. The cat jerked its head up and focused its eye on the pantry, the intact ear pointed forward. A low growl vibrated out of its throat. A real hero had arrived.

"I could, uh. . .catch the cat. . .and put him out." Nick glanced at Carrie as if he was terrified she'd say yes.

"Give him a minute. Maybe he'll eat the mouse."

"He looks like he'd eat you."

"If I close my bedroom door at night, the cat couldn't get me."

Nick shuddered. "You're thinking of keeping it?"

Carrie was seriously sure that, unless the cat cooperated, she couldn't get rid of it. "Sure. If it *is* a cat. It looks more like one of those moth-eaten animals in the Dead Zone."

Nick jerked his head up. "The Dead Zone?"

Carrie nodded. "Great-Grandpa came from a long line of big-game hunters. He personally assisted in placing over a dozen species on the endangered list. There are dozens of moldering murdered mammals upstairs."

Nick's eyes widened. "Cool."

"You can look as soon as you've taken care of the mouse." Bribery. Carrie wasn't above it.

Nick grinned and Carrie filled the silence by studying his dimples until he said, "Got it. Priorities."

"Speaking of priorities, where's your hired man again?"

Nick's smile faded. "Uh. . .I may have made a bad hire."

"Everybody knows Wilkie Melnik is a bum, Nick."

"He didn't seem like a real go-getter, but his name is the same as the town. I figured he was special."

"*Special*—fair description. In fact, I think that was stamped in red ink all over his permanent record at school." Carrie shook her head. "He's got a nasty temper and a complete lack of respect for the law." She suspected she'd just described her cat. "How long has he been working for you?"

"A week. And I need the help. There's a lot of work to do here. Your grandpa already paid me for it."

"Why'd he pay you before you did the work?" Carrie asked.

"Well, that's a funny story." Nick rubbed his forehead again and flinched. "I've been in Melnik six months. The first week I was in town, your grandpa called me and—"

Someone knocked at the back porch door.

"Anybody home?"

Dora Clemson. Carrie would recognize that voice anywhere. Dora was a living, breathing crowbar come to pry loose all her secrets. And Carrie had a big one.

The screen porch door squeaked mouselike on its hinges. Nick obviously knew Dora, because his smile shrank like generic plastic wrap in an overheated microwave. "Hi, Dora." Nick greeted Dora, slipped past her rotund figure, returned to the porch, and resumed hammering.

Some hero. Sure, he might fight a mouse, but where was he when there was *real* trouble?

"Come in," Carrie called—like saying, "Stay out," would even slow the old bat down.

Dora said hi to Nick but didn't pause to talk. Carrie was sorely afraid she was Dora's prime goal. Dora and all her extra chins came through the kitchen door. "You're here, Cindy *Looou.*" Dora dragged the name out, just in case Carrie didn't get the joke. Play a Who from Whoville in the elementary school Christmas play fifteen years ago and live with it forever. That was the nightmare of a small town.

Dora laughed until her chins, ample breasts, and more than ample stomach bounced off each other. Wearing an age-old beige coat, the woman bore an unfortunate resemblance to a really grimy three-tiered wedding cake with a gray dust mop in place of the bride and groom.

Through the porch screens, Carrie saw a police car pull up. Tires scrunched the leaves, newly fallen in the early November weather and blown onto the cracked driveway.

Great—another casserole. Funeral food had been pouring in since Great-Grandma was found dead on Wednesday morning. They figured she must have fallen Tuesday night.

Dora heard the car, turned, and peered out the porch door, afraid she'd miss something good. "Wonder what Junior wants?"

Junior and Cindy Lou. He probably wants a new name. "He probably has another casserole," Carrie said.

Junior Hammerstad. Age fifty-five, a one-eyebrowed, blowhard redneck, born to hassle kids, give out-of-towners speeding tickets, and hold loose dogs for ransom. He'd been employed as chief for thirty years at the exciting Melnik, Nebraska, police department—part-time. Still, that was better than Carrie was doing.

NOSY IN NEBRASKA

The Crown Vic's door opened. Junior emerged clutching a cream-colored file folder five inches thick. He defied the chilly fall wind and only wore his gray police uniform. But he had a substantial insulating layer of fat to get him through the tough times. A puff of white came through his lips, and the breeze blew his comb-over off his head. The thin hairs kept their curved shape and hung like an open lid over Junior's left ear, revealing to all the world that Junior was bald. What a shock.

"I heard Junior was coming over with all Bea's police paperwork," Dora said.

Carrie didn't ask how Dora found that out. It only would have been worth mentioning if something went on in Melnik that Dora *didn't* know about. "Grandpa said the police had a *talk* with him every few months about Great-Grandma Bea and all the crimes she reported."

"I can't believe she's dead. And from a fall." Dora patted Carrie on the back.

"Grandpa said she hadn't gone upstairs in years." A shot of electricity jagged through Carrie, reminding her of the *World-Herald* reporting job she'd started in August right after she graduated from college. She'd felt like this every time she'd latched onto a big story. Her instincts told her that there was something more here than a tragic accident. Of course, her instincts were garbage.

But in spite of that one tiny misstep in Omaha, at Nebraska's biggest newspaper—a mistake that ruined her whole life forever—she decided to ignore her garbage instincts and trust herself. Why had Great-Grandma Bea gone upstairs after refusing to do so for years? If she hadn't been one hundred and three, someone might ask questions—even investigate.

The screen door screeched and Junior came in. "Hey, Nick."

The hammering paused. "Hi, Junior."

Carrie circled Dora—no small journey—and met Junior at the kitchen door. "Hi, come on in. Grandpa Leonard said that someone needed to deal with all of Great-Grandma's complaints."

Carrie leaned forward to see Nick on his hands and knees, next to a pile of lumber perfectly stacked near his right side. He lifted a board and deftly slipped it over the gaping hole in the porch, running his hands over the smooth wood as if he enjoyed touching it. Nick snapped a nail into place, hammered it home with three quick blows of his hammer (i.e., lance), and reached for another board. Carrie could have set it to music.

She wondered what neat, orderly Nick thought of this messy old mansion.

Junior, his cheeks as close to maroon as the human body could muster and belt cinched low to give his belly plenty of room to overlap it, looked back past his bulky shoulder. "You might as well come in, Nick. Beatrice accused you of stealing her lawn mower."

Nick sat back on his knees, a furrow in his brow. "Uh, when was that?"

"Just last week. I hadn't gotten around to arresting you yet. Sorry to be so slow."

"No problem. For the record, I mowed her lawn all summer with my own mower."

"Yeah, everybody knows that." Junior's no-nonsense voice raised Carrie's regard for Melnik's hiring practices.

Dora, eyes gleaming, headed for the kitchen table, the only clear surface in the kitchen—possibly in the whole house.

"I also know she doesn't have a lawn mower. Still, she insisted on filing a complaint." Junior hefted the file.

"Set it right there." Carrie waved him toward Great-Grandma's cherrywood table as Dora pulled up a chair and sat down.

The chair creaked alarmingly. Bless Great-Grandma's heart, she'd always had a knack for buying furniture that, as the years passed, dwindled into junk instead of becoming valuable antiques.

Nick appeared in the doorway, his hammer hanging dejectedly at his side as his gaze slid between the file and Dora.

Carrie lifted stacks of magazines off chairs and dragged them from various corners of the kitchen up to the table. Then she stationed her seat as far from the mouse's pantry as possible, hooking her Nikes on the rungs so the mouse couldn't reach her.

Junior sank into a creaky wooden chair and flipped open the file. Nick rounded the table, dragging his heels (practically a perp walk), and sat beside Dora, straight across from Carrie.

"I've got some old clippers of Nils's that I'll give you to take care of that nose hair, Nick." Dora scooted her chair closer to Nick, the legs screeching in pain over her weight. She folded her arms on the table and turned to, apparently, stare straight up Nick's nose.

Nick flinched but stayed put. He did lay the hammer on the table, as if he thought Dora might back off, knowing he was armed.

In his dreams.

Carrie checked but saw no nose hair. Nick glanced up and caught her staring and narrowed his eyes. She looked away.

"I need a signature on these forms to officially close these cases. For example, when Nick here stole Bea's lawn mower—"

Nick clenched his hands on the table and leaned forward. "I did *not* steal—"

Dora snickered.

"Okay, fine." Nick rolled his eyes. "Is there a paper for me to sign to officially deny it?"

"Nope. Not necessary if Carrie drops the charges." Junior waved a sheet under Nick's nose then slid it in front of Carrie. "Your grandpa told me you're Bea's sole heir and executor of her estate."

That sounded like a big deal. If only Great-Grandma Bea had owned anything but this wreck.

"You've also got power of attorney, so you can clear up all these cases."

This was the first Carrie had heard of any power of attorney. She wasn't even sure what that was, but she was pretty sure she had to agree to it and sign some legal document. But this was Melnik. They'd probably just ignore the finer and more inconvenient points of law. "Show me where to sign. I'm dropping all the complaints."

Junior shook his head at Nick. "Got away with it again, you scofflaw."

Nick grinned. Carrie took a second to enjoy his dimples, and he caught her staring again. He probably thought she was checking for nose hair. She decided to let him think that, since the truth wasn't something she could admit—that he was so gorgeous she could hardly take her eyes off him.

"I'm just going to need your signature on each one of these one hundred and sixty-two complaints, Carrie." Junior shoved the stack in front of her with a twinkle in his eye.

"I've got to sign my name one hundred and sixty-two times?" Carrie flexed her fingers, feeling writer's cramp already.

Dora's lips thinned. Honestly, when she made this face, her lips looked so much like another of her many chins, the woman needed a bookmark to find her mouth. "It won't be the first time."

Carrie cringed. *No, not the story about ninth grade, not in front of*—

"When Carrie was in ninth grade, she had to write 'I will not disrupt class' on the blackboard five hundred times." Dora crossed her arms on the table again and settled into the tale. "The girl in front of her. . ."

2

Nick wondered if Dora was right and he really had disgusting nose hair. He'd never noticed before, but he was such a loser that it'd be about right.

Carrie looked across the table at him and distracted him even further from Dora's story by whispering, "It's the only bad thing I ever did. I promise." She held up one hand, flat, like she was being sworn in to testify in court, then turned back to her legal work.

She pulled a paper off the stack on her left, signed it, and slid it sideways to the right. As she worked, Nick picked up her growing stack of signed papers and tapped them on the tabletop, keeping the pile neat. He should whisper back. Try to convince her he was cool. *Think of something to say, idiot.*

He'd given up sitting in an office, pushing a pencil through complicated blueprints and math formulas, for a reason—to try to make a human connection. Now if he could just speak to the prettiest woman he'd ever seen. A woman who needed a hero. And here he was, completely unafraid of mice. *Look out, Lancelot!*

"It's true," Dora said. "She was so well behaved we worried about her."

"The whole town blew a gasket over the *shocking* event." Carrie clenched her fingers on the pen.

Junior snickered. Dora kept chattering. Carrie sighed.

Nick glanced from Junior to Dora and then at Carrie. "Event?" He'd tuned out Dora's story. He might be new in town, but even he had heard about Carrie, the small-town girl with big-city ambitions. She'd been hired at the *Omaha World-Herald*, with her eye on being an investigative reporter. She'd dreamed of bringing down presidents—but only if they were bad. And, more shocking yet, exposing the seamy underbelly of Cornhusker football—in the event she found a seamy underbelly, which was unlikely, the Huskers being above reproach and far too nearly worshipped.

Nick was going through his first Husker football season right now. He'd never seen so many red and white flags flying. He'd better get one.

"I pulled the chair out from under Amy Clark in English class," Carrie confessed.

Nick arched a brow.

"And then I said to Bea, my best friend even then"—Dora reclaimed possession of the story—"'Carrie'll pull out of it.' And Bea said, 'Don't say the word *pull* around me, Dora.' And I repeated that at the Community Club spaghetti dinner, and before you know it, everyone in town was talking about Carrie 'pulling' a stunt. It even made the *Bugle*."

"Famous sayings in Melnik history. Not exactly 'Give me liberty or give me death,'" Carrie muttered into the police reports. She looked up at Junior. "You know, Junior, I can't find Grandma's skillet."

Junior intertwined his fingers like a man preparing to beg. "Please tell me you're not going to accuse Nick of stealing that."

Being accused of something by Bea Evans was practically a badge of honor. But Nick didn't want Carrie accusing him of anything, not when he was trying to work up the nerve to ask her to be the mother of his children.

Carrie tapped the current complaint with the clicking end of her pen.

Nick read it upside down. "Hey, she accused Leonard of that." Leonard, Carrie's grandfather and Bea's son, a retired carpenter whom Nick suspected didn't have a single black mark on his record, not even for ninth-grade hijinks.

Carrie pulled a paper from the pile. "She accused you"—she jabbed her pen at Junior—"of stealing her cat."

"Not that mangy, bad-tempered, one-eyed, one-eared, broken-tailed yellow cat that just slashed Carrie's porch screen?" Nick glanced at the doorway to the living room, wondering where the cat had disappeared, as he tidied the pile Carrie had knocked askew.

Junior rolled his eyes. "Yep, caught me. My dream pet. I had him in my clutches."

"Great." Carrie looked at Junior. "I can make your dreams come true. Grizzly's yours."

"Grizzly? You're naming the cat?" Nick was pretty sure that meant that Carrie was stuck with the shaggy beast for life.

"You'll have to catch me first." Junior smirked.

Carrie looked back at the complaint she needed to sign. "Grandma always kept her skillet on that nail." She pointed at the heavy-duty nail head sticking out of the cracked plaster just behind the cookstove. "So where is it? In all my twenty-two years, it's never been anywhere else."

"Maybe your grandpa really did steal it," Junior suggested.

Carrie rolled her eyes.

"I remember that skillet." Nick rubbed his forehead. "She nailed me with it the first time I came to the house to work. She'd let me mow the lawn, but she'd come after me if I so much as set foot on the porch. My head still hurts."

"That's motive." Carrie wrinkled her nose at him.

Nick's heart beat erratically. All that white-blond hair and those amazing pastel blue eyes. She weighed just the right amount, too. Catching her in his arms was no hardship.

Junior grunted. "Yeah, you owe Leonard a thousand dollars' worth of work."

"Grandpa paid you a thousand dollars, and you've never done any work except mow the lawn?" Carrie glared those baby blues right at Nick.

He wondered if *she'd* start filing complaints on him now. "He actually paid me separately for mowing the lawn. The thousand dollars was to repair the house. We had a deal. I'd come over, your great-grandma would chase me off in some semiviolent way, and he'd still pay me twenty bucks for trying."

"Which means"—Carrie did the math—"she ran you off fifty times."

Nick shrugged, feeling like the dopey math geek he'd been in junior high, beaten up by a one-hundred-year-old lady. "But who's counting."

"Leonard is. It's costing him a fortune," Junior grumbled.

"I came here twice a week for six months."

"Since there was never any chance she'd let you in," Carrie pointed out, "that was easy money."

"Easy? Before I learned to duck, she gave me a concussion. I spent three hours in the emergency room."

Junior snorted. "You drove yourself. You weren't hurt too bad."

"And Nick wouldn't even really try after that one time she nailed him with her skillet." Dora shook her head. "I was in the kitchen when she did it. I can still hear the metallic clang against his skull. After that, he just walked up, kind of slowly, until she came out and started hollering at him, and then he'd leave."

"Quitter." Carrie grinned at him. "Why didn't you go swear out a complaint of your own? Assault is a felony."

Nick scowled. "Because she was a century old, and I would have been laughed out of town."

"That still doesn't tell me where the skillet is. I loved that skillet." Carrie studied the paper and tapped the pen on the table.

"I hate that skillet." Nick rubbed his forehead again. After six months, he still had a lump. Bea Evans had reshaped the contour of his head.

"I want to know who stole it."

"I didn't do it." Junior raised his right hand as if it was now *his* turn to testify. "I was too busy taking care of that nasty cat I stole."

Grizzly yowled from another room.

"Someone did. I'm not signing this one." Carrie shoved it back at Junior.

Nick eyed the lone sheet of paper, wondering if he'd have to keep another pile in order.

Junior groaned and took it. By the time Carrie was finished, her signature had deteriorated to a scrawl Nick couldn't even recognize as being human. Grizzly could've done better.

Apparently deciding that nothing interesting was going to happen, Dora hoisted her significant weight out of the chair, its squeaking joints groaning in relief. "I'm going to the smorgasbord at Jansson's Diner. I'll be back to help tomorrow, Carrie."

"No need," Carrie said to Dora's receding back. "I'm not sure—"

The door slapped shut.

"So you inherited this. . .uh. . .house." Junior looked around the jam-packed kitchen.

"Dump, you mean?" Carrie's shoulders slumped. "Every countertop, every drawer, every end table, every flat surface in this house, including the floor, except this kitchen table and Great-Grandma's bed, are piled high with junk." Carrie glanced around the room.

Nick could tell she couldn't see the potential. "You've really got your work cut out for you. But it's a majestic old house. The lines and layout are fantastic."

"You might find some valuable antiques." Junior studied the room, flicking the corner of his manila file folder.

Carrie snorted inelegantly, which, when Nick thought about it, was really the only way a person *could* snort.

"My great-grandmother had a knack for only holding on to junk."

Nick's eyes skimmed the papers stacked to the ceiling on top of the refrigerator behind Carrie's back. There was a cardboard box full of magazines on the stove next to the refrigerator.

"But still," Nick said, "old magazines, dishes, furniture that doesn't seem valuable—some might have worth as collector's items."

"It'll take me a year to get it sorted out, listed on eBay, and shipped." Carrie's voice sounded so grim that Nick couldn't help smiling. "And when it's said and done, it's still don't-give-up-your-day-job money."

"Oh, speaking of day jobs, you want a job?" Junior jammed Nick's neat stack of complaints back in the overworked folder with complete disregard for keeping them tidy. He held up the remaining unsigned paper and scowled at it before he set it on top of his folder.

Carrie sat up straight. "At the police station?"

Nick couldn't tell if she was intrigued or horrified.

"No, the job's at the *Bugle*."

Carrie wrinkled her nose. "What position is open there?"

"Editor."

"They've turned over another editor?"

"Yeah, Edith Eskilson had been doing it, but she quit because Marlys Piperson complained about. . ."

Nick tried not to daydream as the two townies chattered away.

"So did you arrest Jeffie?" Carrie snickered.

Nick's mind wandered to the wreck of a porch. He itched to get back to repairing it. A couple of more hours replacing rotten floorboards and then he could. . .

"And then when Marlys called Edith an old. . ."

Carrie leaned in. Nick began a mental inventory of repairs. If he had his way, this would be a showplace.

"And of course Muriel saved her marigolds."

"Well, sure. Muriel isn't going to let anything hurt her flower bed."

Junior nodded. "Got a green thumb, that woman. But still, they. . ."

The screens were in shreds, but Nick loved the graceful way the porch wrapped around all four sides of the house.

"So Edith misspelled Stu Piperson's name?" Carrie asked. "Big deal."

And the complicated, gabled roof—what a nightmare to shingle, but so elegant. . .

"She spelled Stu Piperson 'Stupid Person,'" Junior said.

Carrie gasped and started choking. "She didn't!"

Nick sat up, glad he'd caught that.

Junior nodded. "Mrs. Stupid Person and her son Jeffie were Friday afternoon coffee guests at Luella Hasting's home on. . ."

Nick dropped his head back and laughed.

"She's lucky she just got fired and not hanged." Carrie giggled.

"She didn't get fired," Junior scoffed. "Jeffie's mom threw such a fit that Edith quit in a huff, so now the job's open. Interested?"

Carrie sighed. "Sure, why not. I need a job. Do I go see Gunderson?"

Nick wondered why she'd given up her job in Omaha. He'd heard it was her dream. Of course, he'd given up his job and moved, but engineering hadn't been his dream.

"Nope, I told Viola I'd ask. She knew I was bringing the reports over. Besides, Old Man Gunderson died about a month back. Rumor is his son Sven is coming back to town, but I haven't seen him."

Carrie's brow furrowed. "Maybe Sven will want to be editor."

"I doubt it. His dad got rich collecting rent on all his property. He owns most of Main Street. Why would Sven jump in and take over the *Bugle*?"

"What does it pay?"

Nick wished he'd kept daydreaming. "You know, this is one of the more bizarre job interviews I've ever heard."

"Yeah." Carried turned to glare at Junior. "Is that what this is, a job interview? Why would you interview me for a job at the *Bugle*?"

"I'm not interviewing you. I'm the grapevine."

Nick remembered the infestation and turned toward the pantry. "I forgot about setting your mousetraps."

Carrie shuddered. "This town grows really big mice."

Nick thought of Maxie, stuffed, his black, beady eyes fierce, posed by a local taxidermist and preserved forever in a glass case at city hall. With a shake of his head to dislodge the memory of that gigantic mouse—"The World's Largest Field Mouse" and Melnik's greatest claim to fame—Nick strode toward the pantry, a little spooked by what might jump out at him. Carrie's phobia was rubbing off on him. Prepared to stay and fight no matter how big the mouse, he grasped the handle and yanked open the door.

Wilkie Melnik came tipping out of the closet straight at him wearing Bea Evans's skillet like a cast-iron baseball cap.

3

Nick staggered backward into the table, banged his hip, and rammed into Carrie, who was striding toward the toppling body.

Wilkie tilted in slow motion until the skillet tumbled off his head and clanked to the floor.

"What happened?" Carrie pushed past Nick. Junior came up on the other side.

Wilkie—eyes fixed and dilated—was dead beyond a doubt. Scaredy-cat Carrie approached the body as Nick backed away. She crouched beside Wilkie, reminding Nick she'd worked the police beat at the *World-Herald*.

She pressed two fingers to Wilkie's neck.

"Stay back, Carrie. Call 911. I want both deputies down here ASAP. Tell Sandra to contact the Dodge County coroner, too." Junior knelt by the body. "Whoever's on duty there will need to cover this."

Carrie stood, rounded the body, grabbed the wall phone, and dialed. She rapped out her name, the address, and Junior's orders.

A siren blasted at the police station two blocks away. Carrie laid the phone on one of Bea's countless stacks of papers and knelt by the body again.

"Back off, Carrie." Junior reached across Wilkie's body and grabbed her shoulder. "I'm serious."

Carrie's hand froze inches away from a bruise on Wilkie's forehead. "I know. What's that on his mouth?" Carrie inched closer.

Nick squinted. Junior dropped to one knee and leaned down. "It's hair. It looks like gray fur. Funny we were just talking about big mice, because it could almost be—"

A mouse scrambled out of the closet, and an ear-splitting squeal came from somewhere deep in Carrie's gut. She jumped to her feet and while she was at it just kept going up. Nick grabbed her in his arms.

Junior fell over backward, fumbling for his gun.

"It's a mouse!" Nick shouted to head off the shoot-out. "She's just startled."

"Carrie, for Pete's sake!" Junior rolled onto his hands and knees.

Carrie whispered into Nick's chest, "God, forgive me."

Nick felt kind of sorry for the little sweetheart, who labeled her greatest phobia a sin. That was quite a burden for someone to carry around. He held her close to help her bear it.

The mouse dashed between Nick's feet. The cat snarled behind his back.

NOSY IN NEBRASKA

Nick turned with Carrie in his arms in time to see the mouse zip out the torn screen door on the porch with the cat hard on its heels.

Carrie's arms went around Nick's neck as she leaned to watch the chase. "I love that cat." She sounded almost reverent. True love had come to her while Nick held her in his arms. Too bad it was love for that mangy cat.

Out of the corner of his eye, Nick saw another mouse slip from the pantry into a hole at the base of the kitchen cupboards.

He didn't even consider mentioning it.

"How is it," he asked, pulling her attention away from the porch, "that you can touch a dead body, kneel beside it, and phone 911 all without turning a hair, but a little mouse scares you?"

Carrie said in a tiny voice, "It's a sin, that's all. It's stupid. I'm stupid."

"No, you're not."

"About mice I am."

Nick hesitated. She might be right.

The mouse and Grizzly vanished into the browning leaves of the lilac hedge at the back of the lawn. Carrie twisted in Nick's arms to look at poor Wilkie.

"It looks like you were the last one to see him alive, Nick. That makes you the prime suspect." Carrie narrowed her eyes at him.

Since she didn't show any signs of climbing out of his arms, he doubted she really thought he was a killer.

"You two get outside before you contaminate my crime scene." Junior glared at them. The sirens got louder.

Nick nodded.

"Wait." Carrie tightened her hold.

Stopping, Nick asked, "Why?"

Carrie pointed at the kitchen table. "Take me closer, please."

Ever the obedient pack animal, Nick complied.

Carrie leaned down, still with one arm clinging to Nick's neck, and signed the last complaint. "No need to hunt for the frying pan now."

Shaking his head, Nick carried his little armload of phobia outside.

She tapped him on the shoulder and arched her eyebrows. "You can put me down now."

The wind was sharp but nothing like the wind that whistled through the skyscrapers in Chicago's fall and winter. Nick was grateful for his Windbreaker and wished he'd taken the time to carry her to her coat before they'd come out. But she had a thick sweater on that was the exact color of her eyes, plus blue jeans and black leather boots, so she'd be okay for a while.

Setting Carrie down on Bea's sidewalk, which was so old and broken that it was almost gravel, Nick followed her toward a rickety picnic table. She perched on the top. Paint chips sprinkled off the table, and Nick remained standing rather than get messy. A bit of snow lay on the shaded ground under the table, left over from an early snowstorm. A police car pulled up, its siren shrieking. A second siren fired up across town.

Carrie said, "Rescue squad."

Junior came out, and Nick was touched to see he'd grabbed a coat for Carrie, a denim jacket with brown fur lining. Junior handed over the coat just as the screaming squad car pulled up. Junior walked away to talk with his deputies.

The first curious Melnikite stuck her head out her front door. A second gray head soon followed, and then a third. A screen door slammed a block over.

Carrie started to follow Junior.

Junior glowered at her. "Stay put, Carrie."

Nick noticed a pouty bottom lip, but Carrie stayed. She shook the blue-jean jacket violently as if expecting a mouse to have taken up residence.

"Let me check." Nick relieved her of it.

She gave him that wide-eyed-wonder look again. Nick knew he had the social skills of a swamp rat. He'd never held one in his arms before. A woman, that is. He'd had a swamp rat or two in his grasp during Vertebrate Zoology in college.

To be or not to be a science geek or math geek, that was the question. Nick wanted to kick himself. Internal sarcasm with mutant Shakespearean quotes was a really bad indicator of coolness.

Dear God, could I be cool just this once in my pathetic life?

He ran his hands heroically down the sleeves and into the pockets, even squeezing the whole coat as if he could wring a mouse out of it. Then he handed it back. She practically glowed as she pulled it on.

Say something. *Let's run off and get married. Then I can protect you from mice for the rest of your life since I'll be living in your house.* He clamped his mouth shut for fear of what might come out.

How about dinner? Better. That didn't make him sound like a complete moron.

Unless, when he actually asked, she said, "No, forget it. Ick. You're a complete moron."

But he'd saved her from two mice now. *Slayer of pint-sized dragons at your service.* And she was smiling up at him as if she liked morons.

He could do this. *How about dinner?* Five syllables. He took a deep breath. "How about—"

"Nick, I've got to ask you a few questions."

Nick's eyes shut along with his mouth. He turned to face Junior. His deputies were working at stringing up yellow crime-scene tape.

Junior donned a black down jacket he'd fished out of his cruiser. The coroner had to drive in from fifty miles away, so there was plenty of time for an interrogation. Swell.

23

"You know Carrie's right, Nick. You were the last person to see him alive."

"Oh, I was not." Nick's frustration with Junior's timing sounded loud and clear. *Okay, loser, mouth off to the policeman who thinks you killed a guy. Brilliant.*

Junior looked up from his notes. "How do you figure?"

"Well, obviously whoever killed him saw him after me." Nick's was a logical, orderly mind—except about women. Then the swamp rat took over.

Junior shrugged one shoulder and arched his unibrow. "Good point." The interrogation went on, occasionally lapsing into gossip over Wilkie's many and pitiful indiscretions. Was Junior just killing time until the real policemen got here, or did he actually suspect Nick?

A cold chill danced down Nick's spine at the thought. In Chicago, he'd have called his dad, and Dad would have called in a high-powered lawyer. The closest thing Nick had seen to a high-powered lawyer in Melnik was eighty-five-year-old George Wesley, who handed out legal advice from his wheelchair in the assisted-living wing of Melnik Manor.

Nick wasn't going to call Dad or Wesley. He hoped that Junior just needed to feel productive. Or maybe he loved writing in his nifty pocket-sized notebook.

"Who had the most to gain by Wilkie's death?" Carrie muttered the question as if she were hoping Junior would think it had come out of his own thick skull.

A gray station wagon inched its way through the onlookers and then turned into Bea's driveway. Its tires crackled on the brightly colored fall leaves on the pavement. It pulled to a stop, and the driver's side door swung open. The words DODGE COUNTY CORONER were painted on the side.

Junior turned back toward Nick and smiled down at his shiny new notebook. "So what *did* you have to gain by Wilkie's death?"

Nick groaned. "I had absolutely nothing to gain by Wilkie's death." He gave up on keeping his backside clean and settled beside Carrie on the picnic table.

The whole town was slowly but surely gathering in the street. Music was playing, and Nick thought he smelled hot dogs, like maybe the school's athletic booster club had seized on this perfect opportunity to raise money for new football uniforms.

"What a bunch of vultures," Carrie muttered.

"Now, Carrie, that's not fair." Junior licked the tip of his pencil. "None of 'em wants anything bad to happen. They just don't want to miss it if it does."

Carrie sighed, centered her elbows on her knees, and plopped her chin onto both fists.

Nick watched Junior's deputies gossip with the gathering horde. The whole house was surrounded by twenty-foot-tall lilac bushes, blocking the view of nosy neighbors. So the neighbors just came around the hedge.

The deputies, Hal and Steve, roped the town out and Carrie, Nick, and Junior in. With Wilkie.

Nick suspected that the tape came as standard equipment in a police cruiser and it'd been rolling around in Junior's trunk for years. No chance Junior had bought it. Why would he? There was no crime in Melnik.

A coroner in a white lab coat climbed out of the wagon.

Almost no crime.

"What did you say you had to gain by Wilkie's death?" Junior asked Nick, as if he wished he'd listened closer earlier—but, golly, that crime-scene tape was pretty and shiny, and who wouldn't be distracted?

"Junior, I did not kill Wilkie, and you know it."

"How do I know it?" Junior looked at his pad of paper as if dying to write down "Solved."

"I wouldn't do a thing like that!" And *that* might be the weakest alibi ever given by a human being in the history of the earth.

Junior shrugged again. "True. Okay, who did kill him?"

Apparently it was enough.

Nick looked sideways at Carrie.

"Means, motive, opportunity," Carrie suggested.

Junior stood in front of them, too wise to risk his weight on the wobbly table.

A middle-aged woman gave a no-nonsense wave of greeting to Carrie, Nick, and Junior, went to the back end of her wagon, swung the tailgate down with a creak of unoiled metal, and busied herself inside the vehicle.

Junior scratched his spare-tire belly thoughtfully. "Well, his wife was madder'n sin at him."

Carrie perked up. The table creaked. "Why's that?"

"He got his girlfriend pregnant."

"Whoa." Nick clenched his hands between his splayed knees. "Good motive."

"Great motive." Carrie glanced at Nick just as he looked at her.

"Plus, everybody knows he liked to gamble. Spent time in Iowa at that casino. He might have owed someone money."

Geese high overhead honked as they passed by on their way south. The street held a growing crowd of snoops, all talking quietly behind the yellow crime-scene tape. Well-behaved snoops in Melnik.

Carrie waved at Dora, who'd brought a lawn chair and perched it on the sidewalk across the street. Nick tried not to feel smug about the fact that he'd made the inside of the tape at gossip central, while Dora was cordoned out.

"Not a lot of loan sharks in Melnik, but it's worth looking into." Carrie nodded. "Anyone else?"

"Wilkie did a little time about five years ago." Junior flipped a page in his notebook. "Stole a bunch of riding lawn mowers from farm places in the area before we caught him."

"I remember that." Carrie sat up straight and punched her knees. "He got my dad's brand-new Snapper. Still, Dad's over it by now."

"Not much motive there." Nick rubbed his forehead.

"But Wilkie may have met some lowlifes in the pen. Maybe he still associates with them." Carrie chewed her thumbnail.

"Plus, his girlfriend was after him for child support." Junior jotted on his pad.

Nick grabbed Carrie's arm and pulled her thumb out of her mouth. "You've been touching things in there." Nick shuddered and shook his head.

Carrie glared at him.

He added, "Things mice might have run across."

Her face twisted with horror, and she turned and spit onto the grass. Then, her hands tightly clenched against lapsing into her bad habit, Nick supposed, she turned to Junior. "So if child support is kicking in, the girlfriend already had the baby?"

Nick reached into his pocket and pulled out a wrapped alcohol wipe and handed it to Carrie.

She began by scrubbing her lips and teeth before she focused on her hands. It looked for all the world like she intended to scrub her skin off.

"No, Donette's still pregnant; she's just getting started early," Junior said. "And the rumor is, she wants more than money. She wants Wilkie to dump Rosie and marry her."

Carrie shook her head. "I can't believe it."

"That anyone would be so irresponsible?" Nick nodded in agreement. He reached for the wipe when the scrubbing stopped. Carrie handed it to him. He refolded it and put it back in the foil packet.

"No. Well, yes, that, too," Carrie said. "But what I meant was, I can't believe any self-respecting woman would get close enough to Wilkie to get pregnant. Eww."

Junior stuck his notebook into his shirt pocket and pulled black leather gloves out of his coat pocket. "I think the key word is *self-respecting*."

"Let alone," Carrie went on, "want to marry the bum."

"It's one of life's little mysteries," Nick said. "There's someone for everyone."

Except him. There'd never been anyone for him. Until maybe now. He considered keeping Carrie's alcohol wipe and putting it into a scrapbook. Except that might qualify him as a stalker.

"True." Carrie stood from the table and blew on her hands, rubbing them together, as the coroner dragged a heavy white case in the shape of a toolbox out of her wagon. "I've known lots of slimeballs who are married."

Junior retrieved his notebook and poked at it with his pencil. "I've hardly ever known a slimeball who *wasn't* married."

"So are you listing suspects? A girlfriend and a wife. Loan sharks." Carrie added dryly, "My dad."

"Got 'em all." Junior tapped his shirt pocket containing the notebook.

"I'm Dr. Notchke." The coroner, a stocky woman in sensible shoes and an unfortunate pageboy haircut that made her face a perfect square, approached the table. "They sent me out from the Dodge County coroner's office."

The doctor and Junior went in the house together.

Carrie studied their retreating backs.

"You want in the house bad, don't you?" Nick couldn't remember the last time he'd enjoyed a woman's company this much. Her silly fear of mice, her amazing nerve around the corpse, her silky blond hair, that sassy mouth, and the dreams in her intelligent sky blue eyes.

Carrie looked at Nick, smiled sheepishly, and hunched one shoulder. He was really close. He leaned closer. Five syllables. Seven if he said her name first.

"Carrie?"

"Yes?"

"How about. . ." That sounded rude. He should have said, "Will you please—" No. Bad grammar. Learned that from the semester he considered being a novelist. *Would you like to have dinner with me?* Better. How many syllables? Nick started counting. *Would you like to—*

"What?"

He tried to say it, remembered his nose-hair problems, and forced his jaw to unclench. "Would you like to—"

"No!" A scream with the force of an electric shock jerked Nick around.

"No, not Wilkie, not my Wilkie!" A painfully thin woman, wearing tattered blue jeans and a T-shirt that hung on her skinny body, fought against the grip of Junior's two deputies. Her limp brown hair flying, she collapsed, screaming with grief. She buried her face in her hands. A boy, maybe fifteen, dashed up behind the woman and fell to the ground beside her, nearly knocking her onto her side.

"Mom, Mom, it's got to be a mistake. It's not Dad!" The boy broke into sobs and flung his arms around the distraught woman. A girl around seventeen, wearing low-slung jeans and a tight, short T-shirt faded to a drab shade of army green, edged up beside the two.

"That his wife and kids?" Nick whispered.

"Yeah, he has two with Rosie." Carrie stood and dusted off the seat of her pants. "Shayla was born just after Rosie turned seventeen. Wilkie was twenty-four."

"That's statutory rape." Nick clenched his jaw.

"Only if someone presses charges."

"Wrong."

Carrie nodded. "Rosie was thrilled, and her parents didn't complain when they got married real fast. It was a huge scandal."

"As big a scandal as you pulling that chair out from under your friend?"

Carrie narrowed her eyes. "I won't dignify that with a response."

"Good for you." *Would you please have dinner with me?*

Say it. Say it. Say it, loser.

"I remember how happy Rosie was." Carrie shook her head and her hair swept back and forth, so close, so silky that Nick's fingers itched to touch it. Of course, he didn't.

"And how sure we all were that she'd hooked a loser."

"Probably what she was fishing for." Nick shoved his hands in his Windbreaker pockets to control them. "Should we go help?" He took a step forward.

Junior loped out of the house in response to the screams.

"We don't want any part of Rosie's drama." Carrie caught Nick's arm. "Let Junior handle it."

"Wilkie's dead?" Another woman shoved through the crowd. Little more than a teenager, she wore a blue-jean jacket that was impossible to button, and a stained white T-shirt stretched over her stomach. She was obviously pregnant.

The woman on the ground whirled on her knees and, with a scream that would have humbled a horror movie actress, launched herself at the second woman.

Even pregnant, the new woman was tough. She sank both hands in Rosie's hair and screamed, "You killed him, you. . ."

Dora actually stood up from her lawn chair.

Nick raced toward them, leaping the crime-scene tape. Hal and Steve were there ahead of him, each grabbing a woman. The pregnant woman was giving Hal all he could handle, so Nick caught the woman's hand and pried her fingers loose one at a time from Rosie Melnik's hair.

Junior was one step behind him. "Break it up, you two."

Rosie shouted a string of words no woman should ever say, let alone in front of her children. She drew back her fist.

The pregnant woman bared her claws and yowled. For a second, Nick felt like he'd bought into a fight with Carrie's cat. Trying to protect the pregnant woman from Rosie's punch, Nick got clipped on the chin. Rosie didn't pack a lot of wallop. Nothing like Bea and her skillet.

"Donette, knock it off!" Junior used his significant weight to push between the women.

"She killed Wilkie!" Donette lunged, but the deputy hung on. "He was leaving her for me!"

"He was done with you, Donette." Rosie lashed out with her foot and kicked

Junior in the backside. "You never meant a thing to him!"

"Both of you settle down," Junior growled in a tone that would have cleared the mice out of Carrie's house if they'd heard it.

The deputies tightened their grips on the two loves of Wilkie Melnik.

"You make me sick, Donette." Wilkie's daughter charged into the middle of the riot and jammed her hands on her hips. "I hate you."

Nick rubbed his chin, now puffy enough to match the bump on his forehead, and gazed at Carrie, who shrugged.

"Back off, Shayla." Donette yanked against Hal's restraining hold. "I was in love with your dad."

Rosie lurched toward her daughter and wrapped her arms around the girl. Shayla shrugged like her mother's arms were smothering her. "You were supposed to be my friend. Instead, you were hanging around with me to get to Dad. You're disgusting."

"I didn't go after your dad. He came after me. We were in love."

"Dad didn't know how to love anyone. He used you because you're a—"

"Enough, Shayla." Junior cut her off. "It don't do no good to spread the hate around."

Junior turned to the deputy gripping Donette. "Hal, take Donette home."

Junior shifted his eyes to Donette. "I expect you to let this drop. Fighting don't solve anything. You come at Rosie again and I'll arrest you."

"You belong in jail." Rosie released Shayla and bent over sobbing. "You're a home wrecker and a murderer."

Nick tried to imagine two women fighting over him. It'd never happen in a million years. The many charms of Wilkie had escaped Nick.

Rosie threw her whole self into a weeping fury that struck Nick as more theatrical than truly sad. He wondered just how sorry Rosie was to see her lazy, drinking, cheating, gambling, ex-con husband dead.

Junior turned toward Rosie. "That goes double for you. Any more fighting between you two and you'll both cool off in a cell."

"Let's go." Hal forced Donette away from Rosie.

Donette resisted as Hal pushed her forward. "She killed him," Donette yelled over her shoulder, jabbing her index finger straight at Rosie. "She wanted him dead when he told her he was leaving."

"And Steve, get Rosie home."

"No!" Rosie made a quick move toward the house. "I want to stay. I want to see Wilkie!"

Steve caught her with the finesse of a nose tackle.

Rosie, held securely by Steve, twisted toward Donette. "You're the one who killed him."

The two women were dragged away weeping, occasionally bursting into screaming fits. Nick heard Hal shout in pain as he wrestled Donette into the squad car. Steve had to deal with the distraught son and hostile daughter, too. Once the cars pulled out, Junior returned to the house muttering. Nick heard the words "Worthless Wilkie" but couldn't make out the rest.

Nick smoothed his hair and tucked his shirt back in, trying to recover from the catfight. He wondered how soon would be too soon to try asking Carrie out to dinner again.

Before he could ease into it, a vision in splattered primary colors burst from the crowd. Tallulah Prichard, president of the Melnik Historical Society and keeper of All Things Melnik.

"Wilkie's dead?"

She wore a turban. Nick knew there were turbans, and he'd seen plenty of them in the news—in stories about the Middle East. But he'd never personally met anyone who wore one. Ditto caftans. This turban was bright red, and it matched a giant splash on her caftan.

Carrie muttered beside him, "It looks like a parrot exploded on her."

"Wilkie was going to be the master of ceremonies for this year's Maxie Parade." Tallulah flung her arms wide, playing to the cheap seats.

"That cannot be true." Carrie sidled closer to Nick—the better to whisper. "No one in their right mind would honor a loser like Wilkie Melnik."

Nick thought about the fact that he'd hired Wilkie and decided not to comment.

Tallulah wrung her hands together, rings flashing on nearly every finger. "He and his family were the last of the Melnik line."

"You know, no one in the town was very good to Wilkie," Carrie said under her breath. "Not that he inspired a lot of good. It's amazing that so many people are upset that he's dead."

Nick looked down at her. "If you're keeping score, there are about fifty people in this crowd, and so far, I've counted five that are upset—so Wilkie's not doing all that well."

"We've already got the float half built for the parade." Tallulah laid her hands on her face with great flourish, careful not to smear her substantial layers of makeup. "It's a giant mouse, and Wilkie was going to ride on its back."

Carrie shuddered and inched closer to Nick.

"It's a fake mouse, for heaven's sake," Nick hissed. "You don't get scared over Mickey Mouse cartoons, do you?"

"Mickey is a very obvious cartoon," Carrie retorted under her breath. "Tallulah will make the float look just like Maxie; you wait and see. Ick." She moved closer yet.

Nick knew there was some way to parlay her phobia into a dinner date if he could just figure out the right approach.

"A completely realistic six-foot-tall mouse. That is my own personal nightmare."

Her shoulder touched his, and so far, this was his best day in Melnik since he'd moved here.

Nick grinned and patted her on the shoulder.

Tallulah ranted a bit more. The crowd went back to their own whispered reflections on the unfolding events while they munched on their hot dogs. All in all, everyone appeared to be enjoying themselves. A great day to be from Melnik, unless you were Wilkie or one of the four or five people who cared about him.

Then a hush fell over the crowd. Nick saw eyes focus on the house behind him. He turned to see the coroner emerge through the doorway.

The stout doctor walked down the steps. Junior appeared from the midst of the onlookers to meet her.

Carrie jumped off the picnic table and headed straight for them.

As repelled by murder as Carrie was attracted to it, Nick trailed along to talk to the officials. If he was going to be arrested, he didn't want to annoy them by making them hunt for him.

4

O kay. The preliminary exam tells me that Wilkie died from a gunshot wound and he's been dead several days—I'll narrow that down." Dr. Notchke read from her notes.

"Gunshot?" Carrie heard Junior gasp. "I saw a bruise on his head—there was no blood."

Carrie hung back, afraid they'd clam up if she got too close.

"I didn't see it at first either," Dr. Notchke said. "The wound didn't bleed like it should have. Even moving the body doesn't explain the lack of blood on his clothes. In fact, I suspect an autopsy will show that someone shot him after he was dead. But for a preliminary cause of death, well, we can't discount that he's got a bullet in him."

"Why would anybody do that?" Carrie backed up enough to whisper to Nick. Her fingertips tingled, she wanted to take notes so badly. A leftover habit from working the police beat in Omaha. She didn't dare in front of the coroner, though. Besides, she didn't have any paper. She wondered if Junior had any to spare.

"Any idea about motive at this point?"

"Nick, get over here." Junior turned a dark expression on Nick.

Nick, his eyes wary, approached. Carrie tagged along. If they were going to tell him stuff, then she ought to get to hear it, too. He made room in the little circle for Carrie, which gave her an "us against them" feeling.

"What?" Nick shoved his hands in the pockets of his black Windbreaker.

"When did you last see Wilkie?"

"I told you I didn't do it. You *cannot* believe—"

"Just answer the question." This was Junior in serious-cop mode.

"Fine." Nick sighed. "I hired him around noon on Monday. He worked for me the rest of the day." The crowd, still lingering two hours after the first siren had sounded, murmured into the fall breeze. More geese honked from a bedraggled V far overhead.

"Keep going." Junior wrote steadily.

"I already knew he was going to be trouble by the end of the day, because he was more interested in taking breaks than in working."

"Wilkie never was a hard worker." Junior shook his head in disgust at the ultimate Nebraska sin.

"Then he showed up an hour late on Tuesday. I told him we started at seven and I expected him to be on time."

Junior nodded.

"He didn't come in at all on Wednesday."

"Great-Grandma Bea died Tuesday night," Carrie interjected. The paramedics from the Melnik Volunteer Fire Department had shown up. Some had gone inside, but the rest waited, their blue jackets proudly sporting MVFD.

"Have you looked into Great-Grandma's death?" Carrie grabbed Junior's forearm. "It can't be a coincidence that both she and Wilkie are dead."

The chief's heavy brow furrowed. "I came over when your grandpa Leonard called 911. She was a hundred and three, and she—"

"Oh," Carrie said, cutting him off, "so now it's okay to kill people once they're one hundred and three?"

"I didn't mean that, and you know it." Junior's cheeks turned red. "I just meant that she was old and unsteady. You know there were risks in her staying here alone. Leonard tried to get her to move in with him and your grandma, but she wouldn't budge. There was nothing suspicious about her death."

"Nothing suspicious?" Carrie planted her fists on her hips. "How about another body? That's suspicious."

Carrie looked at Nick for support.

"Seems suspicious to me." Nick moved closer to Carrie.

Carrie shot him a grateful smile.

"Well, I didn't know about this body until now, did I?" Junior shrugged and made a note. "I'll keep it in mind."

Carrie felt her blood pressure rising at Junior's dismissive tone. Given the circumstances, there was no way her great-grandmother's death was an accident.

"Go on, Nick." Junior looked up. "Is Tuesday the last time you saw Wilkie?"

Nick nodded. "I had cabinets to build. A big project. I told Wilkie to come to my place on Wednesday morning. He still hadn't shown up when I heard about Bea's death. I came over here as soon as I could to see Leonard. He was pretty broken up about his mom dying. I offered him all his money back."

Nick turned to Carrie. "I promise I tried to quit. I'd see him on the street, and every week since he'd hired me, I told him I wasn't earning the money he was paying. But he'd say, 'Keep trying,' and when I refused to take his money, he started depositing a check in my account at the bank. I even told the bank not to accept it, but your aunt Lucille is the head teller, and she just laughed at me and said, 'Learn to duck when you're around Bea.'"

Nick looked back at Junior. "I got the impression he wanted me to check on his mom. I know he didn't like her living here alone, and he was over here every day and your grandma called and stopped, and Dora and lots of others visited, but he still worried."

"That sounds like Grandpa." Carrie noticed Grizzly slip through the torn screen into the house. She hoped her scary new pet cleared out the mice, and fast.

"And I think Bea kind of liked swinging her skillet and yelling at me." Nick shrugged one shoulder. "It seemed to make her happy."

"That sounds like Great-Grandma."

Nick focused on Junior again. "When I saw Leonard Wednesday morning, he told me it was time to earn my money. So I went to work. I called Wilkie again to tell him to come over to Bea's. No answer. I figured he'd already headed to my house, so I went back home. Wilkie wasn't around. I gathered up the tools I needed to work here at Bea's and left Wilkie a note in my workshop, telling him to come on over. I never heard from him."

"He was already dead." Dr. Notchke consulted her clipboard. "I'll pin down the time of death better after the autopsy, but I'd guess he's been dead at least three days."

"You mean he's been dead since maybe Tuesday night, the same time my great-grandma died?" Cassie asked.

The coroner nodded. "Certainly when you were hunting for him Wednesday morning, he was already in the closet."

"So I've been working in the house with a dead body?" Nick grimaced at the thought.

The coroner nodded. "We're done here. You can take over, Chief Hammerstad."

"Thanks. Let me know when. . ." Junior fell silent as a paramedic emerged from the house. Wheels clattered as one husky medic lowered the white-sheeted gurney down the steps.

The crowd in the street fell silent. Wheels squeaked down the sidewalk, and the EMTs escorted the ne'er-do-well great-great grandson of the town's founders away.

Tallulah wept loudly. Dora stopped knitting. Carrie noticed Grandma Elsa and Grandpa Leonard Evans, her dad's parents, in the crowd. Grandpa Leonard, who'd been doing his best to take care of his uncooperative mother for years, nodded at her and gave her a little wave.

Most of Melnik quietly watched while Wilkie made a spectacle of himself one last time.

When the ambulance pulled away, Junior clapped the notebook closed. "We're done inside. The coroner's team did a sweep for fiber evidence. You can have your house back."

"Fiber evidence?" Carrie shook her head. "Great-Grandma's house is one gigantic fiber."

"Tell me about it." Junior walked away, snagging the crime-scene tape as he went. The crowd surged forward, Dora at the lead.

Carrie looked at the house and swallowed with a throat gone bone dry.

Nick rested one hand on her upper arm. "You don't want to sleep here. Besides Wilkie, there's the mouse situation."

Carrie didn't admit that the mouse situation bothered her a lot more than Wilkie.

"You can stay with your folks or at your grandparents'. All four of your grandparents live in Melnik, right?"

Carrie turned from staring at the house. "I'm looking for my backbone, okay? Don't make it harder by giving me plausible excuses."

Nick's eyes were warm with concern. "If you're really worried about mice, you stay with your folks, and I'll stay here a few days and make sure they're cleared out."

"You and Grizzly?"

Nick opened his mouth, but no sound came out.

"I didn't think so."

Nick cleared his throat. "No, you didn't give me enough time. I'll team up with Grizzly. You can even help me clear out a different bedroom than the one you were planning to use, if you feel like that's an invasion of your privacy."

"They're all piled to the rafters with junk."

"We've got a few hours of light left. We could clear one out before bedtime."

"We'll help." Dora invaded their conversation.

Carrie knew just how Atlanta felt when Ulysses S. Grant showed up.

"No!" Tallulah, playing the part of Robert E. Lee, shoved her way through the crowd. That wasn't hard. Everyone wanted her front and center where they could watch the show.

Grandpa Leonard came up beside Carrie on the right while Nick stood on her left. Grandma Elsa was close behind her husband.

With a sigh, Carrie said, "Why not, Tallulah?"

"Bea Evans's house is a gold mine of historical information. She's got over one hundred years' worth of newspapers and artifacts in there."

"The main artifacts she has are ten thousand *Reader's Digests* and *TV Guides*," Carrie said, unable to keep the sarcasm out of her voice. "There's no treasure, Tallulah."

"Someone with the correct historical understanding needs to go through that house with a fine-tooth comb."

Carrie closed her eyes so she could roll them without getting caught. "And who exactly would that be?"

"Why, me." Tallulah touched her chest gracefully with five ring-spangled fingers. "Of course."

"Of course." Carrie folded her arms, hoping the body language would help. "The thing is, I don't have time to comb the fine teeth of my house. So we're not going to be careful."

Grandma Elsa eased up by Carrie. "If something has been buried in that house for one hundred years, we can live without it forever. I say let's gather every trash can in town and fill 'em up."

Carrie smiled at the spry little woman who always had time for her youngest grandchild.

Tallulah's gasp of outrage was drowned out by the voices of a herd of bustling housewives, many of whom had been itching to get their hands on Bea Evans's house for years.

"How about a compromise?" Grandpa Leonard asked.

Carrie saw Grandma Elsa's eyes narrow. "Leonard, we're cleaning that house. Don't try to stop me."

Grandpa smiled and patted his wife's arm. "I was going to say, why don't we attack the first floor tonight? My mom kept the first floor pretty clean until these last five or ten years. So there's not going to be any ancient treasure down there." Grandpa smiled triumphantly, as if he'd just arranged world peace.

Tallulah launched the first attack of the cease-fire. "But she could have brought something down."

"No, she never went upstairs." Grandpa shook his head firmly. "She hadn't been up there in ten years at least, ever since she broke her hip. She refused to even try."

Then how'd she die by falling down those steps? Carrie didn't say it. It might be too much excitement for the more elderly Melnikites. But she didn't intend to let it drop.

Grandpa went on. "So we just toss everything on the first floor and decide about the rest later."

Dora came up beside Tallulah. "We can't get more than that done tonight, anyway. So we'll help with the first floor to make the place livable, and if you want us to, we'll come back and help you with the rest of it whenever you say."

People started emerging from their homes all up and down the street rolling huge green trash cans. Sacrificing their own garbage space for her. Carrie choked up. Of course, most of them were senior citizens and only threw one small trash bag away each week, but still, she appreciated it.

Dora laid her hand on Tallulah's exploded parrot shoulder. "And we'll include you, Tallulah. We'll let you examine anything we think is interesting for historical value. That's the best deal you're going to get."

Dora as peace activist. Dora should be turned loose on the Middle East. She'd straighten everyone out. If nothing else, she'd send them running to their own homes just to get away from her. Dora had some good qualities. She wasn't all bad.

"And since Carrie has that same slob gene Bea had, we'll keep at her to clear the place out."

Carrie clenched her fist to deck the old bat.

Nick rested his hand on Carrie's back, and she got control of herself. Trash receptacles rattled past them.

"This is going to be great," Nick said. "Fixing that majestic old house."

"Okay." Grandma Elsa rubbed her hands together as if she'd just scooted her chair up to a feast. "Let's go, ladies!" Carrie knew Grandma Elsa had been dying to clean up her mother-in-law's house for years. She was right behind Dora.

The whole town seemed to stream past Carrie, nearly knocking her into Nick.

"Be careful with the cat," she called after them.

Grandma Elsa looked back. "We'd never hurt your cat, Carrie. Shame on you."

"I'm not worried about the cat. I'm worried about you."

5

As the invading army of neat freaks filed past, Nick stayed at Carrie's side. "Your great-grandma's home is spectacular. Your family lived there?"

His reverent tone stopped Carrie from entering the infested wreck. It was possible she was looking for an excuse. "You must love big old houses."

"Sure." Nick shoved his hands into his back pockets. Carrie noticed that his shirt was neatly tucked in again under his jacket. He'd had a shirttail or two flying after the tussle with Rosie and Donette. His hair didn't show a sign of being mussed.

"I was an architectural engineer in Chicago before I moved here. Form and function was my job, but I was always more interested in form than function. I just love beauty in a building." His eyes wandered over the house. "It's why I quit. All those high-rises, sheets of glass hung on load-bearing walls. I wanted to do something better, something that would make people stop and enjoy a building. My firm in Chicago sent me out to do some engineering work for Valmont, the irrigation company near here, and I loved the area. I fell in love with the houses in Melnik."

"A lot of them were built by my ancestors."

"You must be so proud of that." Nick's eyes sparkled.

She'd never given it much thought, but now that Nick mentioned it, she was proud of her forebearers. She was the first failure in the family.

"I'd gotten so tired of pushing for more beauty in the buildings my company designed. What I wanted took time and money. I was always in conflict with my bosses."

"Boy, I know how that feels." Carrie's ears were still ringing from her last conflict with her boss.

Nick's eyes sharpened as he watched her. "Trouble at work? I wondered why you'd quit your dream job to live in Melnik. I thought maybe you missed home."

Before Carrie could answer, Grandpa Leonard came sauntering back from the house. The fall breeze ruffled his comb-over, which was much thicker than Junior's. Grandpa smoothed it back into place. "Listen, let me apologize one more time for not warning you before I sent you over and Mom crowned you with the frying pan. I should have warned you, but I just didn't think she was spry enough to get you. I underestimated her. Sorry."

Nick winced, but his smile held.

There were still people coming with cans, and Carrie saw a couple of ladies carrying casserole dishes. When the first filled trash can came out of the house, Carrie knew she'd procrastinated long enough. Trying not to think of mice, she headed inside. She sidestepped to let another garbage receptacle out as she crossed the porch with Nick and Grandpa right behind her.

When they got inside, the kitchen counter was already empty, and Tallulah was hugging age-yellowed copies of the *Melnik Bugle* to her brightly colored bosom.

Carrie felt funny watching all the activity, a beehive buzzing on the floor where, only moments ago, Wilkie lay dead. No one looked interested in pausing for a moment of silence, though they probably would if Carrie clapped her hands and demanded quiet so she could ask. But instead, she decided to have her own.

She bowed her head and said a short prayer for poor Wilkie. There'd been rumors about him all his life: hyperactive as a child back when they just called that being a brat; learning disabled in his teens back when they called that being stupid; shades of manic depression self-medicated with alcohol and drugs back when they called that being a moody drunk.

Had the new terminology done any good?

Wilkie had precious little raw material, and what he'd had, he'd squandered.

God, Wilkie is Yours now; You know his struggles and his choices better than I can. Be with his family; heal the scars. Bless his wife and children. Bless Donette and the baby she's carrying. I miss my great-grandma, Lord. Hold her in the palm of Your hand and bless us all. Amen.

A hand rested gently on her shoulder, and she looked up.

"Thinking of Wilkie?" Nick asked, his eyes warm and kind.

"Yeah, and Great-Grandma Bea."

Nick nodded, but then Pastor Bremmen came inside with his usual energy and pulled Carrie away from her somber thoughts. "We just finished a community pastors' meeting, and when we heard about this, we all came over."

He was the minister at the nondenominational Country Christian Church between Melnik and the neighboring town of Bjorn—one of four Swedish capitals of Nebraska, all self-proclaimed. Sweden had wisely not gotten involved. Carrie thought with a sniff of satisfaction that no one else claimed to be "Home of the World's Largest Field Mouse." A true claim to fame, however horrifying.

Grandma Elsa slapped the lid closed on a bulging trash can. She backed up a step and eyed the messy kitchen. "How did we let this place go to rack and ruin so badly, Len?"

Leonard shook his head. "You know Mom."

Nick whispered to Carrie, "Did she use a skillet on everybody?"

"People she didn't know," Carrie said. "But not usually family."

"Everybody knows how Bea was." Carrie turned to see that her mother had shown up. Carrie gave her a hug.

Carrie saw Grandpa Leonard shake his head. Nick rubbed his.

More family appeared when Carrie's mother's parents, Grandma and Grandpa Anderson, came in the back door through the porch. No one had used Great-Grandma Bea's front door in one hundred and three years.

Carrie's grandma Anderson was a classic Swede. Tall and round as a beer keg. Grandma Helga gave Carrie a hug that almost smothered her granddaughter. Grandpa Hermann, a head taller than his wife and as skinny as Grandma was stout, hugged her, too. They were farmers, thrilled when their daughter, the youngest of six—all girls—married a man who wanted to work the land. They'd taken Carrie's dad on as a partner and then retired and moved to town about ten years ago.

The kitchen kept filling with people. Carrie thought she should probably be directing them, but Grandma Elsa was already in charge and Grandma Helga looked eager to give a few directions. Mom was no slouch either, plus Tallulah kept shouting orders, and of course everyone obeyed Dora out of sheer terror.

Carrie had a dictator for every room on the first floor.

"Are you keeping anything, Carrie?" her mom asked.

"No."

"Don't throw any clothes away," Dora ordered. "I'm taking them to Second Time Around in Bjorn to sell. Just bag them and put them in my car. I've already opened the trunk."

Carrie mentally apologized to the young family who had started the tidy used clothing and furniture store. When they got hit with all this, they'd probably turn tail and run.

"Carrie's bedroom needs to be cleaned out." Carrie heard her mother issuing commands. "We'll do that before we tackle anything else so she has a place to sleep tonight."

"Strip the bed first," Grandma Helga ordered. "I've got Bea's washer uncovered. We'll get a load of laundry going so Carrie can sleep on clean sheets."

Carrie barely controlled a shudder at the thought of sleeping in the mouse-infested house.

"You don't have to stay here." Nick patted her back, which meant she hadn't controlled the shudder as well as she hoped.

"And before we go any further"—Pastor Bremmen's booming voice quieted the crowd—"let's say a prayer, remembering Bea and thanking God that Carrie's back."

Nick said, "Say a prayer for Wilkie's family, too, please."

Pastor Bremmen smiled. "Absolutely."

Everyone bowed their heads, and Pastor Bremmen prayed for about ten minutes, a prayer that covered Bea, Carrie, Wilkie, his family, and the whole town. He then outlined the salvation message, threatened everyone there with eternal darkness, and offered a brief altar call. He finished with a flourish, and then everyone got back to work.

Carrie counted at least thirty people in her house. As she worked her way through the crush toward the living room, she found herself pressed against the curved railing of the stairway.

Above the chattering horde, Carrie heard a floorboard creak upstairs. It sounded for all the world like a footstep. They weren't supposed to be cleaning up there yet. She glanced around and realized she'd lost Nick in the chaos.

Carrie started up the stairs, making sure to be noisy to scare off any mice, although the talking and laughing in her home had surely harassed every rodent back into its hole—maybe even scared them into moving out.

Fat chance.

Someone came through from the kitchen holding a turkey sandwich. This was turning into a party. Another green trash can came wheeling in—this time through the front door. Viola Seavers pushed it as she bickered with her sister Alta. Carrie, who had never seen the front door to this house open, stopped on the bottom step to greet her.

"Put us to work." Viola quit complaining and greeted Helga. "We want Carrie settled so we can work her like a slave at the paper." Viola produced a key and handed it to Carrie. "Front door of the *Bugle*. Heard you were going to work with us."

Carrie took the presentation of the key to mean that she was hired. The ladies walked away from her, squabbling. Carrie went back to braving the upstairs.

The stairway was square at the bottom, with about five creaky steps coming down from a landing. Although the bottom was open, the stairs turned at the landing at a ninety-degree angle, and the steps went on up past an enclosing wall. When Carrie reached the second floor, she heard the strange creaking again, this time from the third floor.

Carrie hadn't been up to the third floor since she was about ten. Inhaling the stale, musty air of the second floor, she approached the narrow doorway straight ahead, her hand trembling.

Grizzly dashed up the stairs, and Carrie felt better. She gave the cat a few seconds to scare all the mice into their holes, and then she ascended, step by creaking step. The murky staircase was so narrow that she could touch both walls with her hands hanging at her sides. The air was thick and laden with dust and ancient neglect. Carrie breathed through her mouth to keep from sneezing. She swallowed and tasted dirt.

Her head emerged into a full third floor. Three rooms off the hallway stretched the length of the house opposite where she stood, and two more were behind her. The hall was stacked high with a lifetime of junk.

A flash of movement made Carrie jump. She grabbed the walls to keep from tumbling back to the second floor. After her first frightened reaction, she got mad. "Who's here? What are you doing up here?"

Tallulah jumped from behind a stack of boxes. An armful of papers slipped from her grasp and spewed in a graceful stream to the floor, kicking up dust as they skidded in all directions.

Grizzly, startled by the raining papers, jumped with an unearthly yowl from behind a cardboard box to the top of it. Rotten with age, the box broke, and Grizzly scrabbled for a foothold as old clothing spilled from the box. The cat vanished into one of the rooms on Tallulah's left that stood with its door slightly ajar. Carrie could see footprints in the dust going in and out of several rooms.

As the papers settled, Tallulah, usually a flurry of motion and color, stood frozen like a multicolored deer caught in the headlights of an oncoming semi. One paper floated nearly to Carrie's feet, and she saw what looked like a legal document. Tallulah wasn't just going through old newspapers.

"Carrie, I d–didn't expect you to come up here."

Since she'd been ducked down behind boxes, Carrie doubted that.

"Were you planning to steal those things?" Carrie nodded at the mess scattered on the floor, covering the little bit of a walkway Great-Grandma had left.

"No! Steal? Carrie, don't say that! I—I wouldn't steal anything from you. I was just worried that things of historical significance might be thrown away."

"You were there when they decided to leave the upper floors alone, so you knew nothing would get thrown away up here. And if your intentions are so honorable, why did you hide from me when I came up here?"

Tallulah's mouth opened and closed goldfish-like, but she couldn't seem to think of a good answer.

That's because there wasn't one.

Then Tallulah squared her shoulders and took on an offended look. "Well, I was just curious. I'm shocked that you'd doubt my word."

"Let's go downstairs."

"Of course. Glad to. After you?" The Melnik history buff made a grand gesture toward the steps.

Carrie came fully up onto the third floor and crossed her arms. "No, you first."

Tallulah gave the floor a look of such blatant longing that Carrie couldn't even pretend Tallulah was just snoopy. The woman wanted something from this house, and she wanted it badly.

Eyes locked on Tallulah, Carrie didn't even blink, afraid Parrot Woman would slip a few papers under her caftan. Tallulah went back to her usual dramatic self and flounced past Carrie.

Carrie intended to have it out with Tallulah, but the woman charged down to the first floor so fast that Carrie couldn't catch her.

Her jaw tight with annoyance, Carrie realized that although she'd only learned she owned Great-Grandma's house today, she already felt possessive of the old wreck.

6

Carrie gathered Tallulah's papers, wondering if a mouse was going to dash out at her from somewhere. Grizzly peeked out from the bedroom door. "Hi, guy. Welcome to the family."

Glancing at the old documents, Carrie didn't see anything that jumped out as important, but she wanted to decide what papers to share with the town, and she couldn't do that until she had time to go over them carefully.

Grizzly hissed and slashed a paw at her and then ducked back into the bedroom.

The exact temperament Carrie wanted in a cat.

Carrie, filled with dread, knew there was one place the papers would be safe.

The Dead Zone.

With a little shudder, Carrie went back to the second floor and approached the room on the west end. She twisted the knob. It was stubborn, and so were the rusty, squealing hinges, but she wrestled the door open and stood in the Dead Zone. Deer heads sporting massive antlers, an antelope, a big-horned sheep, a regal elk, a shaggy buffalo, a black bear, a wolf, a coyote, and even a massive moose head. Living creatures that some Supermannish dose of testosterone must have poisoned her ancestors into believing was art.

On wooden display stands with bases that resembled miniature columns from the Roman Coliseum stood pheasants, grouse, a wild turkey with its tail feathers splayed, and every imaginable breed of goose. Carrie looked at the whooping crane with wings extended as if caught in a mating dance. Two bald eagles; one with wings closed as it dove in for the kill, one with wings wide, its beak spread in a grim smile as it soared on an imaginary breeze. Both birds fell into Great-Grandpa's clutches before anyone noticed that they were almost extinct.

A fox seemed to skitter along the floor, as if frozen in midflight. A white ermine, a deep brown mink, and a dozen other furry, ratlike critters crawled along the floor. Fish of every size and color were mounted and left to collect dust as they hung on the walls. A full-sized buck, doe, and fawn stood in one corner. That spotted baby especially horrified Carrie, to think of her great-grandpa wanting that little still life.

Her great-grandpa had been in his eighties when she was born and had no longer gone upstairs much, abandoning this room to the moths. But Carrie had come up here with her cousins whenever they could, especially to stare at the greatest prize of all.

A life-sized grizzly bear stood on its hind legs, its mouth wide open as if frozen forever in a sharp-toothed growl and its claws slashing the air.

Carrie forced herself to enter the room, clutching the papers against her chest like a security blanket. As children, there'd been a strange kind of thrill in coming here with her siblings and cousins and spooking themselves half to death. The thrill was definitely gone.

The single bare bulb swung quietly as she pulled the string that ran from it to an eyehook by the door. That moving light danced over the animals, making their eyes come to life. Shadows made the bear's claws appear to rise.

Knowing exactly where she wanted to hide the papers, Carrie picked her way through the muddle of Great-Grandma's life savings of trash to a swan standing with its neck curved down, looking depressed. Who could blame it?

She tilted the graceful bird up and slipped the papers under its substantial wooden base.

With the papers secure, Carrie picked her way out of the room to find Nick in the hallway.

He smiled. "I lost track of you."

Carrie decided that someone else knowing about the papers might not be such a bad idea. "I've got something to show you in the Dead Zone."

"That's the Dead Zone?" Nick peeked past her shoulder.

She turned back and was glad for his company as she led the way into the room.

Grizzly the cat sauntered into the room dragging a stuffed fox.

"Yuck." Nick crouched beside Carrie.

He snagged the fox and began a tug-of-war that struck Carrie as really brave, considering the noise emanating from Grizzly's throat.

Nick chose that moment to rest one big hand on the feline's head and rub the coarse, matted fur with a gentle caress. Grizzly twisted his head as if to get closer, and Nick scratched the cat behind his ears, murmuring something Carrie couldn't hear. The demonic growl changed to a purr.

"Quite an inheritance, huh, Nick? Do you like trophy animals?"

"Sure. What's not to like?" Nick won the tug-of-war with Grizzly. He held the poor battered fox in his hand.

Carrie glanced back and saw Hal, Junior's deputy, just outside the door to the third story, almost as if he were about to head up the stairs. Her gaze met his, and he looked away and then went downstairs. "I hid some papers in this room. I want someone else to know about them in. . .in case something happens to me."

"Nothing's going to happen to you, Carrie."

"Well, somebody put Wilkie in that closet."

"Whoever did it had a problem with Wilkie, not you."

"They might come back. They might be after something in this house."

Nick set the fox at the feet of the huge bear. "Carrie, I was an architectural engineer before I came to Melnik."

Carrie scowled and jammed her hands on her hips. "What does that have to do with anything?"

"My job was to make a building work."

"Work? What does that mean?"

"I didn't design the buildings. I made sure that the blueprints were feasible, the service elevators were adequate to meet the needs of the structure, the wiring met codes, and there were enough bathrooms to provide service to the projected number of occupants of the offices or stores on each floor. There are hundreds of little details, especially in a big building and with so many building codes. It was complicated and tedious."

"That's very impressive." To her own ears, Carrie sounded completely unimpressed. "And it sounds like a really great job. High-paying, too."

"I did okay."

"And you gave it up to repair porches in Melnik?"

She might as well have added, "Stupid," after that question. She hoped Nick hadn't heard it.

"My work was mathematical. Very detailed and orderly. I employed logic."

Now Carrie knew where he was going. This wasn't just a walk down memory lane. She sighed and checked her fingernails for dirt. Whoa—there was a lot of it.

"When a one-hundred-year-old woman falls, especially in a town with no crime like Melnik—"

"You're forgetting Wilkie."

"Listen, I'm not saying you're wrong. Something happened here, and I'll help you track down any answers you need. But I'd hate to see you get hurt."

Her head came up and her brows arched. "That's my point. Whoever killed Wilkie might come after me."

He shook his head. "I don't mean your being in danger. I mean in getting your *feelings* hurt. It sounds like Wilkie had plenty of enemies. Logically it would seem that none of them would turn their attention to you or your great-grandma."

His brow furrowed as he studied her. She wasn't sure how she felt about him showing this much concern. Kind of warm.

"Nick, I confided in you because I thought you were the one person in this house who might believe me. It's a small-town trait to not believe what's in front of your eyes if it doesn't fit in your tidy little life. You're not a small-town guy."

"I want to be."

"Why? What can you accomplish in a place this small? I mean, you can help people one at a time, and there's nothing wrong with that."

"There's everything right with that."

"But it's so much better in a city. Bigger communication, bigger jobs, a bigger church that can provide a real mission; it takes—"

"It takes God, Carrie. And God always reaches one person at a time. That's the only way a soul can be saved."

With a huff of anger, Carrie snapped, "Tell that to Billy Graham. He'd have been a great, great pastor of a small-town church, but there was more to do. God called him to it. And God has called me."

"Called you away from Melnik?"

"Of course called me away from Melnik."

Nick seemed to shrink—or maybe just shrink back from her. "Okay, let's clear this up about Wilkie and your great-grandma. Where do you want to start?"

Nick's warmth was gone.

She thought again about the break-in. "I'll start by writing a news story for the *Melnik Bugle*. I need to shake a few people up."

"Why?" Nick caught her hand. "Why shake people up in this nice, quiet little town?"

What was quiet worth if it was only a mirage? She tightened her jaw and said what she needed to say. "Because I think someone in this nice, quiet little town killed my great-grandma."

7

Carrie heard scratching in the walls. Of course, between worrying about mice and murder, she was going insane. So the scratching might have been her imagination. Grizzly also yowled from time to time. Carrie was rooting for him.

She survived the weekend by staying mostly at her parents' house, eating with them and going along to church. Despite her mom's urging, Carrie went back and faced that house to sleep every night. On Monday morning, she shook all her work clothes thoroughly. No mice fell out. Then she pulled them on quickly and brushed her teeth as fast as possible, grabbed her purse and coat, and sprinted outside. If she didn't see the actual rodents, she could pretend they didn't exist.

Denial was a beautiful thing.

Glancing back at her new home, she shuddered. "You chicken. You can't let mice scare you. Cindy Lou Who came downstairs Christmas morning and found the Grinch stealing Christmas. And he was a hairy, creepy creature. But was Cindy Lou afraid? No!" She spoke to God through the canopy of Great-Grandma's huge maple trees. "Lord, I'm sorry. I know they're more afraid of me than I am of them."

And that was a cliché that Carrie hated almost more than any other in the world. She hated it especially because it was so stinking true.

She walked to work, leaving her ten-year-old rust bucket Cavalier behind, wishing God would heal her of this strange fear. Yes, she'd admitted years ago that it was going to take a miracle.

She turned at the corner that took her toward Main Street. She'd need to pass the lifelike statue of the giant rodent Maxie the Mouse, preserved forever in granite on the corner of Third and Main. A three-foot-tall, disease-bearing vermin was a questionable decoration for the sidewalk in front of the town's only grocery store, but oh well.

Nick drove up in his black Ford truck. He smiled and pulled to a stop. She walked out on the street toward him, knowing that the chances of an oncoming car were slim.

"Did you get through the night okay? No mice?" Nick leaned farther out the window to talk. The sharp November breeze tousled his hair like fingers running through it. He smoothed it back.

Carrie had already learned he didn't like to be messy. "I didn't see any. But I

. . .uh. . .didn't check the mousetraps you set in the pantry."

Nick rested his elbow on the open window. Even the hair on his forearm looked combed and neat. He wore a knit shirt just like before, only red this time, with black thread in the OC logo just above his heart.

"I'll do it for you and reset them if I find anything."

Her smile widened. "Between you and Grizzly, I almost feel safe."

"Almost?"

"What can I say?" Carrie shrugged and studied her toes. "It's a phobia."

Nick chuckled. "See you later."

Carrie nodded and stepped back so he could drive away. She headed on to work. She rounded the corner onto Main Street, giving the Maxie statue a wide berth, and was caught by the drab block of old buildings.

Her eyes slid down the row of stores, mostly brick, mostly two stories, mostly empty. Their facades were squared at the top, even though the buildings had peaked roofs.

It hurt Carrie's heart to see it. Despite wanting to get away from Melnik, Carrie loved her hometown and hated to see it folding up. She arrived at the *Bugle* office at 8:00 a.m. and let herself in. Viola pulled up in her drab orange Park Avenue and parked so crookedly that she took up all three diagonal spaces in front of the building. It didn't matter. Except for one car parked in front of the grocery store, the parking spaces along Main Street were empty.

"Hi, Viola."

"Hi, honey. Bright and early your first morning. Good girl."

Carrie pushed the door open with a flourish. It screeched as if it were desperate for attention.

Viola followed Carrie inside, sat at the closest of three desks crammed into the little L-shaped room, and shut her purse in a drawer by her right knee.

"What do you think of the old place?"

Carrie was torn between dismay and wonder. This was the newspaper business at its most basic. Also its most depressing. You didn't need a ten-story building, the latest technology, and an army of reporters to put out a good newspaper. But it sure helped.

Viola's desk stood on Carrie's right. The other two desks were bunched in behind that. Shelves lined two walls, all stacked with oversized books that held bound copies of the *Bugle*, going back over a hundred years. The whole town's history was in those yellowed pages, and no one could look at them because the paper was too fragile to touch—although honestly, no one needed to look at them. Everybody knew the town's history by heart.

"Thanks for stopping by Friday night, Viola. I really appreciate all the help."

Viola waved her words away. "It was the best party in town. I wouldn't have missed it for the world. You'll need to put a thank-you note in the *Bugle* this week. They cost six dollars unless you want to get wordy."

"Thanks." Carrie should say she was happy to be here, but she just couldn't wrap her tongue around a blatant lie like that. She caught sight of the equipment, and her stomach twisted. "Uh, how old are these computers?"

Viola wrinkled her nose and her glasses jumped up and down. "Pretty bad, huh? I've got one at home that's a hand-me-down from my granddaughter's college years, and it's ten times fancier than these."

"Are they Windows 98, at least?" Carrie saw the disk slot on the closest computer and suppressed a gasp. It was for the old five-inch floppy disks.

Viola snorted. "They were all old when I started fifteen years ago."

"Are we online?" Carrie knew the answer before she asked the question. These computers were too old to have modems.

"Nope. Your desk is the back one."

To Carrie's left in the short end of the L-shaped room, a rack of wooden easels lined the wall on two sides, each supporting a sheet of paper the size of a newspaper page. The words THE *Melnik Bugle* were a bold masthead on the first sheet. The other seven were mostly blank, although Carrie recognized a few small ads scattered near the bottoms of some of them, ads that appeared in the paper week after week, never changing. The last two pages were covered with fine print with the words CLASSIFIED ADS across the top.

Predictable, eternal, boring. Carrie couldn't read them from where she stood, but she knew in general what they'd say. *Kittens, free to a good home. Garage Sale.*

Carrie suppressed a sigh because Viola was a nice lady and it wasn't her fault Carrie was a failure at age twenty-two.

Viola rose, drawing Carrie's attention away from personal failure to focus on the disaster of the out-of-date newsroom. "C'mon, I'll show you how to run these dinosaurs. We live in a kind of constant fear that something will break, because no one makes parts for these computers or the printer anymore."

"New computers don't cost much."

Viola laughed as her trim form led the way to the back desk. "You either have to make enough money on the paper to finance it yourself or get the new Gunny to kick in. Good luck with that."

"Old Man Gunderson should have invested in capital improvements if he expected his business to have any market value."

Viola gave her a pitying look. "Well, he never planned to sell it, I'm sure. Gundersons never sell anything. He wasn't interested in the market value of anything, only rent money. And now he's dead, so he was right not to put money into the business, I expect."

The place smelled like ink and something else Carrie recognized as intrinsically the *Bugle*, but she couldn't identify it.

"Pay attention, because formatting is a sixteen-step process. You'll catch on to it."

"Can't you just create a master copy and reuse it?"

Viola shooed Carrie into her desk chair. "You're welcome to try, although again, if you break it, we're doomed. And we've never failed to get out an issue of the *Bugle* in one hundred and seventeen years, so you don't want your name on *that* disaster."

Viola plunked some scraps of paper down in front of Carrie. "These are stories that have come in. Since we change employees so often, we've written down all the formatting steps, but I expect you'll have questions, anyway." Viola pointed to a half-buried page of tired-looking paper taped onto the desk. "It's all there. For now, just get the story typed into the computer, and we'll work through the formatting later. Can you type?"

Carrie nodded. "I'm fast and accurate."

"Accurate enough not to call Stuart Piperson 'Stupid Person'?"

Carrie looked up, and they both started laughing at the same second. All the tension and defeat and sense of failure dropped from her, and for now, Carrie could enjoy what was best about Melnik. Everybody knew about the typo in last week's paper. Mixed with the horror of such a thing appearing in print was the laughter, and once the shouting was done, there was the understanding that it was, indeed, just a funny mistake.

Poor Stu. But eventually even he would laugh.

Viola was mopping her eyes, and Carrie had just turned to the Jurassic Era computer. The front door screeched like a rabid parrot and slammed against the bookshelves behind it, and, in another rabid parrot imitation, Tallulah came flying into the *Bugle*, dressed in full plumage.

"Carrie, you have to help me save Melnik!"

8

"Tallulah!" Carrie jumped to her feet. She had to admit that drama queen Tallulah looked distraught even for her. Sniffing the air for smoke, Carrie wondered if even now a fire was burning down Main Street. "Save Melnik?"

"This is the fiftieth anniversary of Maxie being declared the World's Largest Field Mouse." Tallulah flailed her arms and nearly knocked her bright pink turban off her head. She grabbed for it before it could roll away. "I need a book written about it before the festival. And now that Wilkie's dead, I don't have any true founders to honor."

Maxie. Of course.

Carrie realized that she was the drama queen here, worrying about fire when it was only about that oversized rodent.

The only disaster at the moment was Tallulah's fashion sense.

"Wilkie's got two kids, Tallulah," Viola said. "Ask them."

"I already did. I've been after them for months to ride on the float, but they were both angry at their father and refused. And of course there are no other direct descendants."

The door screeched open again. Donette came in, her stomach preceding her.

Tallulah turned when the door alerted her to the newcomer. Her greedy eyes locked on Donette's baby bump. "When's that baby due?"

Donette stopped short. Her hand went to her stomach. "About two weeks."

Tallulah clapped once, loud, as if a bolt of lightning had zapped her with inspiration. "So it'll be born before the festival?"

Donette's chin wobbled, and she covered her mouth. "Yes, but Wilkie won't be around to meet the baby."

Carrie hurried past the insensitive history freak, went to Donette, and wrapped an arm around her. "I'm so sorry, Donette. I'm praying for you."

"Don't bother." Donette jerked away from Carrie.

"You and your baby need a church family, Donette." Carrie hated to see the hardness in Donette's eyes. But girls Donette's age didn't go for guys like Wilkie if they didn't have lives that made them hard. "More than ever with Wilkie gone."

"No, we don't. We have each other." Donette's voice broke. "I'm going to love him enough for Wilkie and me both."

"We can help you. We can—"

"Him? You know it's a boy?" Tallulah raised her hands in triumph. "The name will survive."

"Wilkie's got two kids." Viola exchanged a glance with Carrie. "One of them is Kevin, a son. The name is already going to survive. Refusing to ride on the float isn't the same as not existing, Tallulah. Don't you think you're being a little thoughtless?"

Remembering the fight between Donette and Rosie and Donette's claws, Carrie didn't think bringing up Wilkie's other kids was a good idea. She didn't want to have to call the chief to pull Donette off Viola.

Carrie rested a hand on Donette's trembling shoulder. "Finding out about God would be the best thing you could do for this baby. You'd never be alone if you had God in your life."

Donette scowled at Carrie and then tried to burn Viola to the ground with her tear-filled eyes. "I'd be proud to have my baby on the float, Tallulah. Thank you for asking."

Carrie sighed, determined to try again with Donette. But she wasn't ready to hear it now. *Please, God, give me the right words at the right time.*

"You can ride right there on Maxie's shoulders." Tallulah framed her fingers into an open-topped square as if she were a director, laying out a scene before the cameras rolled.

"You know the float is going to be a giant replica of Maxie, right?" Carrie shuddered as she told Donette. Carrie wasn't the only person in the world with a mouse phobia. "A realistic replica. You're riding a room-sized rat."

"Maxie—is—not—a—*rat*!" Tallulah's voice went so "*Exorcist*," Carrie watched closely to see if her head would spin around. "He is absolutely, unequivocally, fully tested and certified to be of the genus *Peromyscus*. Field mouse!"

Tallulah spoke Latin. How was Carrie supposed to respond to that? *E pluribus insane-um?*

Besides, Carrie knew Maxie's scientific classification as well as any Melnikian. Animalia; Chordate; Vertebrata; Mammalia; Rodentia; Sciurognathi; Cricetidae; Sigmondontinea; Peromyscus. She'd had to learn it to pass the fourth grade.

"Rat jokes could ruin us. If Maxie is a rat, then he's not so big anymore, is he? He's not important. Melnik isn't important. *I'm not important.*" Both fists in the air, Tallulah was one sunset, a silhouetted tree, and a handful of gnawed onions away from bursting into the "As God is my witness, I'll never be hungry again" speech from *Gone with the Wind*.

"Everybody knows how you feel about mice." Tallulah jabbed an index finger at Carrie. "Just because you're afraid of a precious little animal doesn't mean. . ."

Carrie gave Tallulah a minute or two to rant. When she ran short of breath, Carrie jumped in. "So what did you mean when you said I have to save Melnik?"

Tallulah, caught off guard, actually quit yapping. For a second. She got over it fast. "I need someone to write a book on Melnik's history and get it published in time for the Maxie Mouse Golden Anniversary Festival."

"You know, Tallulah, we've always included Maxie in the *Christmas* festival in Melnik, and it's fine to play Maxie up big, but it is *Christmas*, you know. Our Savior's birth? Salvation? The virgin Mary and the little town of Bethlehem? We don't want to lose track of what's really important here."

Tallulah swelled up with indignation. Her face picked up the lovely fuchsia shade of her turban. "We've renamed it to fully take advantage of this historic occasion. The city council approved the change. It could attract state and even national media. I expect the *Melnik Bugle* to embrace the change."

Take another breath, please, Tallulah.

It wasn't to be. "This celebration could be just what we need to put Melnik on the map once and for all."

Tallulah apparently didn't need air.

"I demand that the full power of the *Bugle* be brought to bear to promote this."

Power? The *Bugle*?

"Done correctly, this could attract businesses and new residents to Melnik."

Carrie tried to figure out how she was going to put a picture of Maxie on the front page of the paper without looking at it or touching it. The phobia stuff wasn't just something she did as a hobby. It was full-time.

"This will be Melnik's finest hour. This will be the defining—"

"Tallulah!" Donette yelled. "Enough already. Carrie just started this morning. Viola and I know all about the golden anniversary. Carrie isn't going to fight you on it. I'll be glad to be in the parade. It will be a tribute to my love for Wilkie."

Viola and I? Carrie barely caught that because she was focusing on Tallulah, despite her better judgment. "You know the festival is usually held in city hall, too. A parade in December is kind of a bad idea." And wasn't Carrie just snowing on Tallulah's parade with that reminder. "It gets cold in Nebraska in December, you know."

"Macy's does a Thanksgiving Day parade in New York City every year." Tallulah wasn't going to let a little thing like reality stop her. "People just wear coats. We'll be fine."

"New York and Melnik?" Carrie rolled her eyes. She just couldn't control herself. "Is it worth pointing out the difference?"

Tallulah seemed to run on some recorded speech she'd downloaded from her brainpan to her mouth. She turned, vampire-like, on Carrie, the fresh blood in the group.

"I have compiled data on Maxie, and I want a book we can offer to the media and sell in a booth set up in the city hall for after the parade." Tallulah looked so sincere that Carrie knew that what was coming next was a lie.

"The reason I was so interested in your great-grandma's old papers is because I believe there are photos of the original ceremony when Maxie was first placed in Maxie Memorial Hall."

"Where?" Carrie, Viola, and Donette all said it at the same time.

Tallulah beamed and pointed at the building straight across the street from the *Bugle*. "I've approached the city council to officially rename city hall as Maxie Memorial Hall, since it's housing Maxie's shrine. Isn't that nice?"

The shrine was a cheap, rectangular fishbowl. Carrie didn't mention that fact.

"Going back to the first part of that, what you really want is my permission to snoop through all my great-grandma's papers, right?" Carrie had worked in the city too long. She'd forgotten that straight-talking and Melnik just didn't mix.

"Well, of all things, Miss Big City Newspaperwoman. I was *not* asking for that."

Another lie. "That's good, because the answer would be no."

Tallulah's jaw tightened perceptibly.

"And there's no way to get a book written and published that fast. Maybe we can print up something here at the *Bugle*. Pamphlets or something." Pamphlets with mouse pictures prominently featured. Carrie closed her eyes in dread.

"Pamphlets? I want a book! Hardcover. We'll sell them to Melnik tourists."

Melnik. . .tourists? Those were words that could not coexist in a sentence. The woman wanted something out of Great-Grandma's house, and Carrie needed to find out what. It might genuinely be about Maxie, but it might also be related to Great-Grandma's and Wilkie's deaths. But how in heaven's name could Tallulah be involved in either death? The woman was obsessed with Maxie, but she wasn't a killer.

"Tallulah, bring me whatever research you have. I'll do my best to put it into some form for a book. I'll also promise to search Great-Grandma Bea's house. I—"

"Now, Carrie, I don't mind—"

Carrie raised her hand like a cop stopping oncoming traffic. Tallulah closed her mouth.

Hand signals. I'll have to remember that.

"I said I'd do it."

The rabid parrot's eyes narrowed until Carrie feared she might be pecked to death. Tallulah crossed her arms in a huff, emphasizing a generous belly the caftan covered nicely. Dora ought to look into a caftan.

"If I find papers that have any historical significance, I'll make sure to go over them with you. That's the best offer you're going to get. I don't want anyone taking important papers out of *my* house without me knowing about them." Carrie thought that was the first time she'd called the house hers. She kind of liked the sound of it. She had a house. A mouse-infested, filthy, falling-down house, true. But a house nonetheless.

Tallulah opened her pink-painted lips to complain.

The door screeched and Clara Wickersham came in, dragging her rolling cart. Staring at her feet, Clara mumbled, her words barely audible, and what was audible didn't make a lot of sense. But everybody knew that's just how Clara was, and it was no big deal.

"Anybodywantapie? NoonegoeshungryinMelnik. NotwhileClaraWickersham hasbreathinherbody."

"I'll take one." Carrie interrupted when Clara's singsong ranting broke off so the woman could suck a breath into her body. Carrie's offer distracted the poor woman from the mumbling story, the same story she repeated over and over again to her shoes. Or maybe it wasn't the same story. Carrie didn't listen, so she couldn't be sure.

Everybody knew better than to actually eat Clara's pies, but Viola, Tallulah, and even Donette piped up. "I'll take one."

They had to be sold for Clara to pay her bill at the grocery store, which was sky-high because of all the baking she did. Dreadful, dangerous baking. It was every Melnikite's duty to buy a pie.

Clara began pulling pies out of her cart. They were all squashed because she stacked them five deep. "Thistownwouldn'tsurvive. NotifIdidn'tseetothings."

Carrie clenched her teeth at the sucking sound made as Clara pried the pies apart.

She faithfully produced twenty-five pies for the town of Melnik every Monday. Her family, five grown children, took turns staying with her on the weekends, often luring her into visits at their homes scattered across the state. And the town did its best to pull her into activities, to save themselves from buying pies every day. The routine had settled into a Monday bake sale.

"Wildcatsrunninglooseeatingpieleftandright."

Her children didn't want her locked up. Clara had been like this for the last twenty years, so she obviously had the skills to survive. And the citizens of Melnik helped by pulling together, buying her pies, and then discreetly disposing of them.

"I'm not going to let some oversized mouse get the upper hand." Clara handed out a green bean pie to Viola.

Viola waited until Clara turned her back and then lifted a tater tot up off the top of the pie for the others to see.

Turning back to her metal cart, a low mesh basket on wheels, Clara continued her sanity-challenged food distribution and storytelling.

"NotwhileIhavebreathinmybodyohno. IseewhatIsee. Ido."

Carrie fought down a grimace when Clara gave her a hamburger meringue pie. It had been underneath Viola's and Donette's, so it really looked bad.

"It'sthatMaxieandhisCommunistfriends. They'rebehindallthetrouble. And don'tthinkIdon'tknowit."

Taking the pie, Carrie felt the pinch of handing over her last five dollars in cash. Tallulah gamely accepted something that smelled like it might be mostly lard, looking like she'd be willing to start in on the argument with Carrie as soon as Clara left.

"NowaythatGundersonboygetsapie. Noway. Nohow. Giantmice. Whoever-heardofsuchathing?"

Carrie caught enough of that to agree with Clara, but she didn't say so, afraid the crazed but harmless—well, harmless if you didn't count her cooking—woman would linger.

From here, Clara would go across the street to Jansson's Café. Olga Jansson was the best cook in town. One cup of Olga's coffee and you were hers for life. She was the best cook in town, but she'd still buy one pie, give Clara a slice of safe pie along with a cup of coffee, and then shoo her on her way before quietly discarding the ghastly baked offering.

Everybody knew the drill.

"Somepeoplethinktheyownthistown. I'vegottotakecharge."

Clara talked her way out the door.

"We'renotsafeinourownbeds. Communists everywhere."

Carrie didn't even consider discussing the fall of the Berlin Wall with Clara. The Communists weren't really that much of a threat anymore.

Carrie, holding the door for Clara, saw Marlys Piperson duck behind a minivan parked outside, pulling Jeffie into a crouch beside her until Clara moved on. Marlys obviously wasn't in the mood to buy a pie. It was the only time Carrie had ever seen Jeffie obey anyone. Carrie had personally signed a petition asking Boys Town to drop their age limit and let the child in.

Marlys, the town's postmistress, then headed for the *Bugle* and, bless her heart, thwarted Tallulah's nagging because she wanted to gossip about Edith Eskilson misspelling her husband's name.

Tallulah apparently got sick of waiting to rant some more and went on her melodramatic way. Marlys ran out of steam and went off with Jeffie in tow to gossip about Edith elsewhere.

Donette settled into her chair, and the other shoe dropped for Carrie.

Viola and I? Donette clearly included herself in the *Bugle* staff.

"Uh, do you work here?" Carrie asked Donette.

"Sure. I just started a couple of weeks ago."

"Oh, sorry. I didn't know. Aren't you supposed to be in school?"

"I quit. My name's in the paper every week. Everybody knows I work here."

Everybody knows. Carrie sighed. They should just go ahead and carve that right into the WELCOME TO MELNIK sign out by the Highway 77 turnoff onto Main Street. Right next to the five-foot-tall painting of Maxie—which, Carrie had long believed, did more to scare people away from Melnik than to lure them in.

"Sorry. I never read the masthead."

Donette frowned. "The what?"

"The what?" Viola asked.

Something not everybody knows. "That's the list of names and job titles of those responsible for producing a publication: editors, writers, designers, art directors, sales representatives, publishers, lawyers, and support staff. It usually runs someplace in the first few pages."

"Oh, we've got that." Viola turned back to her typewriter. "I just never had a name for it before. Guess you learned that in newspaper college, huh?"

Journalism school. Carrie was too tired to define yet another term. "That's right."

"Well, knowing what it's called won't help you get the paper out." With those words of wisdom, Donette began clicking away on her keyboard.

And wasn't that just the truth. All the "newspaper college" in the world wasn't going to help her figure out how to work this antiquated piece of junk. Bill Gates would probably be horrified if he knew this old computer was still in use. She sighed, wondering when she would find out the computers had to be stoked with coal. She might as well put her name on the masthead: Stupid Person.

Carrie fought with the balky computer mouse and the Jurassic Era machinery, rehearsing a "You need to go back to school" speech for Donette.

As she typed, Carrie planned how to deal with the news of Wilkie's death in the paper. Poor, dumb Wilkie, the serial statutory rapist. First his wife, now Donette. Had there been others?

She had to make the article show some respect. His family deserved that even if he didn't. Some in town would think that death was an inappropriate topic for the *Bugle*. There was a tendency to avoid anything resembling news in Melnik's fourth estate. But Carrie was determined to print the truth. And she was going to kick over rocks until something crawled out that told her what happened to Wilkie and Great-Grandma Bea.

C arrie wrestled with her computer as Viola and Donette whipped out copy. They were living proof it was possible to master the system, so she clung to hope.

Viola announced that she was taking a lunch break.

"Can I go with you?" Donette asked in a shaky voice.

"Sure, I'll buy you and that baby lunch."

"Thanks, but you don't need to do that."

That was most likely not true.

They both turned to Carrie.

"I think I'll keep typing." Carrie wanted time alone to work on the Wilkie story.

"Take a break sometime." Viola slipped on her light blue cardigan. "This place'll make you nuts if you don't get out of here for a while."

Too late. Carrie smiled. "Okay."

Donette followed Viola out, and then the door swung back open and Carrie heard Donette call out, "I'll be over to the diner in a minute."

"Uh, what you said earlier?" she asked Carrie.

Carrie tried to think of all she'd said earlier, most of it insulting to Donette, Wilkie, Tallulah, and, last—but certainly not least—Maxie Mouse.

"About not being alone if I had faith in God?"

Carrie's stomach twisted as she realized Donette wanted to know more about God. *Give me wisdom, Lord.*

"Yes?"

"What's that mean? How is God with me? I don't get it."

Carrie rose from her chair and circled the desk, making her way to Donette's side, praying every step. "It's hard to explain what it feels like to have God in your life unless you've experienced it." Carrie settled onto a corner of Viola's desk. "But He's with me all the time, Donette. Someone to lead me, Someone to talk to. You're not alone if you have Him."

Donette rested both hands on top of her stomach. "I get so lonely sometimes. Mom's gone with her boyfriend most of the time. Dad's long gone. Wilkie. . . having him in my life was so much better than being alone."

Carrie wasn't sure how plainly to speak. Donette was so defensive about her relationship with Wilkie. "But he left you, too, didn't he?"

Donette bristled. "He didn't mean to. He loved me!"

"But that's the thing about love between people. Maybe Wilkie would have left Rosie and married you."

"He would have!" Donette backed toward the door and reached for the knob.

"But losing someone you love can happen to anyone. When you put your faith in Jesus, He never leaves. That's what makes it so wonderful. God has offered this gift to everyone. All you have to do is reach out and take it."

Donette stared at Carrie for a long, quiet moment. At last she nodded. "I know I need something. I want my baby to grow up and amount to something. I want a better life for him than the one I've had, and now he won't have a father, just like me."

"He can have a heavenly Father, Donette. That gives a baby a really good start in life."

"I want to change. I know I shouldn't have been with a married man. But he loved me, and he was so unhappy with Rosie. Even Shayla hated Wilkie. He couldn't get his own daughter to love him. Wilkie and I needed each other." Donette pulled the door open. Carrie stood and took a step toward her, not wanting to let her go when she seemed so open to God.

Donette held her hand up. "Stop for now, please. Let me think about what you've said. Maybe. . .maybe I'll go to church with you Sunday."

Carrie wanted to grab Donette and hold her until the girl had made a real commitment, but no one could be forced into believing in God. It was a choice Donette had to make for herself. Carrie nodded. "I'd be glad to talk with you more anytime you want."

"Thanks." Donette left, shutting the squeaking door behind her.

Carrie prayed as she returned to her desk. She talked to God a long time before she went back to work. The prayers and Donette's reaching out renewed Carrie's spirit enough that she could treat Wilkie's death with respect but also with honesty. She decided to keep the article to herself until the last minute, knowing that whatever she wrote would cause trouble.

As she clicked away, polishing and revising the story, she heard a soft *thunk* and glanced sideways. A door behind her, one she had assumed was a closet, rattled on its hinges as if shaken by the wind. Wind? In a closet?

She printed out her Wilkie article, walking around her desk to get the story as it rolled out of the massive, decade-old machine. She took it to her desk and settled a stack of books on top of it so no one would notice it and snoop.

The closet door thumped again. As she faced the closet, imagining mice big enough to shake a door. . .her stomach growled, reminding her that she'd missed breakfast and couldn't afford lunch.

Another thud in the closet stopped her hunger pangs. She was busy working up the nerve to touch the knob when the usual murderous scream came from the front door's hinges. Carrie turned to see Nick.

He gave her one quick nod before he began studying the source of the noise. "This is awful. We've got to fix this door."

We? Carrie bit her tongue. Maybe efficient, order-loving Nick would fix the door because it offended his sense of decency to exist in the same town with those rusty hinges. With luck, he'd be done before she told him this was another job that offered no hope of pay.

Nick crouched down, vanishing behind Viola's desk. Honesty overcame avarice. "I don't have to look at the *Bugle* accounts to know we can't afford you. This place runs on a shoestring."

Nick stretched his neck so he could smile at her. "A badly frayed shoestring." He turned away. Swinging the door back and forth, he listened to the squeak as if he were a doctor with stethoscope in hand.

"Don't worry about it. It's on the house. Give me ten minutes, an oil can, and a smoothing plane, and I can minimize the noise problem and save a lot of wear and tear on your doorjamb and hinges."

He stood and turned, apparently to fetch the oil and his tools, and then caught himself. "I didn't come in for that." He shut the door, flinching against the noise. "I heard you were working through lunch, and I came to see if you wanted a break."

Carrie didn't even ask how he knew this. She shot an arrow prayer to God for her finances, because she wasn't going to let Nick pay. "I've got plenty to do here, but I'm hungry. I'd be delighted to take a break."

Nick smiled again and lifted up a white paper sack. "I've got subs from the Mini-Mart." The corners of his eyes crinkled in a way that told Carrie he smiled a lot.

Well, maybe she'd let him pay this once. She headed toward Nick and free food. "Did you find any mice?"

Nick's smile faded.

"Nick, what happened?" Dread scampered mouselike up her spine.

"I've considered all the ramifications." His eyes leveled on her like he was a gunslinger. "I've decided not to tell you."

Carrie felt her hand creeping toward the buttons on the collar of her knit shirt. "Why's that?"

"I told you I worked a lot with math, logic, analysis, right?"

"Yeah, on the skyscrapers in Chicago. What does that have to do with my mice?"

"I've analyzed the situation and concluded that the most effective way to handle it is to refuse to discuss it with you. Think about it logically. If I found a lot of mice, that would be bad, right?"

Carrie inhaled long and slow and crept backward a step. "You found a lot of mice? How many? What if—"

"I didn't say that." Nick raised his hands as if he were trying to keep a maniac calm.

Carrie could almost hear him thinking: *"Step away from the detonator. No one has to get hurt here today, ma'am."*

"If I found *no* mice in your traps, then that would be *really* bad, right?"

Carrie quit backing up. She advanced on Nick and caught two fistfuls of his neatly pressed logo shirt. "You didn't find any? You know there are mice. That means they're all still in there. That means—"

"I didn't say I didn't get any, now, did I?" Nick gave her a pathetic failure of a reassuring smile. "And if I say I got a few, well, you'd know that's not all, so you'd—"

Carrie buried her face in her hands. "That house is still full of mice. No way there were only a few. I can't—"

"And that"—she felt Nick pat her on the shoulder gingerly, like he was afraid to make any sudden moves—"is why I'm not going to talk to you about mice. Because nothing I say will be useful. Right?"

Lifting her face, Carrie grabbed his shirt again and twisted the fabric tight to his neck. "Tell me!"

"So forget about the mice." Nick spoke through his tightly squeezed throat. He put his hands on hers gently, like a caress, but he was really trying to save his miserable life. The jerk. She had to know.

"I can't!" She shook him.

"I've dealt with them for today."

Carrie felt light-headed. How wonderful to have someone to deal with the mice.

"And I'll deal with them tonight before you get home and again tomorrow after you leave for work and every day until there aren't any mice anymore. Not to say there are any, but, well, just forget about them. They're not your worry. I will assume complete responsibility for your mice."

"You will?" Carrie thought she heard music, maybe an angel playing a harp. Maybe a choir singing the "Hallelujah Chorus."

"If you see one, call me, any time of the day or night. I'll come and protect you. I'll even get a whip and chair in case there are any Maxie descendants in the mansion."

"You mean you found oversized mice?" She didn't mean to strangle him, but with a phobia, sometimes these things just happened.

"I did not say that." He used two fingers to gently raise her chin. "I said I'm in charge of the mice. Okay?"

Carrie almost threw her arms around his neck, she was so grateful. Still, a morbid part of her couldn't bear to be kept in the dark. "Tell me! How many did you find?"

"No. Leave them to me. Please?" Nick raised and lowered her chin a couple of times as if forcing her to nod in agreement, and somehow, probably because she was a lunatic, she felt like she did agree.

"Okay."

"Good girl."

"Thank you."

"You're welcome."

"If only I don't see them. I'm pretty good at living in denial if they just stay inside the walls. You can't believe the extent to which a human being can lie to herself."

Nick smiled more generously. "And I've thought about it, and being afraid of mice isn't a sin."

"Is, too." She'd thought about it a lot more than he had.

"Is not. God loves you, and He made you just the way you are. I've decided that you're so close to perfect, God had to give you this one little quirk to make it so the rest of us won't spend our lives feeling inferior."

Carrie went all melty inside. "Wow." To combat becoming a puddle at his feet, she teased him. "Great line."

But it was such a sweet thing to say—she knew that the extent to which she was charmed sounded in her voice.

Nick caressed her chin with his thumb. "It *is* a great line. I've been working on it all morning." He smiled. "I thought it came out okay." His thumb stopped. "So you don't have a phobia. You have a gift. Embrace it and respect it."

"You really are my hero." A soft, tender part of Carrie's heart got a little softer as she looked into Nick's kind eyes and clung to his poor shirt. She already knew he hated wrinkles, but he didn't make her let go. Their gazes locked. The moment stretched.

Nick glanced down near her lips—maybe it was his thumb he was looking at. Then he seemed closer and sweeter. "Carrie, would you like to—"

The door smashed open. Carrie jumped away from Nick but without letting go, so she dragged him back a few feet from the door.

Shayla Melnik stumbled as she came into the *Bugle* office. She caught herself and looked around, wild-eyed, until she found Carrie. She shoved herself off the door and knocked past Nick as a sob wrenched from her throat.

Carrie kept one hand on Nick's shirt, afraid to take her eyes off the distraught girl.

Nick shifted closer. Carrie felt safe just knowing he was there.

Red blotches and swollen eyes told Carrie that Shayla's tears had been flowing for a long time. Last night the girl had been furious. Now grief had finally hit.

"I've come because I need help." Shayla hurled herself into Carrie's arms, knocking her a step away from Nick, tearing Carrie's hand loose from the mooring to her hero. But Nick was here. Nick met Carrie's eyes over Shayla's heaving shoulder. Carrie arched her brows and, feeling like she had little choice, wrapped her arms around Shayla.

Between broken sobs, the girl said into Carrie's neck, "I need you to save me."

"Uh. . ." Carrie's mind went blank. "Okay."

Nick shook his head frantically. "Okay" might be a bad thing to say, but Carrie didn't try to get away. Shayla's grip clearly said that would be a waste of time.

Nick looked outside the door, as if he expected someone to be pursuing Shayla. He closed the door, jerking his shoulders as if the squeak gave him an electric shock.

"Save you from what, Shayla?" Nick asked the obvious question.

"Save me from going to jail."

"Why would you have to go to jail?" Carrie's heart turned over for the young girl, so distraught at losing her father. A man she obviously had just realized she cherished.

"Because I killed my low-life, scum-sucking, dirtbag of a father."

10

Breath whooshed out of Nick's lungs. He watched Carrie stagger and ram into the wall as if she'd taken a hit. Shayla clung like a scared house cat.

Carrie widened her eyes at Nick, silently asking what to do.

He wanted to intervene and put himself between Carrie and Shayla. He'd offered to do it for mice. He'd better be doing it for a murderer. He held back, giving Carrie a reassuring nod that he was here if she needed a rescuer. He lifted the phone and gestured at the keypad.

Carrie shook her head.

Violent sobs shook Shayla; then she released her death grip on Carrie's neck and sank to her knees as if she were begging. "Everybody knows you're really smart. You solved a bunch of crimes in Omaha, right?"

Carrie shook her head. "I worked the police beat. Not the same thing. Although I did some investigative reporting. Not successful at it, really."

Nick caught Carrie's muttered protest, but Shayla didn't. He'd heard Carrie had solved crimes, too. Everybody knew what a great investigative reporter she was. Then why did she quit? What did she mean by "Not successful at it, really"?

Just because you inherit a house doesn't mean you have to live in it. Nick didn't like unsolved puzzles. He wanted things in balance, like a correctly completed algebraic equation. And this didn't balance. Why would Carrie give up her dream job? Then he remembered that she was leaving again—maybe not right now, but that was her goal. She couldn't have been clearer Friday night in the Dead Zone.

"You can help me. I didn't plan to do it. Well, I did, but I didn't mean to do it. Well, I did mean to, but not ahead of time. But, well, a little bit ahead of time. But not. . ."

"Shayla!" Carrie cut off Shayla's ranting.

Shayla looked up from the floor and seemed to get a grip on herself.

"Get up." Nick stepped closer, moving slowly, trying not to set the poor kid off again. He reached down. "Tell us what happened, and we'll help you."

Shayla looked over her shoulder through stringy, dishwater blond hair stuck to her tear-soaked face. "Where'd you come from? Now I've confessed to you. Now everybody will know."

"I won't tell." That, Nick realized immediately, was a stupid thing to say. Not telling was aiding and abetting. Accessory after the fact and. . .what else? He'd spent a semester studying law. He remembered some basics.

The whites of Shayla's blue eyes were bloodshot like a road map. Her shoulders trembled with another hopeless sob.

"Well, I will." Carrie pulled Shayla's attention back.

"No!"

Nick's muscles tensed as he prepared to pull the girl off Carrie.

"Yes. You can't keep this to yourself. We'll talk it through, and then you and I will go see Junior."

"He's a sick, stupid jerk." Shayla howled to humble Grizzly.

Nick stepped closer. "Junior's not so bad."

"I meant my dad!"

Nick decided to quit talking.

"He got my best friend pregnant. I hated him. I shouldn't have to go to jail. Someone needed to do something about him before he hurt anyone else!"

All the starch went out of Shayla. "But I can't quit thinking about pouring that antifreeze in his beer can." Shayla looked up. "He was already so drunk, the big perverted dope didn't even realize he was drinking it."

Nick came around beside Carrie so Shayla could see him and not be startled again. She didn't seem to be able to keep a thought in her head—except for the one about killing her dad.

Carrie slid an arm around Shayla and supported the poor little murderess while she stood.

Nick put a hand under one of Shayla's arms. They steered her around Viola's desk and eased her into the wheeled chair behind it.

Carrie knelt in front of Shayla. "Okay, start at the beginning."

"There's nothing to tell. I hated him. I poisoned him."

Carrie tilted Shayla's chin so their eyes met. "Why?"

"Donette was pregnant, but I didn't know my dad was the father. I caught them together, and Donette laughed. She told me they were in love."

"When was this?" Nick inserted quietly, hoping he wouldn't stop Shayla from talking.

"Tuesday night. The night I killed him. Dad had—he had. . .he said my cat, MacGyver, was going to have kittens, and he threatened to poison her. He said he was going to put antifreeze in MacGyver's food and she'd die before we had six more cats eating us out of house and home. I was scared to death because the cat left footprints all over Dad's pickup that morning. Like that stupid pickup wasn't a piece of junk! Dad was so mad, I thought he'd kill MacGyver with his bare hands. He ended up hitting me when I tried to stop him."

Shayla rubbed her hand over her face as if remembering the pain.

Nick saw the faded yellow of an old bruise at her temple.

"Dad had a bottle of antifreeze when he got home that night, and he said the cat was going to die. I started yelling, and when he started in on me again, I ran out, hoping to find MacGyver and take her to Donette to protect her until Dad calmed down."

"I couldn't find the cat for a while. When I finally did, I went to Donette's mom's house—she still lives with her mom—and caught her and Dad. . .together. He ran out the back door, but I saw him. Donette just laughed and told me that the baby she was expecting was Dad's." Shayla ran both hands through her hair, distraught, staring at the floor as if a crystal ball was unfolding the events of last Tuesday.

Shayla looked up from the floor, her face pale except for vivid circles of violent red high on her cheeks. "Donette spent the night with me a lot. I thought she was my friend."

Nick's heart ached for the devastated young girl.

"I took MacGyver to the park and let her go. I knew she'd come home, but I needed a few minutes alone with Dad first. By the time I got back, he was back home, and he'd finished off a six-pack and was halfway through another one. Just like always. He didn't even act like anything had happened. Maybe he thought I hadn't seen him. He hollered at me to get him a beer the second I stepped in the door, and. . .I don't know. . .him and Donette. . . MacGyver. . . He slaps me and Mom around every time he's drunk. He grows marijuana in the basement and sells it to little kids. I saw that gallon of antifreeze sitting right by the refrigerator. I just snapped! I cracked open his beer, swallowed most of it, and then filled the can with the antifreeze and gave it to him. He was so drunk, probably on some drugs, too, that he'd have swallowed sand if it had poured out of that can. He drained it and then finished off two more and left. I never saw him again."

Shayla threw herself back into Carrie's arms.

Nick sighed. Well, the crime was solved, but it was a terrible shame.

Carrie held the weeping girl, rubbing her back. Nick stepped close and gingerly rested one hand on Shayla's shoulder, hoping that would help calm the poor kid. As he continued his awkward attempt to comfort the little homicidal maniac, the door in the far wall shook. A draft—something else to repair in this historic old building. As the sobbing died, Carrie gripped Shayla's shoulders and pushed, lifting the girl away from her until their eyes met.

"We need to tell the chief. You're a minor; this is a spontaneous act, not premeditated—uh, not premeditated much. We'll fix it." Carrie nodded.

Shayla nodded her head while she sniffled.

"Let's go." Carrie slung her arm around Shayla, and Nick led them outside.

The inner door shuddered again, and Nick glanced over his shoulder. He knew the layout of these old Main Street buildings enough to realize that the door didn't lead to the alley. Instead, it opened into a big, vacant room that had once been a mechanic's workshop. He'd need to check with Sven Gunderson, who had inherited most of Main Street when his father died, and make sure there weren't broken doors or windows that allowed weather to further damage the beautiful old wreck of a building.

Nick ushered Carrie and Shayla through the door of the cop shop, just a half block down the street from the *Bugle*. He'd been in Melnik long enough to know that everybody who saw them would start talking and filling in blanks. Those guesses would be passed on as pure facts. Any questions would be answered by leaps in logic that would have humbled an Olympic pole-vaulter. Normally, that made for some seriously twisted gossip. Unfortunately, this time, the wildest thing they could guess at would be very close to the truth.

Junior looked up from his computer, where Nick suspected he was playing solitaire. Why not? There was no crime in Melnik.

"I killed my father." Shayla broke into sobs again.

Almost no crime.

Junior's eyes widened. He rose from his desk.

"She didn't kill him," Nick said quietly.

Carrie turned to him. "Yes, she did."

"Yes, I did," Shayla wailed between sobs, her face buried in her hands and her whole body shuddering.

"It took me a minute to think of this, but it wasn't enough." Nick quickly explained to Junior about Shayla's confession. "I've heard enough about antifreeze poisoning to make me doubt that a beer can full of it would kill a man."

Junior beetled his unibrow. "Wilkie was drinking heavy. Alcohol can make poison react differently."

Nick exchanged a doubtful look with Carrie, and he was honored by the quick nod of her head and the trust he saw in her eyes. Shayla was innocent, probably.

Shayla's whole body had straightened and her tears had subsided, her terror replaced by hope. "You mean I didn't kill him? I might be innocent?"

"Probably." Junior shook his head. "But shame on you for trying to kill your dad, Shayla, honey."

"Shame on you"—Shayla's punishment for premeditated murder. Not a bad system if you were a murderer. For every potential murder victim, it was kind of scary.

"Well, okay." Shayla started backing toward the door. "Guess I'll go now. I'm on my lunch break from school. If I hurry, I won't even be late for fifth period."

"Hold on just a minute." Junior looked torn. Tardiness? Homicide? What was an overworked policeman to do? "You're not going anywhere except to jail,

Shayla. We're not going to just take Nick's word. We have to have that autopsy report back first and see the cause of death." He pointed a beefy index finger at the chair directly in front of his desk in the tiny office. "And even if it turns out that you didn't kill him, he made you killin' mad."

"I don't know—"

"You may know others he's made that mad. You have information—without knowin' it—that could turn up a killer." He jabbed his finger at the chair again. "Sit!"

She did. Then Carrie sat in the chair next to her. Junior grabbed a folding chair leaning against the wall beside his desk. Nick took it and placed it next to Carrie's chair. All three of them sat like well-trained basset hounds. Very law abiding, Melnikites, even the murderers.

Nick noted how tiny and bare the office was—just room for a small metal desk painted we-have-no-imagination gray; a beige, cloth-upholstered rolling desk chair for Junior; and the two chairs in front for Hal and Steve. In fact, if they didn't position the two chairs correctly, they'd block the door to the outside. Nothing on the wall but a couple of pieces of printer paper. Both looked like they had a week's worth of work schedules on them. There was also a wooden and brass plaque that said OUTSTANDING COMMUNITY SERVICE, with Junior's name, Roland Hammerstad, engraved below. In a town where everybody knew everything, Nick realized he'd never heard Junior's real name before. Oh, the older folks probably knew Junior's father and, using "Junior" as a clue, knew Junior's name. But anyway, according to the plaque, Roland Hammerstad was a man of honors in a teeny office.

Of course, why would there be a bigger office? There wasn't any crime in Melnik.

"I wanted him dead because he got my friend pregnant. Donette's a jerk, but she's still in high school, which makes my dad a child-molesting pervert. And he cheated on my mom, and he hits me and my brother and my mom, and he spent every night drunk, and there's that weed growing in the basement."

Almost no crime.

Junior cocked his head at her. "Now, first, are you eighteen? Because if you're not, we need to get your mom in here. I can't question a minor without a parent or guardian present."

Shayla nodded her head frantically. "I'm eighteen." Then she shook it, just as frantically. "But if I didn't kill him, we don't need to let Mom know."

Junior rubbed his chin. "Honey, you're not walking away from this. You've confessed to attempted murder, and I'm going to arrest you. Maybe Nick's right and your poisoned beer didn't kill your dad. But we can't be sure without talking to the coroner. For now, your confession is enough for an arrest. We'll have to talk to a judge before you can make bail, and out here that's gonna take at least overnight. And then you or someone is going to have to come up with bond money. It doesn't matter anyway. You know this is Melnik. No sense in even trying to keep a secret in this town."

Shayla got a mulish look on her face. "I'm moving away as soon as I graduate, and I'm never coming back."

Nick had heard Carrie say almost the same words about Melnik. Shayla and Carrie, kindred spirits—except for the antifreeze.

Junior ignored Shayla's declaration of independence. "Just tell me what you told these two."

"*Fine!* I'm already eighteen, just last month, so let's get this finished and get me locked up." Shayla retold her story, and it didn't get better.

Nick reasserted that the quantity of antifreeze made it unlikely Shayla had administered a lethal dose.

Shayla was considerably less devastated by the time the interview was over.

Suddenly the police station door slammed open and Rosie Melnik charged into the room, literally breathing fire.

Nick could actually feel her rage heating the room. She took a long drag on her cigarette, and it lit up bright. She dragged it out of her mouth, tossed it on the floor, and left it to smolder. Nick fought down the urge to grab it, extinguish it, and dispose of it properly.

"You killed your own *father*?"

Shayla rose from her chair and backed toward Junior's desk. "Mom, I—"

"Shut up!" Rosie charged toward Shayla. Nick jumped in between the young girl and her enraged mother. Rosie shoved her hands into her lank hair. Her skin, sallow and pitted with acne scars, flushed a blotchy red and her teeth bared; Nick saw she was missing a couple of important ones right up front.

Junior dodged in front of Nick and grabbed Rosie's arm. "She didn't do it. Now settle down."

Rosie turned her fire on Junior. "I heard she did. I heard she confessed."

"Where did you hear that?" Carrie asked. Nick felt more than saw Carrie move to Shayla's side.

"This is Melnik. Everybody knows." Rosie's T-shirt hung on her emaciated body. She shoved Junior's shoulder as if she needed to rough *someone* up.

"No, Rosie," Carrie said. "Not everybody knows. Who told you—"

"Shayla did not kill her dad," Junior interrupted. "I don't care what you heard; it's wrong. She did break the law, though. I'm locking her up, and you'll have to call the county courthouse about arranging bail."

Rosie glared past Junior, Nick, and Carrie to Shayla. Nick shuddered at the rage.

"You can rot in jail for all I care." Rosie jabbed a finger at her daughter. "And if you do get out, don't come crawling to me looking for a roof over your head.

Just stay away from me."

Rosie whirled, wrenched the door open, and charged out of the building, slamming the door viciously.

Dead silence was broken only by Shayla's devastated sobs. Nick turned to find Carrie hugging her. He offered the girl a handkerchief.

At last Shayla swiped a hand over her face and straightened her shoulders. "She always picked him over me and Kevin. I used to try to protect her when Dad started in on her, but sometimes she'd hit me, too, like *she* was protecting *him*. Maybe jail's a better place for me now."

Jail. A better place than home. Nick sighed. It wasn't much of a jail, either, reachable through a door in Junior's office. It was actually more of a steel shed with a chain-link fence—no great security there. But most of the people who did time were sitting out traffic fines they couldn't pay, so they weren't apt to attempt escape, knowing they'd just have to come back later and sit longer.

"Your mom'll calm down. And we know you probably didn't kill your dad, so she'll figure that out pretty soon. Nice catch on the antifreeze, Nick. I've got just a few more questions, Shayla." Junior studied his faithful notebook.

"Forget it. I'm done talking." Shayla grabbed the doorknob and snarled at Junior, as if he'd done something wrong instead of her. "Is the jail unlocked?"

Junior nodded. "Wait a second. I'll come with you."

"I'll get there myself. Just stay away from me." Shayla slammed the office's side door after storming through it. A perfect imitation of her mother's exit. Nick heard the clank of the cell door as it shut.

"Nice to see she's got all her anger issues under control." Carrie stared at the door to the county jail.

"Is there another door out of there? She could have slammed the door without going in and just kept walking." Nick rubbed the back of his neck and then smoothed his hair, worried that he'd mussed it.

"I think she's smart enough to stay put."

"Let's hope she's smart enough to quit trying to kill people, instead of smart enough to get better at it." Carrie laid her hand on Nick's upper arm. "You probably saved her by knowing all that about antifreeze."

"I took a semester of animal husbandry in college when I thought I might want to be a veterinarian." Nick gave a very sweet, humble shrug. "Pets accidentally drinking antifreeze happens a lot."

<div align="center">~~~~~</div>

Carrie almost sighed out loud. It was the kind of modest shrug she expected from a hero. He was the real deal. She knew it, and unless she was mistaken earlier—before Shayla had burst in—he'd almost asked her out. Who was she kidding? He'd almost kissed her. She needed to get him alone and give him another chance.

"Anyway, Shayla couldn't have been convicted." Junior pulled an official-looking stack of papers out of his desk drawer.

"Why not?" Carrie saw the letterhead, DODGE COUNTY CORONER, and forgot about Nick. She leaned forward, hoping to read the report upside down.

"Because even if she'd given him enough, it wouldn't have had time to kick in. Antifreeze kills you slow. Something else got him long before he'd have died of poison."

"Of course." Carrie nodded. "When she first started confessing, I didn't even think of that. The coroner said that Wilkie was shot."

"He was shot." Junior kept skimming the paper that listed possible murder weapons. "But they haven't pinpointed that as the cause of death yet. How about your great-grandma's lethal skillet?"

Carrie twisted her fingers together. "I'm never going to be able to fry an egg in that thing now."

"The skillet isn't likely," Junior added. "Although it's kind of hard to say what combinations went together to finish off Wilkie. Poison, bullet, and skillet aren't the only possibilities."

"What else?" Nick asked. "Maybe I should start a spreadsheet when I get home."

"He was also smothered." Junior pointed to a spot on the paper with his beefy finger. "Again, there are doubts about that being the ultimate weapon. These results are preliminary; no tox screen yet. They don't have a thing in here about antifreeze. Who knows what all else he had in his system."

"Smothered?" Goose bumps erupted on Carrie's arms, and she began rubbing them. "I remember now. There were short, mousy gray hairs on his mouth."

Nick gave her a sympathetic look and glanced at her arms.

"That's right. The autopsy isn't finished. But it's looking like Wilkie might have been smothered." Junior gave Shayla's chair a dark scowl.

"S–s–smothered?" Carrie knew what was coming, but she couldn't deal with it.

"Yes, almost certainly smothered to death by a—"

"No!" Carrie knocked her chair over, jumping to her feet.

"—really large mouse."

11

ick heard Carrie's head crack against the glass in the door. He rushed over, to be handy in case she needed to jump into his arms.

Her eyes were so round and dilated that he could almost see into her brain. She had no color in her face. Her breathing was short and rapid. He could count her pulse by a throbbing vein in her forehead. Her white-blond hair trembled so violently, it seemed alive. But this was Carrie, the mouseophobe. She was doing pretty well.

He watched her closely as Junior stationed himself on Carrie's other side.

Nick asked him, "Are you done with us?"

"Sure." Junior sorted through the file and extended a few pages toward Carrie. "You want the part of my report I can show you? There's mice stuff in it."

Carrie's quaking hand reached past Nick. "I–I–I'll take it."

There was something illogical in being proud of someone just for picking up a form that *mentioned* a mouse, even if the mouse was a murder weapon. And Nick hated illogic.

"You must want a look at that thing really bad." Junior snickered.

Some of the color returned to Carrie's cheeks. "I know it's stupid to be afraid of mice. Okay?"

"Especially the *word* 'mouse' written on paper."

"I've just got this image, this horrible image." The paper crinkled up into a ball in Carrie's hands. "Of a huge mouse stalking Wilkie, holding him down, pressing his sharp clawed paws over his mouth." Carrie backed into the door again.

"You know, if a mouse really killed Wilkie"—Junior was torturing Carrie—deliberately in Nick's opinion—"then we've got no murderer. It's more of an animal attack, like if a bear came after you. Or if you hit a deer driving down the road and crashed and died. No crime there. Of course, there's no reason to think the mouse was big. It'd only need to be big if it attacked Wilkie while the poor guy hid in the closet or if it stuffed him in the closet afterward. And that means this new, supersized Maxie Mouse tried to cover its. . .uh, mouse tracks, you might say—which means it knew that what it was doing was wrong, so there goes its insanity defense. We have to assume. . ."

Trying to stop Junior, who was enjoying himself way too much, Nick said, "Common sense tells us that a mouse couldn't smother Wilkie, which means someone had to *use* a mouse to—"

"Eeek!" Carrie screamed and jumped.

And just like that, Nick had an armful of soft, vulnerable woman. He'd been trying to help. But now that he thought about it, using a mouse as a murder weapon might rank up there with Carrie's worst nightmares.

"Forgive me," Carrie whispered.

Nick hugged her. "You want me to take that paper? Maybe if it wasn't so close to you. . ."

It was trapped between their bodies. Carrie had her hands full clinging to Nick's neck. "No, I'll keep it."

Junior groaned and then reached for the doorknob to help Nick out. "The really weird thing is, because of the reputation of this town and the fairly strange mode of death, I've decided we need to do genetic testing on Maxie. I mean, where in this town would you go if you wanted to kill a guy and needed a mouse as a weapon?"

Carrie buried her face in Nick's shoulder with a whimper. "How about my house? It's full of mice."

Junior pulled the door open. "But they're not handy like Maxie. My gut tells me someone took Maxie out for a. . .walk." Junior covered his mouth while he chuckled.

Suddenly the smile vanished from Junior's face. He quickly but silently shoved the door closed, pushed Nick against the wall with Carrie still in his arms, flattened his back against the other side of the door, reached out, and flicked the dead bolt.

"Peoplewon'tstarveinthistownaslongasI'maroundohno."

"I already bought my pie from Crazy Clara this week. I'm not buying another one. This job doesn't pay that well, my youngest needs braces, and I'm just not doin' it!"

The doorknob rattled. "Giant-sizedmicerunningwildkillingfolks."

Carrie lifted her head off Nick's shoulder. "What did she say?"

"Shh!" Junior waved his hand at her.

Clara turned from the door, exited the building, and pulled her squeaking cart on down the sidewalk.

Junior pulled a handkerchief out of his back pocket and mopped his brow. "Nasty business, those pies."

Opening the door, Junior peeked left and right and then slipped out into the outer hallway where he could get a better view of the street.

"What did Clara say?" Carrie asked again.

"I'd be glad to keep carrying you," Nick said. "But people will see us when we walk down the street. Dora, you know. I don't mind. But maybe you'd rather walk."

Carrie nodded then relaxed her death grip on Nick's neck.

Junior returned. "Coast is clear."

"Are you done with us?" Nick set Carrie down with regret.

Junior laughed. "Except for comic relief."

Nick glared at Junior over Carrie's bowed head.

Junior held up one hand, as if vowing to quit having fun at Carrie's expense. "I've authorized the tests on Maxie. Apparently they can make an exact match even with a mouse. We'll know for sure, but it's slow. I couldn't convince them it was a priority."

Carrie buried her face in her hands. "DNA testing on a mouse? Only in Melnik."

Nick lifted Carrie's chin. "Try to stop thinking about the mouse and think about how many people had access to that glass case in front of the Historical Society Museum. If we pinpoint Maxie as the, uh. . ." Nick almost said *culprit*, opened his mouth to say *murder weapon*, then finally settled on, ". . .you know. . . we can narrow the list of suspects. It's a great lead. Way better than if it turns out that someone killed Wilkie by whacking him with that frying pan."

"Except someone *did* whack him with the frying pan, despite whatever. . . *method* finally did him in." More color returned to Carrie's face.

Nick could almost feel her spine stiffening.

"So narrow the list to whoever had access to the museum and Maxie's case, throw in motive, and the crime is solved."

"Shayla obviously had one." Carrie held up one finger. "And Donette and Rosie and Kevin."

"Not a long list." Nick smiled, hoping to encourage her and distract her from mice at the same time. "It should be easy. This is a sweet little town. How many potential murderers can there be?"

⸻

Carrie had a list as long as her arm by the end of the day. Everyone in town hated Wilkie Melnik, mostly for very good reasons.

Life couldn't get much more interesting—for Melnik. As for anywhere else on the planet—well, don't ask.

And then, back at the office, she met her new boss.

The door gave a screech worthy of a haunted house, and a wizened old man came in. No one Carrie had ever seen before, and she'd seen everybody.

"You're my editor, right?" The man, tall and gaunt, bent with age, balding and gray-haired, his face plowed deep with grouch wrinkles, advanced on her desk with surprising speed.

"I'm Carrie Evans, and you are. . . ?"

NOSY IN NEBRASKA

"Sven Gunderson." The man slammed his fist on Carrie's desk.

Carrie jumped to her feet, startled but not really afraid. She could take him. Of course, he seemed to be furious, so he had rage on his side.

Gunderson wore a threadbare brown suit that hadn't been in fashion. . . well. . .ever. Carrie knew he was rich. Everyone knew the Gundersons were the wealthiest people in Melnik. Like slumlords, the family had bought up most of Main Street three generations ago and held on tight, letting buildings fall into disrepair and charging exorbitant rent. People had tried to buy lots and backed off due to sticker shock.

No cabal of earnest citizens had been able to disabuse the Gundersons of their strange notion that in the great mysterious "someday," downtown Melnik would be worth a fortune. Meanwhile, Main Street buildings deteriorated and no new businesses took on the onerous monthly lease rates.

"I own the *Bugle*, and I'm going to make some changes around here. I'm sick of the way my father ran this newspaper."

Carrie stiffened, wondering if she was going to be fired before the end of her first day of work. That was fast even for her. And since when had Sven's father ever "run" the newspaper? He'd collected rent and left it to succeed or fail on its own.

"Mr. Gunderson, I just started this morning." She went for a little reverse psychology. "I absolutely understand if you want to bring in your own editor."

"I'm not here to fire you. I'm here to tell you what's what." Sven bent vulture-like over Carrie, across the desk. His nose even looked a little like a beak. His dark, beady eyes, shining through gold-rimmed glasses, made him look like he'd feed on the dead.

"This paper is gonna change." He hammered the desk again. "Just because Melnik is small doesn't mean we can't tell the truth. I'm going to blow the lid off this town."

Carrie sincerely hoped he didn't break anything he pounded on, because she had a bad feeling about him paying to replace it.

In an effort to placate him, she said, "It just so happens that I agree with you, Mr. Gunderson. I want to write a real newspaper. Right now, I'm finishing a story on Wilkie Melnik. I don't intend to offer platitudes or whitewash the events surrounding his death." On the other hand, there was no sense in humiliating Wilkie's wife and children. Or upsetting his girlfriend, who had a bad temper and worked five feet away.

Gunderson grunted and fished a piece of paper out of his brown suit pants. "My family goes back as far as the Melniks. I consider it an injustice that this town bears the name Melnik instead of Gunderson."

Carrie didn't mention her family's deep roots. No sense in throwing gasoline on Gunderson's fire.

"Wilkie Melnik was a liar and a thief, and I want him exposed. Dying doesn't end all the wrong he's done." He slapped the paper on her desk. "I want this story in the *Bugle* this week."

Carrie had a nostalgic moment dwelling on the old "Don't speak ill of the dead" rule. Those were the days.

"I'm not going to let the truth die with Wilkie Melnik." Gunderson's fists curled.

Carrie hoped he was going to slug only her desk. "Let me print up what I've got for you to read. I'll go over your notes and add them to my story."

"I don't have time to sit here and do the work of my editor." The man had an almost deranged gleam in his eyes. "You put that information in *my* newspaper word for word or find yourself another job."

Gunderson turned and stormed out of the building, slamming the door so hard that the glass rattled. Carrie's heart pounded with fear, and her face burned with barely controlled anger.

She reached a trembling hand toward Gunderson's exposé on Wilkie, sinking down into her chair. She started to read and knew her career as a small-town journalist was over.

She crumpled the pages of half-truths and character assassination and tossed them in the trash.

Like poor dead Wilkie didn't have enough trouble. The article she'd been planning to write was tough enough. But this? Out of the question.

She'd never print such hogwash. So Gunderson would fire her Wednesday afternoon at about three, when the *Bugle* hit the stands. Two days from now.

One issue. Even for the revolving door of the *Bugle*, this had to be some kind of record. She could see it now: CARRIE—THE WORLD'S LARGEST FAILURE.

Maybe they'd stuff her and put her in a case right next to Maxie.

That's why she believed in God, to avoid something like that. Because spending eternity next to a mouse in Melnik was Carrie's very own personal definition of eternal darkness.

12

Nick squeaked the *Bugle* door open. Carrie knocked page 6 of tomorrow's paper onto the floor and shrieked. She sounded a lot like the door. She whirled around, her eyes wide, clutching her chest.

Great, scare her to death, doofus.

He'd spent Monday and today on her house repairs—and dealing with all those mice. It'd kill her if she knew.

Last night there had been another cleaning party, but tonight she'd had to work, so she would be going in that house alone. Nick had kept at the repairs, hoping to protect her from facing the mice by herself. And it had gotten later. . . and later. . .and later.

He could see the lights of the *Bugle* office from her house—if he stood at the third-floor window on his tiptoes and watched the reflection in the insurance office across the street from the paper. So he'd work awhile and then jog upstairs to check. The light at the paper just kept burning. Before jogging up and down the stairs gave him a heart attack, he broke down and went to see her.

"Sorry." He held up his hands, glad to surrender. "I saw the *Bugle* lights still on, and I thought I'd check. It's almost midnight. I was afraid something might have happened to you, like you fell into the wax machine and were now the World's Largest Pair of Red Wax Lips."

Don't mention lips, idiot.

"I can leave if. . ."

"Stay!" Carrie strode across the room. It looked to Nick as though she didn't run only because there wasn't time to pick up speed.

She wanted him.

Nick smiled. "I can help with the paper so you can get out of here, or I can fix this door."

"Come and see what I've got." Carrie reached his side and grabbed him by the sleeve of his Windbreaker. "Then the door would be great. I'd let you help with the paper, but I'm figuring it out as I go along, mostly thanks to Viola's notes. I can't imagine explaining it to you."

She sank her nails into the fabric of his jacket, and Nick had the strange sensation of being taken prisoner. The woman was definitely glad to see him.

"Okay, I think I've finally gotten it all laid out." Carrie pulled him to the first oversized sheet of paper. The front page lay slanted backward at a forty-five-degree angle on the wooden easel. Seven more stands just like it lined two sides of the little nook of the L-shaped *Bugle* office. The third side featured a flat table that lit up under white glass. The easels had sheets of paper on them about the size of one page of a newspaper. All of them were covered with newsprint and pictures.

The Melnik Bugle blazed across the top of the front page just like it did every week. Under the banner was a picture of Wilkie Melnik that looked about fifteen years old. Below Wilkie's picture, the headline read Descendant of Melnik Founder Dies.

"This was the best picture of Wilkie I could find." Carrie tapped on what looked like a blown-up picture of Wilkie taken out of a crowd scene.

Nick studied the picture. "He's got an I'm-up-to-no-good smile on his face."

"Yeah, he was born with that smile. It's a shame we don't have something a lot less honest to put in the paper." Carrie looked sideways at Nick.

He caught her glance, and they both grinned.

"So how'd the story come out?"

Carrie clenched her jaw. "I'm dreading the moment Donette reads it. I know she'll say that I am betraying her child's ancestry and denying the little tyke of any hope for a full and happy future."

"Wow. Not very nice of you."

Carrie snorted. "Viola voted for not even mentioning Wilkie's death except for a tasteful obituary. Her position was that everybody knows already anyway."

Nick leaned forward and read. Carrie leaned in by his side, going over the article again herself. She smelled great for a woman coated in wax and ink.

After several minutes, Nick straightened. "There's nothing in there to offend anybody. You didn't make reference to Wilkie's problems. You just wrote the facts."

"In Melnik, people don't like facts; they like puff pieces. They like 'Don't speak ill of the dead.' I believe Viola said those very words to me seventeen times."

Nick frowned, skimming the article again. "Where in there do you speak ill of him? You don't mention the illegitimate child with his daughter's friend. You don't mention his battered wife and children, his substance abuse problems, his time in the state penitentiary. You even leave out his threats against his daughter's cat."

"I said he was found in my great-grandma's pantry." Carrie tapped paragraph 2. "I didn't pretend he died peacefully in his sleep."

"Everybody knows where he was found. What's the harm in mentioning it?"

"What indeed?" Carrie crossed her arms. "And yet I know I'm in for trouble."

Nick noticed that her fingertips were black and there were smudges on her cheeks and her arms. She'd really dived into the paper. "So when this comes out, will Donette and Viola quit in a huff?"

"We'll see."

"Well, try to hang on to them. You might have to stay even later into the night if they quit on you. So what's left to do before you can get out of here?"

"I've got to double-check that all the ads we sold are on the pages." Carrie held up a clipboard. "Viola went over it, and I'm sure it's fine, but she said to double-check, so I will. Then I have to blue line it and I'm done."

"Blue line?"

"See those faint blue lines on the paper?" Carrie pointed at the large sheets covered in news.

"Yeah." Nick leaned close.

"I put the whole sheet on the light table." She pointed at the flat, glowing, glass-topped table. "And use those lines to make sure everything is perfectly straight."

Nick ran a finger over a square yellow Post-it Note stuck on the paper slightly below the photo of Wilkie. "What's that for?" He reached for the edge of the note.

Carrie slapped his hand. "Don't touch it!"

Nick jerked his hand back. "Why not?"

"Because it's a picture of Maxie. I can't stand to look at it."

Nick fought down the urge to laugh. He stared straight at the paper, not wanting Carrie to see him.

"Oh, just go ahead. Laugh all you want. I can't stand that awful little rodent staring at me. I had a fight on my hands there, too. Viola wanted the picture three columns wide. I refused because I didn't have a Post-it big enough. Ick. A huge close-up of a mouse on the front page? Why don't I just post a huge STAY OUT sign out by the highway? A mouse is *not* the symbol a town should adopt for itself. I'm not even going to be able to read the front page tomorrow with him on there."

Nick patted her arm. "You're very brave to give Maxie a front-page story when you hate him so much."

Carrie rolled her eyes. "I'm a ridiculous, stinking coward, but I still put him on the front page because it's the right thing to do."

Nick nodded. "That blue lining thing sounds a lot like something I did when working with blueprints. Show me what you want to do, and I'll help you."

"Really?" Carrie laid her hand on Nick's arm.

He leaned down. "Sure."

"Thanks. I know it's late. I really appreciate the help."

Nick felt his face heat up and hoped the rather dim wattage of the *Bugle*'s lighting system covered his embarrassment. "I. . .uh. . .the real reason I stopped in was because I was wondering if. . .if maybe you'd like someone to go into your house ahead of you tonight? There was still a crowd there working on Friday and you weren't home all weekend."

"Yeah, I was. I was gone a lot during the day, but I came home at night."

"Oh, I'm sorry. Were you all right?"

"All right for a lunatic. I never saw any mice."

Nick smiled. "All that cleaning must have scared them away, but tonight, well, if you don't want to go in alone. . .I could help."

Carrie's hand tightened on his bicep. The look of gratitude in her eyes almost made him lean in and kiss her. He backed away before he could do anything stupid. Or would it be smart? He almost asked her out, but the dark circles of exhaustion under her eyes stopped him. "I'll take that look as a yes and get to work."

"Thanks. You really are my hero." She smiled and lifted the front page off the easel then slid it onto the white glass of the light table. She reached for the little switch under the table and flicked it on and off to demonstrate it to Nick. The whole top of the table lit up, leaving the faint blue lines on Carrie's newspaper page clearly visible.

"See, with the light on, you can see right through the paper. Then we can make sure the stories we've waxed and stuck on are perfectly straight."

Nick edged in next to her, really close, as she showed him how to make sure each story, picture, and ad on the page was perfectly straight.

He hoped Carrie would decide that she'd like a hero around her all the time. But he kept that to himself. For now.

⁂

Carrie dropped off the *Bugle* at the post office at noon on Wednesday. The paper normally went out closer to 3:00 p.m., but they pushed extra hard this week because of Wilkie's funeral in the afternoon.

She delivered the bulk of five hundred copies to the mail, tied together in bundles of about fifty each. Then she dropped more bundles off at Jansson's Café, the Mini-Mart, and the grocery store.

She regretted being fired, but she knew it'd be coming just as soon as the newspaper hit the streets.

She'd ignored Gunderson's warning, just like she'd ignored Viola and Donette, and written Wilkie's story her way. And she'd paid tribute to the upcoming Maxie Christmas Festival, set for mid-December and now only six weeks away, without being snide but without slavering either. Which meant Tallulah would be gunning for her.

At least she'd go down in flames on her own terms.

And wouldn't that just look great carved on the brass plate by her shrine in

NOSY IN NEBRASKA

Maxie Memorial Hall. Right below the words WORLD'S BIGGEST FAILURE.

She stepped out of the grocery store, pressing on her aching back. A bright yellow cottonwood leaf fluttered down at her feet, as dead as her career. The massive tree flanked the corner by the grocery store, and a soft November breeze rustled in the branches and made the leaves glisten like raining gold.

A perfect fall day to be unemployed.

Dora drove by in her 1975 Chrysler New Yorker, the cruise ship of automobiles. Dora got about four car lengths to the block and four miles to the gallon. No clue what it looked like at the beginning of its life. But now the New Yorker was a solid red shade of rust. A nice contrast to Dora's general grayness.

Dora waved, not watching the quiet street for way, way too long. The car began driving toward Carrie, who stood on the sidewalk waving back. But Dora finished trying to read Carrie's mind and turned to watch where she was going before anyone was killed.

That defined success anytime Dora got behind the wheel.

Carrie drove straight home. She'd walked to work today but found out it was her job to drive the *Bugle*, in its waxy, one-step-up-from-chiseled-in-stone condition, over to Gillespie to be printed. The Gillespie newspaper owned the only printing press in three counties. She'd loaded the newspaper into its oversized wooden suitcase last night and stopped by to grab it this morning and drive to Gillespie. Inking a paper was similar to coloring in first grade—finding scratches in the negative they'd made of each page.

She watched while they attached her negatives to the massive rollers of the press, ran them off onto newsprint, and folded them on the spinning, room-sized press. Then she'd loaded them into her car, driven back to Melnik, slapped five hundred mailing labels on the papers with help from Viola and Donette, and reloaded them into her car. She began her deliveries at noon and was done at twelve fifteen.

Also, done forever.

13

The autopsy went into extra innings.

The funeral morphed into a memorial service—so Wilkie wasn't required to attend—because the Melnik ladies already had their casseroles done for the dinner.

Nick picked Carrie up at one fifteen on the dot. Not a minute early, not a second late. The man liked order. Carrie suspected that her chaotic house was driving him nuts.

She scaled his truck, careful of her black rayon sheath. She'd added a thin silver belt, small silver hoop earrings, and black pumps—two-inch heels, closed toes—not a strap to be found anywhere. The funeral uniform she'd learned from her sorority sisters. She had her hair pulled back in a French twist, but wisps of blond already escaped.

"Did you catch any mice this morning?"

"You look nice." Nick smiled as he ignored her question, the traitor. He knew she needed the information to guard her sanity. He wore a black suit that made his chocolate brown hair more milk than dark. A crisp white shirt fairly glowed behind the thin diagonal stripes of his red and blue tie. A gold tack held his tie in place, as if even in this Nick was afraid to be out of control. He looked great. But he was still a brat about the mice.

"You've got to tell me how the mouse hunt is going." She pulled her seat belt across her body, clicked it sharply, and then turned to glare at him. *"I have to know!"*

"So did the paper go out?"

Carrie's jaw clenched. She considered not telling him just to get revenge for his stubborn refusal to tell her about his mouse-catching escapades. But what else did they have to talk about for ten minutes until they got to the little country church?

"Fine! Be that way."

Nick grinned.

"I'm going to be fired."

Nick jerked his head around, and his brows slammed together. "Did someone come in and yell at you?" He looked for all the world like he'd hunt them down and pound them. What a sweetheart.

Then he shook his head. "No, they couldn't have. No matter how many typos there were or how badly you insulted someone, the paper hasn't hit the street yet."

"Well, technically it has. I mean, just a few minutes ago. People snag it pretty fast. But it's not for something I put in the paper; it's for something I left out. Gunderson came in to see me the other day."

"He's back in town?"

"Yes, Sven Gunderson is back. He came in with this really nasty smear piece on Wilkie. Plenty of it true, lots of it rumors, none of it necessary. Gunderson told me to run his story or get out. I smiled nice and he left—I hadn't seen what he'd written yet. I figured I could weave enough of his info into my story to make him happy."

"And. . ." Nick pulled off the highway and drove down the gravel road to Country Christian Church.

"It was awful. No way I could use that stuff. I mean, my piece wasn't exactly a whitewash. I certainly didn't tap-dance around the fact that Wilkie was murdered. But I didn't start guessing at possible motives."

"Well, no, of course not. You mean Gunderson did?"

Carrie nodded as she remembered some of the things in Gunderson's story. "He speculated on people in town who had motives. By name. He talked about Wilkie being a drunk and a doper. He said that Wilkie sold grass to kids."

"But there's no proof of that."

"There was no proof of most of what Gunderson gave me." Carrie looked at the charming little clapboard church just ahead. She'd been baptized, gone to Sunday school, attended the youth group, sung in the choir, watched two of her older sisters get married, and seen her great-grandma and other ancestors buried in the backyard cemetery there.

It was home in the way all of Melnik was. Small and boring but part of her. She loved to visit. She just didn't want to live here. This was her past.

Her future lay elsewhere.

"And when he sees you've left it out, you really think he'll fire you?"

Her very near future.

"He was breathing fire in my office. He was dead serious. I'm done."

"We'll talk to him. He'll listen to reason. A young man like that shouldn't be so stubborn." Nick turned into the church's crushed-rock parking lot. The tires crunched, and the cold wind blew dirt past the windshield.

"Young? Where'd you get the idea that he's young?"

Nick pulled up beside a line of three late-model sedans.

"Uh, I guess from him being known only as a son. A son sounds young."

"Well, he's old. Old Man Gunderson was in his nineties, remember. Sven is midsixties at least. And he's so grouchy it's like his face has been cut into these grim, deep lines. No, I'm sure he means what he says." Carrie swung down from the truck and trudged across the graveled parking area.

The church lot was lined with sugar maples, their leaves a brilliant orange-red, dipping and swaying in the breeze. The three cars, parked side by side, formed a line close to the back door of the church. They belonged to the serving committee that Carrie was here to help. A bevy of ladies were already hard at work an hour before the service.

Carrie led Nick to the back of the building. He pulled the heavy wooden door open for her. The church basement steps went down on her left, and a ramp to the sanctuary went up on her right. Carrie and Nick went down.

The basement was cool, but it was nothing compared to the blast of pure ice awaiting Carrie at the bottom of those steps.

"How could you do that, Cindy Lou?" Dora plodded toward Carrie, wiping her hands on her apron.

"D–do what?"

The plump tyrant made a fist, and Carrie took a half step back until she bumped into Nick's solid form. She heaved a sigh of relief that he was there. She might need rescuing from more than mice today. The whole white knight thing must be exhausting for him. Dora, Melnik's answer to the CIA, wore bright green—a terrible fashion choice considering that she'd just had her hair tinted an amazing shade of bluish purple. She wore fluorescent green polyester slacks decorated with small white flowers and a solid green tunic top that reminded Carrie of something she'd seen growing in Great-Grandma's refrigerator.

Carrie had badly misjudged funeral styles in Melnik.

A gnarled finger waggled in front of Carrie's eyes. "You young whippersnappers don't know it isn't right to speak ill of the dead."

Uh-oh. The Wilkie story.

"I'm ashamed of you, Carrie Evans." Another lady, this one adorned in a pumpkin orange blouse sprinkled with appliquéd fall leaves, marched out of the kitchen with her hands jammed on her ample hips. A third woman stormed straight at Carrie.

Dora quit talking, obviously too busy recording the attack with her eagle eyes and steel-trap brain.

And if Carrie once in a while wished that steel trap would snap shut on Dora's—

"I never thought I'd see the day. . ."

Carrie noticed quiet Bonnie Simpson neatly slipping brownies out of a pan onto a plastic platter that looked like crystal. Carrie tried to remember the last time Bonnie, ten years older than she was and a fixture at all community events, had actually spoken to her. Bonnie kept her head bent, her thick round spectacles focused on her work, her blue jumper concealing any hint of the woman's size and shape. No yelling from Bonnie. Carrie decided Bonnie was her new best friend. After Nick.

Nick rested his hands on Carrie's shoulders, and for a second she enjoyed the support. Then it occurred to her that she was the only thing standing between Nick and these furious women. Was he protecting her? Or using her as a human shield? She couldn't decide.

Heavy footsteps pounded down the wooden stairs. "Carrie, I am shocked, do you hear? Shocked."

Carrie whirled around at the deep voice coming from behind. Nick stepped out of the kill zone.

Chicken.

Pastor Bremmen, his face normally the very image of love and forgiveness, had a vein pulsing in his forehead, his jaw clenched, his cheeks florid.

"All right, hold it!" Nick's voice boomed into the crowd.

Silence fell on the basement.

"I read that story. She was fair to Wilkie."

Nick had obviously gotten the message loud and clear, too, without Wilkie's name being mentioned once. And he'd stepped in to protect her. God bless the man.

"You're all overreacting. Now Carrie might not have—"

Pastor Bremmen slapped a folded-up newspaper against Nick's chest. "You call this *fair?*"

Nick unfolded the paper. Carrie looked around his arm and then flinched when she saw Maxie staring at her. Nick must have felt her reaction, because he quickly flipped the paper over and folded it so Maxie didn't show. There was a mug shot of Wilkie in prison garb with a number across his chest.

Ex-Con Murdered screamed in bold, underlined forty-eight-point type across the top of Wilkie's photo.

Nick swiveled his head around to look at Carrie.

She looked up, afraid he'd start yelling at her, too.

"I did not write that." Carrie swept the group with her gaze. "You have to believe me. I. . ." She looked back at the text. Where had this come from? She racked her brain to figure out how this switch could have been made and then realized that she'd never really looked at the paper this morning, avoiding that awful Maxie. She'd figure out who and how later, but the responsibility was all hers.

As she scanned the story, "who" became immediately obvious. *Gunderson!*

This was his lurid tale of rumors and half-truths, every sin, real and imagined, Wilkie had ever committed, in painful detail.

Nick spoke up. "This is a story Sven Gunderson wanted run about Wilkie. Carrie refused. He must have—"

Carrie's nails dug into Nick's forearm. Their eyes met. He fell silent.

Carrie looked at all these old friends and her heart twisted. These ladies and Pastor Bremmen loved her. But she knew her place in this fiasco.

"This is a mistake."

"Sven Gunderson did this?" Pastor Bremmen thundered.

"It's *my* mistake. I didn't mean for this story to be in the *Bugle*. But I'm the editor. Whatever comes out in the pages of the *Bugle* is my responsibility." She *should* have double-checked this morning. That stupid mouse! This was all *Maxie's* fault.

"This is all my fault. It won't happen again." Carrie looked from one lady to another, until finally she turned to face Pastor Bremmen head-on. She might as well face it. In Melnik there was nowhere to run. "An article retracting this and printing the truth will be in next week's paper."

Too little, too late.

Pastor Bremmen still looked grim. "This is going to hurt a lot of people." In all honesty, it'd only *hurt* four. Maybe five since Shayla was still living in the county lockup for trying to kill her dad. Shayla was probably hurting pretty badly these days, but it wasn't about grief. Not even close.

Junior had sprung Shayla for the funeral. The plan was for her to sit through the memorial service, far away from her mother since Rosie was still in a rage, and then Shayla would have a nice lunch and go back to jail. Junior wanted to let her go, but for now, since the poor little confessed-but-probably-innocent murderess had nowhere to go, he was using the jail like low-rent foster care.

But judging from the lynch mob in front of Carrie, these citizens of fair Melnik didn't have to be hurt to be appalled. And they especially didn't have to be hurt to come and scold her. They'd be openly furious, but they'd quietly revel in the gossipy pack of lies. It pinched to know that more copies of the *Bugle* would sell this week than ever before.

She turned and wanted to beseech these ladies not to hate her and not to enjoy the pain she'd caused. "I'm terribly sorry. I should have given the paper a final look before I took it to the printer."

It occurred to Carrie she might *not* be fired. Of course, by the time she was done with Gunderson, she *would* be fired. Her termination would result from screaming at the boss, not from disobeying him.

Nick patted her shoulder. She gave him a grateful look and then turned to Pastor Bremmen. "Would it be all right to say a few words of apology at the funeral, Pastor? I never intended to inflict more pain on this family, and I want to say so publicly."

The road-flare red of Pastor Bremmen faded, and the usual kindness Carrie depended on returned to his eyes. "I'll ask Rosie. We'll go by her wishes."

Carrie nodded. "Now, ladies." She turned to face the septuagenarian hit squad. "Do you forgive me enough to let me help in the kitchen, or am I banished?"

14

Far from being banished, after the funeral Carrie had been given hard labor. And Nick wasn't sure why, but it appeared he'd been sentenced along with her.

He rinsed the one thousandth plate—or was it the one millionth?—while Carrie scrubbed. Wilkie had quite the turnout.

The church had used all its paper plates and china, and still the food line stretched up the stairs and into the parking lot. So Nick and Carrie washed. As the day wore down and the food ran out, the crowd thinned.

They worked silently as long as there were women bustling in and out of the kitchen. But at last even those faithful ladies began to untie their aprons and go home.

"At least they forgave you, Carrie." Nick glanced over his shoulder. There were still a few people left, but they were busy in the social hall.

"I don't think this exactly qualifies as forgiveness. They just see fresh meat. Someone young to do the heavy lifting. That's Melnik for you."

"I love this." Nick grinned at her. They stood shoulder to shoulder by the double sink, their hands in hot water—not unlike Carrie's whole life. "I mean, I don't love that you've become a Melnik pariah. I love helping. This is the purest form of Christian service."

Carrie pulled the metal strainer to let the water go. "You see that dreary dishwater being sucked down the drain?"

"Sure."

"That's my life, Nick." She faced him, and a hank of her fine hair hung in one eye. She blew it away and glared. "And washing dishes is not the purest form of Christian service. Washing dishes is what got Martha in trouble with Jesus."

Nick tried to accept that Carrie hated living in Melnik. He'd found his home here. He'd found the direction God had for his life. So where did that leave them?

Looking back at his rinse water, he scooped out a fistful of silverware and changed the subject to keep himself from begging her to love this town. "You were so brave up there during the funeral. It was the most courageous thing I've ever seen, the way you stood there and let everyone have their say and didn't complain."

Carrie reset the drain plug and let fresh hot water spray into her sink. Nick caught the scent of lemons as she added a generous squirt of soap. Suds bubbled in the sink.

The door between the basement social hall and the kitchen swung open, and a woman Nick knew in passing came in. "Hi, Marian." Nick lifted his dish towel in greeting.

The woman carefully scraped some plates and stacked them on Carrie's left, perfectly positioned to wash. Nick noticed a nervous glance between Marian and Carrie.

"Uh. . .Nick?" Carrie said.

"No, it's okay." Marian blushed, and some dishes clattered as she set them down and fled the kitchen.

Nick slipped a plate out of the rinse-water side of the double sink with a quiet splash and set it on end in the drainer with a soft click. "So Gunderson really changed the—"

"Nick!"

"What?"

"Her name's Bonnie."

"Whose name?"

"Bonnie's."

"Who's Bonnie?"

Carrie closed her eyes. "You embarrassed her half to death. *Marian* isn't her name; it's *Bonnie.*"

Nick's brows rose nearly to his hairline. He looked over his shoulder through the opening above the countertop that separated the kitchen from the hall. "I'm sorry. I'd heard her name was Marian."

Carrie turned around and looked through the same window. "And there are still a few plates on the table. Bonnie never left anything undone in her life."

"I've been calling her Marian for six months. How come she's never corrected me?"

"Do you talk to her often?"

"Well, no."

"And you heard her name was Marian from Dora, right?"

Nick turned back toward the sink. "Right."

"That's because Dora calls her Marian. As in Marian the librarian. It's from *The Music Man* or some old movie. Just like she calls me Cindy Lou, as in Cindy Lou Who from Whoville."

"Marian seems so shy. I must have embarrassed her every time I've talked to her. I need to apologize." Nick straightened away from the sink, intending to run after her immediately.

"Relax. I'm the one who embarrassed her. She knew I'd tell you. She didn't mind. Just like I don't mind being called Cindy Lou. . .much."

"Well, I have to find her and tell her I'm sorry."

"That won't be hard. She works at the Melnik Historical Society Museum, which also contains the closest thing Melnik has to a library. She's the curator and librarian. Thus the nickname."

"Okay, I'll make it right." Nick went back to his wiping with a decisive nod.

"Nick, listen, I really appreciate the kind words about taking abuse. I feel like I took a beating, but it needed to be done. Since the whole town showed for the funeral—"

"Mainly because of your story."

Carrie gave a short, humorless laugh. "Yeah, hoping for fireworks. Anyway, I'm hoping I let them get it out of their system. I'm hoping it'll minimize the long, drawn-out, behind-closed-doors whispering campaign that would have normally followed."

Nick shuddered. "Well, you took it like a. . ."

"What?"

Nick was tempted to just go ahead and drown himself in the rinse water. "I was going to say, 'You took it like a man.'"

Great, insult her.

"You like doing this, huh?" Carrie handed another plate to Nick. She was fast. It kept him hopping.

Nick lifted one shoulder. "Yes, I like this. It feels like I'm God's servant. He tells us to comfort those who mourn. This is a way to do that. And we don't ask for thanks."

"The family always comes in and says thank you."

"Yes, but the service committee doesn't quit if no one comes in."

"True, but they gossip about them."

"Well, we don't insist they pay."

"Actually, a donation to the Women's Auxiliary is expected."

Nick glared at her.

Carrie grinned. "Sorry. I agree with you, actually."

"So you're just arguing with me for entertainment?"

"Of course. This is a great ministry. But nothing like what a big church can offer. In my church in Omaha, we had a casserole committee to prepare meals, freeze them ahead, and deliver them. But we did more than that. There was also a grief counselor on staff. We had someone coordinating the funeral, and using memorial money, we funded Sunday school classes and Bible studies for new widows, parents without partners, and a singles ministry. Even those were targeted—some for traditional singles, others for divorced singles, and still others for people who'd lost a spouse, parent, or child. We did so much for so many in that church. But in Melnik there aren't enough people, so everyone gets lumped in together or forgotten, with nothing available to meet their needs."

"But here people actually know each other by name." How could she not know what she had in this little town? It was filled with people who cared so much for her. "They can give Rosie Melnik a hug and tell her they'll stop by. They can show kindness to Shayla and Kevin as they pass them on the street. They can be a support system for Donette, now and when the baby comes. This is a *real* church. The reason grief counselors and casserole ministries and funeral coordinators exist in huge churches is because no one does that stuff, because no one even knows each other."

Nick quit drying to stress his point. "I moved away from Chicago, and I've never heard a word from my church there. There's no one to notice I'm gone. We had six services on Saturday and Sunday and a nine-piece praise band that recorded albums. We supported a dozen churches in Africa and sent mission teams to build churches and hospitals there every summer. And that's all wonderful, and I don't disparage the work they do. It's a beautiful ministry. But I could go weeks without seeing anyone I knew well enough to say hi."

Nick looked back at his water. "I wish I'd thought to bring a casserole to the funeral."

"Can you cook?"

"No."

"Then thanks for not bringing one."

Nick laughed. He couldn't help but like her. But why would she be interested in a man who wanted to stay in the very place she was itching to leave? A man who was such a dope and so out of the loop that he'd called a nice lady by the wrong name for six months? But that was the whole point, wasn't it? Yeah, he'd done it wrong for six months with Bonnie, but in Chicago he would have never even discovered his mistake.

"I can learn. Living in Melnik will *make* me learn. Maybe I can take food to the Melniks' home." Nick went back to work feeling good about his decision, as if the Lord Himself had put the idea in his heart.

"I'd better phone Rosie and warn her that she might have another Crazy Clara pie-type situation on her hands."

"Hey! You take that back!" An aging china plate slipped through Nick's hands and landed flat on the water, splashing his pristine suit. "I'm a much better cook than Clara." He snagged a nearby dish towel and dabbed at his shirtfront.

Carrie splashed him deliberately, much more dramatically than the plate had. Nick's jaw dropped. "I can't believe you did that."

He made a move toward the water with the flat of his hand.

Dora lumbered in. They both went back to work while Dora told Carrie to stand up straight so her stomach didn't pooch out. She also advised Nick to start dyeing the gray out of his hair and to use a better deodorant.

She launched into the pros and cons of mouthwash just as Tallulah came into the kitchen breathing fire. "Carrie Evans, you have destroyed Melnik and ruined my life's work. The Maxie Festival will be a disaster, and the governor will never come."

Nick braced himself to step between Carrie and Tallulah. Sure, Carrie was tough, but she had to be exhausted after the funeral inquisition.

Before he could protect her, he remembered that this was her town. She was used to it. Carrie belonged in a way he never would. And she didn't even know to be grateful. He went back to rinsing dishes. When Dora had been insulting him, he'd almost felt like a true Melnikite. But now he was back to being an outsider, the loser, the fat kid who spent recess dodging bullies and class time showing up those losers, which only bought him more trouble. He'd never found his place. His home had been nice with three equally geeky brothers and a sister, all younger, and his kindly college professor parents who thought all two hundred pounds of his five-foot-two eighth-grade self were wonderful. But he hadn't been able to take his family to class.

He'd grown past six feet without gaining an ounce, but the awkward nerd was still alive and well. Despite his fumbling attempts to find himself in college and his pivotal role in the engineering firm, he had never fit in. Then his brothers, one by one, had moved out of Chicago. His parents had retired to Florida and left him their big house to live in alone. The solitary life had almost crushed him.

He had hoped he'd finally found a home in Melnik. And now here was Carrie, the prettiest thing he'd ever seen, and all she wanted was to get away from Melnik and—by extension—him.

Nick sighed and took over washing so Carrie could defend herself, something she was perfectly capable of except when it came to mice. *Thank You, God, for mice.*

"How did I destroy Melnik, Tallulah?"

"By assassinating the character of our favorite son."

Nick thought that Wilkie had done a fair job of that without any help from Carrie.

Once Dora and Tallulah wound down and left, Nick and Carrie finished cleaning the kitchen. They headed up the stairs, Carrie clicking off lights behind them with a familiarity of the building that made Nick envious. The rest of the church was dark. As they got to the top of the murky basement steps, Donette stepped out of a dark corner.

Carrie squeaked. Not quite her mouse eek, but close.

"Thanks a lot, Carrie." Donette sneered the words. "You've taught me what it means to be a Christian."

Nick glanced at Carrie.

Carrie's eyes widened with regret. "I'm so sorry about that story. It wasn't supposed to end up in the paper."

"All you are is a nasty gossip. I don't want to be like you ever!" Donette whirled and shoved the door open.

Carrie ran after her. "Donette, wait. Please, let's talk about this."

A rust-bucket Pontiac was sitting in front of the church door, headlights blazing and motor running.

"Hurry up. I'm tired of waitin', babe." A man who must have been one of Wilkie's bum friends from the memorial service swung the passenger's side door open. When the dome light came on, Nick saw the guy leering at the very pregnant Donette. A cigarette hung from the corner of his mouth. Acid rock music, oldies from this guy's era, blared out of the radio.

Donette stalked straight for the car. Carrie ran after the girl. Donette reached for the handle just as Carrie caught her arm. Nick was close enough to see Donette's eyes brim with tears.

"Donette, don't leave. Be angry with me if you want, but don't blame my mistake on God. Talk to Pastor Bremmen." Carrie lowered her voice so Nick could barely hear. "Don't leave with this guy."

"If I don't want to spend the rest of my life alone"—Donette jerked free— "I'm going to have to put up with a few things I don't like."

The distraught girl climbed in. The car tore out of the parking lot, spitting gravel.

Nick prayed for Donette as his heart broke for the defeated look in Carrie's eyes.

"She listened to me, Nick, when we talked about God. Letting that story get published wrecked her chance at finding Jesus."

He urged her toward his truck and helped her inside. "You can't take that on yourself. Donette has to make her own choices. And it was Gunderson, not you."

"I'm responsible. And I'd have caught that story if I wasn't such a coward."

He climbed in, released his parking brake, and started his truck, easing over the crunching gravel onto the dark road home. His headlights cut through the setting darkness. "Do not *ever* call yourself a coward again in my presence."

"Is this about my mouse phobia not being a sin?"

"It's about Donette, Tallulah, Rosie, Pastor Bremmen, the funeral committee, and everyone else in town."

"I know. I stood there and took it like a man." Carrie shoved her fingers into her hair, wrecking what little was left of her neat hairstyle. "I'm going to do some serious payback when I get my hands on Gunderson."

"Sneaking in there and switching the stories late last night was so low, I just can't believe it." Nick pulled his car out onto the road. They were the last ones out of the church. He flicked on the heater as he drove. "Did you really look at what he wrote?"

Carrie nodded, crossing her arms over her seat belt. "Pure yellow journalism at its worst. And what really kills me is, he left *my* byline on it. I deliberately used a byline because I knew there would be trouble and I wanted it to land on me, not the paper. He could have put his name on that story, but noooo, there's my name, Carrie Evans, front and center. He did the whole thing at home, too. The font isn't right in the article. It doesn't match the rest of the paper.

"And he must have cut that picture off a wanted poster. Then he snuck in there, waxed it, and put it on the page. I already had the page packed up, so he had to hunt through the case and find it. What a jerk! And I didn't notice it because I didn't want to look at Maxie when I was inking the paper, so I skipped the front page. I'd have noticed that headline and picture if I'd so much as glanced at the paper."

"Why would Gunderson have a wanted poster on Wilkie?" Nick knew a lot of town gossip, but. . . "I've never heard of Wilkie being on the *run* from the law. If he had been, they might have hung one in the post office. But he'd been arrested. So it must have been a mug shot. Where would Gunderson get that? Would Junior have one? But Junior would have mentioned it if Gunderson had asked for one."

Carrie scowled at the scenery. "I can't decide if Gunderson has some grudge against Wilkie or if he's just got twisted ideas about the newspaper. Gunderson never should have included all that about Shayla and her confession. I can't believe Junior would tell him all that. I'm going to have a talk with Melnik's loose-lipped chief as soon as I'm done with Gunderson."

"When are you going to go after him?"

"Just as soon as I get out of this stupid dress." Carrie looked at Nick.

"No one in town has mentioned seeing him but you. He may not be that easy to find." Nick pulled up beside Carrie's house.

"He can't hide forever."

Rounding the truck, Nick opened her door before she could reach for it. She dug in her little black joke of a purse and found her keys. He took the keys and unlocked the outer door to the porch. He'd installed the sturdy lock without being asked. He crossed the porch. Carrie followed, stomping until the floor shook.

"What's that for?"

"To scare the mice away."

Nick nodded. He banged long and hard on the inner door with the side of his fist. Glancing over his shoulder, he asked, "Enough?"

Carrie smiled. "Yeah, thanks."

He unlocked the door, and Grizzly shot past both of them to beat them inside.

Carrie sighed audibly. "If the stomping and banging don't shoo them away, the cat will."

Nick flicked on lights as he tramped around the kitchen into the bathroom, bedroom, and living room. "You know, this place is looking pretty good."

"Thanks for all the traps you've emptied."

Nick came back in from the living room smiling. "Nice try. I'm not telling."

That growling noise Grizzly was famous for came out of this cute little woman—who needed his protection—since she was all alone—late at night—with the man she'd called a hero.

Say something, loser. Ask her out.

He'd almost kissed her earlier, and she hadn't been running when they'd gotten interrupted. Of course, he was so clueless about women he might not have noticed she was about to run. He took a step toward her, fully expecting to trip over a shoelace even though his shoes were slip-ons, or spill something on her even though there were no liquids within ten yards. She didn't back up. In fact, she seemed to inch forward. So he'd invite himself to stay awhile.

"I've got to go."

Idiot!

Her face fell. "Uh. . .okay, bye."

The good-bye kiss was a classic. Maybe that would be the right way to go. "I've got a full day of work planned for tomorrow." He stepped closer, no disaster yet. "Here at your place."

"With the paper out, I should be home for a change, although I've got a Community Club meeting tomorrow evening to cover for the *Bugle*."

"I'll bet the *Bugle* work will keep you busy all the time."

"Yeah, there's a 4-H Club meeting on Friday afternoon and a senior citizens' fund-raising dinner on Saturday at noon. And there's a mission dinner at the Missouri Synod Lutheran Church after services on Sunday—plus the Catholics are having a Thanksgiving program on Sunday evening, and I need pictures. And I'm sure that people are going to want to drop by and yell, so that will keep me occupied. I've also got to hunt down Gunderson and strangle him, and go have a nice, sharp talk with Junior for giving Gunderson that information and the picture. Plus, I think I ought to visit Shayla in jail, if she's still speaking to me, and try to find Donette and beg her forgiveness—and I'd like to take a casserole to Rosie. But aside from that, I want to spend the day going through the upper floors. To see what I've inherited." She shuddered. "Besides mice."

What Nick wouldn't give for a sword, a shield, and a year's supply of d-Con. "I can help you go through the upstairs if you want. Maybe you'll find some things that will give you a jump start on Tallulah's book."

"And maybe if there are mice"—she twisted her fingers together and her voice got small and high-pitched—"you can scare them off for me?"

Nick nodded, finally close enough to touch her. *Please, God, make me cool. Give me some sweet talk. Give me some poise. Heal me of my dork gene.* But instead of reaching for her, he raised his hand and held out her keys.

"Thanks. I'll appreciate the help." She lifted her hand palm up. He rested the keys on her fingers.

Help me say the right thing, Jesus.

He could think of nothing. He sighed, dropped the keys, and turned to go.

A mouse zipped out of the living room. Grizzly, a shaggy yellow blur, howled in hot pursuit.

In one split second Nick went from walking away empty-handed to holding an armful of warm, soft, clinging, shrieking woman. He looked down, and her eyes, scared, embarrassed, desperate, met his. God hadn't sent a *mouse*, had He? Because this sure seemed like an answer. But would God do such a thing? Would the heavenly Father use a mouse to get Nick a girlfriend? Did God think he was that pathetic?

The mouse seemed to be living proof that He did.

If God, in His infinite wisdom, did such a thing, it would be wrong of Nick not to respect the holy Lord's decision.

"Forgive me." Carrie seemed to be asking it of him, not God, this time.

Nick thought that was progress. "What did I tell you about being afraid of mice?" He hugged her closer.

"That God gave me this one flaw." Dejected, Carrie rested the side of her face against his shoulder.

She fit perfectly. She smelled like wax and ink and whatever wonderful thing she'd used on her hair. "Because you're so close to perfect."

She raised her head, her blue eyes glowing.

He lowered his head. She reached up and met him halfway. Maybe he'd said the right thing at last.

The kiss lasted only a moment. Nick pulled back and saw Carrie's eyes flutter open. Now he'd ask. Now he'd say, cool as Brad Pitt, "Carrie, would you like to have dinner with me?"

Of course she'll say yes. She wouldn't kiss me if she wasn't willing to have dinner with me. Surely a kiss was further along the relationship curve than dinner.

He knew just what to say. In his head, he was smooth, brilliant, and suave. "Would you like to—"

"Let me go!" Carrie pushed at him, struggling to get out of his arms.

"B–but I didn't say anything stupid yet!" He must have a stupid vibe in addition to his stupid mouth. He let her go, suddenly feeling as if he were an attacker she wanted to escape.

Carrie charged toward her stairway. "There's someone in my attic."

Nick heard the creaking overhead, realized what she'd said, turned, and ran after her. If there was a robber or a murderer up there, Carrie would probably be fine. But there might be mice.

15

The intruder dropped all efforts at stealth. Footsteps pounded overhead. Carrie's feet hammered as she raced upstairs with Nick trying to keep up. The attic door crashed open before she rounded the staircase landing.

Nick, just a step behind her, saw a pair of feet vanish to the left of the stairway. Another door slammed shut.

"He's in the Dead Zone." Carrie scrambled faster, Nick keeping pace.

Carrie raced for the door and slammed it open. A man dressed in black and wearing a black ski mask swung his leg over the window, an armload of papers clutched to his chest.

"You get back here!" Carrie took two running steps and launched herself at the man, knocking him into the window frame, and the two of them tumbled back into the room. The papers the burglar clutched went flying. The man grunted as he rolled sideways, scrambling, shoving at Carrie, knocking over a lineup of small fur-bearing creatures. Carrie wrestled with him, clawing at the ski mask.

Nick jumped into the fray as the man twisted loose from Carrie and rammed into the grizzly bear.

"Look out!" Carrie scrambled backward, knocking small animals aside as she dodged the falling behemoth. Nick leapt back just as the bear landed on the man, caging him, its extended paws on each side of the intruder's head and its gaping fangs stopping inches from his face.

Nick reached between the bear's teeth and the crook's face, snagged the ski mask, and yanked it free.

Deputy Hal froze.

Then he raised his hands like he was preparing to put his arms around the bear's neck and accept a big, toothy kiss. "Okay, I'm not running. You caught me."

Nick looked at Carrie and realized that her last-minute dive for safety had nearly buried her in dead animals. A raccoon perched on top of her head as if auditioning for a coonskin cap. She hoisted herself up, resting on her elbows. A mink, a badger, and an otter sat on her lap. A fox and a family of coyotes lay across her nylon-clad legs, and a baby fawn had tipped forward and rested its muzzle on her shoulder. It was almost like wearing a fur coat. Only icky.

He was also pretty sure he saw a couple of sharp teeth peeking out from under her backside. Carrie must have sat on a poor dead predator.

Brushing all those long-dead remains aside with barely a glance, Carrie rose from the furry rubble. Nick wondered why those animals didn't scare her like Maxie the Mouse did. He turned back to the trapped, defeated Hal.

The papers he'd been carrying were strewn across the floor. After thwarting the Cleaning Brigade Friday night, Carrie had let them have at the Dead Zone on Monday. It was clean enough that, except for a few neglected corners, the papers were all that was scattered. If you didn't count the corpses.

Carrie rose to her feet, shedding fur like a mammal in the spring. "What are you doing in my house, Hal?"

Nick noticed a wolverine peeking around Carrie's waist, its teeth sunk into her dress, hanging from her. . .self. He quickly plucked it loose. Carrie never took her eyes off Hal.

"I admit it." Hal looked up, his expression as sick with fear as if the bear had growled at him. "I killed Wilkie."

He lowered his hands, twisted his head sideways, and buried his face in his palms, his shoulders trembling. "Just call Junior and get him over here."

"Go call." Carrie glanced over her shoulder at Nick.

The only phone was downstairs. Nick had a cell phone, but it didn't get a good signal in Melnik. And Nick wasn't leaving her up here alone with her second confessed murderer of the week.

"What possible motive could you have for killing Wilkie?" Carrie asked.

Hal clenched his fists and looked up. "He killed your great-grandma."

Carrie gasped. "You saw him?"

"I saw him standing over her body holding a skillet. When I saw what that lousy scumball had done, I just lost it. I grabbed him, and we struggled. I started out planning to arrest him, but while we were fighting, I remembered all he'd done to my mom."

"Your mom?" Carrie dusted away the mink fur that had shed onto her dress.

Hal ignored her, the better to continue confessing. Nick wondered where Carrie got this gift. The woman could give pointers to a priest.

"I saw your defenseless grandma laying there dead. I—I wrestled the frying pan away from him and just hit him. Hard. Once. That's all it took. He collapsed onto the floor right next to Bea." Hal began pushing at the bear gingerly. Nick bent down to help, and Carrie chipped in, grabbing a fistful of fur. They managed to free the deputy from his bearskin prison. "Your great-grandma was already dead, Carrie. I checked. I'd have saved her if I could. But I couldn't help her, and I hated him enough that I hit him harder than I should. I'm guilty."

Hal rolled onto his knees and stood, his eyes locked on the floor. "Just go call. I'm not running anywhere. Get it over with."

Nick remembered Shayla locking herself in a cell and wondered if they could just send Hal over to the jail to turn himself in. Even the murderers in Melnik were a polite bunch.

"Uh. . .did you put him in the kitchen pantry?" Carrie asked.

Hal looked up, surprised. He obviously hadn't thought of that. "No."

"Did you, at any time, try to smother him with a mouse?" Nick tossed that question in but regretted it when Carrie shuddered.

Hal's lips curled in horror. "Hey, I may be a murderer, but I'm not gonna do anything as creepy as *that*. I'd never touch a mouse. I hate mice."

Carrie straightened, and her expression lightened. "Really?"

"Oh yeah. It's something I can't control."

"I know."

"It's so stupid. I hate myself for it."

"I know."

"It's a phobia."

"I know."

Nick interrupted before they exchanged Facebook names. "I don't think you're guilty, Hal. Wilkie may have regained consciousness and hid in that closet, or someone may have come in and finished him off." With the mouse. Nick knew better than to say that out loud. "And then stuffed him in the pantry. But either way, the autopsy hasn't confirmed that he died of a blow to the head." Nick remembered the gunshot wound and definitely decided to create an Excel spreadsheet when he got home to keep track of the possible causes of death.

"I saw the autopsy," Hal said. "I know it's not settled, but it'll turn out to be me. Wilkie might have been wounded, and he might even have come around after I whacked him, but I know that blow to the head at least contributed to his death. I killed him. I *know* it!"

"You don't know it," Nick said. "I'm pretty sure it'll turn out to be something else."

"Really?" Hal perked up. "Uh, can I go, then?"

"No!" Carrie and Nick spoke at the same instant.

"So what were you doing in here tonight?" Carrie crossed her arms, looking like a stern mother, even though Hal was probably older than her.

Hal shoved his hands into his back pockets and scuffed one toe on the floor. "Sorry about the breaking and entering. I. . .uh. . .I thought I'd maybe left a clue behind or something."

Since the whole town had spent two days cleaning this house, Hal included, Nick very much doubted Hal was worried about dropping an incriminating matchbook. Nick wondered what the guy really wanted. He also wondered how Hal happened to be here to find Wilkie standing over Bea. Maybe they'd find out when they went through the papers he'd been carrying. "*Sorry* is not going to cut it. We're still going to have to call Junior."

"I thought you said I probably didn't kill him." Hal scowled at Nick. "And anyway, I didn't mean to kill Dad, exactly. But I sure meant to belt him with that skillet. I'll gladly confess to that."

Carrie's jaw dropped open. "Did you just say Wilkie is your dad?"

Nick rubbed his still-puffy forehead. "That Maxie Mouse float they've got planned to carry Wilkie's family?"

Carrie looked away from Hal. "Yeah, what about it?"

Nick started mentally sketching out alterations. "It's going to need a sidecar."

16

I can't believe Junior isn't going to charge him with breaking into my house." Coffee sloshed over the rim of Nick's cup when Carrie smacked it down on the table in front of him.

He didn't complain.

He was too afraid.

"Well, there is the murder charge." Nick had shown up early, determined to work quietly outside Carrie's house. He'd let her sleep in but be close if she needed him. He'd listened for *"Eeek!"*

No eeks, but she had eventually come out and invited him in for coffee. He was pretty sure that meant she didn't consider him a stalker.

"Yeah, but the murder charge is weak, and you know it. He's claiming self-defense, even that Wilkie resisted arrest. Hal should have been arrested for burglary. That, we *know* he did."

"At least he's locked up." Nick mopped up the spilled coffee with his own handkerchief. He hated messes. "He won't be breaking in here, at least for a while."

Carrie looked up from her cup as she stirred in a spoonful of sugar. "Shayla was flirting with him through the bars until Junior told her that Hal was her long-lost brother."

I'd like to flirt with you. No, don't say that. If Nick lived to be one hundred and three, he'd still always be a fat, awkward, nine-year-old brainiac who got bullied every day at recess.

"And what's Shayla still doing there, anyway?"

"You heard Junior say that she won't leave." Nick sipped at his coffee. "What's he supposed to do? The door was standing open when we got there. Like he's hoping she'll wander out and he can slam the door quick with her on the outside."

"She doesn't have anywhere to go." Carrie lifted the cup for a sip but set it back down with a sharp click. "And Junior arrested Hal, but he didn't *fire him*. If they call what Wilkie did resisting arrest, Hal may get a commendation."

"Too bad about that confession." Nick hoped he didn't slip up and confess all the stupid thoughts that rattled around in his head. Carrie had a way about her, so he'd have to be on his toes. "I bet Hal's kicking himself for that now."

"I think the bear scared it out of him." The woman who would let a mouse scare her into anything shook her head in disbelief. "Hal could be awarded right there in the cell."

Discussing their kiss over a cup of coffee would have been way more fun than talking about Hal. But *ohh* no. "People don't get fired all that easily in Melnik. I've noticed that."

"And then when I threatened to press charges for burglary, Junior went all 'You're just like your great-grandma' on me. How am I supposed to respond to that, huh?"

It really had backed her down. Nick decided it was the perfect threat. *You know, your great-grandma hated me. You don't want to be just like her, now, do you?*

"And what was Hal after, anyway? I need to go through those papers he left and the ones I got away from Tallulah and everything else on the upper floors. I need to do it right now, today, before anyone else comes. Someone else may have *already* come. I may have missed out on clues that would give us a motive for murder because I'm so. . .so stupid. . .so afraid. . ." Carrie looked up from the cup she hung on to for dear life.

Nick's heart turned over. She wanted to be strong. She wanted to be completely self-sufficient. She wanted to wade in and investigate patricide and burglary and trespassing and not talk about important stuff like kissing. In fact, right now, as her knuckles turned white and she braced herself to ask for his bodyguard services, it was only nasty little rodents keeping him in her life.

God, it wouldn't be sacrilegious to stop by the Maxie shrine just to say thanks, would it?

She got up from the table, tiptoed across the kitchen to the coffeemaker as if the mice were floodwater that was coming up around her ankles, and poured herself another steaming, rich-smelling cup. The aroma almost covered up the years of musty neglect, overridden with Pine-Sol and Lemon Pledge—the Melnik ladies' weapons of choice in their war on grime. And by *almost* Nick meant *not at all.* The place smelled terrible. But it was better than before.

She turned with the pot in her hands. "Want more?"

"Not yet, thanks."

She replaced the carafe and tiptoed back. He noticed she sat facing the pantry. Her feet were below the table, but he could hear her twisting them around the chair rungs to get them off the floor, and she glanced at the pantry door compulsively, watching for mice. Like they didn't come from all directions. The woman had denial down to a science.

"I tried to call Gunderson last night and again this morning. All I've got on him is his father's phone number."

"He'll turn up." Because he couldn't stand to watch her try to be brave a second longer, he offered what she was too ashamed to ask for. "I don't have any pressing work. I'd be glad to take a day off and sift through the upstairs with you."

Carrie's shoulders slumped on an audible sigh of relief. "Thank God. Uh . . .I mean, good, thank you, and God, too. . .uh, I mean, okay. When can you start?"

Nick saw a mouse skitter along the wall behind Carrie's back, and he was very, very careful not to react. It vanished under her refrigerator, only about three steps behind Carrie's chair. If it kept coming her way, maybe he could get his hands on her again. But that seemed so low-down.

"Right now sounds great. Let's go."

He scraped his chair backward, making a racket to scare off the rodent invader. Carrie arched one of her pretty blond brows. Great. He'd acted like a clumsy dork instead of mentioning the mouse. Why not mention it? Why not get her to jump again? Maybe he could reenact last night. Maybe this time no intruder would interrupt him before he could say, "Would you like to have dinner with me?"

Help me, God. Please un-dork me now. I've suffered long enough. The people near me have suffered long enough.

Carrie refilled their cups. Nick saw the mouse slip under the pantry door. He had five traps in that area alone. He was almost sorry that God had seen fit to keep Carrie focused on the burning liquid she was dispensing. Except for third-degree burns for both of them when she jumped into his arms with two blazing-hot cups of coffee, he'd enjoy getting ahold of her. He took his cup and followed Carrie upstairs.

They paused to grab the papers Carrie had taken back from Tallulah and Hal that she'd hidden under a trumpeter swan, species *Cygnus buccinators*, kingdom Animalia, phylum Chordate, class Aves, order Anseriformes, family Anatidea, genus Cygnus.

Nick, thanks to the semester he spent studying endangered species when he wanted to try to save the planet, had memorized that and a thousand other useless facts that he now couldn't forget. He still wanted the planet to be saved; he just decided he'd repair woodwork until someone came up with a good idea first.

Grizzly climbed the steps, moving with heavy, plodding footsteps that didn't become a feline. Nick wondered if the cat had actually nailed a mouse yet. Carrie took the papers out of the Dead Zone and closed the door.

"Let's keep Grizzly out of there. Those poor animals have suffered enough."

Somehow that seemed like Nick's fault, too.

Carrie perched herself on the top step and began sorting through the papers. There really was no place for Nick to sit other than right beside her. And the steps weren't all that wide.

She shoved half the papers into his hands. "These look like legal documents." She tapped on the top paper she held in her lap.

"This is the deed to this house." With a soft crinkle of yellowed paper, she flipped to the next one.

"Wow." Nick was instantly fascinated by what he held. "This is the layout of the house. I wonder if there's a blueprint somewhere. Chances are, there isn't. Back then a builder like your great-grandfather. . ." He paused and looked at her. "Or was it your great-great-grandfather?"

Carrie grinned. "Two greats at least. The Evanses built this for my great-grandpa's parents. Great-Grandma moved in when they were married and lived here with her in-laws and some of their children because Great-Grandma Bea had younger brothers and sisters. Then the two of them had kids. This house used to be bursting at the seams with people. It's a shame it's such a huge, empty hulk now."

It is a shame. A crying shame. You should marry me. We could fill it with kids.

Nick shook his head to clear it and started looking at the papers she'd handed him. He focused on them quickly before he jammed his size twelve steel-toed Red Wings right in his stupid mouth.

"This is a copy of. . ." Nick fished in the inside pocket of his black Windbreaker for his glasses and shoved them on to make sure he was reading it right.

"You wear glasses?" Carrie stared.

Nick flinched. *Nick the Wonder Dork.* Might as well admit the whole truth. "Yeah. I used to have these really thick glasses all the time. I had LASIK surgery so I wouldn't need them, but now for really fine print I have to have reading glasses."

"Tortoiseshell rims?"

Nick shrugged. He hadn't thought much about the rims. They'd just felt good on his face.

"I like them." She seemed to be studying the glasses closely.

She was just being polite. Since glasses had been the bane of Nick's existence all through childhood, he could only imagine how stupid she thought he looked. Or worse yet—how smart.

To make her quit staring, he shook the paper. "Now why would your great-grandma have a copy of the last will and testament of Rudolph Melnik?"

"What?" Carrie looked away from him.

Nick breathed a sigh of relief.

She grabbed the paper out of Nick's hand and stared at it.

Last Will and Testament—in bold writing across the top of an oversized piece of parchment paper. The words, written in heavy ink, possibly with a quill pen, swirled as elaborately as if this were the Declaration of Independence.

Below those words in smaller but equally elegant cursive: Rudolph Melnik.

Then Carrie looked up at Nick with wide, suspicious eyes. "Do you think this is what Hal could have been searching for? Did he somehow think there was a way to claim the property because he was related to Wilkie?"

Nick shrugged one shoulder. "I don't see how. Whatever Rudolph Melnik. . . Where does he fit into this mess, anyway?"

"He's the son of the first founder. Rudolph was the one who consolidated the family's wealth. He bought property and worked like a fiend getting rich."

"Fiend, huh?" Nick curled his mouth into a grimace. "That just an expression?"

"Great-Grandma Bea knew him. 'Worked like a fiend' were her words exactly. Great-Grandma said he'd have worn a crown if he thought he could get away with it. She said he thought he deserved to own the whole town. The Melniks donated a fair share of Main Street to the city in order to get the town named after them."

"But regardless of what Rudolph had, the generations that followed lost everything."

"A lot of it to Gundersons. They now own a good chunk of the old Melnik family holdings."

"How'd that happen?"

"Wilkie was the lowest the Melniks sank. But each generation seemed to be a little more interested in lazing around. A few get-rich-quick schemes and way too much time with a whiskey bottle frittered away the family fortune."

"So what difference does a. . ." Nick pulled the paper around so he could see it. "Fifty-year-old will make?"

Carrie shook her head. "Beats me. This is from the stack that Tallulah had. What does she want it for?"

"Just for the historical record, maybe. It probably should be in the Maxie Museum."

Carrie snorted. "It's the Melnik Historical Society Museum. It's about more than Maxie."

"From what I've heard, Carrie, it's mostly about Maxie."

Carrie nodded and rubbed her head as if it ached. "You know, these probably all belong in the museum."

"Right next to Maxie?"

Carrie glared at him through narrowed eyes. "Don't even suggest it. What I wonder is, would they like this will to be kept there? I should go over and show it to Bonnie."

Nick flinched. "I forgot to apologize to her. I need to do that. If you want, I'll go and show it to her, apologize, and scope out any other historical papers that might help us find some answers."

"Well, I'm not ready to hand them over yet, but you can look around the museum and ask Bonnie if the historical society might want these papers."

"Okay, I'll handle it."

Further examination of the stack that Hal and Tallulah had gathered amounted to yellowed newspaper clippings, including the momentous announcement that Maxie had been admitted to the *Guinness Book of World Records*.

"It was exactly fifty years ago this December." Carrie studied the story. "They featured Maxie in the Melnik Community Christmas Pageant that very year. No one took it too seriously. Grandpa Leonard said it was just for fun, a no-big-deal claim to fame."

As they set the papers aside, Nick, his hands so grimy he could barely stand it, said, "The rest of the second floor is pretty well cleaned by now."

"If you don't count those flea-bitten dead animals."

"You know, those could actually be worth some money. You want me to list them on eBay and see what happens?"

Carrie's eyes lit up. "You think I can convert those disgusting beasties to cash? Really?"

"We won't know unless we try."

"Well, okay." Carrie turned and glared at the Dead Zone door. "I'd part with them for the cost of shipping, so don't play hardball if you get any bids."

Nick laughed. "Your mom and grandma and the other ladies saw to this floor. But they haven't touched the third floor. I think we have to turn our attention there if we want to uncover anything really old." Nick looked up the narrow stairs, a funnel leading them straight to Mouse Heaven. Except he suspected that Carrie would die before she admitted there could be mice in heaven.

He felt Carrie tremble. "There's an attic, too, above the third floor."

"What a great house. I'll go first." He would have rubbed her back to comfort her if his hands had been clean.

"Let's just get it over with." Her head hanging, she plodded toward the stairway as if her feet weighed one hundred pounds each.

17

"Forgive me." Carrie clung to Nick's neck, feeling like a fool.

"I'm starved." Nick held Carrie in his arms.

"Let's quit." Carrie smiled, although she kept her eyes fixed on the stunningly neat piles of paper Nick had lined up on the floor. She'd seen about fifty mice today and spent a good part of the day jumping and screaming. She just hoped she'd seen the same mouse fifty times, rather than seeing fifty mice. And heaven only knew where Grizzly had gone.

"You know, I just used to scream. This jumping-into-a-man's-arms thing is new."

"I'm glad I can help." Nick scanned the floor then set her down next to one of the stacks of interesting papers they'd found.

He'd been a perfect gentleman, and Carrie liked perfect gentleman. She did. She especially liked gentlemen who wore tortoiseshell glasses. She'd just found that out about herself today.

But there might be some room in the perfect gentleman's handbook for a very polite kiss shared with the woman he'd spent a large part of the day holding. Especially since she hadn't exactly fought him off the other time he'd kissed her.

Oh, wait. She had kind of fought him off. Hal's fault. Maybe she should make sure he hadn't taken that personally. She looked deep into his eyes. He looked so gorgeous in those glasses. "Nick. . ."

Nick's arms didn't slip away like they had the other forty-nine times. Instead, he turned her to face him. Pulled her closer. "Would you like to—"

"Carrie Evans!"

Carrie dropped her forehead against Nick's strong chest. The stack of papers at Carrie's feet slid sideways, knocked over by the booming sound waves coming from below. Carrie gasped as they slid dangerously close to the box of Christmas ornaments they'd found. All she'd seen was dust-laden junk. Nick assured her that, once cleaned, the delicate glass baubles would be spectacular. He'd promised to chop down a pine tree and help her decorate for Christmas.

The sliding pile missed the ornaments, which was lucky because Tallulah was here, which left no time to pay attention to anything else.

Footsteps stomped upward. So much for knocking.

"We could hide," Nick offered.

"She'd just go through my stuff." Carrie spoke into his perfect green knit shirt, the logo in place, the fresh smell of laundry detergent still there even after a day in the grime. She sniffed quietly so he wouldn't notice. "There's no escape for us."

"We're up here, Tallulah."

After Nick hollered, Carrie sighed.

Nick patted her on the back. "I wonder what took her so long."

"It's Thursday." Carrie straightened. No sense putting off the inevitable. "Everybody knows that Tallulah drives to her sister's house in Bjorn to get her hair done on Thursdays. Her sister's a beautician. They have lunch and go visit their mother in the Bjorn Elderhostel all afternoon."

"Elderhostel? What is that?"

"The nursing home. Bjorn is the Swedish capital of Nebraska."

"I noticed. They're eyeball deep in Dala horses over there."

"Yeah, you can't move in Bjorn without tripping over a lutefisk and falling into a bowl of muesli."

"As opposed to Melnik, where you can't move without tripping over a—"

Carrie slapped him on the chest. "Don't say it!"

"I'm warning you, Carrie. I have pull in this town." Tallulah sounded like she'd gained the second floor and was heading on up, wheezing but determined. "I can make or break that newspaper with a snap of my fingers."

Nick's eyebrows arched. "True?"

"Nope. She's not even from Melnik."

"She moved here recently?"

"Yeah, she and her husband moved here in a snit from Bjorn when Bjorn's fire department didn't put out the fire in their garage fast enough to suit them."

"But she's not married, is she? I've never seen her with her husband."

"He died the year we celebrated Maxie's fortieth anniversary. I remember because I think Tallulah threw herself into that and created the historical society out of grief."

"Ten years? And they lived here how long before that?"

"Oh, twenty years or so."

"And you say she moved here recently? Thirty years ago is recently?"

"Well, yeah. I mean, her roots aren't here."

Nick's whole face just fell.

"What?" Carrie tried to think what Tallulah moving here from Bjorn could possibly mean to him.

"I'm never going to belong."

"Sure you are." *The poor sweet dummy. Why would anyone want to belong in Melnik?* It did occur to Carrie that maybe she wasn't a good judge of that since she, of all people, belonged up to her eyeballs. "Tallulah belongs—"

"You're darn right I belong!" Tallulah's vibrant pink turban broke the plane of the stairway opening.

Belongs in a loony bin.

Tallulah's mouth and the caftan of the day followed quickly behind the turban.

Nick leaned forward just a bit. "She got her hair done? Why?"

Carrie fought back a giggle. "Hi, Tallulah. Didn't like the article about Maxie or Wilkie in the *Bugle* yesterday, huh? And you didn't quite feel you'd made yourself clear after the funeral?"

That set Tallulah off. By the time she quit ranting, Carrie felt like her ear had been chewed off. The whole town was ruined. The governor would never come—*Like there was a ever a chance that he would*—and Tallulah's lifework was destroyed by a flick of Carrie's poisoned pen.

Carrie kind of liked the way that rolled off Tallulah's tongue. The woman had a bit of poetry in her obsessive-compulsive soul.

A lightbulb went on in Carrie's head. She snapped her fingers. "I'll tell you what, Tallulah. Why don't you start writing a column for the *Bugle*?"

Tallulah fell silent. *Thank You, God, for minor miracles.* Although *minor* might be an understatement. Parting the Red Sea was one thing, but making Tallulah be quiet, well, that was heavy-duty.

Tallulah stood stone still, although Carrie thought the turban vibrated a bit. Tallulah's shock passed, and she flung her arms wide. "I'll do it!"

Big surprise. Carrie nodded, accepting that she'd opened her mouth and now had to live with the results of having a foot inserted. Why not let Tallulah rave about wonderful Maxie from now until the festival? It'd save Carrie having to give the disgusting rodent much thought.

Tallulah clasped her hands in front of her with a loud clap. "Finally, someone who fully understands the true greatness of Melnik will have a hand in reporting the news."

"You can write an article a week, do a big buildup for the festival. Then after that, if you're still interested, you can write a column focusing on the town's history in any way you see fit. Or you can put in a report of the historical society's meetings, if you want. Just send in the minutes of the last meeting. Whatever you think is appropriate."

Carrie knew, way down deep inside, that Tallulah's definition of appropriate and Carrie's definition of appropriate were two very different things. Carrie made a mental note to put Tallulah's byline in big letters.

Tallulah went off on another outburst, this one overjoyed. Carrie tuned the woman out so thoroughly she barely registered Nick saying, "No, we're going to handle that."

"But if I'm writing about Melnik history, all these papers would give me a wealth of information. They would be in far better hands."

NOSY IN NEBRASKA

Tallulah trying to get her hands on Great-Grandma's stuff again. What is going on?

Tallulah might have harassed Great-Grandma this same way, not that Great-Grandma harassed worth a hoot, what with that cast-iron skillet handy. Tallulah couldn't have anything to do with Bea's death, could she? She wouldn't have, for example, sent Wilkie, her favorite Melnikite, in here hunting around, which resulted in Great-Grandma confronting Wilkie, possibly with that blasted skillet in her hand. Which Wilkie took away from her and. . .

Carrie narrowed her eyes and studied the flamboyant woman. Was she obsessed to a degree that crossed over to dangerous? Would Tallulah have sent in Wilkie? Then when Bea ended up dead, would Tallulah be treacherous enough to keep quiet about her part in it? Could Tallulah have been here? Might Wilkie, stunned from Hal's bonk on the head and maybe dopey from Shayla's antifreeze, have called the lady who sent him and asked for help?

Someone had smothered Wilkie, and Maxie Mouse had almost certainly been involved. Who better to have access to Maxie than Tallulah, the mouse-obsessed historian? Carrie would bet anything she had keys to both the museum and Maxie's cage.

Maybe. And maybe—instead of journalism—I should try fiction. A cozy mystery, maybe, about a town full of crazy people planning to spend Christmas worshipping a mouse instead of the baby Jesus.

Nah, who'd believe it?

"Of course you could go through them. They'd still be yours, Carrie. You know, these should be in the museum. We could—"

"Not now, Tallulah." Carrie held up her hand. "*I'm* going to go through these things. I promise to be careful and treat them respectfully. But they're mine. I decide what I share with the world. Chances are, it'll be everything. But I decide. That's final."

Tallulah's face darkened with anger until it was hard to see where the fuchsia turban stopped and her skin began. "Well, I never!" She turned and marched down the stairs in a huff.

Carrie tried to imagine anything Tallulah had never!

She stood next to Nick, listening to the pounding footsteps. It sounded like the residents of the Dead Zone had come to life and were thundering down the steps, making their break after fifty years of captivity.

Oh, if only they would.

The back door slammed so hard that the attic windows rattled.

Carrie heard a loud grunt from outside. She whirled and ran to the window. Nick came up beside her, and they watched Tallulah lean over the edge of the Dumpster. Nick had phoned the city and had it delivered midmorning after his tenth trip up and down the stairs. He hadn't asked, or Carrie would have told him

110

she couldn't afford it. He said he paid for it out of Grandpa Leonard's thousand dollars because of all the building debris. It now sat below this open window so they could drop bags of garbage down into it and save the trips up and down the stairs.

"It's all just old clothes and empty packing boxes, Tallulah," Carrie yelled. "I promise I haven't thrown anything important away."

Tallulah looked up so far that her turban fell off.

Carrie flinched. Tallulah was mostly bald. Tallulah gasped, scrambling after her rolling turban. She retrieved it, shoved it back on, and scuttled away.

"That poor woman."

"You're sure she's a woman?" Nick asked. "That looked like male-pattern baldness to me."

Carrie gasped. "Well, uh, yes. Why would you even think of such a thing?"

"Probably too much big city. You get so you've seen everything."

"No, I know she's got children. I know she had a husband."

Nick shrugged. "She sure yells like a woman."

Carrie smacked him.

Nick laughed. "Let's go wash up and eat something. I'm starving. Jansson's has tacos on Thursday nights."

"I hadn't heard that."

"Really?" Nick turned to her. "I thought everybody knew."

"Wow, clash with the smorgasbord." Carrie wondered if this counted as a date. She'd been wishing he'd ask her. She thought he'd come close a couple of times.

"Not really. They put lingonberries in the picante sauce. But it's drowned out by the jalapeño peppers, so it's okay."

Carrie shuddered. "Well, bless Olga Jansson for innovating. If this were Bjorn, she'd probably stick with strictly Swedish fare, but we can go a little nuts here in Melnik."

"I noticed." Nick picked up three-fourths of the stacks of papers they were keeping, and Carrie got the rest. They headed downstairs. "Where are we going to hide these so Tallulah or Hal or anybody else who might come snooping around doesn't find them?"

"There's really only one place I can think of that's completely safe."

"The Dead Zone again?" Nick stopped on the second floor.

Carrie kept going down. "Nope. Nowhere in there big enough, and the whole two lower stories are too clean. They'd be too easy to find."

Nick fell in behind. "Then where?"

Carrie felt the shuddering start in her belly and spread out to her limbs, her brain, her very soul. She moved quickly down the stairs, afraid she'd get clumsy with terror very soon. "The basement."

"Sounds good." Nick followed closely, sounding casual. He just didn't know.

"Sounds awful!"

"Why?"

"Because my great-grandma's basement is Mouse Ground Zero in the mouse capital of Nebraska."

18

He'd worked up the nerve to ask her out for dinner. It didn't really count because they were filthy and starving and no one had said the word *date* before or during their meal. It would have been hard to say a word of any kind since the good folks of Melnik all but stood in line to tell Carrie they were shocked, *shocked*, at her treatment of poor dead Wilkie.

By the end of the meal, when she never shirked from taking all the blame on herself, he was more impressed with Carrie's honor than ever.

Of course, word had gotten out—thanks to Nick's big mouth—that Gunderson had done it, but Carrie deflected all criticism of Gunderson, taking the whole load of blame on herself. Still, everyone knew the truth.

Once they were clear of Jansson's smorgasbord, Carrie quit being such a good sport. "I can't believe all those people yelled at me like that!"

Nick tried to lend moral support, but when he pictured himself hugging her, there was too much selfishness in it. "Give them a week. They'll get over it."

"Oh, they will not. They'll still be talking about this on Maxie's *centennial* festival, for heaven's sake. Are you kidding? They'll still be talking about Edith typing Stu Piperson's name as 'Stupid Person'. No way will they forget a fiasco like my Wilkie story."

"Well, that's probably right." Okay, could he be any wimpier? "I mean, they'll move on. Yes, they'll remember, but it won't matter and. . ." So the hug was selfish. So what?

Just slip your arm over her shoulder. Classic junior high move. She won't care a bit. She needs a white knight. Have-Mousetraps-Will-Travel. After all, I'm here, she's here. . .

He reached for her shoulder.

"I have to get out of here."

Nick dropped his arm to his side, hoping she hadn't noticed his clumsy move. He had no intention of ever leaving this charming village.

"That's why I'll never settle back in this lame little backwater."

His heart dropped as fast as his arm. He wanted roots. He wanted a small town where people knew him. Carrie was not a match for his dreams. But she was so cute and sweet and smart and funny and *cute*. Maybe if she knew he had enough money to travel a lot—thanks to the consulting he still did with his Chicago engineering firm—she'd be okay in Melnik. But trying to convince her

113

to stay by quoting his bank balance was so bad, even a dope like Nick knew it was wrong. He felt sure God was ready with a lightning bolt if Nick had any second thoughts on the subject.

"It will pass. You're a good writer. You'll know to check up on the paper now, so it won't happen again. The *Bugle* could be a great choice for you. The writing would be personal. You could try everything: news, features, columns, advertising. It's what a newspaper is meant to be—someone's vision, someone's voice." Mr. Pep Talk. "You could make a great career at the *Bugle*." Nick's heart stirred. He could almost hear "Yankee Doodle Dandy" in the distance. He was almost eloquent, almost a poet. Why, running the *Bugle* was her patriotic duty.

"Running the *Bugle* is a waste of my life!"

Carrie apparently preferred to rant. When they got to her house, he scouted for mice—none—too bad—so no leaps into his arms. Nick paused in his fretting. What if the mice moved out? She wouldn't need him anymore.

He turned into a tongue-tied coward—or rather, he turned into himself. He left her without asking for another date or another kiss.

Dope!

For the rest of the week, Nick worked on Carrie's house, loving every minute of coaxing the grand old mansion back to life and hoping she'd come out and ask for protection. She rushed in and out, giving him updates on news stories and the search for Gunderson. He never saw her for more than "hi" and "good-bye."

Even Sunday morning at church he couldn't catch up with her. He picked a pew at church with plenty of room so that maybe Carrie would come in and sit next to him, but Dora got there ahead of her and plunked down beside him. Now, thanks to Dora, he had ten new personal hygiene goals laid out in front of him. He also agreed to repair the cemetery fence, keep the sidewalks scooped this winter—he'd already done the lawn work all summer, so why not—and donate gravel for the parking lot.

When he caught up with Carrie after church, he said, "Wait'll you hear what they're going to let me do. I think I'm really starting to fit in here." Nick recited his list.

Carrie scowled. "They roped me into the funeral committee, the decorating committee, the cleaning committee, the choir, and teaching Sunday school."

"Wow, that's great. The town must be excited to have you home."

"They saw a sucker, just like with you. They're trying to dump every bit of work on the 'new guys.' "

"But you said yes, right?"

"Right. But it's no big deal for me. I'm not going to be here that long." Carrie patted him on the shoulder. "Bye." She joined her parents and grandparents. Nick overheard Carrie's grandma Helga invite everyone for lunch. Everyone in the family. Not him.

Dejected, Nick climbed into his pickup and went home alone to the little house he'd bought when he moved to town. It wasn't his dream house, not by a long shot. But it was old with pretty details. It needed him.

He did hang around Carrie's house later to make sure that Carrie got inside without incident, but no mice gave him an opening to sneak in another kiss. Which just made him the most pathetic human being who ever lived—that he needed a mouse to make that happen.

As he let himself out of her house Sunday night, he wondered if the day would ever come when he could kill off his inner overweight, nerdy bookworm.

And then it was Monday, and the *Bugle* monopolized every minute of her time. By Tuesday morning, desperate to have something Carrie needed him for, he decided to go apologize to Marian/Bonnie and find out if the museum wanted Carrie's old papers.

Nick gathered the papers into a file folder and drove to the Main Street building that now housed the Melnik Historical Society Museum. A very grand name for a fish tank containing a really large mouse. It shared an entrance with the city hall. And right in the entrance stood the Maxie Mouse monument. Someone had done some landscaping, and Nick saw that Maxie had some fake shrubs and a few brightly colored rocks in his aquarium house.

The Melnik city hall boasted an entry area about twenty by ten feet with five doors: the city offices and two bathrooms on the left, the museum on the right, and straight ahead, a door to a large auditorium.

The Maxie monument stood in all its verminy glory. Nick had done a considerable amount of business with the city office, applying for building permits and checking underground power and phone lines. But he'd never gone into the museum. Today, historic paperwork in hand, he tucked his folder under his arm and pushed on the chipped beige door labeled MELNIK HISTORICAL SOCIETY MUSEUM.

He fell in love.

It wasn't pretty or welcoming. It was just books. Oh, there were little displays, too. Old toys and rusty tools from a bygone era. Some slightly bent street signs, a few dozen replicas of Maxie on coffee mugs and stationery, and a few stuffed Maxies. There were also postcards of Maxie for sale. But mostly it was books. He took a deep breath and smelled books. The smell took him back to his childhood. Books and libraries, the refuge of the brainy dweeb.

The small Melnik museum was overwhelmed by ceiling-high shelves laden with books. The lights weren't bright enough to cut through the gloom. An aisle barely wide enough for Nick's shoulders led him to a little desk, where Bonnie

"Marian the Librarian" Simpson sat quietly, reading a dog-eared copy of *Les Misérables*.

She looked up, startled, as if no one had ever come in before. Nick wondered how close to true that was.

"Victor Hugo." He smiled at the memory of the sanctuary that books had been in his childhood. "My favorite. I read that book so many times when I was a kid, I could recite whole passages."

"I like *The Hunchback of Notre Dame* better."

"You identified with Esmeralda?" Nick couldn't see that. Bonnie was a quiet, sweet woman, not given to flashiness à la Esmeralda.

"Nope, I'm more the Quasimodo type."

Nick laughed. Even in the murky museum, Nick could see Bonnie blush, as if she'd never spoken so boldly in her life.

"For me it was more *The Count of Monte Cristo*."

"Alexander Dumas?" Bonnie nodded. "Revenge. One of my favorites."

"Yeah." Nick laughed. "Hey, I'm sorry I've been calling you Marian all this time. I thought—"

"Dora."

Nick nodded. "I apologize. It was the only thing I heard you called, and you answered to it."

Bonnie smiled, and Nick saw that behind the glasses and the plain dark blond hair scraped into a ponytail at her nape, she was a very pretty woman. Probably midforties.

"Well, who's going to fight with Dora over nicknames?"

"I haven't gotten one yet, but I'm new in town."

"So you read the classics?" Bonnie lifted a bookmark off her desk and slid it in place. No folding over corners to mark her spot. No laying the book facedown on the desk. She didn't even stick her thumb in her place and hang on to it. She set the book down perfectly square with the desk. Besides the book, the desk held a small ceramic turkey wearing a pilgrim hat, its tail feathers spread and colored rich orange and red and yellow, a perfect Thanksgiving touch.

"I read everything."

"How come you haven't come in before?" Bonnie slid her glasses into a beige case and then looked around the dingy museum as if she were sitting in the very center of heaven.

"I knew it was the museum, but I never heard about the books. I'll be back."

Bonnie smiled. "Did you need something today, or did you just come in because Carrie told you my real name and you wanted to apologize?"

"I have some old papers here." Nick lifted the manila folder of documents and clippings. "Things that might be of historical interest to the town. They were among Carrie's great-grandmother's things, and she says that if you want them, she'd probably donate them. You could cross-check and see if you already have copies."

Bonnie's eyes lit up as if Nick had brought old Hugo back to life and brought him in for a book signing.

"I'd be glad to help." Bonnie rose from the desk.

"Really?"

"What, you think I look too busy?" She blushed again, as if surprised at her nerve. Nick couldn't help but like the painfully shy woman. He remembered too well countless hours spent in the library as a child, his three brothers and one sister joining him often as not. His scholarly parents sometimes, too. The O'Connor family of nerds. And he'd been the king of them all.

The engineering firm had been more of the same—long hours alone with his computer and calculations. His move to Melnik had been more of a prison break than a career change. Bonnie seemed forever trapped in this lonely wonderland.

Nick felt a deep connection with her. "I'd appreciate it. Thanks."

"Let me show you some of my favorite books that pertain to Melnik history. You might want to study them to see if the information in your papers is already in our collection." Bonnie slipped around the desk, turning sideways to fit between it and the nearest bookshelves. Nick had to back up to let her pass. She led him deep into the literary jungle past displays of Melnik mementos.

"Look at all this stuff." Nick ran his hands reverently down the rows of books. "I like the old ones better than the new."

Bonnie glanced over her shoulder. A beige cardigan sweater draped over her shoulders set off her dark eyes in the dim light. Nick thought he saw mystery in those eyes, and loneliness, as if her thoughts were so private she hated to even think in the presence of others. He wondered how many hours a week she spent alone in here.

"These are all the yearbooks from Melnik High School," Bonnie pointed out as they went down the row. She tapped one book with a white spine. "My senior year."

Nick stopped. "Your year—hey, that's my year. We graduated the same time." Nick was stunned. He'd misjudged her age by over a decade. The poor woman was in her early thirties, not forties. He turned quickly to cover his expression.

"The books about Melnik history are in this section. They are more about the individual families and genealogy research, stuff like that, but put together they really do tell the story of the town." Bonnie led him to the farthest corner of the room and began pulling heavy tomes, their bindings cracked with age, off the highest shelves. "There's one here that has a lot about the Evanses in it. That might be the best if your papers came out of Bea's house."

"Here, let me do that. I'm a foot taller than you."

Bonnie turned to face him. She couldn't get past him in the tight aisle. Nick turned sideways. "Just scoot past."

Bonnie stared at the floor as she approached him. Pressing her back to the shelves, she inched by.

She glanced up, and Nick wondered about her and worried. "I really am sorry about calling you the wrong name. I know that had to hurt."

Bonnie shrugged one shoulder. "It's okay."

"No, it's not." Nick rested a hand on Bonnie's shoulder. She quit pressing herself so solidly against the shelves. In fact, she might have leaned toward him just a bit. She blinked, her lips parted. Nick noticed it all. How pretty she was in an understated way, how lonely. She'd gotten stuck in her world of books while he'd escaped. He still loved reading, but not as a substitute for life. He could help her escape.

"Bonnie, I—"

"Having that stupid mouse outside the museum is like a repellant. No wonder you never have anyone in here. This is the first time I've ever come—" Carrie came around the corner of the shelf, and Nick looked up, forgetting what he was going to say to Bonnie. Carrie's eyes widened. She looked from Nick to Bonnie to his hand on her shoulder.

"Oh, sorry, excuse me." She turned and disappeared.

Carrie thought she'd interrupted. . .something. Nick jerked his hand off Bonnie's shoulder as if he'd been burned and raced after Carrie.

He caught up with her on the sidewalk. It was easy enough.

"NoonestarveswhileClaralives."

Carrie stood in the icy, buffeting wind just outside the door of city hall, forking over money for what looked like a cherry pie.

"Mouseishome."

"Wow, cherry. That looks great." Nick tugged his jacket collar up around his ears and reached for his wallet. Sure, it was probably poisonous. It made drinking antifreeze seem yummy. But still. . . "Cherry's my favorite."

"Marbles," Carrie muttered under her breath.

Nick handed over a five, took the surprisingly heavy pie, and looked closer. Sure enough, red marbles.

Bonnie came out at a near run, as if she were chasing after Nick. He glanced at her flushed cheeks and saw her eyes bright with embarrassment and what might have been the gloss of tears. Before Nick could apologize again, although he wasn't sure for what this time, Bonnie bought a meringue pie garnished with bright yellow cottonwood leaves.

"Areyouamanoramouse?"

Bonnie had a heavy book in her hand. "H–here's that book on the Evans ancestors if you'd like to take it and study it, Nick. . .uh. . .and Carrie." Bonnie looked up as if lifting her chin was too much effort.

"Thanks. Uh. . .do I need to sign something to take this out of the museum?" Nick tucked the file folder under his arm, balanced the pie with his right hand, and reached for the book with his left.

"No, but I can give you a brochure explaining how to join the Melnik Historical Society. It's not required."

"Melnik'sgotitsmouse. ButI'vegotmyownideas."

Nick saw the look Carrie slid between him and Bonnie. He couldn't read her expression now. But she hadn't liked finding Nick with Bonnie in that narrow aisle. It gave him hope. With a glance at Bonnie, who was not nearly as good at covering what she was feeling, Nick saw the same hope he was afraid gleamed in his eyes. Only Bonnie's hope was aimed straight at him.

He knew just how Bonnie felt. She'd found a kindred spirit. Another bookworm. Nick knew they could talk for hours. And Bonnie loved Melnik and had no plans to leave. Ever. She was perfect for him. Well, what relationship ever worked between two people who were perfect? He wanted the mouse-phobic woman who saw Melnik as a giant mousetrap.

"What are your ideas, Clara? Tell me." Carrie shifted the pie into her left hand and slid her arm around Clara's shoulder.

"Giant-sizedmice." Clara's gray hair trembled as she flinched from Carrie's touch. "Runningwildkillingfolks."

"You mean Maxie." Carrie nodded her head toward the glass doors of city hall. Maxie's case was clearly visible beyond them.

"Iknowafewthings."

"We need to talk, Clara. Let me go with you to sell your pies, and we'll talk all about how you take care of the people in this town."

"It'stheCommunists.They'rebehindallthetrouble."

Nick watched in fascination as Carrie walked away with Clara. Listening, cajoling. Being a reporter. But Nick wasn't sure what the story might be.

"So, Nick. Would you like—"

"Give me that book!"

Nick groaned.

Carrie abandoned Clara.

Bonnie clutched the volume.

Tallulah.

"I recognize that." The wind gusted and Tallulah's caftan billowed fit to keep a ship sailing. "I've got everything I need gathered and written—mostly—for the Maxie book. But I was just going into the museum to dig through some of the oldest material."

Carrie snatched the book out of Bonnie's arms. Nick couldn't control a sigh of relief when Carrie gained control of things. Bonnie was too sweet. Tallulah would crush her like a bug. He grinned at the fiery competitive gleam in Carrie's eyes.

"I was here first, Tallulah. I'll go through it and then get it to you. And I've gone through a lot of Great-Grandma Bea's things and found a few interesting documents and pictures. I'll start on the Maxie pamphlet as soon as I get the paper out this week."

Tallulah gasped. "But I thought we'd go with my vision for the book. I only need you to polish it and to give me any pertinent information lost in Bea's house."

"Do you have your book with you, Tallulah? Believe me, I'd prefer editing your work to creating the whole thing myself."

Tallulah nodded, her eyes flitting to the book. "It's in my car in front of Jansson's. I'll get it and bring it across to the *Bugle* office. We don't have a moment to spare. I've even settled on a title. *Maxie Mouse: The Glorious Rodent of Melnik.*"

Bonnie turned and headed straight back into the museum. Nick thought he heard a snicker before the glass doors of the possibly-soon-to-be-named Maxie Memorial Hall clicked shut.

To keep from laughing straight into Tallulah's vivid green turban, Nick began thinking through a particularly complex exercise he'd learned the semester he spent studying physics. He heard Carrie coughing as he examined the variety of conventions for describing vector.

She got control, and with a sincerity that impressed Nick greatly—considering it was completely fake—she said to Tallulah, "I'll look forward to getting the draft of your book. I honestly don't see myself making a lot of changes. I'll just double-check for grammar errors and misspelled words. I'm sure I won't find any."

Tallulah gave a jerk of her chins that set them wobbling and nearly capsized her turban. "We need that book within two weeks so it can be mailed to the media and federal, state, and local dignitaries."

Nick pictured the president waving from the back of a giant mouse and immediately began reciting, internally, the Declaration of Independence, something he'd memorized during his semester studying American history.

When in the course of rodent events. . .

"This is going to be a huge event. I fully expect the governor to attend."

"Maybe if it was an election year, Tallulah," Carrie said. "But I'd hate for you to get your hopes up."

. . .it becomes necessary for one people to use a great big mouse. . . Nick caught himself. That wasn't in there.

"I refuse to be denied this triumph. The governor *will* be here, or I'll know the reason why."

"Uh, Tallulah, the reason *why* might be because he's busy and every town around has some kind of Christmas festival."

"This isn't a Christmas festival; this is a *Maxie* festival."

"But it is *Christmas*. You may be losing your perspective a bit. I mean, it is our Savior's birth. Maybe we shouldn't focus *too* much on Maxie."

We hold these truths to be self-evident, that all mice are created equal. . .except for Maxie, who is gigantic.

Nick shook his head and decided to stay with the bizarre conversation. Reciting the Declaration wasn't helping anyway. Maybe if he paid more attention instead of daydreaming, he'd have figured out Bonnie's name faster.

Carrie headed across the street to the *Bugle*, and Tallulah lumbered toward her car. Nick traipsed along after Carrie for no good reason. Maybe he'd check to see if the *Bugle*'s front door needed more work.

19

Carrie finished with Tallulah, thanked Nick for her perfectly oiled door, and settled into her desk chair, dreading the next part of her day.

She needed to find a Maxie photo. *Eeek!*

The door crashed open. Sven Gunderson stormed in.

Lifting her head to face him, she was actually grateful for the interruption. She'd been wondering when he was going to come in and fire her.

"I read that puff piece you did on Wilkie, retracting the first story." Gunderson jabbed an arthritic finger at her.

The man was her boss. She really ought to be polite. "You sneaking, lying coward!" Okay, forget polite. Maybe the paper in Bjorn or Gillespie was hiring. "It's bad enough that you wrote that garbage. But then you put *my* name on *your* story!"

Gunderson launched into a tirade, *none* of which included the words "You're fired."

Carrie gave as good as she got, and eventually Gunderson stormed out.

"It really is hard to get fired in this town," Carrie said to the empty paper office.

She finished her workday and went home to spend her evening writing something that she hoped marked her as the ultimate professional, unbiased journalist. A flattering story about that nasty, obese mouse.

⁂

Carrie looked at the time in the corner of her computer screen and was shocked to see that it was 9:00 p.m. She sat alone in the mouse house, rope tied firmly around her jeans at the ankles so no mice could run up her legs. She was finished writing *Maxie Mouse: The Glorious Rodent of Melnik.*

"Is it any wonder I've got a phobia?" Carrie asked her living room ceiling.

Grizzly came in howling like a demon-possessed Osterizer and leapt onto Carrie's lap.

She picked up the soft-bristled baby brush she'd unearthed in the bathroom. Grizzly liked having his hair combed.

Grizzly, who was turning out to be *not* the rampaging killer she'd hoped for at all, looked up. Carrie studied him. "Didn't it used to be the other eye that was closed? Are you sandbagging your injuries to get sympathy?"

His unearthly yowl eased into a rugged purr. He twitched his strange, L-shaped tail, and Carrie hugged him.

"Okay, even if you're faking the eye thing, you've had it hard. I'll keep babying you. I hope a diet of mice will give you all the vitamins you need, because I'm not feeding you while I hear scratching in the walls. You"—she tapped him on the nose—"hunt your own supper."

She'd have rather had Nick nearby protecting her, but after a very promising start, he'd pulled back. She kept hearing herself yell, "Let me go!"

"I believe those were my very words, Grizz. You don't think he took them wrong, do you?"

How could he take them any way but wrong, idiot?

"Did I tell you I'm a genius writer, Mouse Breath?" Carrie smoothed the brush over the cat again, finding fewer knots. "A dope about men, but I can really write."

Grizzly rubbed his head on Carrie's knee. "I told the Maxie Mouse story as it's meant to be told. It's a story of freedom and courage and creativity. This book isn't about Maxie; it's about America. It's about a small town's struggle to hold on to their heritage while building for the future, all to preserve a way of life they love." Satisfied with Grizzly's now-smooth back, Carrie set the brush aside. She didn't want the old boy to get irritated with her. Besides, they needed to talk.

"It's really good. The governor really might come. And in writing it. . ." She whispered in his good ear, almost afraid to speak out loud. "I'm going to give the good people of Melnik something to really be thankful for." Carrie hugged Grizzly again, loving the softness of him. Even his coarse growl seemed like an offer of friendship.

"I've convinced myself that Melnik is where I belong, too." And if she belonged and Nick belonged, then maybe, just maybe, she and Nick belonged together.

It was way too late at night, but she reached for the phone.

⌘

"Nick, can you come over for a while?"

Nick's eyes fell shut. This was it. Carrie was going to tell him she'd found a job and was leaving forever. He swallowed and tried to speak. Nothing came out. He swallowed again.

"Did I wake you?"

"No, just. . .uh. . ." Nick couldn't even think of an easy excuse. "What did you need?"

"I have to go up to the attic again and I'm. . ."

He breathed a sigh of relief. This wasn't good-bye. This was mice.

"I'll be right over." He jogged out the door into the frigid wind, tugging on his down-filled jacket. November wound down aiming toward Thanksgiving. The trees were as bare as his future would be if she left him.

Pulling to a stop in front of Carrie's house, sitting alone in his cold, empty truck, he thought of his cold, empty life. "I don't want you jumping into my arms tonight," he said to the cold, empty air. "It hurts too much to let you go."

***

"This time when I see a mouse and jump into his arms, I'll hang on," Carrie said to the ceiling of her cold, empty house.

Quit being such a dope and just tell him you care about him and you've decided to stay in Melnik. You don't need a mouse. Still, a mouse would make things easier. When Carrie realized she was actually *wishing* for a mouse to appear, she knew that either she'd completely lost her mind. . .or this was love.

Nick walked up her back steps, and Carrie swung open the door. The bite of the November weather chilled her, even in her red Cornhusker sweatshirt and blue jeans.

"You called?" Nick smiled at her.

Her heart turned a twisty somersault. Nick's smile was going to give her internal injuries. She stepped back to let him in.

"I've been writing the book Tallulah wanted, and I've come up with some questions. I need to search the attic to answer them. Do you mind keeping me company?"

"It's my pleasure." Nick followed her into the kitchen just as Grizzly jumped up on the table and then leapt at him. Nick caught him by reflex.

Carrie stopped. "Before we go up, I—I'd like you to see something I wrote."

"The Maxie book?"

"I've been working on that, too. But I wrote a story for next week's paper about Maxie, and I really feel like it came out well." Her cheeks heated. "I wouldn't mind a second opinion."

Nick's expression lightened.

Carrie lifted the laptop off the couch and handed it to him. He sat and began reading. The room was still. Carrie's nerves crackled until she was sure Nick could hear them. The moments stretched. She considered making coffee or unsnarling more of her snarling cat or maybe checking the kitchen pantry for new dead guys.

Instead, she sank down on the couch beside Nick and read over his shoulder. About the time she started, he was done.

He lifted his head. "This is beautiful. How did you do this—make a story about a big dead mouse seem important?"

Carrie shrugged. "You like it, then?"

Nick set the laptop on the coffee table. A week ago the table had been buried in refuse.

"I love it. You made the words. . .sing."

Carrie's throat closed. Nick seemed closer than he had before. . .bigger, nicer—which wasn't possible. He'd been the nicest man Carrie had ever met right from the start.

She managed a hoarse "Thank you."

Nick studied the computer screen. "I'm sure the minute you contact them at the *World-Herald*, they'll take you back. It seems like you've been regretting making this move back to Melnik. When you want your job back, they'll jump at the chance."

Guilt and the weight of all she'd left unsaid made it hard to talk. "Sure, maybe."

His blue eyes, lit by the computer screen, shone with the honesty and decency she'd come to expect. "Can you answer a question for me?"

Carrie wouldn't have denied him much right now. "Sure."

"Why are you here? Why did you give up the *World-Herald* for Melnik?"

Carrie's heart pounded. "I got fired." Her face heated until she had to resemble a matchstick, with her hair the white tip on the end.

"Fired? Why? You're brilliant."

Carrie's humiliation morphed into pathetic gratitude. "I accused a man of a crime. A man who, it turns out, was a good friend of my editor. When I took my suspicions to him, I got my head taken off. The worst part is, I was wrong. I looked a whole lot closer and found out I'd jumped to the wrong conclusions. Of course, I didn't know that until I'd faced down my editor and given him a rousing speech about Rich Man's Justice. I burned my bridges at the paper. I can't go back."

She dropped her chin and looked at her hands twisted together in her lap. She couldn't meet his eyes. "I was out of work. I couldn't make the rent, and Great-Grandma's house came along. Instead of admitting I'd messed up, I took the house. I'm not a big success, Nick. I may just qualify for the *Guinness Book of World Records* as the World's Youngest, Fastest, and Most Complete Failure. Maybe they'll stuff me and give me my own case at City Hall."

Nick lifted her chin with one finger, startling her. She forced herself to meet his gaze, braced for his disappointment and his contempt. She deserved it.

"You're not a failure, Carrie. You're a genius."

All she saw in his eyes was kindness. "What?"

"I just read the proof of it on your computer. Anyone who can write like this can never be called a failure."

Carrie felt her eyes burn with threatening tears. "You're the nicest man I've ever met."

His hand relaxed on her chin and eased around to the back of her neck.

Carrie waited for a mouse to jump out or a robber to break in or a neighbor to drop by.

He kissed her.

She made a point of *not* yelling, "Let me go!"

He tilted his head and deepened the kiss.

A loud thump came from underfoot. The cellar. Mouse Ground Zero.

Nick eased back. His lips twisted in a wry smile. "Another home invasion, I suppose. But remember where we were, huh?"

Carrie nodded, not particularly interested in whoever might be robbing her blind.

"Let's go. Maybe we can add a new member to the rogues' gallery in the Melnik jail." Nick stood up and rounded the couch. He wrenched the basement door open with a nasty squeak, and when his feet hit the hollow-sounding boards to the cellar, another crash echoed up the steps.

Carrie came out of her kiss-induced stupor, jumped up, and chased after Nick.

Her feet reached the cement floor of Ground Zero just as Nick clicked on the pull string of the bare bulb and reached down to pull Tallulah to her feet, where she'd stumbled over one of Great-Grandma's ten rusty water heaters.

Carrie hoped the woman hadn't broken a hip.

When Nick pulled Tallulah to her feet—pretty gently, Carrie thought, all things considered—Tallulah's turban du jour dropped off her head and rolled across the floor like an electric blue tumbleweed.

Tallulah, hairless except for a ring of bright red perfect male-pattern-baldness fluff, made a dive for the hat. Nick held on. A gun shook loose from somewhere in Tallulah's voluminous color-splattered caftan, clattered across the basement floor, went off, and shot a dusty canning jar to death.

Carrie jumped and squeaked, but it wasn't as bad as if she'd seen a mouse.

Nick pulled Carrie close to his side, shielding her with his own body.

"A gun?" Nick turned to Tallulah, his brow arched.

Carrie let herself be held for a few seconds and then stepped away to focus on Tallulah, who was struggling against Nick's hold, reaching for her turban. "Leave the gun and the turban. You're not going to be able to keep them in jail anyway."

"Jail!" Tallulah covered her head with her one free hand, as if she had no bigger problem than her hair. Carrie decided Tallulah might be right. It was bad hair.

"Unless they make turbans to match the orange jumpsuits, you're going

126

hatless for a long, long time. This time no one's going to talk me out of pressing charges. I'm sick of you breaking into my house."

"No, not without my turban!" Tallulah waved her hand and an object flew straight at Carrie. With a soft thud, something hit her chest.

Carrie looked down as the little ball of. . .

"Eeeek!"

She landed in Nick's arms, shrieking, slapping at her shirt as if it were on fire. Carrie had just been hit by Maxie Mouse.

Tallulah, free, raced for her turban, ignoring the gun.

Nick stepped well away from the bedraggled, rolling mouse. "Don't cry. Run up and change your shirt, quick. Take a shower if you need to."

Carrie hadn't noticed she was crying. She'd have wiped her face, but her hands had touched her mousy shirt. She buried her face in Nick's chest. She was going to have to boil her shirt, her hands, maybe her whole body. She was pressed against Nick—she was going to have to boil him, too.

Nick carried her to the bottom of the stairway, set her on the first step, and picked up the gun.

"Oh, what's the use?" Tallulah took a second to pick up Maxie and slip him in her caftan pocket and then buried her face in her mousy hands to cry with sufficient drama. "I'm ruined anyway. I might as well admit everything."

Carrie knew what was coming before the woman even opened her mouth. She almost held her ears, but she'd touched her shirt and her shirt had touched Maxie. Still, she didn't want to hear it.

"I did it." Tallulah's sobbing deepened until it didn't even seem like she was acting. "I shot him. I killed Wilkie Melnik."

20

The cell door rolled shut with a metallic bang.

"I'm not like the other trash you keep in this jail." Once her turban was restored, Tallulah's inner diva fully reemerged.

Shayla rolled off her cot and stood, looking like a lifer in a no-death-penalty state. The type of person with no fear of punishment. So why not mop the floor with the lady who'd just called her trash?

Tallulah was too busy emoting to notice that she was insulting a young woman with antifreeze flowing where her paternal love should be.

Hal strolled over to the cell wall that separated him from Shayla and Tallulah and looked through the bars. The women's and men's correctional facilities weren't exactly across town from each other.

"What's Hal still doing here?" Carrie whispered to Junior.

"I think his apartment's being painted. He refused to pay his bail, and then when I told him to just go home anyway, he wouldn't leave. I quit feeding him unless he chips in for meals."

"This isn't a bed-and-breakfast, Junior. Send him and Shayla home."

Junior shrugged. "They're not hurtin' nothin'."

A man lay snoring to humble a sawmill, with his back to the action. Ned Gaskell, the town drunk, sleeping off a brawl he'd had in the local bar. Someone had questioned the skill of the Cornhuskers' starting quarterback, and Ned had defended the honor of one of Nebraska's finest.

Nick knew Junior would have let the man go home. Badmouthing the Huskers amounted to someone begging to be punched. But Ned's wife was too mad to let him in the house, so he'd sleep here a night. . .or two. However long it took Mrs. Gaskell to cool down and Ned to sober up.

Nick glanced at Carrie, still pale even for a Swede. Her hair was wet and slicked back, her face raging pink from the blazing-hot water and scrubbing during her shower. Her clothes were fresh out of her drawer. Nick had her whole outfit from the Maxie incident stashed in the back end of his truck, destined for the burn barrel. Nick didn't tell her he'd seen a mouse dash into her clothes drawer while he was tearing up the kitchen flooring. Amazing that somebody had covered a perfectly good solid oak floor with Congoleum.

"I want a lawyer. I demand a phone call."

"Tallulah, give it a rest." Junior shook his head and rubbed his bare scalp with his beefy hand.

It occurred to Nick that Junior had more hair than Tallulah.

"It's after 10:00 p.m.," Junior went on. "You've confessed to murder, and the only lawyer in town already took his nighttime meds and is out cold until breakfast."

"I know my rights!" Tallulah's fists punched the air. The woman couldn't act her way out of a paper bag, let alone a jail cell.

Ned jerked in his sleep and grumbled something about women and bowling a three hundred. He yelled, *"Giant mice. . .crawling!"*

Hal looked at the man and shuddered. Nick noticed goose bumps on Carrie's arms.

"Actually, I get to hold you for twenty-four hours before I press charges. And it's not that I don't know what charges to file. I've got a list as long as my arm. But it's late, and my wife told me that if I don't get back and help with the slumber party she's having for our son and his twelve best friends, she'd throw away my share of the leftover lasagna instead of letting me have it for lunch tomorrow. But before I go. . ." Junior grabbed a folding chair and plunked himself down in the narrow hallway in front of the two cells.

"You let me out of this cell, Junior Hammerstad." Tallulah wagged the scolding finger of death under Junior's nose. "Or I'm calling your mother!"

"I've quit letting Mom tell me who to arrest ever since she got lost driving the three blocks from her house to mine and ended up in Kansas City. So don't bother her. You're staying."

"I'm leaving!"

"Knock it off."

"I ought to be above suspicion. I'm an upstanding member of this community!"

"Tallulah." Junior scrubbed his face with both hands. "You confessed."

"You said he was already dead."

"You didn't know that when you started spraying him with bullets."

"One bullet!"

"Oh, like that makes it okay."

"You're going to regret this."

"I wouldn't be surprised." Sounding exhausted, Junior scowled at his three prisoners. "Now I want all three of you to listen up. I love my wife's lasagna." Junior glanced sideways at Nick and Carrie loitering in the jailhouse doorway. "Get some chairs in here."

He turned back to the criminal element. "I'd let you out of the cell to talk—just so Ned gets a good night's sleep—but my office is too small for all six of us."

Nick ducked out to grab the chairs. He was the new guy in town. Rule of thumb: The new guy did it. He was glad to be outside the cell.

Junior pulled his notebook out of his pocket. "Now you say you shot

Wilkie—is that right, Tallulah?"

Nick was losing track of the confessed murderers, the motives, and the weapons of choice. That struck him as a bad, bad sign.

Tallulah jammed her fists on her rotund hips. "But you said he was already dead." Tallulah had gotten over her confession real fast when Junior gave her that bit of news.

The turban to cover her hair problems. The caftan to cover her weight problems. Nick wondered if there was anything she could get to cover her mouth.

"I said *most likely* he was already dead. The coroner's report tells me something and then one of you confesses. I ask the coroner, 'Could it have been antifreeze poisoning?' and she says, 'Wow, gunshot wound, blunt force trauma wound. . . I never thought to check for poison.' She's got a limited budget, you know."

"What did kill him, Junior?" Carrie asked, crossing her legs as if they were at a tea party instead of Murderers' Row.

"The results are sketchy. The coroner said all these things contributed. The gunshot seems to be postmortem, but with him unconscious, weakened by the poison, and showing obvious signs of suffocation, there's some question of which came first."

"You said the gunshot *was* postmortem, not *seemed* to be," Tallulah screeched.

Nick wondered if she subconsciously dressed to look like a parrot to match her voice.

"Even if you didn't kill him, Tallulah, you're still under arrest for breaking into Carrie's house *with* a gun. Plus, you've admitted to doing the same thing the night Bea died. That's *four* felonies, so *settle down!*"

"There's a concealed-carry law in Nebraska. I've got a license. I can carry a gun in my pocket."

The top of Junior's head turned red. "*Not if you're breaking into a house.* That's committing a felony with a weapon."

Tallulah sniffed. "A technicality."

"*A felony is not a technicality!* Not even close."

Nick wondered if he should get some duct tape to wrap around Junior's head so it wouldn't explode.

"You want me to walk all the way home just to put my gun down before I break in? That's very inconvenient."

"Well, sitting here talking while my wife rides herd on a dozen junior-high-aged boys is inconvenient, too."

"I brought the gun for protection. I wasn't going to use it on anyone."

"It went off twice. Once into *maybe* already-dead Wilkie and once into Carrie's canning jar. *You stop carrying that gun around until you learn how to use it!*"

Nick thought that maybe Tallulah ought to quit carrying the gun under any and all circumstances.

"Well, fine then." Tallulah crossed her arms, a gesture of defiance somewhat weakened by the bars on the jail.

Junior clutched his hands together in front of his paunchy belly as if he were wrapping them around Tallulah's neck. "And we haven't even talked about you breaking into city hall and stealing Maxie yet. The break-in is a felony. Stealing Maxie, well, I don't know about that. He isn't worth much; probably can mark that down as a misdemeanor."

"Maxie is extremely valuable."

"You *want* another felony count?" Junior's voice rose until it might hurt a dog's ears.

"But I didn't *steal* him. I have a key to Maxie Memorial Hall—"

"It hasn't had its name changed yet, Tallulah. Don't call it that." Carrie clutched her hands together as if she were begging.

"I sometimes get Maxie out and take him home overnight, just so he's not so lonely."

Carrie dropped her face onto her clasped fingers. Hal grabbed the cell bars with a faint nauseous-sounding groan.

Nick asked, "Does anyone else do that? Carry Maxie around? That could explain the mouse fur on Wilkie."

Carrie whimpered. Hal backed away from the bars.

"They'd better not." Tallulah looked affronted that anyone would take Maxie for a sleepover except her. "As for Wilkie, I went in the pantry to hide—"

"With the gun drawn. . . ," Nick said.

"I'd just seen Bea dead and heard a noise. I pulled the gun out of fear. Then I opened the pantry door and Wilkie was in there and—"

"Why'd you wanna kill Dad?" Shayla interrupted.

Nick braced himself. If seventy-year-old Tallulah announced she was forty-something Wilkie's child, he was just going to believe it and add another seat on the Maxie float.

"I told you it was an accident. I went to Bea's house to talk to her."

"That late at night, Tallulah?" Carrie shook her head. "You've been prowling around that house too much. What's so important that you think is in there?"

Tallulah had a mulish expression on her face.

Carrie said, "I'm pressing charges on the break-in, Junior. Give her four felony counts right now."

"Okay!" Tallulah cracked. "It's just that—that there have been rumors about Maxie maybe not belonging to the city. There might be a will lost somewhere that puts his ownership into question. I'd heard that maybe the will is in Bea's house. I just need to make sure. We need to clear up even the slightest shadow on Maxie's ownership."

"What you mean is, you hoped to find proof that it existed and destroy it."

"No, that's not what I mean. And it's not *four* counts. I didn't break in the night Bea died. I saw she'd fallen. I *went* in. To help. Then I heard someone upstairs and it scared me. I decided to hide and accidentally shot Wilkie in the pantry. That's why I didn't call an ambulance for your great-grandma. I promise you, I'd have called if there'd been any hope of saving her." Tallulah gave Carrie a beseeching look.

Carrie nodded, and Nick could tell Carrie believed the woman. Actually, he did, too.

"After the gun went off, I slammed the door. I ran out and didn't look back. I didn't mean to shoot Wilkie. I didn't want him dead. I wanted him to be the grand marshal of this year's Maxie Festival. I had no motive to kill that poor man."

Junior's face had returned to a color compatible with life while Tallulah talked. He exchanged a look with Carrie and Nick then turned to his trusty notebook. "Here's how I see it. Shayla"—Junior jabbed his pencil eraser at her—"served up the antifreeze cocktail, and Wilkie drank it and went out about 6:00 p.m. He spent the evening in the bar. By ten o'clock, he ended up at Bea's. Hal"—Junior looked up and glared at his deputy—"for no good reason I can figure out, was in Bea's house. Care to explain that, Hal?"

The deputy went sullen. "Look, I heard rumors, okay? I was paying real close attention to Dad because I wanted to know everything about him. I knew he was spending more money than he should have, and I heard there might be a lot more. I knew it had something to do with an old will and the will might be hidden in Bea's house. I figured if I got it first, I might be able to keep Dad from getting it. I didn't want the money, but I didn't want him to have it just to gamble away. So I tailed Dad when I had the night off that Tuesday. I was cruising around town, and I saw Dad through a window in Bea's house. He was standing over Bea. I assumed he'd hurt her."

Junior shook his head in disgust. "Hal clobbers Wilkie and leaves him for dead on the floor next to Bea."

Tallulah sniffed. "That was tacky, Hal."

"Well, bad manners are all over murder near about every time it happens." Junior wet his finger and turned a page, then settled his notebook on his stomach as if it were a handy TV tray. "Somehow, between ten and eleven thirty when you say you went there, Tallulah, Wilkie gets in the closet. I'm guessing someone found him unconscious and smothered him to death with Maxie or some other mouse."

Carrie scooted her chair two feet farther from Junior. Nick patted her on the knee and prepared to catch her. Hal backed up. Nick was going to let Hal handle his fears alone.

Tallulah looked appalled. "They could have ruined Maxie. He needs to be treated with care."

Junior rolled his eyes. "Then the murderer set Wilkie in the pantry like a can of cream of potato soup."

"You know, Junior. . ." Carrie sounded the next thing to crazy, in Nick's humble opinion. Which might be why she was glaring at the man who seemed destined to arrest half the population of Melnik. "I've been meaning to tell you, you never should have told Gunderson all those details about Shayla and the crime scene. That's unethical."

Nick decided not to remind Carrie of all the stuff Junior had told them.

Junior sat up, obviously surprised. "What are you talking about? You're the one who wrote that story with all that information in it about the crime. You wrote about Shayla's confession and the autopsy report in that stupid pack of lies about Wilkie."

"I didn't write that article."

"Who did?" Junior lifted his notebook, pen ready.

Nick couldn't believe Junior hadn't heard. Everybody knew who'd written that story. Of course, Junior had been busy arresting confessed murderers. "Gunderson."

Junior and Carrie stared at each other. Nick was adding things up, too. That noise in the newspaper office. Behind the door that opened into a building owned by Gunderson. He'd gotten the information on that hatchet piece on Wilkie by eavesdropping on Shayla's hysterical confession. Why would Gunderson be eavesdropping on Carrie at the paper?

"I'm adding his name to the suspect list. Someone strong had to pick up Wilkie and stuff him in that closet." Junior jotted away.

"Don't forget Mom," Shayla said. "She might've killed Dad because of Donette."

"Or Donette might've killed Wilkie because he wouldn't leave your mom." Junior did some more writing. Then, satisfied with his notes, he gave a tiny jerk of his head toward the three prisoners and went back to his notebook. "My gut tells me the mouse smotherer found Wilkie unconscious from the skillet and the poison, but alive. Finished him off and stuffed him in the closet. Neither your mom nor Donette could've moved his body, Shayla."

Shayla looked mutinous, like she'd fight to prove her mother was a killer. Dysfunctional-family poster child at your service.

"I've got one other detail from the state police detective who's in charge of this investigation."

"I thought you were in charge," Nick said. Although, when he thought about it, that seemed unlikely. Junior was nobody's image of a competent police detective.

"Nope, but while they're waiting around for the autopsy results, I'm looking into it myself. They did check financial records, though. Hal's right about Wilkie coming into money. He was gambling more than usual and spreading cash around for the last couple of months. He had two payments of five hundred dollars. Wilkie kept records."

Carrie said, "You think maybe he was blackmailing someone?"

"Maybe." Junior glared at Tallulah. "But even if someone else smothered him, your reckless gunplay could have finished him off. I'm not about to let you off the hook for murder until we've got a final autopsy report. Right now Dr. Notchke, the coroner, is so fed up with me for phoning her with new confessions that she'll barely take my calls, so that slows everything down."

Junior sighed. "I don't think any of you did it." He pulled the keys off his belt. "You can all go home, but I'll need to ask you more questions, so don't leave town."

Shayla shook her head. "I don't have anywhere to go."

Hal settled into the cot next to snoring Ned. "My apartment won't be ready until the day after tomorrow."

"Everyone in town will have heard about it, and they'll be gossiping." Tallulah crossed her arms stubbornly. "I'm not leaving until you admit you were out of line to arrest me in the first place."

"I want you all out of here. I'm tempted to kick Ned out, too. It's aggravating, hauling in food for the bunch of you."

All three glared at him but didn't budge, not even when Junior threw both doors open. "Fine, stay if you want, but no free meals."

"What it really comes down to is. . ." Carrie leaned forward, her elbows on her knees. Nick saw her eyes lose focus as the investigative reporter added everything up. "There's still a mouse-wielding murderer running loose in Melnik."

Nick sighed. He was never going to get a date with Carrie. "Well, isn't this just going to be a happy Thanksgiving, compliments of Maxie?"

Carrie nodded. "And a very merry Christ-mouse."

21

Four days until Thanksgiving. Maybe more to be thankful for than I'd thought when I moved home to Melnik. Carrie jingled her keys as joyfully as sleigh bells as she opened the *Bugle* on Monday morning.

Her "Maxie makes America great" story had set the town to buzzing with joy last week. This week, Thanksgiving week, she was going to cause trouble. She still needed to transcribe the city charter and Rudolph Melnik's last will and testament.

Tallulah, Hal, and Shayla remained in jail, even though Junior now left the door wide open night and day. Shayla was homeless; Hal's landlord had decided to remodel his bathroom. Tallulah was sneaking home to sleep in her own bed, but she always beat Junior back before he could lock her out of jail.

At least Ned had gone home, bless his heart.

Olga Jansson had taken to dropping off meals, which annoyed her because everybody knew she didn't do takeout. But Tallulah was an old friend who paid for all three meals—and she tipped well—so Olga made an exception.

Junior refused to apologize for arresting Tallulah, citing her confession. He threatened at least five times daily to physically heave all three of them out onto the street, but Tallulah said that if he so much as touched her, she'd whack him with her purse so hard he'd have to arrest her for assault, so what was the point?

Carrie was pretty sure none of those three had killed Wilkie. She was convinced that the killer was the person who had stuffed Wilkie into the closet.

During a quiet moment at the *Bugle* while Donette and Viola were out chasing hot-breaking news—or possibly having coffee at Jansson's—Carrie pulled a couple of documents out of her desk drawer. One of them was the Melnik town charter, the other Rudolph Melnik's will. If she was reading them right, both contained a motive for murder. One about wealth; the other about the ownership of an oversized mouse. Anywhere else on the planet there would be no doubt what the motive was. But this was Melnik. As Carrie read, her hands began to tremble. Finally, she thought, they had the answers they needed.

She reached for the phone to call Nick, knowing he wouldn't be home, but glad for an excuse to try anyway. She didn't bother with his cell. Cell phones didn't work well in Melnik. She needed one of those books from Bonnie's museum, and Nick had it. Knowing he'd drop everything to bring it over warmed her heart.

Not enough to make her blood stop running cold from getting whacked by

Maxie, but it was a start.

Nick didn't answer. She remembered that he had planned to hunt for more historical information at the museum. Shuddering at the very thought of walking past the Glorious Rodent of Melnik, she shoved back her chair and marched out the door. Nick's truck was parked in front of the Melnik Historical Society Museum and the City Auditorium, soon to be renamed Maxie Memorial Hall if Tallulah had her way.

She entered the dingy hallway dividing the museum on the right from the city offices on the left. She tiptoed past Maxie's aquarium, keeping far to the left.

Maxie was in the aquarium looking none the worse for hitting her—Carrie swatted at her chest. She couldn't quit wiping away the Essence of Rodent that now clung to her like a death shroud despite her taking ten boiling-hot showers— the theory being she could change into a whole new layer of skin more quickly if she burned the old one away. Forget that Maxie had never actually *touched* her skin.

She made the mistake of a true phobic. She glanced at Maxie, his teeth bared as if he wanted to go for her throat. He stood frozen in all his rattish splendor, in his case, as if trying to terrify children away from learning about Melnik's past.

She dashed past the wretched vermin, remembering Bonnie and Nick in a very close situation when she went in last time. A flash of jealousy made her swing the door open quietly. She heard the murmur of voices—back in the corner where she had found them before.

Carrie was absolutely sure Nick liked her—maybe. But there was no denying that Bonnie was his perfect match. Bonnie loved Melnik. Nick loved Melnik. Bonnie loved books. Nick loved books. Bonnie was an obsessive-compulsive neat freak. Nick was an obsessive-compulsive neat freak.

Instead of being jealous, Carrie knew she should push Nick and Bonnie together. A little light matchmaking. Instead, she decided she'd invite Nick to her family Thanksgiving right in front of the little poaching OCD bookworm.

She rounded the corner and saw Nick reaching for books off the top shelf while Bonnie stared at him with abject misery, as if all her dreams were just out of her reach on a high shelf.

Jealousy and pity created a toxic-waste dump where Carrie's Christian charity should be. Shamed by her unkindness, Carrie knew Nick really did deserve someone good enough for him.

Too bad.

She stepped forward to stake a claim. Then Bonnie opened her mouth.

"Would you like to have Thanksgiving dinner with me, Nick?"

Carrie clamped her jaw shut. Bonnie had beaten Carrie to the invitation. He answered her without stopping his search, a search that stretched out his long, lean body and reminded Carrie of what good shape he was in and how tall and broad and strong he was. And how he'd been a hero from the first moment she'd jumped into his arms.

"That would be nice. Thank you." Nick pulled a book down, studied the title for a minute, then looked back at Bonnie. "My parents are in Florida, and I dreaded spending the day alone."

His eyes went past Bonnie to Carrie. "Hi. We've found some more interesting information."

Nick the Clueless had just broken her heart, and he was too stupid to even notice.

Bonnie turned, her cheeks faintly flushed. Her eyes met Carrie's, and behind her embarrassment was just the tiniest bit of triumph. Carrie wanted to crush her like a bug.

"I've found something, too. I may have figured out who killed Wilkie. But I need some books and the papers we brought in."

"Let's set these up on Bonnie's desk. Bonnie knows Melnik history forward and backward, don't you?" Nick smiled at the shy woman.

She nodded and stepped closer to Nick, as if she were a moth and he a light in the darkest night.

Boyfriend stealer!

"She'll be a lot of help." Nick turned to leave the narrow book aisle, and Carrie had to go first and then Bonnie. They shifted to let Bonnie take her seat behind her antique desk.

Nick went to the side of the desk and laid his books down. Carrie stood so she faced Bonnie. She outlined her suspicions to both of them and explained what she needed. The pair of Melnik-loving, perfectionist brainiacs went to work.

After much discussion, they had a plan of action.

"First," Nick said, "we have to spring Tallulah from jail."

Carrie shook her head. "She won't go home. She's so determined to punish Junior, I don't think she'll ever leave."

"She'll leave," Bonnie said with confidence.

"She will?" Carrie looked up from her notes. With Tallulah locked up, they'd never spring this giant mousetrap.

"Sure. Right now I'm subbing as the organizer of the Maxie Festival. She trusts me."

"So how does that get Tallulah out?" Nick asked, closing the books and stacking them neatly.

"Simple. I quit. I nominate Carrie to be the chairperson."

"Me? I hate Maxie. I despise that mouse and think we need to emphasize Jesus' birth. I'll even change the name back to *Christmas Festival*. I think the parade is a stupid idea, too. It's freezing cold in Nebraska in December! Everybody knows that."

Nick grinned. "Of course everybody knows. Tallulah will be out of the county lockup before the sun sets."

That pinched. But Carrie had to admit the truth. "Bonnie, you're a genius."

The shy woman grinned, and Carrie had a hard time hating her. "For the rest of the day, I'm in charge. But I'm not touching that raggedy, nasty, flea-bitten, overactive-thyroid *mouse*."

"How do we get the word to Tallulah without making it seem obvious?" Nick asked, as out of touch with Melnik as Crazy Clara would be at a Mensa quiz bowl.

Bonnie stood and brushed nonexistent wrinkles out of her drab cream-colored blouse and her tidy khaki skirt. "Easy. I'll go have coffee at Jansson's."

"Perfect." Carrie smiled. "Dora was just pulling in when I left the *Bugle*."

22

Forget nightfall. Tallulah resumed control of the Maxie Festival by noon.

In a fit of pique, she took Hal and Shayla with her to her house as if she'd opened a foster home just for children of Wilkie Melnik. Hal's apartment had no functioning plumbing, and Rosie, still furious about the antifreeze, didn't want any part of her daughter.

Nick expected to hear that Shayla's little brother had moved in with Tallulah, too. Not because Rosie was mad at him. Just because the Melnik family was gathering like migrating geese.

A flock of Melniks.

Nick had volunteered to help with the parade. He stood now in Tallulah's garage, coating the gigantic replica of Maxie with the gray felt "mouse hair." Maxie would be the crowning touch to a float Tallulah had special-ordered from Mexico for the big parade set during the Maxie Festival, during the second weekend in December. Carrie was right about the float; it was completely realistic. It looked like a real mouse. Hal wouldn't touch it and privately told Nick he wasn't riding on it. . .although he held out a bit of hope to Tallulah. Maybe to get a free place to live. He did agree to ride a hayrack pulled along behind Maxie.

Carrie's sentimental Maxie story came out in the paper. Nick, after some research on the Internet, carefully cut out several copies of the story and, with regret, mailed them away to newspaper contests and some national publications who used syndicated material. If Carrie wanted the big city and a big paper, then she should have it. Even if it meant leaving Melnik. . .and him. . .behind.

Rosie Melnik had been persuaded to ride on the hayrack if Shayla rode on the mouse and didn't speak to her. Shayla wasn't speaking to her mother anyway, so that was easy. Then Shayla found out that Donette and the soon-to-be-born baby were riding mouse-back and threw a fit. Donette and baby had been moved to the hayrack. Rosie balked, although she was okay with Hal riding beside her and Kevin.

Tallulah rigged a sidecar somewhere around Maxie's small intestine for Donette, and the whole feuding family planned to be aboard for the parade.

Tallulah had a special turban made out of faux mouse fur and had a Maxie aquarium created for the parade with the sides made of magnifying glass because, World's Largest or not, Maxie was still pretty small.

As he worked, Nick thought of Bonnie's Thanksgiving dinner invitation. How lonely must she be to ask a near stranger to Thanksgiving? Nick knew she had three brothers—one a lawyer in Omaha, two others still in college. Bonnie had dropped out of college to raise them after their parents died. None of the ingrates were coming home for the holidays. He felt sorry for her, but he'd been praying for Carrie to ask.

Nick inserted teeth fit for a horror movie into Maxie's felt mouth and muttered, "Jurassic Park IV—*The Verminator*."

Carrie stepped into Tallulah's garage. "Eeek!"

Nick rushed to her, hoping she'd jump.

Instead, she backed away. "You've got mouse fur on your hands—stay back!"

"It's gray felt." Nick couldn't hold back a grin. "C'mon, let me save you." He remembered that kiss right before they'd caught Tallulah. It had been a long time since that happened.

Carrie smiled, a little pale but coping. "I can't believe you can stand to build that disgusting mouse."

"Boy, Tallulah was sure right to fire you from the festival."

"Absolutely. When I handed in my crown—"

"The one with the foot-tall picture of Maxie's face?"

Carrie shuddered. "That's the one. Guess what? I never put it on."

"There's a shocker."

Carrie managed a smile, and most of the color returned to her pretty, fair skin, pinking up her cheeks. He couldn't even see the whites all around her eyes anymore.

"When I handed in the vermin crown—apparently Tallulah wears it at all the historical society meetings—I told her I thought we ought to at least let the baby Jesus go first. You'd have thought I asked her to toss Maxie into a wood chipper."

"The Catholic church made a really nice nativity scene float, too." Nick wiped his hands on his pants and realized he was actually thinking that if he got all the mouse-colored felt off his hands, he might try to sneak in a kiss. "Father Calvecci asked Donette to let them use her baby in their manger and it was a total no-go."

"I heard that. They're using a Cabbage Patch doll instead."

Nick nodded. "Might be for the best. Tallulah said that the doll they used last year rolled out of the manger and off the float, and the hayrack rolled over its head."

Carrie winced.

Nick stepped closer.

The door banged open and Tallulah stormed in. She saw Carrie and stopped in her tracks. She came over to them, now friendly again, with her power and turban fully restored.

"That was a beautiful story, Carrie. Thank you so much for writing it."

"Did you like the final copy of the book?"

"Yes, but I don't think we need all those pictures. One of Maxie on the cover is enough. Ink costs a fortune." Some of the pictures included a photocopy of the Melnik town charter they'd found in Carrie's great-grandma's house and the slightly altered version that hung in city hall. They'd also put Rudolph's will in. The same things that would show up in this week's *Bugle*.

"Whatever you say," Carrie agreed, exchanging a furtive glance with Nick.

Nick tried to remember one single instance of this festival where Tallulah had worried about the cost. Just maybe Tallulah was taking the bait.

"I'm just double-checking that the float really resembles Maxie." She pulled her hand out of the pocket of her exploding-parrot-of-the-day caftan and, lifting her hand up to her nose, opened her lightly closed fist to reveal Maxie.

Carrie landed with a shriek in Nick's arms.

Tallulah rolled her eyes. With a huff of contempt, which struck Nick as a little arrogant for a woman who'd shot a corpse recently, the woman went into the room she insisted on calling the Artistic Vision Studio.

Carrie opened her eyes. Nick held her close.

A long, drawn-out moment passed as their eyes met.

"If you kiss me, it's just like you're begging someone to break into my house." Carrie grinned.

Nick said, "I'll risk it." Their lips met. He pulled away after far too short a time. "I didn't want to have dinner with Bonnie. I wanted to be with you."

A mouselike squeak grabbed their attention. Carrie grabbed Nick more tightly around his neck. They turned to see Bonnie standing in the doorway— her cheeks flaming red, her eyes brimming with tears. "The in—" Bonnie's voice broke. "The invitation is withdrawn." She whirled and stormed out, slamming the door.

"Oh no." Nick set Carrie down.

Her feet swung to the floor while she clung to his neck. "I thought you liked her."

"I do like her."

"No, I mean. . .I thought you *liked* her."

Nick quit looking after Bonnie. "Not like I like you."

Nick's heart leapt at the longing in Carrie's eyes, and he pulled her close again.

"Nothing like you." No one came in until he was good and done showing her just how much he liked her.

"Have dinner with me?" He'd done it. He couldn't believe he'd said it, and it hadn't even been that hard.

Carrie nodded, as agreeable as he'd ever seen her.

"But I've got to apologize to Bonnie. And if she'll have me, I'm going to her place for Thanksgiving dinner. Not for a date, but she's alone. Accepting her invitation was always about sharing a lonely meal."

"And that, Nick O'Connor, might be why I lo—like you."

Nick smiled. "Friday night. We'll drive out of town, go to the big city, and find something great to eat."

"Omaha?"

"I was thinking of Bjorn, but Omaha works for me."

Carrie laughed. "Bjorn, population one thousand and seventy-two."

"Big compared to Melnik. We could go to the Dairy King." He pulled Carrie back for a long hug.

"It closes for the winter."

Nick came to his senses, or as close as he ever got since he met Carrie. "We've got the community Thanksgiving dinner Friday. How about Saturday? We could leave early and make a day of it. Dinner and a movie?"

Carrie shook her head. "Pastor Bremmen wants us at the young adult potluck. He thinks he needs us to help the group get off to a good start."

"He's right; he does need us. We're the only people coming except for him and his wife."

Carrie's smile spread. "Sunday, then?"

Nick shook his head. It didn't matter about dinner; they were spending every evening together, even if it wasn't at a nice restaurant in Omaha. "You know we can't do it on Sunday."

It took a minute, but the dreamy look faded from Carrie's eyes. Nick thought it was a really good sign that he'd driven most of the thoughts from her head.

"That's right. We can't leave town."

Nick rubbed his hands together in anticipation. "Because sometime this weekend, one of our suspects is going to walk right into our trap."

23

After consulting Junior to make sure she didn't end up in jail, Carrie made a pea-and-Spam casserole and spent Monday in the late afternoon with Rosie Melnik, spreading Christian compassion and dropping a few hints about what would be in the newspaper that would scare her good if she was a killer. Except, instead of acting guilty, Rosie bemoaned the death of Wilkie the Wonder Jerk.

Nick's job was to make sure Gunderson would read the *Bugle* articles when they came out Wednesday. Gunderson either wasn't home or didn't answer the knock. Nick slid a note under the door of his decrepit old house.

Carrie met Nick back at her place. He kissed her hello just as if he had the right to. Carrie kissed him back and led him inside.

Nick hooked up his computer printer to Carrie's laptop so she could do all the work at home on the story they were planning to use to expose a killer. Carrie would later sneak it into the paper without anyone, especially Donette, knowing.

Carrie flexed her fingers and reached for the keyboard. "Let's get started."

The back door slammed open. Nick stood. Carrie loved a man of action.

Donette charged into the room, her face soaked with tears. Her hair was scraped back in a ponytail. She wore blue jeans and a stained white maternity T-shirt with the words THERE'S A PEA IN MY POD across the front in green sequins. Carrie had just barely finished reading the shirt when Donette threw herself into Carrie's arms. A child having a child. Carrie wanted to cry, too.

"He dumped me." Donette flattened Carrie against the back of the couch.

"Who, the guy from the funeral?" Carrie held on and closed her eyes to pray that she could somehow undo the damage from the story about Wilkie.

Donette nodded. "I—I told him I'd had enough of guys treating me like dirt. I told him I wanted some respect and. . .and that God loved me."

Carrie's eyes flew open, and she stared over Donette's shoulder at Nick.

Nick gave Carrie an encouraging nod.

Tightening her arms around Donette, Carrie tried to apologize. "I'm sorry about that awful Wilkie story. I did *not* put that in the paper. I took responsibility for it because I'm the boss. But it was sneaked in when I thought the paper was done. I've been heartbroken to think you would give up on God because of me."

"I forgive you."

Donette jerked upright with a little scream.

Carrie looked frantically for mice. "What is it?"

"I–I'm not sure. But I think my water just broke."

Nick jumped up from the couch and fell over the coffee table.

Carrie stood up and pulled Donette to her feet. "Are you going to the Bjorn hospital?"

"Nope, Gillespie."

"Nick!" Carrie tried to break through the panic she saw in his eyes. She expected him to say *"Eeek!"* and leap into her arms. She regretted that her hands were full of Donette.

Nick's eyes focused—some.

"Get Donette to your truck. I'm calling the hospital and telling them we're on our way. She could go fast."

"I'm not letting her drive."

Carrie sighed. "I mean, go fast as in having the baby, not go fast driving your truck."

Donette groaned and clutched at her stomach.

"Is she having a labor pain?" Nick's eyes went wide. Carrie could see white all the way around his pupils, like a scared horse.

"They're called contractions now, not pains. I think it's so an expectant mother won't know that having a baby might hurt—like they want it to be a surprise or something."

"It hurts to have a baby?" Donette grabbed Carrie's arms.

Wrenching loose, Carrie dashed to the phone and called the hospital quickly, thanks to Great-Grandma Bea having one thousand numbers posted by her phone.

Nick supported the apparently-now-made-of-china Donette out the door. Carrie was beside them before Donette scaled the truck with Nick boosting for all he was worth.

When Donette had two contractions before they'd gotten out onto the highway, Nick set out to break the land speed record getting to Gillespie. Another Guinness entry for Melnik.

As the nurse hustled Donette away in a wheelchair, it occurred to Carrie just who ought to attend this birth. She phoned and then waited with Nick until. . .

"This baby is a gift from a providential God!" Tallulah flew into the ER like a flapping, squawking parrot descending from the treetops. "I demand to be the birthing coach!"

Carrie waved her hand toward the maternity ward, and Tallulah fluttered off.

Donette and her doctor must have agreed, because Tallulah never came back.

"So much for baiting our trap, right?" Nick sighed and settled into a utilitarian brown chair in the waiting room.

"A large percentage of our prime suspects are busy doing Lamaze breathing." Carrie shook her head. "We'll just have to push back the timetable a bit. We don't really turn up the pressure until the *Bugle* comes out, anyway."

"We still haven't managed to have a dinner date." Nick seemed really glum.

Carrie's heart warmed irrationally. "Let's leave this baby to the pros and go have pizza."

"Are you sure we should?" Nick sat up straight and smiled.

"He's destined for greatness!" Tallulah shouted from the depths of the extremely shallow Gillespie Hospital. "And I will be his mentor!"

Carrie shrugged. "We can't compete with that."

Nick smiled, and they ran.

On Wednesday afternoon, Carrie lugged the newspapers over to the post office then took twenty-five copies each to the Mini-Mart, the grocery store, and Jansson's Café. The deliveries took ten minutes; everybody would know the news in fifteen. Mission accomplished. Article written. A niggling fear had grown in her stomach until she felt like she'd swallowed a bucket of mice.

She swiped compulsively at her dirty black T-shirt. She always came away from Wednesdays coated in printer ink.

She hopped into the Cavalier and tore away from the café like a kid who'd batted a ball through a picture window. She'd sure tried to break things wide open.

Donette's baby boy only made it better—or worse—if you happened to be a murderer.

Nick waited at her back door. "How was your day?"

Carrie almost heard him add "dear." Like they were a real couple. Her heart beat harder. "I did it, Nick. I wrote the story just the way we planned."

"Good. Come on in and see what I did to the kitchen linoleum."

Carrie wanted to talk crime and punishment.

Nick wanted to talk vinyl.

Her heart slowed to normal.

Then she saw Great-Grandma's kitchen. No, *her* kitchen. He'd been working on it for days, making a terrible mess, but Carrie could see the finished project at last. "It's beautiful." The linoleum was no more. Instead, bare wood was in its place.

Carrie crouched down and slid her hand over the sleek, honey oak floor. Then her conscience stood up and she followed it. "Nick, I love what you did—"

"It still needs wax and polish. Wait'll you see it after it's finished."

"—but you have to have worked off all Grandpa Leonard's money. I can't afford you."

Nick smiled. "I am completely in love with this house. I'd be glad to work here for free in my spare time."

Carrie's hands left black smudges on the oak. What had she come to? She was dirtier than Great-Grandma's kitchen. She pulled her hand back and went to wash up at the kitchen sink. Confession time. "As for that, you seem to have a lot of spare time. I can't ask you to give up whole days to work for me. You need the money, and I can't—"

"Have I ever mentioned that I'm rich?"

"No." She looked up from the flowing tap water. "I'd have remembered."

"I made really good money in Chicago, and I lived in my parents' house because they travel constantly. So I didn't spend much. Plus, I still do consulting work for the firm. They pay really well, so I haven't had to touch my investments, which were extensive."

"How could you quit such a well-paying job?"

"I have enough money to live on for the rest of my life. Now I'm doing what I love. Sanding and waxing this floor is what I love. Restoring beautiful old things feeds my soul." Nick shrugged as if he were embarrassed.

It sounded like poetry.

"I find time to pray and meditate. I'm closer to God using my hands and the gifts God gave me. Please don't make me stop."

"I can't even afford the wax." While she was admitting things, she added, "I'm living on what the *Bugle* pays, which is next to nothing. I'm already worrying about property taxes. I might agree to let you invest your time, but I can't ask you to spend your own money."

"Okay, then don't ask. Just let me do it. Please."

Carrie stared at him. The man was preparing to beg—beg to do something she seriously needed done. She still felt like a leech. "Okay, for now. If I ever get ahead, I'll pay you what I can."

Nick's shoulders rose as if she'd lifted a weight. "Great, because I need to strip the rest of the floors and paint the walls and varnish the woodwork. I want to strip the paint off the kitchen cupboards. They're solid oak. Who painted them? What were they *thinking*? Then next, I'll—"

"Wait!" Carrie raised her hand like a school crossing guard. "That all sounds wonderful. But first, we've got a murderer to catch."

"And I know where we have to start. Maxie Memorial Hall."

Carrie shuddered. "Stop calling it that!"

"I promise. You'll never have to touch him. By the way, welcome home." As if it was their home, not just hers. Then Nick pulled her close and kissed the living daylights out of her.

146

They finished deep cleaning the living room together and put up a Christmas tree. The freshly cut tree almost made the room. . .not stink. It would be better than that when Nick was done. He saw the majesty in the old house, and he wasn't going to settle for less than complete restoration.

They moved out Bea's ugly furniture and hauled away the cheap area rug that had to be fifty years old. Next, they centered the white Douglas fir Nick had chopped down in front of the living room picture window. They'd brought down the Christmas ornaments from the attic that Carrie told him she'd never seen before. Cleaned and polished, the delicate glass figures of Santas and angels and nativity scenes and shining balls were truly beautiful. They probably didn't have any great antique value, but from the shine in Carrie's eyes, Nick decided Bea had saved something precious after all.

Nick knew they didn't need to do any of this tonight. But they did need to wait for darkness to fall.

When even Dora had probably—hopefully—gone to sleep, so she didn't notice them slinking around under cover of night. Nick knew better than to underestimate Dora.

They slipped out the back door and scurried like mice down alleys and between buildings until they got to the back door of the city hall. Nick produced a key.

"It's no wonder we can't pin down who had Maxie. Everyone in this town has a key to this building. Why don't they just leave it standing open, for Pete's sake?"

Nick grinned at her. "You think anybody saw us?"

"I don't think so, but this is Melnik."

"If we get away with it, it'll be the caper of the decade." Nick moved quickly through the high-ceilinged city hall to Maxie's case. He pulled out another key.

"You're sure this is okay with Junior?" Nick asked before he inserted the key.

"I talked to him. He said that since you're on maintenance, he could call it cleaning Maxie's cage."

"Good, because it'd really be embarrassing to have to tell my mom and dad and younger brothers and sister that I'm doing hard time for grand theft mouse." Nick unlocked Maxie's cage.

Carrie stayed back about fifty feet.

Nick had rubber gloves and a Ziploc bag for Maxie. Dropping the mouse in, he zipped the yellow and blue into green to close the bag, Carrie gritted her teeth, and in the dim light of city hall at midnight, Nick saw her bite back an "*Eeek*!"

Nick put the first bag into a second one, tucking his gloves into the second bag before he zipped it and put it in his jacket pocket. "Are my hands mouse-free enough?" Nick extended his fingers in front of her.

"As long as you don't touch me."

Nick chuckled. "We'll see about that."

They left the hall the way they'd come and were back home in minutes.

Nick stuffed Maxie into the battered bear in the Dead Zone. There was a nice opening in his stomach cavity, thanks to Hal's collision. Grizzly—the cat, not the bear—had followed Nick into the Dead Zone, licking his lips at the huge mouse in the sandwich bag. Who could blame him for thinking dinner was served?

Worried about the cat's mouse-eating binge that had turned him from a lean alley cat into a fat pig, Nick stuffed a wad of newspaper—somehow overlooked by the Compulsive Cleaning Housewives League—into the bear's belly to keep Grizzly out.

Grizzly turned his back with a flick of his bent tail and pouted his way out the door. Nick firmly closed the door on the Dead Zone and followed the cat downstairs.

Carrie had insisted on being in on the Maxie Heist but refused to escort the mouse a step farther once the "cage cleaning" was over.

Nick washed his hands eight times while Carrie looked on. He said, "They've already read the paper, which should tip off a murderer that the truth is out there. Tomorrow the town will discover Maxie gone."

"Or Friday. The city hall is closed tomorrow. The crime might go unnoticed."

"And soon after—" Nick dried his hands and turned to her.

"I still can't decide who," Carrie interjected.

"But we've got a really short list. Hal, Tallulah, and Shayla are out."

"Probably," Carrie said with some skepticism.

"Rosie had a motive, but she couldn't have moved Wilkie's body." Nick was envious of Junior's notebook.

"Unless he was semiconscious and she somehow coaxed him to get in the closet before she smothered him. Or she had help."

"Let's don't start with conspiracy theories. I can barely keep the suspects straight now. And don't forget Gunderson." Five suspects? That was four too many. "He had to want Wilkie's name blackened for some reason, or he'd have never given you that story."

"He's an awful man, but that doesn't give him a motive for murder. Maybe he enjoys printing hateful things."

"Gunderson is strong enough to hide a body. And if that will was forged, Gunderson stands to lose a fortune. He's the only one except Tallulah in this mess who could afford to pay blackmail." Nick shrugged. "Anyway, someone is going to make a move, and that's when we'll catch him. . .or her." Nick gave her a long look. "Uh. . .are you going to be okay in here with Maxie?"

"Look, I'm never going to like that glandularly challenged rodent, okay? But I'm phobic, not stupid. I can handle it."

A mouse dashed out from under the couch and raced on its teensy, clattering claws straight toward them.

"Eeek!"

She found herself in Nick's strong arms as the mouse ran toward them. Carrie, looking frantically to keep her eye on the danger, saw the evil little beast run up inside Nick's pant leg.

Her next scream almost peeled the ancient cabbage-rose wallpaper off Great-Grandma's living room walls.

Nick stomped his foot several times, acting as unconcerned as if his leg had just gone to sleep. The mouse ran back out and vanished into the kitchen with Grizzly hot on his disgusting, long, dragging, pointy tail.

Carrie quit screaming and looked at Nick. In horror, she said, "You're going to have to live with that for the rest of your life!"

"You mean live with knowing a mouse ran up my leg?" Nick tilted his head, considering. "Okay, no problem."

"And so am I!"

"Honey, you're strangling me."

Carrie loosened her hold. "Uh, is that what mice always do when they run up your pant leg?"

Nick shrugged. "I suppose. What else?"

"I figured they ran all the way up and crawled inside my underwear and got stuck in the elastic and started biting and squeaking and. . ." Carrie buried her face in his chest.

"And yet none of that happened."

Carrie thought Nick sounded a speck impatient. Couldn't blame him. "It's my lifelong dream to live on the fifth floor of an all-glass building."

"I'm an architect. There aren't any of those. I know that for a fact. What if someone threw a rock? Five stories of dangerous broken glass raining down on everybody? Nope, bad idea." Nick pressed a quick kiss onto the top of her head.

Carrie looked up.

"Before I leave, how about I make sure you've forgotten all about mice?" Nick smiled and leaned down.

24

Kissing hadn't worked, but not for lack of trying. And to give Nick full credit, it *had* worked during the actual kissing, but he'd had to quit eventually.

After Nick left, Carrie lay awake for hours shuddering over the stupid, disease-bearing vermin crawling inside her walls, under her furniture, and even in her bed, for all she knew. She fell asleep and dreamed of mice running up her leg, squirming in her unmentionables.

She woke up screaming twice.

She had Thanksgiving dinner with her family and heard talk of how boring the special section of the paper was, the one containing the fine print of the town's charter and Rudolph Melnik's last will and testament. The one who wasn't bored was guilty of murder, so impatient though Carrie was to solve the crime, she was glad her family was bored.

Carrie had printed the exact words of the charter that hung on the wall in the museum and then printed the words from the one in Bea's house, knowing that only someone who really cared would notice. Someone who'd figured out that Wilkie had a legal claim on all the Gunderson property. One of his heirs could end up rich. Or Sven Gunderson could end up broke. Excellent motives for murder.

She had a great family time with one thousand cousins and two big feasts, one with each grandma. Being with all of them almost controlled the jealousy she felt over Nick spending Thanksgiving with Bonnie. Almost.

On Friday Nick showed up at Carrie's house neat as always, in a knit, two-button, hunter green shirt that didn't have his company logo on it.

He'd gone casual.

"How was Thankgiving?"

"Fine. I had to do some fast-talking to convince her to still let me come. But it was okay. Bonnie knows. . . I mean, I told her I wanted to be friends. That. . .I'm . . .uh. . .well. . .seeing you." Nick shrugged. "Bonnie's a good cook."

"You really told her that?"

"Well, sure. We. . .uh. . .are. . .aren't we? Seeing each other?"

"Oh yeah." Carrie wasn't jealous. That was an unworthy emotion. She just wanted to know every detail. Every word. Every look Bonnie and Nick exchanged.

He didn't tell her a thing, but he did kiss her until she was convinced that

Nick and Bonnie had shared nothing more important than turkey and pumpkin pie. Which didn't take long. After all, she trusted him.

He refinished the living room floor while Carrie gingerly pulled junk out of kitchen cupboards. They got a lot done despite Carrie being a spaghetti-spined coward.

But it was Friday night and time to face the music. On Wednesday, the paper had come out with the articles that few people would notice contained a motive for murder. On Thursday, Thanksgiving Day, the city hall was closed, and word of Maxie being missing never hit the street. On Friday morning, however, the atrocity had come to light.

Time to attend the community Thanksgiving potluck at city hall. The place had been in an uproar all day over Maxie.

Tallulah took over the microphone and raged.

Pastor Bremmen tried to calm her and talk about giving thanks to God and preparing their hearts for the holy season.

It almost turned into a fistfight.

Carrie got scolded for the first Wilkie article, fawned over for last week's Maxie Festival article, was informed of a few typos in this week's *Bugle*, and heard the word "boring" a lot.

Donette was there with her baby, accompanied by Hal, of all people. Dora whispered that if they got married, Hal would be his brother's father, his wife's son, his stepsister's stepfather, and his own uncle. Or something like that.

Nick was coerced into washing dishes. Carrie wiped tables.

Rosie Melnik, the most injured Melnikite of all, approached her. Carrie braced herself to be told off yet again.

Whispering a prayer for the right words, Carrie turned to face the music.

"Can I talk to you, Carrie?"

Interested in the frightened voice as opposed to anger, Carrie said, "Sure, but before you say anything, please let me apologize again for the article about Wilkie. That never should have gone in the paper. I'm so sorry."

Tears welled in Rosie's wounded eyes.

Yell at me. Please don't cry.

Carrie patted Rosie's slumped shoulder. "Is there anything I can do to help?"

"I—I want to put a few personal touches on the Maxie float. I just—I know you hate mice, but I don't want to go in there alone. If I go when there's a crowd, I'll have to face them. If I go alone, it's spooky. Would you please come with me?"

Carrie's arm got a gentle tug. "You mean, go now?"

In the night? To that garage containing a giant mouse?

She pumped up her courage.

NOSY IN NEBRASKA

I did ask if there was anything I could do to help.
I am a stupid, loudmouthed idiot.

"It won't take long. I've already told Nick I was going to ask you, and he gave me his key to Tallulah's garage." Her open hand displayed a brass key. "I told him we'd only be gone a few minutes."

Carrie knew this was a perfect opportunity to talk about faith and repentance. Rosie couldn't move a body. With a prayer of thanks to God for opening this door, Carrie nodded, snagged her leather jacket, and walked out of the hall.

Controlling a shudder, she glanced over her shoulder, looking for Nick to wave good-bye. He had his back to the room, hard at work scrubbing casserole dishes.

It was two blocks to the garage. Shivering in the November cold, Carrie hurried along, praying for the right words.

"God loves you, Rosie."

"There's no God. How can you believe that stuff?"

Carrie jumped a bit at the harsh response. Where had Rosie's tears gone?

Lots of people in small towns didn't go to church. A small town was no guarantee of faith. But most of them acknowledged that God existed. And even if they didn't, they were a little too afraid of God's wrath—should they turn out to be wrong—to say so out loud.

"Sure, there's a God. His Son, Jesus, died for all our sins, and if we believe in Him, we can be saved." It sounded a little rushed, not the sincere testimony Carrie had wanted to give. But this might be her only chance. She'd better get the basics in.

"I don't want to hear about what a sinner I am." All the quiet fear from earlier had vanished.

"We're all sinners. Me, Nick, you, Pastor Bremmen, everyone. We all fall short of perfection. That's just part of being human. And since we're all going to die someday, we need to live this life in preparation for the next."

"I'm not going to die for a long time. Then when I do, they'll stick me in the cheapest coffin they can find and throw dirt over me."

They reached the garage at the rear of Tallulah's huge, tree-lined lot. Carrie unlocked the door and pushed it open. Carrie waited, but apparently she was supposed to go in first. Fumbling around the wall, Carrie found the light switch, and the garage lit up from one small bulb. The small room being used for the float was partitioned off. Carrie had avoided it up to now, coming in no farther than this. She gritted her teeth and marched across the chilly building filled with storage boxes, with barely room for a car. Right now, the car must be at the Thanksgiving party.

Rosie twisted the doorknob. Something about her demeanor made Carrie's stomach jump.

"After you."

Taking a deep breath and calling on all her courage, Carrie stepped in this tiny room full of giant Maxie. Just as she crossed the threshold, she stopped and looked back. Her stomach sank as she realized something she should have noticed right away. Rosie was empty-handed. "Weren't you going to include some mementos in this float? Where are they?"

The smile had turned to gritted teeth. A hard shove sent Carrie stumbling forward, and the door slammed shut. Carrie heard a lock click before she could open it.

Carrie fought with the doorknob then pounded on the door. She yelled, "What is going on?"

"Just shut up." The voice rose unnaturally high. "I'm not letting you ruin everything we've planned."

"What do you mean? What plan? Who's we?"

The outer garage door closed, leaving Carrie's question to echo in the silence.

And then the echoing was replaced by something else. Something rustling and skittering. Like a thousand frantic mice.

25

"Where'd Carrie go?" Nick hung up his apron and tossed his dishcloth onto the pile of towels and rags he'd offered to take home, launder, and return.

Dora handed an empty pie pan to Crazy Clara. "Excellent pie, Clara."

"Pecanpieismyfavorite."

Nick moved casually to the trash and dropped a stack of used paper plates over the upended pies. Clara had brought five of them, bless her heart. Near as he could figure out, instead of pecans she had chiseled bark off a tree and broken it into pecan-sized pieces.

"I haven't seen her, Nick." Dora handed out another container and another as the ladies finished up their cleaning. Nick looked through the big window into the social hall.

Carrie's chair sat empty, and her coat was gone. He glanced around the kitchen. Everything was in order. He picked up the bundle of linens, and with a quick good-bye to Dora and the other few ladies still chatting in the kitchen, he headed out. Carrie wouldn't have walked home without him. Not with that most recent mouse-up-the-pant-leg experience so fresh in her mind.

She wasn't out in the hallway. A quick look at Maxie's cage reminded him of what Carrie had written in the *Bugle* and how it ought to trap a murderer into revealing him- or herself.

He hurried outside. They'd set a trap. Carrie wouldn't have gone anywhere with their main suspects. If someone dragged her out, there would have been a scene.

"Micerunningloose. Nobearbigenough."

Nick turned to look at Clara. How had she known about the bear? Maybe God whispered in his ear, using the mouth of a crazy woman.

"Clara, tell me about this big mouse."

Clara looked past Nick to the cage. "BetterthanSvenrulingthistown."

"Sven Gunderson rules this town?"

"Ownsitdoesn'the? Lockstockandbarrel. DeathofMelnik."

"Gunderson owns the town, but why would that kill Melnik?"

"Thinksheownsthetown. Melnikthoughtdifferent."

Clara headed for the door, pulling her cart, which was empty because she'd donated all her pies to the Thanksgiving dinner. A woman fixated on feeding a dying town. Or was it a dying town? Maybe she meant it was a dying Melnik. Wilkie Melnik.

"Clara." Nick caught Clara's arm before she meandered off. "Did Sven Gunderson kill Wilkie?"

"Everybodykilledhim."

Nick knew that was the absolute truth. Everybody had killed poor, worthless Wilkie. But right now Nick couldn't focus on that. He had to find Carrie. He prayed a quick prayer for help and then looked at Maxie's empty cage. He guessed that solving the crime would lead him straight to Carrie.

Then another thought struck Nick like one of Clara's pies in the face. Whoever had killed Wilkie had used Maxie as a murder weapon. Nick died a little inside as he imagined someone coming after Carrie with a mouse. Carrie in danger was bad enough. But her phobia was well known. If whoever did this enjoyed cruelty. . .

Clara tugged at Nick's hold, and Nick realized he'd been hanging on tight enough that he might have bruised the addled old woman.

"I'm sorry. Did I hurt you?" He massaged her wrist carefully as he released her. She went out the door, and he followed, trying to catch every word she muttered.

"You *saw* everybody who killed Wilkie? Can you tell me who?"

Clara listed three people he expected and one he'd pretty much eliminated. Rosie Melnik.

⁓

Carrie turned to face the pitch-black room, fumbling for the doorknob behind her. It held as if it were made of iron. The tiny, clawing footsteps came closer. Had the slamming door scared them into their holes, but now, in the silence, they felt bold?

Something raced over her toe.

"Eeek!" Of course, she had shoes on, but she felt it. She was sure she felt it.

A weary voice sounded from the farthest corner.

"Carrie, is that you?"

Carrie screamed and staggered backward into the wall. It wasn't her mouse scream. It was one she'd never heard before, one that she'd been saving for if she wanted to curdle someone's blood.

Unless the Maxie float had learned to talk, there was someone else in the room.

Please, dear Lord Jesus, let it be someone else.

"Yes, it's me. Who are you?" She braced herself to hear, "It's Maxie, and I'm your worst nightmare."

True, all true.

"It's Tallulah, honey. Someone hit me."

Carrie realized that it was just barely possible that the horrid, teensy, clawing, zipping footsteps had been Tallulah moving around. No one could fault Carrie's ability to imagine mice in every situation.

Carrie edged toward the voice, trying to avoid colliding with Giant Maxie while dodging countless electric lawn beautifiers. "Talk to me, Tallulah, so I can find you. Who hit you?"

Carrie realized that she knew very well who. The same person who'd lured her here.

"I don't know. All I know is that I heard footsteps and turned just in time to see a rolling pin crashing toward me. I woke up with a throbbing head when I heard the door slam."

Carrie slowly slid her feet forward, the cement floor scratching under her tennis shoes as she closed in on Tallulah. A soft object on the floor rolled as her toe connected with it. It felt turban-like. She was getting close.

"I'll help you. I'm locked in, too, but we'll find a way out."

A moan of pain almost directly under her feet stopped Carrie in her tracks. The black in the windowless room was absolute. She crouched and reached forward, hoping for Tallulah's silky caftan instead of the felt of a Maxie suit.

Her fingertips touched a slippery bulk that could only be the elderly fanatic. "I'm here." Carrie fumbled for Tallulah's hand.

Tallulah reached out, her breath broken and ragged. Their hands met and they clung to each other for a few seconds. Carrie was desperately glad there was someone else in there. Even Tallulah.

"Thank God you came. I've been praying and praying for help. It's so dark." Tallulah's voice broke, and weak sobs set the caftan wiggling like Jell-O.

"I'm glad you're here, too, except I'm really sorry that either of us is here." Carrie toughened her voice to brace Tallulah's backbone. "Now how do we get out?"

"We can't. This room has one door, with a good lock, and no windows. I designed it specifically to house the Maxie float. I wanted maximum security."

Since Carrie couldn't quite picture anyone stealing a six-foot-tall mouse float, she changed the subject. "What about these tools I bumped into along this wall? Is there an ax? We could chop a hole in the door or the wall. Or a crowbar— maybe we can pry the door open."

"There's a weed whacker."

Okay, not useful for beating down a door. "Why did Rosie bring me here? Why would she lock me in here with you? It's awfully cold, but not cold enough to kill us. We'll get out and get away and tell everything."

Tallulah interrupted. "What's that smell?"

Carrie inhaled once, and that's all it took.

"Smoke."

N ick pounded on Gunderson's door. The house was dark. There was no sign of life. Nick knew the old goat was in there. Maybe.

"Burntpies! Burntpies!"

Nick quit pounding and stared at the mad baker sitting in his truck. He turned to pound some more. "I know you're in there, Gunderson! I want some answers!"

An orange light caught his eye from the far side of Gunderson's privet hedge. *Burnt pies? Fire?* It looked as if Tallulah's garage, where the Maxie float was being assembled, was on fire.

Nick had a frantic second to wonder if the fire was the result of Tallulah—in some mad experiment involving lightning and spare parts she'd stolen from the Melnik Cemetery—trying to bring Maxie back to life.

That'd make the Christmas parade special.

Nick knew—as well as a man can know anything that he doesn't really know—that this fire had something to do with Carrie's disappearance.

"Carrie!" He ran for his truck, jumped in, and roared out of Gunderson's driveway.

⁓⁓⁓

"Tallulah, stay down. I'm going to find a way out of here, and I don't want you to be hurt if I knock something over." Carrie flailed her hands along the wall of the garage, searching for anything heavy enough to knock the door down. Even a weed whacker might be enough. Tools clattered down around her feet, barking her arms and shins and toes. Finally, she caught hold of some wooden handle that seemed to have enough heft to be useful. She rushed her hands down the circular wood and found a hoe at the end. She made her way as fast as she dared the few feet to the door.

Orange light gleamed through the door frame. The dim light lifted the gloom in the float room, but now Carrie glanced over her shoulder to see the huge, skulking mouse and wished for the dark.

A crackle of fire sounded on the other side of the garage. Something whined as if it were under pressure. Who knew what? Aerosol cans, gas—garages were notoriously full of flammable liquids.

Something exploded and slammed against the door, sending Carrie staggering backward into the float. The mouse seemed to reach for her as if he needed a snack.

Carrie's "*Eeek!*" barely registered, even with her. She approached the door again and gingerly touched the knob. Jerking her hand back from the burning-hot metal, she knew that knocking down the door would just let the flames in.

"Start praying again, Tallulah. We need a miracle."

"I'm way ahead of you." Tallulah's voice sounded as if she'd stood.

"Stay back. I'm going to swing this hoe."

"No, I can see the fire from here. We can't get out that way."

"There's no other way!"

"I know! I know!"

Carrie turned back to the door, scared to death, and swept the hoe back to take a swing.

———

Nick laid on his horn the whole three blocks to Tallulah's house. He saw a light flicker on in Dora's house as he roared past. He skidded into Tallulah's driveway and saw the flames.

"Clara, can you stay in here and keep honking?"

Nick noticed Tallulah's car parked behind the garage and knew a way to get inside that building. He should make sure Clara was safe, but there wasn't time. The flames had circled the structure and were eating their way up the walls. Nick knew the fire wasn't accidental. A jagged line of flames danced across the lawn like an arrow pointing straight to Tallulah's outbuilding. Nick caught the whiff of gas among the smothering smoke.

The side containing the Maxie float wasn't nearly as engulfed as the other. If Carrie was in there, he prayed she was in the small room. Alone with Maxie. Terrified. Nick prayed. He threw open the truck door and poked his head out. "If you're by the garage door, get back! Get back from the door!"

The sound of a fire siren streaked through the night. Help was on the way, but Nick didn't have time to wait for the experts.

He reached over and clicked Clara's seat belt then turned back to the raging fire. Something exploded with a deafening roar. One corner of the garage door blew open. Nick grabbed the steering wheel with both hands. He jammed his foot on the accelerator. His truck spun out, and the back end slewed. Nick aimed for the garage. And the fire. And Carrie, burning alive.

His front bumper smashed into the garage door. Wood snapped. His windshield shattered. An iron brace jammed with a sickening thud into the seat between Nick and Clara. Sparks erupted. Ash filled the cab of his truck. Fire crackled down from the ceiling. Suffocating smoke choked him. Clara screamed. Nick coughed, his eyes stinging, his lungs roasting. He had to get the elderly woman out.

He shifted into REVERSE, shoved the accelerator to the floor, and barreled backward. Wood and metal clattered off the roaring truck. He slammed on the brakes as soon as they were far enough away for Clara's safety. Nick's safety wasn't high on his agenda.

Nick leapt from the truck and raced toward the billowing smoke.

He ducked under the fire, his arm covering his mouth and nose. Flames reached like greedy fingers toward the sky, out of the destroyed garage door. The inside walls were consumed by the ravenous inferno. Lungs burning, Nick nearly fell to his knees.

Shrill sirens grew closer. He could barely hear them over the snapping, snarling inferno.

"Carrie! Carrie, are you in here?" There was no sign of her in this side of the garage. He heard something bang into the door to the Maxie float room.

"Carrie?" Dashing for it, he shouted, "Carrie, is that you?"

"Nick!" The fear in her scream cut his heart.

"Get back! I'm coming in!" Nick noticed the heavy padlock on the door, snapped shut. Fury blazed as high and as hot as the fire.

Carrie shouted, "Okay! We're away from the door."

We? Nick had a split second to catch that. He drew in a short breath full of gritty, hot ash. He lashed out a foot. The blackened door smashed open. The padlock ripped from the burning door frame. Carrie stumbled forward into his arms.

"Tallulah's in there."

"Go! I'll get her."

Carrie shook her head. "She's close to unconscious from the fire. It'll take both of us."

There wasn't time to argue. They charged back into the room that was clogged with the overpowering fumes and smoke. The fire was now so loud they couldn't talk. Carrie kept a hand on Nick's arm and led him straight to the corner where Tallulah crouched behind Maxie. They lifted her.

"We've got to save Maxie. We can't let him burn!"

Nick and Carrie exchanged an incredulous look. They towed the woman out the door, cinders raining down on their heads.

"No, save him. Save Maxie!" Tallulah fought them.

They dragged her outside while she was screaming for Maxie.

A blast of cold water hit them in the face.

It served to calm Tallulah down.

The valiant men and women of the Melnik Volunteer Fire Department raced toward the building with their hoses cannoning water ahead of them.

"We've got everyone!" Nick shouted at Marc Swenson, who led the charge. Deputy Steve was right behind Marc, his yellow fireproof suit and hat askew. Hal came next. Just because he was a confessed murderer didn't mean he couldn't fight a fire.

The two men took over supporting Tallulah as the Melnik ambulance shrieked into the yard. Tallulah screamed for Maxie as they dragged her away.

Two other paramedics grabbed Nick and Carrie.

Carrie waved them off then began coughing until Nick had to hold her up.

"Let them help you. Just to give you some oxygen."

"I'm fine. I'll go with them in a minute, but first I need to talk to Junior."

Junior huffed up to them, his pajamas sticking out of his unbuttoned uniform shirt. "Is everyone all right?"

"They're seeing to Tallulah. She took a blow to the head." Nick patted Carrie on the back and held her. He'd come so close to losing her.

Carrie broke in.

"Rosie Melnik tried to kill Tallulah and me."

The governor came to the Maxie Festival. So did both Nebraska senators and a congressman, two state senators, ten area newspapers, news crews from six television stations, and a reporter and photographer from the *Omaha World-Herald*.

The festival came off in grand style. It was a fairly balmy twenty-degree day. Everyone dressed for the cold, there was no wind, and they were Nebraskans. It was lovely.

The Country Christian Church float, the St. Bernard Catholic Church float, the Swedish Covenant Church float, and the Lutheran church float led the way. Each had a nativity scene, and each had a different piece of the Christmas story immortalized with chicken wire and spray-painted facial tissues. Jesus had made it into the starting lineup of the Melnik Christmas Parade after all.

Of course, Maxie wasn't to be forgotten. Carrie understood that. She just wanted some perspective.

Nick glanced at Maxie's aquarium, centered on the quaint gazebo from Melnik Park. Today it had been rigged with wheels so it could carry Maxie in style.

After the parade, Carrie went into city hall, and members of the press started shouting questions at her. She climbed up on the stage in the front of the auditorium so she could see who was yelling and give them answers.

Before Nick followed Carrie in, he offered to help Tallulah carry in Maxie's display case from the gazebo.

"No." Tallulah flinched as if he'd attacked her, her turban pulled on more tightly than ever. "I've put new locks on Maxie's home, and no one has a copy of the keys but me."

Nick thought that was for the best. The mouse needed to stay put.

He left the woman to it and quietly slipped into the press conference, staying well back. He got there just as Carrie got the news that her Melnik and Maxie article had been named as a finalist for six Nebraska Press Association Awards. The crowd broke into applause.

She stood on the stage in front of the social hall, near a microphone. Nick watched her furrow her brow.

"That's not possible. I never entered anything. I've only been in my job a few weeks."

161

The *World-Herald* reporter shrugged. "It must have made the deadline."

She looked up and her eyes met Nick's, and that's when she knew what had happened. She mouthed, "Thank you," and Nick touched his forehead in a two-fingered salute.

"So what exactly was Rosie Melnik's motive?" A reporter shouted out the question.

Nick saw Carrie's shoulders raise and lower in a deep sigh. "Wilkie was blackmailing Sven Gunderson. Wilkie found out that Gunderson had forged an old will and stolen the Melnik fortune. The truth was in the real town charter, now posted in the Melnik Historical Society Museum. The one formerly posted there was switched by one of Sven Gunderson's ancestors."

"But why is that a reason to kill her husband?" someone shouted. "Why not help him claim his rightful inheritance?"

"She didn't know about it until the very end." Carrie shook her head. "If Wilkie died and Rosie married Sven, he could keep everything. He began manipulating her. She decided to work with Gunderson when Wilkie asked for a divorce to marry Donette."

"When Chief Hammerstad arranged for Maxie to go missing and for the original charter to appear in the paper"—she glanced at Junior, who gave her an encouraging nod—"he knew it would provoke someone to go to great lengths to protect their secret. He knew someone would fall into his trap."

Nick saw Carrie glance at Tallulah. They'd thought Tallulah was a strong suspect, but she hadn't been their first choice. They'd stolen the mouse to force Tallulah's hand, if she was the culprit. The charter was to goad Shayla, Hal, Rosie, and Donette, all possible heirs to the fortune, if owning Melnik Main Street could ever add up to a fortune. And since Gunderson stood to lose his inheritance, it would have brought him out to destroy the new charter, too, before someone got a good look at it.

Donette had been a long shot to get caught, what with a new baby to care for. But Nick hadn't been all that suspicious of her anyway.

They'd all had their eyes on Gunderson.

None of them had suspected poor, distraught Rosie.

"Rosie's pretty mad about Gunderson tricking her into killing Wilkie, so she's talking. That's filling in a few blanks. It looks like Wilkie found the original town charter a few months ago while sneaking around in my great-grandma Bea's house, before he started blackmailing Gunderson. He went back the night of his death to snoop around some more. Rosie followed him, thinking he'd drink himself into a stupor, which he did most nights, and she could strike. She saw it all. Wilkie frightened Great-Grandma into falling. Hal knocked Wilkie cold with the skillet. Rosie sneaked in and urged Wilkie, groggy from the blow and the poison, into the closet, where she wedged him in and smothered him."

"With Maxie the Mouse?" the reporter from Channel Six asked.

"Not really." Carrie's voice faltered. "Rosie always liked the mouse's. . . ."

Nick bit back a smile. All this horror, and the only thing that fazed her was that stupid mouse.

"Rosie had a key to city hall."

"Maxie Memorial Hall," Tallulah interjected as she approached the front carrying the heavy aquarium. Nick again offered to help and was rejected. Tallulah made her way forward, obviously determined to take center stage.

"And she liked to visit Maxie and take him home for the night. She'd been petting him. . ." Carrie's eyes filled with dread, and someone snapped a picture.

Nick definitely wanted a copy.

"So there was mouse fur on her hands, and she left some behind on Wilkie's mouth." Nick edged nearer Carrie. He'd try to catch her if she jumped and went flying off the stage.

"Miss Evans?" the *World-Herald* reporter called out. "My boss mentioned your name when that award was announced. I have it on good authority that he's ready to offer you a job in the *World-Herald* feature section."

The crowd gasped aloud, but with dismay rather than joy. Nick wanted to join in. But she'd never be his if she didn't have a real choice. Nick didn't want her to make a commitment to him because she needed money or her life was boring or she'd given up on her dreams.

He prayed quietly because he knew that, if necessary, he'd give up his own dream of small-town life. If she'd have him, he'd follow her anywhere.

"Gunderson is now in jail as a coconspirator in Wilkie's death, and the will has been broken." Carrie kept talking, but her eyes were fixed on the approaching Maxie. "The Main Street businesses revert to the city and are all for sale or rent at a more reasonable price. Six of the empty buildings are already under new ownership."

Nick had bought one himself.

"Plus, a good-sized chunk of the Gunderson estate will be divided up between Wilkie's heirs," Carrie concluded.

Tallulah unsteadily made her way up the three steps to the stage. Carrie had her eyes locked on Maxie, so Nick suspected the interview was over. Just as Tallulah got to the top step, she wobbled, her fingers slipped, and she shrieked. The aquarium tumbled to the stage, shattering into a thousand pieces. Maxie bounced out of the shards of glass, rolling straight for Carrie. Nick jumped onto the stage to save her.

Out of nowhere, Grizzly leapt onto the stage and swallowed Maxie in one gulp.

Tallulah shoved her askew turban out of her eyes and screamed loudly enough to shatter crystal. Good thing the aquarium was already destroyed.

The whole crowd yelled. Carrie relaxed immediately and Nick put her down.

The cat hunched, opened its mouth wide, gave Tallulah a look of absolute contempt, and regurgitated Maxie onto the floor.

Carrie's ear-splitting shriek was like a warning that screamed, "Incoming!"

Nick caught her, marveling at her perfect weight and size. She looked at him and smiled.

"Are you taking the *World-Herald* job? Let me know so I can start packing." She smiled and held him tighter.

"I've already got a job I love, in a town I love, near a man I love."

Tallulah's screams faded away as Nick got lost in Carrie's beautiful blue eyes. Or maybe, now that Maxie had reappeared, Tallulah just quit screeching.

"I love you, too, Carrie Evans. I want you to marry me."

"Can we live in my house? Will you take care of the mice in there for the rest of your life?"

Nick frowned. "You're not marrying me just to protect you from mice, are you?"

Carrie giggled. "Not just."

Nick looked at Maxie, who was lying in an unmentionable condition with Tallulah kneeling beside him, her hands clenched. Grizzly stood nearby. Maxie was in the center. No crying he made.

Nick shook his head. "We're one star, a heavenly host of angels, and a herd of sheep away from an extremely twisted nativity scene." Nick looked past the little scene and saw the real nativity set in front of the twinkling Christmas trees.

Pastor Bremmen hustled up on the stage and pulled Tallulah to her feet. "Really, Tallulah, there are limits." He gently but firmly urged her toward the manger and helped her back onto her knees. "I think a few moments of prayer would do you good." He left the stage.

"Much nicer." Carrie patted Nick's chest. "You know, I think Maxie actually looks a little better. He's got a nice sheen to his coat."

Nick conceded the point with a one-shoulder shrug.

Carrie turned to look out at the reporters, her family, and almost everybody in Melnik. "I'm not taking the *World-Herald* job," she announced, loudly enough for them all to hear. "I'm staying right here. I'm going to keep living in Great-Grandma's house. Nick's going to turn it into a showplace, and I'm going to make the *Bugle* the best small-town newspaper in America. Oh, and Nick and I are getting married."

Dora snorted, emphasizing an unfortunate resemblance to a member of the hog family. "Everybody knows that."

The crowd broke into cheers. Carrie saw her mother and two grandmothers mopping their eyes and smiling.

Carrie exchanged a look with Nick while Tallulah finished what looked like a sincere prayer; only God knew for what. Then she tore a sleeve off her caftan and lovingly returned to Maxie to dry him off.

"Feel free to keep jumping in my arms," Nick whispered, stealing a quick kiss.

"I want to be there." Carrie kissed him back. "But I much prefer it to be for some reason other than mice."

Nick nodded. "Or murder."

PRIDE AND PESTILENCE

In honor of the mouse obsession that rules Melnik, I'm dedicating *Pride and Pestilence* to my sisters, Ruth Moore Diedrichsen and Nila Moore Novotny, and my lifelong friend, Joanie Kroger Rogers.

Ruth was driving the car. Nila had a mouse run up her leg and screamed until it's a wonder Ruth didn't crash and kill us all. Joanie, in her attempt to escape, shoved me out of the car while it was still rolling.

I tumbled to a stop in a ditch and managed not to die, no thanks to Joanie. After the car stopped moving, Joanie and Nila jumped out. We made Ruth get another car and drive home. It was the bravest thing I'd ever seen.

These are the types of events that make a woman write a series of books about a town that has a really big field mouse for a mascot.

W omen cry. Men have heart attacks.

Bonnie Simpson laid the advice-filled women's magazine down. So if women didn't cry, were they destined to have heart attacks? Checking for chest pains, she regretted that she wasn't much of a crier.

Thunder like an explosion jerked Bonnie out of her mental electrocardiogram. The noise almost gave her a heart attack. It didn't, however, make her cry.

She needed to work on that. Maybe she should chop more onions.

The lightning ripped across the sky.

A glance at her wristwatch—nearly midnight.

Why did I stay so late?

Evening hours at the Melnik Historical Society Museum ended at 8:00 p.m.

You stayed because you've got nowhere else to go.

Setting her magazine down on top of this month's copy of *The Smithsonian,* Bonnie took a second to wish for a teensy, miniscule fraction of the grandeur in the Smithsonian for her little museum. She looked at the stuffed replicas of Maxie the Mouse. They were for sale for $4.99 each, plus tax. Nope, not even close.

She'd locked the museum door at eight, but she hadn't headed home. Instead, dreading her insomnia and that quiet, empty house, she'd settled in with the stack of April magazines that had arrived right on schedule—the first of March.

Lightning streaked across the sky like an incoming missile.

She braced herself.

It hit.

She shrieked as the building shook. Not just noise this time. Lightning had hit something close. Spooked, she realized she'd forgotten to lock the outer door that led to Melnik Main Street. Anyone could come in.

Bonnie liked storms, but this one was too much.

Thunder rolled and struck like a whiplash. Her door shook. That was more than thunder. Someone was pounding on her door.

Her heart sped up, but her logical mind overruled her fear. It must be Junior, come to shoo her home. Sheriff Junior Hammerstad, her second cousin, did a late-evening round and knew her well enough to come into the outer hallway that separated the museum from the city hall offices and look for a crack of light under the heavy metal museum door. He only pounded like that to be heard over the storm.

"I'm coming. Hold on."

The hammering grew louder and more insistent. Thunder detonated. Rushing for the windowless door, Bonnie twisted the lock and pulled. A flash of lightning hit right on top of a thunder clap. A fuse box in the hallway exploded.

The lights blinked out. The sparking fuse box lit up the menacing face of a stranger.

The man yelled something, his words drowned out by thunder.

Bonnie swung the door at the man, but he slammed his forearm against it then shoved it open.

Spitting light sizzled like fireworks from the fuse box. The glass door that opened onto Main Street shattered.

The man shouted words Bonnie couldn't understand and caught the front of her blouse in both his fists and lifted her off her feet. The whole north side of the building exploded.

Screaming, she caught the man's hands. He pushed himself inside with a roar that sounded like part of the storm. He tackled her and pulled her to the floor.

"No! Help! *Help!*" They thudded to the floor hard enough to knock her breathless. She hit at him, frantic to escape.

The man clutched at her and shoved her, head first, between one of the ceiling-high rows of shelves.

No one could see them. He could do his worst.

"Help!"

If only Junior would come. She screamed at the top of her lungs, sucked in a chest full of grit and smoke, and started choking.

She punched at her assailant.

Shout, struggle, don't be a victim.

His iron hold crushed her.

"Don't fight me!" He stretched out on top of her and wrapped his arms around her neck as if trying to finish strangling her.

"Let me go!" The pandemonium of the storm drowned out her cries. She opened her eyes and looked up, past his shoulder. Sick fear overcame her battle to be free. A metal bookcase containing thousands of pounds of books yawed. As it tipped, the whine of distressed steel added to the bedlam. They'd be under that crushing weight if the bookcase collapsed. Now she struck at the man's shoulders, kicking and twisting, screaming for another reason. To get out from beneath the falling steel.

Another furious shout from him added to the deafening noise. She hit harder, her closed fists whaling on his head. She wouldn't be a victim. She'd read too many books where the heroine fought back and lived.

"Stop that." His grip tightened until she thought she'd smother.

The shelves tilted farther. Books fell. She ducked her head, using her assailant's body for protection. The impact of the books striking the man's back matched the pain on his face. He flinched as they rained down. His arms covered her eyes as a huge volume tumbled straight toward her face. Bonnie felt the book hit him, and his forearm smacked her in the nose.

Burying, attacking books were out of Bonnie's nightmares. Books were her best friends, and now they turned on her. The falling books rained on and on and on.

Then, suddenly, it was over.

Silence reigned.

The quiet froze Bonnie in place. She quit trying to wriggle free. The man lay still. Maybe he'd been knocked unconscious.

What seemed like hours passed; then the man groaned. Bonnie braced herself to fight again.

Then Junior was there. "Bonnie! Are you all right? Answer me."

"Here. Help! Get him off me!"

The man let go of her and slid backward.

Bonnie swung her fist hard at his retreating face and connected with the man's nose.

"Hey! Ouch!" He scrambled backward, books shedding off his back. He kept an eye on the books and carefully sheltered her from the ones sliding sideways off his broad shoulders.

A light flickered on overhead as he scooted, unable to rise because the bookshelf trapped him. Bonnie saw her oak library desk, donated to the museum when it was found in the back room of the old Esso gas station building. The desk had saved her by holding up the shelves. The very top of the case had smacked into the shelf on the other side of her desk. The desk and that still-standing shelf and the massive tilted bookcase created a triangular cave. Had it fallen flat, the weight would have killed her and the man.

Her attacker vanished, leaving her in the tomb alone. Bonnie raised her head, but there wasn't room to sit up. She saw Junior kneeling, his face pale, his comb-over flapped open like a snap-top ketchup lid.

"Can you get out?"

"Where did he go? That man attacked me!"

"I did not!" A voice stormed from above and behind Junior.

Bonnie slid on her back, feet first. Aware of her skirt riding up, she pulled at the hem as she moved.

Junior disappeared. Bonnie's heart shuddered. That horrible man had done something to Cousin Junior. She cleared the shelf and rolled onto her knees amid the rubble, every muscle aching.

"Dora, don't move. The ambulance will be here in a few seconds."

Dora? What did Dora Clemson have to do with this?

Bonnie rose to her feet in thick, choking air lit by an eerie red emergency light. The dark stranger caught her arm. Some wild fight-or-flight reflex roared to life, and she chose fight. She wheeled back to slug him.

Her fist stopped dead with the slap of flesh on flesh. He caught her hand in midair, and it felt like his fist was encased in iron. She looked at him, coated in white, his nose bleeding red through the grit caking his face.

That gave her some satisfaction. She'd done good work. She'd fought back. A sense of pride kicked her heart up. He had a trickle of blood running down from his scalp just in front of his left ear. His hair was standing up in all directions, wild and white like the rest of the world.

She realized the white was plaster dust that filled the air, which explained his Einstein white hair. Their eyes locked together.

"Leave him be, Bonnie." Junior smoothed his comb-over into place. "He's with me. This is Joe Manning."

The man glared at her, his eyes dark as storm clouds in his plaster-powder-coated face. He towered over Junior, but now his eyes looked less like those of a vicious predator and more like those of. . .a cranky schoolboy. "Yeah, I'm with him. Are you done beating on me yet?"

Bonnie didn't answer. She heard thunder again, reminding her of how this had started. An approaching storm.

He let go of her fist.

"B–but y–you attacked me." The fuse box in the hall fizzled and shot more sparks.

"I saved you, you ungrateful little—"

Bonnie shook her head. Her brain must be rattling, because nothing made sense. "I thought you were—"

"Get me out of here!"

Bonnie turned at the outraged voice coming from behind her.

Dora.

Dora was in the museum. No big surprise there. Dora was active in the historical society. She came in once in a while. The surprise was that she was inside her 1975 Chrysler New Yorker.

Bonnie looked at the enraged senior citizen, apparently unhurt, fuming in the rubble of Bonnie's museum. Bonnie reached out to steady herself on a shelf. Of course, there wasn't one.

She sank. Joe Manning, busy dabbing the blood off his face, caught her and pulled her against his side. She looked up, her vision blurred.

He swung her up in his arms. "Call an ambulance for her, too."

Junior looked away from Dora. "We've only got one, but it'll sleep two long enough for the ride to Bjorn."

Bonnie's head cleared as soon as she didn't have to depend on herself for legs.

She blinked her eyes at the savage, attacking beast, bleeding and trying to take care of her at the same time. That didn't seem right.

"I'm sorry, Mr. Manning." She said it by reflex.

"Call me Joe." The man tilted his head as if what she said might make more sense if his brain were shifted around a little. "What are you apologizing for?"

"For beating you up."

The man sighed, his dark brown eyes seeming less thunder, more lightning. "Me, too. Sheriff Hammerstad told me you were still at the museum. He let me into the outer hall, and I was coming to the museum to ask for a book about Melnik history. I wasn't trying to hurt you. Just as you opened the door, I saw that car veer and head straight for us when the lightning hit the building. I was trying to save you."

"Really?" Bonnie breathed the word. She looked deeper in his eyes, the only dark part of his plastered face—except the blood. "Thank you for saving me. I *am* sorry."

He held her just a bit closer.

The ambulance siren kicked on, which was silly, since the ambulance was parked in the back of the same building as the museum and just had to back out and come around to the front door. But rules were rules. And you had to run the siren when you were on your way to the scene of an accident.

Honestly, Bonnie was pretty sure the brave members of the Melnik Volunteer Fire and Rescue Department just really thought it was fun to turn on the siren.

"What's that?" Junior straightened away from Dora so suddenly it pulled Bonnie's attention away from her hero.

With cop eyes Bonnie had never seen on Junior before, he looked straight past Bonnie and Joe. Then he surged forward and shoved past them.

Joe turned, Bonnie still in his arms. Junior raced toward the door to a little storage room that had been locked for about a decade—ever since Bonnie had lost the key.

Joe dropped Bonnie's legs. He might have dropped all of her if she hadn't grabbed hold of him the minute she saw—

"It's a dead body." Joe looked at the corpse then leaned closer and stared harder.

"How did he get in here?" Junior knelt beside the man and checked his neck for a pulse.

"I. . .I don't know. I've been the only one in here all week." It was Wednesday, so that didn't speak well of the number of tourists coming to the Melnik Historical Society Museum. Bonnie was forced to admit that the number of people willing to look at an oversized mouse was proving to be limited.

Bonnie let go of Joe to hug herself. Her own arms were far inferior. Chills raced up her spine as she recognized who it was.

"That's Sven Gunderson," Joe said.

Sven Gunderson—town miser and crank—lay stretched out on the floor, clutching a book to his chest. It touched Bonnie's bookaholic heart to think that the man's dying act was to cling to a book.

Junior turned on her. "You sure about that?"

"That it's Sven?" Bonnie glanced at Joe. "How do you know Sven Gunderson?"

"No." Junior didn't give Joe time to answer. "Are you sure that you're the only one who's been in here."

Bonnie shrugged. She'd have remembered a visitor. "During the hours we're open, yes, I'm sure."

The ambulance pulled up outside, its lights strobing red inside the museum. A buzz and a flicker of light overhead pulled Bonnie's glance up at the rectangular fluorescent fixture, now hanging from wires, swinging over the rubble where her desk used to be. She looked at the destruction, her crushed desk, the massive weight of the shelves and books.

If she'd been sitting there, as she had been just seconds before Joe had hammered on the door, she'd be dead. The man had saved her life, pure and simple. She imagined him—despite his chalky white face smeared with blood and his I've-just-received-electric-shock-therapy hair—astride a prancing warhorse. His sword and shield glinted in the sunlight, or in this case they glinted in a dangling fluorescent fixture, aided by the red emergency spotlight in the hall and the flashing ambulance cherry.

"Of course I'm sure." Bonnie heard her voice, breathless, entranced, charmed, as she looked at her chivalrous warrior. She rested one hand on her chest to steady her thudding heart. She read a lot of books. The man made a fine Sir Lancelot.

Could it be that she was trying to impress the man with her intellect? She had no illusions she could do it with her personality or looks, so instead, in a voice Marilyn Monroe might well have used to sing "Happy Birthday, Mr. President," she stood ready to show how smart she was.

Yes, Sir Lancelot, I am brilliant, and I'm sure that I accurately counted to zero this week.

"Get me out of here. I'm suing this town," Dora snarled from behind them.

"It's Sven Gunderson all right. Looks like he's been dead a day or two," Junior pronounced as he knelt beside the corpse. He looked about two days dead to Bonnie—stiff, his eyes fixed on the ceiling. But then, the few times she'd seen

Gunderson walking around he'd been really stiff, too. So it was probably best to let the coroner get involved.

"How do you know Sven Gunderson?" Bonnie asked Sir Lancelot, just to get him to talk to her, look at her instead of staring at the corpse.

"If no one else has been in here all week besides you—" The storm flared again in Joe's eyes as he glared at Bonnie.

Not the loving look and chivalrous words she'd hoped for.

"—then you just confessed to killing my father."

2

I did not!" The curator of this pathetic excuse for a museum stumbled backward.

Joe caught her before she ended up in a pile of books and shelves and artifacts. Another part of the wreckage. He'd known her now for—Joe checked his watch—twelve minutes. It looked like keeping this woman from catastrophe was a full-time job.

Joe wasn't applying.

Thunder rumbled again, but Joe saw the lightning in the curator's eyes and thought the thunder might have come from her. His gut told him this lady was no murderer, but anyone could kill in the right circumstances. He also knew enough about his father that it wouldn't be hard to imagine just about anyone gunning for him.

"Confessed?" Sheriff Hammerstad lurched to his feet. Joe couldn't figure out how the man could catch any bad guys. He was too fat to run after them. Of course, these days, chances were the criminals were all fat and out of shape, too, so maybe the sheriff held his own.

"Your father?" The blue-haired lady in the demo derby car squawked like a hen. An old hen.

Steam suddenly blasted out the front of her hood, shooting a huge book into the air. It smacked the ceiling and bounced until it fell open at Joe's feet.

A headline screamed.

EX-CON MURDERED.

The letters stood so huge they virtually roared off the front page of the *Melnik Bugle*. The book must contain bound copies of the local newspaper. Joe looked at the mug shot and the shocking headline for a little town, especially since it appeared to have happened again. Had they caught that murderer? Could he still be loose? Could the killer have struck again?

Joe looked at the town cop. "Did you catch—"

"Sven Gunderson was your father?" The woman who drove the wrecking ball on wheels shouted at him. "Everybody knows Sven never married and never had children."

An old biddy hen.

And she kept squawking. He decided to ask about that EX-CON MURDERED headline later. Joe turned from the biddy to the body. Not a lot of struggle there

176

to set priorities, even if he didn't care whether Sven "The Bum" Gunderson, aka dear old Dad, was dead or not.

The whole room was lit by the swinging fluorescent light overhead and emergency spotlight in the hallway. The spotlight did more good than it normally would have, Joe observed, thanks to the convenient absence of the wall between the hallway and the room.

As he turned, something caught his eye on the old lady's car hood. Among the broken bricks and settling silt and mangled metal shelves and destroyed books sat an odd gray lump so out of place Joe had to look closer.

"What's that?" He approached the small, dusty object on the hood of Biddy's car.

He felt more than saw all three of the other people involved in this mess turn to look where he was looking.

The biddy screeched and started fighting with the crumpled car door as if the vehicle were on fire.

Sheriff Junior waddled toward Joe from behind, knocking aside debris.

The curator came up beside him with a long gasp that turned into a cough when she inhaled the grit thick in the air.

Then, over the squawking and waddling and coughing, all three of them yelled, "Maxie!"

The curator, belying her earlier knack for falling over, ran the few feet forward like an all-pro tailback dodging a defensive line. She even jumped onto the hood of the car as if getting to Maxie—whatever that meant—equaled recovering a fumble and saving the game.

"Oh, Maxie. . ." Museum Girl picked up the little lump and cradled it in both hands, pulling it close to her face.

"Is he all right?" Junior shoved past Joe as Museum Girl climbed off the car, cradling Maxie-the-lump.

"Get me out of here." The squawk was morphing to a roar.

Three men in black jackets raced into the building. They rolled a gurney into the hallway outside the destroyed museum. One of them yelled, "Who needs help?"

Junior looked up from the lump and jabbed a thumb at Dora. "She seems okay. Just get the Jaws of Life and get her out of the car."

The closest EMT nodded. "Awright! The Jaws of Life. Cool!"

All three men ran out the building from the direction they'd come.

Junior yelled after them, "And shut off the stupid siren. I can't hear myself think."

The car, a rust-bucket Chrysler big enough to raise a family in, was inside the museum up to the back doors. The trunk straddled the sidewalk and the street. Joe noticed the left turn signal blinking. The whole outer wall of the museum and the front doors of the entrance had been obliterated. The hallway opened onto city hall on the left, and on the right, this miserly Melnik Historical Society Museum—a name far too grand for this little hole-in-the-wall.

The door Joe had been standing near when he'd seen lightning hit the ground and the driver head straight for him was gone.

And the lump? Who in the world was Maxie?

And why were they all more worried about it. . .him. . .whatever. . .than the dead body?

"He's okay, Bonnie." Junior pulled a handkerchief out of his back pocket and dusted at the little lump. Curiosity drew Joe forward. Junior moved aside as if he were a proud father eager to let others see his precious newborn son.

Joe came up beside Curator Bonnie and saw. . .

"That's a mouse."

Bonnie looked up, brown eyes shining with affection for the lump. Joe had never had a woman look at him that way. Well, his mom, maybe, but looking at Bonnie's shining eyes didn't bring Joe to thoughts of his mother. He'd saved her. It had felt. . .heroic. He thought he had grown a couple of inches. Except those eyes weren't for him. Save my life? Big deal. You want to be my hero, you've gotta be. . .

"A dead mouse," Joe added.

Bonnie drew one finger down its matted, dirt-encrusted fur. Gross.

"Sure, he's dead. He's over fifty years old, for goodness' sake."

"A really *big* dead mouse—maybe a rat?"

"No, he's definitely a mouse. A field mouse. Maxie is the largest of his species. A world-record-sized Animalia; Chordate; Vertebrata; Mammalia; Rodentia; Sciurognathi; Cricetidae; Sigmondontinea; Peromyscus. We've had genetic testing done." Bonnie said it like she was boasting instead of revealing herself to be insane.

"How did you ever learn all that scientific babble?"

"We have to learn it to pass fourth grade." She turned those soft, concerned, kind eyes back on the disease-bearing vermin in her hand. Joe felt a pang of self-pity, maybe even jealousy. Bonnie the Insane stroked its fur again, restoring it to order as much as a creature that probably helped spread the Black Plague could be restored. The woman obviously liked fur. Joe wondered if he should grow a beard—and ask her to wash her hands. And he wondered if he'd ever met a woman who had him quite so torn between attraction and revulsion before. No one came to mind.

"Did you check to make sure she was okay?" A voice sounded from inside city hall, from the direction the EMTs had gone.

"We've got to get her out before we can examine her, Chief."

The EMTs were back, but there was no Jaws of Life unit.

"Did you even try yanking on the door, Hal? You like getting out the Jaws of Life too much, and it takes awhile to set up." A tall, dark-haired man emerged from the still-gritty plaster-filled air. Like a tidy, scholarly Sea of Tranquility in the midst of madness, he came up to the car in his official team jacket. All the rescue squad members—a number now growing to a half dozen—wore them. True, some wore them over pajama pants, but still, the EMTs matched. One woman came in with her jacket on and pink sponge rollers in her hair.

The tall man asked through the window, "Are you okay, Dora?"

"Nick, you get me out of here now. Maxie's hurt!"

Since it was clear to Joe that Maxie was beyond being hurt, he said, "There's no rush."

Nick pulled on the door handle and jerked the frame. The door groaned in metallic distress and gave an inch. A brick rolled with a clatter off the car's roof and down the trunk, onto the floor.

Hal, of the Jaws of Life, grabbed the door's edge and threw his muscles into yanking.

Joe decided since he'd already rescued one fair maiden today, why not go for two? Although Dora the old biddy hen was kind of a stretch for a maiden.

He got his hands in low on the now slightly open door. It made sense to help. His father wasn't going to get any deader.

Together the three of them got the door open over the screaming protest of bent hinges. Dora flapped out. Joe was tempted to see if she was cackling because she'd laid an egg.

Just then the ambulance siren and strobe lights cut off. Junior climbed down from the ambulance, which had been backed into a parking space right outside the building.

"Dora, you shouldn't move." Nick said it like he'd had training and had listened and remembered.

A short, elderly woman, Dora knocked everyone aside.

"You could be hurt," Nick protested as she rushed past, as unhurt as anyone Joe had ever seen. "You need to let us check."

"Be careful with him, Marian." Dora rounded Nick like he was just another piece of rubble.

Joe tried to figure out who Marian was. Maybe Junior's real name?

Dora shoved her way to the dead mouse. Joe *knew* the mouse was Maxie, so that left. . . But hadn't the sheriff called her. . .

Bonnie opened her hands so Dora could have a good look.

"He's okay," Bonnie/Marian cooed. "I'll clean him up."

Dora nodded her blue-gray dust mop of a head, and grit flew in all directions. "Good. He'll need a new fish tank. Tallulah will pay for it."

The two women exchanged a delighted smile.

Joe was starting to have a serious problem with this town.

"Uh. . .what about the dead guy?" He didn't put too much energy into encouraging proper police procedure. He had a bad feeling about what a car smashing into the crime scene did for trace evidence.

"What dead guy?" Nick looked up as if he'd just noticed Joe, even though Joe had helped wrestle the door.

"Wow, dead guy, nine o'clock," Hal said.

Everyone—Joe thought maybe even Maxie—turned to look at the Bum.

Nick's eyes sharpened as he looked from the Bum to Joe to the car. "I've got to call my wife."

Which Joe thought was the most unlikely reaction to this situation anyone could have. Well, except for caressing a mouse carcass like Museum Girl was doing.

"I'm here." A young, pretty woman, blond as sunlight in the emergency beacons, pushed through what Joe realized was a growing crowd. None of the newcomers were wearing EMT jackets, so this was just a bunch of snoops.

Blondie waved a camera.

"This is a crime scene!" Joe hollered to make himself heard above the chattering bystanders. People seemed to surge closer as if Joe had yelled for them to crowd around. More came from the street every minute, most of them in robes and slippers.

The young lady rushed forward.

Curator Bonnie/Marian held up her cradled hands. "Don't worry, Maxie is going to be okay."

The blond squeaked so loudly Joe was sure she took a layer of skin off his eardrums. She jumped straight up and Nick caught her in his arms, grinning down at her with affection that lit up the room far better than the spotlight ever could. Joe sure hoped this was Nick's wife. Otherwise there might be more trouble before the night was over.

Joe tapped Junior on the shoulder. "Shouldn't we clear the crime scene, maybe?" Joe had seen that on *CSI*, so it had to be true.

Junior seemed to get his concern for Maxie under control. He nodded and gave Blondie a disgusted look. "When are you gonna get over bein' scared of mice, Carrie?"

Carrie shrugged from her safe spot in her husband's arms. "Never, most likely."

Junior turned to the crowd. "Get out of here, all of you."

"Why's Sven Gunderson dead in there, Junior?" Carrie asked. She lifted her camera and took a picture of the corpse.

Joe was impressed. He'd have bet a lot—if he was a betting man, which he wasn't—that she'd have snapped her first picture of the mouse. This woman had some sense at least, except for the fact that she was being held by her husband while she chased down the story of the century for this little town. Joe glanced down one more time at the open newspaper page. Maybe not the story of the century. Maybe people got murdered in this town all the time. Maybe that's why no one was paying attention to. . .ho hum. . .just another boring old corpse. This week's dead guy.

"Don't forget to get a picture of Maxie," Bonnie said. Obviously completely out of her mind.

Carrie shuddered visibly. "No way."

Nick turned and toted her out into the hallway like he was used to it.

"Take me back there. I've got to get this story."

"It's a crime scene." Then Nick lifted his voice. "We've got to get outside. Junior needs to work in there."

Somehow the town obeyed. This guy must be some really respected community leader. Maybe he was just the old guard. He'd been here forever, something like that. The whole town followed him like he was the Pied Piper and they were a bunch of rodents. Oddly enough, the only real rodent in the room didn't follow him. Just because the mouse was dead wasn't reason enough for Maxie not to get up and walk. Not in Melnik.

They all left but Junior and Bonnie. Joe turned back toward the Bum.

A bloodcurdling shriek sounded from the street.

Joe whirled around.

Another ear-splitting squeal of agony.

The kind of scream usually reserved for someone getting a gangrenous leg amputated—with a dull saw.

The scream cut through the crowd again.

A dull, rusty saw.

"Maxie!"

With no anesthetic.

Joe was tempted to find a bullet to bite on just to stop the pain in his ears.

"Maxie! No! No! My Maxie!"

"Tallulah Pritchard's here." Junior gave Joe an apologetic shrug. "Now things are going to get weird."

Joe almost started screaming himself.

3

Gunslinger eyes.

Bonnie swallowed hard every time she looked at Joe's cold, unemotional eyes. Grouchy, quick on the trigger. They had a gunslinger in Melnik. A grouchy gunslinger who'd accused her of murder like a quick draw.

Not a good thing.

Not a chance on the chivalry she thought she'd glimpsed earlier, either. A real shame. Yes, he'd saved her. Traces of knight in shining armor there. But it hadn't lasted. Bonnie sighed. If it were easy to find a Sir Lancelot, they'd have never written a book about him, now, would they?

Bonnie watched the gunslinger's eyes swing away from Tallulah's screaming and catch her looking at him. She turned away quickly, feeling her cheeks warm. He'd told Junior she was the prime suspect in Sven Gunderson's murder. The jerk.

"Get back! Let me through!" Tallulah charged past the crowd and the rubble. "I have to save Maxie!"

The crowd parted like the Red Sea; then they surged back in on Tallulah's heels.

Bonnie extended her hands so Tallulah could be reassured. The town's precious mascot had been spared.

"He's okay, Tallulah. We'll fix up a new case and he'll be just like before."

"Carinthemuseum. Bodyinthemuseum," came another voice.

Bonnie looked past Tallulah's brightly colored shoulder and saw Clara. The Red Sea parted again, this time probably because they were afraid madness was contagious. Or maybe Clara just smelled bad.

Bonnie liked Clara but not the sickening pies she made. The last one Bonnie had bought was—near as Bonnie could tell—turkey jerky and dryer-lint meringue. And the pies' stench tended to linger on Clara long after she'd gotten rid of them.

Everybody in Melnik knew it was their responsibility to buy Clara's awful pies. It wasn't like they had to eat them, just wait until she moved on and then throw the things away. The woman needed money—mainly to buy more groceries for more pies. Insanity wasn't contagious by purchase, now, was it? It didn't hurt a thing for the citizens of Melnik to help Clara out.

"Shouldn't you people be worrying about the dead body?" Gunslinger Joe just would not give them a minute to deal with what was really important.

Bonnie glared over her shoulder at him. "Sven Gunderson isn't going anywhere. We have to make sure everyone is okay."

The man's dark brows, liberally dusted with plaster and grit, slammed together. "You mean the lady in the car or the dead mouse?"

Since Tallulah wanted Maxie so badly, Bonnie gently laid him in the Melnik historian's hands and turned to deal with this stubborn man.

Tallulah started cooing a lullaby.

Bonnie stepped up to Joe, her heart thudding, not with fear, but with indignation. "You need to calm down."

She took a split second to wonder if she was flooded with adrenaline from Dora's near miss, because she was *never* confrontational. As she stood in front of Joe, her throat went dry and her teeth clenched on grit.

He glared at her as she stopped, her nose turned up so it was only inches from his. Only he towered over her five-foot-seven, so he must have leaned down to meet her.

"Getmybook!" Clara shoved past Bonnie with sudden desperate strength.

Bonnie let herself get moved aside, and when the smell hit Joe the Grouch, he backed up a step, too. Clara swooped down on the body.

"Clara, don't!" Bonnie yelled.

Junior blocked Clara. "You can have that book when you pry it out of Sven's cold dead fingers."

Clara made a surprisingly agile move for a seventy-year-old crazy person and dodged past Junior. She shouted at Gunderson, "Letgo!" With one grab, she yanked the book free.

Crime scene violation there.

"Clara, you can't take that!" Junior reached for the book.

"Needstobestopped." Clara pulled the book to her chest until she was holding it a lot like Sven had been, minus the rigor mortis. "Hewon'thurtMelnik. He'sdead. Goodhe'sdead."

Bonnie recognized the book. "That's *The Melnik Centennial Cookbook.*"

"You're tampering with a crime scene, lady." The Gunslinger reached for the book.

"You can't have that, Clara." Junior made a move for it, too.

There was only one thing to do. Bonnie turned away from the murder on the west, the car on the east, and the jumble of books fallen helter-skelter on the north. She turned to the south, where shelves still stood neatly, proudly upright in the midst of chaos. Though she regretted it, because it was her last copy, she pulled down a book.

Before Clara found herself doing hard time for grand theft cookbook, Bonnie said, "Clara, here's *your* book."

Flinching, Bonnie realized she sounded as if she were talking to a child. Poor Clara. "That's Sven's. Leave it with him, please."

Clara, in a tug-of-war with the Gunslinger and Junior, turned and saw what Bonnie held. Easing her determined expression, Clara released the book and took the one Bonnie offered. "Mylife. Mylife. Inthisbook. Gladhe'sdead. Wantedhimdead. Idid. Idid. Idid. Idid."

Clara hustled out of the rubble as if afraid they'd try to take the book back.

"Did she just say, 'I did'?" Joe asked. "As in—'I killed him'?"

"Clara didn't kill anyone." Junior picked his way through the mess toward Sven.

Bonnie knew Clara used to be a caterer and one of the most admired cooks in Melnik. A lot of her favorite recipes were in the old cookbook. That must be what the poor addled woman was talking about. Bonnie let Clara leave even though the museum really should have a copy. They used to have a stack, but over the years they'd been sold until they were down to this single copy.

Bonnie's eyes fell on the book Gunderson had been hugging. Maybe when they were done dusting that one for fingerprints, the museum could have it. She shuddered to think of Gunderson's cold dead fingers on the book.

"I'm pretty sure I just heard her confess to murder." Joe swiped at his hair, and bits of dust and plaster poofed out. Bonnie decided his hair was brown instead of white.

Junior looked doubtfully at the mangled shelves lying on top of Bonnie's desk. "I've got to call in the coroner. I'll go use the phone in the city hall office."

Joe pulled a small black phone off his belt. "Use mine."

Shaking his head, Junior said, "Cell phones don't work in Melnik."

Tallulah broke off cooing over Maxie and spoke from behind Bonnie's back. "Try sitting on top of the school slippery slide. It'll work up there."

"Out back of my house, if you're on the second step, for some reason you can make calls." Carrie O'Conner snapped another picture of Gunderson. "But you don't get good reception." Bonnie sincerely hoped Carrie would have enough good taste not to put a plaster-dust-coated corpse on the front page of the *Bugle*.

Bonnie noticed Carrie was still perched in Nick's arms. A little twist of regret reminded her that one of the sweetest guys to ever pass through Melnik had also passed over her and picked Carrie.

Of course.

Carrie was pretty and brave—not counting mice—and funny and a really talented writer. Not the shy, plain, bookworm curator of a tiny museum no one ever visited.

"Drive out of town west to the second hilltop," someone yelled out of the crowd. "Cell phones work there, but you've got to pull over; you can't keep driving 'cause you'll lose your bars."

Bonnie knew the hot spots, too.

Junior growled, "Forget it. I ain't got time for all that." He looked between Bonnie, Tallulah, and Dora. "Do any of you have a key to the city office?"

Hands went up all through the still-growing crowd. At least twenty people said, "I do."

Bonnie half expected Maxie to raise his paw.

Junior shook his head as he took Tallulah's key and left the museum for the city office straight across the hall. Bonnie heard him mutter something about changing the building's locks. Getting new locks might actually be on the agenda now, seeing as how the front door to the building had been ripped completely away and the building was being held up almost entirely by the trunk of a Chrysler.

The New Yorker was absolutely up to the job, incidentally. They'd built that car to last.

"Get out of this crime scene," Junior roared. Tallulah jumped and crushed a fist around Maxie then opened her hand and began shrieking again.

Bonnie watched Junior display surprising authority as he shooed the citizens of Melnik, who were only here to rubberneck at this point—and that included the rescue squad—out of the building. Neither Joe, Bonnie, nor Dora wanted to go to the hospital. Apparently Maxie did. Tallulah gently laid him down on the gurney.

"If someone straps that mouse in and starts an IV," Joe the Grouch grumbled, "I'm getting a net for this whole town."

Tallulah scowled at Joe and shifted her considerable weight as if to block him from harming Maxie. Then she wheeled the mouse away. The town dispersed once Tallulah left the building with Maxie. Dora agreed to take a ride home with Nick and Carrie and walked away slowly, as if she might miss something.

Just as the crowd was thinning down, Jeffie Piperson came tearing up the middle of Main Street on his bike, toward the battered front entrance of the historical society museum. Bonnie frowned. Jeffie was six. He shouldn't be out at this hour.

Dora stopped. Nick, too, no doubt expected—considering Jeffie had arrived—that the skills of an EMT would be needed very soon.

Jeffie jammed on his brakes and slid the bike along sideways, slammed into Dora's trunk, and fell. Still sliding, he vanished under the car.

Joe shouted with alarm and rushed past Bonnie. He crouched at the trunk of the car and said, "Be careful; you could have broken a bone."

He sounded so kind and concerned. Jeffie was already scrambling free of the wreckage. Of course Jeffie was uninjured. The boy had a knack for cheating death. If they needed Nick's paramedic skills, it would be for someone wiped out by Jeffie's antics.

"Are you okay?" Joe ran his hands down Jeffie's arms and legs so quickly and efficiently, Bonnie wondered if the man was a doctor. "We need to call your mom. What are you doing out so late? Do you need help?"

Jeffie gave one bloodcurdling scream right in Joe's face. Joe rose to his feet and stepped back from the wild little boy.

Then Jeffie yelled, "You're a stupid-head! I hate you!"

Joe reacted as if he were a gunslinger again. With a quick draw, he produced . . .a sucker from his pocket.

Jeffie froze. "For me?"

"Sure, I just wanted to make sure you weren't hurt. I'm proud of you for not letting a stranger get close to you without yelling. And you're right not to just take the candy, too. Good boy."

Jeffie looked from the sucker to Joe, then to Junior. "Is he a bad man?"

"Nope, and I'm watching him real close even though he's okay, so you can have the sucker, Jeffie."

Jeffie narrowed his eyes then reached out and snatched the candy. "Uh. . . thanks, I guess."

"You're welcome."

"You're still a stupid-head!" Jeffie ripped the paper off, stuck the sucker in his mouth, then jerked his bike free from the car and tore away from the scene.

Joe turned to look at Bonnie. She grimaced, feeling the need to apologize for Jeffie. He was the town's mini-maniac.

"I love kids." Joe sounded almost reverent.

Bonnie's heart softened at Joe's kindness toward Jeffie the Terror. Try as she might, Bonnie had never been able to get close to the little boy. Most children loved her and her books and all the odd, interesting artifacts in the museum. The museum did double duty as Melnik's only library, too. During the summer the town had a reading program, and Bonnie read the children stories and checked out books to them from the meager collection.

Children frequently came in and wandered the shelves. She tried to let them touch everything under her careful supervision. Jeffie never came in except to cause trouble. She'd never heard him say thank you before, either. She knew everyone in town would be watching for him to make sure he got home, but the kid would be sure to get loose again.

Joe was a miracle worker. And a white knight. And a grouch. With gunslinger eyes.

Leaning on Nick's arm, Dora left the museum, so used to Jeffie that she didn't even bother to insult the child or gossip about him. "We'll talk again in the morning, Marian," she called over her shoulder.

Bonnie accepted Dora's nickname with her usual patience.

As Dora, Nick, and Carrie—the last of the crowd—walked away, Bonnie heard Dora ask if they could take the ambulance and run the siren.

"I don't want to wake anyone else up, Dora," Nick said.

"You've got that look again, Nick."

"What look?"

Bonnie could tell from twenty feet away that the question was practically torn out of Nick's throat.

"You need fiber and lots of it." Dora turned to look at Carrie. "You need my recipe for bran muffins, Cindy Lou."

Carrie was Cindy Lou, thanks to a part she played in an elementary school program a decade and a half ago. Bonnie was Marian, as in Marian the librarian. Bonnie was grateful. In earlier years she'd lain awake nights rhyming words with *curator*, and it wasn't pretty.

Dora never seemed to notice that no one else laughed at her nicknames.

"Who was that kid? Is he going to be all right?"

"Jeffie is indestructible." Junior waved the Melnik Terror away. "And whatever damage his parents do by spoiling him rotten, I'm sure can be fixed once he's been sent to Boys Town."

Bonnie turned back to the Grouch. "Sven Gunderson is really your father?"

Joe nodded.

Bonnie then spoke to Junior. "Everybody knows everybody in Melnik. But Gunderson left when he graduated from high school and never came back until his father died and he inherited all his money, including the Gunderson mansion. I'd never heard he married or had children."

"He wasn't married to my mother. He was a bum who abandoned her and me. I've never met him. Out of curiosity, when Mom died, I tracked him down."

Bonnie felt a stir of compassion. She stifled it. "So on the very night you come to town looking for a man you hold a grudge against, he turns up dead." Bonnie arched one brow and said nothing further.

"I have no motive to kill a man I barely knew."

"Oh, and I suppose I do have a motive?" Bonnie crossed her arms. "Maybe he had pilfered old books about Maxie the Mouse, and I decided it was payback time?"

"Look, you're the one who said you were here alone all day. You're the one who said no one else came in. You as good as confessed to having the only opportunity."

"You take that back!" Bonnie jammed her hands on her hips, surprised at herself for being so rude, but the man was infuriating. "You're the one with the motive in this room."

He took two long strides and vultured over her. "I didn't, repeat *didn't*, have a motive to kill my father."

"Well, neither did I," Bonnie yelled. Her throat hurt a little.

The man held her gaze. She could see sharp glints of fury in his brown eyes.

Then the glints cooled down. He straightened away from her and shook his head. "As far as that goes, I'm inclined to believe you. You don't seem like the type."

Bonnie dropped her fists from her waist in surprise. "Really? You believe me?" She hadn't been afraid of the accusation—it was just too outlandish. But now that he'd backed down, she realized part of her anger had been fueled by fear. She rested one hand flat on her chest and heaved a sigh of relief.

"I said I'm inclined to. No one who cares that much about a stuffed dead animal has got a real killer instinct. Unless they're insane, of course." His eyes narrowed.

Bonnie watched, expecting the man to whip out a magnifying glass to study her for clues. But any resemblance to Sherlock Holmes didn't seem to extend to his powers of deduction.

While they waited for Junior, Bonnie took inventory of the damage to her museum. It wasn't totally destroyed as she'd first thought when choking grit filled the air. One quarter of it, the quarter with the car in it, was toast. Dora had knocked the shelves over like dominoes. Each one had tipped, crashing into the one next to it.

There were three tall shelves that didn't begin to reach the high ceilings of the historic old building. The third one to topple had landed on Bonnie's desk and reached far enough to slam into the first of three more shelves on the other side. That first shelf had tipped and landed on the second, but the second shelf held, and the third in the row was unscathed. On the south side of the building, the shelves stood upright like good soldiers. The last corner, occupied by the unused storage room—and Sven Gunderson's corpse—took up the remaining space. The door had popped open after the impact, but the little room was intact.

Junior came back from calling the coroner. "I talked with Dr. Notchke and explained the situation. She told me we should get Sven out of here. This building isn't stable."

"It's fine, Cousin Junior." Bonnie patted him on the arm.

"*Cousin* Junior?" Joe's voice rose.

Bonnie narrowed her eyes at him. "Yes, he's my cousin—well, second cousin actually—my mom's cousin. But we call him Cousin Junior to differentiate Uncle Junior and Grandpa Junior."

Joe shook his head hard, like a dog shaking water off his fur, then looked back at the sheriff. "Moving the body will destroy any evidence that's left."

"Having a museum collapse on him will do that, too," Junior pointed out.

"It's not going to collapse," Bonnie reassured him.

Nick came back in. He must have thought there was still work to do. Nick was a responsible man. "Actually, it could. Dora smashed two main support walls."

Nick pulled an empty gurney behind him. Bonnie wondered where he'd delivered Maxie.

"I asked Nick to help us out." Junior grabbed one end of the gurney. "We've got to move the body."

Joe looked at the ceiling above their heads. "See that crack around the light fixture?"

Considering her whole life's work lay in rubble around her ankles, Bonnie hadn't looked up.

"I don't think that was there before."

Junior moved a little faster. "Okay, let's get him out of here."

Nick didn't help. Bonnie saw him try. But he kept flinching away from the body. Bonnie thought it was sweet and normal to not want to touch a corpse, not like that jerk Joe who didn't bat an eye.

"Get out of the way, Bonnie, honey," Junior said. "We need the space to get Sven and the gurney out of here."

Bonnie stepped into the hallway and Nick came along, looking sheepish for not helping.

Joe and Junior lifted Sven, one of them on each side. Sven was so stiff it was easy. They sidled out of the little room and picked their way to the gurney and laid Sven down. Then all four of them, five if you counted Sven, were in the hall. They turned back—all but Sven—to look at the mess.

"We're going to have to leave Dora's car there for now." Nick crossed his arms and studied the room. "I'm afraid it's holding up the building."

Red bricks decorated the roof of the car. The tail of it stuck out into the hallway and through the front door, onto the sidewalk and street. "So we can't board up the building."

"I'll just go home for my camp cot and sleep in here," Junior offered. "I'm afraid Melnik is going to be without a museum for a while."

"Nonsense." Bonnie dusted her hands together, already getting organized. "It just needs to be cleaned up, and the community can pitch in and refit the bricks. We can even reuse most of the ones that are there. We'll have this fixed in no time."

An awful, distressed-metal sound pulled their attention toward the museum.

Bonnie saw the upright second shelf tremble. The metal whined; the shelf shifted and stopped. She breathed a sigh of relief. "Okay, that was scary, but it's going to be just fine."

"You're a real cockeyed optimist, aren't you?" Joe looked away from the wreckage. "No way is this building going to be 'just fine.' It's over a hundred years old from the look of it."

"They built things to last back then."

Joe snorted. Just like a rude pig. "The roof is probably undermined. The floor may have been distressed, and the whole building will most likely end up being condemned. I hope this town and the driver have good insurance."

"Stop looking at the worst-case scenario." Bonnie rounded on the Voice of Doom in their midst. "The museum will be fine if we give it some TLC and a little elbow grease."

Joe rolled his eyes.

Bonnie hated that. Especially when *he* did it.

"How can you say—" Joe stopped talking when the shelf on the far side of Bonnie's desk rumbled again. They all turned.

The shelf moved as if in slow motion, tilting, tilting, tilting an inch at a time. It hit the third shelf in that row and stopped. The books and artifacts didn't stop, though. They slid off the shelf, one, then two, then ten, raining down in the space between the two shelves. Then the third shelf gave with a loud *snap*. It fell faster than the second one and hit the outside museum wall. The wall crumbled and the third shelf fell out into the night, the other shelves crashing after it.

"Three support walls." Nick could do a good Voice of Doom himself. "That's bad."

Bricks crashed down from the space above where the third shelf had hit; then the museum ceiling collapsed on top of the whole mess. Dust kicked up.

"Get out!" Joe shoved her ahead. They all dashed out of the building.

Junior grabbed Sven and rolled him along. As they rushed out to the sidewalk, the back bumper of Dora's car tilted upward. Bonnie saw the front wheels break through the floor of the museum into the musty, neglected basement. Bonnie had been down there only once. It was a bleak and filthy place fit to breed an entire army of oversized rodents.

The car's trunk tipped up and up, then slid forward, like it was being swallowed, a gulp at a time, by a building-sized snake. The Chrysler vanished into the bowels of the Historical Society Boa.

The sign outside the entrance to the city hall snapped its anchor as the first floor of the old brownstone building collapsed. Sparks flew from a nearby power pole. Bonnie was dragged by Joe out into the middle of the street as the sign, a ten-foot-by-two-foot stretch of painted sheet metal, bolted above the entrance, sheared on one corner, swung down, snapped the bolt on the other corner, and dropped. The sign bounced on end with the rather pretty vibration of a musical band saw, flew up again in a graceful arc, and impaled itself through the front window of a cherry red Jeep Cherokee.

Bonnie had never seen the snappy-looking SUV before, but she knew without being told whom it belonged to.

But she was told.

"My Jeep!"

Instantly.

Joe took two steps toward the vehicle, his arms thrown out at his sides. He stopped. They all froze. Even Sven, lying there dead, strapped to the gurney, seemed unnaturally still.

Dust curled up from the building as the rumbling finally stopped. It was done. The disaster was complete. Right out of the center of the old buildings that made up Melnik Main Street, the ground floor of one disappeared into a pile of rubble. Bonnie held her breath, hoping the rest of the buildings wouldn't collapse, too. The second floor still stood overhead. A brick dropped off it, but the rest seemed to hold.

The museum was her life, and her life was now utterly destroyed. The books might be saved, but the building, an old one that would have qualified as a national historical monument if anyone had done the paperwork to arrange that, was now nothing more than a footnote in Melnik history. Tears flooded Bonnie's eyes as she realized things just could not get any worse.

The sky opened up. Angry little needles of rain sliced down on them. Bonnie remembered this whole chain reaction had started with a lightning bolt that caused Dora to veer onto the sidewalk.

"I hate this town." Joe's voice sounded like he was grinding up rocks with his throat.

"Bad for trace evidence." Junior pulled off his jacket and covered Sven as best he could.

"My artifacts!" Bonnie dashed toward the museum. An arm clamped around her waist and stopped her in her tracks. The Grouch had her.

"You can't go in there." The arm gave her a little shake. "It isn't safe."

Bonnie struggled, but the grip was iron, as was the logic. She couldn't risk her life for a bunch of old books, old wood, old metal. The rain mingled with Bonnie's hopeless tears as she watched her museum receive the final insult. A good soaking.

The arm loosened until it was almost a hug, and the Grouch, still behind her, brushed her hair off her face. "I'm sorry about your museum, Marian."

He actually sounded kind. It only made her cry harder.

As she sobbed, she hoped at least she might be heading off a heart attack.

Headlights fell on them and Bonnie couldn't quite bring herself to move out of the way of the oncoming car. It had to be past 1:00 a.m. This was Melnik. There were no cars on the street at this hour—Jeffie on his bike, maybe—but no cars. A white station wagon stopped as Bonnie turned to look into the glaring headlights, blinding her through the rain.

Joe released her gently as if worried she might collapse just like her museum. They all turned to see windshield wipers whapping. The car's motor seemed silent with the roar of the rain, as if it were a ghost car. But then, *everything* was silent compared to the last hour, and since the whole night had Bonnie spooked, she suspected the car wasn't much like a ghost at all.

The headlights snapped off. The car door swung open. The words DODGE COUNTY CORONER were visible in the dim streetlight.

A stocky woman emerged wearing a white coat and sporting an unfortunate Little Dutch Boy haircut. Maybe the white coat was a warning. Bonnie wondered if they were coming to take her away. Ho-ho.

"Well, Junior," the square little coroner began. "How many people have claimed to kill this one?"

4

Bonnie's world had collapsed.

Why wasn't she surprised Dora the town meddler had brought that on?

She wasn't one to wallow in despair, though. After she got home, her hard-core insomnia was delighting in this excuse to keep her mind churning. She showered off about a pound of plaster dust then spent most of the night online, researching museum grants.

She finally slept for a couple of hours but woke at her normal 6:00 a.m. Her eyes gritty from lack of sleep, her head fuzzy from exhaustion—both things she was very used to—she headed for work at the crack of dawn, fully armed with short-term, medium-term, and long-term solutions to Melnik's historical society crisis.

Short-term? Save the books and artifacts. She would have done it last night, but no one would let her back inside. Today she wore her oldest beige slacks and a worn-out beige knit shirt so she could get dirty.

Medium-term? She'd find a temporary location for the materials while applying for grant money.

Long-term? Melnik was going to have a brand-spanking-new historical museum, and she was just the one to raise the money.

Joe emerged from the wreckage of her museum, saw her coming, must have read the determined expression on her face, and held up his hands.

"You're not going in there. Are you crazy?" He cleaned up good. Bonnie had heard Junior invite Joe home last night. Junior had a wife and two teenage boys in a small house, so it couldn't have been comfortable. But his plaster coating was gone—and the blood.

Bonnie noticed his front-windowless Jeep parked across the street from the museum. Bonnie had parked next to him. The city hall sign lay on the sidewalk next to bricks and jumbled debris.

"Can anything else really collapse?"

"You're kidding, right? The whole back half of the building is barely standing. It could still fall, as well as both buildings beside it."

Bonnie came even with Joe and looked at the line of buildings that created the south side of Melnik's main business district. They stood shoulder to shoulder, with shared outer walls. It was absolutely true that if one collapsed, the whole south side of the Main Street business district was in danger. Was it possible for one small woman to destroy an entire block of buildings?

With Dora, anything was possible.

It was a pretty bleak business district to begin with, but there were signs of renewal. The buildings were all similar, worn redbrick mainly, with one beautiful granite facade close to the east end. A couple had tidy siding and awnings, nice and modern, but were an unfortunate contrast to the charming, if decrepit, historic buildings. Most had squared-off roofs and were two stories high but of different designs, their very difference giving them harmony.

Anchoring the west end of Main Street was a lawyer's office that had at one time been the Melnik National Bank. The bank now had a modern building a few blocks east of the business district. The old pinkish granite building was on the east end of the block. It rose in a grand peak Bonnie had always loved.

Next to it was a brick building with an overhang that used to hold letters spelling out this week's movie, reminding everyone it was a former theater. Nick now owned three of the buildings, the only ones that were unoccupied, and was renovating them.

Joe seemed to be studying the layout of the town along with her until he looked at the grocery store. "What's that?"

Looking where he pointed, Bonnie smiled fondly at the statue. "That's Maxie."

"No, it isn't. He's way smaller than that."

"It's a tribute statue."

Joe looked at her nervously. "Do you personally think it's a good idea to put a four-foot-tall statue of a rodent outside the town's only grocery store?"

"Oh yes. It's exactly the message we're trying to send."

"That the grocery store is infested?"

"No, of course not." Her smile curled down. "The message is that our town's pride and joy is Maxie, the World's Largest Field Mouse. He's our claim to fame."

"Y'know, I don't think 'field mouse' and 'fame' can really go together in the same sentence."

"Of course they can." Bonnie sniffed at him and crossed her arms. "In fact, I'm spearheading a summer arts festival in which a dozen statues of Maxie will be placed around the town, each painted in a unique way."

"You mean brown fur, gray fur. . .what else? What other colors do mice come in? White, maybe?"

"No, each artist will be given complete freedom to express him or herself artistically with the mouse statue. Olga Jansson has already announced plans to have her mouse painted like a Dala horse."

"Dala horse? What's that?"

"It's Swedish. Olga is Swedish and runs a café." Bonnie pointed down a few doors on Main Street to Jansson's Café. "She'd be expressing her Swedishness and her love for Maxie in the same statue."

"Rat grocery store, rat diner. Why not?"

"Maxie's a mouse. He's Animalia; Chordata; Vertebrata; Mammalia—"

"Got it." Joe cut her off. "Fourth-grade graduation test. I remember." He ran his hands into his hair as if he were checking to make sure his skull was still there.

His thick brown hair was distracting Bonnie from this morning's project. She turned away from him and noticed movement through a hole in the wall of her collapsed museum. "Is Junior in there?"

"Yes. He's determined to go over the crime scene. He's hunting for the Melnik cookbook Sven held. We managed to drop it last night. He's also photographing the place Sven was laid out. I couldn't stop him, but—" He turned to her and stood in her way. "I can stop you."

He stood there staring; then a grin quirked the corners of his lips. Last night his plaster-coated hair had inspired a resemblance to Albert Einstein. Now that Joe was clean, there was no comparison. The golden brown hair looked as soft as Dora's mink coat. It was the only mink coat in town, and Bonnie had touched it once. She would kind of like to compare the feel of Joe's hair—her fingers itched to just test its softness. He had a straight nose, eyes that looked as soft as his hair, and a square chin with an amazing dimple right in the center.

Bonnie's heart clutched, and that scared her enough to stop the staring. She leaned sideways to study the building, blocked by his broad shoulders.

"It looks about as down as it can be, at least the museum side." She pointed and he turned to look. "The city hall side is actually another building. We converted some space to create a shared entry when we opened the museum."

Joe seemed satisfied that she wasn't going to make a break for the building—so naive—and turned to stand at her side, his arms crossed.

"The rest of the building looks pretty good. In fact, the city clerk is already at work. If he can go in there, and you, *and* Junior, then so can I. You're just being nitpicky. Everything that can collapse, has."

Joe nodded. "Probably."

"So can I borrow your Jeep?"

Joe looked at his battered vehicle and his forehead furrowed. "No."

"Fine, whatever. I'm going in there to save my historical artifacts and the library books. I'd like to load them in your Jeep, something bigger than my trunk. But I'll just fill my car and take everything to my house. It will take more trips, but so what? When we figure out where to put the new museum, I'll have all the books dried out, all the artifacts clean. We can begin putting things out for display immediately."

"New museum?"

Bonnie nodded. "In the meantime, there are still one or two empty buildings on Main Street, right? And now that they've been taken away from Gunderson and are selling at a more reasonable rate, I'll just use the insurance money to rent one and start hauling the books in."

"Taken away from Gunderson?" Joe asked.

"Yes, a very old will came to light that proved the Gundersons stole a lot of property from the Melniks. The police confiscated the property. A judge's ruling returned some of it to the Melnik family and some of it to the city of Melnik. Now the city's share is up for sale, but a lot of the buildings are still vacant. I'll use one as a temporary museum."

"That won't work. I looked at the abandoned buildings on your Main Street. They aren't in good shape, and they aren't handicapped accessible. Bringing them up to code will cost more than building."

"Nick. . .you remember Nick from last night, right?"

"The one with the screaming wife?"

"That's him. He's already working on most of these buildings. He's an architect and he'll make sure they're safe. Renting is only a stopgap solution. The museum can open here while I apply for grants and start a local fund drive. Then this town is going to build a new museum."

"A museum in honor of an oversized mouse? Seriously?"

Bonnie glared at Joe. He wore dress pants and a white button-down shirt, and he was shaking his head at her. "Well, you don't get to vote, thankfully."

At that moment, Junior emerged Phoenix-like from the ashes. A section of the roof on the museum half of the building drooped nearly to the ground. The city office half was in good shape. It was like God had wanted the museum—but only the museum—destroyed. Bonnie prayed for some answers.

Junior shook his head, dislodging a cloud of dust from his meager hair and ample body. Then he approached them, holding up a book in a Ziploc bag. A cookbook.

"Interesting reading."

"Of course it is." Bonnie reached for it.

"You can't have this, Bonnie." Junior pulled it away so she couldn't get ahold of it. "This is evidence from a crime scene."

"That means don't touch it," Joe added.

"I know what it means."

Joe arched one eyebrow and looked pointedly at her extended hand but didn't answer.

Bonnie put her hands on her hips. "That book contains more than just recipes. It's full of family lore. Town history. Household hints passed on from mother to daughter for generations. And it's the last one we have in the museum."

"You can't use this one anyway. There are a lot of recipes scratched out." Junior stared at the book thoughtfully. "And every one of the mutilated recipes was submitted by Clara Wickersham."

"What?" Bonnie and Joe asked at the same time.

"Either Clara did it herself in some act of self-loathing. . ." Junior paused in speculation.

Self-loathing? Bonnie was beyond impressed with Junior's psychobabble.

"Or someone who hates Clara's guts is involved in this murder."

Bonnie knew from Junior's tone that he believed the latter, but then, he might not know what *self-loathing* meant.

"I've got the keys to Gunderson's house. I need to get in there and have a look around. You'd better come with me, Joe. You're his next of kin."

"I don't want to help with this." Joe shoved his hands into his pockets. "I'm not a cop and I'm too closely involved. Gunderson was my father."

"Plus, Joe's a suspect," Bonnie reminded Junior.

Joe turned on her, his brows slammed together. "I am not."

"You are, too."

Joe jabbed his index finger at her. "You're the suspect around here. You and Clara Wickersham."

"That is so rude."

"Well, whoever killed dear old Dad was as rude as snot," Joe growled.

"I wouldn't kill anybody." Bonnie made a *humph* sound that she thought fit this occasion perfectly. "Just like someone from the big city to say such a thing."

"Oh yeah, right. Big cities have a corner on murder. I saw that paper last night—someone else was murdered in this town not that long ago."

"Neither one of you killed Sven, and neither did Clara." Junior cut them off.

That was a shame, because Bonnie was getting ready to make a great point. She hadn't thought of it yet, but she would. Any minute.

"That's a big house. I'm not searching it alone. I want someone there when I do it, and Hal and Steve are off today, so I'm deputizing you." Junior jabbed his finger at Joe then headed toward the corner, diagonal from city hall. His house was half a block over, and he'd obviously walked to the crime scene. But Gunderson lived on the edge of town, nearly six blocks away. Junior needed his car. He called back over his shoulder, "Quit accusing each other of murder. Joe didn't know Sven well enough to hate him."

"Sure I did." Joe crossed his arms.

"Want a ride?" Junior called over his shoulder.

Joe rolled his eyes and followed him.

Bonnie started for the museum.

"Don't even think about it," Joe yelled.

Bonnie froze in her tracks.

Joe and Junior watched her.

"Leave it, Bonnie." Junior crossed his arms, a perfect match for Joe. They'd teamed up against her. Junior sounded nice enough, but it was pretty obvious that he wasn't budging until she abandoned her poor museum.

"I mean it, Bon." Junior had a mule-stubborn look on his face. "We've got to get an insurance adjuster in here and then get an engineer to make sure it's not too dangerous. Nick's probably qualified to do it, but there's some paperwork he's got to complete or the city could be liable if something happens."

"I'm just going to pick up a few books. I'll be careful."

"No!" Junior shook his head.

"You let him go in there." Bonnie jabbed her finger at Joe.

"That's it." Junior stormed back toward her. "I'm deputizing you, too. You're helping us search, because I'm not taking my eyes off you."

"I need to save the museum, Cousin Junior!" Bonnie realized she sounded about eight years old. She saw Joe smirk and felt herself blush.

Junior came and wrapped an arm around her shoulders and guided her along. "Come on, honey. You *know* it's not safe. And I didn't let him go in there. He just went in when I wasn't watching. I kicked him right back out. Hal's coming down before he starts his shift at the de-hy plant to seal the area off so no one can get in."

"What's a de-hy plant?" Joe asked.

"It's the hay mill north of town. It dehydrates hay and turns it into pellets. Hal can't make a living being a part-time deputy." Bonnie turned back to Junior. "How are you going to seal off the building? Nothing stops Jeffie."

"You're talking about that cute little boy from last night?" Joe asked.

Bonnie turned to stare at him. The man was out of his mind. "Yes."

Junior scratched his chin. "Maybe his mom'll let me lock him in the hoosegow until things are boarded up. Heaven knows the woman needs a break."

"She won't. You know Marlys. Try asking his dad."

"You can't put a child in jail."

"I s'pose not. Stupid rule. But a sheriff's gotta obey the law. It don't matter, anyway; Jeffie's got nine lives. We'll figure something out. Now let it go. There's no more rain forecast for today. No more damage can be done."

Bonnie looked back at the museum helplessly.

"We'll get in as soon as we can. And we'll get the whole town to help. You don't have to do this alone."

She sighed all the way from the soles of her feet then turned away from her precious collection. "I'll take my own car."

Junior studied her with narrow eyes. Then he looked at Joe. "Go with her. I don't trust her."

Joe scowled but climbed into the passenger side of Bonnie's beige Taurus.

They drove to the Gunderson place in silence. Joe's eyes widened as they pulled up. She parked her car.

Her passenger climbed out and whistled in amazement as he looked across the roof of the car at the eerie old mansion. He leaned his forearm on the car top. "I hadn't seen it in the daylight before. It's even uglier than I thought."

Bonnie noticed how riveted he was by the wreck of a building. He watched it. She watched him.

Unfortunately, neither of them watched for Jeffie.

The little boy and his bicycle slammed into Joe's door and shoved it as far shut as it would go with Joe's body in the way.

Joe grunted with pain and surprise.

Jeffie screamed.

Bonnie dashed around the car to help Joe dig a Taurus out of his chest.

Jeffie, of course, was fine, already regaining his feet. Bonnie grabbed the bike before the little marauder could get away. He'd fight for the bike awhile before he ran off. Bonnie had learned she could gain a few seconds of his attention that way.

"Jeffie, you have got to be more careful."

"I crushed him like a bug. I made a pancake outta him. I'm going to tell my mom you took my bike. I. . ."

Joe quit audibly fighting for breath and closed the door. He pulled another sucker out of his pocket.

Jeffie grabbed for it and it vanished. Bonnie was watching, and the sucker just popped out of sight. Jeffie froze midsnatch then looked from where the sucker used to be, to Joe. His eyes widened, fear and fascination showing in equal parts.

"Where'd it go?"

Joe smiled and slid his right hand over his left, and the sucker was back. Jeffie grabbed. The sucker vanished.

Then the fear was gone and only fascination remained. "Show me how you did that."

Joe crouched down so he was at eye level with Jeffie. "I'd like to teach you how to do that. But you need to pay me for it."

Jeffie scowled. "I'll ask my mom for money."

"Nope, I want something besides money. Now you heard Sheriff Hammerstad say last night he knows me and I'm a good man. I don't want you to ever let a stranger talk to you. Okay?"

Jeffie nodded. The sucker reappeared. Bonnie couldn't help but grin. However Joe was palming the thing, he was very good at it.

One move from Jeffie's hand and the sucker was gone.

"First, if you want a sucker from me, you've got to say please."

A twisted expression on Jeffie's face told Bonnie no one ever made Jeffie say please for anything. It was like Joe had asked the boy to speak ancient Greek.

"Okay, fine! Please." Jeffie might as well have delivered the words with spit attached, they were so rude.

Joe shook his head. "You've got to mean it to get the sucker. And you've got to speak politely to me all the time to get magic lessons." A sudden *pop* came from Joe's fingertips and smoke puffed up in the air. The sucker was back.

A gasp of delight wiped the cranky expression off Jeffie's face.

Sounding more genuinely polite than Bonnie had ever heard, Jeffie said, "Please can I have the sucker?"

Joe handed it over.

"Thank you. And please teach me to do that."

Joe looked from Jeffie to Bonnie. "Do you know Bonnie really well?"

Jeffie nodded his head frantically. "Sure, she lives just four blocks down from me."

That was over halfway across Melnik, but Bonnie didn't point that out.

"We can work on the magic trick if Bonnie is with us. And we have to get your parents' permission. Or if Bonnie can't come, we'll meet at your house, with your parents around."

"Awright!" Jeffie waved the sucker in the air like it was a sword.

"And, Jeffie?" Joe fell silent until Jeffie quit dancing around.

"Yes?"

"The first time you're rude to me or Bonnie or your parents in front of me, or hurt someone because you're reckless, then the lessons are over, understand?"

Somehow, without raising his voice or frowning, Joe made Bonnie believe absolutely he meant what he said. Jeffie must have believed it, too, because he almost knocked himself over nodding his head and promising.

"Okay, good. Now please be a little more careful riding your bike."

"You swung your door open in front of me!" Jeffie was already pushing his luck. But a lifetime of brattiness wasn't overcome in a day.

"When you're out riding, part of being grown-up and smart is being careful about what *might* happen. A car door *might* open in front of you. A car *might* not see you and pull out in front of you. It's called defensive driving, and you have to learn it, to protect yourself and everyone else."

"I'm smart and grown-up."

Jeffie was six and in all ways an immature brat.

"Good." Joe mussed Jeffie's hair. "I can see that you are. I'll call your house and talk to your mom about magic lessons, okay?"

"Yes, sir. Thank you."

"And you left a big scratch in Bonnie's door."

Bonnie's car was older than dirt and not worth a second thought, but Bonnie didn't mention that.

"I'm sorry." Jeffie turned to Bonnie. "I'll be more careful next time, I promise. Can I have my bike back, please?"

Stunned, Bonnie handed it over. Jeffie rode off at half his normal pace.

Bonnie watched the little delinquent ride away then turned to Joe. "How did you do that?"

Joe was watching Jeffie, too, with a fond smile on his face. When Bonnie spoke, he looked back at her. "Do what?"

"Uh, you've heard of Boys Town, right?"

"I grew up in Omaha. We lived about two miles from Boys Town. Sure, I've heard of it."

"'He ain't heavy—he's my brother'?"

"Yes, I've seen the statue."

"Father Flanagan?"

"My grandpa actually met Father Flanagan."

" 'There's no such thing as a bad boy'?"

"I remember that quote very well. I love it."

"Well, Father Flanagan never had to tangle with Jeffie."

Joe looked down the street in the direction Jeffie had ridden.

"Will Rogers never met a man he didn't like, right?" Bonnie looked in the same direction, but Jeffie was long gone.

"Bonnie, I don't think—"

"Will Rogers never met Jeffie."

Joe flinched. "That bad, huh?"

"Ever watch *Mr. Rogers' Neighborhood*? You know how it was always a beautiful day in the neighborhood? Remember that it was always a beautiful day for a neighbor?"

"Okay, okay. I get it."

"Well, Mr. Rogers was never neighbors with Jeffie."

Joe held up his hands in surrender.

"You really have a way with children."

Joe shrugged. "I know, but it worries me. I don't want Jeffie or any child to think it's okay to accept candy from strangers. I've worked with kids. It's gotten to be a habit to carry the suckers and the little exploding smoke stuff. I thought he might be hurt and I wanted to calm him down. I wasn't thinking. I'd better talk to his mom and make sure she warns Jeffie to be more careful."

"A word to the wise on that," Bonnie said. "Whatever you do, don't speak a single critical word about Jeffie. His mom won't hear of it."

"Why would I speak a critical word about that great little kid?" Joe seemed genuinely bewildered. Or maybe *certifiably bewildered* was a better way to put it.

"Let's get this done!" Junior shouted from the porch.

Approaching the ghastly old wreck, Joe said, "Whoever built this obviously didn't spare any expense." Joe looked from one end to the other of the masssive building. It was at least a hundred feet long and two stories high.

"It was Sigfrid Gunderson. Everybody knows he liked to show off. But succeeding generations have leaned more toward being tightfisted. They've let it fall into near ruin. I've always been scared of this awful old house."

"I don't blame you."

The house sat in the middle of a large lot. Leafless trees surrounded it on three sides, leaving it open toward the street. The spring hadn't progressed enough to soften them into anything less than a sky-high KEEP OUT sign. All they needed to complete the image was coiled barbed wire running along the top branches.

Both corners of the huge brick house were square, sticking out farther than the center, like sentinels on guard against happiness. A porch, one story high, ran between the two towers. The roof between the two square wings was A-frame, but centered in that normalcy was a strange tower about eight by eight feet, with an ornate metallic roof, inset with windows on all four sides, like a gabled lookout post for incoming pirates—in Nebraska.

Bonnie suspected that the original Gunderson had possessed a streak of paranoia.

An elaborate picket fence of wrought iron ran along the top of the porch roof between the towers. The towers had square roofs, flat on top, in a style Bonnie knew was French provincial, but she only knew that because someone had told her. Architecture wasn't her strong suit. The whole house, in its grim grayness, had too many flourishes for any decent Melnikian.

Whatever the style was called, to Bonnie it just looked ugly.

The white paint had peeled away from red bricks to make the house a dull pink, which might have been pretty if it wasn't so bedraggled. Windows were broken and boarded over. The three front steps sagged, and she wouldn't have stepped on them if Cousin Junior, with his significant weight, hadn't survived the climb. As she got closer, that weird center tower with its broken window resembling jagged teeth seemed inclined to lean down and swallow her.

Even in the full light of day, the house sent shivers up her spine. She heard a crow caw—or was it a vulture? The trees bent in the stiff spring breeze; the bare branches clattered together and reached for her with their skeletal fingers.

She expected Lurch to greet them at the door.

Joe went up the steps ahead of her. Junior opened the door himself, and although the hinges screamed like movement was torture, no Lurch made an appearance. Bonnie quickly prayed a thank-you to God and quit dragging her feet so she could go inside within save-me distance of the two men.

She intended to stay close.

Junior had his hands on his hips as he looked around the cobweb-shrouded entry to the house. The right side of the room had double doors, pulled shut. A narrow open stairway hugged the wall on the left. A door just before the stairs opened into what looked like a library. Bonnie's heart sped up with excitement. She'd brave this spooky house for a library full of what looked like really old books.

The hallway they stood in had a wooden floor, mostly clean in the center, with dust along the edges. A spider scurried up the wall by Bonnie's side. Two mice skittered out from a hole along the baseboard that ran alongside the stairs.

The sight of the mice reminded Bonnie that it was a Gunderson who had raised Maxie as a pet. Was it Sven or his father? Bonnie had it all recorded in the history books, but right now she wasn't sure. She also remembered that the Gundersons, never ones to give anything away, had *loaned*, not given, Maxie to the city of Melnik.

Whoever inherited this estate also inherited the town's only claim to fame.

"Who owns this house now, Cousin Junior?"

"Well, I've already called the nursing home," Junior said.

Bonnie came up beside Joe as the three of them studied the nooks and crannies in the entry.

"George will call when he's done watching his game show. That man gets testy if I ask him to do any lawyering during *The Price Is Right.*"

"So he's got Gunderson's will?"

"Honestly," Junior said with a shrug, "I have no idea. But after Wilkie died—"

"Wilkie?" Joe asked.

"I'll explain later," Bonnie whispered.

"—and the Gunderson family's scam to cheat the Melniks came to light, Sven lost a lot of his property. Surely the man made some arrangements after that. And I know George Wesley is third cousin to Old Man Gunderson's second wife—Sven's stepmother. He's about the only family Sven had left in town. So if George didn't update the will, he might know who did."

Junior turned to Joe. "And if there isn't a will, it looks like you'll inherit everything."

"Fat chance." Joe snorted. "My mom had to take him to court to get child support out of the old miser. That old tightwad wouldn't leave me a dime."

"His wishes don't come into it if there's no will," Bonnie said. "You're the next of kin by law. In the absence of specific provision to the contrary, the property is yours.

"All the Gundersons were tight with their pennies. That could include not giving your mom support and leaving you the estate."

Joe reached up to swipe at cobwebs hanging from the library door.

Junior grabbed Joe's raised arm. "Stop!"

Joe turned back. "What?"

"That cobweb might be a clue. It's obvious that no one's been in that room for a while, and that cobweb proves it."

Bonnie pointed to a pattern in the dust on the library floor. Footprints and something else, thin lines that she couldn't recognize as anything obvious. "Someone's been in there."

"Okay, it's obvious no one *tall* has been in that room for a while."

"Unless they ducked." Bonnie gave Cousin Junior an apologetic look for pointing out his flawed logic.

"Okay, yeah, they could have ducked." Junior crouched and reached one hand toward the messed-up dust. "Definitely footprints, but not enough to clean the floor like there are in this hallway. I noticed Gunderson was tall, although I didn't note the size of his feet. These footprints are most likely too small to be his."

Bonnie leaned over Junior's shoulder. "Gunderson was a recluse. He never had company. Whoever made those tracks is probably who killed him."

Joe's brows lowered. "He was really that much of a loner?"

"He'd lived in Melnik since his father died nearly two years ago." Bonnie nodded. "In that time he spoke to no one except Carrie O'Connor at the *Bugle*. Junior arrested him, and it wasn't easy because the old coot wouldn't come to the door for the longest time. Then he called a lawyer and was out of jail fast. He brought new meaning to 'the right to remain silent.'"

"Gunderson didn't buy groceries or fill up his car in town. The lights didn't even come on at night, so there's always been some doubt that he really lived here. But I think he was just too cheap to turn them on."

"I arrested Sven for Wilkie Melnik's murder." Junior stood from examining the prints. "But then, I also arrested Hal."

"The Jaws of Life guy?"

"Yep, and Tallulah."

"The woman who rolled that oversized mouse away on the gurney?"

"That's her. And Shayla."

"I haven't met any Shayla."

"You're lucky. She's an odd duck; tried to murder her father."

Joe winced.

"And I should have probably arrested Carrie and Nick, too. They were suspects after all. I just didn't think they were the type, so I didn't take 'em in."

"The rest of them *were* the type?" Joe rubbed his stomach as if it ached.

"Not really. Rosie, Wilkie's wife, was the one who did it."

"Wilkie Melnik's wife *and* daughter tried to kill him?"

"If you knew Wilkie, you wouldn't be all that surprised." Bonnie patted his arm.

"All in all, I'm glad I didn't know him."

"But Sven should have gone to prison, too." Junior stared at the tracks in the dust. "Wilkie's wife said the whole idea to kill Wilkie was Gunderson's, but Rosie wielded the mouse and smothered him."

"Wielded the mouse?"

Bonnie swatted her kindly cousin on the shoulder with a grin. "She didn't use Maxie to kill him. She just had Maxie's fur on her hands. Stop telling him all about Wilkie. Joe's going to start thinking we're weird."

5

T oo late."

Bonnie caught the smirk on Joe's face.

Junior went on. "Rosie was the one who actually committed the murder, and Sven bought a good lawyer—"

"George from the nursing home?" Joe asked.

"No, of course not. George isn't a good lawyer." Bonnie pitied Joe. The man just could not keep up.

"So Sven ducked the conspiracy charge. He spent a few hours in jail and had to appear in county court a few times, but once he was out from under that, he never spoke to anyone in town again. But he definitely lived here. I checked this morning. He paid his utility bill on time. And there was a trash can set out on his curb once a week."

"People have mentioned seeing him back out of the garage behind his house. They'd see him drive away, but he never spoke or waved or even looked around." Bonnie shrugged.

"I need to get pictures. We might be able to match prints if the shoes have an unusual tread. I'll go get a camera. I have one in my office. Don't touch anything." Junior trundled away, leaving Bonnie alone with Joe and the haunted mansion.

"Let's go see what else is in this mausoleum." Joe reached for the double doors opposite the library.

"Don't touch anything. Junior said—" Before Bonnie could stop Joe, a stair creaked and they both whirled. Bonnie had been behind Joe when he faced the double doors; now she was front and center of. . .nothing.

Bonnie backed up closer to Joe and whispered, "What was that?"

"It seemed to come from beneath the stairs." Joe rested his hands on her shoulders. He was so close his quiet words ruffled her hair and warmed her ear. "It sounded like someone moving."

Bonnie shivered, not from fear, but from Joe's nearness. She decided she'd better put some space between them. "Let's see what's under those stairs." She took one step toward the kitchen, the most likely place for a door to the basement.

"Are you crazy?" Joe grabbed her arm. "What are you trying to do, act out a horror movie script?" He pitched his voice high in the worst mockery of a female airhead Bonnie had ever heard. "Oh, I hear creaking in the black and creepy cellar of the house where a man was murdered."

She had to fight not to grin at him.

He fluttered his eyelashes at her and tipped his head from side to side until he nearly hit his ears on his broad shoulders and almost sang the rest of it. "I've got a good i-dee-yah. Let's go see what's down there."

She covered her mouth, but a giggle still escaped.

Joe smiled. The dimple in his chin was a matched set with the two in his cheeks. Bonnie was enchanted. The only real look she'd had at his straight white teeth had been when they were practically bared in anger. . .at her. The smile made him impossibly attractive, like a forties movie star. His shoulders were broad and square, his hair a bit flowing and dark, his face sculpted as if God had found extra time to work on a masterpiece.

"No one's ever accused me of being overly brave, Joe. If you say it's a bad idea, I'll trust you." They heard another creak. It sounded exactly like a footstep on a stairway. A chill of fear raced up Bonnie's back, and she found herself pressed against Joe's side.

His arm came around her waist protectively. "We really ought to go check that out." He sounded as if he were pronouncing his own death sentence.

"My whole life is so tame." Bonnie whispered as if there might really be someone down there listening. "I spend my time reading and dusting. That's pretty much it. Searching this house comes close to being the greatest adventure of my life. I kind of want to go down into the basement."

She looked over her shoulder at him. Joe's eyes met hers. His grew warm, maybe with approval. As if he liked the fact that she was brave. Well, she had some bad news for him. This was a fluke. Brave she was not. But for today, faced with the collapse of her whole world at the museum and all that lay ahead of her to fix it, she felt particularly courageous.

Still, she felt compelled to be honest. "I'm sure this show of courage is temporary. The right response here is to run away screaming."

"I agree." His hand flexed on her waist just a bit. She felt every fingertip.

Bonnie shook her head. "You don't seem like the screaming type."

"I've done some screaming in my life. I mostly keep it to football games, but I can scream."

"Shall we check?"

Joe shook his head. "Let's wait for Junior. We might as well obey the law since we don't want to go down there anyway."

Bonnie snickered. "Okay." Silence fell between them. Bonnie tried to think of something to say. "So you're from Omaha, right?"

Joe nodded, watching the hallway that led to the kitchen. He answered absently. "Born and raised."

His hand left her waist and he rubbed his palms together as if wiping the touch of her off. More silence. Bonnie felt her cheeks heating up. Small talk. She was the worst at it. The weather, the Nebraska Cornhuskers—what else was there to discus with a stranger?

"You already know I'm the museum curator, I read, and I dust. Oh, I forgot, I'm an insomniac. Now you know everything. So it's your turn. What do you do for a living?" There, that was safe.

Joe's gaze sharpened and he looked away from the kitchen to glare at her, as if the question annoyed him.

Not so safe after all. Bonnie wanted to punch herself in the head. He probably earned his living doing something he wasn't proud of. Except his clothes were nice and his Jeep was shiny and a lot newer than her car. And anyway, there was no shame in hard work. Not everyone could be a captain of industry. If he said he flipped burgers, she'd congratulate him. He probably made more working with those burgers than she did being a museum curator. The Melnik Historical Society was neither rich nor generous. She'd inherited a house, and there'd been enough life insurance money from her parents to send Bonnie's younger brothers to college. It also helped fill in the gaps between her modest expenses and even more modest income.

Bonnie said a quick silent prayer for something to say. Could God miraculously make her a sparkling conversationalist? True, if He did, the feat would rank up there with the top miracles: parting the Red Sea, turning water into wine, raising the dead, Bonnie being scintillating. But it could happen. At last, feeling embarrassed, she murmured an apology.

She was a chronic apologizer, and she was really sorry about that.

"If you don't want to talk about your job, that's fine. I'm sorry if I was being intrusive."

"Look!" Joe scowled at her. "I'm kind of between jobs right now. I had something for the last three years or so that, well, I thought would go on longer, but. . ."

Bonnie took a step toward the kitchen, hoping to find a murderer in there just to shut her stupid self up.

Joe grabbed her arm. He managed to turn her to face him. "Stay here. I didn't mean to snap at you."

"I think you did."

Joe looked at her and his expression softened. "You really want to know what I did for a living? Most people think it's kind of weird."

"Look, I sit in a museum guarded by an oversized mouse. Is what you do really weirder than that?"

He smiled. "Well, if you put it that way, no. What I did was pretty normal, sort of. I was a manny."

"A what?"

"A manny—a male nanny." Joe's hand relaxed on her arm and he let her go, but she didn't back away like she probably should have. "I was a day-care provider for a little boy. I'd taken care of him since he was about four months old. He's three now. I really love that little guy. And I miss him."

Joe stared at the floor and kicked the dust around a little. "I just don't know if I can handle doing it again. Getting so attached, then getting the boot. His mom had another baby, and until about two weeks ago, I thought I had job security. Two kids now instead of one. Then about the time her maternity leave was up, she decided she couldn't leave them. She quit her job to stay home, and of course that means they don't need me anymore. I'm proud of her, but that doesn't make it any easier for me."

"Wow. Was the little boy—"

"Stetson."

"They named their child after a cowboy hat?"

Joe shrugged and slid his hands into his pockets. "Welcome to the brave new world."

"Was Stetson sad to see you go?"

"Yeah. In fact, he was so sad, I think it's best I'm not there anymore. I didn't realize it until I told him good-bye, but I can see now that I was bad for his relationship with his father." Joe looked at her intently. "I'm not sure what I'm going to do with my life now."

Bonnie thought of the collapsed museum. She had plans, true, but did she really know what she was going to do with her life if it didn't work out to rebuild?

"I just stumbled into the manny job. Stetson's folks went to our church, and Stetson had severe asthma. His mom knew I'd been taking care of my mom, doing a lot of medical stuff for her. Mom died of cancer three years ago. I was at loose ends, and this nice couple asked if I'd stay with their sick baby. It was supposed to be short term, but it worked out. Like I said, I was there for three years."

Bonnie thought of what Joe was doing in Melnik. A man torn by his love for a child and his feeling that he might have been messing up a family. "And now you're in Melnik looking for your father."

"Mom and I lived with my grandparents all the years I was growing up and even during college." Joe shrugged. "My grandparents died; then Mom got sick, and I dropped out of college to take care of her. When she died, I became a manny. After my job ended two weeks ago, I started going through some of her things, and I found my father's address here in Melnik. I also found out she had to fight for every dime he ever gave her. So I don't have any illusions about Sven Gunderson. I wasn't kidding myself that we'd be close. I guess I just wanted to meet him."

Bonnie kept her expression neutral, but she knew without a doubt that Sven Gunderson would not have cared about a son.

She might not have been as neutral as she'd hoped, though, because Joe must have seen something in her eyes that made him turn away and look toward the kitchen. "Junior's taking forever. I say let's go down in the dungeon and wrestle with a murderer."

Bonnie knew things were tense when she decided that was a good idea.

The hall led to a huge kitchen that could have stepped out of the early 1900s. The opposite wall was lined with appliances and cupboards. On the right end was a short refrigerator with a rounded top; the sink in the middle was porcelain with a dripping faucet corroded white. To the left of the sink stood a stove so filthy Bonnie refused to believe anyone would let food touch it. A hot plate sitting on the tattered black countertop supported her theory.

The cupboards, woodwork, and walls were all painted the same dull shade of olive green. Several doors led out of the room. Joe turned to the one directly to their left and tugged it open, the warped wood wailing against the frame.

Bonnie saw a pitch-black rectangle. "You found the basement. Great." She came up close enough to peer over his shoulder, not easy. He was so tall she had to stand on her tiptoes.

He glanced over his shoulder and they were nose to nose. He froze for a moment. Bonnie lost her train of thought—or maybe her mind.

She looked in his eyes. Then, as if startled awake, he jerked his head around. Fumbling, he found a string hanging inside the door, and with a quiet *click*, a single bare bulb lit up to show a steeply descending staircase.

"You really think we heard someone moving down there?" Bonnie whispered in his ear.

He turned back to her. Too close. Bonnie seriously needed to back up, so why did she step closer?

With a shrug, he whispered back, "I doubt it—probably just an old house creaking, but who knows?"

"So then why are we whispering?"

Joe smiled.

His attractiveness hit her so hard she found the sanity to take that step back. She forced herself to speak aloud, to break up the intimacy of the moment. . .an intimacy she was pretty sure she was inventing all in her own head.

She spoke normally. "So are we going down?"

"No cobwebs." Joe pointed at the top of the doorway. "Now why would there be cobwebs in the library doorway, where there are obvious footprints, but none here?"

"Someone's been using these steps. Look, no dust."

Joe nodded. "No dust even on the edges. These steps have been used a lot."

"So Gunderson stores canned goods down there." Bonnie shrugged, even though the otherwise untended house made that seem unlikely. Why store food in the basement when there was a huge kitchen that was no doubt full of empty cupboards?

"Or he has a furnace that he likes to keep an eye on." Joe took his first step downstairs, and they both heard a creak that sounded exactly like the noise they'd heard earlier.

Bonnie grabbed his shoulder. "I think we should call the police before you go down there."

"Bonnie, the police is Junior. I don't think he'll be that much help."

Honesty prevented her from defending her cousin. Still, her fingers tightened until they sank into his button-down shirt. No shoulder pads needed here. This was all Joe. "Even cops need backup. He can call Hal. And they can search after Hal's done with his shift at the de-hy plant."

"How about instead, I play the cop and you be my backup. We'll be a team. Starsky and Hutch, Melnik style." He smiled again and she wished he'd stop. It was just too distracting.

Bonnie liked the sound of being on a team with Joe so much she let him go. Best to face death immediately rather than make a fool of herself with a man whose primary reactions to the world seemed to be grumpy and grumpier—despite this sudden rash of smiles.

"I've got your six. Let's roll."

His forehead crinkled. "Where'd a nice curator learn that lingo?"

"Books. No real-life experience at all."

He shook his head and started down into the belly of the beast. Bonnie slid right down the house's gullet behind him.

Another louder creak stopped them short. Distinct footsteps came toward them from the kitchen. Joe wheeled and brushed past her, to be ahead of her if someone attacked. To shield her body with his own. To take a bullet for her. To mount his trusty steed, take up his shield and sword, fight to the death for. . .

"There was a preliminary autopsy report waiting from Dr. Notchke when I got back to the office."

Junior was back.

No life and death. No shield required. Just Junior. Bonnie was oh-so-faintly disappointed.

Junior consulted a sheaf of papers in his hand as first Joe, then Bonnie emerged into the kitchen. "I just printed it off my computer and grabbed it."

Flipping pages, Junior mumbled, "I haven't had time to read it yet. It looks like. . ." Another page turned.

"He was killed by. . ."

Bonnie had a feeling Junior was stunned speechless or maybe embarrassed to speak the words out loud.

"Pie."

6

And who in this town made lethal pies? Joe knew one person right off the bat.

"If Sven ate one of Clara's pies, he's so stupid, his death cannot possibly be blamed on Clara. So it's not murder." Bonnie shook her head.

"She can't just walk around poisoning people. It's against the law." Joe couldn't believe he'd had to say that out loud.

"Not in Melnik, it's not. Not when it's Clara." Junior wrote "Solved" in his notebook then tucked it away in his breast pocket.

"So they really found Clara's pie in Gunderson's stomach?" Joe shuddered at the thought.

"Well, not exactly. They found poison in Gunderson's stomach, and he had a pie smashed into his chest that contained the same poison. These are still preliminary results."

"One of Clara's pies was smashed into Gunderson's chest?" Bonnie grimaced as if being touched by the pie was unbearable. Joe wondered how the guy managed to attempt to eat one. Not real likely. If Joe was in charge, he'd erase the word "Solved."

"Yep. We'd have seen it if we'd opened his coat last night."

"So she's the culprit, then?" Joe asked. "You're sure? Have you arrested her yet?"

"Don't figure to arrest her." Junior looked at Joe with contempt. "We got no law saying Clara can't bake. Anyway, it's like a deer wandering out in front of a car. Sure, it's bad for the deer, but no one's gonna arrest the driver."

"It is nothing like a deer wandering out in front of a car. You at least need to bring her in for questioning," Joe reminded the lawman. "And we did hear footsteps in the basement. Shouldn't we go down there and check?"

"Old houses creak. I'm sure it's nothing." Junior visibly shuddered. "I'd rather go down there, though, than question Clara. She don't work or play well with others."

Joe opened his mouth to throw a fit. He thought it was called for under the circumstances. But he didn't have to.

"Rat poison?" Junior read a little further into the autopsy report, scowling. "The ingredients for the pie were egg whites, Spam, Chinese elm leaves, and d-CON."

Betty Crocker was rolling over in her grave.

"We'd better pick her up." Junior looked unhappy.

Joe had smelled Clara last night. He was unhappy, too.

The door closed as the three left his house.

His house.

His!

No one was taking it. Not Sven. Not Sven's long-lost son. Who could have imagined there was a son?

He slumped down on a mildewed packing crate, sick of the dampness of this cellar. Fear mixed with anger as he hid in the dark.

Hid for now.

Well, killing Sven had been easy. And pinning it on the pie lady was a cinch. And he'd liked it. Liked killing. Doing it again had been tempting, but there was no one else left at the time who needed to die.

Except now there was.

The son.

The Poisonous Pie Lady of Melnik didn't take being arrested well.

Joe figured no one would. But this was ridiculous.

She was a fairly happy little murderess as long as no one told her where to go and when to come along quietly. Joe almost confessed to the murder himself just to get some peace.

The Melnik jail was a nice quiet place under normal circumstances. But Clara Wickersham really ruined the homey atmosphere.

It was like being trapped in a. . . Joe shook his head. Metaphors escaped him. Only through sheer willpower did he prevent himself from holding his ears and humming "Yankee Doodle" to drown out the noise. After all, couldn't the woman scream something useful? Like how on earth she got Joe's idiot father to eat a Chinese elm leaf pie?

Joe's hope for any good news in his genetic history was dashed.

He'd never heard this kind of noise before. There was a temporary respite when Bonnie, who'd vanished after she'd helped them find Clara wandering aimlessly in the local park—no doubt poisoning pigeons with her cooking— returned with a copy of *The Melnik Centennial Cookbook* and used it to distract Crazy Clara from her new home behind bars.

Joe had a feeling the old woman was going to have to get used to it.

Junior, to his credit, went into the jail and frisked her. It was as courageous as anything Joe had ever seen. The woman had pockets full of. . .stuff.

Junior tossed a notebook at Joe. "Keep an inventory. We need to make sure she gets all this back."

Joe shook his head and poised a pencil over the paper.

"Ham sandwich." Junior tossed it aside.

An extremely old and green ham sandwich.

"Mine. Givememysandwich!" Clara's voice could shatter crystal. Fortunately, there wasn't a square inch of crystal in Melnik's jail.

Joe saw Bonnie back out of the doorway.

"You get back here! I can't go frisking a woman without another woman present. In fact, you ought to be doing this." Junior looked stern, but Joe suspected this wasn't about police procedure. Junior's attitude was more about, *If I have to search her, I'm not letting anyone wimp out and leave.*

"No, please, Cousin Junior, don't make me!"

Joe knew just how Bonnie felt. He'd have begged, too, if Junior had volunteered him.

Junior reached in again and lifted out his next find.

"Roll of toilet paper."

Well, Joe decided, that wasn't so bad. Handy, in fact.

"Grocery store flyers. One. Two. Three. Four. Five. Oh, forget it, they're all outdated. I'm not giving them back."

Clara's screaming got louder. "Mine! Mine!" She hit at Junior, but she didn't pack much punch—except with her pies, obviously. Those could kill you.

"Two pocket calculators, both dead. Shame on you, Clara. They both say MELNIK HIGH SCHOOL on them. Did you steal these calculators?"

"More likely she dug them out of the trash," Bonnie said.

Junior nodded.

Joe tuned out all but the inventory. Eighteen stubby, eraserless pencils.

An empty Coke can.

A jar of garlic powder.

A jar of maraschino cherries.

"Mine! Mine! Mine!" Clara clawed at Junior. "Melnikwillstarve!"

Joe flipped to page 2 of the notebook, then page 3. He saw something alive in Junior's hand, but Junior yelped and dropped it. It, whatever it was, vanished under the cot, and Junior didn't chase it down. Joe couldn't decide if that was a good thing or not, but he sympathized.

"There," Junior called out over Clara's screaming. "I'm done with one pocket."

An hour later, Junior straightened from where Clara was still slapping him silly, but doing no real harm apparently, because Junior hung in there and took it. He held up a key.

Joe noted the dangling white tag that said MUSEUM STOREROOM.

Junior's eyes fell closed, and Joe could tell the man didn't want to believe it.

But he was an officer of the court. They had means, motive, and opportunity. The pie, Clara's enmity toward Gunderson, and the key.

"Clara," Junior said.

Joe heard real, sincere regret in Junior's voice. And Joe didn't think it was because she was going to stay here with him. He thought Cousin Junior really kind of liked the old lunatic.

"You're under arrest for the murder of Sven Gunderson."

"I'mgladhe'sdead. I'mglad. Badman. Idid. Idid. Idid."

The same words she'd said last night.

So now they had means, motive, opportunity, and a confession.

She took a swipe at the key in Junior's hand and batted at it, as if to slap it away from her. It was the first thing she hadn't tried to grab back.

"That'snotmine. Badkey. Badkey. Badkey."

Clara reached down the front of her dress—farther in than Junior had dared to tread—and dug around, searching through who knew what.

"Badkey. Badman." Clara's frantic hand made her housedress, under a ragged sweater the color of pink and dirt, vibrate until it looked like a sack of cats heading for the river. Joe seriously hoped there weren't more living creatures in there.

"Badman. Badplace." Clara produced a key. "Goodkey. Secretkey. Secretrecipe."

Junior swiped the key from Clara and compared it to the key he'd found in her pocket. There was no tag on the key, but there was no denying they were a perfect match. Clara attacked for real now, trying to retrieve the good key.

Junior howled in pain and ran out of the cell with the keys, leaving a stack of garbage behind, along with shrill screams. "Badkey. Ididit. Secretrecipe. Ididit." She frantically stuffed all the things Junior had left back into her pockets. Then she dropped to her knees and scrambled under the cot, possibly to retrieve her pet. . . ?

Joe watched, but Clara didn't reemerge. It looked like she was planning to stay under there, screaming.

Junior looked exhausted. "I'll call the county attorney and tell him to file charges. Clara's nuts, but she's always been harmless nuts, as long as you were careful not to eat anything she cooked. But now. . ." Junior's shoulders slumped.

Bonnie came closer. The little coward had stayed as far from the action as possible. Joe knew because he'd been standing right beside her.

She patted her cousin's shoulder. "I suppose they'll lock her up. That's a shame. She's been reasonably happy wandering around selling her pies."

Junior nodded. "They'll have to. Gunderson's death could have been an accident, even with the rat poison, I mean. That's a formality, right? The pies are poisonous no matter what's in 'em, so I'd still blame Gunderson for eating one. But how'd he get into that storage room? She has the only two keys in town. She had to put him there, and that means she knew he was dead. That means she

215

attempted, in her own crazy way, to conceal the body. Which actually rules out the insanity defense, even though anyone could spend two seconds with Clara and know she's crazy as a loon."

"Remember those strange tracks in the dust in Gunderson's house?" Joe asked.

Junior nodded. "The ones by the library door."

"Didn't Clara have a cart she was pulling last night? I'll bet we find out they match the wheel tracks in the dust."

"So she somehow scooped Gunderson up and put him on her cart and wheeled him across town with no one noticing, then laid him out in that little locked room with her book in his arms?" Bonnie asked. "That's impossible. Someone would have seen her. This is Melnik. No one makes a move in this town without everybody knowing."

"And why'd she want that book back so badly last night? If she gave it to him, it figures she'd be okay with him having it." Joe looked between Bonnie and Junior.

"He's right. The recipe book pinpointed Clara more than any other detail." Junior pulled his notebook back out. "So that means someone planted evidence on Sven to implicate her in the killing."

"And they could have somehow planted the key on her, too," Bonnie added.

"Then what? Stolen her cart and left fake tracks?" Junior shook his head.

"Melnikwillstarve! Ihatedthatman! Idid! Idid! Idid!"

"I'm afraid she really *did* do it." Junior's lips tightened into what almost could have been a smile, but there was no humor in it. "But how could she make Gunderson eat the pie? Who would do such a thing? The man was a cheapskate, though. If he got the pie somehow, he might have decided he couldn't let it go to waste."

"D-CON à la mode," Bonnie said, looking sad. "Crazy Clara's pie of the day."

⟶

Bonnie didn't gag. She considered that a major success. Junior had insisted she stay during his search of Clara for propriety's sake. She'd stayed, but she'd also stayed back. Even so, her hearing was never going to be the same.

The phone rang as she led the way into Junior's office. "Get that, Bonnie, honey."

Bonnie picked up the phone.

"Put that young Joe on the phone!"

Bonnie jerked the phone away before her eardrum shattered. George Wesley. The man was deaf as a post. Which meant he did all the talking when you were dealing with him. Loud talking. And Bonnie hadn't recovered from Clara yet.

"I heard he was at the police station!" George must have news about Gunderson's will.

Bonnie knew there was only one way George could hear her. She roared, "Joe wants to talk to you!"

Joe jumped like she'd stuck him with a hatpin.

Bonnie wrinkled her nose. "Sorry. George is deaf." She spoke normally, even though George was right there on the other end of the line. He couldn't hear her.

"You tell that young whippersnapper they're serving coffee in the dining room in five minutes and I've got a few things to say to him! We're having snickerdoodles with coffee, and if I'm late, that old bat Frieda Curzinski eats everything on the table!"

Bonnie, her ears ringing, held the phone out to Joe.

Joe, obviously quick on the uptake, yelled, "This is Joe!"

Joe yanked the phone away from his ear as George shouted. Bonnie heard every word. Who was she kidding? Clara, under the cot in the back room, heard every word.

Joe had been named in Gunderson's will. Everything was his. George said a packet would be coming in the mail soon. Except for his deafness and the general frailty that came from being in his eighties, George seemed to be in good shape. He and his wife had moved into the assisted-living wing of the Melnik Nursing Home, and he kept files and even held client appointments right in his apartment.

"There goes Frieda! There go my snickerdoodles. That woman would eat through the tabletop and right down into the carpet on the floor if her teeth were strong enough!" George even hung the phone up loudly.

Joe stared at the phone, the expression on his face one of complete confusion. Bonnie wasn't sure if that was due to George and his volume-control issues or to the inheritance.

"Why would he ignore me all his life, then name me in his will?"

The inheritance won.

Junior grunted as he rose from his desk. "Prob'ly you were all there was. It was either leave it to you or let the state take it, and if Sven was anything like his dad, the man would kill someone before he'd let the government have it."

Joe slammed Junior's phone down viciously but kept a grip on the receiver as if it were Gunderson's bony neck. He glared at Junior and spoke through gritted teeth. "I don't want any part of his money."

He looked at the phone and lifted his hand from the black receiver. "It broke Mom's heart when I dropped out of college to take care of her." He slapped it twice, hard. "She hated being a burden on anyone, but most of all me. I found the court papers she filed to try to force my bum father to pay for my college. He fought it and won. Now he leaves me everything."

Bonnie thought Joe might pick the phone up and throw it through Junior's window. She saw him fight the rage.

Trying to slip inside his anger, she said softly, "You did the right thing caring for your mom. Even if there'd been a fortune, you'd have wanted to be there with her, wouldn't you?"

Joe raised his eyes. His face was flushed with anger; his dark brown eyes had gone harsh, gleaming black.

For a second Bonnie thought Junior's phone and his window were goners. Then Joe pulled in a long, steady breath and nodded.

"You're right. I'd have been there." Joe shook his head. "That was three years ago." He shook his head again as if his temper were water dripping off his hair and he needed to get it off. "It's all over."

He straightened. "I'll figure out what to do with the money. Something generous. That alone will ruin my father's chance at eternal rest because he'll be busy spinning in his grave."

Junior snorted. Joe closed his eyes then looked at Bonnie and smiled.

She nodded. "I'm not sure about the biblical passages related to grave spinning, but it's kind of fun to imagine annoying the old coot. His father, your grandfather, helped drag this town almost all the way down. And once Sven inherited, he picked right up where his father left off. You won't find anyone with any sympathy for Sven Gunderson in this town."

Clara's screeching hit a note that penetrated the cement block wall.

"No one," Junior added with a nod.

Joe jabbed a thumb at the noise. "Okay, what do we have to do to help that poor woman in there?"

"I need to call for a mental health evaluation." Junior reached for the phone.

"I'll start right now using dear old Dad's money to hire a lawyer for her so she gets a good defense."

"She may be crazy," Bonnie warned.

"Letmeout! Melnikwillstarve!" Clara's scream carried from under the cot, out the cell, through the cement blocks, and into Junior's office.

"Okay, she's *definitely* crazy." Bonnie had to face facts. "But I can't believe either of you are satisfied that you've solved this crime."

"Now, Bonnie, honey—" Junior lifted his hands as if to ward off words that might mean he'd have to pull out his notebook and go back to the brain-wrenching business of detecting.

Bonnie cut him off. "You know Clara's harmless."

"But the Chinese elm leaves—who else could—"

"And if she's harmless, that means only one thing." The chill in her spine threatened to escape and shake her whole body. "There's still—"

"Don't say it." Junior held up a hand that could stop traffic. "Dr. Notchke will kill me if I come up with a bunch of suspects."

"—a murderer running loose in Melnik."

7

"If you're done with me here, Junior, I'm moving into my new house." Joe couldn't believe he was going to live in the old wreck.

"Give me a few hours to go over the place. I've got both deputies coming to work, and I've asked the Dodge County coroner to get a special forensics guy. They thought the stomach contents were so interesting, they agreed."

Joe turned to Bonnie. "Nick was going to go over the structural integrity of the museum. If he's done and gives the okay, we can go pick up books until Junior is done."

Bonnie looked at him with wide eyes, the kind of sweet brown eyes a guy might be tempted to write ballads about. She was a pretty little thing, but in a quiet way. No makeup, no flashy clothes. But perfect skin and dark blond hair that reminded him of a jar of honey, golden in places, darker in others, depending on the light and the sun. Last night she'd been coated with grit and the light was dim. He hadn't noticed much but her temper and her affection for that stupid mouse.

Today she wore her hair pulled back in a no-nonsense ponytail that made her look like a kid, midtwenties at most. But her expression—at least when she thought about Melnik memorabilia or murder—was serious. Life had left a few tiny lines at the corners of her eyes. He suspected she was closer to his age, thirty-five. He'd done eight years in the army, gotten out, and spent three years in college. Two with Mom dying. Three as a manny. Always, while he did each job, he wondered, *What next?* Where was he really meant to be? What was the Lord's plan for him? Nearly half done with a normal man's working life, he still hadn't started a career. There was no IRA growing steadily, no years ticked off toward retirement, no college degree to boost him toward that brass ring. He didn't think that whatever he was searching for he was going to find in Melnik, and certainly not in a shrine to a fat mouse.

Then he thought of Bonnie's eyes. He wouldn't mind searching deep into them for a while. He decided to try to make those sweet brown eyes glow. "You can have books from Gunderson's. . .uh, that is. . .my place. There might be a whole library's worth of books. Maybe there's Melnik history in that house. I'd gladly contribute that."

"Your father would hate that."

"All the better."

Her eyes sparkled. *Bingo.* And she gave him a genuine smile. She'd smiled a time or two when they were waiting for Junior at the house, too. He liked her smile almost as much as he liked her eyes.

Joe got to the museum and found his Jeep windshield repaired by Melnik's efficient glass repairman. Nick was finishing his inspection, and he suggested they move the books and artifacts to a building he'd bought on Main Street. Nick also gave them the go-ahead to enter the museum. They started with some old glass bottles and wooden toys.

"Look at this." Bonnie held up a round hunk of rusty metal. "This is a piggy bank owned by the first settler in Melnik."

Joe looked closer. "It's a pig. A piggy bank that's a real pig." He laughed. "It's cute. How old is it?"

"At least two hundred years old. The Melniks brought it with them from the east. It was already old back then. Melnik National Bank used it for a model and for years gave a plastic version of this away each Christmas."

Joe began to look closer at the bric-a-brac in the room. "A lot of this stuff is really interesting."

Bonnie beamed at him. "Yeah, it is."

He'd done it again. A woman with a ready smile. He liked that.

Melnik citizens began to stop by to snoop; then they stayed to work. A growing work crew loaded historical papers into plastic wrappers that saved them from the rain—a little late, but it was worth a try.

Then they turned to the waterlogged books. They hauled them to Nick's building—just three doors down from the historical society—and laid them out to dry. The whole town worked like old-time firefighters running a bucket brigade, handing things one after the other down Main Street to the new building.

Jansson's Café brought sandwiches, and the moving turned into a party that lasted until the sun sank low in the western sky.

Finally, everything that could be saved was moved. The noisy, talking crowd wandered off, leaving Joe and Bonnie in the cavernous building—formerly the Melnik Mercantile, now the temporary home for the Melnik Historical Society.

"This building was owned by Wilkie Melnik's family before they lost most everything to hard liquor and the conniving Gundersons." Bonnie the historian kept giving him background information.

Junior finally came and told Joe he could move into his house.

When Junior left, Joe turned to Bonnie and spoke, his voice echoing in the big, high-ceilinged room. "Would you like to look around the house with me?"

"Sure. But don't you want to get settled in?"

Joe shrugged and darted around the truth. "I'd like to go through the place a little better, and I thought it'd go faster with two of us."

"Admit it. You're scared."

Joe smiled; then he laughed. "Okay, maybe a little spooked. That is one creepy house. I keep hearing those stairs creak." He felt his eyes widen. "You don't suppose it's haunted, do you?"

Bonnie tilted her head as if she were thinking it over. "Seeing as how I don't believe in ghosts, I'm going to have to go with no."

"I don't believe in them, either. But I'm thinking of making an exception for the Gunderson Mausoleum."

Bonnie's giggle brightened the gloomy store. Joe hoped she did the same thing for his new house. He suppressed a shudder at the thought of moving into that huge, foreboding old dump.

※

"A little spooked, huh?" Bonnie climbed out of her Taurus and turned to watch Joe emerge from his flashy Jeep.

He turned and looked at the house, slamming his door loudly, maybe to warn the ghosts to vaporize. She forced herself to face the old heap, too.

She didn't charge right toward the derelict mansion, though. All she had to do was go slower than Joe. Let him go in first and scare *whatever* away.

The sun set to their left. The house cast shadows that deepened its general gloom—as if that were possible.

Joe kept stopping to wait for her. "At this rate we're never going to get in there."

Bonnie finally realized she wasn't the only one dallying.

She narrowed her eyes. "You don't want to go in there any more than I do."

Joe's jaw tightened. Bonnie suspected she'd stepped on his ego somehow. With three little brothers, she'd gotten pretty comfortable abusing men—when she wasn't letting her shyness stop her from talking altogether. The combination of shyness and man abuse most likely explained her lifelong inability to get a date.

Her parents had died, and she'd raised her brothers until last year, when the last one had gone off to college. Now she lived alone when the boys weren't around, with her books and her artifacts and her little bungalow—the family home. An insomniac who wandered the house, vampirelike, until the early morning hours. In those hours she read and delicately cleaned artifacts. A life dedicated to Melnik . . .except not to this house. *Ick.*

"Okay, fine. I admit it. I dread this." Joe's shoulders slumped. He muttered for a few moments then stood up straight, drew in a breath of courage, and stomped up the sidewalk.

A rattling noise from the house stopped him cold. Bonnie looked for the source of the spooky noise—of course, at this place there were no sounds except spooky ones. It seemed to be coming from the central tower that rose out of the roof.

NOSY IN NEBRASKA

The stretching fingers of shadows cast by the winter-dead trees now wrapped their skeletal digits around the watchtower. Bonnie came up beside Joe, willing to be nearer the house if it meant she could have Joe close at hand.

They both stared up, silent, scared, just barely too adult to run for their lives. Seconds ticked by in silence. The rattling grew, the shadows deepened, the sun gave up its last grip on day and settled into dusk.

Joe's shoulders rose and fell as he breathed for the first time in too long.

A nightingale sang and Bonnie relaxed. "I guess the wind or something must have—"

Black exploded from the sentinel tower.

Bonnie shrieked and jumped sideways, ramming into Joe. He caught her as a startled yell escaped from his macho lips. He dragged her behind his Jeep and ducked them both down.

By the speed he applied to get a barricade between himself and the house, Bonnie wondered if he'd have just deserted her if she hadn't been clinging. She buried her face against his chest as they crouched.

After a few seconds, Joe peeked over the hood of his SUV, and inspired by his bravery, Bonnie turned to look, too. The explosion turned to a flurry of rattling and black and movement. A dark line spread and stretched as if the ghoulish fingers of the tree branches had come to life and reached out. It seemed to Bonnie inevitable that the hand would dart at her, grab her, and drag her screaming back into that house.

Reflex made Bonnie duck. Then she gathered her courage—when ghost fingers didn't snatch her—and looked again. That black line stretched and spread and grew and—and—and flapped its wings.

Finally, it made sense. "Bats."

Joe shook his head slowly and stared. "Bats?"

Bonnie shuddered. "You know I've got to say this, right?"

"What, that I've got bats in my belfry?"

Nodding silently, Bonnie grinned at him then went back to staring.

"I am *not* sleeping in that house." Joe rubbed his mouth as if he wished he could gag himself before he said more wimpy stuff.

Bonnie would have died before she stayed. But since he had admitted it first, she felt comfortable acting brave. "They're probably gone for the night. You'd be fine."

Joe turned his back on the house and sank to the pavement with a sigh, his knees bending until they came up to his nose as he leaned against his Jeep's front fender. "Great."

"You know, Dracula and other vampires have really given bats a bad name. Bats are our friends."

"They *are not*. They are mice with wings. They are disease-bearing rodents.

They are fanged vermin."

"They eat insects like mosquitoes, their. . .uh. . .by-products. . .fertilize the soil—they are very useful creatures. In some cultures bats are—"

"I know, I know!" His forearms on his knees, Joe sighed and bent until he almost rested his head on his arms, or almost buried his face in his hands, if you wanted to put a really wimpy spin on it.

"They're a creepy, neck-biting, rabies-carrying part of the great big *slimy circle of blood-suckin' life.*" Joe was yelling by the time he was done. Then he turned and glared at her. "Just give me a minute to get my heart beating again, and I'll burst into song and celebrate that fact."

Bonnie laughed.

"This isn't funny." Joe's eyes narrowed. "I've got to live in that house."

Dropping to her knees beside him, taking a second to be grateful for the complete lack of traffic on this quiet street at the edge of Melnik, as well as the complete lack of bats at her house, Bonnie offered, "You could sleep with me."

Joe's neck snapped around so fast Bonnie thought she heard the tendons whip. He looked at her, his eyebrows raised nearly to his hairline.

Bonnie realized what she'd said. Her face heated to around the boiling point.

"Uh. . .that is. . .I meant. . .you could. . .could *live* with me."

Joe started coughing as if he'd swallowed something the wrong way, like maybe his tongue. "Bonnie. . .I. . .I. . .don't think. . .I mean, I'm. . .uh. . .we don't know each other. . ."

"I live with my *brothers.*" Bonnie said it so fast she almost gave her brain whiplash—maybe Joe's, too. "I *meant* you could *stay* at my place, with me *and* my two brothers, who got home today from college for spring break." Her face blazed hot.

Despite the humiliation of blushing, she hoped the chipper crimson tone of her skin told him she didn't mean it the way it sounded. She was just being her usual socially moronic self.

Idiot!

"Okay, got it. You had me going there for a minute." He chuckled. "I've never seen anyone turn that color of bright red. Hello, fire engine."

Bonnie clapped her palms over her cheeks, which kept her hands occupied so she didn't kill him or dig a hole in the street to crawl into.

He turned back to the bat house. "I think if I'm going to call myself a man, I've got to go in there." He glanced at her, and his dimples popped out like joyful flowers in the spring. Bonnie did her best not to stare. "But you definitely took my mind off the bats for a second. Thanks."

With a little time to think, Bonnie did have some ideas. "Since we were lucky enough to see the bats leave—"

"Lucky?" Shaking his head, Joe gave her a look that seemed to measure her IQ and come up with a single digit. "I can think of a lot of words to describe seeing those bats, and *none* of them is 'lucky.' "

"We now know exactly how they get in your house." Bonnie jerked her head at the tower. "The roofing of the house has no doubt pulled away from that lookout post. That's pretty common."

"It is?"

"Sure." It sounded good and Bonnie forged on so he wouldn't ask her exactly how she knew that. "So if you had a long extension ladder, a hammer and some nails, some boards, and maybe a caulking gun and some caulk, we could lock the bats out easily."

"To my knowledge, I have none of those things."

"No, but Nick has a ladder and he's a carpenter. It's a few minutes' work. He'd probably come over right now and do it for you."

"So I can get rid of the bats, keep my manhood intact by sleeping in there, and still have your house as a fallback if I. . .uh. . .change my mind?"

"You mean get *scared* out of your mind."

"Whatever." Joe sighed as if a huge weight had been lifted off him. "What's the curfew on that invitation to sleep with you?"

Bonnie swatted him on the shoulder, and he gave her an unrepentant grin that did something warm and tingly to her insides.

"I'm an insomniac. Come over anytime before 2:00 a.m. And after that, check to see if there's a light on in the living room. If it's on, I'm up. If it's not on, there's a key under the doormat at the back door. Sneak in and sleep on the living room couch."

"You don't have one single survival instinct, do you?"

"Sure I do."

"You just told a complete stranger where you hide your key."

"Oh, well, do you want me to move it or what?"

"No, leave it there. Just in case." He pulled out his cell phone. "Insomnia, huh? Bummer. My grandma could never sleep. It drove her crazy. I'll call Nick."

He studied the face of the phone. "Hey, I've got reception."

Bonnie leaned close and saw three bars. "Well, don't tell anyone. They'll be coming from all over town to crouch behind your Jeep and make calls."

Joe laughed. "Send 'em on. I can use the company."

Bonnie rattled off Nick and Carrie's number.

Joe dialed and explained the situation.

Nick must have explained things to Carrie, because Bonnie thought she heard Carrie screaming, maybe through the phone, maybe just across town.

They only lived three blocks away, so within minutes, in the quiet of a town busy eating dinner, Bonnie heard the clanging of Nick's ladder when he loaded it and the roar of his pickup when he turned the engine over.

"Get up, quick." Joe stood, gave Bonnie a hand, and dusted off his backside, then his knees. "Don't tell him we were hiding."

Bonnie pointed straight across the street at a small ranch-style home. An old lady's face was framed in the window of the front door. "She'll tell. Give it up."

Joe flinched.

Nick pulled his huge black rig in behind Joe's Jeep and emerged from the truck, staring at the mausoleum. "I love this old house. It's neglected, of course, but with some hard work and time, it could be a showplace."

Bonnie looked hard at the house then exchanged a glance with Joe.

"Not seein' it," Joe muttered.

They exchanged a grin.

Joe helped unload the aluminum extension ladder.

Bonnie stood aside, the good little maiden letting the big strong men do the hard work. Truth was, she could slap a ladder up against a house and do some work herself. She knew how to drive a nail, too. But it was kind of fun to step aside. Maybe she could bake chocolate chip cookies in a housedress and pearls while they worked. Of course, that would mean she'd need to go inside—not to mention buy a housedress and pearls. She decided to skip the cookies.

Joe and Nick had the bat hole patched quickly.

Bonnie heard Nick talking the whole time they worked. She moved close enough to catch most of it. House talk about bricks and siding and architecture. It sounded like he had only glowing words for the craftsmanship of this nasty old dump.

He and Joe reloaded the ladder and Nick drove away.

"Who was that masked man?" Bonnie stared after Nick the Lone Ranger.

Joe grinned. "I didn't even get a chance to thank him."

She appreciated that he got her weird sense of humor. She wasn't exactly famous for her wit. She jabbed a finger at the front door. "Now we're going in there."

Nodding, Joe marched toward the house. "Nick offered to stay and hunt around the house with us, but I told him he didn't have to."

"You're feeling that brave?"

"No, I'm afraid I'll start shrieking like a little baby, and I don't want him to witness it."

"Just me?" Bonnie was oddly touched that he'd let her see him so vulnerable.

"Well, I had to balance my fear of shaming myself and my fear of going in there alone. I figure I'll have a better chance of begging you to remain silent."

Bonnie wasn't completely opposed to Joe begging. With that intriguing image in her head, she started toward the house. She took a second to wonder where the bats were going to sleep and asked God to keep them from finding any cracks in her house.

"I just hope you aren't infested with anything else."

Joe faltered, glared at her over his shoulder, then muttered something dire sounding as he went on inside.

Bonnie stepped through the doorway just as overhead lights popped on. A filthy chandelier, heavy with dangling crystals, ornate twisted brass, and dozens of tiny lightbulbs, gleamed to life. About half were burned out, but the room, though gloomy, was visible in the deepening dusk.

"Wow." Bonnie had never been in this house before today, and they hadn't turned the lights on earlier, so she hadn't noticed the beautiful fixture. Fact was, almost no one in town had been in here. "Even with the cobwebs, that's beautiful."

"It is." Joe stared upward. "While we were on the roof, Nick talked nonstop about the architecture and workmanship of this building. I've started to think more kindly of this place. Of course, it's badly neglected, but it's really a lovely old home."

"If you're a Munster."

Snickering, Joe quit studying the light fixture and flashed those dimples again. "I'm glad you're here. I'll get through the night somehow. I mean, good old Dad did it, right?"

Bonnie didn't mention that good old Dad was dead. Probably murdered in this house.

"And his father before him?"

Another dead guy. Bad trend.

"So let's have a look around and see if there's anything the Melnik Historical Society can use. Are you really going to try to raise money to build a new museum?"

"I'm not going to *try*. I'm going to *do* it." Bonnie's surge of self-confidence surprised her. Confident wasn't her normal state. But she'd read enough on the Internet last night about funding big projects to know it was possible. There were a lot of grants and endless creative fund-raising ideas. Plus, she'd read enough to know the effort was worthwhile. Melnik would be better. She had statistics to prove this kind of commitment to a town's heritage drew new residents and businesses.

"It will be a lot of work." She led the way into the library. The light switch was a push button. The huge room took up part of the east side of the first floor, probably thirty by thirty feet. Bonnie looked for a door that would lead to the rest of the east wing, but there was no door—only a wall lined with shelves separated by tall, thin windows. The room was crammed with little tables overloaded with statuettes and other oddities. Everything was coated with decades and decades of dust as if a mad collector had hoarded his treasures then locked them away for eternity. A monument to greed, obsession, and neglect.

A fireplace dominated the left end of the room, and a massive desk faced inward by the window on the street side. The desk chair had its back to the outside as if the Gundersons had turned their backs on the world to look at their own wealth. And that, Bonnie decided, described the Gundersons perfectly.

"The museum you're going to build can have most of this stuff. I'm not into antiques." Joe strode toward the south window, a massive bay that looked out on his shiny red Jeep.

Bonnie thought Joe's SUV looked almost science-fictionish when viewed from this house-that-time-forgot.

"That's great. Some of this stuff is valuable, though. I won't accept it until you've had time to think it all over."

"Fair enough." Joe spun a massive globe set on a small table near the desk.

"I'd love to help you go through things, clean them, research them, and catalogue it all. If we find anything with real value to Melnik's history, the historical society will definitely take you up on your offer." Bonnie saw that the few places on the wall that weren't either window or door or bookcase held small paintings and wall hangings.

Hanging over the fireplace was one massive, grimy portrait Bonnie suspected was the original Gunderson. The family had an extremely unfortunate nose, which appeared to be delivered by a gene that was beyond dominant. It hooked down so far Bonnie wondered if the Gundersons had trouble with nose burns when they tried to drink hot coffee. Maybe the beakish nose was the source of their hermit tendencies, not to mention their general crankiness. She looked at Joe's perfect profile. His mother must have had a nose the size of a kidney bean.

Below that scowling portrait on the north wall was a mantel overloaded with tall, thin candlestick holders of matching style but different heights. The furniture, as best she could tell under the dust, was old and solid oak. Everything in this room had sat and waited, quietly converting into antiques with the passage of time. The house and its contents might be the find of the decade.

She reached for a lace doily spread across the back of an upholstered wingback chair. It was coated in dust, but the fabric looked unworn. As she touched it, a barely audible scratching noise sent a chill up Bonnie's spine. She had the sensation of being watched, although she couldn't ever remember having such a feeling before in her life. So how did she know what that feeling was?

Turning, she studied the fireplace, where she thought that miniscule sound had originated.

Nothing. Unbroken expanses of dust and cobwebs. No movement, no bats, no nothing.

She glanced at Joe, afraid to turn her back on the north side of the room.

Joe bent over the desk, opening noisy drawers. Could she have heard a drawer squeak? Could her imagination have provided the rest?

Most likely.

Her eyes searched shadowed recesses. Each window had a seat shrouded in darkness. The floor-to-ceiling bookcases loomed. Each nook became a hiding place for whoever had killed Gunderson.

She shuddered to think of Joe staying here alone. Even now, with her at his side, it didn't feel safe here. But at least they were awake. Swallowing hard, Bonnie clearly visualized just how easy it would be to sneak up on a sleeping man.

The forensics had suggested Gunderson had been killed here, although that wasn't definite. The coroner had informed Junior that Gunderson's body had been moved.

Bonnie looked at the picture of the Gunderson patriarch, almost expecting eyes to follow her. Nothing. Dust and plenty of it, but no living eyes.

"Joe?"

Joe fought with a warped drawer. He looked up, wary, no doubt warned by her tone. "What?"

"I. . .uh. . .feel like. . ." Stupid to dump such a vague impression on him. It added to his worry, and that wasn't very nice. But there *had* been a murder. Bonnie didn't accept safely-locked-up Clara as the culprit for a second. "You should find somewhere else to sleep, I think. Offering you my home. . .well, that was a spur-of-the-moment idea, not one of my best. With my brothers there it gets pretty noisy. All their friends hang out. Nick and Carrie have a lot of space. And if you want privacy, there is a house for rent near the Catholic church. I'm sure we could crouch behind your Jeep and phone—"

He crossed the room, his eyes faintly amused. "What is it? Did you see a mouse? A bat? I was spooked at first, but now I'm calm. I can handle a few household pests."

Her mind flashed to the sight of Gunderson clinging to that cookbook, stiff and—however oddly it happened—very definitely dead.

Tingling with fear and dread for absolutely no reason beyond that tiny creaking noise, Bonnie couldn't shake the feeling of being watched. She opened her mouth to admit it then shook her head.

There was no one. "But someone killed Sven Gunderson."

"Clara. Case closed."

Bonnie rubbed her hands up and down her arms and warmed the goose bumps away. "No, I don't buy it."

"Well, whoever killed him wanted *him* dead. No one hates me."

"Unless they killed him for some reason other than hate. Don't you ever read books? Revenge."

"I can't see how I've hurt anyone, especially not in Melnik. I just got here yesterday."

"Then to silence a witness."

Joe raised his open palms. "I haven't witnessed anything." He seemed calm now, accepting of the house and its grim shadows.

"How about greed? You are now the sole heir to Gunderson's fortune. A murderer could have killed him, thinking the body wouldn't be discovered in that little room. He'd have complete freedom to rob this house. Sven Gunderson could have been missing and dead for a long, long time and no one would have noticed."

Joe's eyes locked with hers. She saw courage and strength. Two things she lacked. "Then I'd better stay here and guard all this treasure, huh?"

They both looked around. True, there was valuable furniture in here, but it would take a lot of hard work to go through it. Not an easy treasure. And most thieves preferred easy.

Bonnie leaned closer. She couldn't let him stay. She couldn't! "Are you familiar with the feeling of being watched?"

"Yes. I was in the service, so we had some training in surveillance, and I've got a few paranoid reflexes."

Paranoia. That could explain it.

"Well." The fireplace creaked again and Bonnie's goose bumps came back with a vengeance. "Just because you're paranoid doesn't mean someone's *not* out to get you."

Joe looked at her arms and arched his brows. "You want to look in another room for a while?"

Bonnie looked at the old Gunderson painting and had a bad, bad feeling. There was no room far enough from whatever was bothering her.

"Sure. Let's go." She was probably the one who had bats in her belfry. What an idiot.

8

What a sweetheart.

Joe smiled as Bonnie left the room. She was scared for him in this spooky old house. Well, he'd survived two tours in the army, a long, tough stretch tending his mother while she died, and three more years chasing after a toddler.

Not much scared him.

The long evening exploring his house had calmed down the whole bat experience. And after last night's craziness with the dead bum's corpse and the decimation of the historical society museum, tonight was a snap by comparison. He was pleasantly tired. Not even this spooky old derelict could stop him from sleeping.

A footstep sounded right behind him. He whirled. No one.

Swallowing hard, he fought to regain the steadiness an evening with Bonnie had brought on. Would she be flattered or insulted to hear she had a sedative effect on a man?

Joe was a high-energy guy, which helped him keep up with kids. But all that energy tended to spill over and make him restless. As a kid, he'd been a human bouncing ball, as his mom and grandparents had told him on countless occasions. And he suspected that if he'd been a few years younger, they'd have pegged him as ADHD and drugged him to get him through elementary school.

Joe-the-Hyper meets Bonnie-Human-Ritalin.

Deciding that being alone was making him imagine footsteps, he followed after Bonnie and saw her going upstairs. He tagged along and found a room his father must have slept in because it was slightly less dust coated than the rest.

"Here are some clean sheets." Bonnie dragged them out of a closet in the upstairs hallway. "They aren't fresh, but there's no dust on them. I'll take another set home with me tonight and launder them."

Joe stripped the bed and helped Bonnie remake it. "I wonder how long these have been in there?"

"You probably don't want to know."

When they were done and the last possible excuse for keeping Bonnie here was gone, Joe squared his shoulders. He could do this. He could live in this house.

No problem.

"You have my number?" Bonnie stood at the doorway outside, chewing her bottom lip as if she were scared for him.

What a sweetheart, again.

She recited her number and Joe programmed it into his phone.

"I live in a bungalow, white, right next to the park with the big tank in it. First house to the east. Do you think you can find it? You could follow me home, just so I could point it out."

"I've been in town twenty-four hours, Bonnie. I know exactly what you're talking about."

Bonnie smiled, looked nervously around, and, her shoulders drooping, said for about the twentieth time, "Are you sure you don't want to find somewhere else to—"

"I'm fine." Joe cut her off. "I appreciate the offer, and if I need to bail out, I'll come."

"Promise?"

Smiling, Joe nodded. "I promise."

With a sigh so demoralized Joe felt like he'd shouted an insult at her rather than promised to come to her in his hour of cowardly need, Bonnie said, "Good night, then."

Joe watched her go, in all her beige glory, down the sidewalk, glancing behind her several times.

He swung the door shut as soon as her car started then turned to face his brand-new home. He almost ran after Bonnie.

No, he'd be fine. Good grief, so it was a spooky old house. Big deal.

He headed up the stairs, and as he reached the second-floor landing, that same eerie footstep echoed like someone walked down the stairs to the basement. They'd never gotten down there.

Joe shook his head to clear his imagination. That was probably the furnace switching on. Of course, it was a warm night. The furnace wasn't switching on and off. But maybe a water heater or a fuse box, something simple. Joe refused to jump at shadows. . .unless they really caught him by surprise.

Shaking his head, Joe opened and closed doors on the cavernous upper floor of the house, noticing that the end of the upstairs hallway was blocked. There should have been an opening to the west wing of the house, but a blank wall stood there, as if the house ended.

Weird.

Well, he wasn't going to worry about it tonight. By the time he finished cleaning up this house, he'd know all its secrets.

He'd collect his inheritance and consult Nick on renovations. He'd donate generously to local causes, especially if it was something his father was known to hate. Then he'd get out of Melnik. With his newfound wealth, he'd go back to college. Finish his degree. Start a life he'd put on hold for too long.

Staying in town was out. He had no interest in getting stuck in a one-horse town that worshipped a disease-bearing rodent.

Bonnie was sweet, but not enough to make him consider—

He caught himself. Why had his head even gone there? It was just that crazy slip of the tongue about living at her house. Otherwise he'd had no such thoughts about sweet, beige Bonnie. Well, maybe a couple of thoughts in the hall when Junior left them alone this afternoon. And sure, he'd noticed how well she fit in his arms when he'd scooped her up last night. He even liked the idea of having younger brothers.

Shaking away the errant thoughts, he went into his new bedroom. It was so dreary he almost went and slept in his car. The four-poster bed was centered right across from him. There were countless dressers and cabinets, all bulging with junk, judging by the slightly open drawers and the things hanging out of them. And there were six doors. He and Bonnie hadn't gotten to them.

Curious, he started swinging them open. One led to a converted bathroom . . .obviously put in by a cheaper generation of Gundersons, because it was utilitarian beyond belief.

One door led to a catchall room—which had been catching all for most of a century. Stacks and stacks of boxes and furniture had been crammed in and piled high.

One door stuck. Joe tugged, trying to decide if the door was locked or just warped shut. He'd found a key to lock the front door, a skeleton key of all ridiculous safety measures—maybe that would work in this door.

He'd peek behind the rest of these doors then go lock up the house and get to bed.

He tugged on the stubborn door again. There was no give. Joe wondered again if his single skeleton key would open this, too. He'd bring it up when he finished downstairs.

If it wouldn't open, Joe would worry about it tomorrow. He'd explore with Bonnie. Maybe he'd ask her to bring her brothers. . .and a big stick.

Joe reached for a white porcelain knob on a door that must be a closet. Before he got a good grip, the knob twisted and he jerked his hand back, his heart going into overdrive in a split second.

The door rammed open, bashing him on the forehead with a thud that made his ears ring. Stunned, he staggered backward. His heel caught on a throw rug.

Falling, he felt his head crack against a bedpost.

Comets of light blinded him. The room dimmed. He forced his eyes open as vision faded. He saw two of everything, then one, then a blur. Shocked, Joe realized he wasn't alone. Someone leaned over him and snarled.

"Get out of my house!"

The man reached for Joe's neck and squeezed, laughing, his eyes vicious and mad with the power to kill.

"Get out of my house!"

Struggling against the strangling and the double blows to his head, Joe heard a laughing whisper.

"Get out of my house!"

Joe caught at the gripping hands.

"Get out of my house!"

An almost electric shock hit Joe.

"Get out of my house!"

He recognized his attacker.

"Get out of my house!"

At the same moment, he knew he'd never seen him before.

"Get out of my house!"

He was groggy, his lungs dying for air. One senseless, desperate thought came absolutely clear.

"Get out of my house!"

He'd been too quick to agree with Bonnie that there were no such things as ghosts.

"Get out of my house!"

Because Joe had just been attacked by a dead man.

Bonnie hammered at the door, embarrassed to come back, but it had to be done. She couldn't stand knowing Joe was in this house alone.

She heard a cry and a loud thud. She shoved the door open.

Unlocked. Joe was a city boy. Wouldn't he have locked up?

A second shout from above had her dashing up the stairs. "Joe!" Bonnie screamed. "Joe, are you all right?"

Gripping the stair rail, she sprinted. A door slammed. Bonnie raced toward the sound, scared but determined.

She found Joe unmoving on the floor. Alone. As still as a corpse. Looking around, she saw nothing; then she dropped to her knees. She quickly touched his neck, feeling for a pulse. It was there. He was alive.

He moaned when she touched him, and his eyes flickered open.

"Joe, what happened?"

"I don't know." His voice sounded raw as he rubbed his head and tried to sit up.

She pressed down on his shoulders. "It looks like you fell and hit your head."

"Fell?" Joe reached for the back of his head and winced when he pulled his hand back, covered in blood. His eyes focused more sharply as he touched the wound.

"We need to get you to a doctor." Bonnie leaped to her feet.

Joe snagged her arm, and she fell back to her knees beside him. "No, hang on."

"Let me call an ambulance. You could have neck injuries."

"I'm not calling an ambulance for a bump on the head."

"How about for being knocked out? You could have a concussion." Bonnie felt like she was dealing with one of her stubborn-as-a-mule little brothers. Joe got unsteadily to his feet, and Bonnie rose from crouching beside him to support his arm. As she touched him, the resemblance to one of her brothers ended.

He smiled down at her, those blasted gorgeous dimples fully in place. "Thanks for worrying about me, Bonnie."

Bonnie didn't answer. He was too close for her brain to function at such an advanced level as speech.

"You're a sweetheart, aren't you?" His head was bowed, no doubt in pain, but it brought him really close to her. Then he was closer.

So was she. Her gaze lit on his lips as he lowered his head. She lifted her head and their lips grazed once, twice. He pulled back mere inches and his eyes met hers; then his arms went around her.

And she noticed his neck.

"Joe!" She grabbed for his shirt collar.

He jerked back. "What?"

"What happened?" She used two thumbs to raise his chin and study his neck. "You're bruised."

"From the fall probably. Somehow." He gingerly touched where Bonnie stared.

"No, those are—Joe, those are *fingerprints*. The kind of bruises you'd get if someone tried to—"

"Someone tried to strangle me!" Joe looked around, spied a mirror, and rushed to look. "I remember now. I uh. . .uh. . .I mean. . ." He fell silent as he looked closely, his eyes narrowed with anger. "I remember it all. Someone tried to kill me."

"Someone?"

Joe swallowed hard. Bonnie noticed his bruised Adam's apple working.

Joe shook his head. "It's crazy."

"So is being poisoned with pie."

Joe nodded. "That's right. I'm in Melnik now."

From his tone, Bonnie thought he might as well have said, "I'm in Oz."

He pulled his collar wide and studied his neck before locking eyes with

Bonnie in the mirror. "It might have been a nightmare—in fact, it must have been. But it seemed very real while it was happening."

"While what was happening?" Bonnie had a strong urge to stop him. Somehow she didn't want to hear what Joe had to say.

"While I was being attacked. . ." The look in his eyes, the way he so blatantly dreaded saying whatever came next, made her want to cover her ears. To run away. Or better yet, to slap her hands over his mouth and yell, "Don't say it!"

"By the ghost of Wilkie Melnik."

9

J unior, you have *got* to do something about him!"

Joe was about to do something about Bonnie the protective mother. He didn't want another mother. He'd already had a perfectly good mother. And if he *did* want one, he sure wouldn't pick pretty, comforting Bonnie. Not after he'd kissed her.

Joe shook his head. Identifying a ghost as his attacker was tricky since he didn't believe in ghosts.

"He cannot sleep here."

"I'm staying in the house, Bonnie. I shouldn't have said that about the ghost."

Junior patted overwrought Bonnie on the shoulder. "It's not all that uncommon to see crazy stuff when you're passing out. You've heard of people having their life flash before their eyes."

"What about those bruises on his neck?"

Joe wished Junior would go away for just a little while. Maybe Bonnie would abandon this supernatural murder theory she'd cooked up and consider kissing him again. Since the sheriff had, to all appearances, settled in for good, Joe worked off some of the tension by stepping right in front of his valiant little protector.

"I can only think of one person who has tried to strangle me lately."

She grabbed his arm. Her brown eyes nearly shot sparks of excitement. "You've thought of someone? We have a suspect in the murder attempt?"

"Well, no, but I have a culprit for the bruises."

Her fingers clung to his upper arm. "Who?" She wanted to save him. Bless her heart, she was a little beige warrior.

His heart softened, but not enough to stop him from saying, "You."

Her fingers turned into claws in his bicep. "Me? When did I do that?"

"When I was saving you from Dora? You fought with me."

"I thought you were attacking me."

"Which is the reason you fought with me."

"I didn't strangle you."

"Are you sure? I don't remember you pulling any punches. You could have gotten your hands around my throat at some point." Since he'd thought of it, Joe decided it was probably true.

"Maybe when I tugged on that door, it stuck. Maybe I pulled hard and it popped open, bonked me on the forehead. I stumbled," Joe explained, pointing at the messed-up rug, "whacked my skull against the bedpost, dreamed a crazy dream about a man whose face I saw in the newspaper less than twenty-four hours ago with a big 'Ex-Con' headline. Bingo, the ghost of Wilkie Melnik. Supernatural killer at your service. Neck bruises compliments of—" He poked her in the cheek with his index finger and smirked. "You."

"It makes more sense than a ghost." Junior stared at his notebook, stubby pencil handy.

Joe nodded. "The Gundersons and the Melniks have hated each other for generations. It's probably programmed into my genetic code by now to suspect a Melnik of attacking me."

"You've never met a Melnik or a Gunderson. How could you have any strong feelings about any of them?" Bonnie plunked her hands on her hips.

"You're arguing with science here, Bonnie." Joe wondered why she was so fond of the ghost idea. Or was she just protecting him again? His eyes flickered to her lips. "Wilkie starring in my semiconscious nightmare probably came straight from the Gunderson half of my DNA."

"And if it didn't, then someone attacked you—not a ghost. It makes some sense that you'd project Wilkie's features onto whoever came at you in the dark."

"It wasn't dark. The light was on."

"This place would be murky at high noon in the middle of July on the surface of the sun."

Joe had to give her that.

"I still think those bruises came from you." A shiver of memory spooked Joe. Wilkie Melnik bending over him, laughing.

"Get out of my house."

Crazy dream. He refused to consider anything else.

"Listen, Bonnie." Junior chewed on his pencil. "Wilkie was killed because he found out Gunderson had stolen a huge inheritance."

"Really?" Joe asked. "I don't really know the motives."

"Yeah, his wife thought if she killed him, she would make Gunderson happy enough to marry her. She didn't know Wilkie was snooping around hoping to overturn Gunderson's will and regain a lot of money. That's why Gunderson manipulated her into committing murder." Junior looked around the gloomy room.

Bonnie had dragged Joe outside to crouch behind his Jeep and phone Junior. Then they'd braved the house again and she'd bound his head wound with the gentle hands of a born caretaker. Joe had cared for little Stetson for three years, so he knew how much a soft touch helped when someone had an "owie."

Then Joe had changed his shirt, which had an alarming amount of blood on the back. But head wounds bled a lot, he knew, even teeny scratches. And now he was fine.

"I'm sure that's why I thought I saw a dead guy. I'm living here now, and I have really conflicted feelings about the inheritance from dear old Dad." Joe shrugged. "Projecting Wilkie Melnik attacking me fits."

He didn't mention those frightening flashes of memory. Wilkie bending over him, those hands tightening on his throat.

"Get out of my house."

He'd nail the closet door shut before he went to bed. Maybe the windows, too. No, he'd leave those open as an escape hatch.

Exhaling a near scream of frustration, Bonnie said, "Fine! But you're not sleeping here." She almost poked him in the nose. "If you won't leave, I'm telling."

"You're telling? What? Are you a fourth-grader now? A tattletale?"

"Believe it, buster. I'm telling my brothers, my entire young adults group at church, plus Dora and Tallulah. They're all going to stay with you here." Bonnie snapped her fingers as if inspired. "And Jeffie Piperson. No one scares Jeffie. He could clear the ghosts out of this house in a heartbeat. And while I'm at it, I'll tell the rest of Melnik's first grade, along with their parents. I'm going to get them to sleep in this house with you tonight."

"You could come down and sleep at the jail." Junior spoke in a low voice, as if not to interrupt Bonnie from listing every known resident of Melnik whom she was inviting to Joe's slumber party.

"Is Clara there?"

"No, her daughter came and got her today. I released her to spend the night in the hospital. I'll put you in the other cell. It's got the best mattress. I sleep there sometimes when my wife's mad at me, so I bought a good mattress with my own money. And with Clara gone, it don't smell too bad."

Joe shrugged. "That could work." Truth be told, he wasn't all that wild about staying here alone.

"Jeffie alone would scare away all the bad guys, real and imagined."

Joe pulled his phone out of his pocket and offered it to Bonnie. "Go crouch behind my Jeep and start inviting people."

Bonnie nearly glared him into two pieces then looked at the phone. "Hey, it's got four bars." She looked up at Joe. "You should charge money for people to make calls from your second floor."

"Invite them to bring their cell phones. No charge." Joe rubbed the back of his neck. He'd been told he had a good smile, and he'd used it to his advantage many times. Why not now? He smiled.

She quit keying in numbers and stared.

"Aren't you going to call anyone?"

"Call them what?" She looked in his eyes; then her eyes drifted back to his smile.

Joe wished Cousin Junior the Watchdog would go investigate someone else's ghosts and give him just a few minutes alone with Museum Girl.

Bonnie's cheeks suddenly flushed pink and she turned sideways, as if that was the only way to make her eyes behave. Joe's smile widened. Except for the ghost and the cut on the back of his head and the bruise on his forehead and the finger marks on his neck and the murder and his deadbeat dad and the bats, he was really starting to like Melnik.

"I am calling my brothers. I was bluffing about the rest of it, but they'll run everything out of this house, human and ghost alike. In fact, they might run *you* off. They're like a couple of zoo animals."

"Scary, huh? Like the lions and tigers? Something ferocious?"

"Apes. The smell of them is what will clear this place out. If that doesn't do it, their manners will."

"Big sisters." Joe shook his head and laughed.

"I'm done here," Junior said, tucking his notebook away in his shirt pocket. "I want you to come down to the station and sleep. Your brothers will already be asleep, Bonnie. You're the only one in that family with insomnia."

Joe touched Bonnie's dialing hand. "Wait and get them tomorrow. I'll sleep in the jail." Joe was pretty sure he'd never said those exact words together before.

"Good," Junior said. "Then in the morning, you can make a formal statement."

"You already know what happened."

Junior snorted. "*You* don't even know what happened. How'm I supposed to be sure?"

The man had a point.

"He should see a doctor." Bonnie stopped calling. Her brow furrowed.

Joe hated to think he was giving the poor woman premature wrinkles.

"And, Bonnie. . ." Junior jabbed his pencil at his cousin. "I saw your name on the city council agenda tomorrow night about raising money for a new museum. Are you ready for that?"

Bonnie jumped. "No. I've got a lot to do before that."

"Get on with it, then. All your worryin' and fussin' is slowing down my investigation."

Bonnie said, "I'm still calling my brothers."

"I'm telling them you called them smelly apes." Joe couldn't wait to meet them. He wasn't that excited about staying here alone. He wouldn't complain if Jeffie stayed and the whole first grade—along with their parents. Running, screaming kids and harassed, scolding mothers had a knack for taking the "spooky" out of a place.

"I call them that to their faces all the time, so they won't be surprised." She glanced at her wristwatch, gold with a large dial face, a cheap one like Wal-Mart sold. She rushed out.

Joe watched her go, fascinated. She was so lively and determined and bold and pretty.

"Such a shy, scared little mouse, our Bonnie." Junior tucked his pencil away, too. "Let's get on with this."

As they left the room, Joe asked Junior, "Do you ever have the feeling you're being watched?"

He slid the patch of wood back into place. The faint *scritch-scratch* echoed in his ears, but the Son and his policeman friend never heard it. It was only because he was so careful, so conscientious, that he heard the sound.

Watching them.

He toyed with the tickle of pleasure.

A watcher.

A spy like in a movie.

Someday he'd let the world know how smart he was. How stupid the Son was. How dull-witted the Cop was.

He buried his face in his hands so they couldn't hear his satisfied laughter. Even then he knew he was overcautious. But that was as it should be. A smart man was cautious. Better to be too quiet than let them hear. Let them know he was watching.

He made his way to his room and pulled the whiskey bottle off his bedside table. He could relax. Nothing more would happen tonight. The Son had lived, but that wasn't a mistake. It was too early, anyway. He'd never have attacked if the Son hadn't stumbled on his hiding place. And in the heat of the moment, he thought to end things then and there. But then the pleasure would end.

There was time. There was nothing but time.

The Watcher.

The Spy.

The Winner.

The Ruler.

He toyed with the name that captured him best. Perhaps the True Heir.

He enjoyed the burn of the whiskey and laughed at his mental games and planned when he'd strike next.

And where.

There was no question of who.

The Son had to die.

10

Together we'll create something Melnik will take pride in. Something that will be part of a more vibrant future. Something to enhance, energize, and inspire people and businesses across the state and across the nation. Thank you."

Bonnie's hands were shaking as she sat down next to Joe. She clasped them together in her lap so no one would notice; then, fidgeting, she wiped her sweaty palms on her very best beige skirt.

"Can we ask a few questions?" The mayor had taken notes on the tidy handout she'd distributed to each member of the city council. She'd brought extra in hopes a few interested citizens would show up, and she'd needed them all.

"Absolutely."

The meeting went well. Bonnie had spread the word far and wide. Or rather, she'd told Dora, and there'd been the best turnout of all time at the city council meeting. A crowd of nearly twenty.

Bonnie couldn't believe she'd managed to give an actual speech. And in front of all these people! And the questions the mayor and others peppered her with were good ones that showed a lot of interest. And she could answer all of them. She'd spent all last night and most of today online, researching.

"This'll be a big fund-raising effort, Bonnie." Junior had even jotted notes in his official police notebook. Bonnie was honored he'd used his paper for her.

"If we get the grants I'm hoping for, it won't be hard."

"I think we ought to pick a historic building already in existence and refurbish it." Nick had come. Carrie moved around the room taking pictures. . . . Ugh! A picture of Bonnie on the cover of the *Bugle*. . . Bonnie knew she did not have a front-page face. She planned to speak with Carrie later. Carrie was gun-shy about putting too many pictures of her husband in the paper, but if Nick agreed to donate blueprints, maybe Carrie would admit he deserved the front page this once.

"The grants are specific for new construction, Nick. I checked, and there are some funds for historic reclamation projects, but it's far more difficult to qualify for them. If we pick an existing structure, we'll stand a far better chance of having to fund it ourselves. You know how expensive it is to bring old buildings up to code."

Nick nodded. Everyone knew he was working hard on several abandoned

Main Street buildings. One of those would be a good choice, but they'd already been claimed by businesses eagerly waiting for him to finish. And Main Street needed those businesses. The building the museum had been transferred to wasn't spoken for—and it was beautiful. But it was also condemned. Safe enough to use for storage, but getting it in shape for use by the public was daunting.

"Without outside help, I'm afraid the museum project is beyond our reach. We're going to have to build. That's what the historical society has set as its goal." They'd held an emergency meeting this afternoon and Bonnie had convinced them to go along with her. She couldn't remember persuading anyone to do anything before. But her enthusiasm had overcome her shyness. She looked at her shaking fingers. Almost overcome her shyness.

Nick nodded, but Bonnie knew him pretty well, and she could tell he wasn't fully convinced. Nick loved old buildings.

Bonnie suspected she knew exactly what he was thinking. There'd be no better house in town for this museum than the one he and Carrie lived in. It was big enough, it had real historical meaning, and it was beautiful. But he and Carrie loved their home. It had been a mouse-infested wreck when they'd gotten married. He and Carrie had poured their hearts into refurbishing it.

When the meeting broke up, Bonnie walked out with Joe. "Did my brothers show up?"

Joe smiled that sneaky, beautiful smile. "Yeah, I left them there along with about ten of their friends. They'd ordered five pizzas from the Melnik Mini-Mart and were talking about the good old days in Melnik High School like they were all in their eighties."

Bonnie giggled.

Stupid sound.

She never giggled. How humiliating.

"Come home with me."

She looked up at his dimple. Her ears quit working while she thought of that fascinating invitation.

"See what we did this afternoon. Your brothers know how to work."

Bonnie stopped short and could barely get her jaw to stop hanging down. "Really?" She crossed her arms, her daydreams completely forgotten. "Well, *they're* busted. They've been telling me for years it would kill them to pick up their socks or wash a dirty dish."

Joe laughed. Those dimples. It just wasn't fair what they did to her. She hurried to the car before she could reach out and touch the one on his chin. They drove separately to Joe's.

He was right.

With light blazing from every window, music blaring, and cars jamming the driveway, the spook factor at the Gunderson place had been reduced to zero.

Bonnie went inside to see the proof of her brothers' hard work and came face-to-face with filth. "I thought you said they helped you clean."

"They did. It's great."

"What did they clean?" Cobwebs and dust were everywhere. With the addition of pizza boxes, pop cans, empty potato chip bags, and a dozen sprawling man-children, it was worse than ever.

But not spooky.

"We got boxes from the grocery store and filled them up with all the old papers that were stacked everywhere in here. Now they're stacked in the library. Ready for you to sift through for historical stuff. It all looked pretty old."

She looked away from the chaos in the front room and saw a thousand boxes stacked in the library. In other words, they'd left it all for her. She opened her mouth to say something scathing to her little brothers; then she noticed an unlikely addition to the group.

Her brothers were nineteen and twenty-two, both still in college at the University of Nebraska in Lincoln. The guys in here with them were their high school classmates, the same crowd that had been in and out of her home for years.

Except for Kevin Melnik, who sat slumped down on a threadbare couch.

He was sixteen at most. He'd been living with Carrie's grandparents ever since his father had been murdered and his mother, Rosie, had gone to jail. A ward of the state, Kevin landed in clover to Bonnie's way of thinking. There were no better people in Melnik than Hermann and Helga Anderson. There were a lot just as good, but none better.

But Kevin had never hung out with Bonnie's brothers, and Kevin had a lot of reasons to hate the Gundersons. In fact, if anyone had a motive to kill Sven Gunderson, it was Kevin Melnik. If he was a little older, Bonnie might consider him a suspect.

Kevin looked up and met Bonnie's gaze. Cold, angry eyes. A chill danced up Bonnie's spine. The boy wasn't having a relaxed, noisy, fun time with old friends. So why was he here?

Sixteen was late in life to throw a child a life preserver. Kevin had been drowning for a long, long time with his alcoholic, abusive father and codependent, homicidal mother. Despite the hot food, new clothes, firm limits, and generous love in his foster home, he was still a very troubled boy.

Bonnie was also struck by how much Kevin looked like Wilkie. Joe had seen a dead man. Was it possible—

"Hey, Bon-Bon." Her brother Greg, twenty-two and ready to graduate this spring, grinned at her.

"Long time, Bonnie baby." Her brother's friends had always flirted outrageously with her. It was all just high spirits, and near as Bonnie had ever been able to figure, they thought they could get more food out of her if they flirted.

"Missed you, Baby Mama." Brian tipped his Dr Pepper can at her.

Bonnie giggled—again.

Stupid sound.

"Baby Mama." She sniffed at her dorky brother. "Like I'm a gang member and all you boys know so much about street life and rap lingo. I know for a fact you're a lot more likely to be listening to Kenny Chesney than Snoop Dog."

The boys had all called her that and other silly nicknames when they'd hung around her house. She was struck by how quiet her life had become since her last little brother had gone off to college.

"Better go before she calls your moms." Greg stood with the grace of a lazy lion and slapped one of the guys on the back. Greg looked like her, dark blond hair and brown eyes, but an athlete with all the confidence in the world. He looked even more like their brother Tyler, who was grown and married with two young children. Tyler was a lawyer in Omaha. His wife was from Omaha and she hadn't seen the charm in Melnik when Tyler wanted to open his law practice here.

Or maybe Bonnie just thought Tyler had intended to come home when he graduated. He'd always said that was his plan. But maybe Liza had given him the freedom to chase his true dream of living in the hustle and bustle of Omaha.

As the years had passed, Liza had cut Tyler off slowly and steadily until now Bonnie only saw him once or twice a year, and only then if Bonnie invited herself to their home and endured Liza's cool disdain for all things small town.

Brian jumped to his feet, buzzing with his usual energy. He patted his stomach as if he was loaded with pizza, but Brian never really relaxed. He was the different one in the Simpson family. He was dark with flashing blue eyes. He was a natural-born charmer and a leader, although he didn't always use his leadership skills for good.

Bonnie had received a lot of phone calls over the years from the principal, complaining about harebrained schemes of Brian's that had usually ended in disaster. She was twelve years older than Greg, fifteen older than Brian, and she'd been their mother to the best of her minimal ability after their parents died.

As the boisterous crowd shuffled out, leaving all the trash behind, she realized none of these boys had to phone home and ask permission to stay out late.

Her throat clogged.

Her years as a mother were over at the age a lot of women were just starting.

She got a hug and kiss and some teasing from nearly every boy on his way out. They were all taller than her these days and razzed her about being a shrimp. She'd known them all since the days when they'd come to her with scraped knees or bragging about losing a tooth.

Except Kevin. He went out last and didn't get near her. As he passed, he shot a quick defiant glance, as if daring her to mention that he didn't fit with this crowd.

"Hi, Kev. It's nice to see you." He came with the Andersons to church, so Bonnie knew him fairly well. It was a small town; she knew everyone fairly well.

The boy shoved his hands in his pockets and shrugged his slumped shoulders. Bonnie remembered how Shayla, his big sister, had moved away from Melnik without a backward glance after their mom had been arrested.

Bonnie hadn't been much older than Shayla when she'd taken over and raised three little brothers, but near as Bonnie could tell, Shayla hadn't given Kevin a second thought.

The boy scowled then followed the others out the door, leaving it wide open.

Bonnie went to close it. Her brothers stood outside saying good-bye to their friends and making plans for the rest of the week. But Kevin headed in the general direction of his foster home. In a few minutes she'd crouch behind her car and phone the Andersons to make sure he got home.

"What's up?"

Bonnie jumped then turned to find herself nose to nose with Joe.

Joe reached past her to shut the door. Imagine that, a man who closed a door. He'd shown no talent for cleaning. Bonnie had two brothers who could be expected to close doors and clean when pigs flew. If a pig managed to fly at all, Bonnie wasn't about to complain; after all, the pig didn't stay up very long, so she enjoyed the closed door and didn't ask for more.

Her eyes locked on Joe's for a second. He looked kind and interested in what was going on in her mind. And there was that dimple. Her finger itched. A throat cleared and snapped her out of the trance. Brian had come back inside. Bonnie must have missed the squeaking door. How long had she been standing there looking at Joe?

Now Brian watched them with narrow, speculating eyes. When he caught her gaze, he arched his brows but said nothing.

"That was Kevin Melnik." Bonnie stepped aside so she wasn't quite so close to Joe right in front of Brian the brat.

Greg appeared in the doorway behind Brian. Brian whispered something to him. Greg turned and shifted his eyes between Bonnie and Joe.

Well, they weren't going to change the subject. "How did Kevin end up here?"

Greg shrugged and looked at Brian. "He came with someone, I think. Lots of people came and went. Jeffie was here for a while, too."

"Jeffie?" Bonnie turned to Brian.

"I phoned his mom and made sure she knew where he was. She said he could stay."

Bonnie shook her head. "That woman. She lets that boy run wild."

Greg, Brian, and Joe all nodded.

"Did Kevin say much?"

"No, nothing, I don't think. He didn't even have pizza, unlike Jeffie. Just sat there and listened. I'm not sure when he came. He just showed up. A lot of the guys did. It's not like there was a formal guest list or anything. I feel sorry for the kid, and he didn't cause any trouble. So there was no point in chasing him off."

Bonnie looked at Joe. "You said Wilkie Melnik attacked you last night. It couldn't have been Kevin, could it? Wilkie's son? He looks a lot like his dad."

Joe didn't answer right away. Bonnie realized he was giving her suggestion serious consideration. First the city council and now Joe. It was a red-letter day in her quiet, largely-unnoticed-by-anyone life.

"I don't think so. That blow to the head that we're blaming everything on could have twisted a boy into a man, I suppose. But it seems like the nonexistent attacker was older."

Bonnie looked back at her brothers. "Did Kevin stay in the room with the rest of you? If ever a kid had a reason to want to snoop around this house, it'd be Kevin. Besides losing his parents and his sister because of Sven, a lot of his family's wealth and history was stolen by the Gundersons. He might think there was some payback to be found in here."

"Money? Hidden in this house?" Joe looked around the room.

"Cool." Brian's eyes flashed. "Treasure hunt."

Bonnie's stomach sank. She knew her brother when he got an idea. On the other hand, hunting for a pot of gold would keep him busy, and Brian hadn't been that good a sport about staying in the haunted mansion. He had friends to see during this break. Only the chance to snoop around had convinced him. Gunderson's house had always been the most forbidden place in Melnik, and no teenager had grown up without daring others to sneak in and look around. But Old Man Gunderson had kept a sharp lookout, and anyone brave enough to attempt it had been scared away. Sven had been the same.

Now, with the suspicion of buried treasure, the boys would gladly stay and snoop. So she decided to encourage Brian's foolishness—as if she could stop the brat anyway. "Gunderson was a wealthy man and a miser. I suppose he could have a safe behind some picture or stuffed his mattress full of money."

"Cool." Brian, Greg, and Joe all said the same word at the same time in exactly the same tone.

"So did you guys explore every corner of this house tonight?" Bonnie sincerely hoped they had.

"We meant to. But we got to talking and never went past that room." Brian pointed at the front room, and Bonnie's heart sank. She'd hoped the boys had brought noise and activity to every room and scared the spooks away. She was a little vague on the rules of scaring off ghosts, especially since she didn't believe in them.

"Why not? Once in your life you get a shot at exploring the Gunderson house, and you sit around and eat?"

Brian grinned. "We're going to live here for the rest of the week, right? We've got lots of time to explore."

Bonnie rolled her eyes. "Let's get the mess cleaned up. I've got a lot of work left to do at home." She threaded her way past Brian and Greg into the front room.

Greg caught her arm, gentle but firm. "So have you been sleeping?"

Bonnie's heart melted a bit at Greg's concern. He'd always been the one who'd let her hold him and cuddle him, right from the time he was born. Not so much when he got older, but they had a special bond. Tyler, only four years younger than she, had stepped in and done a lot of co-parenting at first. But he'd been nearly grown and had left for college a year after her parents had died. No one had seemed to notice the unfairness of Bonnie having to stay behind. Bonnie had, of course, but self-pity was something she was too busy to indulge in.

Brian had always kept her hopping. He was the baby and he was spoiled, not horribly, but the plain fact was, he was the smartest of all of them, and he had a knack for using that charm and intelligence to get his own way. Greg had been quieter, more openly lost and grieving. When Bonnie had quit college and moved home, he'd turned to her more than the others had.

She smiled at him. "Don't ask."

"I've been seeing ads for sleeping pills that are supposed to be good. I think you should ask a doctor about it."

"I'm pretty used to living on four hours of sleep. I've been this way all my life. I think it might be normal for me."

"Then why are your eyes bloodshot? Why do you yawn all the time?" He leaned closer. "You weren't this bad before Mom and Dad died. I think you should see someone. Why not at least ask?"

"I might." She would when she needed to see a doctor for some other ailment. But she wouldn't make a special trip just for this. Of course, she was disgustingly healthy. She hadn't seen a doctor in years. Bonnie noticed Joe come up behind her.

Bonnie smiled her bossiest smile at her brothers. "And you guys are going to help me clean this up or *nobody* sleeps. You know the rule."

Greg let it go, let her change the subject, but she saw determination in his eyes. She wasn't about to tell him that she avoided the doctor if at all possible because her meager health insurance had such a high deductible that she had to pay for all medical care out of her pocket. An office visit cost a hundred dollars— if they didn't do anything but talk to you—and she'd asked a pharmacist about the new generation of sleeping pills. They were way out of her price range.

The truth was, she couldn't afford a good night's sleep. Maybe if they ever went over-the-counter *and* generic, she'd try them. She'd read up on it. Patents lasted seven years. She'd sleep when she was thirty-nine.

"You know the rule." Brian groaned. "When Bonnie ain't happy. . ."

Greg chimed in and they spoke together. "Ain't *nobody* happy."

"You'd better believe it, bucko."

Joe laughed. She had to take a peek at his dimples.

That weird creaking sounded from the basement stairs again. She could laugh it off now. Having her brothers here was a great idea.

They went into the living room and worked. Her brothers wasted time stacking pop cans four high and balancing them like circus jugglers as they dumped them into a sack Joe had scrounged.

Joe worked at her side, though. How had his mother managed to teach him that?

When the house was tidied of the take-out mess, it was still filthy. Bonnie had a sudden awakening. She was going to have to clean this house herself. Rather than start crying, she told the menfolk good night and headed to the lonely house she'd lived in alone since Brian left last fall for the university. He didn't come home much, and she respected that. She didn't want any of her brothers to curtail their college experience by worrying about poor old Bonnie back in Melnik.

She went into her empty house, forcing herself to focus on the paperwork she had ahead of her tonight to start the grant application project. She took a second to be glad her darkened house wasn't a spooky old place like the Gunderson derelict.

11

Joe caught up with Bonnie at Jansson's Café.

He'd left her brothers sleeping. Like most college students, they had a night-owl gene and slept until noon unless a tornado blew them awake—or they had a final.

Joe knew that Bonnie, even though her job was buried under a pile of rubble, would be up and going early because of her insomnia. So he came to the teensy downtown area to hunt around for her. It took him two minutes to find her. Her beige Taurus was parked on Main Street. He parked his Jeep beside her car in front of a diner with JANSSON'S CAFÉ painted on the front window, next to a horse painted bright blue and red.

He went in and slid into the booth across the table from her, where she sucked on a cup of coffee like it was her only chance for survival. She drained the cup and reached for a brown insulated pot. Her hand trembled slightly as she lifted the pot.

"Did you get any sleep at all?" He'd heard what Greg had said about bloodshot eyes. Joe added dark circles and heavy lids. She'd spoken casually of insomnia, but Joe hadn't paid that much attention. Now he wondered if it were more serious than she'd let on.

Bonnie smiled as she refilled her cup. A chubby gray-haired lady brought Joe his own pot of coffee, as if she knew better than to expect Bonnie to share.

"Joe, this is Olga Jansson, the best cook in a town full of great cooks."

The woman patted Bonnie on the shoulder. "Bless your heart. You look exhausted, honey." Then Olga flipped over a white pottery cup resting in front of Joe. She was so quick and efficient it was almost musical.

"I really don't—"

Olga bustled away before Joe could tell her no thanks. He'd already had some coffee and didn't need more. He wondered if he'd have to pay for it if he didn't drink it. Who knew the rules in a small town?

Bonnie reached over and flipped his cup back over. "There. You're safe. Best not to drink Olga's coffee anyway."

"Is it bad?"

"No, it's fantastic, almost addictive. Once you've had a cup of it, you're hers for life."

"Okay, thanks for the warning." He smiled. She stared at him the same way she had several times when he'd smiled. These stupid dimples. He'd been fooled before into thinking that women who liked his dimples also liked him.

"Your brothers snore like maniacs. It was like trying to sleep while surrounded by hibernating grizzly bears. They had their own rooms, too, so it's not like they were that close to me."

Bonnie nodded and rolled her eyes. "Tell me about it. I blamed my insomnia on their racket for years. Then they moved out and—I'm still wide awake."

"So, any sleep?"

"It was pretty bad. I think your house has me on edge." Bonnie arched her brows comically. "I kept *hearing* things."

Joe frowned. "What kind of things?"

Bonnie opened her mouth, glad someone wanted to share her little fears.

Dora came toward them like Sherman rolling toward Atlanta and slid in beside Joe, bumping him over with her ample. . .seating area. "Marian, the historical society voted, and we need you to take Maxie into your care from now on." Dora opened her purse and set the dead mouse on the table.

Joe flinched. "Don't put that thing there! The health department could close this place down!"

Bonnie giggled.

Joe loved the sound, light and sweet. He watched her pick up the mouse, and after looking the rodent in the eye for a second, as if giving him a proper morning greeting, she slipped him into the patch pocket of the beige tunic top she wore this morning. Joe tried to remember if he'd ever seen her in any other color. And now she wore boring beige *and* had a dead mouse in her pocket. And he still thought she was cute.

Joe needed to get started on a real life.

He needed to claim his inheritance and use it to go back to school. Make his mother proud. She'd sacrificed her life for him, wanted so much for him, hurt so badly when he'd given up college to care for her. This was his chance to make it all right. He didn't have time to think about cute small-town girls with weird pocket contents.

"I think Melnik should invest in a carrying case for Maxie." Joe thought the case might also head off a health-code violation. "Something small and easy to carry. It can't be good for him to be handed around like that. Doesn't he shed his fur?" He was considering calling in a complaint to the board of health personally, because he'd planned on breakfast, but he wasn't eating off this table.

Bonnie perked up, which made her red-veined eyes all the more visible. "He's held up really well over the years, but a carrying case isn't a bad idea."

Dora swatted him on the arm. "Especially until we get the new museum built and he has a permanent home again."

Dora didn't know her own strength. Joe barely resisted rubbing his tender elbow.

"Were you going to have breakfast, Joe? I ate at home, but I don't mind waiting."

Joe was starved, but there were visible mouse hairs on the table. "Nope, I'm looking for you. We need to talk about the papers and books in my house. Junior caught me on the street and told me I've got an appointment with George Wesley as soon as *The Price Is Right* is over to read my—that is, Sven's will." He'd never called the man his father, unless he could add "the Bum," and he couldn't in front of everyone, not when they were still wondering who killed the old man.

"You look a little pale to me." Dora jabbed him in the bicep. "Flabby, too. I'll bet you need iron. Have one of Jansson's liver doughnuts. Cure what ails you."

"Liver doughnuts?"

"Sure, she mixes the liver in with the prune filling. Can't even tell it's there." Dora laughed until her entire body bounced. Joe wondered if that meant the liver doughnuts were a joke.

"Liver and prune?" Joe thought of Clara. Could the woman have been a former baker at this café?

"Y'need the prunes, too. Keep you from getting bound up. And don't be afraid to have two. People come into this town anemic and constipated, but they don't leave that way. It'll help your bones, too. You're stoop shouldered, probably headed for a humpback at this rate."

Joe sat up straight and rubbed his neck, reaching back to see if he could detect a hump.

He saw Bonnie control a grin and decided he might not have a problem. After all, Dora had rammed her car into a building. She wasn't exactly someone with unerring judgment. Although Joe had to admit that hadn't been her fault. The lightning would have caused anyone to swerve.

Bonnie said, "Let him up, Dora. We've got a lot to do before his meeting with George."

"Gonna be rich. Even after the town took back all Gunderson had stolen, there was a lot left." Dora kept up a steady chatter while she hoisted herself up out of the booth. She told Joe he needed to start exercising and work off a few pounds, tighten up some muscles, maybe consider a breath-freshening mouthwash.

She had a few choice words for Bonnie, too. All cruel and none true, except for the bloodshot eyes. Dora had that one right.

Dora slid back into the booth after Bonnie and Joe got up, settling in to insult the waitresses. Olga Jansson came over bearing two pots of coffee for her and Dora's morning gossip session as Bonnie and Joe paid their bill and left. Bonnie was right, no charge for the coffee.

Joe, traumatized, walked across the street to his Jeep.

Bonnie walked on his left and patted the arm Dora had nailed. She had a much softer touch. Bonnie could pat his arm all day if she wanted to.

"Don't listen to her. She doesn't mean a thing by it. And Olga's doughnuts do have prune filling in them. They're *kolaches*, which is ironic, because that's Czech, and of course Olga is pure Swede. Dora's joking about the liver."

"She doesn't mean it when she tells me I have bad breath and I'm fat?"

"Well, there's a difference between meaning something and being right about something." She patted him again. Very reassuring. Very sweet. "She might mean it. It's hard to tell with Dora. But even if she does, you shouldn't listen to her. You have fine breath and you are in great shape."

"Thanks." Joe glanced at her, grateful for the kind words after the ego pounding.

Bonnie's cheeks turned a nice shade of pink that coordinated nicely with her red eyes.

Then he remembered the mouse in her pocket. "Let's put Maxie in the temporary museum and go back to my place."

Bonnie looked sideways at him, her brow arched.

Joe's mind went wide open to the possibilities. He hadn't had Bonnie alone long enough to see if the moments they'd shared could become more. He had places to go. College, a career, but he wouldn't mind exploring his feelings for Bonnie just a bit. Except, of course, for their very own eagle-eyed chaperones. Bonnie's brothers.

It just wasn't meant to be. "I need to settle up this inheritance and get back to school."

Joe spoke out loud, wishing he knew if he meant it.

⌁

He obviously meant every word.

Bonnie had gone from being charmed by the personal tone of his voice when he said, 'Let's go back to my place,' to a bit stunned at realizing she'd been weaving stupid little pipe dreams about gorgeous Joe Manning and herself.

Idiot.

"Let me put Maxie away; then we'll go." Why not just wish for Brad Pitt to stop by Melnik and sweep her away? Except she thought Joe was cuter than Brad, and nicer probably—Joe was no pampered Hollywood actor.

A blush she couldn't control snuck up her face, and she increased her speed, walking toward the temporary museum so he wouldn't see her. She hated her stupid reflex to turn bright pink when she was embarrassed. And this time she hadn't even *said* anything moronic. It had all gone on inside her head. But there had been that kiss last night. Granted, the man was semiconscious at the time. Even so, since then, there'd been a lingering moment or two.

"Sounds good. Let me drive, okay? I can bring you back to your car. We don't need to move both of them."

"Fine." She'd let herself believe those moments were mutual. If the man was going to college, of course she'd imagined it all. Had he noticed? Was he right now cringing at the thought that she might cling to him? He was still so nice, but that might be pity. She knew more people in town pitied her than didn't. Why not Joe, too?

Stupid, stupid, stupid!

Her cheeks cooled. A quick glance at Joe told her he was lost in his own world. Of course, she probably barely registered with the poor guy.

The temporary museum was half a block down from the diner. She went in, knowing she should take the time to set things up and start running regular museum hours again. But not yet. She could take a few more days. Exploring the Gunderson house for Melnik relics could really enhance the museum, and since no one came to the museum anyway, there was really no hurry.

She realized her heart was beating faster because she was almost alone with Joe, and that foolishness made her rush to set Maxie on a stack of packing boxes and leave.

As Joe pressed his remote, the Jeep door audibly unlocked. The man locked his car on Melnik Main Street. How odd. Of course, if she had one of those cool remote door locks, she might do it, too, just for fun.

She pulled her door open, and as she slid in, she felt composed enough to talk again. "So tell me about school. Where do you go?"

Joe looked up, startled, as if he'd forgotten she existed. "Well, when Mom was sick—"

A fist hammered on Bonnie's window so loudly she jumped and hit her head on the roof. She looked sideways and saw a tidy little cage. And behind that, a turban.

"It's like he's a pet rock or something." Joe twisted the key then rolled down the window.

"I heard Maxie needed a cage, that he might be shedding his fur. You'd better hand him over before you destroy the First Citizen of Melnik. I'll take better care of him than you."

Bonnie had a sudden urge to start yelling at Tallulah. She'd like to tell Dora to stop insulting her, too. And she could only imagine what her brothers, always good at tormenting her, had said to Joe. As if Joe needed anyone to point out her shortcomings. Of course she didn't yell.

"I left Maxie in the temporary museum. You can pick him up there."

Tallulah whirled off like a primary-colored tornado. Most likely planning to cage Maxie up then take him to coffee.

12

Sven Gunderson's last will and testament was unfolded on George Wesley's bed at the Melnik Nursing Home.

The only chairs had wheels. Joe opted to stand, and George didn't try to convince him otherwise. He informed Joe and Bonnie at the top of his lungs that they had gingersnaps for morning coffee break and it started in fifteen minutes.

"So I wonder what the tight old buzzard was worth," Joe said aloud.

Joe had figured out instantly that he could say anything in front of George, who was both deaf and nearsighted in the extreme. But the man knew his gingersnaps.

"I can step out of the room if you—" Bonnie took a step away.

Joe caught her wrist. "Stay. I'm not planning on keeping it a secret and hoarding it. The way my luck goes, my whole fortune is invested in stock for some company that builds pedal sewing machines and buggy harnesses."

Not so, as it turned out. Joe's bum of a father might have been a miser and a semihermit, but the man knew stocks and bonds. The amount staggered him. Joe could now go to school for as long as he wanted without worrying about money. And when he was done with school, he didn't have to get a job.

Shouting his thanks to George's back while George hustled his walker down the nursing home hallway toward the dining room, Joe led Bonnie outside and they drove to his house together.

As they walked inside, Joe said, "Okay, let's sit down and figure out how much money the Melnik Historical Society needs. You're hoping for a grant of a quarter of a million dollars, right? The grant will be in the form of matching funds. So the grant will double any money you raise."

"That's right. I've filed the grant application already, and my understanding is that we've got a good chance."

"Well, plan on me donating the full amount to match it. So plan on a five-hundred-thousand-dollar building."

Bonnie shook her head, obviously overwhelmed. "But—but you can't give the whole thing. I don't expect that." Joe grinned when she staggered on her way to his front room couch and slumped against the cushions.

Joe sat beside her and put his arm around her, afraid she might faint. Her face was white. Joe would have felt bad except he knew she'd recover eventually and be thrilled.

"Nick's an architect, right? Let's hire him right now to design something that will capture the history of Melnik. Do you want a building shaped like a giant mouse, or what?"

"No!" Bonnie sat up, some color returning to her cheeks. She shoved against his chest as if she could stop the horror of a Maxie-shaped museum.

"What's going on here?" Brian appeared at the door just as Bonnie yelled and shoved.

He strode across the room, grabbed Bonnie by the arm, and pulled her to her feet. He shoved her behind him and faced Joe.

Joe rose to his feet to face the assault standing and wiped the smile off his face. Later Brian would regret his temper, but right now Joe was one wrong word, or one grin, away from getting punched right in his dimples. He'd been battered enough for one week.

"Bonnie, tell your brother I didn't hurt you."

"Shut up. Bonnie doesn't take orders from you." Brian's fist clenched and Joe braced himself.

Bonnie shoved Brian to the side. "Will you knock it off?" She punched him in the stomach. Brian grunted and rubbed his belly, glaring at his sister.

"You leave Joe alone. He didn't do anything."

She had a pretty good right cross. Joe figured she'd taught it to Brian. He felt lucky to escape.

Brian scowled at his big sister, who was five inches shorter than him. "Don't protect him. I saw you shoving him. I saw the way he looked at you earlier."

Rolling her eyes, Bonnie placed two hands flat on Brian's chest and shoved him. "You mean like that?"

"Yes, exactly like that."

"I did it because I couldn't believe he was going to contribute so generously to the museum fund and he suggested we build it to be mouse-shaped. Now that you've pointed out how rough I was with him, I owe him an apology. Joe," she said, turning to him, "I'm sorry I—"

"I just had a unit in my psych class about women in abusive relationships. They're always covering for their abusers. Don't pretend—"

Bonnie looked at the ceiling and raised both hands in sincere prayer. "Please, God, save me from college psychology courses."

Joe snickered.

Brian glared at Joe.

Bonnie looked back at Brian. "I told you I'm starting a fund-raiser for the new museum. Joe just inherited a bunch of money from old tightwad Gunderson. He's going to give a lot of it to the museum."

"Mainly because I know it would drive my father crazy." Joe didn't want to come out of this sounding like some humanitarian saint. "My motives aren't exactly pure. The old miser did his best to hurt this town and me. I'm going to use his money to make up for that with the town; then I'm going to take the rest and finish college. Something I put off, mainly because my mother was sick, but my father wouldn't help out and that made it even more impossible."

Brian studied Joe. Joe let him look. And what had Brian meant by, "I saw the way he looked at you"? What way? How had he been "looking" at Bonnie? Joe struggled to make his expression bland and composed, to give no more "looks."

"Now is this settled? Because I've got a lot of work to do today." Bonnie plunked her fists on her slender, beige-swathed hips.

Joe noticed her sparkling eyes and shining intelligence. Then he wondered if what he'd just done qualified as a "look."

Joe focused on Brian. Since the kid wanted to play white knight, maybe he'd help with the house if it benefited his big sister. "If you're really staying here, Brian, I need some help going through this place. Do you realize I haven't even been in either wing of this house yet? I've opened a lot of doors, but none of them have led to the wings. Whatever is to the east of the library or the west of this front room is blocked. I'm starting to think we'll have to get a ladder and break a window to get inside."

Bonnie turned, her brow furrowed. "You can't find the way in? That's weird."

"Why don't we just list the things about this house and my father that aren't weird? That will take less time. There's a door upstairs I couldn't open. It might lead to the east wing. It might just be warped shut, but it felt locked to me. I want to hunt around for stray keys. If we can't find any, I might need help breaking into my own house. What do you say? Are you and Greg up for exploring a haunted house?"

The animosity faded from Brian's face. "Sure, every kid in town wants a crack at this place. I grew up listening to ghost stories all based on the old Gunderson place. I'll boot Greg out of bed."

Brian turned to leave then, his shoulders slouched. He tucked his fingers into his back pockets and turned back. "Look, I'm sorry about before. I just heard Bonnie yell 'No.' I came in as she shoved you. I jumped to conclusions. I should have known you wouldn't go for my geeky big sister."

Bonnie pulled back a fist.

Brian laughed and ran out of the room.

Bonnie went after him.

Joe had to move fast to catch her around the waist. "Let him live. He adores you and you know it."

Looking back, she narrowed her eyes. Joe let her go, raising his arms in surrender. "Okay, kill him if you want. I don't know the rules brothers and sisters live by."

Bonnie shook her head. "I have a zillion things to do about the grant. I need to start a petition drive and draw up plans for a series of fund-raisers. Even though your donation is going to make this all very easy for us, I want the town to chip in. They need to have ownership of this project. Besides, the block grant asks for the community's input and requires their involvement, so we have a lot of work to do."

"Too bad you're so busy. I'd like help exploring this house. You'd be a lot better at discovering. . .uh. . .Melnik artifacts"—Joe covered his desire to laugh with a carefully cleared throat—"than any of us."

"Maybe I could call the historical society. Those women would be glad to come over and help."

Joe hesitated. He wasn't sure why. "I don't think I want the whole town in here going through stuff I haven't had a chance to see yet. I mean, if someone stole something, I'd never even know."

Bonnie's shoulders squared in indignation. "No one in Melnik would steal anything."

"Of course they would, some of them."

"They would not. This is an honest town."

"This is a town full of human beings, some good, some bad. I don't know which is which, so I'm not throwing the doors open to everyone."

"You've lived in the city too long."

A crash from the kitchen had them wheeling around and dashing toward the noise. They heard the back door slam before they got in the room. A drawer had been pulled all the way out and lay on the ugly cracked tile of the kitchen floor. Papers had exploded in all directions. Joe dashed past the mess to get to the door that had slammed. He saw a young boy—the one who had been there last night—dart between the bushes in his backyard.

Bonnie came up beside him. "That's Kevin Melnik." The boy was visible through the thin branches of the neglected privet hedge.

"No one in this town would steal anything, huh?"

Bonnie stood with Joe at the back door, staring after Kevin. The boy obviously had his arms full, but of what, Joe couldn't tell.

"Well, almost no one. I'd have told you to keep your eye on Kevin if he came to a cleanup. Not because he's known to steal, but because he's got a lot of reasons to hate the Gundersons. I suppose he might be in a street gang if he lived in the city. But out here we take care of our own. No one with any sense would give this up for Omaha."

"Here's a newsflash, Baby Mama: Everyone lives in the city these days. Little towns like this are dying. I admire your efforts to slow that down, but you can't stop it."

"Sure we can. And don't call me Baby Mama. It's ridiculous."

"Your brother called you that last night and you laughed."

"Well, you're not my brother."

Joe turned to face her, saw her soft, kind brown eyes, and lost his train of thought. No truer words were ever spoken. He didn't have one single brotherly feeling for Bonnie Simpson. He did an internal face slapping to get his mind back on what he'd intended to say. "I did the math. You became a mother when you were twenty-one. Your oldest brother was what?"

"Seventeen."

"So you would have had to give birth at age four. You're a baby mama."

Bonnie's lips quirked. "Well, put like that, I suppose you're right."

Joe felt like he had had a lucky escape from her temper. She was so mild mannered, but underneath was a little fireball. She was also a hopeless optimist, but he didn't see the point of forcing her to admit the obvious.

"Anyway, sorry if I've hurt your feelings about Melnik, Home of the World's Largest Field Mouse, but if you could postpone your fund-raising binge for a few hours, I'd appreciate the help."

"I'd like to help. This old house is fascinating. Thanks. I'll stay."

Her shoulders were still a bit stiff, and she didn't give him her usual quiet smile, but she was staying.

Joe counted himself a lucky man.

─────

Bonnie couldn't believe her luck!

Going through the old Gunderson house was every museum curator's dream. Well, sure, some of them wanted King Tut's tomb, but most of them would rub their hands together at the chance to go through an old house that had never been cleaned out, having been in the same family of hoarders for one hundred fifty years, *and* have the blessing of the new owner to take anything of historical value.

And Joe was right. There seemed to be no way into the two huge wings of the house.

"Maybe they closed them off. Took out the doorways and just boarded over them and plastered the entrance."

"But why?"

Joe shrugged. "I don't have a good reason, but when no good reason presents itself for an odd situation, you have to start makin' stuff up." He grinned at her. Those unbelievable dimples. She wondered if he knew just how. . .distracting. . . they were. When he turned them on her, it was as if every other thought drained straight out of her head.

They sat together in the library. A pile of books and papers had built slowly into a mountain. Her brothers had done good work rapping on walls and trying every door, but they'd found nothing, basement to attic, that led to the two towers.

They'd left to see friends, promising to return with tools to pry that one last upstairs doorway open. It had to be that door. If not, they were going in through the windows.

"I'm almost hoping we have to break a window to get in." Joe sat with his back resting against the fireplace. He had a teetering stack of papers on his left that they'd hauled down from the attic. "That's more of an adventure."

"What do you think we'll find over there? Gold? Museum-quality furniture? Empty rooms full of dust?"

"Bones?"

Gasping, Bonnie set a box full of toys aside.

Joe laughed. "If you could see your face."

Bonnie relaxed and her temper sparked. She hadn't even known she possessed a temper until she'd met Joe. Well, sure, she'd lost her temper with her brothers, but that was different. "You're just lucky I have too much respect for artifacts to toss these at you."

She pulled a piggy bank out of the box. It was just like the one that was now buried in the rubble of the museum. She pulled her arm back as if she were going to hurl it at him. "This is solid iron. It could do some real damage."

Joe set his papers aside and rolled onto his hands and knees to look in her box. "This is great stuff. Look at this little rocking horse with a pull string." Joe set it on the floor and pulled it slowly. The brightly painted iron horse tipped forward and backward as if it galloped, the tinkling of tinny music accompanying each turn of the wheels.

"Look at these." Bonnie opened a wooden box containing metal disks. Joe leaned closer. Bonnie pulled one of the disks out and handed it to him. Joe was so close she could smell him. He should smell like dust and mold considering all the old boxes they'd dug through today. But instead he smelled like some brand of masculine soap and shampoo that none of her brothers had ever used.

"'Roosevelt for President'?" Joe lifted the disk and held it so the light shined on it. "Teddy Roosevelt?"

"Yeah, there are lots more."

Shaking his head, Joe took the box. "These might be valuable."

Bonnie's heart trembled a bit. She hadn't thought of how much they were worth in cash; she'd thought of—

"I'll donate the whole bunch of them to the museum. If there's more stuff like this, the Melnik Historical Society could actually become quite an attraction in the region. It could take off and make real money."

Bonnie's soft gasp of pleasure interrupted him. He looked up from the button, way too close to her, and saw her excitement.

He smiled.

Oh, that blasted gorgeous smile. It faded. His eyes flickered to her lips.

A creaking sound that had to be someone walking up the basement steps sounded clearly in the room.

"There it is again." Bonnie shuddered.

"I've almost gotten used to it," Joe said, but she thought his jaw was a little tense.

"And do you ever get the feeling you're being watched?" Bonnie regretted saying it the minute it was out of her mouth. Talk about paranoid.

"You feel it, too?" Joe looked away from the direction of the noise.

A sigh of relief almost made Bonnie glad she sounded like a fraidy cat. "Yes. What is that? I've never felt anything like it before."

"When I was in the army, we were trained to be alert to the area around us. It's like someone is. . .almost. . .touching your back. Very weird. You can't *feel* anything really, no bony fingers."

"Joe!" Bonnie shook her head. "Stop it."

He laughed. "But it's usually not your imagination. There are subtle clues, noises, changes in shadows that your mind registers subliminally. It's a feeling I've learned to trust."

He looked at the walls of the room, obviously empty except for them. "But how could anyone be watching us?"

Shaking her head, Bonnie remained silent.

"Maybe," Joe said, grinning at her, "it's someone living in the wings of this house. Maybe the Gundersons locked up their crazy relatives." He got a spooky, wavering tone to his voice and had a sly look in his eyes. "Maybe they sneak out at night to feed on stray *cats*!" Joe yelled and jumped at her.

Bonnie squealed. Joe started laughing his head off. Bonnie growled and went for his throat, and he caught her hard against his chest. When their eyes met, the laughing and growling ended like someone had switched off a light.

Time passed in silence while she looked into his kind eyes. A long time, yet not enough time.

"Bonnie, I—"

"It's so—"

Talking on top of each other, they stopped. Joe leaned closer. His lips touched hers, and in the middle of a musty room filled with neglect and grime and years of isolation, Bonnie found something she'd given up on as the years passed, with her whole heart being given to raise her orphaned brothers.

She didn't regret that. They'd needed her. She'd needed them just as badly. But she'd paid a price and given up her dearest dreams. And now maybe there was still time to make some dreams come true.

Joe deepened the kiss and wrapped his arms around her waist just as her arms encircled his neck.

The front door slammed open.

"We got the crowbar."

They jerked apart.

"My brothers." Bonnie's eyes momentarily fell closed. Then she noticed she was sitting on Joe's lap. How long had they been kissing?

Not long enough, that was for sure.

She practically jumped to her feet and charged the door, putting space between herself and Joe.

She glanced back to see Joe studiously sifting through papers, apparently unaffected by that kiss. A kiss that had changed her whole world and altered everything she knew about herself.

Thinking back, she realized she'd practically thrown herself at him. He'd been too polite, probably too sorry for her, to push her away. He'd made it more than clear that his life didn't include Melnik and its mouse and certainly not her.

If he felt anything, it was probably embarrassment and regret.

Brian came into the library before she got to the door. With a grin on his face that said he was excited about busting stuff up, he held up an iron bar. "Let's get that door open."

His grin faded when he looked at Bonnie. She wondered what on earth the brat thought he saw. She couldn't visibly look like she'd been kissed, could she? His eyes went from her to Joe and back.

Bonnie realized that darkness had fallen while she and Joe sorted papers. The lights in the dingy library had been on from the beginning, so she'd never noticed the sunset. But the hallway behind Brian was shrouded in darkness.

Greg followed with two flat white pizza boxes. "Let's eat first. I'm starving." He looked at Bonnie and his eyes narrowed. No way. She didn't believe they could tell they'd interrupted her and Joe. She knew her brothers. There wasn't a sensitive or insightful bone in their bodies.

Joe came up behind her. "I want that door open before we quit for the night. I don't like thinking I'm locked out of over half my house. I feel like my ghosts, or whatever's back there, own part it." Then he sniffed long and loud. "But we could eat first."

Brian waved his arm as if to shoo Bonnie and Joe past. Joe slipped past her.

"We've got work to do." Bonnie crossed her arms and tapped her toe.

"C'mon, Bon-Bon," Brian wheedled. She'd heard that tone a zillion times before.

"I want that door open."

"Get your priorities straight. Ghost busting? Pizza?"

"Joe might be in danger. And I sent you boys over here."

NOSY IN NEBRASKA

"Quit calling me a boy, Bon-Bon," Greg called over her shoulder. "I'm a grown man."

Bonnie snorted at the little punk. The little six-foot-two punk. "*You* might be in danger."

Sure, she wanted to kill them herself several times a day. But no one *else* was allowed to hurt them. Until they'd explored every inch of this house, she'd never rest. And did she ever need *rest*! Her eyes burned. Her lids weighed a hundred pounds each. She could blame it on dust, but nobody was fooled. She needed sleep. She didn't hold out much hope she'd get it until she was sure this house was safe. She should call Jeffie and his first grade class.

"No contest—let's eat." Brian deserted her.

Bonnie watched Joe and Brian follow Greg as if he were the Pizza Pied Piper and they were a couple of rats. As far as the comparison to rats, it was too close to call.

"Let's eat in the kitchen," Joe said. "We've got the table cleaned off now. We can dig into this house tomorrow. You know we're just going to find more dust and cobwebs."

She heard a click inches from her on the right. She looked and saw only a tall shelf. She felt that crawling feeling on her neck again, too. Just like Joe had described it.

She was hearing noises everywhere now. This was why the house had to be searched top to bottom. To help her shake off this feeling that the paintings were watching her and the bookcases might swing open to hidden rooms.

She remembered those bats exploding out of the gabled tower and the impression that a hand was going to grab her and pull her into the bowels of this awful house.

She wanted to yell at Joe and her brothers. Force them to deal with that door. If it didn't open to anything but another closet, then they'd go into those wings through a window. Those lazy, pizza-eating, mule-stubborn men—

A long, loud yawn stopped her from yelling. Another creak barely registered. She was hearing creaking here and at home; she'd probably hear creaking at Jansson's Café if she wasn't careful. Good grief, old buildings creaked—everybody knew that.

With a shake of her overly imaginative head, she ignored the creepy paranoia that plagued her, no doubt a direct result of exhaustion and starvation. She realized the pizza *did* smell great. She hadn't eaten for hours. Maybe she was weak from hunger as much as exhaustion.

Smiling, she abandoned her plans to attack and followed her nose.

The hand lunged forward and missed.

Disappointed, he eased back into the shadowy corner created by the window seats and slipped into the bookcase passage. He'd almost had her.

He'd been completely exposed for a few seconds, right after she'd heard the click. The risk of stepping out of the shadows thrilled him. He would have had her before she could call out. . .or maybe right after.

He shivered, thinking of the fun.

His door clicked shut and he made his way along the narrow walkway to his peephole in the kitchen. How he would have loved to just—presto!—make her disappear. The shock, the desperate search, the fear building and building. They deserved it for taking what was his.

He put his eyes to the crack in the kitchen wall and relished the power.

He muffled his laughter, and the woman looked over her shoulder straight at him. She couldn't see. None of them could. He was a ghost after all. *That's it! A worthy name.*

The Ghost looked back at those he haunted, and smiled.

13

Thanks for inviting me to church. I'd have never found it. I hadn't had time to think about where to find the church."

"*The* church? Try four churches." Greg barreled down the gravel road.

Joe peeked at the speedometer. Forty-five miles per hour. It seemed closer to eighty.

"Four? In this tiny town?"

"Well, they're not *big* churches."

Joe rode in the backseat next to Brian, who must have pulled his brother into some plot, because the young men had immediately claimed their seats, assuring that Joe and Bonnie couldn't sit together. Like riding together in the backseat of Brian's Grand Am with the brothers in the front seat was within a country mile of romantic.

"We're getting that room open this afternoon." Joe was determined not to sleep another night in that house without exploring the wings. The creaking in that place was driving him crazy. He'd had the sense of someone standing over his bed in the night, but now he couldn't remember if he'd even come fully awake. The whole thing was probably a dream.

"And I want to ask Nick's advice about refurbishing."

"He goes to our church. We'll ask him there."

The dust kicked up past the windows as Greg tore down the road. Joe had the admittedly paranoid sense that the Brothers Grimm were taking him out in the country to dump him. But Bonnie wouldn't let them, would she? She'd sure jumped away fast when he'd kissed her, and she'd practically run to the safety of her brother. As if they were playing hide-and-seek and Brian had shouted, "Olly, olly, oxen free!" instead of "Crowbar."

"So. . ." Bonnie looked at Greg then twisted to see Joe behind Greg, and Brian straight behind her. The move was worthy of a circus contortionist. "Since we're on our way to church and we're Christians here—right?"

"Yeah." Joe heard her brothers echo him.

Bonnie continued, "And none of us believe in ghosts—"

"Well, there's the Holy Ghost." Brian shrugged one shoulder.

Bonnie reached back between her seat and the car door and grabbed Brian's shin. She must have sharp fingernails, because he yelped.

264

"In general, we agree there's no such thing as a ghost, *right?*" She said it in a tone that threatened anyone who didn't agree with her.

"Yes." The three men were some kind of a barbershop quartet now. Minus one.

"So how come the whole time I'm in that house, I feel like I'm being watched?"

Joe looked at Brian and was a little surprised to see a shiver of fear. "You feel it, too?" Joe asked as he looked Brian in the eye.

"I just figured I was spooked by that creepy house." He glanced at Joe. "No offense."

"None taken. I own it, and I think it's creepy."

"It's weird." Greg drove the car across some wicked washboard bumps. He had one wrist balanced on top of the wheel. Joe decided then and there he was never riding with this reckless kid again.

"Joe?" Bonnie looked him straight in the eye.

"I feel it, too." Joe caught Greg's eyes in the mirror and saw relief.

Bonnie stared forward. "So is it the rumors all the kids in Melnik have cooked up over the years?"

"It must be." Greg sounded relieved.

"Yeah, we're trained to think it's spooky, so we're imagining things." Brian nodded.

"I've never even heard those rumors."

Brian and Greg glared at Joe.

"Work with us here," Brian muttered. "We don't want to be chickens."

Joe wished he could blame it on childhood fear, but it just didn't wash.

"Maybe it's those ugly old paintings on the wall." Brian pulled on his lower lip. "You know, you hear about artists who paint so that the pictures seem to follow you everywhere. Maybe the Gundersons' paintings are like that."

"Maybe. But I don't like it." Bonnie sounded firm and in charge. Joe could well imagine her running these boys all through their growing-up years. He had that same gift with children. Firm but kind.

"I want that house searched from top to bottom. No excuses." Bonnie slashed the air like she was karate chopping the ghost. "Joe, I know you're worried about losing your stuff, but turn forty people loose in that house, Melnik citizens who fight grime like Eliot Ness fought the mob, and there'll be no spooks left. They will have been cleared out by the bright light of day and Lemon Pledge."

"I've been wondering what Kevin Melnik took out of the house. I looked into that drawer he dumped earlier, before he got there, and there wasn't much important I could see. That's why I didn't bother chasing him down or calling the police."

"He'll be at church today. His foster parents, the Andersons, attend Country

Christian." Bonnie pointed at the white clapboard church Greg was hurling the car toward. "We'll corral him and ask."

Joe shrugged. "I've heard you talk about all the kid's been through. I'd like to offer him part of the inheritance. Just enough to get him through college, give him a chance at a good start."

"Well, college is no guarantee of a good life. His dad and mom were bad news, and his ancestors have been bad news back five generations—so Kevin is fighting long odds to make something of himself. Money might make things worse instead of better if he's got his dad's drinking and drugging problems, plus Wilkie's love of the casinos."

"I'll think of something."

"So what about the cleaning party?"

Joe was silent as they turned into the church's parking lot, tires crunching gravel. A ring of trees surrounded the church, and Joe saw a quaint cemetery behind the steepled building.

It's like a church out of some peaceful dream. Simple, beautiful, welcoming.

Joe's heart softened to the town of Melnik just for having this little church. He'd been raised in a church like this. Even in great big Omaha there were little churches. His grandparents had faithfully attended with his mother and him. During his time in the service, he'd moved around a lot and learned to enjoy a more contemporary service and all the programs big churches offered, but Melnik's Country Christian Church looked like home.

A lonely, empty place in his heart seemed to fill up as he studied the modest building. He was suddenly in absolutely no hurry to get his house in order and leave town. No college semesters started until fall anyway. Well, ignoring summer school, but Joe could ignore it if he wanted. Maybe he should stay at least that long. Clean out his house, help Bonnie with her museum. Get her brothers out of town and see if she'd be interested in sitting in his lap again, trying another kiss.

God, thank You for this time in Melnik. Bless these people and bless this little church and all who go here.

As if God answered the prayer by putting a longing in his heart, Joe decided he'd prolong things by sifting through his creepy inheritance on his own. And while he sifted, he'd attend this church and maybe learn to worship closely with others.

He gave Bonnie a heartfelt look and prayed silently that she'd embrace this little bit of a dream. "I want more time with the house." Surely God would speak to her heart. She'd see the wisdom.

"That's dumb."

Or not.

Bonnie's mouth scrunched up. "You'll be safer if we get the whole place opened up and cleaned. If someone attacked you that night, they'll be less likely to come back with so many people around. Maybe we'll find a broken or unlocked window. We can repair it and he won't have a way in."

"Or. . ." Brian gave his best imitation of a spooky ghost, ruined by laughter. "Maybe we'll find a secret passageway. Maybe it'll lead to the cemetery and all the undead who walk the night." Brian laughed too hard to go on.

Joe backhanded him in the stomach.

Brian clutched his belly and laughed harder.

An only child, Joe had never had a brother to beat up on. If his mom had picked somewhat less of a lowlife to fall in love with, there could have been some brothers and sisters. It might have been like this. Irritating, but kind of fun.

Greg braked the car to a crunchy halt on the gravel. Bonnie unbuckled her seat belt and opened her door. "One more day, Joe. Then I'm calling in the big guns to clear that house of the undead who walk the night and anyone else who's annoying me."

Joe hoped that didn't include him. "Big guns?"

"Yeah." Bonnie's eyes narrowed.

Joe felt like a gunslinger had come to Melnik.

"Tomorrow I'm telling Dora."

Chills ran up Joe's spine.

He hadn't made a single one of the personal hygiene changes Dora had recommended. She'd be sure to notice. Worse yet, she'd be sure to comment on it.

He felt safer sticking with the undead who walked the night.

⁓

Bonnie always felt restored by her morning worship.

She'd enjoyed singing the old hymns side by side with Joe. He'd visited with the other parishioners and had a long, friendly talk with Pastor Bremmen.

Even her brothers seemed to have let their hackles down. Once they found out Nick and Carrie were going back to the house with Bonnie and Joe, they'd agreed to let a carload of old friends lure them away.

When they got back to Joe's mausoleum, Bonnie itched to get on with battering down that door, but Nick was in love with the architecture and Joe was enjoying the company. Nick slowly circled the outside of the house, telling Joe about the unique qualities of the structure.

It took half an hour before Joe and Nick even went inside. Bonnie and Carrie followed the menfolk around quietly. For Bonnie that was normal, but Carrie usually thrust herself into the center of things.

Not today. Carrie was too busy glowing.

She caught Bonnie's arm as soon as the men disappeared. "I have to tell someone. Nick's making me wait, but I'll explode if I don't tell. We're going to have a baby."

Bonnie couldn't look away from the glow of pure joy on Carrie's face. "Congratulations!" Bonnie gave her a fierce hug. She was happy for Carrie. She was.

It had hurt that the nicest guy Bonnie had met, one who shared Bonnie's love of books and old things and small towns, had picked cute, smart, ambitious, courageous—well, courageous except for mice—Carrie over her.

For a few precious days, Bonnie had dreamed that she'd met her soul mate. Nick loved the same things Bonnie did, but Nick also loved Carrie.

Bonnie couldn't blame him. She'd been disappointed but not hurt or jealous. Everyone in her life had picked someone or something over her.

Of course Tyler picked his wife. If he hadn't, Bonnie would have been furious.

Of course Greg and Brian went to college. She'd have chased them with a skillet if they hadn't.

Of course Nick picked Carrie.

"Why hasn't he let you tell?"

"We just found out Friday. He wants it to be a big event. He's organized a party. We've invited the whole family over for supper tonight."

Bonnie's eyes widened. "Your *whole* family? *Both* sides?"

Carrie nodded. "His side, too. His brothers, his sister, and his parents are all flying in. They're meeting at the airport in Omaha and driving up together. They should be here about five. He hinted that it's something big to get them here, so maybe they've guessed, but he hasn't told. It'll be great. Potluck. He's already got a thirty-pound turkey and two hams roasting."

Another thing Bonnie would envy Carrie for was her huge family and the fact that a lot of them lived close at hand. But envy was a sin, and Bonnie wasn't going to indulge in it.

They let the men get ahead of them so they could whisper about every detail of the pregnancy. Then finally, after the men had long gone inside, they caught up. The two women tried to look innocent while the men talked about crown molding and the difference between plaster and drywall and a bunch of other things Bonnie had trouble being interested in—since she was busy wallowing in self-pity.

It might have gotten out of hand if a mouse hadn't chosen that moment to run out from behind the kitchen stove. Carrie screamed and launched herself straight up. Nick caught her on the way down and laughed.

Joe gave them a strange look then arched a brow at Bonnie. She shrugged and crossed her eyes at him. He smiled that perfect smile, and Bonnie looked away before she did something stupid, like launch herself into Joe's arms.

Since the house was completely infested with mice, they proceeded to tour the house with Carrie either in Nick's arms or close enough to jump there if necessary. The screaming definitely took Bonnie's mind off her troubles.

Nick stopped in front of the locked door in Joe's bedroom. He jiggled the knob and crouched down to stare in the empty keyhole, frowning. "This isn't locked." He tugged on the door. "The door swings out; nothing heavy resting against it would matter. Maybe it's barred from the inside."

Bonnie saw Joe and Nick exchange a look.

"Someone would have to do that deliberately, right?" Bonnie asked. "They'd have to be in there to bar it."

Nick nodded.

"Do you think this leads to the wings? It's strange that the entrance to them would be up here in a bedroom. Why not downstairs? Why not at the end of the upstairs hall? Why not both? Why not a big, obvious entrance? Double doors, even."

Nick shrugged. "There's a blank wall in the library and the living room that are the obvious places for doors. I'm guessing they closed the wings off. Maybe there was a time when they didn't want to pay to heat this much space. Maybe there weren't doors, just open passageways. They could have framed in the openings and plastered over them."

Bonnie came up beside Joe. "They could have made any number of changes. As far as I know, no one has ever been in Gunderson's house."

"No one who's still alive," Carrie added.

Bonnie and Carrie exchanged a look. The men were newcomers, but Bonnie and Carrie had roots in this town. Carrie's went deeper, right back to the founders. But Carrie was a farm girl. Bonnie's family had been here a long time, and she'd grown up in town and knew the eccentricities of all the inhabitants as well as anyone, even Dora.

"It's been a long, long time since this house has been a welcoming place, if it ever was. Almost from the first the Gundersons have been reclusive snobs." Bonnie stared at the door.

"I want to know what's back there." Carrie's nose for news twitched.

"Me, too." Joe rose and crossed his arms. "Are we going to have to chop through this door with an ax?"

Nick shook his head. "This is a valuable door, solid oak—it matches the woodwork. I'd hate to ruin it, and it would be a lot of work. The wood is thick, and if it ages well—and this has—oak chops about as well as iron."

"So what do we do?" Joe asked. "I'm not letting another day pass without getting to the bottom. . .and the top. . .and the wings of this house."

Something creaked behind the door. Her eyes riveted, Bonnie asked, "How many times have we heard that exact sound?"

"Way too many." Joe pressed his ear to the door. "Way, way too many. That is *not* an old house settling."

The creak came again, this time several, steady, like someone walking. Joe straightened with a jerk. He turned to the rest of the group. "Someone's back there."

"But who? Kids? If they can get in, why can't we?" Nick shook his head. "We were all over the outside of this house. There's nothing that looks like an outside entrance to those wings."

"I don't know who, but whoever it is attacked me that first night."

"But I thought you got hit by the *closet* door, not this one." Bonnie gnawed her bottom lip, giving Joe's bruised forehead a close look.

"Maybe I did, or maybe I got it mixed up. Right now, I'm not so sure just what happened."

"Give me a minute to think." Nick studied the room then opened the closet door right beside the locked door. He stepped inside. There were clothes hanging on both sides of the expansive walk-in closet. "This is huge for the time. A lot of houses this age didn't even include closets. Even rich people had only a few changes of clothing."

Nick shoved a rack of moth-eaten suits to the side with the distinctive scrape of wire hangers on an iron rack. He ran his hand over the blank wall behind, then knocked. "I think this is one narrow layer of plaster and lath. We can go through the wall faster than we can go through solid oak. I hate to tear up your house, though."

He and Joe exchanged a long look.

The floor creaked again.

Joe's eyes returned to the wall. "Get the ax."

14

Nick came back upstairs only seconds later. No ax, but he had the sheriff. Joe turned away from the wall at the grim look on Junior's face.

"Joe, I need to you come right now."

His gut twisting, Joe wondered if Junior had changed his mind about hanging his father's murder on the new guy in Melnik.

"What's the matter?"

Junior caught his arm. "George Wesley had a heart attack. He's in the hospital in Gillespie and he's not expected to make it. They just phoned. He's asking for you, hollering that he needs to talk to you before he dies. It's really riling him up. The doctor asked me to bring you down fast. If talking to you will calm him down, there's a chance he could make it."

Joe was already moving down the stairs fast at Junior's side.

"Bonnie, honey, you coming?" Junior looked over his shoulder. "I might have to stay; there's some legal stuff George wants cleared up. Joe'll need a ride home."

Glancing back, Joe saw that Bonnie had followed, as well as Nick and Carrie.

"Sure." Bonnie jogged after them down the stairs. "I'll lock up here then follow along."

Joe heard Nick and Carrie say something about company coming over as he jumped into the squad car. Junior backed out of the driveway so fast that rocks spit and the tires squealed. He turned his siren and lights on, shifted into DRIVE, and floored the black and white.

Joe looked back, and for a split second, a face appeared in the upper window of the west wing.

Joe blinked and the face was gone.

"Junior!"

"What?"

Before Joe could say anything about it, or even be sure he'd seen it, Junior took the nearest corner on two wheels. Then he floored it again.

"What is it?" Junior drove like a pack of wolves were on his tail.

"N–nothing. I guess." What had he seen?

"Get out of my house."

They cleared the city limits within seconds. Junior stomped on the accelerator. Joe locked his seat belt tight with a loud click. He grabbed a leather strap above the car door. There was no sense talking with the siren shrieking, so Joe just held on tight.

Junior radioed they were coming. A nurse met them at the door. She grabbed Joe's arm and ran. "He won't settle down. Just let him talk."

"Get Gunderson's son here now!" Joe heard George, loud even for the deaf lawyer, long before they got to the room.

"Here he is. Here he is, Mr. Wesley," the nurse shouted as she dragged Joe forward.

Joe almost skidded into George's bed. The gaunt old man grabbed at his arm. The heart monitor beeped its loud, shrill proof-of-life. Too fast, unsteady...George's life reduced to electronic rap music.

Joe caught the arthritically gnarled hand and leaned close.

The old man roared, "I've got papers for you, Joe."

Joe stumbled backward at the eardrum-shattering volume. Leaning close had been entirely unnecessary. The lawyer's grip held or Joe might have fallen over backward.

"I gave you the will, but I have more. Gunderson wanted them delivered after you'd been in town a few weeks. But I have to talk to you before I hand them over. Destroy this town. Gunderson wanted to. They're in my files in my room at . . ." A coughing fit stopped the onslaught of words. George let Joe loose to grab at his chest.

"The future of the town, the future of every—" A gasp of pain cut through the shouting.

A nurse pushed Joe aside. George's hand groped again for Joe's.

"Melnik is in your hands. You've—"

"Tell him what he needs to hear!" The nurse hit a button that set a loud buzzer off. "And yell!"

The woman whipped back the white blanket pulled up to George's chin.

"We'll find it, George," Joe shouted as he looked George in the eye, over the nurse's shoulder, and saw George nod. "We'll get it. Everything will be okay."

A doctor entered and began shouting questions at the nurse. Next came a man running with a rolling cart.

The nurse injected something into George's IV line.

"We'll do it, George. Don't worry," Joe hollered as the old man gasped in pain then let his eyes flicker shut.

The injection, combined with hearing what Joe shouted, calmed the old man down, and the coughing and gasping eased. Chaos reigned as the nurses and doctors talked fast and moved faster. Junior pulled Joe out the door as two more people passed them going into the room. As Joe backed against the far wall to get out of the way, a loud, solid alarm went off—the cry of a heart monitor that had lost the beat.

Joe gave Junior a wild look. Junior shook his head, grim with worry. The hospital main entrance doors at the end of the corridor slid open with a *whoosh*. Joe saw Bonnie running.

By the time she reached them, a doctor came out of George Wesley's room, pulling a surgical cap off his head as if he barely had the strength.

He came up to them. "I'm sorry, folks. He didn't make it."

The medical smell and the sad-faced doctor reminded Joe too much of his mother's last painful days. "If he hadn't been so agitated, you could have saved him. I'm sorry there was something about my legal business that upset him so much."

The doctor clapped a gentle hand on Joe's shoulder. "His heart has been failing for years. Being agitated probably kept him alive longer."

The doctor looked at Junior. "His kids have been informed that he was admitted. They knew the end was near. If you want to stick around, make sure they take the news okay and get home safely. . ."

Junior nodded. He looked at Joe. "I heard what George said about the paperwork, but we can't just go rummaging around in his confidential files. When he was alive, with his permission, yes. But now that he's dead, we'll need to do it right. The only other lawyer in the county is on vacation, fishing in Canada. He's from here, Gillespie, and he's also the county attorney. I'll call the courthouse and leave a message. They'll have someone covering for him, but no one will even check the machine until tomorrow morning."

Bonnie spoke up. "I could call Tyler. He'd know what to do. It's kind of late. I don't know if he'd come up."

"You can at least ask him." Junior nodded.

The entrance door slid open. An older woman, leaning on the arm of a gray-haired man, came in, her face buried in one hand, crying. The doctor caught Junior's eyes and jerked his head toward the couple.

It struck Joe that these people, who looked beyond retirement age, must be George's children. It was impossible not to compare that to the age he'd been when his mother died. Bonnie had lost her parents even younger.

Junior nodded to the doctor then looked at Bonnie, frowning. "I don't know if there could be any trouble, but someone in Melnik killed Sven Gunderson—maybe it was Clara, maybe not. If Sven was killed over money, there might be something in those files a killer might want. Can one or both of you go to George's room and make sure no one gets to his files before I have a chance to secure them?"

"I'll do it," Bonnie quickly agreed.

"Thanks." Junior headed for the crying woman.

"That's George's oldest daughter." Bonnie's eyes filled with tears, and Joe marveled at her sympathy. He hardly knew anyone well enough to cry for them.

"He's got four kids and they all live close by. We might as well get out of the way."

Bonnie hugged both newcomers and expressed sympathy. Joe hung back, and although the couple gave him a curious look, they headed quickly down the hall in the direction of George's room.

Joe and Bonnie headed for Bonnie's car.

She slid into the driver's seat and pulled out her cell phone. "Tyler's my brother, the oldest of the three boys. He works at a big law firm in Omaha. He'll know what to do."

Bonnie keyed in a number, and Joe listened quietly as Bonnie explained the situation.

"Are you sure? You don't have to come if you don't want to. Could you do it from there?"

A long silence stretched.

"Well, that's great. Yes, we'd love the help. I don't want to cause trouble, though."

Silence.

"Oh. Yes, sure, I'd really love to see the boys again."

She sounded so sad. Joe looked at her, the downturn of her lips, the furrow between her brows.

"That's great, Ty. I love you. Thank you."

She snapped the phone shut and stared at it in her hand.

"What was that about?"

Bonnie started, as if she'd been so lost in thought she'd forgotten he was there. Her bottom lip trembled, but she firmed it as she tucked her cell into her purse. "Nothing. It's just—Tyler doesn't get up very often. He's so busy. I haven't seen the boys in a while."

Joe knew there was more to it. "How long?"

Bonnie started the car and reached for the lever between them to shift into Drive. "We were there last Thanksgiving for an hour or two."

"He lives in Omaha and you haven't seen him in almost six months and then only for an hour or two? What's up?" Joe couldn't believe how snoopy he was. He knew better than to invade someone's privacy like this. But she just seemed so upset. It might help to talk.

Bonnie shrugged one shoulder as she pulled out onto the four-lane highway that cut through Gillespie. "His wife thinks we're. . .oh, Green Acres or something. She acts like our small-town ways will turn her boys into hicks."

"It's not like you're living in an undiscovered tribe deep in the rainforest."

"I know." Bonnie nodded. "We all know that. She just wants Tyler for herself. 'A man will leave his mother and be united to his wife.' That's scriptural. I need to respect her wishes. To fight with her would just cause trouble in their relationship."

Joe noticed that Bonnie stayed in the slow lane and drove cautiously. Yeah, she'd be a real bad influence on a child.

"I needed Tyler so badly when Mom and Dad died. He got married the Christmas of his first year of college. He and Liza just fell madly in love and got married really fast. I felt so abandoned, and I guess Liza could tell." Bonnie steered her way down the hilly, winding two-lane highway. The ditches were heavy with lush green grass. The fields were striped with the green of newly sprouted corn.

"I'm sure I was rude to her and clingy about Tyler. I got off on a really bad foot with her, and it's my own fault." A farmhouse popped up, surrounded by windbreaks and outbuildings. As they drove along, a herd of black cattle appeared, baby calves gamboling among their mothers, who grazed in rocky meadows.

"Tyler has been trying to keep the peace ever since. And I've learned not to intrude." In the midst of this pastoral calm, Joe felt his hackles rise. As if sweet, shy Bonnie could be rude. He even doubted clingy. If anything, the pillars of her character were generosity and self-sacrifice. He bet she'd bent over backward to be careful of her new sister-in-law's feelings. And meanwhile, Bonnie had little brothers to raise alone. Where was Liza? A new adult woman in the family should have helped, not made things harder. Why was bringing up those two little boys Bonnie's job alone?

Tyler abandoned them.

Bonnie stuck with them.

Nagging wife or not, Tyler should have helped with Brian and Greg. He probably should have taken over, taken them into his home. As a married man, he had a more stable life than Bonnie. When did Bonnie's turn come to go back to college, to have some freedom, to recapture her lost young womanhood?

Joe realized how angry he was getting and gave his head a tiny shake. It was none of his business. In the city he wouldn't have known or cared about the trauma of his neighbors. Privacy was far more important than a snoopy bunch of neighbors who knew every time you took a wrong step.

Melnik the fishbowl—no, thank you.

Trying not to get involved in Bonnie's personal trouble, he got back to the point. "So Tyler's coming to help us find out what had George so upset? That's great."

"Yeah, Liza has a meeting that will last all afternoon and evening."

"On a Sunday?"

Bonnie nodded. "So Tyler can come up—he didn't say this, but I read between the lines—then get back before Liza catches him."

"Catches him? Like coming to Melnik is a crime and she's a cop?"

Bonnie smiled as she gave a slow-moving tractor time to pull off onto the shoulder so she could pass the wide rig. There was no one else on the highway for as far as Joe could see. They'd met maybe two cars since they'd left Gillespie.

Bonnie gave Joe a smile that struggled to turn up on the corners. "It's all right, Joe. I'm used to Liza. They've got a solid marriage, and I'm not going to interfere with it by being a burden."

Joe didn't know much about having a solid marriage. His grandparents were great, but what couple from that generation wasn't? His mom had never, to Joe's knowledge, so much as dated another man after her disastrous relationship with Sven Gunderson.

They arrived back in Melnik in short order.

Bonnie offered, "You want to go home? I told Tyler I'd wait for him at the nursing home, but it'll be awhile."

"I'll wait with you. If Junior's suspicions are right, whoever killed my f–father"—Joe said the word then felt a little sick, as if he'd uttered a profanity before God—"may have some interest in those files. We might not be the only ones who want them."

"You really think Sven's killer might try to get in George's room?"

"I think it's a strong possibility." Joe quit studying the gracious colonial brick structure of Melnik Nursing Home as Bonnie pulled into its parking lot. He turned to her. "You might go in there and find yourself alone with a murderer."

15

N o killer yet. But Frieda Curzinski was going to bore her to death, so it
was kind of the same.

Bonnie wished she had the spine to run the woman off. Of course,
the old bat's walker made any running unlikely. But Frieda was lonely and
unaffected by subtle hints.

Bonnie wouldn't have been opposed to spending a little time alone with Joe,
just in case he had a notion to kiss her again. But making out in a nursing home
was a little revolting anyway, so Frieda talked and Bonnie and Joe listened.

The senior citizen lived next door to George, both of them in the assisted-
living wing of Melnik Nursing Home, and was, to hear her talk, alive when Melnik
was settled in the mid-1800s. Of course, that made her around one hundred and
seventy-five years old. But she was still going strong. The woman had a whole long,
truth-challenged version of Melnik history. She'd been pestering the historical
society to adopt "the truth according to Frieda" for years. Bonnie had heard it all
before. . .a thousand times. . .literally.

Bonnie noticed Joe nodding off and envied him his total lack of insomnia.

When Tyler appeared behind Frieda, who had settled onto her walker,
conveniently convertible into a chair, right in front of George Wesley's door so
there was no escape, Bonnie almost wept with joy. Help had arrived.

"Hi, Tyler!" Bonnie nudged Joe awake.

Tyler might have wiped the dust of Melnik off his feet when he married Liza,
but that didn't mean he was stupid. Bonnie could see it in her brother's eyes.
He remembered know-it-all, tell-it-all Frieda very well. He wisely stayed behind
Frieda, knowing his only escape could be cut off if he let Frieda get between him
and the door.

Joe rubbed his eyes as he stood from George's creaky La-Z-Boy with the
electric ejector seat—slow-motion ejector, mercifully.

Bonnie waited until Frieda was distracted by Joe's movements to dart around
the elderly guard dog and hug her brother. "Where are the boys?"

"I left them with Brian and Greg. What's with their phones working?" Tyler
squeezed her until she squeaked and lifted her off her feet.

Bonnie knew how much Tyler looked like her. Only, on him it worked. Dark
blond hair and huge brown eyes that were a window into his gentle soul. On
Bonnie the same coloring was beige and lifeless; on Tyler it glowed. He was nearly

six inches taller than she, and he'd been her rock after their mom and dad had died, for a year.

And then he'd vanished from her life.

All that sweetness had made him a perfect mark for Liza. Bonnie had seen through Liza right away. If Tyler hadn't been able to, Bonnie figured he deserved whatever happened to him.

Too bad it had happened to her, too. She'd lost her brother when he married, and she'd needed him so desperately.

But this was all old news. Bonnie had learned to enjoy whatever bits and pieces of her brother she got. Now she laughed and swatted Tyler's shoulder. "Put me down."

He smiled impishly at her but obeyed. He was dressed casually for once. Bonnie had learned to expect him in a suit. But he wore a polo shirt and khakis with sturdy sneakers. They had all cost a fortune, no doubt. Good thing Liza enjoyed dropping designer names, or Bonnie would never have known she was in the presence of such haute couture.

"Are they at our house?" Our house. With a pang, Bonnie realized it was no longer anyone's house but hers. And it hadn't been Tyler's house for a long, long time.

Tyler tipped his head toward Joe. "I managed to get Brian on the phone on my drive in. I left them at that spooky Gunderson house—I assume it's yours. You're Joe Manning?"

Joe squeezed past Frieda. The woman stood and turned, one click of her walker at a time.

Tyler backed into the hall.

Bonnie followed with Joe right behind her.

Bonnie looked over her shoulder and saw Frieda was following. If they timed it just right, they could get inside George's apartment and lock the nosy old lady out.

She took Tyler's elbow and pushed him a little farther back. At his arched brow, she gave Frieda a significant look, and Tyler got it and moved. Bonnie towed Joe in her wake.

Frieda came outside, still talking. They were saved from strong-arm tactics by the bell.

"Dinner!" Frieda headed down the hall, one surprisingly quick step after another.

Bonnie remembered George and Frieda and the snickerdoodles and ginger-snaps. It was possible that the most dangerous place in Nebraska was between Frieda and the nursing home dining room.

Tyler sighed in relief and led the way into George's room, closing the door firmly. "As Sven Gunderson's heir, you have a right to the files that concern Sven.

You can't so much as touch anyone else's, but lawyer/client privilege laws give you legal access. I'm acting as an officer of the court, and Bonnie is the witness to testify we didn't tamper with the files of other clients."

After a quick look around at George's surprisingly spacious living area, Tyler headed straight toward a cluttered oak desk and the filing cabinet behind it. "I had my secretary fax me the affidavit we all need to sign saying this was done in accordance with the law."

"You've got a fax machine in your car?" Bonnie asked, amazed.

"Yes." Tyler stopped just as he reached for the third drawer of a four-door file cabinet and looked back at her. "I really love you, Bon-Bon."

"Because I'm so far behind the times?"

He smiled. "Because you're smart." He reached for the handle and clattered the drawer open.

"Smart? How so?"

Tyler shrugged. "It's just nice to be around someone who still realizes it's very cool that I can get a fax in my car. To me, that's smart." He flicked down the alphabetized papers and withdrew a file so slim it didn't look like there was anything in it, then opened the second drawer and pulled out a slightly thicker file.

"These are the files of Sven Gunderson and Joe Manning owned by recently deceased George Wesley." He spoke very formally, putting it all clearly on the record for Bonnie the witness to attest. "As Sven Gunderson's sole heir, Joseph Manning has a legal right to these files and he falls within attorney/client privilege statutes."

Laying the files on George's desk, Tyler flipped the thicker one open. It had Gunderson's name clearly printed on it. Bonnie saw "Last Will and Testament" written across the top. A copy of Sven's will. That was all the file contained.

"This is the paperwork you'd expect from a cheapskate like Gunderson." Tyler didn't sound so formal now.

Bonnie snickered.

He handed the contents of the folder to Joe then flipped open the second file. This one clearly had "Joe Manning" printed on the tab, and it contained a single sheet of paper. Tyler picked it up, read silently the very few words, then whistled. He raised his head to look between Joe and Bonnie, concern etched in every line of his face.

"What?" Joe reached for the paper.

Tyler stepped back in a way Bonnie could tell was a reflex. Tyler didn't want to hand over that paper.

"What does it say?" Bonnie felt a chill that could not be explained by the temperature in Melnik Nursing Home, which was always kept at a balmy eighty-five degrees.

Tyler shook his head, as if in denial. But he gained control of himself, and Bonnie saw his lawyer face fall back into place. He extended the document to Joe.

"You are now the proud owner of Maxie, the World's Largest Field Mouse."

"I inherited a dead mouse?" Joe shuddered.

Bonnie gasped and covered her mouth, as if afraid she'd say something awful.

Tyler grimaced as if he'd just had a client receive the death penalty—for jaywalking.

Joe had to fight not to laugh. Then he remembered George, clinging to life. "This can't be what George wanted to tell me."

"Of course this is what George wanted to tell you." Bonnie threw her arms wide.

"It has to be something else. Something big, important."

"This is huge." Tyler patted Bonnie on the shoulder.

"This is ridiculous." Joe read the page. Two sentences. His eyes boggled at the instructions. First that Gunderson owned Maxie and was leaving him to Joe. And second that. . .yeesh.

"We need to seal this room so no one gets access to these files without permission. I've already talked to the nursing home administrator and Junior."

Joe wasn't sure, but he thought Bonnie was crying. She kept her head down, but he saw her filch a tissue out of a box on George's desk and press it to her lips, then her eyes. Tyler closed the filing cabinet drawers, retaining the two manila folders, and led the way out of the room.

Bonnie sniffled.

Tyler exchanged a few legal-sounding words with a man who met them as they exited, the hospital administrator, Joe surmised. Then the three of them left the nursing home.

Once outside, Tyler leveled eyes on Joe that almost made him confess to things he'd never done.

I'll bet he's a good lawyer.

"We need to discuss the legal ramifications of—"

A white car came around the corner of the highway, the tires squealing, the speed dangerous.

Tyler looked up and froze. All that lawyer cool melted off his face, and he looked like a little boy caught with his hand in the cookie jar.

"Liza." Tyler's Adam's apple bounced, probably almost as much as the original Adam's did when he'd taken his bite.

The cranky wife who had been rude to Bonnie after she and Tyler were first married.

The car, a sporty Mercedes, skidded to a stop. Bits of gravel kicked up from the paved parking lot. The driver's door flew open and a vision of loveliness stepped out of the car. . .lovely, that is, except for the expression on her face. That was downright scary.

"This is the last straw!"

"But, Liza, honey, Bonnie needed my advice. I was planning to be home before you got back."

The cool, professional lawyer was completely gone, and in his place stood a scared child, making excuses, preparing to grovel. Joe had to shake his head in wonder. Tyler had *married* this woman?

"Where are Benetton and Giancarlo?" She stomped her way around the car, whipping off stylish sunglasses—the better to kill her husband with her laser-gun eyes. She wore a pure white suit, perfectly fitted and accessorized. Joe noted a diamond flashing on her balled-up fist so large there was no missing it. Dark hair, perfectly styled, seemed to be nearly standing on end from fury. Her fair-skinned, perfectly made-up face was mottled with rage. Perfectly aligned teeth were bared like those of a rabid she-wolf. Joe was tempted to tell her that she was *not* achieving the lovely, gracious appearance she was no doubt going for.

"The boys are with Brian and Greg." Tyler flinched as if he'd just confessed a grave sin but was too frightened to lie.

"You went off and just left them with your brothers? Who knows what those two hayseeds are teaching our sons? You've ruined any chance I had for signing this contract today."

"Liza, you didn't have to come up here. You didn't need me for a—"

"Get your stupid brothers on the phone right now!"

Joe noticed Bonnie's cheeks turn pink. He saw her lips clench and her hands ball into fists. He waited to see who would call this horrible old bat on her insults. Neither Bonnie nor Tyler did.

Bonnie stood silent and Tyler quickly dialed his phone.

"I've got no signal." He looked up sheepishly.

"This little dump of a town. I'm surprised they have running water."

"I'll just drive over and get them. You can follow me if you want them to ride home with you."

"I'm going back to Omaha right now. I'll expect you to be ten minutes behind me." The wolf-lady turned on Bonnie. "I've told you not to be such a leech."

Liza advanced on her.

Bonnie backed up a step. "We had a little crisis, Liza. We really needed a lawyer's advice. I'm sorry if—"

Since Joe was behind Bonnie, she backed into him and he steadied her, ready to throw himself into the breach if the shrew actually started swinging.

"I'm sorry!" Liza singsonged the words like a little child. "I'm so sick of your stupid excuses. This is the end! Don't you come whining—"

"Enough, Liza!"

Joe was surprised to see Tyler grow some version of a spine.

Liza whirled to face him and Tyler's spine seemed to shrink away. He looked at his shoes. "This is between you and me. Leave Bonnie out of it."

Liza charged forward until her nose practically pressed against Tyler's. "Don't you dare speak to me that way. We'll settle this at home."

She gave Bonnie a last furious look, wheeled, and climbed back into her car, slamming the door with vicious force. She left the parking lot like she had a rocket strapped to the underbelly of the Mercedes.

Silently, they watched her tear onto the highway. An oncoming car's brakes squealed as she pulled out in front of it. Liza laid on her horn and roared away. Road rage personified.

"You're *married* to her?" Joe couldn't help asking.

Tyler looked away from his fast-vanishing wife. "She's got every right to be upset. I shouldn't have come up here on the spur of the moment."

Joe shook his head, pure pity warring with contempt for the way Tyler let his wife treat sweet-hearted Bonnie. Contempt won. "Nice choice, Einstein."

Tyler gave Joe a narrow-eyed look, but he didn't stay to defend his wife's behavior. Maybe because it was indefensible, more likely because the clock was ticking. The man practically ran toward his car without so much as a good-bye to Bonnie.

"He named his two sons Benetton and Giancarlo?"

"Liza's Italian."

Joe thought that over. "She has dark hair, but she really didn't look all that Italian. What was her maiden name?"

Tyler's car raced out of the nursing home parking lot.

"Barnston."

Joe snorted. "You mean Barnstini?"

"It was back a few generations. . .five, I think." Bonnie, her faced flushed with anger, watched until Tyler's car vanished. "My brother is the sweetest man I've ever known."

"Your brother is a world-class wimp, and he's sure not very sweet to you. Maybe the town should forget about Maxie and make your brother their mascot. Tyler Simpson, the World's Most Henpecked Husband."

Glaring at Joe as if all of this were his fault, Bonnie said, "He's softhearted."

"He's a wimp."

"He's easygoing."

"A pansy."

"Nice."

"Gag," Joe said. Really, he had to do something to cheer her up; why not mock her family?

"He'd make such a great husband for someone who appreciated him. Instead, he's married to that awful. . ."

Joe decided words must have failed her—no surprise there. They were failing him, too. He'd run out of synonyms for Bonnie's sissy brother. So he decided to change the subject.

"So what's the big deal that I own Maxie, the World's Largest Field Mouse?"

Bonnie gave him a horrified glance and burst into tears.

16

Joe made soothing sounds, feeling as awkward as a lummox, and herded her toward her car.

He settled her into the passenger seat and drove quickly to his house.

"Oh, good, they're here."

Bonnie couldn't quit crying. "Who's here?"

Joe ushered her inside. "Greg! Brian! Get out here!"

Brian appeared out of the library, took one look at Bonnie, and launched a fist at Joe.

Joe expected it and ducked behind Bonnie. Brian had enough sense not to aim at Bonnie, so he missed.

"Get away from her." Brian drew back another fist.

Greg came thundering downstairs. "What did he do to her?"

"Listen, I did not make her cry." He leaned forward so his head was over Bonnie's shoulder. This was completely different than being a sissy.

"If I had, I'd step right out from behind her and take my beating like a man. But I've got no idea what's wrong with her, and I don't want a broken nose to deal with while we try to fix whatever it is."

"Was it Liza? Ty just dragged his kids off. He barely spoke to us, so we figured Liza caught him."

"She was at the nursing home. Wow, what an old bat."

Greg and Brian nodded. Bonnie even managed to nod. Joe tucked a handkerchief in her hands to replace the now-soaked Kleenex.

"But what seemed to push Bonnie over the edge was finding out that Gunderson has always been the owner of Maxie Mouse, and now he's left it to me with instructions to take the mouse back and throw him away or the whole inheritance will be left to the American Nazi Party."

"Throw Maxie away?" Brian came at Joe again. Greg grabbed Bonnie and pulled her away from her human-shield position.

"Look!" Joe held up his hands in surrender. "I'm not going to throw Maxie away. She never even gave me a chance to say that. How about if I formally 'throw' him out my back door, then one of you pick him up and claim him for Melnik. I mean, what does that mean, anyway, 'throw him away'? C'mon. And why are you all ready to cry and fight over a dead mouse?"

"Because Maxie's important to this town, and we hate Nazis."

"Everyone hates Nazis, moron. It's only the *mouse* I'm talking about. Doesn't this reaction seem a little insane to you? How obsessed is this town with that stupid mouse, anyway? Maybe I *should* throw him away so you can all come to your senses."

Bonnie quit crying and wheeled to face Joe. She took two giant steps so her shiny red nose was right in his face. "Don't you dare hurt Maxie! Why, this town would die if we didn't have him. You. . .you big, dumb—"

Her phone rang to the tune of the "Hallelujah Chorus." She froze. "That's Tyler." Then she clawed at her pocket and pulled the phone out, whipping it open with a snap of her wrist. "Hello?"

There was a pause; then suddenly Bonnie's face went ashen. "No!" Her knees gave out and Joe caught her or she'd have hit the floor. The boys shouted and rushed to her side. Joe kept his arm around her back as he pried the phone out of her white-knuckled grip. Her fingers were ice cold.

"This is Joe Manning. What's going on?"

"There's been an accident. Liza's dead."

Joe's stomach twisted.

Bonnie cried harder. "It's my fault. I never should have asked him to help. I knew how she felt."

Joe looked at the boys as Tyler explained. Greg and Brian had already had a lot of loss in their lives. He wondered which one of them was steady enough to handle this. Bonnie was out of the question. He repeated the basics of what Tyler was saying. "Liza died in a traffic accident. This is Tyler. He just drove up on the scene."

Joe turned his attention back to the phone. "What do you need us to do? Where are you?"

After another extended silence, he said, "We'll be there in twenty minutes." Joe hung up and looked at the two young men. "I need one of you to go with me to bring Tyler's car back. Brian, you're it. Greg, take care of Bonnie."

"No, I have to go." Bonnie leaned more heavily against him.

"No, you don't. I'll get Tyler and the boys. Brian can drive them back here. I'll bring Tyler's car. Tyler said it's bad. We need to get them away from the scene; there's not time for a family gathering out there."

And from Tyler's broken rambling, Joe knew Bonnie didn't need to see the wreck.

Bonnie got through the next few days by living one moment at a time.

Joe kept her going for the first day, until the shock eased enough that she could obsess about her guilt. She saw to all the details of the funeral because Liza had no family, and Tyler didn't seem able to make a decision. She barely slept. Her head ached, and she began to hear a buzzing noise in her ears.

They laid Liza to rest in the country cemetery beside Bonnie's parents. Liza would hate it, but Tyler didn't protest. He just went along, his face white, every muscle tight and grim. The boys clung to him, their usual high spirits drained away by the loss of their mother.

The funeral ended with a brief graveside ceremony. Bonnie stood by Tyler's side, wearing her most somber beige pantsuit.

"Tyler, the ladies have a meal for us in the church basement," Bonnie murmured in his ear as Melnik citizens gave him awkward words of condolence on their way out of the cemetery. She had stayed as close as possible since the wreck, but she'd quit touching her brother. He flinched and pulled away every time she did, as if being close to her now violated his marriage vows. As if he couldn't summon a single thought, and Liza still ruled him with her disdain for Bonnie, Greg, Brian, and all of Melnik.

"I have to go home."

"You need to eat, Ty." Bonnie rested her hand on his arm and felt him recoil, but she held on. "You've hardly taken a bite of food since the accident. I don't want you to drive home in this condition."

The boys clung to him, one on each side.

"I'll be fine." His lips barely moved. They were white with strain. Dark circles underlined his eyes. Were there tears in him to shed? Did he truly grieve for his tyrannical wife?

"What about the boys?" Bonnie rested one hand on Benetton's head. "They need a meal. You'll have to cook the minute you get home. Let them eat and spare yourself that chore at least."

"I can take care of my own children, Bonnie." Tyler glared at her, almost the first emotion he'd shown.

"I know you can, Ty." Bonnie's heart ached for him, but she couldn't push him. He was too close to the breaking point now. Stepping back, she watched him rest his hands on his sons' shoulders and begin walking, as if the three were one being, toward the parking lot.

They got in the car and Tyler drove away without a backward glance. Greg and Brian stayed long enough to eat a quick meal; then they hugged Bonnie good-bye. Spring break had ended Monday, and it was Wednesday now. They had to return to school.

Bonnie walked out with them then stood in the churchyard, their dust settling around her. Frantic not to think about her quiet house, she decided to think about Joe, who stood quietly beside her. He'd stepped in repeatedly these last three days until she'd started depending on him too much. Well, she wasn't quite ready to quit doing that this second. But in the hectic aftermath of the car wreck, they hadn't given a thought to his house or its closed-off wings.

Joe was particularly good at keeping Tyler's boys occupied. They were too upset to learn magic tricks, but Jeffie came over for his lesson and Tyler's boys watched Jeffie practice, which diverted them from clinging to their father every second.

"We never even checked the wings of your house. Has anything else happened?" Brian and Greg had stayed with Joe, and no one had given his troubles a second thought.

Now Bonnie badly needed something to think about, before she started crying.

"Don't worry about it. You need to get some rest and get your life back to normal."

Bonnie caught his forearm and sank her nails in to keep him from leaving. "Don't make me go home and rest."

Joe ran one finger gently under Bonnie's eye. "Have you slept at all?"

Bonnie could imagine the dark circles. Her eyes burned, and her brain felt thick and slow. But every time she stopped moving, she saw Liza, screaming, furious because of Bonnie's phone call. Driving away in a rage. The guilt was driving her crazy.

"Some. A little." She shrugged one shoulder. "Not much."

"You haven't had a good night's sleep since the accident, and before that you hadn't had a good night's sleep since Dora collapsed the historical museum. You need to see a doctor, get some medicine."

Bonnie shook his arm. "Listen, let's knock the wall out of your closet. In fact, let me do the demolition. I think smashing something to bits might do me as much good as a sleeping pill."

Joe looked at her a long time, and Bonnie prayed silently, a bit desperately, that he wouldn't refuse her. He finally glanced down at his wrist. She followed the direction of his eyes and saw his hand had turned red. She let go and gasped at the finger-shaped welts on his arm. Each welt was tipped by a crescent dent from her nails.

"I'm sorry." Bonnie felt tears cutting her bloodshot eyes like acid. She didn't dare start; she'd never stop.

"Maybe you do need to release some tension." He nodded toward his Jeep. "C'mon. I'll call Nick and see if we can borrow a sledgehammer."

Bonnie was so relieved she almost hugged him.

J oe was so relieved he almost hugged her.

The last few days had been awful. Bonnie's devastation, her guilt, her exhaustion. Tyler, so dazed he could barely respond to his children, had only made it worse by dumping everything on Bonnie. They played their roles so easily Joe suspected they were falling into a pattern set by their parents' death.

There had been absolutely no possible way on the whole stinking planet Joe could have added to their burden. But the truth was, his house was driving him crazy. He'd considered just running off from the creaking and the ghostly footsteps. Travel around on his newfound money until it was time to start college in the fall. In fact, he'd looked into starting school this summer. Now that money was no object, he didn't need to spend the summer working to raise the cash.

He might have done it if not for Bonnie. She needed help, and instead, everyone looked to her to take charge. If her brothers hadn't been so traumatized, Joe might have seen if he could pound some sense into them. Tyler, sure, he was in shock, but there was no reason Greg and Brian couldn't have helped out more.

Now she was half asleep on her feet and wound so tight he could hear her brain cells squeaking, and she wanted to hammer on his wall.

Well, fine.

With her brothers gone, he didn't know if he could sleep there. She needed the outlet; he needed those walls down. He ran by her house and waited in the car while she changed into a stained pair of khakis and a well-worn beige polo shirt. Then when they pulled up to his house, he got out and crouched down to phone Nick.

"He's coming." Joe snapped his phone shut. "Before he does, I've got an idea." He'd had a lot of time to think during the last few sleepless nights. He might be catching Bonnie's insomnia, but he didn't add to her guilt by telling her that.

He led the way into the library and went straight to the section of shelves on the east wall. "This is where the entrance to the east wing has to be." He tugged on the shelves, but they were as immovable as their age and the dust suggested.

Bonnie studied the eight-foot-high shelves, loaded with heavy, moldering books. "You're right. It makes sense that it's here. There's a set of shelves like this in the living room, too. Right where the entrance to the west wing ought to be."

Joe ran his hand down the sides of the shelves, feeling for a lever or a gap between the shelves and the wall.

Bonnie knelt and pointed at the floor. "Look at this line in the dust."

An arc cut through the dust. The room had been trampled in for days, so the line was almost blurred out of existence, but it was there. Joe's eyes narrowed. "I was thinking they just put in shelves, maybe permanently installed them, but this line tells me this swings open." He rubbed his chin as he studied the massive cabinet, then began touching, sliding his hands, tugging.

Bonnie went to the other end and imitated Joe's search.

Joe began pulling out books, setting them aside, not wanting to damage the leather-bound volumes. He grabbed the fifth book on the shelf right at eye level, and rather than sliding out easily as the others had, it tipped onto its spine with a quiet click. The shelf came silently open an inch.

Bonnie turned at the click. "I've heard that sound before."

Joe pulled on the door. "This is absolutely silent. These hinges should squeak if this door—" Joe dropped to one knee. "Will you look at that."

Bonnie came to his side as he swept the shelf wide, opening an entrance to the east wing of the house. It was a perfectly furnished room an inch deep in dust and obviously neglected for years. Except for the footprints.

"Your ghost looks to wear tennis shoes, about size eleven." Bonnie looked up from the floor to Joe.

Their eyes met. He suspected his eyes matched hers as far as being red-veined from exhaustion. But this was real, and there was no time to sleep now.

Joe took a step into the room that time forgot.

Bonnie jerked her head in the opposite direction. Before she spoke, Joe smelled it.

Smoke!

He turned and ran toward the smell.

He heard her fumbling for the old phone sitting on a table near the front entrance. No time to run for the second floor or crouch behind his Jeep. She rapped out the request for the fire department as he reached the kitchen and saw smoke coming from the basement door.

He wrenched the door open and she caught his arm. "Is there a fire extinguisher around here?"

Joe came to his senses about running down into the smoldering cellar. He looked wildly around the room.

"I've seen one. I'm sure." He dove for the cupboard under the sink and brought out an extinguisher.

Bonnie threw herself in front of the door. "Don't go down there. Listen, the sirens are already going."

Joe heard them and knew exactly how long it would take for Nick and his crew to get here. Sixty seconds. The siren was getting closer right now.

"You're right. Let's let them handle this."

They stood looking down at the basement. No flames, just choking smoke. Joe pulled Bonnie away from the open door. "It just started. We could have probably put it out ourselves."

"Pretty convenient timing, huh?" Bonnie looked toward the library.

The door burst open and Nick and at least five others came barreling through the door carrying heavy hoses. Joe pointed at the basement. "I don't think it's serious. But it's really smoky. Be careful."

Nick nodded, pulled on his face mask, waited until the rest of the team did the same, and then led the brave men and women of the Melnik Volunteer Fire and Rescue Department down into the dark.

Joe caught Bonnie's arm and led her toward the library as more people raced in and cars began to gather outside to watch the action.

They reached the room to find the shelf pulled back into place. "Yeah, pretty convenient. Look, the book that worked the lever is gone and the lever's been snapped off."

"Whoever it is has to know we'll get in there now." Bonnie ran her hand over the rough edge of the broken metal lever. "He's only buying himself an hour or two while we fight the fire then pry the shelf open."

"Maybe all he needs is time to get out of the house." Joe heard footsteps behind them and saw Junior come into the library.

"What's happening here?" Junior pulled out his notebook.

"I just found out that I've got a roommate." Joe poked at the lever uselessly.

"A roommate?"

"Yeah, I just found out my ghost is flesh and blood."

"What's that have to do with the fire trucks?"

Bonnie crossed her arms just like she was getting ready to scold one of her brothers instead of a pesky ghost. "He's not only flesh and blood. He's an arsonist."

"And," Joe added, "probably a murderer."

Junior scratched his head, making a mockery of his comb-over. "I'm gonna have to phone the hospital and tell 'em to let Clara go. Then we're all gonna have to go back to buying her stupid pies!"

*

They still hadn't gotten into the closed-off wing by the time the fire trucks started packing up.

Joe called Nick in, and along with Junior, they threw themselves into breaching the shelf barrier.

"Bonnie, honey, don't you have to give a museum progress report to the city planning committee tonight?" Junior looked up from where he was lifting a pry bar on the bottom of the shelf.

They'd already checked the living room and found that lever snapped off, too. Joe had declared he was getting in before one more day passed. Junior was pretty sure the intruder had just sealed off the entrances so he could have time to make an escape and that there was no longer another resident in the house.

"That's tonight?" Bonnie panicked.

"I'll drive you home." Joe straightened away from his shelf project.

"No, there's a fire truck still here. I'll catch a ride with them. I want you to get through that door."

The three men promised to attend the meeting.

They didn't make it.

Bonnie didn't need them.

She put on her best beige dress and was greeted with great enthusiasm after she told the city council about Joe's promise of a generous donation. She didn't mention that Joe now owned Maxie. With Brian and Greg gone back to college, no one in town knew the truth except for her and Joe. Since Joe had assured her he'd do the right thing, she saw no reason to start a panic.

Her part of the meeting was short. When she left, the sun was still up, and though she was cheered by her success, her exhaustion felt like a heavy weight pressing her eyelids closed. It was a feeling she recognized. A feeling that preceded a good night's sleep. She decided Joe, Nick, and Junior could handle things at Joe's house. She'd go home and sleep. As she packed up her file folder of information, she closed her eyes for a second and had to fight to get them open.

Thank You, God.

Sleep. She was going to be blessed with sleep for one perfect night.

She emerged from the city office, took a second to give a drowsy look at the devastated remains of the historical society museum, and turned to face Shayla Melnik.

"Shayla, hi. It's good to see you." Had Wilkie's daughter come back to try to get custody of Kevin? Bonnie would have been encouraged if the selfish young woman did such a thing, but honestly, Kevin was better off with the Andersons.

"Can I ask you a question?" Shayla looked worse than when she'd left a year ago. She'd gained weight, and her hair, bleached until it was coarse and broken, had grown about an inch of dirty blond roots. Her fingernails were painted black, and she had a tattoo of her name spelled in cursive on the left side of her neck. Bonnie noticed a pierced nose and eyebrow and what looked like a new scar on her chin.

"Shayla, how are you? Are you back to stay?"

Shayla sneered, shoving a stick of gum into her mouth. The action made the diamond stud in her nose glint in the setting sun. Very festive.

"I'm back because I heard Gunderson died. I wanna know if this town is gonna do the right thing and give me some of the money he stole from my family over the years."

Bonnie frowned. "You got a settlement after your dad died. The city took all of Gunderson's local property holdings except his house and split the proceeds between you and Kevin and the city of Melnik. Kevin's is in a trust fund that he can't have until he's older. But you got a lot of cash—it was thousands of dollars. Don't tell me it's gone."

"That was nothin' to what he owed us. And now that he's dead, we oughta inherit. He got rich on us. I heard some mystery son showed up and killed him and took everything and this town is letting him get away with it."

Bonnie suddenly wondered where Shayla was "hearing" all these things. As far as Bonnie knew, no one in town was in touch with the young woman. It occurred to Bonnie that someone had been living in Joe's house. Shayla? Biding her time? Lying low while the search for Gunderson's killer was at its peak? Wilkie had skulked around that house. Could Shayla have known some of the secrets her father had discovered, like where the secret entrances to the blocked-off rooms were?

Shayla's appearing right now—the same day Joe's ghost had been exorcized, was a bit too much of a coincidence.

"Is the city council in there right now?" Shayla nodded toward the building from which Bonnie had just emerged.

"It's the planning board. Only one city council member is in there."

Shayla threw her scraggly hair over her shoulder and narrowed her eyes. "I'm just gonna go in and see if any of them can make this easy. If they can't, then we'll do it the hard way. I've got a lawyer who's going to see I get my share of what's been stolen from my family."

"Shayla, come with me. Don't start right in fighting with the whole town. Let's go see Kevin. Let me make you some supper. Are you hungry? Have you got a place to sleep tonight?"

Shayla's lips twitched as if Bonnie had made a bad joke. "I'm not interested in seeing my loser brother. And I'll eat steak with the money this town is going to hand over to me, not your handouts. And my house has never sold, so I'll just stay there." She marched into the building.

Bonnie knew how much trouble nuisance lawsuits could cause. Melnik didn't even have George Wesley to handle its few legal problems anymore. A week ago she'd have phoned Tyler to ask for help. Guilt over her part in Liza's death vanquished the triumph of the city planning meeting.

Her pleasant tiredness took flight.

She knew her insomnia well. Rather than go home, she got in her beige car and headed for Joe's haunted mansion.

"Well, whoever was here is gone for good." Joe dusted his hands together.

He, Nick, and Junior had been over every inch of the house.

"I hope." Nick packed his tools away so neatly Joe couldn't help admiring him.

It had taken awhile to get in, but once the swinging cabinets were open, they'd gone through the whole place thoroughly. They'd found plenty of evidence someone had been living in this part of Joe's house. . .for quite a while. Disturbed dust, a bed that had the covers thrown back, a bathroom with a wet shower, food containers. The guy had been living better than Joe.

A passageway led between the wings. It also led to the basement, to the barred upstairs door, and to a little shed out back, which explained how Joe's intruder had gotten in to begin with.

That entrance was now solidly locked, and Joe believed he'd be able to sleep soundly for the first time since he'd come to this town.

That sense of being watched had faded. His living, breathing ghost was gone.

Bonnie found Nick, Junior, and Joe in the backyard, looking at the little shed, now fitted with a shiny new padlock.

Joe saw her first and grimaced. "Is the meeting over? Bonnie, I'm sorry we didn't come. I lost track of time."

Nick and Junior chorused their apologies. Bonnie waved them off with a bright smile, but Joe saw the lines of fatigue around her eyes.

Nick glanced at his watch. "I'm late. Good luck sleeping tonight, Joe."

"I owe you for your time, Nick. I expect a bill."

"Expect all you want. Just give me a chance to make a bid when you decide to renovate." Nick jumped in his truck and drove the three blocks toward his home.

"It went well. I didn't need your help." She waved a lofty hand at them. "The committee is full speed ahead for building the museum. What did you find here?"

Joe and Junior took turns telling her and even led her through the wings. Joe noticed her intelligent, bloodshot eyes cataloguing the perfectly preserved antique furniture and the desks and file cabinets full of time-yellowed documents.

Bonnie pulled a file that looked like it held financial forms out of the cabinet. "These things are valuable, Joe. You need to get them under lock and key right away. Which reminds me, I saw Shayla Melnik uptown."

"She didn't offer you a swig of antifreeze, did she?" Junior shoved his hands in his pockets.

"What?" Joe asked.

"She looks angrier and more ruthless now than she did a year ago when she tried to kill her father."

Bonnie gave Joe the bare bones of Wilkie's murder. He'd already heard most of it. "I didn't realize there were so many suspects. Lots of potential murderers in this peaceful, law-abiding town."

"It *is* a law-abiding town," Junior huffed at him. "With the single exception of Wilkie and Sven—"

"That's not a single exception; that's two exceptions. Plus whoever killed Sven. That's three exceptions. Plus Kevin breaking into my house. That's four—"

"Whatever." Junior cut him off. "With four exceptions, there is no crime in Melnik. An occasional dog gets off its leash; sometimes a kid shoots up a stop sign out in the country. Speeding tickets. That's it."

Junior scratched his stomach. "I wondered where Shayla's been all year. I haven't heard a whisper of new gossip about her, and you know how gossip is in this town. Far as I know, she didn't stay in touch with anyone in town, not even her brother Kevin."

"She tried to kill her father and she's more ruthless now?" Joe's eyes narrowed, and he noticed goose bumps on Bonnie's arms. "Do you suppose she's been staying here?"

"It occurred to me that her father had done a lot of snooping around this house. If anyone learned a way to sneak in, it'd be Wilkie. And he could have passed that information along to his daughter."

"Or his son," Junior added. "Or anyone his son or daughter talked to."

"Well, whoever it is, it's not Clara. Did you call the hospital and tell them to let her go?"

"Yeah, I called the hospital then phoned her daughter. Her daughter wasn't even upset. She said the lockup in the psych ward was good for her mom. Got some solid food into her. That pie smashed on Sven had to be a setup. Whoever did that was trying to cast suspicion on Clara. Someone else fed him that poison— ground it up and slipped it into his morning coffee or something, easy to do if you were living in his house and watching him. And easy to see Clara wandering all over town with that pie cart, even if the guy was hiding in this house. She'd be a natural to pin the murder on. When Gunderson died, our ghost snuck out and borrowed Clara's cart and moved Sven in it to that little room. He plastered Sven with the pie then planted that key on Clara."

"Where'd he get the key to begin with?" Bonnie crossed her arms, trying to fit the pieces together. "I'll accept that Clara had one all these years. The one she called the 'good key.' But the 'bad key' someone planted on her, probably not dreaming she had another one. So our ghost had to have the key somehow."

"When did the key disappear?" Junior licked the tip of his pencil.

"Years ago. I've been working at the museum for over a decade now. We almost never looked in that room. I have no idea when or how we lost the key."

"Could the ghost have stolen it way back then?"

"Is that important?" Joe asked. "He or she had the key somehow. In fact, having the key is probably what made our ghost think of that room. There were no fingerprints on it, so it figures Clara didn't use it—she's not sane enough to wipe away prints."

"Why not just leave the body in here?" Junior pulled out his notebook. "The murder might have gone unnoticed for years."

Junior tapped on his notebook, frowning. "Clara's in the clear. In a way it's too bad that we don't have enough to get her committed somewhere. Someone might be able to help her, get her on medication or something."

"Anti-baking pills?" Bonnie shook her head.

"It doesn't make any sense." Joe started wishing for his own notebook to keep track of the twisting clues. "Unless that's the whole point."

Junior looked up from his reading.

Bonnie's brow furrowed. "What's the whole point?"

"Living in this house secretly. Staring at people through the peepholes we've found. That's not normal criminal behavior."

Bonnie grimaced as if bracing herself for what Joe was going to say. He didn't blame her. He felt the need to be braced, too.

"What it is, is crazy. We're trying to blame Crazy Clara, but what if we're trying to blame the wrong crazy person?"

Junior tilted his head as if wondering whether to make a note of that. "But Clara's the only crazy person we have."

"That we know of."

Bonnie nodded.

Junior made a note.

Joe suddenly realized he didn't want to be right. He was better off with a ghost than a murderous lunatic.

He slapped his hand over his mouth to control the laughter. They were confident they were alone now, the fools. He had plenty of hiding places in this old crypt of a house.

Let them think he was crazy. It suited him. He had to give it to sonny boy, though. Sven probably should have been left to rot in this place. But it bothered him to have Sven in this house lying dead in here. The Ghost wanted him banished completely. The corpse was a reminder of all that old miser and his family had stolen.

NOSY IN NEBRASKA

How many years had the Ghost held that museum key? He'd used it dozens of times and no one had known.

In a town where everybody knew everything about their neighbors, he'd floated through them unseen. And he'd been ready to claim what was rightfully his. Then the Son showed up and snatched it right out of his jaws. That wouldn't be too hard to fix. All sonny boy had to do was die.

A laugh escaped between his fingers. He moved quickly to his peephole. No one had noticed, not even plain, boring Bonnie. Many times he'd watched her from the locked museum room. His fingers tingled when he thought of how close he'd come to grabbing her that day.

Sweet Bonnie. Boring Bonnie. Lifeless Bonnie.

The Ghost needed that. He needed sonny boy gone.

How to start?

Who to start with?

Who'd be most fun?

Decisions, decisions.

They thought he was gone. The Ghost wanted to keep it that way.

For now.

18

J oe was safe.

For the first time since he'd moved into this place, he knew for sure he was completely safe.

When Bonnie and Junior left, he stood in the hallway entrance to his home, so isolated, so utterly alone, he almost ran after Bonnie to beg her to stay. But she needed to sleep. He needed to sleep.

A somewhat sleep-related thought—completely inappropriate for a single Christian man—invaded his thoughts and was quickly banished. The only way he could think about Bonnie like that was to marry her, and that wasn't going to happen. He'd made a promise to his dying mother and to himself. Now, with the inheritance, there was no financial barrier.

Of course, a huge part of going to college was about financial security, and now he had no need for that, either. But there was more to it than that. He felt God leading him in his desire to work with children. Becoming a teacher would fulfill that longing.

Looking from side to side, he saw his home with those shelves swung open. The structure was now almost three times the size it had been that morning. It had always been a mansion from the outside, but now it was a mansion on the inside, too. A ghost-free mansion.

The loneliness was so bad he actually missed the feeling of being watched. He even missed his bats and thought of driving to the twenty-four-hour Wal-Mart fifty miles away, buying a tall ladder, and pulling open that crack in his siding to let the creepy little beasts come home. Ghosts and bats—spooky company was better than no company at all.

Maybe Junior would let him sleep in jail again. That hadn't been so bad.

If he wasn't planning to move as soon as he got everything settled here, he'd get a pet, a dog maybe. He'd never had a dog.

He didn't dare go after Bonnie. He was afraid that would end with him getting his face slapped.

Or not.

If she didn't slap him, if instead she let him kiss him again, it would be even worse, because he wasn't staying, and Bonnie was a staying kind of woman.

Joe thought of the Lord's Prayer.

"Lead us not into temptation."

NOSY IN NEBRASKA

Going after Bonnie right now was not the Lord's leading. Joe didn't need a crack of thunder and a voice from heaven to tell him that. He turned from temptation and headed upstairs.

The only creaking was the lonely sound of his own footsteps.

He wanted his ghost back.

The whole town turned out to watch Clara come home.

Her daughter brought her to jail to officially see the charges dropped. Bonnie held the old lady's arm. Dora was there with baking supplies so Clara could get back to cooking. Carrie snapped a picture for the *Bugle*. Nick had a stepstool—which he opened and set on the ground so Clara could climb into his truck. Jeffie almost ran several people down.

Joe had his first chance to visit with Jeffie's mother, Marlys Piperson. A revealing conversation.

Joe kept expecting Maxie Mouse to come strolling down the street to watch the festivities. Then he saw Tallulah, shining like a beacon in a caftan splashed with tropical flowers, most of them orange, and a turban that held an unfortunate resemblance to a basketball. Tallulah held the new Maxie Taxi. So Maxie was in attendance, too.

Clara rambled, with only a rare word understandable, but Bonnie hung on every word and talked back. Nick nearly lifted Clara into his truck. Carrie snapped a picture. Dora handed Clara a sack of groceries; then Nick closed the door.

Joe would have mocked them all for coming, except here he was, too. Of course, the woman had been accused of killing his father. Joe might be the one person here expected to truly care about the Bum's death. True, he'd never met his father and didn't like him, and everybody knew that, but still, Joe had a legitimate personal interest in this case. It figured he'd be here. Besides, he was lonely, and this was the only action in town.

What would Clara do once she was alone? Attack? Curl up on the ground and scream? Bake? Her daughter just smiled indulgently. The rest of the family was on its way for a visit. Clara wasn't allowed to leave town until the case was settled. Junior held the theory that if she hadn't killed Gunderson, she might be a witness. And if she had a lucid moment—that happened occasionally—Junior might get important information from her.

Shayla Melnik showed up. Joe figured out who she was when a buzz hummed through the crowd like an electric current. Kevin was there with the Andersons, just another part of the rubbernecking throng. He knew enough about the town now to realize Shayla and Kevin were brother and sister. Shayla walked up to her brother and the two stepped away from the gathering to talk privately. They looked angry and seemed to be arguing, but they were far enough away that no one could hear a word.

It was driving all of Melnik nuts, Joe included.

"Hey, Nick, wait a second." Carrie waved her camera like a starting flag.

Nick nodded and walked to his wife's side.

"Before you all leave, I've got news. The article I wrote in last week's paper about the lightning strike and the museum collapse got into the *World-Herald* on Sunday."

"Everybody knows that, Carrie." Dora's voice sent a chill of fear down Joe's spine, and he quit slouching.

"Then the AP Newswire picked it up, and just last night I drove to Omaha and did an interview about the museum and our identity as Melnikians. That was supposed to be for the Omaha station, but I got a call this morning and it's going to be on the national news tonight."

That got everyone chattering. Carrie waited until the noise died down.

"And *Current Events*, the TV show, is coming to town to do a human-interest piece about us. They should be here later today. I might be phoning some of you for interviews. They're going to particularly want to talk about the historical society museum." Carrie shuddered visibly. "I'll need one of you to help them get pictures of Maxie."

A gasp of delight rose higher this time.

"Wait, there's more. Bonnie?"

Bonnie stepped beside Carrie. "We've had some interest from several small manufacturing companies about Melnik."

Joe's heart swelled with pride as he watched Bonnie speak to the town. He saw the pink in her cheeks and the sparkle in her eyes. She was in her element as Melnik's biggest cheerleader.

"If they decide to locate here, it could mean dozens of jobs for Melnik, maybe even hundreds." Bonnie smiled until Joe needed sunglasses to look at her.

A shout of delight went up.

"I can quit commuting to the city?" a man shouted over the babble.

"Maybe there'll be part-time work so I can be home with the kids after school," a woman said.

Happy voices. People making plans, excited, wanting more of their home-town, not less.

Joe couldn't figure it out. If they wanted to work near their homes, why didn't they just move?

Bonnie went on, the crowd now hanging on her every word. "And that could mean other new businesses, like restaurants and retail stores, which in turn would mean more jobs. More services could open here, like accountants and law offices and construction for new homes. This news story, if this comes out well, could kick off a new, exciting era in Melnik, Nebraska."

Tallulah raised Maxie in the air with a scream that would have backed down a Viking warrior.

Carrie shrieked and jumped into her husband's arms. No one gave her a second look as they talked and cheered.

Joe waited for a conga line to break out.

⁓

Bonnie refused to take part in the snake dance, led by Tallulah and Maxie.

She pushed herself to Joe's side. She tugged on his arm until they were far enough from the riot to speak in private. Her head was heavy with fatigue. Still shaking from standing up in front of the crowd, she needed to settle one huge worry. She'd slept a total of three hours last night, and those hours had been plagued with ghosts and bats and secret doors opening and dragging her into the bowels of the earth.

"We need to talk about the fact that you own Maxie."

"Oh yeah. I forgot. Let's go get him and I'll 'throw him away' like the will said."

Bonnie's eyes burned, and she had to make a conscious effort to hold them open. "I think we need to do it right. We need to make sure the terms of the will are satisfied. At the very least, that means we need witnesses. When Greg and Brian were here, they might have been enough, but now, with them gone, we need someone else. Right now, no one else knows about it. If we ask anybody, this mob"—she tilted her head at the celebrating crowd—"could turn on you, and you'd end up under the museum rubble. Let's keep it quiet for now and figure it out after *Current Events* goes home."

"Sure, no problem."

He just didn't get it. "Of course it's a *problem*. Can't you see how everyone loves Maxie?" They turned to watch the dancing switch over to the "Hokey Pokey."

When Tallulah put Maxie's "left foot out" to "shake it all about," the mouse got too close to Carrie, and even safe in Nick's strong arms, she screamed. Nick swept her toward his truck, lifted her in, and drove away.

"Almost everyone," Bonnie amended.

"Well, maybe we should tell the truth, then. It might add a dimension to the story."

"Not a chance!" Bonnie glared at Joe.

Joe grinned at her.

Those dimples should be outlawed. She tried to remember what they were talking about.

"It's so fun to watch you all fired up about that stupid mouse. You practically run this town, don't you, Bonnie?" His eyes flickered to her lips.

She remembered that he'd kissed her that time in his library, when she'd threatened to hurl a cast-iron piggy bank at his head. She'd been teasing and acting like she was bold and confident. At that moment it hadn't been an act, but in the normal course of things, it was completely out of character.

Bonnie, shy and beige, didn't interest him. But this fake Bonnie, the one who couldn't last and wasn't real, caught his attention. Joe hadn't seen her worrying or blushing, tongue-tied and awkward. At least not much. He seemed to think she was influential and powerful.

But that wasn't her.

And he had no interest in the beige Bonnie.

She wanted to slug him.

She should.

He might kiss her again.

"I know you don't take Maxie seriously. But just go along with me on this, okay? I. . ." She looked over her shoulder and dropped her voice lower. "I'm afraid if Shayla sues for Gunderson's property, she could come out of this somehow owning Maxie. I don't trust her to do the right thing. And I want to go through some of those old files. I'd like to do that before the TV show turns up. Did Sven really own Maxie? I was sure his ancestors donated him to the town. I'd like to nail that down before we do some bogus 'throwing Maxie away' stunt."

Bonnie looked around. "Where'd Shayla go? Junior wanted to talk to her. See if she'd let anything slip about her dad and the Gunderson house. We might be able to prove she or Kevin have been sneaking in there. You know Shayla's now the prime suspect for killing Sven. Antifreeze, d-CON, both poisons."

"She'll turn up," Joe said with his usual disregard for the vital importance of Melnik in general and Maxie in particular. "And don't worry, I'll play along about King Rat."

His smile widened, and Bonnie turned away before the dimples hypnotized her into doing something stupid. . .like hoping.

19

Once *Current Events* got wind of Sven's murder, the story about Melnik's hopes and idealism threatened to become a lost episode of *Twin Peaks*.

Joe didn't know what do to when they asked to interview him. He tried to speak of the kindness and simplicity of life in Melnik. He also tried not to lie. He was a Christian, after all.

But talking about Melnik in glowing terms? He knew Bonnie expected it, and that helped him to do it.

"The best thing and worst thing about a small town is the same thing. Everybody knows. Everybody knows if you mess up; it's true." Honesty forced Joe to say, "That can feel like an invasion of privacy, and in the city, with people everywhere and neighbors so close you can see in each other's windows, privacy becomes very important.

"But in a small town, if something bad happens to you, everybody knows that, too. People in Melnik are ready with emotional, physical, and spiritual help because they *know* you. They know who you are and what you need. Since my father's death, this town has opened its heart to me."

Joe thought of Bonnie's sweet, courageous heart. Was it open to him? Did he want it to be?

Joe thought of Clara. In the city she'd most likely be locked up or living on the street. "If your family has health problems. . ."

He thought of Kevin Melnik. "Or needs help during hard times. . ."

He thought of the funeral dinner for Liza Simpson "Or in the event of a death in the family. . ."

He thought of the town helping move the contents of the collapsed museum. "Or if there's a storm. . ."

He thought of how the whole town pulled together to keep Jeffie from killing himself or others.

In fact, what *had* happened since he'd come to town that wasn't wrapped in kindness? He thought of Dora, but he moved on.

In the bright TV lights, he concluded, "The people here know each other. They care about each other. They help each other. This is what America should be. This small-town kindness and support is the backbone of America, the *best* America, the *real* America."

Bonnie sniffled and wiped her eyes. Well, she ought to. Joe had turned into a poet right in front of her bloodshot eyes. It had been easy, because he believed every word. He did his best to pay attention to the interviewer's next question when what he wanted to do was go hug Bonnie.

The reporter concluded. By the time he packed up and left, Bonnie's tired eyes were dry and Joe had missed his chance.

⸻

"We've been through all these files. There's nothing here to find, Bon-Bon."

Bonnie started, looked up, then grinned. "Don't even think of calling me by any of my odious brothers' nicknames."

Joe smiled. He knew the power of his smile—he'd heard about his dimples too many times in too glowing of terms. He tried to use his power for good. "There were some boxes in the attic. It looked like they might have belonged to whoever was living here. They weren't covered in dust. Junior set them aside to go through later, but we could have a look."

"Sounds good." Bonnie dusted her hands on her beige slacks.

She was still wearing the same thing she'd put on for the television camera, her best beige outfit. Joe wanted to tease her, but he refrained. "You want to go home and change? It's filthy up there."

"No, these will wash."

Joe suspected Bonnie didn't own anything that wouldn't wash.

"I'd like to get a look at the attic." Bonnie looked up the stairs. "I think that once we're through up there, it'll be time to call in the town and let them help clear this place out."

Joe nodded. "Sounds great. Just the thought of cleaning this place myself is overwhelming."

He followed Bonnie up the stairs, thinking about the future. He thought of the words he'd said to the reporter, and it settled in his heart that every word was true. His promise to his mother wasn't what mattered. What his mother really wanted was for him to be happy. And he'd just decided happiness meant Melnik and this house and Bonnie.

He didn't even let it bother him when his house creaked.

⸻

A companionable hour later, Joe realized the sun had set.

The lights were on and the only windows were so dirty they didn't let much sun in, but the streetlight blinking on through the nearest window caught his attention.

Joe sifted slowly down through the last stack of old clothes. They most likely were hiding nothing, but he checked every pocket. Whatever else kind of slob had been here, whether this house had been a hideout for Kevin Melnik, or had been Shayla's home for the last year, or these were things left behind by Wilkie, the intruder hadn't left his name behind.

Bonnie emptied the final box.

She lifted a picture. "This *has* to belong to Wilkie. This is an old picture of his family. Wilkie's father, a notorious drunk, died young. His mother died when Wilkie was about sixteen, I suppose. I remember Wilkie dropped out of school. Not too many kids in Melnik do that, so it was a big deal." Bonnie showed Joe the photo.

A beleaguered woman held a blond-headed little boy on her hip. A man who looked much older than her stood at her side, a cigarette in his mouth, a toddler clinging to his knee, frowning at the camera.

"Which child is Wilkie?"

"The one being held. The older one is his brother, Melvin. They were really close in age. Melvin died in the military. He's the only one in that family who had dreams and goals. He got out and started to make something of himself. And he ended up dead. Ironic, huh?"

Joe nodded. He set the clothing aside. There was nowhere else to search. Only the pictures remained, so he scooted closer to Bonnie as she flipped through pictures of Wilkie that seemed to document his wasted life. His father vanished from the pictures while Wilkie was still a toddler. The lines in his mother's face deepened.

The brothers grew up by jumps—there weren't that many photos. One photo was disturbing because the older brother had one arm slung around Wilkie's neck. Melvin had a cruel smile. The little brother looked angry and scared, like this wasn't an embrace he welcomed.

Wilkie in a school picture as a skinny high school kid, a phony smile that didn't reach hostile eyes.

Melvin alone, sneering, a cigarette dangling from his lips, saluting the camera with a brown bottle in his hand.

"Melvin made something of himself?" Joe tapped on the picture. "Are you sure? He looks like he's cut from the same cloth as his father."

"Compared to his parents and his grandparents, joining the army was outrageously productive. He's probably ten years older than me, but I remember we had an assembly at school. The principal spoke. The band played. We all sang "When Those Caissons Go Rolling Along" and "The Star-Spangled Banner." Melvin led us in the Pledge of Allegiance. It was really patriotic and inspiring. I was proud Melvin came from my town. He died in some accident just weeks after he left for basic training. Shortly after that his mother died; then Wilkie quit school and began a life dedicated to underemployment."

"That's too bad. Maybe Wilkie would have followed Melvin into the service if Melvin had lived."

Bonnie nodded and rubbed her eyes.

"So did you sleep last night?"

Bonnie looked up as she flipped to the next picture. "Not really—a little. Maybe tonight."

"It's getting late. As soon as we finish these, go on home and rest."

Bonnie looked up at the window. "It's dark out." She laughed softly. "When did that happen?"

She looked back at Joe. He'd made a point of leaning closer when she was distracted. "That speech I gave this afternoon to the TV reporter really opened my eyes to some of the best things about Melnik."

Bonnie's laugh settled into her usual generous, quiet smile. "It was wonderful, Joe. I hope they use every word of it. Thank you."

"You don't need to thank me. Everything I said came straight from my heart."

"Really?"

He saw hope in her eyes. Joe said a silent prayer that Bonnie's hopes matched his.

"Yeah, really. I've decided. . .that is, I wondered. . .if maybe you. . ." He didn't know how to put it into words. It was an all-new dream and he had just settled on it.

"Maybe I what?"

Joe reached for her then stopped. "I'm filthy. I don't dare touch you."

Bonnie caught his hand and smiled. He lowered his head. Their lips met.

Joe lifted his head. "I thought maybe you. . ."

Bonnie looked down as if too shy to meet his eyes. He loved that about her. Her courage and her shyness.

"I thought maybe you. . ."

"It can't be."

"Sure it can." Joe decided to use his smile to hypnotize her quick before she ran off.

She didn't get the smile because she focused on something on the floor. "Will you look at that?"

Joe wondered what she saw that could be better than another kiss. He followed the line of her gaze as she reached for a picture she'd dropped on the floor.

The attic plunged into darkness.

Joe sat up straight. "What—"

A floorboard creaked. No ghost, no old house, a footstep. Right behind him. He whirled to put himself between Bonnie and whoever was up here.

A soft whoosh of air warned him and he ducked, but something glanced off his temple and sent him backward into Bonnie. He felt her warm body as he knocked her flat.

"Joe, are you all right?" Bonnie's hands caught at him.

He struggled to sit up. . .to block the next blow with no idea where it might be coming from. Bonnie, right behind him, was suddenly gone. Her scream was cut off.

Joe struggled against unconsciousness. Head throbbing, he scrambled to his hands and knees. His hands reached wide. Where was she? He had to protect her.

She was nowhere.

A sudden wrench of pain arched his neck back. Heavy fingers anchored his head. Joe clawed at the restraint. Something hit his hands so hard he jerked them away. A voice, eerie, like nothing he'd ever heard before, whispered in his ear.

"The Ghost has her."

"What? Who—" Joe's neck arched so sharply it cut off his words. He reached toward the hands that restrained him. There was a blow to his fingers again, hard, maybe a metal pipe or a crowbar. Darkness pulled at him. Warmth ran into his eyes near where he'd been hit in the temple. He smelled blood.

His own, he knew.

"The Ghost wants her."

"No." It wasn't real. The pain in his head had him confused.

The whisper seemed to come from inside him.

"The Ghost needs his fun."

"No, please. Please don't hurt her." *God, please protect her.*

A soft laugh, rancid breath, made Joe shudder. He reached for the restraining hand again. He'd been in the military. He knew self-defense. But his head spun and his hands weren't coordinated.

The pipe struck his fingers and glanced off his head.

"I'll give you one more chance." The voice echoed, wavered, laced with madness.

"One more chance for what?"

The whisper faded. The fetid breath washed over Joe's face. His neck twisted. He couldn't breathe.

Joe focused all his strength on remaining conscious. He had to get free, to save Bonnie.

"To get out of my house!"

Joe's head slammed forward and struck the hardwood floor.

There was no sound from Bonnie. No cry for help. Footsteps creaked away. Joe, dazed, blinded by the darkness, prayed for the strength to keep going. Each inch was a battle as his throbbing head tried to stop him. His body begged him to stop. He crawled in the direction of those steps. He was too dizzy, too slow, too stupid. The footsteps sounded burdened as if they carried a load, a body. Bonnie.

Whoever it was clearly went down the stairs. Joe reached the top of the steps and began dragging himself down.

20

Joe slid on his belly down to the second-floor landing, praying every inch of the way. There he tugged his cell phone out of his pocket. It worked up here. He dialed 911 and took ten seconds to report the attack and Bonnie's disappearance. At the operator's instruction, he kept the phone line open but continued moving. His fumbled the cell on the stairs and it went clattering down ahead of him.

The footsteps faded, but he heard them go all the way to the ground floor. Joe didn't try to stand, afraid he'd fall. Crawling on his belly, like a failure, a weakling, stupid, he kept moving as the footsteps gained distance.

A siren came on at Junior's house. A truck roared to life at Nick's. The cavalry.

Thank You, God. A small town. Help just seconds away. Thank You.

Joe listened. Where had the Ghost taken Bonnie?

Once down the steps, Joe staggered to his feet. The back door squeaking open drew him toward the kitchen.

The siren grew louder and tires slid as someone stood on their brakes. Joe got to the back door. The lights were dead all over the house. The doorknob slipped under Joe's hand, and he realized his hand was slick with blood.

"Joe, where are you?"

Nick. The siren cut off and another car door slammed. Junior.

"Back door!" Joe stepped out into the murky darkness of his backyard and stumbled down the steps. Running footsteps came toward him from the street.

He stopped when he saw her.

Bonnie. Laid out on the grass. Her beige clothes shining white in the moonlit night. On her back, motionless. Like a human sacrifice.

"Bonnie!" Falling to his knees beside her, he carefully gripped her shoulders. She groaned and tried to roll to her side.

Joe's heart missed a beat when she moved. The Ghost hadn't killed her.

"One more chance. Get out of my house."

Whoever had done this had hurt Bonnie because he wanted Joe out.

The guilt came at him in waves. Toxic waves as he thought of his selfishness.

He hadn't known or cared about his father. He hadn't wanted this house or the money. But he'd stayed. Selfishly, he'd stayed. Stupidly, he'd stayed.

Stupid, stupid, stupid. He should have just gone to college. He'd promised his mother. He'd promised, and then he'd considered breaking that promise, and if that didn't make him stupid, nothing did.

God, I'm so sorry. Please don't let her be hurt because of me.

Nick rounded the house with a flashlight and was beside them in an instant. He started examining Bonnie. Junior came next. Another siren fired up. The Melnik Volunteer Fire and Rescue Department.

"What happened here, Joe?" Junior shined a light in Joe's eyes, and Joe lifted a hand to block the glare.

Junior gasped and came to Joe's side. "You're bleeding."

Nick looked up from Bonnie.

"Thanks for coming." Joe reached across Bonnie to make contact with Nick, Junior, anyone—he was so glad to see a familiar face. So grateful to live somewhere that the neighbors would come running to help.

His hand gleamed red, blood soaked, in the light. He lifted his hand toward his temple.

"A ghost. We were attacked by a ghost." He was barely aware of collapsing.

***

Bonnie saw his eyes flutter open and quit praying.

She'd been beseeching the Lord to let Joe be okay for the past hour. She practically dove toward him. She leaned until their eyes met.

Thank You, Lord.

She barely touched his tousled hair, brushing it past the white gauze that protected his stitches. He was stretched out on a hospital bed.

Bonnie had prayed nonstop all through the ambulance ride. They'd made her go along, but the bump on the head hadn't bled, hadn't left her with anything more than a headache and a knot on the skull.

Joe reached for her, groaned in pain, and let his hand drop to the bed. "Why did I stay here? Why didn't I get out of town the second I knew there was danger? Done. Done with Melnik and that house. Stupid, stupid, stupid." Joe's eyes fluttered closed.

Bonnie's stomach sank. She'd expected words of love. He'd been on the verge of saying them in the attic, she was sure. But instead he talked of leaving, and he certainly made no mention of her.

But did he know what he was saying? Maybe the blow to his head had addled his words. Or maybe it had cleared out all his manners and reason and he was left with only the stark truth.

Bonnie hit the CALL button and told the nurse Joe had been awake momentarily. The nurse said it was a good sign. Bonnie dozed off a couple of times in the orange vinyl recliner by his bed. Nurses woke Joe every hour to make sure his concussion hadn't pulled him into a coma. Between that and nightmares of being attacked by the ghost of Wilkie Melnik, plus her insomnia, Bonnie's head throbbed the next morning more from exhaustion than the attack.

Joe lay awake, subdued, until the doctor examined him and discharged him from the hospital.

Nick and Carrie had brought Bonnie her car so she could drive Joe home. Except Melnik wasn't home. He barely uttered a word.

They pulled up to his house because Junior had ordered them to meet him there. The awful old mausoleum seemed to sneer at her, daring her to come in.

"I'm getting my stuff and getting out. Stupid idea to stay here. Stupid. You could have been killed." Joe glanced at her then looked immediately away.

He didn't invite a response, so Bonnie kept silent.

They approached the house as Junior came out carrying a Ziploc bag with a paper inside.

"It's a note." He lifted it high. "I want a statement from both of you, separately and together. And I want you to see what else I've found."

"Not inside. I'm done with that place." Joe grabbed Bonnie's upper arm and pulled her to a stop.

Junior shrugged and showed both of them the note. The ink was red, the handwriting wavery and bottom heavy as if it dripped blood. Five words.

Get out of my house.

"Let's go down to the station and talk, then. I need to go over this. Whoever attacked you has to be the same person that killed Sven. I'm not buying a ghost and I'm not buying Clara. She'd have never been able to carry Bonnie down those stairs."

Bonnie felt a shudder go through Joe, and he dropped her arm.

"For that matter, I don't see Shayla doing it. She's a little bit of a thing."

"There was something I—I saw something—right when the lights went out." Bonnie's eyes narrowed. "What was it?" She rubbed her head.

"Let's go." Joe turned toward his Jeep, obviously determined to drive himself. Which he shouldn't do in his condition.

Bonnie hesitated for a second; then she got mad. It gave her the courage to follow him and climb in beside him. She slammed the door, and Joe gave her a startled look.

Her instincts to protect herself almost overwhelmed her, but she couldn't let them. She'd backed down when it was obvious Nick preferred Carrie to her. But she'd never wanted Nick like she wanted Joe. And there was no pretty young blond in the wings waiting for Joe.

She crossed her arms as Joe turned the key. He waited while Junior lumbered toward his squad car.

"Before the attack last night." Bonnie leaned closer to him, praying for courage. . .praying for the right words. It would take a miracle, because she'd never before in her life come up with the right words. So if this was God's will and not her own foolish daydream, whatever words she spoke would be blessed.

"Last night, Joe, before that man attacked—"

"He could have killed you." Joe gripped the steering wheel until his knuckles turned white. "I got greedy. I wanted that money from a man I don't respect. I endangered everyone. Stupid."

"Forget the attack for a second, Joe. I thought. . .some things you said. . .I thought maybe you were going to say—" She fell silent. Praying he'd take the hint, pick up and finish her sentence, and finish what he'd started last night.

He stared straight out the window at the house.

Bonnie took every ounce of her courage and plunged on. "You said those nice things about Melnik to the reporters."

Joe snorted and shook his head. He muttered, "Stupid."

Bonnie's heart clutched, but she continued. "Joe, I. . .uh. . .we. . .we like having you in Melnik." She'd meant to say "I"—meant to and chickened out.

Joe turned on her, his eyes narrowed, anger, even contempt on his face. "Yeah, things have been great since I came back. The museum is destroyed."

"That was the lightning. And Dora."

"My father is dead."

"Joe, no one blames you—"

"Your sister-in-law is dead because your brother came to look at my will."

"You can't take responsibility for that."

"You were nearly killed."

"No, I wasn't."

"Only because the Ghost decided to let you live. I couldn't have stopped him. If he'd vanished the way he's done so many times before. . .with you. . .he could have done *anything, anything* to you. I *hate* this town. It made me want things I can't have. Easy life, money, a mansion. *Stupid!*" He slammed his fist on the steering wheel. "That's not my dream. It's not what I want out of life."

For one sickening moment his eyes were blazing with rage—hate, even. Bonnie felt it all the way to her heart. The rage was aimed straight at her. She couldn't look another second. She turned away.

Bonnie stuffed all her courage back down inside. Dumb idea to be honest, to speak from her heart. It struck her that the feeling she had right now was a lot like what had swamped her when she'd gotten word of her parents' deaths. This numbness, this lost, empty feeling that was too big and too awful. Unbearable. So she'd refused to feel it. Just deal with the details, like she'd done for Tyler with

Liza's funeral. Deal with one thing at a time. That was Christian, right?

Strength sufficient for the day. . .

Don't lay up treasures on earth.

The lilies of the field and the birds of the air don't worry and God provides.

Of course Joe was leaving. Only an idiot would believe a man with those dimples would be interested in her. Oh, he'd been a little interested. Bored, probably, in this small town. But of course he had dreams. And of course they didn't include her. What an idiot she'd been. Idiot.

Tears burned her eyes and she cut off the self-contempt. No energy for that either. No tears.

No heart attack.

Just one foot in front of the other. She squared her shoulders and forced her lungs to work. Okay, lungs working, what next?

"Let's go answer Junior's questions, then, so you can get out of here and get on with your life."

Joe shifted into REVERSE and backed onto the street. He aimed the car at the police station and Bonnie kept breathing. Right now that was all God gave her the strength to do.

21

J oe tossed his duffel bag on the floor of the Melnik Bed-and-Breakfast, Minus Breakfast.

The only reason he was still in town was because Junior threatened to arrest him if he tried to leave.

He sank down onto the bed in the empty house. He had to get out of Melnik. He'd locked the house up tight so the Ghost could have free rein. He'd fired Nick from the renovation project to keep Nick from getting hurt.

Then Joe had moved in here. He hoped this only lasted one night.

Staring out the upstairs window of the tidy house, he thought about college. His mother's dream. . .no, *his* dream. His. Of course it was his. He'd finish. Only a couple of semesters left on his anthropology degree, except now he thought he might want to be a teacher, work with kids. He enjoyed teaching magic to Jeffie. He felt a powerful need to reach a troubled kid like Kevin. He even appreciated Bonnie's rowdy brothers. He'd been out of school so long he couldn't even remember what a person did with an anthropology degree, but it had interested him, and when he was in the army, it had seemed like a good idea to try to understand civilization.

He sat there and planned and claimed his dream, and then Dora drove past. He could just barely see her gray head through the leafed-out trees. She had a new car. Another Chrysler New Yorker. This one only ten years old. Her old one was still in the basement of the Melnik Historical Museum. He'd heard rumors that it might just be left there.

Dora. Bonnie. The Ghost. This stupid town, his stupid dream of belonging and knowing his neighbors and finding a home.

"No!" He said it out loud to force himself to quit thinking nonsense. This town, belonging, wasn't his dream. His dream was college, making his mother proud. But he'd left things in a mess. Whoever had attacked him last night wasn't just dangerous to someone in that house. He was dangerous to everyone in this town. Joe had to fix this before he left. Fix it so no one else, ever, was in danger.

Shayla? Maybe, if she had help.

Kevin? He was big enough, strong enough to carry Bonnie. He was Shayla's brother. They could be working together.

Clara? Impossible. But completely impossible? Joe's head ached just thinking about it.

He surged to his feet and moved close enough to the window to watch Dora ride her brake down Main Street. She was going to Jansson's for coffee. She lived on the north side of town, and she'd already passed her intersection if she was headed home. Joe marveled that he knew that.

He stormed down the stairs, ignoring the persistent ache in his head as he made his plan. A plan that began, of course, with Dora.

He'd have coffee, start a rumor, end this tonight.

He jumped in his Jeep to drive the few blocks to Jansson's.

Joe walked boldly into his house.

Not for long his house, but for now. . .

He announced in a voice meant to carry through walls that have ears, "I did it, Ghost. I found a way to drive you out. I donated this house to the Melnik Historical Society. Starting tomorrow, this place is going to be open to the public. It's going to have people in and out all day, every day. And I told them who you are, too. I figured it out. There's going to be no place for you to hide inside or out. You don't know it yet, but you've just been exorcized."

Joe laughed.

He hoped it sounded as gleeful as he felt, because this was going to work. He'd hand the Ghost over to Junior—Joe touched the handcuffs he'd bought at Wal-Mart just hours ago—and leave this town to heal, without any help from a murderer who would kill to keep a stolen roof over his head.

Joe had a flashlight in his utility belt. No one was unplugging a fuse and sneaking up on him. He had a thermos of coffee to ward off sleep. He had the buzz going all through town that even a reclusive ghost couldn't fail to hear. Joe settled in, choosing the living room because the stone fireplace didn't show any signs of secret panels, which Joe hoped would keep anyone from sneaking up on his rear guard.

He kept his back to the stone wall, his flashlight close at hand, and his mind on his plan.

He let the light from the windows fade and he waited. He knew the arrogance of this pseudo-ghost. This insult to his pride couldn't go unchallenged.

"Joe!" the front door crashed open. "Are you all right?"

The hairs on the back of Joe's neck stood on end. He jumped to his feet and ran to the entry. "Get out!"

"No! I heard about your donation. I heard you'd figured out who killed Sven. Joe, I know—"

A creaking floorboard almost sent him into a panic. He'd never get her out of here in time. Joe clamped his hand over Bonnie's mouth and dragged her by the wrist into the living room. He plunked her down in his secure corner.

"Shut up!"

Bonnie froze, her eyes wide.

Joe resisted the urge to grunt, caveman-like, with satisfaction at her obedience. He whispered only inches from her ear, "What are you doing here? I'm trying to catch a ghost. Now he can use you against me."

Bonnie jerked her head sideways in a little shrug. "I came to save you."

Joe rolled his eyes. "Fine, just what I need."

She whispered, "You know, he attacked before when we were talking. What makes you think he needs quiet? You remember I told you I saw something upstairs in the attic. I want to go back up there and look again at those pictures. That will jar my memory."

"The Ghost jars people's memories with a crowbar. We are absolutely not going up there. Are you insane?"

"If it's so dangerous, then what in heaven's name gave you the idea to come in here alone? This is a stupid plan."

That zinged straight to his ego. "Don't call me stupid."

"I didn't call you stupid. I called your plan stupid."

A board creaked and the gloom of dusk made every shadow a hiding place. Bonnie fell silent.

"Go on home, Bonnie. Get out of here." In the dim light, Joe noticed that she wasn't wearing beige. She had on a red sweater. It distracted him from panicking. "You look nice."

"I do?" She smiled; then her eyebrows slammed together. "Don't change the subject. You started that rumor so you could ride to the whole town's rescue and then leave?" She practically hissed at him. His little kitten had some claws. "What's that, the code of the West? The Love Ranger?"

Joe had been scanning the room, trying to locate the source of the creaking noise. He jerked his head around. "What did you say?"

"Lone!" Bonnie shouted, and even in the murky light Joe saw her face redden until it matched her sweater. "*Lone* Ranger."

Joe fought his fury. Fought his fear. Fought his love. Then he wondered why anyone would fight against love. If he did that, he probably really *was* stupid.

Bonnie leaned close. "It was a slip, but only because I. . .I. . .didn't want to tell you."

Wide, vulnerable brown eyes were all he could see.

"You love me?"

Bonnie nodded.

Joe laughed. "The small-town curator has more courage than the big bad soldier."

"That's not true. You're not afraid of Jeffie."

314

"I can't let you get away with beating me on courage." He wrapped his arms around her and pulled her against him and kissed her. Then kissed her again. Then she was kissing him back.

When he came up to breathe, he whispered, "It's true for me, too. I love you."

Her arms wound around his neck and his mouth slanted.

Sudden movement in the shadows drove him to his feet, and he shoved her behind him. Joe leaped at the dark figure and tackled him. No ghost. Solid, human. Flattened onto the floor, Joe grappled with the Ghost until he lay still; then he clicked on his flashlight and identified Kevin Melnik.

"Kevin, no!" Bonnie came up beside them as Joe fished his handcuffs out of his pocket and snapped one wristlet onto Kevin. "You killed Sven Gunderson?"

Kevin lay facedown. He took one wild swing at Joe with his free hand. Joe ducked. Good thing. His head didn't need another whack. He still hurt from last night.

"Let me go. I'm just looking for what's mine. I heard you were donating this place to the town and I knew this was my last night to search. Gunderson stole everything from my family. I know I can prove it if I just go through this house."

Bonnie knelt beside Kevin. "Joe, he's only sixteen. He couldn't have killed anybody."

"Yeah, right." Joe struggled to try to lock the wiry kid's other hand in the cuffs.

"Gunderson tricked my mom into killing my dad. Dad told us there was proof in here that Gunderson had stolen from our family. Dad said there was a lot more than just that Main Street property, and that's all the town paid us for." Kevin wrenched away.

All this wrestling gave Joe back his headache. "So you kept searching after your father was dead, and when Gunderson caught you, you killed him and tried to pin it on Clara."

"I didn't kill anybody! I just started searching after Gunderson died. I wasn't going to come in this place while Gunderson was here. All the kids knew he slept with an ax in his hands."

Joe almost smiled at the spooky lore built up around this house.

"Stop fighting," Bonnie scolded.

"Your schoolmarm voice might not work that well with murderers, Bon-Bon."

"You're going to have to go talk to Junior, Kevin. Whether there is something of yours in here or not doesn't change the fact that you're breaking and entering. Now settle down."

The kid went limp, his face squashed against the floor.

"'Now settle down.'" Joe smirked. "Why didn't I think of that?"

A hard thud knocked Joe forward. His last thought was, *Kevin isn't my ghost.*

⸻

Bonnie screamed and scrambled backward from the man who loomed over Joe. "Wilkie?"

A laugh, ghostly—deliberately ghostly, Bonnie knew—erupted from the lips of a man who was *not* Wilkie Melnik, but he looked enough like him to be his. . . brother? "Melvin?"

The laughter grew louder. In quick movements, the man clipped Kevin's loose handcuff to Joe's wrist.

Kevin wasn't fast enough to escape. "Uncle Melvin?"

"I'm the Ghost. I'm no one's uncle."

Kevin pulled against the restraint. With Joe's deadweight, he was pinned in place. Bonnie jumped to her feet and whirled toward the living room door.

A heavy weight slammed her to the ground, and Melvin Melnik—he was no ghost, and Bonnie wasn't believing anything different even though everyone knew Melvin was dead—dragged her across the room on her stomach.

"No, what are you doing?"

The attacker tied Bonnie's hands with a speed that would impress a rodeo cowboy. He flipped her onto her back and she kicked at him, shouting. She landed a solid blow that brought him to his knees. It wasn't enough, though. His eyes blazed with fury—no, Bonnie thought, with madness. He lifted her by the front of her red sweater, and Bonnie braced herself for a brutal fist. Instead, he pushed her against the heavy oak end table. With a few quick motions, he secured her to it then stood and upended a wastebasket on the couch only inches away from her.

He laughed as he pulled out a book of matches and struck a light.

"No, stop! I'm your nephew! Wilkie was my dad—you can't do this! You can't leave me here!"

The man hesitated as the match burned. He looked down at the boy. "You've got the Melnik looks, no doubt about it." The man's laughter returned. "You'll be one less person wanting to share this property. With sonny boy gone and you, I'll only have Shayla to deal with."

"But if you burn the house down, you won't get it." Bonnie squirmed against the ropes.

The man's eyes narrowed at Bonnie's reasoning. "I've lost it anyway. If he's donating it to the town, I'll never have it. Now no one can. And there's more property. I'll wait, bide my time until they get over hunting for a ghost; then I'll come back and stake my claim."

He dropped the match.

"No, you can't do this!" Bonnie screamed. Kevin kicked at his uncle, and Melvin just stepped aside so the boy couldn't reach him.

When flames began leaping from the couch, Melvin lifted a burning cushion and tossed it toward the far side of the room, into a stack of papers. The papers caught fire with a *whomph* and ignited the drapes nearby. The fire crackled and grew.

Melvin watched. Bonnie saw his hungry eyes enjoying the flames. Where had he been all these years? From the ugly, crudely drawn tattoos all over his arms and neck, his heartless brutality, and this sick love of burning things, Bonnie would bet prison.

Finally, his appetite for destruction seemed to be sated. Melvin looked at the ceiling with one last maniacal laugh and walked out of the room.

Kevin jumped to his feet and tried to battle the flames on the couch. With Joe anchoring him, it wasn't easy. Bonnie thought fast. "Joe's got his phone. See if it works."

A clatter off to the side pulled their attention away from the fire, and they saw, out the front window, in the dim streetlight, Melvin march straight out the front door of the house. Bonnie looked past Melvin to see Clara pulling her cart, talking, ranting like always.

Clara shouted, "Didit! Didit!" She pointed at Melvin, who stormed toward her.

The crazy woman tossed something at Melvin, a small object Bonnie couldn't identify. It must have landed straight in Melvin's path, because the man slipped. One foot flew high in the air. His ghostly voice had vanished and he howled like an angry wolf then landed with a crack that could only be made with his head on the sidewalk.

"Clara! Help us!"

Joe stirred and groaned.

"Joe, you've got to get up." Bonnie fought the rope binding her.

Kevin turned to Joe and tried to help him up as the flames grew and spread.

Clara came inside, pulling her pie cart, talking to herself. Bonnie's stomach swooped with nausea as she realized that Clara wouldn't be able to help them. By calling her, Bonnie had just consigned Clara to a horrible death, too.

Then Dora and Tallulah charged into the house, both armed with fire extinguishers. They lived closer than the fire station and had seen the flames, was Bonnie's best guess. She was glad to see them.

"I already called 911!" Dora yelled. A siren fired to life across town. Dora and Tallulah wielded their foaming swords like knights of old and had the fire out within seconds.

Joe was awake enough now to fish his key out of his pocket. Bonnie had never thought of a key. Of course Joe had the key; they were his handcuffs. He unlocked Kevin and the boy ran.

"Don't step on Maxie!" Tallulah screamed and ran after the boy. Joe had Bonnie untied in time for her to turn and see Tallulah pick Maxie up from right in front of the sprawled form of Melvin Melnik. That was the little form Clara had thrown—or maybe Maxie had leaped all on his own. Bonnie just loved that big mouse.

Maxie had saved the day. Tallulah carried him back into the house, smiling proudly at him.

"Piesforsale."

Maxie and Crazy Clara.

Joe pulled Bonnie into his arms as the fire trucks pulled up with Junior in his squad car hard on their heels.

Dora turned toward Bonnie and Joe. "I told you she'd be here with him, Tallulah. I told you something was up between those two."

"You were spying on us?" Bonnie asked, not really all that surprised. And not one bit upset since it had brought them running with fire extinguishers. She looked at Joe and he winked at her. There *was* something up between the two of them after all. Dora had it exactly right.

"And Clara was carrying Maxie around?" Tallulah lifted Maxie up to eye level and fussed with his extremely rumpled fur. "I'm changing the lock for good this time. No one is going to be able to get Maxie out of his cage but me."

"NobodystarvesinMelnik. NotwhileI'mhere."

By the time Tallulah was done fussing, Maxie looked better than ever. Apparently he'd needed a good fluffing, and Melvin's boot slipping on him had been just the ticket.

Dora, Tallulah, Joe, Bonnie, Junior, and Hal each bought a pie, wiping out Crazy Clara's supply. She headed home to resume baking. Tallulah, who lived just over the hedge, volunteered her garbage can for pie disposal.

Nick finished rooting out sparks in the carpet and sent the fire trucks home. Carrie took pictures. Dora snooped.

"So is anyone curious about why Melvin Melnik isn't dead?" Bonnie asked.

Junior had loaded the unconscious Melvin in the ambulance and sent him to Bjorn. No one was wasting the gas to take him to the big hospital in Gillespie. "You shoulda gone to the hospital, too, Joe. Two blows to the head in twenty-four hours is bad business. You should spend the night under observation."

"Forget it. I'm fine." Joe rubbed his head sheepishly and looked at Bonnie. "I'm sorry. My reckless plan almost got you killed."

"But how did Melvin hear the gossip? He never left this house." Bonnie looked from one to the other. "Something doesn't add up here."

Junior pulled out his notebook. "He confessed to killing Sven clear as day;

you all heard him. And he was bent on killing all of you. We don't need a lot of investigation. I've spent the last few minutes on the phone with the county sheriff, and he plugged Melvin's name into his computer."

Bonnie snapped her fingers. "That's it. That's what I've been trying to remember. Right before Melvin whacked me last night, Joe. Up in the attic."

"What?" Joe came to her side, listening to her, supporting her, respecting her, admiring her sweater. Bonnie would have cried from the sweetness of it if she didn't have such big news.

"I saw a picture of Melvin. A picture like a mug shot, with numbers across his chest. It fell out of that stack, and I caught a glimpse of it just as the lights went out."

"You two were up in the attic with the lights out?" Dora sounded gleeful.

"We were being attacked by a murderer, Dora. Nothing romantic about it." Except that wasn't exactly true. Right before things had gone so badly awry, something very romantic had indeed happened. Then Joe had chickened out. But not for long. He'd found his courage again tonight.

Dora sniffed as if she didn't believe a word of it.

"You did see a mug shot, Bonnie. Melvin had more of them than some kids have school pictures. Instead of dying in the service like Wilkie told everyone, Melvin went AWOL and stole a car on his way out of the barracks. High-speed chase. Pulled a gun on the military police and took someone hostage. He spent ten years in the brig for that mess, and he's been in and out of jail ever since. He's spent most of his life in prison."

Junior flipped a page. "He just got out a couple of months ago, heard about the fuss over Wilkie's death, and sneaked into town scheming to reclaim his family's wealth—which is stupid. His family didn't have any wealth to reclaim, going back four generations. . .at least. And if he had reclaimed the wealth, he'd have drunk it up or gambled it away. Idiot Melniks—shame we named this town after them."

"Everyone knows it should have been named Evans." Carrie snapped a picture of them all standing in the smoke-stained room.

"Get over it, Carrie." Bonnie shook her head. "It's too late to change the name."

"You're right. Especially now that we're on that TV show. I phoned them, by the way, when we arrested Melvin. They hadn't gotten on the plane in Omaha yet. They're coming back to add this mess to the story." Carrie shrugged. "If I play it right, and I will, Kevin Melnik can come out a hero, and we can restore some dignity to this town and its name."

"Good. It sounds like you've thought of everything." Bonnie smiled at Carrie.

"That kid broke into my house to rob it. You can't make him a hero." Joe ruffled his hair.

Bonnie had come very close to finally seeing just how close Joe's hair came to mink. And she intended to come much closer before she was done.

"Oh, Joe, let him be the hero. It'll be good for his self-esteem. I mean, if you'd have known his parents. . ." Dora shook her head in disgust. "Trashy, trashy people."

"Kevin needs this." Tallulah produced Maxie's cage from her voluminous caftan. She opened her hand to reveal Maxie.

Carrie squealed and landed in Nick's arms.

Tallulah snorted and settled Maxie in his cage.

Nick said, "Well, the party's over. Carrie and I'll go on home now." He toted her out, grinning at her while she looked over her shoulder.

Bonnie knew Carrie very well. She was keeping her eye on Maxie in case he made any sudden moves.

"Why does Carrie do that jumping and screaming thing again? I forget." Joe winced when he touched the sore spot on the back of his head. His forehead bandage was gone.

Bonnie could see a bruise and his stitches in the front. She wondered how badly his head hurt and patted him on the arm. "You'll get to know how things work in a small town."

Joe turned to her. "Yeah, I will, because I'm staying. I'm keeping the house, and instead of donating it to the historical society, I'll buy that pretty marble building on Main Street and donate it. Nick will fix it up—and this house."

"No, we're building a new museum, Joe. It's all settled." Bonnie narrowed her eyes at him.

"I think we should use an old one."

"It's not handicapped accessible. A new one will be better."

Joe leaned close. "We'll figure it all out later. For now, why don't you marry me and we'll live here—plenty of room for all your brothers to come home for Christmas."

Dora whooped and laughed until her stomach bounced up and crashed into her chins. "I knew it." She headed out to spread the word.

Bonnie, her eyes wide with shock, said, "You should never have said that in front of Dora. She's got ears like a bat. Now the whole town will know before I've even had a chance to think about it."

"Not if you think fast."

Bonnie smiled. "We really haven't known each other long. I don't think we should get married before we've. . .for example. . .had a date."

"We can take awhile to get married, then, Miss Cautious. I just. . .well, I'm thirty-five. Not some kid who doesn't know what he wants. I know I'd be the luckiest man alive if I could get you to marry me. If you want to wait, we'll wait. But just so you know exactly what we're waiting for. The decision is already made in my heart to marry you. I love you, Bon-Bon."

A loud sigh from the hallway informed them that Dora hadn't gone to spread the word as Bonnie had assumed. She was still eavesdropping.

Bonnie leaned to within a fraction of an inch from his ear. "Here's my answer. Yes."

Tallulah giggled.

Maxie might have squeaked in satisfaction.

Then Joe did something no one could hear. He pulled Bonnie into his arms and sealed their promises with a kiss.

THE MICE MAN COMETH

1

Melnik, Nebraska—Population 1,138
Home of Maxie, the World's Largest Field Mouse

Tyler Simpson pounded his head with his fist, hoping his brain would start up.

Think, think, think. He knew the boys were behaving terribly, but he didn't know what to say or do to stop them. He struggled with every decision as if he still needed his wife to dictate every move he made.

Being dead was a huge stumbling block to her being in charge. Not insurmountable, though. He could still hear her nagging in his head. It had been burned into his brain.

Benetton roared into the room, his arms spread wide, pretending to be a plane. Skidding into a box of breakables. Tyler upgraded his son from plane to dive-bomber. Benetton sprinted up the open stairway to the second floor of the new law office.

In Melnik.

Tyler Simpson's law office.

There's one decision he'd made.

Liza had to be spinning in her grave.

In addition to operating a private practice, Tyler was the new attorney for the city of Melnik, and he had been appointed county attorney to fill a vacancy.

That screamed conflict of interest.

What if the city and county had a legal dispute? No one but Tyler seemed to care, and since the city and county were in complete agreement with the first case coming to trial—as was Tyler, who wanted to crush the defendant like a slimy cockroach—he'd signed on.

Melvin Melnik had tried to kill Bonnie, Tyler's sister.

Tyler's younger son raced up the stairs, and Tyler followed. Who knew whether the second floor was safe? He saw Giancarlo's blond head disappear. Tyler was as blond as most Swedes, and his boys had taken after him.

He reached the upstairs and looked to the right, past a door to the building that shared a wall with his, past a ceiling-high cupboard, and out to a window overlooking Main Street. To his left he saw a mountain of dust-covered boxes of junk. The walls were lined with tall oak cabinets, painted seasick green, most with doors sagging on their hinges.

The door to his right opened, slamming into his face.

He sprawled backward, landing with a crash, the pain blinding him. A cloud of dust kicked up when he hit, nearly choking him. All he could think of were the stairs.

He clawed at the floor. Fear of plunging down the steps he'd just ascended overrode the pain. He stopped skidding. His head dangled over the steep drop. The ringing in his ears eased enough that he heard the boys still shouting and running as he scooted on his back to solid ground. His eyes blinked open.

Lying there, ground into the dirt, in agony, his brain blurry, he saw. . .the prettiest woman who ever lived. Leaning over him. Her eyes wide with worry about him. She cared about him.

"I'm so sorry." She. . .lilted. Her voice was accented, British. "I say, are you all right, sir?" She dropped to her knees and blinked concerned eyes, almost lost under a pair of glasses with small rectangular black frames. Black hair pulled back at her nape. Creamy white skin with rosy cheeks, blue eyes that seemed to sing. . .or maybe he'd just been hit so hard that little birds were flying around his head tweeting. He'd been assaulted by a bespectacled Snow White.

His eyes focused on. . .pencils. . .stuck in her hair. Too many to count. The blow to his head must have been harder than he'd thought.

Her hands went to his face, and a long ponytail rained over her shoulder. She brushed soft fingers over his cheeks, a furrow between her blue eyes.

"Sir, sir, answer me, please." She dropped her *r*'s. It was cultured. Like Princess Diana. Or Princess Snow White.

Please, Lord, don't cast me as a dwarf.

"Shall I summon a physician?" That voice—she might have been singing. Or casting a spell.

Fairy tales, princesses, magic. . .he tried to think. "I'm. . .I'm okay." His jaw worked under protest. "No permanent damage."

He wasn't absolutely sure about that. His nose throbbed like a sore tooth; his forehead did, too. As a matter of fact, his teeth throbbed like sore teeth. And the worst damage was that he didn't want her to quit touching him. He might not recover from that.

She leaned back, still kneeling. Still pencil-adorned. "So sorry about that. I didn't know anyone was about until I heard the ruckus." She pointed with one thumb over her shoulder at his rampaging sons. "I'm letting the flat next over, the whole building actually." She pointed at the door she'd nailed him with, which had to be an entrance to the old opera house, abandoned for even longer than Tyler's building.

"You live in Melnik?" He had to ask. Two and two were not adding up to four. Why would a magical fairy princess move to Melnik? Maybe she was under a spell and had been cast out of her palace and into—Nebraska.

She didn't answer. "I'd barely noticed that door. I heard voices." Sliding an arm around his back, she leaned so close her silken hair brushed across his neck.

What was she doing?

He shivered. His breath caught. His heart hammered.

And how could he help her do it?

"Come, my good man, let's get you up." She lifted.

He figured it out, jumped to his feet, and sent her staggering into the edge of the open door. She banged her head and rubbed it, but didn't cry out or scold him. In fact, except for the rubbing, she acted as if a blow to the head were nothing.

Tyler could relate.

He reached for her. "I'm sorry. I didn't mean to hurt you."

Ducking away, she smiled. "We're even, then. Well, ta-ta." She turned to leave in a whirl of clothing. Now that he saw all of her, he realized she wore a ridiculous outfit, including khaki pants that came almost to her armpits. A white blouse, tucked in but so baggy it could have come out of Tyler's closet, and he was at least five inches taller than her, although she was tall, five-seven maybe. She was filthy. Most likely her building matched his for dust. The mannish clothes swallowed her whole but did nothing to conceal how lovely she was. Not even the pencils detracted. They only made him curious.

Out the corner of his eye, Tyler caught something whizzing toward his head. He ducked. The object shattered against the wall. He was grateful for the distraction, because he hadn't thought of a woman—as a woman—since Liza died. Honestly, it had been long before that, because he hadn't seen anything attractive about Liza for most of their marriage.

What had he been thinking to marry so young, have children so young?

"What are you thinking, to let your boys destroy these artifacts?" She hadn't minded getting knocked into an oak door, but now the woman glared at the broken object with intelligent, cranky eyes. His attraction died a sudden and complete death. He was done with cranky women.

Done with all women.

Tyler realized he'd been standing still too long.

Thirty years too long, but that was another story.

"Boys, come here, please."

They kept running and shouting. There was another crash.

"I've a surprise for you, lads." The woman's crisp, accented voice drew them. It drew him, too.

She was the Pied Piper.

Her voice was a flute.

He was the King of Rats.

NOSY IN NEBRASKA

The boys raced over, Benetton hopping from foot to foot. Giancarlo, filthy even for a kid playing in a room coated with dirt, ricocheted into the tall cupboard beside the open door to Snow White's building. The cupboard door cracked. Mercifully, it was made of solid oak, so it held—barely.

"What are your names, lads?"

Tyler hoped she'd keep talking. He was enchanted by that Pied Piper voice.

Benetton must not have liked it as well. He shrieked in her face. A roar, bared teeth—it reminded Tyler of a movie he'd watched about a woman who lived in Africa with a herd of gorillas.

And if his new neighbor was Jane Goodall, that made his son an ape.

Giancarlo reached for the pocket of her clown pants. He must have thought the surprise was there and he had a right to it. Her pants dropped from her armpits to her hips, and she tugged them back up.

Giancarlo searched. She stared at him in apparent fascination. The boy came up empty-handed. Benetton screamed again.

"Where is it?" Giancarlo, rude as his big brother, Benetton, was a bit quieter and more dangerous. "Where's our surprise?"

Little Brother Syndrome, Liza had called it, as if labeling it made it okay for the boy to be such a brat.

Snow White had a pencil behind her ear, besides the ones in her hair. She grabbed it and tugged a small spiral-bound notebook from the breast pocket of her blouse. She dropped the notebook, bent to get it, and cracked heads with Giancarlo. The boy staggered back, shrieking in pain. He crashed into the cupboard again. It tilted ominously, and Tyler watched it, coiled to dive for his son and drag him to safety. The cupboard stayed upright.

"Oops, so sorry." Snow White said it like a knee-jerk reaction. Tyler wondered how many people she'd knocked into in her life. He'd met her about two minutes ago and she'd already gotten him and Giancarlo. He resisted the temptation to push Benetton behind his back.

Retrieving the notebook while Giancarlo screamed in mock agony, Snow White tore off her glasses, thrust them into her breast pocket, and started jotting. Leaning close to her paper, she worked in rapt concentration. She flipped to a new page and hurried on with her writing.

Within seconds, she tore the pages out of her notebook and handed one to each boy. Giancarlo was interested enough to quit screaming.

Tyler was beside Giancarlo, so he saw it. A drawing. A caricature of his son, looking a bit too real. Benetton's mouth open, his teeth gaping. Fanglike, but there was no mistaking that it was Benetton.

Giancarlo looked like a pig, his nose a little snouty, but the grime was a true depiction.

The boys laughed.

"Draw one of Dad," Benetton yelled.

Giancarlo took up the chorus.

She glanced at Tyler for no more than three seconds, then drew. His took longer. The boys stood still the whole time. A first.

She tore the page off and stuck the pencil back in her hair, missing her ear. He suspected she'd never find it. He looked at the picture.

Grief and loneliness.

It wasn't true.

He hadn't grieved for his wife, and he wanted to be alone. The boys pulled on his arms and snatched the picture away, hooting and making jokes about how dumb he looked.

That was nothing compared to how enraged he felt.

It took all his willpower not to snatch the paper back and rip it in half. Furious—irrationally furious—his cheeks heated and his temper roared. He kept it all inside. Liza had made him an expert at self-control.

The woman turned away without realizing she'd just detonated a bomb and said to the boys, "I'm Dr. Stuart. How do you lads feel about Maxie the Mouse?"

"Max-ee, Max-ee, Max-ee!" Benetton chanted like a cheerleader whipping up team spirit.

"We love him!" Giancarlo grabbed her baggy pants and used her for balance as he jumped up and down. He smeared her already-filthy clothes with more dirt. Her pants sagged. Tyler thought they were going all the way to her ankles. But the belt held low on her hips.

Tyler felt a whoosh of relief; then a second later, he realized he was staring at those hips. He tore his eyes away. It was so hard, he could almost hear the tearing sound.

"Excellent. You young lads want to come over and see my flat? Lots to destroy over there."

"What's a flat?" Benetton shoved past her.

"It's an apartment. *Flat* is an English term."

"We speak English and we've never heard of it." Benetton whirled toward the door. A new world to conquer.

Dr. Snow White scratched her forehead. A red welt had appeared where she'd cracked heads with Giancarlo, and now the bump had dirty fingerprints on it. "I'm going to be living in the upstairs and working downstairs."

With shouts of joy, they leapt toward her. . .flat? They bounced off him and the messy doctor and the oak cupboard then charged through the door and were gone.

"Wait, they can't—"

"They're going to make a great case study." Her eyes glowed with fervor usually reserved for Dr. Frankenstein during a lightning storm. She turned and followed the boys, snapping the door shut in his face.

"Case study?" Tyler spoke to an empty, dust-choked room. He reached for the knob. His first thought was Stranger Danger. But in this case, the stranger was in more danger than his boys.

Something—a body—thudded against the wall, right next to the door. Was it Dr. Snow White or one of his sons? His sons bounced without breaking their bones, but the doctor might be more fragile.

A thud came again, this one right beside that tippy cupboard, and Tyler heard something crack. The cupboard had two doors, floor to ceiling. One of them swung open an inch, but they were latched and padlocked and the lock held.

Dr. Snow White emerged from her kidnapping and shut the door behind her. "You mind if I step back in here until they've finished exploring?"

Exploring struck him as a very polite word for it.

"What are your sons' names?"

"Benetton and Giancarlo."

Her dark brows arched above the glasses she'd put back on. "Their names are Benetton and Giancarlo?"

Tyler felt his cheeks flush. "Yes."

"So. . ." She studied his dark blond hair for a bit. "You're Italian?"

"My wife was."

"Was?"

"Yes."

"I did two years of anthropological undergrad studies in Italy. Perhaps I researched her family. What was her maiden name?"

"Barnston."

She turned and frowned at him. "Excuse me? Italian?"

"On her mother's side. . .back a ways. . .like five generations."

"And yet she gave her sons Italian names? I say, how odd."

Tyler decided it was his turn. "Case study?"

Another crash echoed through the adjoining wall. Her smile, vague and lovely, reappeared. She seemed to be in complete accord with him. As if she'd read his mind, knew the boys were dangerous, and had come back in here to save herself.

He should have been insulted. Instead, his respect for her blossomed, and he caught himself staring again. Her skin was flawless. Filthy, but flawless. It was milky white, and those rosebud cheeks, even smudged with dirt, were impossibly beautiful.

"Yes, didn't I mention I'm here in Melnik to study—"

Another crash interrupted her. The single thin wall—all that separated him from this lovely, lovely woman—vibrated.

The cupboard cracked again and the padlock popped off.

The door blasted open, pushed by the weight of. . .

Melvin Melnik's. . .

Dead. . .

Body.

2

Maddy Stuart jumped and squeaked, colliding with her neighbor.

The corpse landed on a box directly in front of the cupboard and cartwheeled over it, smashing his legs out the window before he quit rolling.

Tyler's strong arms went around her for just a second, one surprisingly pleasant second.

Shocking how pleasant.

Considering the corpse, pleasant should have been beyond her. Then the father with the sad brown eyes and a pillaging horde for children surged past her and knelt by the obviously, utterly, indisputably dead man.

He pressed two fingers to the man's throat then looked over his shoulder. "Call 911."

Excellent; she needed an excuse to run.

A resounding crash in her flat stopped her from reaching for her own door. No reason to go in there, anyway. "I don't have a telephone. My mobile unit doesn't work here, I've discovered." It might have quit working altogether since she hadn't paid the bill for two months.

"There's one on my desk downstairs."

Glad to leave the corpse, Maddy hesitated for a second. "What's the number?"

The new neighbor looked up. "For 911?"

"Yes."

His head tilted as if his brain didn't work on the level. "It's. . .uh. . .9-1-1."

"Oh, well, that explains why you Americans call it that." She turned and ran, reaching the ground level without mishap. Refreshing, that. Stairs were her nemesis.

It took a matter of seconds to reach the dispatcher, and before she was done talking, she heard a siren go off in what sounded like the next building. Why hadn't he just told her to run next door? What an odd little village.

She turned her thoughts away from the man. . .men. . .upstairs. The living one almost as interesting as the dead. Well, more interesting actually; after all, he was alive. Of course, the dead one was dead, and that was extremely interesting— in a horrifying kind of way.

The man—the live one—called down, "Can you come up here and occupy the boys so they don't walk in on this?"

The rabble he called sons would most likely adore seeing a corpse. She was delighted to run across these lads, who were entranced even at their young age by the mighty rodent this village seemed to worship.

What an opportunity!

She hoped to enhance her résumé enough to be considered for a full professorship at Oxford by the time she was done with Melnik and Maxie the Mouse. Those boys were a good place to start.

The police car pulled up before she could return to watch the boys. She let a man in who was uniformed and balding. She saw the notebook in his breast pocket and liked him immediately.

"You found a dead body?"

"Yes, Officer, follow me. The deceased is upstairs."

The man lumbered behind her. "I don't s'pose there's a chance on earth he died of natural causes?"

Madeline tripped on the first stair and fell forward, catching herself and hardly missing a step. She tugged up her pants, wondering why they wouldn't stay at her waist, and looked back as she walked. "I suppose it's possible he did, though I doubt he stuffed himself into that cupboard, and it's even less likely that he padlocked the door from the outside after himself."

The older man's shoulders slumped. Madeline heard him mutter, "There is no crime in Melnik. There is no crime in Melnik. There is no crime in Melnik."

Add a pair of ruby slippers clicked together, and perhaps a Good Witch of the North, and who knows where the man might end up. Madeline reached the top of the stairs, saw the gaping eyes of the departed, and doubted any amount of wishing would erase this crime from Melnik.

Her neighbor, crouching by the side of the corpse, looked up. "Okay, good. I can watch the boys now."

Madeline shivered from her proximity to the cadaver. "I'll help."

"I'll need to talk to you, Ty. And Melnik's gonna need a prosecutor on this."

Tie? What kind of odd name was that? Benetton? Giancarlo? She'd assumed Swedish from their name and coloring. So if his Swedish sons were named after Italians, perhaps he was named after an ascot.

Americans. Such an odd lot.

"No kidding." Tie rose to his feet and stepped back. "I checked for a pulse even though it was obviously too late. Other than that, I didn't touch a thing. He fell out of that cupboard." Her neighbor pointed. "We both saw the padlock pop off."

"We?" the constable asked.

"She and I." Tyler nodded in Madeline's direction.

"I'm Dr. Madeline Stuart," Madeline said to the hefty officer of the law.

"Yeah, I know."

"How could you know? I've only been in town two hours, and I haven't spoken to anyone except"—she couldn't say "Tie," too odd—"him and his sons."

Glass shattered in the next room. The father with the sad eyes, who referred to his wife by saying "was," dove for the door and rushed in.

Madeline followed.

"Miss?"

She turned back to the constable.

"We heard someone had rented that building from Joe Manning, but no one knows what for."

"It's no secret." It was a secret. If the town knew the whole truth, any information would be tainted. But the basic information she was willing to share. "I'm an anthropologist."

"An. . .an. . .what?"

"I'm studying small-town life in America. Your charming village came to my attention because of the news stories about your Melnik Historical Society and your world-famous mouse. I'm here to write my doctoral thesis."

"Don't antheologists dig up Egyptian tombs?"

"That's archaeologists. I'm an anthropologist, completely different, I assure you. I'll do no digging. I promise not to get underfoot. We can surely talk more after you've. . ." She jerked her head at the corpse.

"Oh, sure. What's your name again?"

Weren't lawmen supposed to listen to details? She'd already said her name. A bloodcurdling scream sounded from her flat. She had next to nothing in there as of yet, but she'd soon need sturdy furniture if those boys were going to be regular visitors. And since she'd just decided to center her case study around them, they most likely would be dropping by.

She extended her fingers, intending to shake hands, and managed to smack her knuckles on the constable's enormous silver belt buckle. Withdrawing and taking better aim, she managed to connect with his hand this time. "Dr. Madeline Stuart. I'm planning to live on the upper floor of the building those boys are right now dismantling brick by brick, so you can reach me easily enough."

The man nodded. "I'm Sheriff Hammerstad."

The downstairs door crashed open. Refreshing, that—to have something crashing around in someone else's building.

"He's dead?" The cry, euphoric, shook dust loose from overhead. It drifted down on Madeline, Constable Hammerstad, and the dead man. Madeline couldn't get any dirtier, and the dead man was beyond caring. The constable, though, seemed annoyed as he swiped at his gray uniform.

Madeline decided that the boys had learned their manners from others in town.

"The man who tried to steal Maxie Mouse from this town is dead? Hallelujah!"

A vision in primary colors appeared at the bottom of the steps. A turbaned woman, rotund, swathed in a caftan that looked like Technicolor fairies had splashed her with their wands, charged upstairs.

"Tallulah, stay down there. This is a crime scene."

Tallulah? Madeline had made note of a woman named Tallulah. She'd planned to interview the woman. With her outrageous name—the town seemed to be rife with them—Maddy decided this had to be her. And the woman's mention of Maxie the Mouse was as good as a signed, notarized confirmation.

By the time the constable had quit scolding Tallulah to stay away, she stood at his side. Presumably, since she hadn't quit prattling the whole time she climbed the stairs, she hadn't heard the constable's order. Maddy noticed an odd-looking purse in the woman's hand. It looked rather like a birdcage, only not domed. A lovely, wired, rectangular shape. Before Maddy could figure out what it was, another woman appeared, slower, but fast enough for someone who appeared to be eighty.

"Dora, not you, too? Both of you, get out of here." The officer waved his arm, shooing Tallulah and Dora like they were a flock of chickens.

Dora looked at the corpse, then at Madeline. Her dust mop of gray hair quivered as if she couldn't decide who was more interesting. Madeline felt pinned by the beady, inquiring eyes and hoped the woman chose the corpse.

Tie poked his head through the door. He looked straight at her, and she forgot all about Melnik.

Those sad eyes.

His wife had certainly died. He needed comfort. He needed compassion. He needed gentle touches. He needed. . .

"I need you."

"You do?" How lovely.

"Yeah, my boys may have destroyed something valuable. You'd better come and check."

He needed a whip and chair.

Since she didn't have anything valuable except her computer, which was still in the boot of her car, Madeline wasn't concerned. But Tie had told her to come. She feared she'd follow him anywhere.

She didn't ask for permission; she just left the dead body she'd helped discover, barely noticing several more people trooping up the stairs while the constable scolded them all.

Her upstairs was mostly empty, unlike Tie's, which was piled with dust-covered boxes. She experienced a pang of jealousy for all those boxes Tie got to sift through. She'd have loved to be in possession of all those artifacts. She'd carried up a few boxes of clothing. Unbreakable, but strewn about now, thanks to the boys.

She knew little about the town except what she'd read in the paper, but she knew anthropology. She knew every town had its roots, its eccentricities. Any small village made a good case study. But she hoped to find something more here. Something enduring and valuable that would be printed again and again in textbooks—each paying substantial royalties.

A small, isolated civilization within America that had evolved into something completely unique due to the people's adoration of a giant rodent. She'd already named it.

Maxie Madness.

Catchy.

Not just a dusty thesis, bound and buried in a college library. A book, a *New York Times* best seller. She might be British, but she could smell the interview on *Oprah*.

She followed Tie's broad shoulders and the noise to her lower level. She'd left a few things when she'd come to town last week. She'd spent the winter in Omaha, teaching and researching for her thesis. She'd planned to write the paper on the unique psychology of a small American village. That's when she'd found Melnik.

Her neighbor had found a broom.

He swept glass shards while the boys rummaged. She suspected Tie spent most of his life doing exactly this same thing.

She stared at his sons, her mind given to thinking in caricatures. Hyperactive ferrets came to mind. Her front door opened and a very pregnant woman wearing a bright red dress, obviously maternity, strolled in.

"Ben! Johnny!" One clap of the hands, and the boys were right in front of her, quiet, attentive. Madeline marveled.

A tall, good-looking man followed her, watching her closely. Apparently his only duty in life was to make sure this woman didn't stumble and take a fall.

"Do you boys want to go swimming?"

Screams of joy erupted from the lads.

"Then we can go for ice cream. Jansson's has chocolate today."

The boys jumped up and down. The pregnant woman clapped those magic hands. "The ice cream is off if you get rowdy."

The jumping stopped. They chorused, "Yes, Aunt Bonnie, we'll be good. Hi, Uncle Joe."

"Hi, boys." The man smiled at the children as if he took pure delight in them. Something Maddy hadn't seen from their father. All things considered, Maddy decided Tie's reactions made more sense.

The kindly man looked at her and waved. "Hello, Dr. Stuart. Hope you're finding everything here to suit you."

"It's fine. Thanks." Though why this man should care, she had no idea.

"I'm Joe. You rented the building from me."

Oh, well, that explained how he knew her. They'd done their business over the phone and through the mail. He'd even sent the front door key in a parcel.

Maddy, being a scientist and of an analytical nature, studied the extraordinary effect of the chap on the two boys. She pondered his facial expression, not discounting the bribery, and planned to duplicate it.

She extracted her memo pad from her blouse pocket, hunted for a pencil behind her ear, and found none. She was forever misplacing pencils. She grabbed one the boys had knocked off her battered metal desk and made a note.

"Go on ahead, then." Bonnie shooed the boys out. "Your swimsuits are in my car out front."

"I'll walk with them to the pool, honey. You can drive down or go home and rest."

Bonnie smiled, so delighted you'd think the man had just discovered sliced bread. He leaned down and gave her a quick kiss, resting one hand on her stomach, his eyes glowing.

His gesture made something hard clog Maddy's throat. No man had ever, in her long, clumsy life, looked at her that way.

"I'm going to take a nap. If you're not home when I wake up, I'll drive down to the pool and give you all a ride home. See you later, Tyler."

Tyler, not Tie. It made sense now. And Bonnie was certainly a respectable name. Also, it was another name that had come up in Maddy's research.

The boys raced out, quiet now, but no less energetic. Through her huge front windows, Maddy saw them swinging open the doors of a red Jeep.

Tyler looked up from his broom, scowling. "I've told you not to call them Ben and Johnny."

The newcomer had been turning to leave, but she stopped and laughed in the grouchy man's surly face. "Yeah, keep at me. I'm sure I'll remember one of these days." Aunt Bonnie adjusted a red headband that perfectly matched her dress as she came farther into the room to give Tyler a hug. She turned quiet, intelligent eyes on Madeline.

Maddy saw the resemblance between Bonnie and Tyler. Add the huge "Aunt Bonnie" clue from Tyler's sons, and Maddy deduced that these two were brother and sister. Really, was what Sherlock Holmes did such a big trick?

"Hello. You're Madeline Stuart, then. Joe, my husband, who just ran out of here, didn't introduce me. I'm Bonnie Manning, Tyler's *biiiig* sister." She patted her rounded tummy and laughed. "Welcome to Melnik. I work in the building on the other side of Ty. I'm the curator of the Melnik Historical Society Museum."

Yes. Bonnie Manning! Her day was off to a smashing start. Well, except for the corpse. Maddy had stumbled onto the very person she'd hoped to work with most closely. And Bonnie was the boys' aunt. Perfect.

"I hope Ben and Johnny didn't wreck your stuff."

"No, nothing of any value."

"Bonnie, those nicknames—"

Bonnie turned back to Tyler. "You hear yourself, right? That's coming straight out of Liza's mouth, not yours, Ty."

"I just think we should—"

"Hush." Bonnie hugged him again, not that easy with her extended middle. "I heard about Melvin; that's why I came to get the boys. Joe can watch them at the pool; then they can come over to the building site."

"How's the new museum coming?" Tyler asked.

"Great. We should be ready to move in by the end of summer, I hope. So I suppose Cousin Junior will want to ask you some questions."

Cousin Junior?

Tyler nodded and took a step back. "Sure, I suppose. Melvin died in my building. But I don't know much."

"Well, the important thing is, he's dead." Bonnie ran a loving hand over her enormous belly, seeming quite chipper, considering her bloodthirsty pronouncement. "He can't haunt anyone anymore and he can't take Maxie."

Madeline felt her ears perk up at another mention of the mouse. Maxie had already come up several times. Excellent. There was a good chance these people were as crazy as she suspected.

Tyler clasped Bonnie's hand. "I was scared for you and Joe. I had hoped to convince a judge to revoke Melvin's bail, but now there's no need."

So Tyler had actually been more concerned with human beings than the mouse. Madeline discarded him as a possible subject, but Bonnie was still at the top of the list, as well as Tyler's boys.

Bonnie nodded at Madeline as she turned toward the door. "Nice to meet you."

Madeline hurried forward. "It's Dr. Madeline Stuart, and I'm here in town to study the history of Melnik, and that, of course, includes Maxie, the World's Largest Field Mouse. The Historical Society Museum will most assuredly be a vital resource for my work. And I'd love a chance to visit with you, too."

Bonnie nodded. "That's great. Maxie has brought this town back to life. He's the hero of Melnik."

Tyler snorted.

Madeline shoved him even further off her list.

"He's a symbol of everything great about Melnik. I'm always happy to talk about him."

Bonnie smiled and waddled out of the building, one hand resting on the small of her back.

Madeline was exuberant. She'd only been in town one day and she'd already befriended, in a nonsuspicious way, one of the most strident Maxie worshippers. Bonnie's name had figured prominently in many of the papers she'd read, along with Tallulah, the colorful, turbaned woman from upstairs, and a newspaper editor named Carrie O'Connor. Two down, one to go.

She reached behind her ear, realized she'd lost her pencil again, and found one on her desk. Retrieving her notebook from her pocket, she began jotting.

"What made you draw that picture of me?"

Madeline had forgotten Tyler was there. She looked up. Into the saddest eyes she'd ever seen. "I draw what I see."

His eyes flashed, anger over top of the grief. "And you see sadness when you look at me?"

Madeline's heart turned over with compassion. Not only sadness but denial. A classic case of arrested grief. He must have loved his wife very much. And of course he would. A young man like this, with two beautiful boys who were obviously showing signs of rebellion, no doubt based on their own grief. A tragedy.

"Did you see sadness when I showed you that picture?"

"You drew it. You put it there. You heard about my wife dying and projected that onto me."

Madeline wasn't sure how to proceed. Her specialty was the study of civilizations. She was quite proficient with papers and artifacts, but actual human beings were beyond her. Rather a fatal flaw in an anthropologist. That's why this Melnik paper was so crucial. A well-done thesis that turned into a well-received book could make her faltering career.

"I didn't mean to hurt your feelings. I won't be drawing any more pictures of you. I promise."

"That's not the point." He pulled the picture out of his back pocket. He'd folded it. Obviously not planning to cherish her work of high art.

He stuck it in her face. "The point is, you are a very talented caricaturist."

Maddy marveled at his use of the big word. She hadn't expected much of an intellectual bent in a small mid-American town.

"That gives you the power to hurt. You gave my sons insulting animal characteristics."

"I did not."

"You put a frowning, lonely face on me." He reached up, tugged on her hair, and, like a magician—abracadabra—produced a pencil. Now she remembered, she'd stuck it behind her ear but obviously pushed it a bit too far in. Then he drew an ugly circle around the picture and put a slash through it.

Madeline took the paper from him and turned it around so he could see it. "There's no frown."

His face flushed, his eyes flashed, and his jawline was so taut she wasn't sure he'd be able to open his mouth to talk. If she drew him now, she'd draw a wolf, a hungry wolf, a sad, hungry wolf. He looked at the picture. He looked back at her.

She said, as kindly as she knew how, "If you see sadness, that's you, not me.

If you look at your sons and see insulting animal characteristics, you're projecting all of that. You need to figure out why a father would see that in his sons."

That wasn't the right thing to say, obviously. Tyler looked up from the sketch, his face a toxic mix of sadness and fury. "Don't tell me—"

"Ty, Doc, get up here." The constable's voice boomed down on them. "The coroner showed up. I need to talk to you both."

Tyler looked at the stairway; then he turned back, the sadness and confusion gone, leaving only rage. He leaned down until his nose almost touched hers.

"You stay away from my sons." He spent ten seconds apparently trying to burn her to a cinder with his eyes; then he turned and charged up the stairs.

Madeline trailed along, dismayed she'd alienated him. Just more evidence of her lack of people skills. Preoccupied with mentally giving herself a thrashing, she tripped on a step. She barked a shin, but her firm hold on the railing saved her from falling. Honestly, she hardly ever actually tumbled all the way to the bottom of a staircase.

She reached the top to see Constable Hammerstad whispering to Tyler, talking fast. The constable looked at her over Tyler's shoulder and abruptly ended the conversation.

Madeline approached them, wary of the officer's sharp eyes. As she got to Tyler's side, the constable caught her arm and turned her around. He took one wrist and she felt something cold, heard a metallic click.

"Dr. Madeline Stuart, you're under arrest for the murder of Melvin Melnik."

3

"Y ou have the right to remain silent."

Maddy didn't even consider exercising that right.

"Whatever makes you think I killed that chap?" Handcuffed securely, she looked over her shoulder, expecting the constable to smile. This had to be a joke. She'd just gotten to town and the man looked as if he'd been dead for a while. Days maybe. . .quite stiff.

Maddy remembered that she'd been in town briefly several days ago. "I've never seen him before in my life. I only know his name because you said it."

Constable Junior didn't have one tiny cell of teasing on his face. Her stomach twisted as she realized the man was serious.

"We have reason for our suspicions." The constable finished shackling her and turned her to face him. They were still in her building, but through the door stood a crowd of onlookers. The caftan lady was in the forefront, smiling almost like she wanted to come up and thank Maddy for doing away with that man.

"You have the right to an attorney. If you cannot afford one—"

"I insist you unhand me this instant. I did not kill that man." And she couldn't afford a solicitor. As she faced the constable and the small gathering behind him, she saw Tallulah again immediately—hard to miss the explosion of color. Tallulah clutched the odd purse to her chest and. . .she seemed to be whispering to it. Most odd.

Beside Tallulah, a squared-faced woman in a white doctor's coat crouched in the doorway, obviously inspecting the body. What could this officer be thinking to accuse her?

The coroner lifted something up in a plastic bag. Maddy blinked when she recognized her favorite locket. She'd brought it with her other things a few days ago. Her parents' picture was inside; her name was clearly engraved on the back.

She remembered what the constable had said: *"We have reason for our suspicions."* Now Madeline was looking at the reason.

"Let's go, Doc. We'll talk about this more at the station."

Madeline's heart stuttered as she walked into Tyler's building and slipped through the crowd, escorted by a firm grip on her elbow. She glanced back to see Tyler following and noticed Tallulah and Dora right behind him. Everyone fell into step. She was leading a parade. To jail. But once they got there, she'd be the only one on the business side of the bars.

NOSY IN NEBRASKA

A fair-haired woman snapped a picture. A tall man—so tidy Maddy's envy almost made her forget the handcuffs—stood at the blond's side. As Maddy led the parade downstairs, one curious person after another stared at her. Some said "hi" in such a friendly way that Maddy expected to be offered tea and crumpets.

At the base of the stairs, a gaunt vampire eyed her neck. She blinked her eyes and turned to the constable, whispering—although, as she recalled, vampires had excellent hearing—"Does Dracula live in Melnik, too?"

Her feet got twisted thanks to turning and walking at the same time. Predictable, really, upon reflection.

The constable, with the unlikely name of Cousin Junior, caught her arm. Tyler was behind Junior on the narrow stairs. He grabbed her around the waist to stop her from pinwheeling down the flight of steps. Once more upright, she again looked forward and realized she was face-to-face with the odd man, awake in the daytime, so that was a good sign. No, up close, definitely not a vampire, simply pale and dressed in black. A bit of a widow's peak. Not the walking dead at all.

Maddy hoped she wasn't developing a melancholy streak and seeing ghosts and monsters surrounding her.

The vampire said, "Hello." He reached out one hand—rude, that, Maddy thought, what with the handcuffs and all. When he realized she wasn't going to shake, he dropped his hand awkwardly. The bloodsucker turned to Junior.

"So who's dead? Can I have him? I'll bury him cheap." The man produced a card from the pocket of his black suit.

It wasn't "I vant to drink your blood," but it was very upsetting in its own way.

"Town mortician," Junior whispered in Maddy's ear. He must have sensed she was getting ready to run away screaming. "New here. Just digging up business. I admire a go-getter."

Junior took the card and moved her along. She didn't drag her feet a bit as they passed the vampire or as she greeted several men wearing denim shirts and farmer caps. Jail was beginning to seem like a respite.

One of the men tugged on the bill of a green cap with a bright yellow deer on the front and said, "Hey, miss. Welcome to Melnik."

"Yes, a fine welcome." She frowned and the man smiled, mistaking her crankiness for wit, apparently.

Another man, with far too few teeth for his own good, and what appeared to be a bright red handkerchief tied over the top of his head like he was planning to protect his hair from paint—she'd heard them called do-rags—held her gaze. Not in an unfriendly way, but rather as if he had a partiality toward felonious women.

Thankfully they kept moving before he could ask for a wallet-sized copy of her mug shot.

As they passed him, he screamed. Maddy turned and saw the man gazing in horror at Tallulah's purse.

The do-rag man yelled, "Get that rat away from me!"

Maddy wanted to inquire as to the meaning of that, but Junior towed her onward.

They reached the door to the outside. She heard Tyler mutter to the constable, "New people in town. Dracula and the Hillbilly. And a hillbilly that doesn't like Maxie. How's he gonna make a living?"

"Carrie hates Maxie, and she's doing okay."

"Yeah, but Carrie's got roots in Melnik."

Junior grunted. "There are other new folks, too. Melnik has really been growing."

Then Maddy saw the police car parked directly ahead.

She forgot about the odd townspeople as the reality of her waking nightmare returned. She'd heard of being arrested in a foreign country and locked away, no charges, forgotten in vermin-infested cells for years. Of course, those were usually third-world countries. But still. . .

"It occurs to me that you're not an American citizen, is that right, Doc? I'm not sure you have the right to an attorney."

Here it came. The gulag. The rats. The gruel. The torture. It scared her enough to make her testy. "Well, I definitely want one, and I can't afford one. So I'm not answering any questions until you figure that out."

"Fair enough. Tyler, I'm appointing you." Junior gave her a satisfied smirk. "Now I can question you."

Tyler stormed up alongside them. "I don't want to be her attorney, Cousin Junior. And it's a waste of time, anyway. You know she didn't kill Melvin."

Junior opened the door of his black-and-white car. Maddy stumbled, but for once she wasn't being clumsy. This was from surprise.

"What is that?" She stared across the street.

"A grocery store." Junior stopped bustling her along.

"No, that statue. Is that Maxie dressed up like a—a—"

"He's wearing a T-shirt that says CUDELAK'S FINE FOOD GROCERY STORE." Tyler sounded proud.

"And pushing a shopping cart." Junior smiled fondly at the odd display.

"Do you think that's wise?" Maddy was rooting for Maxie to be important in this town, but really, mice did help spread the Black Plague—wouldn't that hurt sales?

"Of course it's wise. We're having an art festival. Look at what Olga did in front of the diner."

Junior courteously turned her, since her handcuffs made her movements awkward. Maddy saw a mouse, the same in size and shape as the grocery store statue, but this one wearing a chef's hat and apron. It stood proudly just down the sidewalk from Maddy, in front of a building that said JANSSON'S Café, with the word SMORGASBORD painted beneath.

"Was that statue there when I was in town last Saturday?"

"Nope, we put him up on Sunday—it was the start of the art display." Junior nodded in satisfaction, pleased, by all appearances, by the massive rodent outside the diner. Only in Melnik was that an accomplishment of which to be proud. "We've got a whole bunch of 'em all over town."

"Well, that's charming, I'm sure." She was far from sure, but good manners seemed to require her to deviate from the truth in this instance.

Junior ushered her into his patrol car, using one hand to protect the back of her head. Madeline looked out the car windows. She knew the town had about a thousand residents. Half of them appeared to be filing out of Tyler's building to stare at her.

Once she was settled, Junior turned to Tyler. "We do not know she didn't kill Melvin. He had her locket clutched in his hand. That's conclusive evidence to me." Junior glared at Tyler. "You don't have the legal right to turn down a court appointment. Now get in the car."

"I do, too. I'm the acting county attorney. That means I'll be trying this case. I can't be the prosecution and the defense on the same case."

Junior scowled then brightened. "We'll appoint a temporary county attorney. You're not even really official yet, anyway."

"I am, too. I got the appointment."

"You haven't had to try a case yet; that means it's not official. And I need a lawyer right here, right now. You're handy, so you're it. Get in."

Tyler crossed his arms.

Madeline noticed the car doors didn't have inside handles. "I don't want him as my solicitor. He doesn't even like me."

"Solicitor. Nice accent; I like it." Junior smiled at her, quite friendly, considering he'd just arrested her and accused her of murder. "Your agreement isn't required. You request an attorney, you get who I give you. Besides, he doesn't have to like you. No court-appointed attorney likes his clients."

"Forevermore, why not?" Madeline scooted toward the open door. If no one else was getting in, she'd just as soon stay outside, too.

Junior blocked her. Heading off an escape attempt, no doubt.

"Because they're all guilty." Tyler peeked into the car through the front passenger window.

"I'm not guilty!"

"I know."

Madeline leaned back in her seat, trying to figure out how she'd come to this. "How do you know?"

"You're not the type, that's how."

Was he saying she was too spineless to kill someone—even in a pinch? Offended, Madeline forced herself not to speak. What was she going to say—"I say, I'm tougher than I look. I could have done it"? No. Stupid. And her PhD—she was currently working on her second one—was a clear indication that she wasn't stupid. Except here she sat in handcuffs.

"So you're an anthropologist, huh?"

Maddy waited for Tyler to make some comment about digging up bones or pyramids. That's what she usually got. Perhaps an Indiana Jones question or two.

Before he could expose his ignorance, the constable jerked his thumb at the seat beside Maddy. "I've got another pair of cuffs, Ty. Defying my court order to represent her is actionable."

"Have you been watching *Law & Order* reruns again?"

Junior stepped aside. "Get in."

Tyler slid in, grumbling. He turned to her, the anger directed at the constable now, not her. But she remembered very well his order to stay away from his boys. Well, a jail cell ought to help her obey him.

He hated her.

Now he said she was innocent.

Madeline kept her head from spinning by sheer willpower.

"How do you know I'm innocent?"

"Well, anyone can look at you for two seconds and see you're a real nice lady. You'd never do a thing like that."

As a defense against a murder charge, it was quite weak. But it was so sweet. Her eyes filled with tears. "Thank you."

Constable Junior lowered himself behind the steering wheel. The car tilted to his side. The town clustered about so closely that Madeline wondered if Junior would have to threaten them before he could move the car.

"I didn't even know that man. Why would I have killed him? Don't I need . . ." Madeline searched through her mind for the word. She didn't watch much *Law & Order*, and most of a person's knowledge these days seemed to come from the telly.

"A motive," Tyler whispered. He raised his voice. "A motive, Junior. She was in town one day. The only possible motive she could have would be if Melvin just flat-out attacked her or something, and that would be self-defense. She'd just run out onto the street screaming if that happened. C'mon. And means."

"Means?" Maddy whispered. "What is that?"

"Means is the weapon." He shook his head as though he found her hopeless as a murderess. To the constable he said, "You don't even know what killed him yet. There was no sign of a struggle. No gunshot wound. No outward sign of murder."

"Poison. In this town it's poison often as not."

Madeline turned to Tyler. "You have a preferred style of murder in Melnik?"

"No, of course not." Junior spoke too fast. "There's no crime in Melnik."

"This is the third murder in four years." Tyler shrugged. "But it's been the kind of murders that don't really count."

"What?"

"You know, personal. Not just general random murder like you'd have in a big city. And everyone who's dead had it coming to him, so they don't count."

Madeline cleared her throat. "So you're saying you only get killed in Melnik if you're bad?"

Junior and Tyler nodded.

"So just behave yourself and you'll be fine?"

"That seems to work for most people." Junior backed the car up with complete faith in the survival of the fittest. The crowd, obviously highly evolved, stepped aside.

"I've behaved myself all my life, and I'm not fine. I'm in handcuffs in the back of a police vehicle."

"Well, handcuffed isn't the same as murdered." Tyler looked at her, his eyes softening. "And I'll make sure you're fine."

The tears threatened again. "Thanks."

One spilled down her cheek, and Tyler wiped it away with a gentle thumb. "Don't cry. You're going to be all right. Trust me."

And she did. Why she trusted him, she couldn't say, but it was the absolute truth that she did. And that probably meant she was stupid despite her PhD, and she deserved to be under arrest.

No doubt if she'd been standing outside, she'd have remained in the same spot and let Junior drive right over her.

That's when she realized this might be the time for someone she trusted even more.

She closed her eyes and whispered a prayer. Nothing fancy. She had no time for eloquence. "Dear God, please be with me."

"You're a Christian?"

Madeline's eyes flickered open. "Yes."

"They have Christians in England?" Junior asked from the front seat.

Maddy narrowed her eyes at him. "Of course."

"I wasn't sure." Junior shrugged. "We hear weird things about Europe. Nude beaches, legalized drugs, rampant bad behavior."

"England is a lovely country, full of fine, upstanding people, many of them Christians, including me."

"That's good." Tyler sighed doubtfully. Or maybe he believed it about her, but not about the rest of England.

Madeline frowned. "It is good, since it's looking like I'll need a miracle to keep from going to prison."

"You don't need a miracle. You've got me, and you'll be fine. But praying wouldn't hurt. Do you have money for bail?"

They pulled up to the police station, and Junior hit the curb hard enough that she didn't get his question answered. It had been a drive of one and a half blocks. Americans! They drove everywhere.

Junior dragged his bulk out of the car and yanked open the door for them.

Madeline didn't have the money for bail. She'd impoverished herself with this extended trip to America.

Tyler got out and took her elbow. She tried to get to her feet with her hands restrained. Predictably, she fell on her face. Tyler's grip slipped, and she head-butted him in the stomach and knocked him backward into Cousin Junior. She sprawled flat on the ground, her fall broken by Tyler's body under hers.

Her glasses skittered off her face and she looked down at Tyler, nose to nose with the aggravating man. He shook his head and grinned. Her glasses were for distance, so having them off gave her a very clear view of his face. He really was adorable. A perfect specimen of the American male. She'd like to spend some time researching his smile. She looked closer because she hadn't seen much of it up to this point—not from such a short distance. But it was definitely more interesting than that ridiculous stuffed rodent.

She suddenly levitated. The constable had her by the waist. Tyler had her by the shoulders. The two of them set her on her feet. Junior fetched her spectacles and handed them to Tyler. He perched them on her nose while Junior shut the car doors and led the way inside.

Her vision was blurred, but she was certain that was from the constable's thumbprint on the lenses, rather than a concussion.

She remembered she was under arrest. She leaned closer to Tyler. "He won't hurt me, will he? I've heard of you Americans and your interrogation techniques. Beating people while others watch through two-way mirrors."

Tyler laughed. "Where'd you see that? A movie?"

"I'm not sure. Maybe. But everyone knows it's true."

"You'll be fine. Melnik can't afford a two-way mirror. Besides, it's my job to protect you, and Junior isn't inclined toward hitting anyone, least of all a pretty woman."

Pretty woman? She wasn't pretty; she was clumsy and studious and bad with people. A pariah, honestly. She wanted to ask him about it, maybe get him to say she was pretty again, just so she could store it in her memory to live on when times were tough. Like the time she'd set the university chancellor on fire, or spilled her coffee down the blouse of an elderly benefactor being wooed to donate to the college, or spent the entirety of a faculty party with a small piece of Swiss cheese stuck on her forehead.

Tyler had her upper arm in his grasp. It could be to block an escape attempt, but she rather thought it was to keep her on her feet.

"So do you have the money for bail?"

"That's an extremely rude question. You shouldn't inquire into my finances."

"Well, this is a murder investigation, and those have been known to stray into the area of rude. So don't tell me about your finances. Just tell me, if Junior gets the county judge to set your bail for a hundred thousand dollars, can you write a check for 10 percent of that?"

"No."

"Do you have a house to sign over as security so we can keep it if you skip town?"

"Of course not. But couldn't I just promise I won't run off?"

Tyler looked sideways at her. All his anger and grief were gone. The distraction of her being charged with murder had lightened his spirits. Well, she was glad to be of service. As they stepped up on the sidewalk, she noticed yet another large, decorated mouse. "Why is there an enormous mouse wearing a constable's uniform standing there?"

"It's a statue of Maxie."

"Forevermore, why?"

"Pay attention to the murder charges for a minute. I can tell you about the summer arts festival later. The reason we can't just take your word that you won't run off is, you'd be surprised how many murderers are liars, too. I've never heard any studies done on it, but I'm guessing it's, like, one hundred percent. So you might be a flight risk." Tyler held the door for her without letting go of her arm. The door opened into a small hallway with a door to the left that opened into a small, bare office with a boring gunmetal gray desk.

"No budget for a two-way mirror, indeed."

"You have no ties to the community."

"I've rented that building. That's the only home I've got right now. I've got a nonrefundable ticket to return to London in early September and no money to buy a different ticket or even pay the fee to have the departure date changed."

"Still, unless we can convince Junior to drop these charges, you'll have to pay bail or stay in custody."

Tyler settled her into a chair and only released her arm at that point. He pulled up a matching folding chair with a dull scrape of the legs on the cement floor and sat beside her.

The constable unlocked her shackles and sat behind his desk. "Now how well did you know Melvin Melnik?"

Maddy groaned.

4

Tyler could feel his will weakening.

He'd have to put up bail. He had a house. He had plenty of money. But that wasn't the way a savvy lawyer worked. Still, Dr. Snow White was innocent, and his conscience wouldn't allow him to leave her locked up.

If he didn't pay, she might spend the night, possibly the whole summer, locked up awaiting trial. On the other hand, rustic as it was, the jail cell looked more comfortable than that building she'd rented. He'd noticed an inflatable mattress, twin-sized. That was about the extent of her creature comforts.

Then Dr. Notchke came into the police station with her preliminary report and started right in talking. "When is this town going to get good cell phone service?" The doctor didn't wait for an answer. "Based on the condition of the body, I'd say he's been dead twelve to twenty-four hours. And I suspect his hand was pried open after death and the locket stuck in deliberately. Someone framed Dr. Stuart."

Tyler saw tears well in Dr. Snow's eyes. He resisted the urge to give her a hug.

"I can absolutely prove I wasn't in Melnik twelve to twenty-four hours ago." She sniffled, and he handed her a handkerchief. "I was doing final exam work at the university. My study group and I have worked day and night for the last week finishing a project that was overdue. I wasn't alone for a second."

"I've gotta go." Dr. Notchke set her handwritten notes on Junior's desk. "It's pinochle night at the VFW Hall in Fremont. Try not to find any more dead bodies for a while, eh, Junior?" Dr. Notchke didn't wait around for a protest.

Junior studied the papers, looking disgruntled. "Well, I'm not buying your alibi just because you've said you have one."

"Oh, rubbish. You should be thrilled I can prove I'm innocent." Dr. Snow rose to her feet, sounding testy.

Tyler braced himself to save her. Any little distraction on her part and she usually ended up knocking someone over. The woman just needed to concentrate full-time on staying upright.

"Why's that?" Junior looked up from his scribbling.

Maddy laid both hands flat on Junior's desk with a muffled growl. "Because I'm innocent, you daft man! You don't want to arrest someone who's innocent, do you?"

"Well, closing a case is always nice." Junior tapped his notebook with his stubby pencil.

Tyler did his best not to laugh. Junior really preferred to run a tidy police force. He and two part-time deputies. If there was a dog off its leash, Junior was there. If a carload of teenagers did wheelies on the football field, Junior put a stop to it. If someone threw a punch over a bowling score, Junior had a jail cell, and he wasn't afraid to use it.

But murder? Tyler knew his second cousin Junior Hammerstad—or possibly his first cousin once removed; there was some dispute over that—had never signed on for this. The fact that he'd closed two earlier murder cases in quick time had given him a false sense of his own detecting skills, which, to Tyler's way of thinking, were nonexistent.

Tyler had been a lawyer in Omaha for five years before Liza died, and mostly he'd reviewed contracts for his firm's huge corporate clients. That was the kind of lawyer Liza had wanted him to be. But in the year before he landed that job, he'd done a lot of cases as a court-appointed attorney for the city of Omaha. Tyler knew about real crime and real detective work. The crime here, murder, was real enough, but the detective work. . .not so real.

In an abandoned room like the one Melvin was in, Junior should have had good luck finding trace evidence. But he'd allowed—or rather been unable to stop—the whole town from marching up to take turns looking at the body. There should have been footprints in the dust. Of course, his boys had been up there, but those prints would be easy to identify. Tyler's and Dr. Snow's had only been in that one corner. But Junior hadn't kept the good citizens of Melnik out, and now anyone could claim that any matching hairs or prints came after the crime was discovered.

Tyler hoped whoever had stuffed Melvin in the cupboard came forward and confessed. Otherwise, this could be a hard crime to solve and a failure that would make poor old Junior feel bad.

Tyler felt bad, too. "So why my building? Was someone trying to frame me and Dr. Snow?"

"Who?" His client's dark, perfectly arched brows lifted above her glasses.

Tyler moved on fast. "If Dr. Stuart's locket was put there postmortem, maybe it started out to be a frame-up on me. Then they found her stuff and had a better idea."

"Or maybe"—Junior consulted his notebook—"Melvin was living there and that dictated the site of the crime. He hid out in Gunderson's house a long time. Maybe he came back to town, saw Joe and Bonnie had that house opened up wide, leaving him nowhere to ghost around, so he immediately picked another deserted building and just snuck in. He's only been out of jail a week."

"Then whoever killed him must have known he was there or found him there. We need a motive."

"Lots of motive for killing Melvin. Everyone in town hates him for filing that suit to gain custody of Maxie."

The clumsy doctor leaned forward. "Custody of Maxie?"

Why would this woman care about Maxie? Tyler sure knew he didn't, despite Bonnie's loyalty to that dumb, obese vermin.

"Someone is trying to take possession of that rodent you all worship?"

"We don't worship him, for Pete's sake." Tyler stood beside her. Better to catch her when she fell. "He's a town mascot. We use him to try to draw attention to Melnik. It gives us an excuse to have a summer celebration and a Christmas parade. Every little town has something like that."

She smiled. "Poor choice of words. So sorry."

Tyler needed a pocket calculator with a memory function to keep track of all of Dr. Snow's "So sorry's." "Let's get back to the case. I'm sure the doc was just a convenient patsy."

"I say, that sounds ominous." She adjusted her glasses. "Very Cosa Nostra, actually."

"Yeah, right. The mob." Tyler laughed. "Anyway, we've accused so many people of murder in this town, they're starting to resent it. Joe, Tallulah, Shayla, Hal. You even suspected Bonnie for a while, remember, Junior?"

"All of them but Joe and Bonnie confessed." Junior scowled. "It's not like they've got a reason to resent being suspected. And they all did kill Wilkie; they just didn't kill him dead."

"What?" Dr. Snow adjusted her glasses and nearly knocked them off her face.

Tyler and Junior both ignored her. It just took too long to bring her up to speed.

"Besides, I never believed for a second Bonnie killed Gunderson, and you know it."

Tyler nodded. "Still, I think we should proceed with caution. The obvious suspects are, again, Tallulah and Bonnie. I mean, no one was more upset about the thought of losing Maxie than they were."

"Bonnie? Your very pregnant sister?" The good doctor regained her seat and crossed her legs, resting her right ankle on her left knee. Her baggy clothing almost swallowed her as she leaned forward, her wrists resting on her ankle, her expression ridiculing him and Junior both. "You think she tucked Mr. Melnik up inside that cupboard and left him there for you or your young lads to find? Quite rude, actually. Plus heavy lifting for a woman in such an advanced state of pregnancy."

Junior scratched his pencil in his notebook. Tyler had a sneaking suspicion he was crossing off Bonnie's name. Grudgingly, Tyler gave Junior credit. The man didn't list suspects based on personal feelings.

"Physically, she isn't capable of packing him away, even if she killed him up there. But she had a motive, Ty. Plus opportunity. I'll bet there's a key in city hall, and Bonnie's in and out of that building all the time."

"Give it up. She's innocent and so is Tallulah. Tallulah's a drama queen. That means she can act, or thinks she can. You heard her screaming with joy over Melvin being dead. No way does a murderer choose that for her false reaction."

"So who?" Junior chewed on his eraser. "Everyone and no one."

"Who stands to gain from this poor chap's death?"

Tyler almost grinned. He really was enjoying her company. And she was cranky. He'd noticed that and still enjoyed her. Although she wasn't cranky when she was in handcuffs. She'd been vulnerable and sweet and teary-eyed then. Liza had known how to fake being sweet and sad and vulnerable, too. She'd proved it before they were married. She hadn't wasted much time wheedling afterward. She just issued orders.

Tyler smirked. "You have been watching American movies."

"England has a movie industry, too, you know." She scowled.

"Anthony Hopkins acting stiff. Old ladies named Dame Whatever imper-sonating some queen. Shakespeare. No interrogation techniques there. What else you got?"

"The case, sir? Have you forgotten?"

Strangely enough, he had forgotten. Tyler turned back to Junior. "Melvin got a piece of the town's settlement after we took Gunderson's ill-gotten gains. He didn't get it at first, because we didn't know he was alive. When he turned up, Shayla had already spent hers, so we cut a portion from Rosie—she's in jail; what does she need money for?—and took a chunk out of the trust funds for Donette's baby and Kevin. Plus we made Hal give some of his share back. All of them were mad about coughing up the cash."

"Melvin thought the city should have made up the last slice Shayla owed him, but we weren't about to." Junior nodded. "And Joe had Gunderson's money, but he wasn't liable, and since Melvin killed Gunderson, letting Melvin profit from his death was illegal. He'd been using the money he did get to pay his lawyer to delay the murder case. He was also suing Shayla for her share, and he filed papers to get custody of Maxie."

"Melvin wanted the mouse?" The fairy princess doctor rested her chin on her hand and folded up over herself, studying him and Junior like they were lab rats.

Tyler ignored her. "Now that Melvin's dead, unless we find a will, his money—whatever's left of it—should be divided between Kevin, Hal, and Donette's baby."

"Shayla might want a cut. She didn't kick into the pot, but she's family, so it might count legally as an inheritance rather than just paying back his cut of the settlement." Junior shook his head. "Kevin didn't do it. He just graduated from high school this spring. He got a scholarship to Wayne State. Since he's been living with the Andersons, he's turned into a fine young man."

"The apple doesn't fall far from the tree." Tyler leaned back, pondering. His metal chair creaked.

"And those Melniks are one twisted fruit salad, no doubt about that." Junior nodded and made a note. "I'll talk to Kevin, but I hate to upset him. Doubt Donette's little one did it; he's only four."

"Since Hal and Donette are married, they'd stand to gain the most, though, since they had two shares. Hal's and the baby's."

With a grudging look on his face, Junior made a note. "Hal's all right. No way he did this, but I'll leave his name on the list."

"That leaves Shayla. She's got the spine to kill someone; we know that."

"How do you know that?" The doctor was paying rapt attention, leaning forward over her bent knee, hanging on every word.

Tyler found her interest unusual. Except for those few minutes when she was accused of the crime, why did any of this matter to her? Didn't she have a paper to write? "We know that because she poisoned her father, Wilkie Melnik, when she was eighteen. Someone else killed Wilkie before the poison could finish him off, but Shayla had the cold in her blood to pour that antifreeze into her father's beer."

Junior nodded. "As far as I know, she's not in town. I heard she's living over in Gillespie. The coroner's doing a toxicology report, and she suspects poison. Why not antifreeze?"

"Gillespie is close enough for Shayla to have driven over here. She could have even been in contact with Melvin. They could have conspired to gain custody of Maxie with plans to extort the town. Lots of people would pay generously to keep that mouse."

"Joe knows how much it means to Bonnie."

"Bonnie, your sister, right?"

Tyler felt a little sorry for the good doctor. She was trying to keep up. "Yes, pregnant Bonnie, the one you met a little while ago. Her husband, Joe, inherited Maxie then donated him to the town before Melvin sued for custody."

"Well, it's a little more complicated than that," Junior interrupted.

"Of course it is." Maddy sounded resigned and exhausted. Who could blame her?

"Joe actually had to throw Maxie away."

"What?"

"I fished him out of the trash." Junior said it with such pride that Tyler didn't point out that he sounded like a lunatic. "It gave the whole case some shaky points, and Melvin was exploiting that."

Tyler went back to the crime. "Melvin might have been planning on holding Maxie for ransom. Joe might have paid, too. He'd do anything for my sister."

"Isn't *custody* a term used between divorcing parents?" Maddy asked. "Surely there is no custody of a dead mouse. And ransom—that's about kidnapping. . .a human being."

Tyler almost snickered. They'd left the doc behind, and that was a fact.

She must have detected his amusement, because she got huffy, and that reminded him of Liza. She unbent her long legs, so slender she should have been as fleet and graceful as a gazelle. As she stood, she stepped on the cuff of her baggy slacks, cut in manly tailored lines but insanely loose, and fell forward against Junior's desk, knocking his notebook straight into his ample gut.

"So sorry." She reached for the notebook, caught a pencil holder by accident, and sent pencils and pens clattering to the floor beside Junior.

Junior reached for the sky in surrender. "I'll get the pens."

She stood upright without assistance. "So, you've decided it must be this Shayla person, then?"

Tyler looked at Junior. Neither of them answered.

"You've just said she's the only serious suspect."

Junior nodded. "Well, she's serious all right. But it's a little early to be setting our minds on one person. There are other new folks in town."

"Besides me?" The doc stood straighter as if she didn't feel so alone.

"What about the vampire mortician? Hard to forget him." Tyler shrugged one shoulder.

"Hard is right. Believe me, I've tried. Weird dude. Name's Dolph Torkel. But a guy's not a murderer just because he looks goofy. I've heard he's fresh out of undertaker college. We needed him in Melnik, but we only know what little he's told us about his background. I could sniff around there."

"Dolph?" Maddy asked. "As in Adolph?"

Junior shrugged. "I suppose. Funny how the name Adolph fell out of favor after Hitler, huh? Just wrecked the name."

"Funny," Maddy said dryly.

"And how about that antique shop?" Tyler wanted to stay on track. "That lady isn't normal. I've only met her a couple of times, just in passing, but she seems to have a vacancy in her brain. Always singing and dancing—she looks high as a kite to me. Like the flower child that time forgot. Name's Moonbeam something. Ask Dora. If she's drug-involved, she could have some connection to Melvin through prison. They might have mutual acquaintances."

Junior made a note. "The new plumber has only been here a couple of months, and Dora can't get a thing out of him."

"The guy with all the missing teeth?" Tyler asked.

"Yep."

Tyler couldn't control a shudder. "I was ready for him to start twanging the *Deliverance* theme on a banjo."

"Jamie Bobby Wicksner, and don't be calling him Jamie or Jim or Jimmy. He likes the whole Jamie Bobby. Nice enough guy, I suppose, if you can keep from staring at his teeth." Junior grimaced. "He graduated from tech school and he's already done a few plumbing jobs around town. Nick double-checked his work and said he knows what he's doing."

"Well." Maddy dusted her hands. "Good to see you've got lots of people to investigate. Am I free to go? I need to settle in."

"You're still going to live up there?" Tyler could still see Melvin's body, stiff, eyes open, dead as dead could be. He wasn't even sure he'd be able to practice law in that building, let alone sleep there as Dr. Snow planned to do.

A little worry line appeared between her eyebrows, but she shrugged. Her blouse flowed over her body, and her pants dropped from her armpits to her hips. She tugged them back up. "Where else? I can't afford to rent another flat."

"But you'll be sleeping right next door to a crime scene. Whoever murdered Melvin might come back. Your door isn't that sturdy. If you'd have moved in there yesterday, you might have been killed, too, just to silence you as a witness."

Dr. Snow's eyes widened, her shoulders slumped, and her pants dropped. "I hadn't thought of that." She shook her head. Her ponytail holder must have broken, because her hair cascaded around her shoulders. She scraped it back, hooking the dark silk behind her ears and leaving a new trail of dirt with her fingertips. She found several of the pencils, stared at them, and stuck two behind each ear. Then she turned to the door. "Well, let's hope whoever killed him was a one-off, because it's the only home I've got."

She opened Junior's door without incident and left.

"Piesforsale."

Tyler leapt to his feet. "She'll either fall into Clara's pies or not know she's supposed to buy one. Either way, Clara will get mad."

He ran outside.

"Noonestarveswhilel'maround." Crazy Clara, the Mad Baker of Melnik, stood with her cart full of horrible pies.

Tyler knew his duty. He bought a pork chop and coconut shaving cream pie. Junior got a radish and paper clip meringue. The anthropologist gagged and hurried up the street with her hand over her mouth, nearly falling over the Maxie statue in the process. Tyler straightened Maxie's police cap and chased after her.

She stepped off the curb and nearly fell down a gutter into Melnik's sewer system. It wasn't big enough for her to slip through, but somehow Tyler thought if anyone could manage it, it'd be Maddy. She saved herself before he got there, and Tyler had to admit the woman had grown to adulthood somehow.

He extended a key ring to her. "This is for my building. Your cell isn't going to work."

"Cell? Are we talking about biology?"

"Cellular phone. You're really cut off from everyone. Nothing is open on Main Street in the evening. You don't have a home phone and cell phones don't work. You'd have trouble getting help."

"I don't need help."

"Anyone might need help. This is the key to the front door of my building. I think it works in the upstairs door, too. But we might have left that unlocked, anyway." Tyler couldn't remember. Locking doors wasn't a high priority in Melnik. After all, there was no crime in Melnik. "There's a phone downstairs. My home number is taped to the desk. If you need anything, call me."

She looked from the key ring to Tyler and back. When her eyes lifted the next time, he thought he saw a gleam of tears. Why would access to a phone make a woman cry?

"And don't forget in an emergency to call 911."

"Oh yes. What was the number again?"

Tyler shook his head and told her. "Seriously, try to memorize it."

"I will. Perhaps if I write it down. Thank you very much. I doubt I'll need it, but it's very kind of you."

Tyler almost regretted his generosity, because looking in those shiny, bright blue eyes, framed with lashes so long they fluttered in the breeze, made him forget all the hard lessons he'd learned about women. "Well, I'm your lawyer, so I'm the logical one to call if you need anything."

She looked at the key in her hand. "Oh, right, my lawyer. Of course." The silence lasted too long. She dashed at her eyes and smeared dirt, now damp enough to qualify as mud, on her cheeks and nose. "Well, thank you." She turned and hurried off.

Tyler couldn't tear his eyes away. She reached the intersection with Main Street. Tyler held his breath, hoping she didn't cross the street at the same time Dora drove by. Not exactly the irresistible force meeting the immovable object. More like the clumsy princess and the blind bat.

In short, a fractured fairy tale—with real fractures.

Dr. Snow rounded the building, and just before she disappeared, she stopped and glanced back. For a second, or maybe three seconds or ten. She looked him right in the eye.

Tyler's heart hurt from that pretty, klutzy doctor looking at him.

She turned, smacked her shoulder into the bricks of the old furniture store, and vanished around the corner in a cloud of sparkling fairy dust. Or maybe that was mortar from the building she'd almost knocked down and the sparkles were in Tyler's eyes.

He'd had seven years of college, he'd passed the bar and worked in a high-pressure corporate office for five years, and still. . .he didn't have a brain in his head.

That wasn't a discovery he was making right now. He'd known for a long, long time. He'd suspected before the end of his honeymoon. He'd only known Liza two months when they eloped. He'd phoned Bonnie and told her after the fact.

The fact that hurting Bonnie hadn't shamed him was a cross he'd always bear. The fact that Liza had started with her slights aimed at his family and his embarrassing hometown had been major clues to his idiocy.

But then, a month into their marriage, Liza had announced she was pregnant.

That feeling of being trapped after four weeks of marriage hit him like a two-by-four. If he'd been a coyote, he'd have gnawed his foot off to get away. But he was a man; he'd made vows before God. And here was a defenseless baby. That's when he knew how badly he regretted his choice for a wife. He'd married quicksand, and Liza had sucked him under hard and fast.

The hurt in his chest right now, from the doctor's glance, reminded him how fast he'd fallen in love last time, how stupid he was about women, and how completely he couldn't trust his feelings. He was grateful for the reminder. He turned back to Junior and, since Clara had gone on her way, extended his pie to his cousin. "Toss this for me, okay? I'm going to find the boys."

Junior balanced his own pie on one hand. "Do it yourself. You bought it; you throw it out. You know the rules."

Those really were the rules. Unwritten, but known by everyone. You had to buy a pie because Clara needed the money. And you had to throw it away yourself. Tyler hadn't been out of Melnik that long.

Junior leaned forward to sniff Tyler's pie. "You've got to give Clara points for creativity. I think she used menthol shaving cream on this one. Kind of refreshing."

Tyler rolled his eyes.

Junior smirked as he bounced the radish and paper clip pie on his fingertips. Not one bit worried he might drop it. "The doc sure is a pretty little thing. Clumsy, though. A man could keep busy his whole life saving her from one disaster or another."

Tyler wondered how long he'd stared after Maddy. Maybe Junior, the old coot, had some detecting skills after all. "Are you done assigning me to cases I don't want?"

Junior shrugged. "For now. But don't leave town." He laughed at his cop humor all the way back to his office, leaving Tyler with an aching heart, bitter memories, and a pork chop and coconut shaving cream pie.

There wasn't enough menthol in the world to make him feel better.

What had he been thinking to come home? Just more proof he was an idiot.

5

Moving to Melnik was a stroke of genius.

The town was fascinating and growing on Maddy with each passing second.

Even the arrest had been quite educational. Now, without the handcuffs, she was able to see the benefits of the experience. The constable had taken her word on an alibi. He might well check it out, but mostly he seemed to have decided to let her go because Tyler said, "She wouldn't do a thing like that."

How trusting. What a lovely little town.

She finished her settling in, double-checked the lock on her adjoining doors to Tyler's building—she found a second door downstairs as well and locked that—and headed to Jansson's for supper. A community gathering place. She'd begin getting to the heart of this town full of lovable mouse-worshipping lunatics.

As she emerged from her building, she studied Melnik's business district. One block long. To her left was Tyler's law office. She lived straight across the street from the grocery. She strolled along, reading storefronts. Melnik Historical Society Museum, Melnik City Hall and Fire Department—where the ambulance had originated, most likely. Next, a lovely shaded rock garden scattered with benches. Odd to have a gap like that in a row of buildings.

Next she passed O'Connor Construction, the words neatly painted on the window. O'Connor was the name of the other woman Maddy wanted to meet. Carrie O'Connor. Could this be her family? Was it possible that everyone worked within a few feet of her? Well, why not? Honestly, the whole town was within a few feet of her.

Maddy noticed a building across the street with THE BUGLE painted on the front window. The town newspaper where Carrie O'Connor worked. The building looked dark, so Maddy didn't cross over.

The next business past O'Connor Construction was an antique store. A plain rectangle of cheap printer paper, hand-lettered with MOONBEAM'S ANTIQUITIES, was taped to the glass front door. That was the only identification of the business. Through the window, a woman dressed like an aging hippie danced as she flicked a feather duster over glassware. Maddy saw her raise one arm and open and close her hand. There were tiny cymbals on her fingers.

Next was a rather ghastly front window display. A casket. On sale. A large handprinted sign taped to the coffin said:

THE MICE MAN COMETH

$499 Plus Tax
Embalming, Hair, and Makeup Not Included

Startled, she stopped to stare. Read the fine print.

Maddy had never heard of a coffin sale before. After she'd stood far too long, she raised her eyes, jumped, and heard herself squeak, quite embarrassing. The local vampire stood behind the coffin. With a quick smile—which he returned with a little wave—she moved on. As she passed his door, she read Torkel's Funeral Home painted high on the window. Oh yeah, little Adolph. Not a vampire. Not a sign of fangs anywhere when he'd smiled.

She remembered Dolph was a suspect, although based on absolutely nothing except his oddness and newness in town. Not fair, that. He moved so he could see her through the door and waved at her more vigorously. She was struck by the notion that he might be lonely. She could certainly relate.

She waved back, suspecting God would have her invite the chap to dinner. Well, she didn't rule it out for the future, but not tonight. She moved quickly on, embarrassed to be caught staring. Yet if a bargain-basement coffin stood in your window, you had not a single leg to stand on if you complained about people staring.

The next building was the restaurant. Food and coffins—not a comfortable marriage.

Jansson's Café and Smorgasbord. How utterly charming. A Swedish eatery, decorated with Dala horses. Maddy had traveled to Sweden and recognized the little wooden carving of a horse, painted bright red and decorated with a harness and saddle in ribbons of blue, green, and yellow. A lovely bit of Europe in middle America. It was delightful, except for the four-foot statue of a mouse wearing a chef's hat standing on the sidewalk.

Bad show all around, that. An appalling lapse of judgment, really. This close she noticed a spatula tucked in Maxie's little paw. Setting her disgust aside, she knew it would add color to her thesis, so she determined to come back and take pictures. No one would believe her if she just wrote the details in her paper.

On the door, right above a wooden sign that said Välkommen, was stenciled a cartoon of a stout man wearing red overalls and a red cowboy hat. The words Herbie Husker rather ruined the Swedish effect, but Maddy had been in Nebraska long enough to know that the University of Nebraska football team's mascot, Herbie Husker, was far and away more of an iconic figure than Maxie Mouse. Perhaps she'd study him for her next doctorate.

She had a few quid in her pocket, American dollars, of course. She wasn't stone-broke. Even though her present flat was reasonably priced—with first and last month's rent and a damage deposit—she didn't have funds to rent another flat. But she could eat a meal out now and again if she so chose.

NOSY IN NEBRASKA

A bell tinkled overhead as she entered the establishment. The tinkle for some reason reminded her that Tyler had called her Dr. Snow. What in heaven's name had that been about?

She forgot all about it when a mouth-watering aroma greeted her like a mother's hug. Pastry and roasting meat, sautéed onions and brewing coffee. Heavenly.

Maddy realized she'd yet to eat today. The quiet murmur of voices and steady clink of silverware stopped. A fair-sized crowd, scattered about at the square tables and booths, turned and stared. Beastly rude in most places, but apparently not so in Melnik. Maddy had been stared at virtually nonstop since she'd arrived. She reached for her notebook to document the "staring allowed" culture and found the book missing.

Right when she needed to take notes most! Well, she was a twit and that came as no surprise, even with papers saying she had a PhD and the bills saying she was paying to earn a second one.

She wondered how hard it would be to find folks in this charming hamlet who would allow her to interview them. Awfully hard, she suspected. She'd heard small towns tended to be cliquish. Made worse by her implication in murder. Add in her dismal record with interpersonal relationships and the fact that, while she might have God's grace in her soul, she lacked grace utterly in all other ways. When God had been splicing in the coordination gene, Maddy had obviously gotten in the wrong line and picked up two left feet. This summer promised to be one long struggle. One long, lonely struggle. Much like her whole life.

A handprinted sign told her to seat herself, so she slid into an empty booth, depressed to be eating alone. Wishing she had her notebook so she could sit and doodle and ignore her loneliness.

A woman charged the table. It took Maddy a second, but she recognized her from the murder scene.

"Hi, I'm Dora."

The plump matron sat down across from Maddy, turned, and bellowed, "Coffee, Olga!"

A woman, taller and broader than Dora but just as gray, was already approaching the table with a thermal pot. "I'm way ahead of you, Dora."

The aproned woman smiled a motherly smile at Maddy. She limped as if her joints hurt. "First cup of my coffee's on the house. Then you'll be hooked, and you're mine for life."

Olga and Dora chuckled—an inside joke, it appeared.

"Do you want the smorgasbord, or do you want to order off the menu?" Olga finished filling the cup, and the fragrant coffee made Maddy—a tea drinker in the normal course of things—suspect "being Olga's for life" wasn't a joke.

"I. . .I. . ." Maddy had never been in a restaurant before when she hadn't had plenty of time to think, unless it had golden arches.

"Give her the smorgasbord; she'll need her strength." Dora reached across the table and patted Maddy's hand. "Now tell me about yourself. Did you kill Melvin? He had it coming. I heard Junior let you go. Got away with it, huh? Bad business killing people. No sense making a habit of it. But Junior didn't like Melvin. Must have decided to look the other way this once. Providing you stop, I expect this'll be the end of it."

Maddy shook her head. "I didn't kill him. I've been set free. I had an alibi."

Dora beamed. "Good thinking. Honestly, with all the murders in this town, it'd be wise to keep someone with you at all times. To protect yourself if you're the next victim and to have a handy alibi if you look suspicious. Unless the person you kept with you was also the murderer." Dora fell silent, rubbing her chin, trying to solve the alibi dilemma. A quick glance at Maddy sharpened Dora's already-keen focus. "Pencils in your hair, girl."

Maddy felt her cheeks heat. She'd always blushed like a schoolgirl. She began plucking the pencils out, astounded at how many she found.

Leaning close, Dora added, "You really could use one of those whitening toothpastes. What was your name again? You're a doctor? This town could use a doctor. Madeline, right? I've got bursitis in one shoulder that's the bane of my existence."

Maddy closed her mouth then tried to talk and conceal her yellow teeth at the same time. "I'm Dr. Madeline Stuart. I'm not a medical doctor."

Maddy had seven pencils on the table in front of her. She quit talking as she contemplated the disaster of her being put in charge of fragile, sick people. It didn't bear thinking about. "I've spent the last half year in Omaha studying for a second doctorate in anthropology. My first doctorate was in cultural—"

"Dinosaur bones?" Dora nodded. "It's a wonder they haven't found all of those yet. I mean, how many can there be? Good grief, it's like you can't turn around without tripping over a tyrannosaurus."

Maddy opened her mouth to straighten that out, aware that her yellow teeth must be glaring like a caution light.

Another woman slid in beside Dora. The caftan lady. Tallulah. Maddy couldn't believe her luck. Except for her horrid teeth and the pencils, this was going well.

"I heard Junior let you off on the murder rap." Tallulah seemed to suggest Maddy had gotten away with it, rather than being found completely innocent.

"I didn't kill him."

Tallulah shrugged, adjusted her turban, and lifted one open hand.

Maddy jumped.

A mouse. A very large mouse—his nasty teeth bared—sat in Tallulah's hand.

NOSY IN NEBRASKA

"You've saved Maxie." Tallulah spoke with the melodrama of a Broadway actress, projecting her voice to the cheap seats. "And you've saved the town of Melnik." Tallulah's arms swept wide and buried Dora's head in flowing fabric.

Dora batted at the curtain of rayon hanging in her face. "Can't you at least put elastic on the wrists? You've got mashed potatoes and gravy on your arm again. And just because they've invented deodorant, Tallulah, there's no reason not to take a bath now and then."

Maddy noticed Tallulah didn't even react to the insults. Perhaps it wasn't only Maddy who caught the sharp edge of Dora's tongue.

Focus on the rodent. The famed Maxie, at last.

Maddy realized she wasn't particularly fond of mice. She hadn't been around that many, not outside a lab, and she'd never given them much thought. She could abide them, but not as dinner guests. And yet here was the renowned mouse of Melnik. What an opportunity!

She'd just eat later, perhaps at a different table. Which table had Tallulah come from? She wished she could be sure so she could avoid that table, too.

"So tell me about Maxie. It seems. . ." She chose her words carefully, remembering how Tyler had snapped at her when she'd said "worship". She believed they did worship this mouse, or at least held him in awe to an extent that bordered on religious zeal. Not Tyler, perhaps, but many of Melnik's residents.

"It seems that you. . .revere him."

A bell sounded, and Maddy heard the door open behind her. She planned to stare, since it seemed like the town tradition. But Tallulah drew her attention with a wide flourish of Maxie.

"He is the symbol of our greatness." Tallulah lifted Maxie over her head, and her voice rose in triumph and wonder and, yes. . .worship. "He has brought the town back from the brink of the grave. Maxie single-handedly snatched us from the jaws of death."

"Oh, surely not." Maddy glanced at Dora. With a start she realized the older woman seemed intent on boring a hole into Maddy's brain with her eyes.

Tallulah continued emoting. "He has rejuvenated our businesses, given the town youth, and is helping build a future for one and all."

He has given the town youth? Like some fertility symbol? Well, mice were known to be fruitful and multiply to an appalling extent, so as a symbol it made an icky kind of sense. Maddy longed for her notebook.

"His life, his eminence, his regal size are—"

"Get that mouse out of here, Tallulah, or I promise you, I'm calling the county health department." The slim blond woman who'd taken Maddy's picture at the murder scene stood far back from the table, turned, and yelled at the kitchen. "You hear me, Olga? You tell her to put Maxie back in his cage at the museum. I've got the number on speed dial and you know it. I'll march right down to Bonnie and Joe's and crouch behind his car and phone. You know I'm serious; I've done it before."

The patrons chuckled and settled in to watch the show.

Mice, yelling, threats—quite odd.

Tallulah rose before Olga said a word. The young blond backed up until she pressed up against a tall, dark-haired man who had a towheaded toddler on one hip. The man, neat as a pin and handsome as a knight in shining armor, slipped his spare arm around the blond's waist. Maddy had noticed him before at the arrest, and the blond had taken a snapshot.

The man spoke quietly. "Carrie, you're going to have to hold Heather if you jump."

"Please, Tallulah, go up the far side of the diner. Nick has his hands full." The blond had her eyes riveted on the mouse as she spoke.

Despite a gleam of temptation in Tallulah's eyes, she kept well away from the newcomers. Once Tallulah headed for the exit in a huffy swirl of fabric and mouse fur, the blond turned her attention to Maddy.

"Do you mind staying and eating with us. . .at another table?" Carrie twisted her hands together and glanced nervously at the spot where Tallulah and Maxie had been, then looked right back at the retreating Tallulah as if her eyes were drawn to the mouse by powerful magnets.

Dora snorted. "Maxie is perfectly clean, Carrie. Stop being silly. You need to spend time with Maxie if you're ever going to get over this foolish little fear. I thought you'd been working on it. Are you any better?"

"I hate mice with the fire of a thousand suns." Carrie still watched the mouse.

Maddy doubted that Carrie thought the mouse would jump at her, but she had no such confidence in Tallulah.

With a sniff of disdain, Tallulah swung open the door, working her exit like she was onstage at London's West End, bucking for an Olivier Award. "You remind me of your great-grandma Bea more every day." She slammed the door on her way out. The tinkling bell rang joyfully.

Carrie settled at a table across the way and gave Maddy a hopeful look. Of course, Maddy didn't hesitate. She turned to Dora. "If you'll pardon me?"

Without waiting for an answer—afraid of what Dora might find fault with now—Maddy picked up her pencils, gratefully abandoned the mouse hairs, and walked to the new table. This had to be the Carrie O'Connor she was looking for. What luck! All three of her primary targets in one day. Although Carrie's reaction to the rodent didn't bode well for her being one of the believers. And honestly, Maddy was quite sure she'd met nearly everyone in town in one day. So why not her primary targets?

Nick sat beside Carrie, still holding the baby. The child picked up the silverware and tried to put the fork in her mouth. Nick grabbed it before the tike could put her eye out.

Dora slid in beside Maddy, using her ample bum to shove Maddy sideways. "You need to try harder to keep that baby clean, Carrie. It'll be a wonder if she lives to adulthood. Germs, germs everywhere. Nothing will kill them better than a good pine cleaner."

"This from a woman having coffee with a mouse." Carrie rolled her eyes.

"We're using pine cleaner, Dora." The man chucked the little girl under the chin, and the toddler twisted to give him a heart-stopping grin. "And lots of bleach and that antiseptic hand wash and—"

The little girl patted the man's chin, imitating him. He hugged her and kissed her neck. She giggled. Carrie watched, her smile as wide as the child's. Maddy noticed her own smile, and Dora's.

Maddy felt better about her teeth when Dora insulted the very tidy parents of this very tidy baby. Which reminded Maddy that she wasn't a bit clean. She hadn't thought to change after the arrest.

Bother. Did jailbirds have an aroma? She rather thought she'd heard of such a thing.

She was probably a bigger threat to the sanitary conditions of Jansson's Café than that mouse, and nowhere near as popular. She shoved the pencils behind her ear, not caring if she missed by a bit. Who had room for seven pencils behind their ears after all?

"I'd hoped to visit with you." Maddy didn't have time to scrub up now.

"Me? Really? Because I'd hoped to talk to you. You were a witness when they found Melvin's body. Tell me what—"

A bit surprised to find herself being interviewed, Maddy decided the best route to interviewing Carrie was to be accommodating.

They talked all the while they went through the smorgasbord line. With a steady stream of insults from Dora sprinkled in, Maddy laid out the entire encounter with Melvin and the constable. Carrie seemed delighted, and Nick paid for Maddy's dinner.

A bit too broke for pride, Maddy thanked them as she ate the great pile of delicious food. Crispy fried chicken, mashed potatoes, and gravy. Tender slices of roast beef, a corn casserole, macaroni salad, coleslaw, and a variety of beans floating in a tart yet sweet white dressing. Carrie called it three-bean salad, but Maddy counted six beans and a few other things, so if Carrie was right, the salad was badly misnamed.

Over warm apple cobbler with ice cream, Maddy explained about her thesis paper—at least the part she was willing to admit—and Carrie agreed to be interviewed and granted full access to the newspaper's archives, conveniently stored in their temporary home at the Melnik Historical Society Museum, just a few doors down from Maddy's building. Maddy also learned Nick was building the new museum in the empty lot a bit farther down Main Street. The museum was run by Bonnie Simpson Manning—Tyler's sister.

Maddy's heart was light and her stomach full when she left Jansson's. Several strangers said good-bye; all of them called her Doc. She'd made a friend—three friends actually, if she counted Nick and Dora. Tallulah seemed pleased with Maddy, too; at least she had when she'd thought Maddy had killed that man. Of course, if Carrie or anyone from Melnik knew the truth about her thesis, they'd no doubt chase her out of the village with torches and pitchforks. But for now, Maddy enjoyed the human contact.

Her dinner companions climbed in their cars and drove away. No doubt they had nearly a block to go. She walked the half block to her building, waving at the lonely vampire again. She'd learned that her building, combined with Tyler's, had at one time been an opera house. It had stood decaying for decades until Nick O'Connor had refurbished it and Joe Manning had bought it to rent out. The first floor had twenty-foot ceilings. Other than that, nothing about its present condition hinted at its origins. Maddy didn't care. She unlocked her front door and stepped inside. When the door swung shut, with the dead bolt firmly in place, she should have felt safe.

Instead, she felt like she'd just locked herself in with the ghosts of Melvin Melnik and long-dead opera singers of yore.

The floor overhead creaked.

It was an old building. Of course it creaked.

Good heavens, it was to be expected. Feeling complete empathy for the lonely vampire, she trudged toward the stairway.

She had to go up there, where the creaks were, right next to the door where Melvin had lain dead. Then inflate her mattress and sleep.

Good luck.

⸻

"I cannot believe my bad luck."

Tyler shoved his fingers into his hair in frustration. "What did I do to make you drag me into this mess?"

"You're handy, and Hal can't help. He's a suspect." Junior pulled into his reserved parking slot in front of the police station. It was the only car on the block.

"Oh, he's no more of a suspect than I am. Hal wouldn't do a thing like this."

"Well, honestly, you oughta be a suspect, too. The dead body was in your building."

Rolling his eyes, Tyler went back to making his case for being acquitted of his sentence—one zillion hours of community service helping Cousin Junior with this stupid case.

He'd probably get a lighter sentence if he'd actually committed the crime.

"And Steve's got to work at the de-hy plant overnight. Summer's their busy season."

The factory, three miles out of town, dehydrated hay and made it into feed pellets. It was one of the area's best seasonal employers. It took a dozen men to run the big alfalfa choppers, hauling hay to the plant and dumping it, then going back to a new field for more.

"I know that. I worked there a couple summers in high school. But I'm the court-appointed defense attorney for Maddy, if you'll remember. I can't help you question people. It's a conflict of interest. It's unethical. It's illegal. And besides, I need to take over with the boys. Bonnie's gotta be tired of babysitting them by now."

Junior swung his cruiser door open—Tyler had been as good as arrested by his own cousin. "Bonnie's fine. She's better with them than you are."

Tyler knew that for the honest truth, and it hurt his feelings. "Bon-Bon's gonna make a great mom."

"And you're not the defense attorney. You got the doc off, and now you're out of a job. So you might as well help me. You're being paid to act as Melnik's legal counsel."

Tyler glared. "*Paid* is a strong word. I haven't seen a cent yet."

"We can't afford much and you know it, so stop whining."

Tyler reflected on all the high-powered corporate types he'd done legal work for in Omaha. Not a single one of them had ever told him to quit whining.

Home—gotta love it.

Hard to get respect from a guy who'd been the high school star athlete and homecoming king when Tyler was in diapers. Cousin Junior was Tyler's second cousin. Junior's father was a first cousin to Tyler's mom. They'd called the elder Hammerstad Uncle Junior. The whole town had called Uncle Junior's father Grandpa Junior, including Tyler, and Grandpa Junior had, in fact, been Tyler's great-uncle—Tyler wondered what they'd called Grandpa Junior before he had grandkids.

When Tyler's folks had died, Cousin Junior's wife had been a real solid help to Bonnie. She and Junior probably would have taken the family in if Bonnie hadn't been so strong and determined to care for her family.

And Tyler had abandoned her for Liza.

It made him sick every time he thought of it.

Junior led the way to the Andersons' front porch and knocked despite the handy-dandy bell. Helga Anderson, Carrie O'Connor's grandmother, came to the door.

Tyler could never look at Helga without thinking, *It's not over till the fat lady sings.*

The woman needed only a helmet with horns to complete the vision of a Viking wife. Of course, all Tyler's information about Vikings came from reading the *Hagar the Horrible* comic strip in the *Omaha World-Herald*. So what did he know?

Helga started talking before she had the door swung open. "He didn't do it, Junior, and you know it. I won't have you upsetting him."

"Now, Helga—"

"Everybody knows the time of death." Helga turned to her husband, a foot taller and half her width, with half her iron will. "You tell him."

"Twelve to twenty-four hours, right?" Hermann pulled his glasses off and cleaned them with a handkerchief, watching like a hawk for smears while he talked. "Starting at about noon today—that when you found him, Tyler?"

"That's right."

"And the poison had to be administered within twenty-four hours of that."

Tyler didn't even ask how Hermann knew all these details. It was Melnik. Everybody knew. The best thing and the worst thing about a small town was the same thing.

Everybody knew.

If you needed help, lost a job and needed money, had a death in the family, an illness, everybody knew and came to your aid. If you messed up, everybody knew and discussed every detail of the trouble. Tyler wondered what they'd said about Liza. He'd always hoped, because Tyler and his family had never come to Melnik, that no one knew how much she hated them all.

"Well, he was out at the farm all day Sunday, Monday, and today. He's throwing bales for my boy, and his hay was ready on Sunday with rain in the forecast, so they missed church to work."

Hermann Anderson's boy was his daughter's husband, Gus Evans, Carrie's dad, midfifties and still referred to as "my boy." That was one of the things Tyler loved best about Melnik.

"There from sunup to sundown. He came home, and you know baling hay."

Tyler did know baling hay. The kid would have been dead on his feet.

"Sunday night he took a shower, ate about a side of beef, and barely had the energy to wipe the gravy off his chin before he fell asleep. Helga and I were still up when he went to bed. The boy snores like a jackhammer, and he woke me several times in the night. I almost needed the Jaws of Life to pry him out of bed Monday morning, and this morning it was the same thing. Helga fed him and sent him on his way. When he got home, he fell asleep right after a late dinner and went back to his snoring. So he's accounted for all day, every minute of those twelve to twenty-four hours."

"The boy's got adenoid problems," Helga interjected, "but find a doctor who'll take out tonsils and adenoids these days. Didn't hurt any of my kids to have their tonsils yanked out."

Tyler swallowed, glad he'd hung on to his tonsils, just to avoid any yanking.

"And that takes care of the time of death, right? Melvin still alive Monday morning and dead as a carp by midnight, and Kevin's accounted for. I even looked in on him," Junior said.

"You shouldn't have come here." Helga crossed her arms across her ample middle. "He's a good boy, and you'll hurt his feelings by questioning him. We all know Kevin wouldn't do a thing like this."

Junior nodded. "I'd still like to talk to him. I'm sorry, and I believe you, so he's off my suspect list, but Melvin was his uncle. I need to know if the bum ever tried to contact Kevin."

Helga sniffed. "Fine. He's already asleep for tonight. Throwing bales all day again today. Can this wait? Gus is done with his first cutting, so with a good night's sleep, the boy might be less likely to get his feelings hurt."

"I'll come by in the morning. I don't suppose you're planning to have streusel for morning coffee?" Junior grinned. He seemed neither offended by Helga's scolding nor intimidated by it. Tyler was impressed, because he'd dated one of Carrie's older sisters for a few months in high school, and Helga Anderson had scared him to death.

Gus Evans had had a word with him, and so had his wife. But that wasn't enough. The town was lousy with Evanses and Andersons. Hermann had a knack for referring to his hunting rifle collection, casually, no connection between those rifles and the poor soul who might mistreat one of his granddaughters. The man had actually gotten out an old bayonet and shined it while they'd visited.

Tyler had spent the entire two-month relationship looking over his shoulder.

"We'll see. Maybe a good coffee cake will sweeten you up before you injure my boy's feelings."

Junior nodded. "I'll give him a chance to catch up on his sleep, then. Maybe around ten."

Junior scratched in his notebook while he and Tyler walked back to the car. "Okay, one of my main suspects is off the list."

"So are we done for the night?" Tyler shook his head. "No, of course not. Who am I kidding? You want to go try to get a batch of cinnamon rolls out of Donette and Hal? We could bribe food out of every suspect on the list. I wonder if Shayla can cook. We could track her down in Gillespie if you're hungry. I wanted to take my kids home, but Bonnie told me earlier that if I didn't show up, she'd just keep them overnight."

"Then what were you caterwauling about earlier? You aren't going to see them anyway."

"Yeah, but they wouldn't be staying with her if you hadn't called."

Junior grunted and studied his notebook. "I found a phone number for Shayla. I called earlier and a man answered. He said him and Shayla got married. They ran off and eloped when they found out she was pregnant. He mentioned both of them working at the hospital. He's an orderly, and Shayla's got her LPN and works full-time; she's even got insurance benefits. It sounds like the girl's getting her life together."

"Is Shayla's orderly husband strong enough to move a body?"

Junior looked up at Tyler. "You're a suspicious man, Tyler." Then a smile bloomed on Junior's face. "I think I'm starting to like you."

Tyler laughed. Junior had always liked him. But Junior liked everybody.

"I think we're done for the night." Junior dropped Tyler off at his car, which was sitting in front of his law office. They both noticed the little rusty wreck of a Toyota sitting beside Tyler's gleaming SUV. And they could see that every light in Maddy's building was on. The woman was spooked, no doubt about it.

"I wonder how the doc is holding up? Is knowing there was a dead body in there giving her night terrors?" Junior gave Tyler a calculating glance. "Checking would be neighborly."

Tyler swung the car door open, reaching for his keys. Nothing. He remembered. He'd given Dr. Snow White his keys, just handed the whole ring over. Law office, house, car. Tyler shook his head. If that wasn't a Freudian slip—arranging another get-together—nothing was.

"I think I will say good night. If she's spooked, she could spend the night at Bonnie's."

Tyler slammed the door in Junior's chuckling face. He stood there until his cousin drove off then approached the good doctor's door.

She had it open before he'd knocked twice. She must have been watching from inside. With two huge front windows, he should have seen her, but the streetlights made a glare that turned the windows opaque. And maybe she hadn't been there waiting. Maybe she'd watched from the upstairs windows and come running.

She'd cleaned up, put on a new set of baggy clothes—black walking shorts and white blouse this time. Bare feet. Her hair was loose, a bit too curly, as if she'd showered, and whatever control over her hair the ponytail had given her was lost.

No pencils.

"Can I come in?"

"Please do." She said it a little too fervently. Her blue eyes flashed gratitude and nerves. "So did you find out anything more about what happened to that man?"

"Melvin Melnik. A lowlife if ever there was one. The man will not be missed.

And no, we haven't found out anything."

Swinging the door wide, she whacked herself in the forehead then stumbled back. She had a firm grip on the doorknob, though. Tyler suspected the woman had learned to hang on to something at all times.

Rubbing tomorrow's bruise, she said, "How sad someone would die with that as his epitaph."

Tyler nodded as he passed her. She got too close as she swung the door shut and hit his foot.

"So sorry."

She smelled great. Her smile—well, she looked very happy to see him, and he couldn't imagine he'd made a good impression. So she must be afraid enough that any company was welcome. He couldn't leave her here, he couldn't stay, and he couldn't take her home.

"So how's it going? Does this place go bump in the night?"

"It's a little strange, what with the cadaver. I mean, it's gone but not forgotten, as it were. But I'm fine." She looked sad and less open and friendly than before, completely un-fine.

Tyler wondered what was going on in her head. He'd yelled at her. Told her to stay away from his sons, kicked up a fuss about being her lawyer. She most likely preferred the ghost's company to his.

6

Maddy had never been so happy to see anyone in her life.

She wanted to grab him and hang on. Then she remembered his keys. They made a good-sized lump in her pocket, and when she'd showered in the nasty little bathroom upstairs, she'd laid his keys on her air mattress and noticed there were too many. What looked like a car key with one of those automatic lock and unlock buttons on the key chain, and a few other keys he'd need. She'd noticed his car out front and hoped and prayed he'd stop by. He had to get home, after all.

She'd prayed for a lot of things. The dead man's soul. His family's grief—should there prove to be a family, and in case they grieved. Her own fear of every creaking floorboard. Her shaky financial future. Her work. She'd never lied to anyone, but she certainly hadn't told the whole truth to the good people of Melnik. Did God honor a prayer for her work that included falsehood?

While she pondered and prayed, well, since thinking didn't keep her hands busy after all, she'd curled her hair and put on a bit of makeup—not usual for her at any time, but certainly not before she went to sleep. A certain keyless lawyer stopping by was a definite factor in her decision to primp. Her best black walking shorts. A white blouse she went to pains to keep clean for once.

A spritz of perfume.

And now here he was, and she had no idea what to say. She certainly couldn't keep him here permanently, and his temporary presence, although it allayed her fears for the moment, wasn't going to do so after he left. Which could happen at any moment, especially if she stood here without talking. And so what if he was here for his keys? He was her lawyer. That was all. And a reluctant one at that.

"I saw you and the constable—"

"Junior and I ruled out—"

They both stopped and laughed awkwardly. Maddy noticed her hands were clenched together so tightly her knuckles were white. She wished desperately for something better than a folding chair to offer him. She just had to get some furniture.

"Go ahead." Maddy tore her hands apart and gestured toward the gray metal desk, older and uglier than the constable's, but similarly built. It and the chairs had been in here when she moved. "Why don't we sit down? Tell me about the investigation."

Tyler crossed the echoing room. Each footstep on the bare wood bounced off the four walls and towering ceiling, underscoring to Maddy how big and empty and spooky this building was. He settled in a metal folding chair, and because it was the only other place to sit in the room, she took the equally uncomfortable metal chair behind her desk. Folding her arms on the paper-strewn desktop, she leaned forward. This was almost an interview. Perhaps he'd give her background on Melnik.

"So are your roots deep in Melnik?"

"I'm not going to be part of your anthropology thesis, so don't start."

Maddy had to control a sigh. She masked her frustration. "That's fine. So sorry. Old habit to begin asking questions."

"You mean it's an old habit to treat people like lab rats?"

"Most likely. I'm actually a total bore for the most part."

"No, you're not."

He seemed so sure, Maddy wanted to believe him. But she had years of evidence to the contrary. "Well, thank you. But I spend too much time studying people and not enough befriending them. I had a few people talk to me at the diner, but that was just general chatting. In fact, Carrie O'Connor interviewed me, more than the other way around. I may have my face tucked inside the *Bugle* somewhere next week."

"Are you kidding? You'll be on the front page, above the fold."

"Right next to the deceased Mr. Melnik? Splendid—the whole town will remember I was arrested, and now we'll be linked for all time."

"They'll remember anyway."

"At least there was no mug shot taken of me."

"So are you going to be able to handle this?"

"This?" she asked, knowing full well what he meant.

Tyler just waited.

The silence defeated her. "I'll handle it. . .somehow."

"Creepy, though, huh?"

Maddy nodded.

Tyler seemed to shift the possibilities around in his head for a long time. At last, looking almost. . .apologetic, he said, "I've got an idea that might help. The boys are at Bonnie's for the night, so they won't notice."

Maddy stiffened. "Notice what?" Was he getting ready to make some smarmy offer to stay with her?

"They won't notice if their dog is gone."

A burst of air escaped her lungs. "A dog?" She was charmed. "You've got a dog that would share my flat for tonight?"

Tyler nodded. "You won't be spooked, but you'll probably be exhausted. He's a puppy, a golden retriever puppy named Riley. I've only been back in town a month. We moved right after school let out. The puppy was the first act of madness after we arrived. He's doing okay on house-training, but he needs to go out at least twice a night, and he'll whine until you take him. He's so hyperactive he makes my boys seem catatonic. He's a wiggling, licking, yipping, ADHD dog. But he's really cute. And you won't have a second to think about little creaking floorboards."

Maddy's heart melted. "I'd like that very much. This place is a little eerie at night. I just got to town today."

"I know."

Of course he knew. Could she be any more of a twit? "So the night was stretching long in front of me."

"Can I have my keys?"

The question didn't seem to fit in their conversation. "What?"

"My car keys. I left them with you when I gave you the keys to my office so you could use the phone if you needed to."

"Oh yes, those keys." She was a bit lost in his kindness and his handsome eyes. She didn't move.

"I'll go get him if you give me the keys." Tyler smiled. "You can ride along if you like."

"I'd like that." Maddy leapt to her feet so fast her chair went skidding backward, folded up, and collapsed with a clang of metal on wood. "Very much."

Tyler smiled as Maddy fished for his keys in her pocket. They'd hooked into a dusty handkerchief, and a half-wrapped stick of gum glued the whole mass together. Maddy fought the keys free of her pocket contents.

Looking up, she saw an amused tolerance on Tyler's face, as if her ridiculous clumsiness didn't drive him mad. She had the nearly uncontrollable urge to hurl herself into his arms. Instead, she handed the keys over and they went to pick up her new guard dog.

A few minutes later, with the puppy wiggling in her arms, Tyler drove past Maddy's home. "Let me take you on a brief tour of Melnik."

She couldn't control a sigh of relief. "That would be splendid, thank you."

"That's the statue of Maxie the high school football team created."

Maxie in pads, a helmet, and a uniform. The school colors were gray and white.

The Melnik Mice.

Maddy wondered if they'd ever won a game in their lives.

"And this one was decorated by the VFW."

Maxie in a soldier's uniform, holding a rifle. Maddy thought it looked real. Could the town just leave a rifle lying around like that?

Tyler wound around a corner about three blocks from Maddy's wretched flat. "This is my sister's house."

"Good heavens, who built this thing?"

They slowed and Tyler rolled down a window. Maddy thought she heard the caw of a crow, or maybe a raven—*nevermore*.

"It's awful, isn't it? But it's nice inside. Bonnie and Joe have turned it into a real home. They're going to sandblast the white paint off, and it won't look quite so much like it's dripping blood."

"Well, that might help." Maddy was extremely doubtful.

Looking through the large window near the center of the house, Maddy saw Tyler's children sitting beside Joe. He was reading to them.

"You should be with your sons instead of me."

"They like Bonnie more than me." Tyler sounded so glum Maddy wanted to cry for him. "I can't make them behave. I can't even make them like me. My wife was in charge of discipline. I've got a lot to learn."

Maddy didn't comment, but she didn't think the boys had been taught much discipline. No one, not even a child, could so completely forget their teachings. Maddy soothed the sniffling puppy and he settled onto her lap. As she petted him, Riley went to sleep, as relaxed as a baby.

Tyler kept driving, past a mouse in the huge house's front lawn.

"Is this your sister's mouse art contribution?"

A mouse, plain, just sat there. Well, it was on its haunches really. All of the statues were of the same design. The mouse didn't really look like it was sitting so much as it looked for all the world like it was standing up on its hind legs.

"Yeah, she's using her artistic expression to decry the exploitation of the natural world by man." Tyler studied the mouse through narrowed eyes.

"Honestly, that's a lovely sentiment."

"It is, but no one believes her. They think she's just too lazy to fix up her mouse."

"Well, all great artists are misunderstood."

"Yeah, plus when I told her that, she got mad. I try not to upset her in her condition."

Tyler showed her more mice. He was particularly fond of Junior's. Tyler wasn't absolutely sure, but he thought Maxie had on one of Junior's uniforms. Maxie was shorter, but with some hemming of the pants and shirt, Junior wasn't shaped unlike a mouse.

"It strikes me as odd that you've chosen to give me a tour of mouse statues. But I appreciate seeing them. Especially the one outside the day care center dressed like a clown and the one by the nursing home with a walker. That was lovely." In an extremely creepy and shut-down-by-the-health-department kind of way, but Maddy didn't say that out loud.

Tyler took far too long getting her home. Maddy wasn't about to rush him. With the windows open, the cool evening air ruffled Maddy's hair.

"I can't remember ever being anywhere this quiet."

Maddy had lived in London and Omaha, and she'd done a bit of traveling, but never to a rural area. No cars, no chattering people, no planes overhead or sirens in the distance. Just the silence of people settled into their homes for the night.

Tyler finally pulled up beside her car. "Can you handle it? Bonnie would let you stay with her."

"The puppy will help. I'll make it."

Tyler was out and around the car before Maddy could switch the sleeping puppy around and free a hand to grab the door handle.

He let her out and walked her to her door. It took everything Maddy had in her not to grab him and beg him not to leave her. She might have even done it if she hadn't found him so attractive. A friend she could stay with, but not this handsome man.

"Good night, Maddy." Tyler lingered.

Maddy knew he was worried about her. So she said, "Good night. Thank you for the tour." She turned and boldly went inside her spooky building.

Lying in bed an hour later, with Riley's gentle heartbeat warming her, Maddy decided, even with the dead body and being arrested as sour notes, this was one of the nicest days of her life.

⁓

The hammering on her door woke her to full daylight. The puppy licking her face came an instant later. An exhausting night. The puppy wasn't one for long, unbroken sleep. Tyler had in fact lied to her about the little retriever's hyperactivity. He had grossly understated how active the pup was. Still, the baby fuzzball had saved her life. . .or at least her sanity. Her heart tugged at the thought of giving him up.

Sleep dragging at her eyelids, she fought through the cobwebs in her brain and pulled on her clothes in record time. She couldn't answer the door in her nightgown. After all, the whole front of her building was open to the street. She ran downstairs, tripping when she almost stepped on the frolicking puppy. Only her firm hand on the railing saved her. She'd learned to never forgo that.

The knocking continued. It sounded like someone was beating on her door with the side of his fist. She saw Constable Hammerstad at the door, and a twinge of fear surprised her. She'd never feared an officer of the law in her life. Always a law-abiding person, she'd never had so much as a traffic citation or even a warning. Of course, she'd never owned a car in London. The public transportation system suited her.

But in America, she'd acquired a fifteen-year-old Tercel and had been the picture of care behind the wheel.

"I'm coming!" She trotted toward the door, dodged the puppy, and fell forward, close enough to fall against the door and almost brain herself, but her head impacting wood saved her from falling to the floor in a heap, so on balance she was grateful. Twisting at the lock, she saw the flushed anger on the constable's face.

"What happened?"

Constable Junior shouldered past her partially opened door. "Dr. Madeline Stuart, you are under arrest for the murder of Melvin Melnik."

"What? Not again."

Tyler's big car pulled up, his brakes locking. He skidded into the curb and bounced. He was out of the car with the door slammed before the vehicle stopped rocking.

"Sorry, Maddy. I—"

"You have the right to remain silent and I suggest you exercise that right." The constable pulled her wrists behind her, and she heard the metallic snick of the cuffs on her wrists. He stepped up beside her, and she saw the fire of anger in his eyes. "You played me yesterday, and I don't like it. You have the right to an attorney, and here he is."

Junior jerked his thumb at Tyler. "But it's not going so easily for you this time."

"What in the world happened?" Maddy looked at Tyler.

His expression was cool concern. The professional lawyer was back. "I don't know. Junior just phoned and said he was arresting you and to meet you at the police station. But I was driving by and saw this going on."

A crowd gathered, Dora in the forefront. Down the block, Olga Jansson stood outside her diner and wiped her hands on a towel as she stared. The vampire was outside, too. Obviously awake and moving in the sunlight, but no matter how many times Maddy saw him, she couldn't quite remove her suspicion that he was the walking dead.

The hippie lady stepped out, pirouetted, and stared. She was already fitting into Melnik. How early was it? Did these people arise at dawn for fear they'd miss some bit of gossip?

The puppy escaped between Maddy's legs, making her jump sideways and knock her shoulder solidly into the door frame. Constable Junior caught her arm. Insulting, that. Why, she'd never made one tiny escape attempt in all these hours of their acquaintance.

Tyler snagged the puppy and cuddled the little fellow close to his chest, all the while watching Maddy with those cool eyes. He was her lawyer again, no longer a too-handsome friend with a puppy to share.

Maddy walked to the cruiser. She called up the street, "I'm innocent."

Many in the crowd on the sidewalk nodded and waved. Maddy was unable to return those waves. She hoped they understood and didn't think she was unfriendly.

Junior cupped the back of her head when she lowered herself into the backseat, resigned to another block-and-a-half ride.

7

"C'mon, Junior, couldn't you just ask the woman where she was before you start arresting her? It's embarrassing for her." Tyler unlocked her cuffs. "And you'll be embarrassed, too, when you have to let her go."

"She goes nowhere until this is confirmed."

Tyler snorted. "And that'll take what? A half hour? She had Riley last night." Tyler held up the squirming puppy. "She could have used some more sleep. You heard her say she'd only been in town a couple of hours before we found Melvin."

The dog started licking Tyler's face. Not enjoying the dog slobber, Tyler set the cute little pest on the floor.

"I didn't ask about the right time." Junior glared at Maddy as if that was her fault.

Tyler crossed his arms and leaned back in his chair.

"Dr. Notchke just phoned and said the body showed signs of being chilled." Tyler jerked forward. "What?"

"Which means Melvin cooled down a lot faster than he would have otherwise. They're still examining the evidence, but it appears now that he'd only been dead a few hours. And I don't know exactly when she got to town. I'm going to double-check the gas receipts she got when she filled her car in Fremont and see if anyone remembers her."

"I wish you chaps wouldn't speak about me like I'm not here."

Tyler thought she'd been a pretty good sport up to now, but she was looking at the jail cell door as if it had fangs and a healthy appetite.

"I'm sorry." He patted her now-unshackled wrist. "I'll have you out of there faster than we can arrange a bail hearing. The judge works in two counties, so to get bail set, I'd have to go to the next county over from here, which could take half a day—the drive's not bad, but he's hearing court cases, so he's busy. He'll be in this county tomorrow, so if things don't work out with your alibi, I'll arrange bail tomorrow."

"Tomorrow? You mean I might have to spend the night in jail?" She looked down at his feet. Little Riley grinned up at her, wagging his tail. Which Tyler believed was proof positive that the friendly, goofy dog was dumb as a rock. There was nothing to smile about here.

"No, no, of course not. Junior's going to start phoning people right now."

Tyler glared at his cousin as he escorted Maddy into the cell.

"Look, this isn't my fault." The poor excuse for a detective swung the door shut with a loud clank. "The doctor said the time of death was sooner. Melvin had her locket in his hand. That gives us a solid piece of evidence and opportunity."

"You said yesterday there was evidence that his hand had been pried open after his death." Maddy clenched the bars like a seasoned felon.

"Dr. Notchke suspects it, but it's not conclusive. His hand was definitely injured postmortem, but maybe you knew he had the locket. Maybe you were trying to get his fist open when you heard Tyler come in downstairs."

"Oh, rubbish." Maddy released the bars and rubbed her arms. Tyler noticed she had goose bumps.

"Are you cold?"

Maddy looked at her arms and back at him. "No, I'm scared to death I'm going to end up in one of your awful American prisons for killing some man I've never seen nor heard of."

"American prisons aren't so bad."

Maddy made a sound Tyler would expect to come from a wounded, cornered mountain lion.

"Not that you'll ever know that," he added quickly. "You'll be out in no time." Tyler turned to Junior. "You've got no motive. Why would she want to kill Melvin? There's absolutely no link between the two of them."

"A motive might turn up. For one thing, what are the chances some anesthesiologist from England would pick Melnik to write a paper on? Maybe she knew Melvin before."

"I'm an anthropologist, actually."

Tyler ignored her. "Melvin came straight from prison to Melnik and went straight back to prison. Where do you think she met him? On the campus at Oxford?"

"I don't teach at Oxford either. There are other universities in London, you know. Although Oxford is my dream. I hope someday—"

"Like I said, I'm asking questions." Junior got a mule-stubborn look on his face.

Tyler had known his cousin long enough to know arguing with the man at this point would just make him dig in his heels.

Using his best "professional attorney" sneer, Tyler said, "I'd like privacy to confer with my client, please, Officer." Riley tugged at Tyler's shoestrings, and it was hard to keep his professional demeanor intact. He saw Maddy trembling. "Privacy and a sweater. She's freezing."

Junior grunted and slid past Tyler into the narrow hall that ran in front of the two jail cells, one for women, one for men. There was no one in either of them—not counting Maddy—who did count, but not really, because she was innocent.

379

Why would there be anyone locked up? There was no crime in Melnik.

Tyler thought of Melvin and Gunderson and Wilkie. . .all murdered.

Almost no crime.

Junior left and returned in a second with a gray hoodie sweatshirt with the word HUSKERS printed in huge red letters that stretched all the way across the front and onto the sleeves, dissected by a zipper. Judging by the size, this was Junior's.

"Now I'm going to go search your building for evidence." He handed Maddy the sweatshirt, glared at Tyler, then turned and gave them their privacy, closing the door behind him with a solid thud.

"I did not kill Melvin Melnik."

"I know you didn't." Tyler waved his hand at her then centered a folding chair and sat down. "Now since they've changed the time of death, and you don't have as good an alibi as before—"

"I have a rock-solid alibi. I worked round the clock with my study group up until testing time on Monday. The test went late and my group went out and celebrated the end of the class. I went straight home to sleep in the wee hours. I must have awakened my landlord when I pulled up, because he came and scowled at me and reminded me I had to be out early the next morning. I slept just a few hours then loaded the possessions I hadn't moved here days ago and handed my key to my landlord. If I drove straight here, I'd have still been too late to kill that man."

"Well, borderline."

The look she gave him made him glad there were steel bars between them.

"But as I told you, I didn't drive straight here. I stopped to buy tea at a little shop in Omaha and ended up chatting over oolong and scones for nearly two hours. The owner is the sweetest little British woman, and we've gotten to know each other over the past few months. She'll definitely remember me."

"Do you have a receipt with a credit card record of the time you stopped there? Junior called that shop and there was no answer."

"She's probably closed. She talked a lot about her health. And the tea shop is just something she does for a hobby. If she has a doctor's appointment or something, she just locks up, and she doesn't take credit cards. I paid cash for my tea."

"Well, until we find her, she's not much use as an alibi."

"Then I stopped for gas in Fremont. I used my credit card for that. I don't have that receipt, either, but there will be a record. It will prove—"

"Look, I know. That makes it no longer borderline. You didn't get here until hours after the latest possible time of death. You don't have to convince me, but Junior's insisting on checking with the credit card company. It'll be fine. Like I said, you'll be out in a few minutes."

"And in the meantime, Junior is ransacking my flat looking for a nonexistent connection to that horrible dead man. I think that's shockingly rude."

"Yeah, sorry I couldn't head that off."

"You don't seem like you're all that good a solicitor, frankly."

Tyler had been mulling the ins and outs of murder, but her highbrow accent and her snippy insult drew his attention and he smiled.

Mistake.

"Nothing about this is remotely amusing."

"Now, Maddy, don't—"

"Get me out of here. Go earn your money."

Tyler rolled his eyes. "Junior will never cough up any cash."

She sniffled.

"Fine, I'll go try to stop him from making a mess in your place."

Her lips quivered. Her eyes closed. For a second, he was sure tears were inevitable. He hunched his shoulders, determined to stay and comfort her.

She swiped one hand over her eyes. "Can you leave the puppy?"

Tyler hesitated. He kept expecting the boys to show up. Eight-months pregnant Bonnie was bound to get tired of chasing them. So far they must be okay, unless they'd killed her and no one had noticed yet.

In Melnik, it was possible.

The boys would notice their dog was missing. But. . . He eased the chubby pup through the bars and Maddy grabbed the little fluffball, sat down on the cot, and pressed warm fur to her cheek.

"I'll go, then. Tell Junior to phone me if you think of anything you need. Junior can take Riley out for a walk, too. Serves him right for arresting you."

"Get out of here." The words were tough, but they lost their intensity when the first tear rolled down her cheek and the puppy licked it away, his feet peddling. The little doofus didn't seem to realize he was in midair instead of running.

Tyler couldn't go. "You know I won't let anything happen to you, Maddy. I'm a good lawyer. Junior's got nothing, and we just have to force him to admit it."

Maddy stood and approached the cell door. Tyler couldn't resist meeting her right across the steel bars. He reached and touched the soft gold of his puppy. His fingers found hers.

"I do appreciate your help, Tyler. I do. I shouldn't have spoken so sharply. I'm so sorry."

Another tear fell. This was so different from Liza's crying. Lots of noise when his wife cried, screaming—sometimes she threw things. She'd even slapped him a few times—more than a few. He'd learned to stay put even though he wanted to run. The storm seemed to pass more quickly if he stayed, and a niggling seed of doubt told him she might turn on the boys, although she never had.

And when had Liza ever, ever apologized?

He couldn't stop himself. The metal bars were magnetized. He was pig iron. He leaned forward. The bars kept them apart except. . .the bars were just wide enough that he could reach her lips with his own.

One healing kiss, a sympathy kiss.

Comfort, reassurance, friendship, support.

Just good manners.

Great manners.

Great kiss.

The dog licked his face and he pulled back. He couldn't go far. She'd reached one arm through the bars and had it wrapped around his neck.

He reached up to help her let go and realized he had his arms through the bars and around her waist. It took some untangling to get away. And that was slowed down by another kiss. . .or two. If the puppy and the jail cell door hadn't been there, he might have kissed her all day. He thought for a few seconds he might anyway.

His brain engaged, and he stumbled back and nearly fell over his folding chair. She backed away from him as if he were a rattlesnake. With one hand over her mouth, she hit the hard cot and sat down abruptly. Riley jumped down and ran out of the cell.

"Please don't leave—"

Tyler didn't think he could.

"—with the puppy."

Oh, the dog, of course.

Tyler returned the mutt. She took him without touching Tyler.

He saw tears welling again, and she buried her face in Riley's thick coat. He was positive Dr. Snow White didn't want him here to watch her cry.

Whether that was his yellow belly talking or not, he ran.

8

"Look at this, Ty."

Junior met him at the door to Dr. Snow's building with a fistful of papers. "Look what she's got planned."

Tyler scowled at Junior. "You didn't need to keep her locked up. You know she didn't kill that bum Melvin Melnik."

Junior slapped him in the chest with the papers. "She's trying to make laughingstocks out of all of us. Worse than that, she's trying to prove we're a cult or something, worshipping Maxie. If she writes this paper, the whole town will be ruined."

"What are you talking about? Worship?"

"She asked us just yesterday if we worshipped Maxie, remember?"

"Someone is trying to take possession of that rodent you all worship?"

Tyler remembered. He'd called her on it, and she'd backed right off. He looked at the papers, and as he read, he mentally drafted his letter of resignation from her case. He'd turn in his law license before he'd spend any more time with this dishonest, insulting, arrogant little Brit. Tyler refought the whole American Revolution while he read. And America won again.

Junior returned to the stack of papers on her desk. "She wants to prove we're all victims of mass insanity. Her anarchiology paper is going to be about a town that is suffering from delusions and worships an oversized mouse."

"Anthropology." Tyler corrected Junior under his breath. Anthropology, the study of civilizations. Like Margaret Mead, only instead of researching some tribe cut off from the modern world, Dr. Snow White was studying the people of Melnik like they were savages.

"She's got newspaper clippings from the *Bugle*, the *World-Herald*, and one from *Newsweek* from when Carrie got that story printed in there." Junior lifted a flat plastic DVD case. "She's got a copy of the *Current Events* program they did about us."

Tyler well remembered those stirring pieces about how all that was great about America was reflected by Melnik and the citizens' efforts to save their hometown. And that story about Melnik on *Current Events*. It had happened right when Liza died, so he hadn't seen it air originally, but Bonnie had sent him a DVD of it a couple of months later. Melnik depicted beautifully, full of people who cared and loved each other.

He'd always loved his home, but he'd let Liza convince him Melnik was an embarrassment. The shame of how he'd let her dictate every breath he took still clung to him like a bad odor. And he still had a terrible time making decisions, waiting for Liza to tell him how it was going to be.

Carrie, despite her loathing for mice in general and Maxie in particular, had seen in Melnik the foundations of freedom and ingenuity and dignity that were the backbone of America.

The woman was a wizard with words, and her work had won state and national awards and been widely reprinted. Bonnie had always sent him clippings from the paper, especially ones that mentioned her, and as the museum curator, she'd been featured prominently in any Maxie Mouse news.

Liza wasn't there anymore to ridicule it, as she'd ridiculed everything about Melnik. And without her denigrating opinion influencing him, that paper had lit a fire that had never gone out.

His marriage to Liza had long been over—in his heart—before she died. But vows were sacred, and he'd have kept them all his life. Now with her dead, that story had reminded him of his childhood, his roots. Bonnie and his little brothers he'd so cruelly abandoned. The boys were grown now, no thanks to him. Bonnie had done it all alone.

He'd have never acted on any of those stirrings if Liza hadn't died, killed in a wreck by her own road rage while she was furious at Tyler for driving to Melnik to visit his family.

After her death, Tyler had been too stunned to think clearly. But finally the fog cleared. That DVD came from Bonnie. Carrie's articles reminded him of his love for home. Without Liza there to remind him of Melnik's unworthiness, his desire for home took root. He'd grown up with the safety of knowing everyone by name, and their parents and grandparents and great-grandparents. The experience had shaped him, and he wanted it for his children.

He'd been weak to let Liza alienate him from all that was wonderful about small-town life. He'd been less than a man, less than God wanted him to be. He'd hurt his children, himself, and even Liza by his actions.

For the first time he realized that he'd allowed her to be a tyrant. It had been easier to just take her abuse than to be a man. And he'd been less than a man with his children, allowing them to run wild, calling it sympathy after Liza died, when it was really weakness. Even though she got her way in everything, he now knew Liza had been miserable, and he had to take responsibility for that, at least in part.

The shame stung as he realized another woman held Melnik in contempt. And he'd just kissed her.

He was a fool.

But he didn't have to stay one. "I want off her case."

"No." Junior got all bulled up, his brow lowered, his jaw clenched.

Tyler knew that stubborn look. "I refuse to represent her."

"Too bad. You know her alibi will check out."

"Then why'd you lock her up?" Tyler knew why well enough.

"Because it made me mad when Dr. Notchke changed the time of death and I realized the good doctor could have done it."

"Well, it's not Maddy's fault that Dr. Notchke made you mad." Plus, it was probably an abuse of the office—illegal, and they could be sued.

"True, but I'm glad it happened or I'd have never found her notes about her plans for Melnik."

"So am I." With this evidence of her disdain for Melnik in front of him, Tyler would have arrested her, too, just to let her know how mad he was.

"I realized she could have very carefully planned that killing, knowing full well we'd misjudge the time of death and she'd have an alibi." Junior's excuse sounded like he was practicing his testimony before the judge. "By the time we got done questioning her about this dumb oolong tea she bought, I knew she was innocent. Who makes up a tea flavor like oolong? But arresting her, plus having this building adjacent to the crime scene, gave me probable cause to search this place."

Tyler was momentarily distracted from his anger by the words *probable cause*. Maybe he'd underestimated Junior.

"I want to do this investigation right. I want proof of her alibi before she's released. I never even followed up before. Like a sap, I just took her word for it. But I'm done trusting."

Junior shook a new stack of papers he held in his hand. "This proves the woman's a skillful liar. I'm doing this by the book. Once her alibi checks out, I'll let her go, and as soon as she's off the suspect list, we can run her out of town on a rail. It looks like she has to do a lot of interviewing to complete this paper. As soon as people realize what she's here for, they'll refuse to work with her. She'll have to move on. Maybe she can go to that town in Kansas with that gigantic ball of twine. Maxie is no different than that."

"This is all confidential, Junior. We can't just go out on the street and tell everyone what we found here." A creak turned Tyler around. He saw Dora staring straight at him; then she whirled and left with a speed that belied her age and weight.

Junior laughed. "Well, that solves that. Consider the word spread."

Tyler had a twinge of pity for poor Dr. Stuart. This town could close ranks like nobody's business. But then he looked down at her handwritten comments on the photocopy of Carrie's beautiful article.

Delusional? Cult? Uneducated? Low intelligence? Inbreeding? Mass insanity?

NOSY IN NEBRASKA

As if being from Melnik equaled being stupid. As if the people here weren't people of faith who worshipped God, not some oversized mouse.

His pity died, replaced by anger. And that soothed the fear in his heart. Fear mixed with hope, awakened by the pretty, clumsy doctor. Hope that had grown when he'd kissed her and held her in his arms.

Hope. He thought he'd outgrown it, but obviously a spark remained.

Well, he'd just had another growth spurt.

He looked up at Junior's flushed, glowering face. "I want to be there when you unlock that door."

Junior jerked his chin down in a taut nod. "You bring the tar. I'll bring the feathers."

Junior came in and Maddy almost cried.

She'd been here for hours. The constable had been in here only once all day. He'd taken the puppy. She'd asked him questions, but he seemed furious about something and hadn't responded. She wondered what they'd make of her research notes and hoped they didn't look too close. Her project was private, but nothing she was ashamed of. She was light-headed from not eating. Weren't they supposed to feed you in jail?

This morning, Junior had awakened her and brought her straight here. Thank heaven he'd given her a moment in the loo before locking the door. She hadn't eaten all day, and the afternoon was nearly past.

He jerked open her cell with that same suppressed anger and stepped aside. "Your alibi checked out; you're free to go. I recommend you get in your car and start driving."

"What?" She saw Tyler standing in the next room. She hurried toward him until she saw his face.

Rage. Pure and simple.

As she passed through the door, her knees wobbled and she stumbled. Not from her usual lack of grace, but from weakness brought on by hunger mixed with fear. What were they both so angry about? They wouldn't be letting her go if they seriously thought she'd killed that man.

"What's the matter?"

Then she looked past Tyler and saw more people, and more and more. She thought she'd drawn a crowd before, but that was nothing compared to this. Through the open door, she saw the sidewalk was packed, and the street beyond the sidewalk, too.

Tyler leaned close, and she smelled him and remembered that kiss. She'd hardly kissed anyone in her life. She'd been an awkward, bespectacled bookworm

386

with no people skills from birth. Who was going to kiss her? And then Tyler had, and she'd begun to believe something wonderful was happening to her.

She'd felt like a butterfly emerging from a cocoon. Maybe she'd found someone who saw past the worm.

What a joke.

That joy, despite hunger and Junior's anger, had carried her through this awful day in jail. She'd thought Tyler would come and set her free, maybe kiss her again, say lovely words.

Instead, his expression took a fly swatter to her newborn butterfly.

She wanted to run from all the glaring eyes. Get in her car and get out. But she had nowhere, absolutely nowhere to go, and no money to get there.

She stopped. "What is going on? I'm not leaving town, and I'm not budging from this spot until one of you tells me."

She saw Tallulah in the crowd. For once the woman wasn't shouting. But her furious expression said more than words.

Tyler stepped in front of her, his shoulders so broad she couldn't see past him. "I'll tell you what's going on, Dr. Stuart."

"Dr. Stuart?" The contempt lacing his voice made her step back.

"Yes, Dr. Stuart the anthropologist. We found your research papers."

Instantly Maddy knew. They'd searched her building. Of course they'd found her out. She fumbled behind her for the wall and slumped against it and then felt cornered, which she was.

"I. . .I don't know what you think about my research, but there's nothing in it to upset the whole town." Which wasn't true. She'd known they'd be upset, which was why she'd withheld the full truth.

"Don't waste any more time lying."

"L–lying? I didn't lie."

"I read it all, Dr. Stuart."

"You had no right—"

"Junior had a search warrant, and you sent me over there. That's the very definition of the word *right*. The contempt you feel for Melnik. The insults dressed up like scientific research. We worship a mouse instead of God. Where'd you get a stupid idea like that? Is that what passes for education these days?"

"No, I mean the word *worship* isn't. . . I never intended to write a paper questioning your faith, just looking into the. . .somewhat. . .obsessed devotion to your town's—"

"Idol? Fertility god? Your words. Do you think we believe Maxie has some supernatural power?"

"No, of course not!"

"Well, that's not what your research paper says."

"You're quoting a list of questions I found interesting. I intended to study all aspects of your town. Just because I said it doesn't mean I believed it."

"Well, if believing what you say isn't a requirement, then you can say any insulting thing you want, can't you? But what you can't say to us right now is that you cared one bit if your scientific research would damage this town."

"Damage the town? How could I—"

"We've got companies"—he cut her off—"considering us for small factories that would bring good jobs. We've got young people who have picked Melnik to call home, even though they commute to bigger towns to work and have to drive through four other small towns to get to Fremont and five small towns to get to Sioux City. The school has grown, our tax base has grown, the business district is being revitalized. A nasty little smear piece like your research paper would destroy all of that. But you don't care because you don't care about us." He leaned down until his nose almost touched hers. "None of us."

He meant, *You don't care about me.* And that was absolutely, patently untrue. She cared about him so much it scared her all the way down to her two left feet. Two minutes ago it had thrilled her. But now she saw that her caring was only going to hurt.

She looked down. She'd done it again.

The worst ever.

As always, she'd alienated people. Her career was ruined if the paper wasn't written. Her future looked bleak. Her heart was quite possibly broken. And worst of all, when he put it this way, she knew Tyler was right. It was a stupid, insulting paper that didn't begin to rise to the level of serious research. A paper that, if she'd have written it and promoted it as she'd planned, would glorify and enrich her while hurting the people of Melnik.

Which meant that God was disgusted with her, too.

And she deserved all of this.

She looked up, her eyes locked on Tyler; then she scanned other faces, surprised how many were familiar after one day in town. And she told them the total and utter truth. "You've made your point. I didn't consider the harm that could be done to your town when I decided to write my paper. So I agree to drop the thesis." Which meant she'd drop her chance at a second PhD and her chance at a job.

None of the faces in the crowd softened. Which made it harder to tell them this next thing. "I can't leave town until September. I've got nowhere else to go. I'm so sorry."

Those words, those stupid, stupid apologies. She was so sick of uttering them with every clumsy step she took and every insulting word she spoke. She was smart. She had the paperwork to prove it. But what good were book smarts if you lived your life like a fool?

God, forgive me. Please. Please. Please.

And she knew instantly that He did, because He always had. God was her resting place. The only one she'd ever found. The only friend she'd never alienated.

Only God had enough patience and love to abide Dr. Madeline Stuart.

She threaded her way through the crowd. No one accosted her, although she feared they might. The street was packed all the way to the corner. She slid this way and that to get through, although mostly they moved back to let her pass, as if touching her would infect them with something.

She came face-to-face with the strange man with no teeth. She sidestepped.

He blocked her, glaring as if she'd personally insulted him. "I moved to this town because everyone made it sound so nice. I should have never come. Your paper's gonna ruin everything."

"I'm not going to write it. I promise." She raised her voice. "I promise."

No one responded, and she went around the man, though he moved so his shoulder bumped hers hard enough that she staggered.

No one else interfered with her progress, though.

Once she'd passed them all, she walked swiftly toward her home for the next three months. She'd paid the rent for June, July, and August. She owned a nonrefundable plane ticket home dated for early September. Beyond that, she had about two hundred dollars in her bank account and a student visa that made it illegal to get a job.

She couldn't afford to go elsewhere. She stopped at her door and looked back. The townsfolk had rounded the corner to watch her, but they were also talking among themselves. Tyler was toward the back of the crowd, but she picked him out without a second's effort. His anger pinged like a sonar beacon, bouncing off her, warning her away.

She turned and entered her building.

Just another prison.

9

Junior came into the diner and sat down across from Tyler in the vinyl booth. "The boys okay?"

Tyler nodded. "I can't get them away from Bonnie. I thought we'd gotten past some of the old problems resulting from Liza's death. The boys had to get used to me being in charge because Liza was the disciplinarian in the family." A disciplinarian who never disciplined the boys and never let up on him. The boys still treated him with the contempt they'd learned from their mother.

"But they've taken to Bonnie and they're crazy for Joe. That guy is a genius with kids."

"Yeah, Jeffie Piperson is his best friend."

"Jeffie is hanging around Joe? So that means Jeffie is hanging around my boys?" Tyler's heart started pounding with fear.

Junior waved his hand at Tyler, brushing aside his worries. Yeah, right, the words *Jeffie* and *worry* were synonyms in Melnik.

"Bonnie said Joe's almost earned a teacher's certificate. The kids' favorite elementary school teacher retires next year and they've already offered Joe the job. He'll be perfect for it."

"So he might be my boys' teacher. And Bonnie's as good as become their mother." Tyler sighed. "I don't know if I can talk them into coming home. They were with me, or rather I was with them, all afternoon. I sat with them at the swimming pool."

And they now insisted on being called Ben and Johnny, which Tyler had to force himself to do. He could hear Liza slicing him to bits every time he didn't say their full names.

"They're staying the night with Bonnie again. I may have to move in to spend time with them." Tyler said it with a smile, but it was the truth, and there was nothing funny about it.

"You'll work it out." Junior leaned forward a bit and spoke quietly, which Tyler found ludicrous, because Dora was in Jansson's and she had ears like a bat—a bat with long-range, high-tech eavesdropping equipment. "I finally caught up with Shayla. I think she's ducking me, which doesn't look good. But I asked the Gillespie police to watch her place, and they saw her come home about ten minutes ago. They picked her up. Want to ride over with me?"

Tyler shrugged. "Sure, it beats my empty house."

"I'm doing background checks on a few other newcomers in town to see if they have any connection to Melvin. Luna Moonbeam has a few minor arrests for drug possession."

"Who?"

"The new antiques dealer. I'm waiting for more details. Melvin went to prison for arson, but he had some drug involvement, so they could be connected somehow."

"And Dolph Torkel, the vampire guy, a few weird things there, but no crimes."

"Weird how?"

"Well, he's real quiet about himself. And he comes and goes at odd hours, sometimes for days at a time, and no one knows where he goes."

Tyler grimaced. "So he visits his mother and guards his privacy. There's no crime there."

Junior snorted as he consulted his notes. "The plumber, Jamie Bobby Wicksner, had to come from a hard background to have teeth like that. I haven't dug up much on him yet."

"I don't think you can seriously suspect a man just because he has poor dental hygiene."

Junior shrugged. "You know, having a bunch of new folks in town has made my job a lot harder. We probably need a larger police force. The city has to be making more money with the property taxes on new houses and the refurbished Main Street buildings. They could at least make Hal and Steve full-time, maybe pay for some good training programs."

They debated crime and punishment in Melnik all the way to Gillespie, but they had to quit once they picked up a very pregnant—and very cranky—Shayla from the police station. Tyler had never met the girl before, but he'd known Wilkie and Rosie Melnik, Shayla's parents, and Shayla favored her father. Lank dishwater blond hair, blue eyes, bad attitude.

A perfect next-generation Melnik.

Her husband had been called and was on his way to the police station. Cell phones worked in Gillespie, and the police promised to contact him and redirect him to Melnik.

Tyler and Junior drove Shayla back to Junior's office. The girl was so sullen, Tyler expected Junior to toss her in jail just for annoying him.

"Where were you from midnight Sunday till Tuesday morning?"

She scowled at them. "I don't have to talk to you."

"No, you don't. You can get a lawyer and have him present for questioning. But I'm locking you up until the lawyer gets here. Hunting for you all day just wore my patience clear to the nub. It's enough to make you a suspect, and I can arrest you and hold you for up to forty-eight hours, waiting till a lawyer can sit in on questioning. I'm not letting you walk out till I get some answers."

"I was home in bed from midnight to six Monday morning. I had the early shift at the hospital and had to be there by seven. I worked all day. My husband was home, and we stayed up pretty late Monday night, nearly until midnight, I'd guess. He'll vouch for me."

"I can check the time sheets at the hospital, but that leaves midnight Sunday to Monday at 6:00 a.m."

"I'm a married woman. My husband was with me." Shayla ran her hand over her rounded belly. She wasn't as far along as Bonnie, but the young woman was very definitely expecting.

"He was asleep." Junior shook his head. "Not good enough. Did you get any phone calls, wake up in the night and log on to your computer? Anything?"

Shayla shook her head. "I didn't even know Uncle Melvin was alive until he turned up here and killed Gunderson. Then they locked him up about an hour after people found out he was in town, when he set Bonnie and Joe's house on fire. Why would I care about him?"

"Because he was fighting for a share of the money you got when your dad died and the town repossessed Gunderson's property. That's money Melvin would have taken from you, Kevin, Donette's baby, and Hal. You'd have had to pony up your share, and you've already spent it. The courts could have garnished your wages. Plus, you've got a history of killing people."

Shayla leaned forward and pounded a fist on Junior's desk. "I've never killed anyone."

"Not for lack of trying."

"As for that money, Melvin should have been suing Joe. Suing me would have been a waste of time. Squeezing blood out of a turnip. We should have gotten more." Shayla clenched her fists. "Gunderson was rich. You took away the property his family had stolen from mine but none of the money they'd earned on it. We should have split up everything he had."

"Don't start this again." Junior waved his hands in disgust. "The court decided that, not me, and you got plenty."

"Mine's all gone. Joe's still rich."

"That's because you blew yours and Joe saved his. No one's fault but yours. And all this mad tells me you've got a motive for killing your uncle, and since you poisoned your father, who you lived with all your life, I don't think you'd hesitate long before poisoning an uncle you've never met."

"But knowing Dad is what made me want to kill him, and that was a spur-of-the-moment thing. I'd have never pre. . .premed. . .premmy-tate. . ."

"Premeditated?" Tyler supplied.

"Planned ahead on a thing like that." Shayla gave Tyler a sneering look that said, *Don't call me stupid.*

Note to self: Don't make the little killerette mad.

The phone rang, late in the evening though it was. Junior listened, then, covering the mouthpiece of the receiver, said, "It's the coroner."

He listened intently, grunting on occasion, then began scribbling in his notebook.

"Thanks, Doc. Appreciate it." Junior hung up. "They did thorough testing on the poison. It's definitely antifreeze that killed him, but there's one problem."

Tyler seriously doubted there was only one.

"Turns out antifreeze isn't poisonous."

"Then how'd it kill him?" Tyler tried to fit that piece of information into this mess.

"Modern antifreeze isn't poisonous. Someone gave him an old formula. And the doctor said the change in antifreeze's makeup was made awhile ago. It's getting hard to find the old stuff."

Junior stared at Shayla.

"Don't look at me. My dad brought that stuff home to use on my cat. I don't know where he got it."

A loud rap at the door turned Tyler around. A hulking man turned the knob and came in partway, holding the door open.

"Can Shayla leave yet? I'm telling you, she was with me all night."

Junior rolled his eyes. "You were asleep."

"Hi, honey." Shayla turned and smiled at her husband.

Tyler saw genuine affection in Shayla's cold little eyes.

"Take her. We're done here." He jabbed his pencil eraser at Shayla. "But the next time I want to talk to you, you get over here. It makes you look guilty to hide from me the way you did today."

"Whatever." Shayla flounced out.

When they'd exited the building, Tyler asked, "Are you sure you should have done that?"

Junior's eyes hardened and he tucked the pencil and notepad in his pocket. "I didn't tell you everything."

Tyler sat up straight.

"You know how the coroner told me the body had been chilled to hide the time of death?"

"Yeah."

"Well, turns out he was chilled, but before that he was heated up."

"What?" Tyler felt his brows arch to his hairline.

"Yep. Someone was messing around with the time of death."

"But wouldn't those two things offset each other?"

"Not necessarily. It took a lot of testing to figure out there was cell damage indicating a fairly warm heat was applied to the body for about twenty-four hours; then the body was chilled for just a few hours. The coroner tried to explain it to me, but honest, I couldn't understand much of it. I hope she explains it better to a jury."

"So when did he die?"

"About two days before Doc Stuart moved to town."

"Two days—but wasn't that when. . ."

"That was twenty-four hours after she was in town for a day, leaving off her stuff. And antifreeze takes awhile to kill, up to twenty-four hours. She's back at the top of our suspect list."

Tyler felt such hot satisfaction at the thought of locking up that Melnik-destroying snob, he knew he shouldn't even be involved with this. He also knew he wouldn't be this furious with Dr. Snow if she weren't so beautiful, and if he didn't enjoy rescuing her all the time, and if she hadn't tempted him to forget about swearing off women. He needed revenge for that even more than he did for her character assassination of Melnik.

"But what about the old antifreeze?"

"I quit searching her building after I found those papers. That building has stored a lot of stuff over the years, including supplies for the mechanic who used to rent the building just behind it. Wanna bet there's some old antifreeze in the basement?"

Tyler wouldn't take that bet even if he was a gambling man. Which he wasn't. He'd found marriage enough of a risk. He'd never been tempted to add slot machines.

"You're back on as her lawyer."

Tyler shook his head. "I'll quit. I'll renounce my law license."

"Well, that'll take awhile. Surely you've gotta file papers to do that. Until you get notice you're disbarred, you're either her lawyer or her cellmate. I'll lock you up, and I can make the charges stick. You'll really lose your law license then. You'll lose custody of the boys, probably do some real time in jail, be publicly disgraced and penniless before I'm done with you. You pick."

Tyler sat frozen in his chair.

Junior rounded his desk and held the door open for Tyler.

Tyler didn't move.

"Well?"

"You told me to pick. I'm still thinking!"

"I can't arrest her alone. I want to wring her neck too bad. Get up."

"I'd perjure myself if you did, cover for you."

Junior chuckled and jerked his head toward his car. "And this time I'm not letting her go. I'm personally giving her a life sentence just because this case is so aggravating. And if Dr. Notchke doesn't quit changing the time of death, I'm throwing her in, too."

"You've got no grounds to hold Maddy, Junior."

"There you go, being her lawyer. Can't control yourself. And I do have grounds. She's a flight risk, and the way this thing keeps coming back around to her, this time, I'm convinced she did it."

"She's not a flight risk. For Pete's sake, she's penniless. Flight costs money. You heard her—she can't even leave town."

"Well, she's an accomplished liar. She proved that in spades with that stupid Maxie paper. So she just might have some money socked away, too. I'm holding on to her. Now come on. She might have already skipped town and hopped a plane for England. Then we'd have to extradite her." Junior froze.

Dr. Snow might indeed have flown the coop. The hurt caught Tyler by surprise, which made him plow into Junior's broad back when Junior stopped suddenly. "What now?"

"The closest I've ever come to extraditing someone is calling the Gillespie police to watch out for Shayla. This is a big case for me." Junior turned, looking worried. "You think extraditing people is expensive? I'm on a limited budget."

Tyler shrugged. "Probably. At least I'll bet you have to pay to fly her back."

"I say if she left the country, we just let her go." Junior scratched his chin.

"Might as well. This is Melvin Melnik after all. It's not like she killed anyone important." Tyler flinched when he heard himself say that.

Junior furrowed his brow in pain from thinking. "Well, we can decide that if she's gone. C'mon."

Tyler's hunger for revenge overwhelmed his desire to avoid Maddy. "Fine, but this time, I'm slapping on the cuffs."

Junior nodded as Tyler passed him. "Deal. But that'll come back to haunt you on appeal."

Tyler stepped into Junior's car and had to fight the urge to turn on the siren so everyone in town would come and see what was going on.

10

W hat is going on?"

The pounding broke into her tortured thoughts. No puppy to get through this night. Her house was creaking like a whole family of ghosts lived in the walls. Maddy was tucked in bed. Well, *tucked* was a little strong. She was lying on her inflatable mattress, tormenting herself for being such a twit and insulting all these nice people with her idiotic theory about worshipping a mouse.

Where had she ever gotten the notion this would make a good paper?

Of course, just studying small-town life had merit. But that would never land her on *Oprah*. Which meant her motives had been purely selfish, which made her a twit for insulting all these nice people with her idiotic theory about worshipping a mouse, which meant her motives had been purely selfish, which made her a twit for insulting all these nice people with her idiotic theory about worshipping a mouse, which meant her motives had been. . . The circling of her thoughts was driving her mad, until she wanted to bang her head against something really hard.

And then the fist on her door had interrupted the torment.

The pounding was so familiar that she took the time to dress before she ran downstairs. She wanted to be comfortable in her cell.

Junior and Tyler glared at her as she swung the door open.

"Dr. Madeline Stuart. . ."

Maddy ignored the rest and just turned her back with her hands behind her. "What happened this time?"

The cuffs clicked on. Maddy noticed the touch and the familiar scent, and she glanced behind her back to see Tyler doing the honors.

Her feelings were hurt, but she did her best not to show it. "You know, you really shouldn't do this and then pretend to be my lawyer. Any case they bring against me will collapse on appeal."

Tyler smirked. "I'll risk it, Dr. Stuart."

He took her arm and led her to the cruiser.

"You both know I didn't kill that man. You know it. I've got no motive. I've got no means. What poison do I have? And you just found out my alibi clears me for the time of death. So I've got no opportunity." Maddy was rather proud of herself for remembering all three. "Why on earth are you arresting me this time?"

"The time of death has changed, and we think we've got means, too." Tyler opened the back door of the squad car. "The basement of this building you rented is a strong possible source of the very unusual and specific poison used to kill Melvin."

"You changed the time of death again?" Maddy looked over her shoulder and glared. "Can't you people ever settle on anything?"

Tyler shielded her head as she lowered herself into the car. She looked back at him. "You don't need to worry about my head. I'm getting good at it." She tried to shake off his hand and whacked her skull on the door frame.

Tyler's hand slipped, catching a bit of her hair between his fingers. She kept glaring, but his eyes changed. His fingers caressed her disheveled head. Gentle now, too gentle. His eyes focused on his hand in her hair. He looked enthralled for a second; then his expression turned to stone.

Maddy could read his mind. He liked the way her hair felt. And he blamed her for that. This all had more to do with the disturbing effect they had on each other than her perceived character assassination of Maxie Mouse or Tyler's belief that she was a killer.

"So whatever the new time of death is, I'll probably have been working then, too. I've been very, very busy. For a long time. And you still have absolutely no motive. Why would I kill a man I've never met?"

Tyler stared down as she settled in the backseat of the squad car. Then his eyes brightened. He snapped his fingers. "How about Melvin was snooping around in your stuff and figured out what you intended for your thesis? What if you knew he'd ruin your chance of getting your project finished? You've already admitted you're broke and need to finish this paper desperately. I wonder just how desperate you are."

Maddy's heart broke as she stared at him. He looked so pleased with his warped reasoning. That heartache, more than anything, proved to her that she'd begun falling in love with the big dummy. She shook her head and stared straight out the front windshield.

"I didn't kill Melvin Melnik. Take me to jail, Junior. I don't wish to have an attorney provided for me. I'll just wait until sanity prevails and you have to let me go."

"That won't be anytime soon," Tyler muttered.

"That sanity prevails in this town? Now why doesn't that surprise me?"

Tyler slammed the door and got in the front seat.

And that hurt, too.

He'd always ridden in the back with her. Getting arrested and riding to jail was the closest they'd come to a date.

And she was such a dimwit that she deserved to go to jail. Actually, that cot was more comfortable than her inflatable mattress, anyway. And no dead men had been near it. . .at least none that she knew of.

They pulled up in front of Junior's office. "Don't you Americans ever walk anywhere?"

Remembering that she'd been left for the duration before, she managed to talk them into unshackling her and letting her have a minute in the loo.

She looked at the idiot who had kissed her through the cell bars so gently just hours ago and who now escorted her to her cell. Wanting to remind him of how stupid they'd both been, she narrowed her eyes at him and blew him a kiss through the bars.

She didn't even flinch when the cell doors clanged shut. The noise was so familiar she'd come to think of it almost like an art form.

Heavy metal music.

"Hear that, Tyler? They're playing our song."

Tyler actually convinced the boys to come with him the next morning.

He knew he needed to go consult with his client, but Junior was running down all her alibis and that'd take awhile, so Tyler gave himself the morning off. Sure, he could have rushed in there with bail money. And he could have strong-armed Junior and probably gotten Dr. Snow out. But he didn't.

No way.

He and the boys turned their attention to cleaning the upstairs of his building. Which meant he cleaned and they ransacked. He walked down to the city office and arranged for a Dumpster to be set outside his alley window so he could drop stuff two floors down into it. His boys were looking forward to that.

He started sorting and the boys ran wild. Once the Dumpster arrived, they discovered they enjoyed listening to stuff crash, so they actually were some help.

Junior interrupted him around noon. "I've got the information on your client, as if you care."

Ben careened into one of the tall cupboards. Tyler held his breath and realized he should have checked them all for bodies before he let the boys in here. The cupboard door swung open, full of garbage, but corpse-wise, it was clear.

"What have you got?"

Junior pulled out his notebook. "She's got an alibi, but it's thin. She admits to being in town last Saturday for about three hours. I've got fairly solid evidence to support that. Dora saw her, of course, although the old battle-ax worried she'd help clear Dr. Stuart if she told me. Still, she couldn't control her urge to blab, so she admitted she'd seen the doc come, unpack, disappear inside for a long time, then drive away."

Tyler read the notes. "So Maddy was here Saturday morning. When did Melvin die?"

"The coroner—that Dr. Notchke is a testy woman, by the way; I'm not the one who keeps changing the time of death—suspects now that Melvin gave up the ghost late afternoon on Sunday. She won't officially narrow it down past a twenty-four hour window, noon Sunday to noon Monday."

"And is that about how fast the antifreeze works? So Maddy could have dosed him with it Saturday?" Tyler pictured Maddy offering a deadly cocktail to Melvin. For some reason, Tyler pictured her in a slinky red evening gown, long slit up the thigh, low-cut, a cigarette holder about a foot long in her hand. She'd brush up against Melvin with a martini glass—tinged bright blue with antifreeze.

Mata Hari with a doctorate.

It made him sick to think of it. No way she killed anybody. She'd have dumped the drink down her red dress before she got him poisoned. "She'd have been out of town, safely surrounded by other students, before he died."

"Yeah, except it works faster than that when it's given in a strong dose, and Melvin's was strong. The doctor said so."

"Wait a minute—which doctor?"

"Dr. Notchke. This case is just lousy with doctors and lawyers, isn't it?"

"Hey! Leave me out of this."

"Dr. Notchke said, based on the content of Melvin's stomach, he'd been given too strong a dose to take that long killing him. If she'd given it to him Saturday morning, he'd have died before Sunday noon. The coroner thinks Melvin must have been poisoned late Saturday night, possibly even early Sunday morning, for the poison to kill him when it did, and Dr. Stuart has a rock-solid alibi from Saturday afternoon at two until she showed up here Tuesday."

Tyler pointed at one of Junior's notes. "She was in another all-day, all-night cram session with five other people."

Junior nodded. "The students even commented on her taking off Saturday morning. Her landlord wanted the place cleared out about the same time her class final was done. She had two carloads of her possessions. So she had to haul that stuff up here, go back, and repack her car. She was studying until her Monday evening test. She slept in her stripped apartment Monday night and took off for Melnik Tuesday morning."

"So you have to let her go again?"

"It's close. The coroner is sure it was a stiff dose of poison, but what if she's wrong? Or what if Melvin did something to delay the effects? Alcohol can alter the effects of medicine and poison. Maybe it slowed down Melvin's reaction."

"Did Dr. Notchke say it was possible?"

"No."

"You're reaching. She's innocent." Tyler sighed with relief and then felt guilty. He didn't want to be rooting for the sneaky little anthropologist. But then, just because he hated her didn't mean he wanted her to go to jail for a crime she didn't commit.

Well, maybe a few years wouldn't hurt her.

Junior got that mule-stubborn look on his face. "Letting her go and arresting her again is getting embarrassing. Let's go search her basement for the antifreeze first."

"Junior, she's innocent. You can't keep her locked up just because you're embarrassed."

"Why not? That's the best part of being sheriff."

"It's not even that embarrassing. The town likes to see her arrested. If you need to haul her in a fourth time, no one will give you a hard time."

"I suppose you're right. And she didn't do it, which makes me inclined to let her out." Junior mulled over his notes and then looked up at Tyler. "So who do you think did?"

Tyler shrugged. "That's your job. I've got an old building to clean."

Johnny fell against a box of papers, which exploded. The boy rolled into another old cupboard.

"You oughta go through this place for dead guys before you let the boys play up here." Junior slapped his notebook shut and went downstairs, grumbling.

11

Next time just phone, okay? No need to drive over and arrest me. I'll walk over. And I didn't need a ride home, either."

Tyler couldn't hear Junior's deep voice respond, but he must have agreed to un-arrest Dr. Snow, because he heard the front door to Maddy's building slam. Even the slam sounded sarcastic. He hoped she'd just leave him alone. Write her stupid paper and leave town.

Her feet pounded on her stairway. His stomach sank even before she shoved open the door to his building. He stepped out of the kill zone—a good thing, because she would have nailed him with the door. Just like their first meeting.

A tale to tell their grandchildren.

Tyler about choked on that thought.

"And as for you. . ." She was beautiful, a fuming, dangerous, hair-triggered fairy-tale princess with him in her sights. He hated how much he wanted to go calm her down, cheer her up, kiss her out of her rage. It occurred to him that he had never, never, ever, not for one single split microsecond in all their years of marriage, been interested in teasing Liza out of a bad mood.

Or brave enough to try if he had thought of it.

She's a sneak, a liar. She hates your hometown. Liza hated Melnik. Remember Liza.

He was a bona fide idiot, and no wall of framed diplomas and degrees could convince him otherwise. He took a step toward her but she was charging, so he barely moved before she had her nose stuck right up to his.

The boys had tried her door a thousand times this morning and it was locked tight. When they saw her come in, they whooped and raced for the opening like a pair of hogs heading for a hole in the fence. Ben tripped over a box and sent it tumbling, almost knocking Tyler on his backside. Bowling for Fathers. The sport of his kids.

"Are you about done arresting me?" Her hands were fisted at her side, but Tyler knew she'd never throw a fist.

She hates Melnik. Remember that.

"Look, I know you didn't kill Melvin. I've known that from the first second I saw you. But the evidence has pointed to you three times. We have to look into it."

"You're my lawyer. You're supposed to be on my side."

Oh, he was on her side.

Stupid, stupid, stupid. Remember why she's wrong, wrong, wrong for you, stupid.

She calmed down—not all the way down, but enough to confirm his theory that she wasn't going to pound on him. She jabbed him in the chest. "I am not going to write that paper."

Okay, she just took away a huge part of the reason to avoid her. Still, she hated the town.

"I love this town." Her voice broke. She squared her shoulders and went on. "It breaks my heart that no one likes me anymore. They were all so kind. I've always been such a clumsy oaf around people, and for the first time, even after only a day here, I thought I could find friends, not be a pariah."

Another big reason gone, but not the biggest one. You barely know her, and you married Liza too fast. And you're a moron about women.

"I am such a moron about people." She slung her arms straight out at her sides and almost nailed him when she spun away to pace.

Tyler ducked then braced himself to save her. Her hands and feet really should be registered as lethal weapons—at least lethal to herself.

She'd never throw a punch, but she might manage to kill him by accident.

"If I had written that paper, I would have hurt your fair city, and because my idea was so ludicrous, I'd have also been the laughingstock of the academic world. But no one in this town will ever believe me."

She kicked a stack of paper into the air as she stumbled along. "If they'd forgive me, I might be able to get approval for a new topic. I'd write a simple study of life in a small town. It wouldn't be groundbreaking, but it would be a legitimate thesis, and it could earn me my degree."

She whirled back toward Tyler and took his hand, her eyes big and deep and shining blue against her milky white skin. "Could you help me, Tyler? Everyone loves you. They'd trust you, and I'd promise to let them all see the paper, every word, before I sent it in. I'd even let them watch me put it in the envelope and mail it."

She hugged his hand, held in both of hers to her chest, practically tucked under her chin. The woman was begging. She was so beautiful when she begged.

Tyler had been thinking about something important, but when her hand touched his, he forgot everything except how sweet and clumsy she was and how kindhearted, and the way her eyes filled with tears and how she said, "So sorry," every single time she almost killed someone.

She'd come in here furious, and she couldn't even sustain that. She'd turned her wrath on herself before he'd had time to resent her temper. He even figured out why she was so clumsy. Her mind was working at a hundred miles an hour because she was such a genius—book smart, not people smart, but even the things she did badly completely occupied her mind. Not leaving her time to watch where she was going.

He got lost in those pleading eyes for a second too long. She must have taken his silence for a no—better than taking it for him being mesmerized—because her chin dropped, her shoulders slumped, her pants slipped low on her hips. "I don't blame you." She turned away.

"Yeah, I'll help you."

She whirled around, her eyes on fire with excitement and intelligence and hope and something warm and alluring. But happy or not, she was still a klutz. She tripped on today's pair of baggy pants, the same ones she'd been arrested in, and fell over backward.

He'd known her two whole days. He thought he was ready. He grabbed, but she even fumbled that. They both went flying over.

She grunted as she landed smack on top of him. Papers exploded into the air then began raining down on their heads.

"You'll really help me?" She rolled off him. "I'd be so grateful."

Tyler imagined Maddy grateful.

He forced himself to stop imagining and speak. "Well, I said I'd do it because I believe you. I'm glad you've abandoned your thesis."

He was very glad.

Thrilled.

He had no reason except common sense left to hate her now, and he'd proved to have a very short supply of that.

They lay side by side, his arm resting on her stomach.

It would have been romantic if dozens of strewn papers hadn't still been floating down on their heads, along with a cloud of choking dust. Add in boys screaming in the background who could burst in on them any second, and the fact that they had landed square on top of the place Melvin Melnik's rigid corpse had been a couple of days ago.

But except for all that, it would have been romantic.

His eyes focused on her lips. He pushed himself up on one elbow and leaned closer. A wafting sheet of paper drifted down and slipped between their faces.

Lab Test Results Questionable as to Field Mouse Species.

"Maxie!" Tyler grabbed the paper. He pulled his arm away from Dr. Snow, barely noticing he had slid it behind her neck.

He heard her head thud onto the floor as he jumped to his feet, reading.

He regretted the thud, but this was important.

Further tests necessary.

Maxie might not be a field mouse? Tyler knew there were a lot of species of mice, but surely. . . He dropped to his knees just as Dr. Snow stood up.

"What are you doing?"

Tyler didn't even look up. "Here's a page, and here's one." He sorted and saved and discarded. "Get down here and help me find the rest of this report."

Something crashed in Maddy's building. Tyler barely reacted. "This isn't on old paper. Well, not too old." Tyler held up the sheet of paper next to another one that had fallen from the same box. "Most of this is yellow and faded, but I can. . ."

He quit talking to read, and read, and read, and pray. "This is a disaster."

Only barely aware that Maddy had dropped to her knees and was picking up and discarding papers, setting a few on the floor where they knelt side by side, he finished reading the sheet in his hand.

Turning, he faced Maddy, who was still frantically hunting for something she couldn't possibly understand. "Maddy, you may have your thesis paper after all."

She sat back on her knees. "Why? I don't understand."

"We had Maxie genetically tested about four years ago when Wilkie was killed. It had to do with mouse fur found at the site of the murder."

Maddy's brows arched. "You genetically tested a mouse?"

"Well, not me, exactly. Liza didn't like Melnik." Didn't like? Try loathed, despised, ridiculed, sneered at. . . "So we weren't real involved with the town when this happened, but of course, everybody knew about it."

"Of course?"

"Sure, everybody knows everything about everyone in Melnik."

"They didn't know about my thesis paper."

"You'd been in town, what—a day—before they found out?"

"Point taken."

"So how come these papers, dated four years ago, are up here in this building, abandoned for decades? The building where we just found Melvin Melnik? How come nobody knows about this?"

Maddy, her eyes almost crossed in confusion, shrugged.

"Someone knew Maxie was a fake."

"He is for sure? He's not a. . .mouse? Because I saw him, Tyler. He's most definitely a mouse."

Tyler read the next paper. "No, it's not that he's not a mouse; it's that there's some question whether he's a field mouse."

"I'm lost. It matters if he grew up in a field as opposed to—in a hedge or a flower bed or a house?"

"No, no, no—where you grow up doesn't matter. Try to pay attention, for heaven's sake. This is important. Field mouse is a specific species of mouse. Maxie is the largest of his species. A world-record–sized Animalia; Chordate; Vertebrata; Mammalia; Rodentia; Sciurognathi; Cricetidae; Sigmondontinea; Peromyscus. In other words, a field mouse."

"How do you know that?" She shook her head in disbelief.

He could tell she was impressed. "You'll just have to be patient. I don't have time to help you memorize it now."

"What? I have no desire to memorize—"

"We studied it in school. We had to memorize it to pass fourth grade." Tyler had enough to do without explaining every little detail. "Anyway, Maxie is really big for that species."

"Does the state of Nebraska require that? I've heard of No Child Left Behind, but this seems ridiculous."

"No, the state doesn't require it. That would be stupid. Only Melnik requires it."

Maddy arched one of her beautiful dark brows at him. "Has anyone actually been left back for failing this test?"

Her brow almost diverted him, but not quite. This was too big for even slender, lovely, graceful eyebrows. "Of course not. Oh, they've been held back, but not for this. Everyone learns this. Don't you understand? Maxie's not all that big for some other species of mouse."

"Like what species?"

"I don't know. How am I supposed to know about species of mice? No reasonable person wastes their time memorizing a bunch of species of mouse."

"You knew Maxie's."

"He's special. But if he was, say. . .a grasshopper mouse?"

"A what?"

Tyler shrugged. "That and house mouse—mice—mouse—whatever—are the only species I know of. And he's too big to even possibly be a house mouse. So if he's some other species, then he's not special, and this whole town is built on a lie!" Tyler surged to his feet so quickly Maddy tumbled backward.

Tyler was too upset to try to save her. It probably would have ended in disaster anyway. Most of his dealings with Maddy did.

He ran into her building, followed the shrieking and shattering sounds, and found the boys in the dank, high-smelling basement, surrounded by mountains and mountains of boxes and cans and unidentifiable refuse.

"Boys, go down to the museum. You need to stay with Bonnie for a while." The boys, to a degree that was completely disloyal, screamed with joy and raced up the stairs. Tyler turned to follow as he heard them run outside. But before he could move, Tyler spotted a case of antifreeze. It was noticeable because it was the only thing not an inch deep in dust. The case was torn open and one bottle and a cup sat on the floor beside the box. And right next to it, a manila envelope, clearly addressed to Dr. Madeline Stuart.

Maddy.

No way is she a murderer.

That was his male side talking. His inner lawyer had a different opinion. How much evidence needed to point to the woman?

NOSY IN NEBRASKA

No way is she this stupid to leave clue after clue, the man said.

She's a klutz; of course she'd leave clues everywhere, the lawyer replied.

But she just wouldn't do it. Impossible. The clumsy woman upstairs just doesn't have the makings of a murderer, and besides, she wouldn't kill to protect her research paper.

Look how easily she's given it up. The man had a kind heart.

After she'd been found out. What other choice did she have? The lawyer had a functioning brain.

And now she wanted to research Melnik about something else. She said she'd show them her thesis, but who could force her to show them all her work? Who could be sure she wasn't writing a hit piece on Melnik for the college while writing a nice rah-rah piece on Melnik to appease the dim-witted natives, of which he was king?

Tyler took a moment to think about running for office. The mayor of Suckerville. . .he'd win in a landslide.

He looked back at the envelope. Her fingerprints were going to be all over it, of course. It had to be planted, but it wasn't his job to find clues and then cover them up for his client. That was a complete violation of the law, and he could be disbarred, even jailed for it.

But she was so pretty and sweet. Tyler's fingers itched to hide the evidence, grab Maddy, and run.

Maddy and his sons.

And Riley.

Running for your life when you were an adult with responsibilities was incredibly inconvenient.

Besides, Tyler knew he'd found the murder weapon right in Maddy's possession. If he covered that up to protect Maddy, he'd also be covering up a possible clue to the real killer. He had to tell Junior.

He sighed and then lured Maddy to the car. Innocent little murderess that she was, she climbed right in. He drove her straight to jail.

Maybe Junior could just give her one of those electronic ankle bracelets. It would save everybody a lot of time if they could just keep track of her. Hopefully they wouldn't have to dart her like a rogue elephant and put a radio collar on her; although she was so aggravating, Tyler might volunteer for that job.

"Why are we at the jail, Tyler?" Maddy seemed calm.

"Well, the thing is"—Tyler turned to her, his arm stretched across the gap between their bucket seats—"you're under arrest."

W hat now?" Maddy snarled as she opened her door.

The car hadn't stopped rolling yet.

Worrying she'd fall out and get herself run over, Tyler misjudged the curve and smacked his car into the Maxie statue with the police uniform that stood outside the station.

Bad day to be a mouse in Melnik.

Tyler got out quickly, thinking she might be making an escape attempt. Instead, she just walked, her shoulders slumped, sighing deeply, into the police station.

He had to hustle to keep up with her. Say the word *arrest* to Maddy, and anymore, she had a Pavlovian response.

Good girl. Well trained. Head straight for the cell or we'll whack you with a rolled-up newspaper.

Junior was doing a crossword puzzle at his desk. Tyler caught up to Maddy in time to see Junior lift his head and scowl. He must have been doing well on the puzzle.

"What now?"

"I found the murder weapon." Tyler entered the office.

Maddy turned to him. "In my basement?"

"Yes, sorry, but the antifreeze is sitting there, a cup beside the bottle, and an envelope with your name sitting beside it. Your fingerprints are going to be all over that."

"This is ridiculous!" Maddy threw her arms wide and smacked him in the chest.

"Well, you know we were looking for means, motive, and opportunity."

"I have none of those."

"You have all of those."

"I do not!"

"The motive is to silence Melvin after he discovered your report."

"That's a bunch of codswallop!" Maddy stepped forward.

Tyler braced himself to be accidentally knocked over. *Codswallop* was such a cool word. He loved her accent. "The opportunity is a little touchy, but your presence here in Melnik is close enough to the time of death."

"It is not!"

"And now we've got means. The poison is there. You knew about it because your fingerprints are on something right beside it."

Maddy poked one finger at him and managed to jab him in the neck, vampire-like.

"Ouch!" It reminded Tyler that they hadn't followed up on all the town's newcomers.

"I'll tell you something you haven't considered, Mr. Master Sleuth."

"What's that?" Junior had come up beside them. Tyler noticed he'd stayed back far enough to be safe from the doctor's fingernails. Smart man.

"That report you're so upset about, bringing into question Maxie's true genetic makeup—"

"What?" Junior's curiosity overcame his cowardice, and he stepped closer.

"—was in Melvin's possession. And someone in town found out about it."

"No one's said a word."

"Report?" Junior came even nearer, but Tyler saw his cousin watching Maddy's flying hands like a hawk.

"You told me earlier everybody knows everything about each other. Therefore, it is absolutely reasonable to assume the word got out. Therefore, that gives a lot more people than me a motive to kill Melvin Melnik. People who were actually in town. People who know what in the world antifreeze is. What is antifreeze, by the way?"

She turned on Junior. Her hair whipped Tyler in the eye, and he considered wearing protective goggles around Dr. Snow from now on. Perhaps an entire line of protective gear. Flame-retardant suit. Hard hat. Steel-toed boots.

"Is the cell door open?"

"No." Junior produced the key from his pocket.

She snatched it. "I'm keeping the key this time. You chaps forget to let me out when I need a break. I might go to Jansson's for lunch, too."

Junior nodded and Maddy stormed into the jail.

The cell door slammed with a vicious metallic clank.

Tyler filled Junior in on what he'd found. Junior had a thousand questions, and they debated the possibilities for disaster.

The cell door gave its metallic clank, and a second later Maddy appeared. "I'm going to run back to my building and get some paperwork. I might as well be doing something productive while I'm under arrest."

Junior shrugged and gestured toward the door to the street.

Tyler respected a hard worker. "Hang on a second and I'll give you a ride."

"I'll walk!" Maddy left, but Tyler heard her muttering. The only words he could make out were ". . .driving one block. Americans!"

She was so furious Tyler thought he saw storm clouds rumbling over her head.

She was so cute.

"We'd better go after her." Junior reached for the door.

"She won't try to escape." The fact that he had absolutely no concern about an escape attempt didn't mesh with arresting her for murder.

"I know, but we need to look at that basement without giving her time to mess around down there."

"And I was in such a hurry I left the lab result papers behind."

Junior gave a disgruntled look at his crossword puzzle; then he and Tyler went out, climbed in his car, and drove over to Maddy's building.

They got there just as Maddy stormed in her door.

Junior hoisted himself out of the car. Tyler didn't unlock his law office because he hadn't locked it. Why would he? There was no crime in Melnik.

As they entered the old opera house, someone crashed into him from behind. He looked back, expecting to find Maddy. Instead, he found—the whole town.

Tallulah in the lead, clutching Maxie's travel carrier to her chest. "It's a lie. A lie!"

She would have bowled Tyler over if he hadn't gotten out of her way. He rushed after her when something else clicked. Tallulah's name had been on those documents. They'd been sent to her. She had to know about them. And maybe she had the best motive of anyone to kill Melvin. She was committed to Maxie with a zeal that bordered on fanaticism. Even worship.

Tyler flinched. What would Dr. Snow White make of this mob? There were twenty people coming up the stairs behind him, all worried sick about Maxie.

When they reached the second floor, there stood Maddy. "I'm glad you've all come."

No one could hear her over the noisy crowd.

Tyler stepped to her side in case Tallulah attacked.

"I want to announce once again that I am not writing that paper about Maxie."

Everyone froze. Dead silence prevailed. They turned toward her like robots, all controlled by one huge joystick.

Even though, to his knowledge, no one but he had known about these strange genetic testing papers, somehow the whole town knew. And now not a one of them missed the quietly made announcement.

"I have reconsidered my paper, and of course, I can see how ridiculous my focus was on thinking you were obsessed with Maxie."

A crowd of one hundred people and growing, frantic to track down the news about the World's Largest Field Mouse, all exchanged guilty looks.

"I have already contacted my professor at the university in Omaha and asked if I could change my basic thesis question and deal with the general history and anthropology of your town, a classic example of many small American towns. Of course, his approval is required, but I expect to receive a favorable response soon. Also, even with his agreement, I'll understand if I've alienated all of you to the point you don't wish to speak to me."

Into the silence, Dora whispered loudly enough to wake bears, hibernating a thousand miles away in the Rocky Mountains, "What'd she say about being an archaeologist?"

"No, not archeologist. Anthropologist." Maddy smiled hopefully at Dora. "I don't usually explain anthropology because it's a less well-known field of study, and I find people aren't interested in hearing about it."

Tallulah clutched Maxie. "You're not going to make a skeleton out of this mouse!"

Maddy shook her head. "But I believe in this case it would be worth my while to try to explain it to you. Anthropology is the field of holistic study with the intent of examining all aspects, both physical and mental, of humans, both living and dead. I received one doctorate earlier in my career in biological anthropology."

"Did she say they found dinosaur bones in Melnik?" This was Olga Jansson's father, deaf as a post, although no one could convince him of that. It was possible he couldn't hear them trying to convince him.

Maddy soldiered on. "My goal now is to earn my second thesis by studying the sociocultural disciplines. Anthropology, unlike the many other social science disciplines, is distinguished by its focus and emphasis on context, cross-cultural comparisons, and the importance it places on long-term, experiential immersion in the area of research, often known as participant observation."

The old man kept yelling. "I thought she was trying to tell people we were all nuts. Dinosaur bones could make us all rich."

Tyler saw Maddy lose the thread of her explanation. Just as well. He'd had seven years of college, and none of what she was saying made a lick of sense.

Unfortunately for them all, she gathered her thoughts and continued. "Naturally, an in-depth examination of all of these societal factors is integral to my anthropological dissertation."

"Tallulah, these papers have your name on them." Junior had obviously tuned Maddy out. Probably the wisest course of action. "What's going on? They're dated over four years ago from when Rosie Melnik smothered her no-good worthless husband while she had mouse hairs on her hands."

"Eek!"

Tyler didn't even turn around.

The *Bugle* was here.

Nick pressed through the crowd with Carrie in his arms. He grinned down at his wife. "Good thing your mom took Heather for the day."

Tyler felt a pang of jealousy. Not because he had feelings for Carrie, but because everybody knew how ridiculously happy the O'Connors were.

"I've also embraced the subdiscipline of applied anthropology." Maddy forged on. "My intention was to spend a short time with on-site analysis, because the general societal structure inherent in your hamlet has been well documented in case studies such as —"

Carrie snapped a picture of Junior shaking the papers at Tallulah, who hugged Maxie, while Maddy yammered in the background.

Tyler loved being home.

"All right! I'll tell you what I did!" Tallulah flung her arms wide, and since she was holding Maxie, she almost smacked Maddy in the face with the cage. Maddy fell backward, but Tyler snagged her like Derek Jeter going after an infield fly.

Between ducking the incoming mouse and Tallulah's sheer volume, Maddy shut up.

"When that lab report came back, it definitely had Maxie's hair tested as being that of a field mouse. But the lab said the specimen we'd sent had been compromised. There were field mouse hairs, as was to be expected when testing Maxie's DNA. But there were also house mouse and grasshopper mouse hairs in the sample we took off of Wilkie's face."

Carrie's scream peeled a layer off Tyler's eardrums. Even Olga Jansson's father heard it.

"And there were a few stray hairs mixed in with the sample we took off Maxie's body, too. Now, of course, I realized immediately that the other hair came from that mouse-infested house Bea Evans let go to rack and ruin. So even though the lab tests brought into question Maxie's authenticity, I knew it was a bunch of hooey. So I tucked that part of the report away before I took the pertinent part to Junior."

"These are legal papers, Tallulah." Junior shook a handful of them in her face. "If we had taken that case to court, we'd have been in big trouble. By your hiding part of the report, a good lawyer could've canceled out the whole paper."

"But it didn't matter. It didn't go to court."

"Before this goes any further. . ." Maddy had more to say.

Tyler groaned aloud.

"Now you just hand Maxie over, and right this second." Junior stuck out his beefy hand. "We'll get these tests redone."

"Since you're all here, I just want to reiterate—"

The woman needed to drop the big words or no one would ever listen to her.

"—that I now see I was utterly wrong in my assessment of this community."

"Stay back! Maxie is a hero. You all want to destroy him! But I won't let you."

"I postulated the thesis that your interest in Maxie rose to the level of obsession, possibly even worship." Maddy smiled just as if she thought people knew or cared about what she was saying.

Poor deluded fairy princess.

"I can see now that you're all perfectly normal, rational, lovely people with a quaint mascot."

"I'm not gonna be the sheriff of a town with a fake giant mouse. That's just embarrassing."

Tyler flinched. Obsessed? What possible reason could Maddy have for suspecting that?

Tallulah hugged Maxie, and Tyler gave thanks for the cage, or by now Tallulah would have made mincemeat out of that mouse.

Tallulah backed away from Junior's outstretched hand.

"Don't do anything stupid, Tallulah. Nobody has to get hurt here today."

Tyler wondered where Tallulah thought she was going if she made a break for it. Mexico? Or perhaps she planned to take over a small Central American country and install Maxie as king and her as queen? Maybe she could buy an island and write a seriously disturbed Declaration of Independence.

Tyler started mentally writing a little thesis of his own.

"You'd've been guilty of. . .of. . ." Junior furrowed his eyebrows and looked at Tyler.

"Obstruction of justice, aiding and abetting in a felony, falsifying court documents, conspiracy to commit murder, an accessory after the fact, perjury, offering aid and comfort to the enemy. . ." Tyler stopped. He was pretty sure that last one had to do with treason. He didn't think Tallulah could be charged with that, at least not until she got started on her own country. There was definitely a thick layer of dust. . .not only in his office, but also on all his lawyer skills except contract law. Still, rusty or not, it felt good to use them, and no one seemed to notice the dust.

"Tallulah, give me that mouse. Now I know I seem like a hard-boiled cop—"

Tyler had to adjust his head on that one. Junior? Hard-boiled? It was possible the universe had a rule against those two words being in a sentence together.

Well, except Junior was shaped a lot like a hard-boiled egg, so maybe—Tyler noticed Junior's comb-over was askew, as it so often was—nope, that detracted too much from the general ovalness. Junior was a big, affable, slow-moving, lasagna-loving teddy bear. No one could even imagine accusing him of being hard-boiled.

"But I am first and foremost an honest man. A Christian man, just as I know all of you are." He swung one pudgy, pointing finger at the town. "We aren't gonna base something this important to our town on something that ain't true. We're not gonna be a bunch of sneaking, lying, no-account, low-down weasels." Junior gave Maxie a sudden look as if he'd just thought of another species the mouse could be.

Tallulah inched backward, ready to flee.

Tyler refused to be any part of that car chase.

Whether or not she would have run was never known, thanks to the clumsy fairy princess in their midst. Maddy stepped aside to avoid the enormous approaching backside of Tallulah.

Honestly, Tyler decided, there oughta be a law requiring people as big as Tallulah to beep when they backed up.

When Maddy moved, disaster was inevitable.

Big surprise.

She stepped on one of her cuffed pant legs and fell. Tallulah retreated again and tripped over Maddy's prone body and went down in acres of fluttering fabric.

Maddy's grunt of pain made Tyler move before waffle marks appeared on her from the pressure of Tallulah's cellulite. Diamonds were created under less pressure.

Maxie somehow ended up on top.

The mouse had survival skills; no one could deny it. Really extraordinary in a dead animal. Tyler took the cage and handed Maxie to the side.

"Eek!"

"Oops, Carrie, sorry, wrong side." He switched hands as Tallulah tried to snatch the mouse back.

Junior took possession.

Tyler and three other willing—and brave—Melnikians helped a furious, shouting, struggling Tallulah to her feet. Tyler felt sorry for Maddy, but she seemed unhurt.

Flattened but unhurt.

And considering Tallulah was of the age to break a hip, it seemed best that Maddy had softened the older woman's fall.

Tyler helped Maddy up. Her hair had come out of its sloppy ponytail. There were pencils hanging here and there around her head—dreadlocks PhD style. She'd only been out of jail a few minutes, and she'd been pencil-free when they'd locked her up.

Maddy swung her dark hair. Tyler brushed her tousled tresses back so her face appeared. Her rosy cheeks had turned bright red, either from humiliation or from Tallulah's sheer weight.

Tyler began plucking pencils before she put somebody's eye out.

"So sorry." Her chin wobbled, and Tyler patted her on the back. He didn't want her to cry, but honest, if Carrie could scream and Tallulah could emote, why couldn't Maddy be the town crier?

He couldn't help grinning at her.

She scowled back. "I don't believe I have fully explained myself to the good people of this village." She turned away from him and faced the crowd, who didn't notice, because it was more interesting to watch Junior fend off Tallulah. Junior had one beefy arm wrapped around Maxie's cage and the other stuck straight out. Add a helmet and the man would look exactly like a life-sized, obese Heisman Trophy.

"Save it for a quiet moment," Tyler whispered. "You're never going to get anyone to listen." He went back to plucking pencils, but she didn't seem to notice. She'd said she was short of money. He tried to imagine her pencil budget. She could probably get by pretty well financially if she just quit needing a new case of pencils every day and a half.

Maddy frowned and whispered to Tyler, "I feel just dreadful. Everyone hates me and it's my own fault. I thought of most of those questions before I ever came to town. And for the first day or so, I thought I saw evidence to support my obsession theory."

Junior tucked and dodged. The former football hero and homecoming king ran behind Olga Jansson and her father, his very own offensive line. Tallulah came after him like she was the entire defense of the Nebraska Cornhuskers. She weighed just about as much.

"Now I can see that the thesis can't be denigrating." Maddy continued to whisper. "I had hoped to build on the eloquent work of the *Bugle*. I thought I could give real insight into the culture of one small hamlet in the United States of America. I had no intention of doing anything hurtful to this lovely town, even with my original paper. But I see now that the direction of my thesis was going to do just that. As usual, I've managed to alienate everyone. I belong in a lab somewhere, not even a lab with animals. Just computers, waterproof computers, strapped down to the table so I can't knock them to the floor. I'm a complete failure." Her chin wobbled. Her eyes filled with tears. She looked back at the crowd. "I had hoped to make friends here." Her voice broke, and she pressed her fingers to her lips and fell silent.

As always, when someone whispered in Melnik, everybody paid rapt attention.

Tyler noticed Carrie's expression soften. She was a newswoman, so of course she was listening. He also saw Dora's curiosity bloom. The woman would need to forgive Maddy, if only to wring every drop of gossip out of her. Tallulah even paused from grappling Junior to give Maddy a calculating look—possibly realizing that a thesis paper about Maxie that made the mouse and the town sound good could be used in her master plan.

Tyler realized that Tallulah had a master plan and shuddered at the unavoidable chaos.

The pretty, klutzy, fairy-tale princess doctor had a chance.

Maddy was too lost in admitting all her faults to notice. And exactly when had Liza ever admitted she had any faults? Tyler removed the last pencil, and even with the whole town looking on, he might have stolen another kiss. His boys were even uniquely qualified to have Maddy in their lives. They had strong bones and didn't break easily. He'd up their milk consumption just as a precaution.

Junior shouldered past Tyler and stopped any potential kiss. Tyler returned his attention to the Maxie escapade.

"I'm going to take this mouse and have it tested." Junior held up Maxie's cage in one hand.

Tallulah's indrawn breath rose to near scream decibels.

"I'm going to lock these papers up tight so no one can steal them or alter them until the new tests arrive." Junior waved the documents with his other hand.

"I'm going to search the doc's building from top to bottom, and I'm not stopping until I've been everywhere just so I don't get any more surprises. I'm sick of surprises!" Junior reached the door and turned, glaring at the whole town.

Ben and Johnny raced out of Maddy's building, nearly knocking Junior down the flight of stairs. It was a good thing he caught himself, because at that moment Bonnie appeared at the top of the stairs and said, "I'm taking the boys swimming, Tyler."

Ben and Johnny raced up the stairs toward her then skidded to a halt, beamed, and ran back down.

Bonnie looked at Tyler and smiled. "Let me know when you're done here, and I'll give them back."

Joe was with her and nodded at Tyler, holding Bonnie's arm firmly as his very pregnant wife turned and followed the screaming boys, threading their way through the curiosity seekers.

Tyler marveled at his sister. She seemed oblivious to this disaster. Joe had definitely given her life perspective.

"No one else is allowed through this door. Except Tyler. You're helping me. Doc, you're still under arrest. Both of you get in here." Junior turned and stomped into Maddy's building.

Tyler realized he'd left his hand resting on Maddy's slender waist. He steered her in the direction Junior had disappeared.

"I really do most humbly beg your forgiveness." She looked over her shoulder at the crowd.

Tyler hustled her forward. She'd made some progress with her earlier apology. He was afraid she'd use her foot-in-mouth disease to lose the ground she'd gained.

He opened the door and gently but firmly shoved her through, closing it behind them. Junior was there to lock the town out.

He and Junior sighed with relief.

13

Maddy sighed with despair.

"I really should go back and try again to make them see how sorry I am." Maddy took a step toward the door. Tyler and Junior blocked it. She looked at Maxie, grinning at her from his cage, grimaced, and backed off. It wasn't that she was afraid of mice, just—ick.

Tyler held up both hands. "I think you softened them up a little." He looked like an elementary school crossing guard. And what did that make her?

She pulled up her pants and crossed her arms to keep them in place. She'd paid a fortune to have them tailored to this perfect fit. "Very well, let's search this building and find proof that I didn't do whatever it is I'm supposed to have done to whoever this man is.

"It really is outrageously rude of you to make me help convict myself of a crime I didn't commit. But I've got nothing else to do. You say this evidence that proves I'm the murderer is in the cellar? Well, let's go."

Tyler led the way.

Maddy was in the middle. "I can't help but feel you have me surrounded deliberately, as if I've attempted escape after escape in the past. The truth is really quite to the contrary."

Tyler glanced back at her. "We don't have you surrounded to prevent an escape attempt."

"Nope." Junior spoke from behind her, and when she turned to look at him, she missed a step and fell into Tyler, who nabbed her in midair like he was a goalie for the Manchester United soccer team.

He set her back on her feet. "We have you in the middle so we can catch you."

They reached the ground floor. "Well, that's quite gallant of you chaps, I'm sure. But as you can see, I've reached a ripe old age without killing myself."

"It defies belief, but what you say is true." Tyler pulled the door to the basement open. He looked at her, then past her toward the constable. Some sort of communication must have been contained in that look, or else Junior held up a flashcard behind her back, because without a word exchanged—save a most unattractive grunt from Constable Cousin Junior—he passed them both, snapping on a pair of rubber gloves as he walked through the basement door.

"Maddy." Tyler stopped her by gently catching her arm. "I need to clear up about three things with you, considering I had you arrested a little bit ago. I hope you'll listen and give me a fair chance."

"A fair chance at what? Having me convicted and thrown into some American gulag?"

"Uh, that's the Soviet Union that had those, and since the Communist Bloc broke up, the gulags are supposed to be closed. I have my doubts—trust but verify, you know?"

Maddy didn't speak. She had no idea what he wanted, but she was sure it wasn't a debate about the current state of Russian politics.

"The thing is, I'm. . .I never should have. . ." He stepped closer.

She considered stepping back, but with her clumsiness, she might end up tumbling down the stairs to the cellar.

Tyler reached past her, intending to pull her close, she hoped. Then he shoved the door shut, and she knew that he, too, was worried about her possible descent, tail over teakettle.

Then he pulled her close. "I hope you'll give me a fair chance to tell you I care about you, Maddy." Before she could quite process his intentions, he kissed her. And then her processing ability short-circuited until she was really only capable of hanging on. His arms were the sure-footedest place she'd ever been.

He'd said three things. She couldn't wait for the other two.

She wasn't sure how long she'd been standing there, feeling utterly graceful for the first time in her life. But it wasn't long enough. Junior opened the door and hit her in the back of the head. She bumped her face into Tyler's. She was pretty sure she bopped him in the eye with her nose and possibly bit him. He ducked his head and brought his hand quickly to his lips.

Constable Junior looked tired and disgruntled, which was, for the most part, his usual expression. But perhaps this version was a bit more grim.

He held up a plastic Ziploc bag containing a manila envelope. Her address was written clearly on the front. He had a second bag containing a small paper cup. He must have brought the bags along, maybe tucked in his pocket, because she hadn't noticed them before. "Dr. Stuart, you're—"

"I'm already under arrest."

"Oops, that's right. I forgot."

She put her hands behind her back.

⸺

Junior didn't cuff her. He insisted she needed her hands free to help search for more evidence to convict herself.

He actually seemed to have no real interest in her as a suspect. But the evidence was fairly condemning, she knew. They went downstairs together. The cellar was poorly lit, one bare bulb, a few small, dirty windows up high.

"It's mildewed in here. It smells terrible and it's filthy. I'm going to demand a reduction in rent."

"What are you paying now?"

Maddy told Tyler and he snickered.

"It is quite reasonable for anywhere else on earth, isn't it?"

"Yep."

She ignored his amusement and focused on getting herself un-arrested. Nuisance, that.

"Since I have never even been in the cellar, I can't believe you'll find my fingerprints anywhere down here. They should at least be on the railing. You know I hang on for dear life at all times."

Junior had made her don gloves. She felt like a surgeon entering the operating room. She was very, very careful to keep them on so as not to leave a single print. "And that envelope, well, someone obviously brought it down here. Yes, it's mine, and my fingerprints will most assuredly be on it, but that doesn't prove a thing except whoever killed that man was trying to throw suspicion onto me."

"He believes you, Mad." Tyler was on his knees, checking the contents of cases of long-forgotten auto parts. "Just keep hunting through these boxes. Especially look for anything that doesn't fit, isn't as old or dirty. Like those documents we found about Maxie in the upstairs of my building."

Tyler stood suddenly. "Hey, Junior, someone's been down here. Look at these empty cans and bottles; they've been here for a few days."

Junior came and studied the trash heap. "It could be that Melvin was holed up in here, but we can't just assume that."

Maddy looked up. "Do you think he was down here when I unloaded my car last Saturday?"

Junior held up a copy of the *Bugle*. It had a prominent picture of Tyler on it. Headline: SIMPSON APPOINTED COUNTY ATTORNEY. "This is last week's paper. It came out on Wednesday. Melvin got sprung from jail a few days before that. I'd say he came straight here."

Tyler lifted an empty brown bottle. One of many. "And celebrated his freedom. He was in jail for over a year but never came to trial thanks to his lawyer's delaying tactics. He had plenty of time to plan what he'd do when he got out. If he sneaked in here and found those papers of Tallulah's, he might have started hatching a plan to use them to stir up trouble."

"He was spiteful enough." Junior bagged the *Bugle* and went back to sifting. "He thought he could get rich extorting money if his claim to Maxie held up."

"Yeah, but it wasn't going to hold up." Tyler bagged the beer bottle. "His case had nothing to support it. He had to know he was going to end up in prison and without a claim to Maxie. If he'd have quit plotting revenge long enough to just think, he'd have admitted that."

THE MICE MAN COMETH

"Perhaps." Maddy looked in a box labeled Spark Plugs. Since she wouldn't know a spark plug from a hair plug, she had no idea what the little metal gadgets were. She couldn't imagine recognizing something important. "Perhaps he thought if his claim to Maxie became threatening enough, the people of this town would drop the charges against him for murdering. . ."

Maddy looked up. Her eyes found Tyler's, and her brain quit working.

"Gunderson. Sven Gunderson is who he killed. And maybe that's right." Junior paused to scratch his rotund stomach.

Maddy barely heard him speak. She took half a step toward Tyler and fell over the spark plug case that she'd just set down. Tyler caught her and kept her upright.

The constable cleared his throat loudly enough to be diagnosed with whooping cough, catching Maddy's attention. As she turned toward the constable, she noticed Tyler looking sheepish. He'd been staring right back.

"Keep your heads in the ball game, you two." Junior smirked. "So, Ty, it makes some sense, huh? Melvin figures he's got a shot at scaring Melnik into dropping the charges?"

Tyler shook his head. "You can't drop the charges on a murder once the count has been filed."

"Yeah, but you can plead it down; witnesses can refuse to testify. There's a lotta ways we could have helped him beat this if we thought it would save our town."

"May I interject something?" Maddy asked as politely as a schoolgirl.

Junior nodded.

"Unless I misunderstand this town greatly, which is possible," she added quickly before both Tyler and Junior could do it, "Melvin Melnik's plan to take Maxie away gives a lot of people besides me a motive for murder. I will, of course, add that I have no motive, except the very slim one you two have made up out of whole cloth. Whereas the villagers, many of whom are extremely worried about losing that chubby mouse, might see themselves as saving the town by killing the man. I believe we even mentioned your sister, Tyler. She seems sweet, but honestly, I'm sweet, too. Clumsy, stupid about people perhaps, but fairly mild mannered, not the murderess type at all, I daresay. If you don't suspect Bonnie, then you just have to stop this rubbish about suspecting me. I insist."

Junior stared at her a long time. "I really don't think you killed Melvin, Doc. It's this confounded evidence. I mean, I'm a lawman, and I can't keep finding proof and just ignoring it. It all points to you."

"Nonsense."

"It's not nonsense. I've arrested you and let you go and arrested you and—"

"I'm well aware of the arrests." Maddy held up one hand to stop him. Why, she'd make a fine crossing guard herself, and what did that make Junior? "Although I suppose I've lost count. I might start some kind of spreadsheet on my computer to keep track."

Tyler snickered.

Maddy narrowed her eyes. "You know, the first arrest was because he had my necklace. Might I point out that if someone was going to frame me, they needed access to my possessions. How about him?" She jabbed her index finger at Tyler.

"Hey!" Tyler protested.

She smiled. "I'm just using you as an example. I don't want you arrested."

"Oh, okay." Tyler smiled in a way that reminded her that their kiss had been interrupted.

Maddy forgot what she was saying for a moment.

Junior cleared his throat and woke her up.

"Tyler could have moved my envelope downstairs. Didn't Melvin threaten your sister, Bonnie? Someone told me he burned a house down with her tied up inside. You two chaps have to admit that revenge is an excellent motive."

"You have the cutest accent."

Maddy scowled at Tyler and went on. "And now you find Melvin back in town, maybe hiding in your building; that's opportunity. You could have gotten into my building. That door to my flat wasn't locked the first time I came through. And you know more about automotive parts than I do, I'd imagine. So you'd be more likely to recognize poisonous liquids." She turned to Junior. "Means, motive, and opportunity, right? Half the town had better of all three of those than I did. Why aren't you arresting them? Because I'm the newcomer? Because 'Tyler wouldn't do a thing like that'? It's a bunch of codswallop and you know it."

Junior stared at her. He then looked at Tyler.

Tyler looked at her. "I didn't do it."

"I know."

"She's right." Tyler turned to Junior. "You really need to quit arresting her. You're just doing it now to be spiteful."

Junior shrugged.

"You could have the keys to my car and my checkbook, pathetic though my financial status is. That's almost the same as arresting me."

"Melnik—Like Being in Jail." Tyler spoke to the ceiling of the dingy cellar.

"What's that?" Junior pulled out his notebook.

"The town motto after Maxie's lab tests show him to be an undersized, anorexic kangaroo rat."

Junior nodded and went to jotting. Maddy had a wild urge to grab his notebook and see what in heaven's name was in there.

"The trouble is, I don't think you did it, Doc, but I don't think Tallulah, crazy as she is, did it either, and she's the craziest person in town."

"Except Clara," Tyler said.

The pie lady. Maddy fought down her gag reflex.

"That leaves Shayla, and, well, her alibi is pretty tight. I guess she could have snuck out in the night, drove over here, found Melvin."

Tyler nodded. "She could have been in contact with him. Meeting up with him wouldn't be that hard to arrange."

Junior tapped his pencil. "But I've got no physical evidence placing her at the scene of the crime. No fingerprints, no nothin'. Not even a snoopy Melnikian who saw headlights late at night. If it's Shayla, I haven't found a single thing to prove it. I'll take prints off that envelope and cup, but the way that was staged, I'm thinking the killer was mighty careful. I doubt we'll find anything. Or maybe we'll find your prints, Doc, if he got the cup from your boxes."

Maddy did recognize the cup and her stomach twisted.

"So we've got exactly nothing, right?" Tyler's shoulders drooped.

Maddy wanted to perk him up. Perhaps she could offer to be arrested again. He'd found that cheering a time or two. Or maybe she could let his boys come and destroy more of her possessions.

Junior had his hands full of evidence bags. He reached one finger toward the circular ring on top of Maxie's cage but couldn't quite latch onto it. He bumped it and Maxie rolled, cage and all, onto the floor. "Ah, rats!"

"I don't think, considering the shaky status of Maxie's genetic makeup," Maddy advised, "you ought to risk saying 'rats' around the mouse."

"I'll get him, Junior."

"Okay." Junior flourished the Ziploc bags. "This will keep me busy awhile. Bring him along when you come."

"Sure."

"I think there's an attic in this place, too, but I want to get going on these evidence bags, then start the paperwork to have Maxie retested. I'm quitting here for today."

"We can poke around up there."

"Considering she's a suspect and you're her lawyer and I saw you kissing her earlier, that's probably not a good idea."

Maddy felt her cheeks heat up. She always blushed too easily with her ridiculous fair skin.

"I wouldn't tamper with evidence. You know that."

"Okay, have at it. We missed today's mail, so Maxie won't go out until tomorrow, anyway. Bring him along when you're done." Junior plodded up the stairs.

Leaving Maddy alone in the dark with Tyler. He took a step toward her, then another.

She didn't even think of stepping back. "Tyler, I want—"

Tyler walked straight past her and crouched in a dark corner of the cellar where Maxie's cage had landed. "There's something about this. . ." Tyler dropped to his knees. "It's almost like the mouse is pointing at something."

"A pointer rodent? Part mouse, part English setter? That genetic testing needs to be redone and redone fast."

Tyler gasped, fumbled in the corner for a few more seconds, then jumped to his feet. "Junior, wait up! I think I know why Melvin was killed." Tyler sprinted up the stairs without a backward glance.

Maddy studied the empty stairway then turned to look at the corner where Maxie still. . .pointed? Squares of clean floor. In this filthy, stinking basement, that was significant. She approached the spot where Tyler had knelt, mindful not to get too close and allow her clumsiness to erase any remaining evidence.

Something had obviously been here, and something had been removed, but what? And how could something not being here reveal a murderer? What had Tyler taken with him?

She waited a few seconds, thinking Tyler would come back down with Junior in tow. Surely the constable would want to see the. . .nothing. . .that Tyler had seen. They didn't return.

A floorboard creaked overhead and Maddy decided she'd just go along to them if they weren't coming to her.

She made her way upstairs and found both men gone. Technically she was still under arrest. She knew she had to go turn herself in but decided to shower and put on clean clothes before she went. Taking her time, primping a bit—God forgive her, she went back downstairs and noticed the sun had set. As she stepped out with her overnight bag in one hand—a precaution against another arrest—and Maxie in the other, she saw that Main Street was deserted.

She knew she'd been in America too long when she climbed into her Tercel to drive around the block.

A hard, cold piece of metal pressed into the small of her back.

She turned and caught a glimpse of a person crouching in her trundle seat. In the streetlights, she made out a dark hood pulled over someone's face, but forgot about that when her eyes focused on what was poking her.

A gun.

"Face forward and stay on this street. It'll take you straight out of town."

14

I t's drugs." Tyler burst into Junior's office.

Junior looked up from the padded mailer he was preparing for Maxie. "What?"

"That basement—it stunk, you noticed."

"Sure, old basements smell bad."

"Not that bad. It was meth. I smelled it once before a long time ago. And . . ." Tyler produced the pieces of evidence that had tipped him off. A matchbook stripped of its cover, a striker plate from a matchbook, and an empty box of cold pills. "These things are used by meth-heads. I found them in the basement in the corner where Maxie rolled. They're what clued me in. Once I saw them, I recognized the smell."

"You think that pretty doctor is running a meth lab?"

Tyler snorted. "Pay attention, Junior. Melvin was running a meth lab. There isn't enough stuff there, though. He must have stored things down there, maybe smoked it, too, but I'll bet he's got a real lab somewhere. Probably with someone else, and that someone else killed him."

Junior opened an evidence bag. Tyler dropped his find in. Junior's usual good spirits had vanished. "I'm sending these to the lab for prints. I've had some special classes on recognizing meth addicts. It's a growing problem in rural areas, but I haven't caught anyone with it around here. That lowlife Melvin was bringing it into town."

With surprising knowledge, Junior explained what he'd learned in his training about meth. Then he phoned the county sheriff, who offered to call the crime scene techs in from Fremont. Junior phoned the state penitentiary and the state police. It was a maddeningly slow process, because it was after hours and no one with any clout was working late.

When Junior had finished, he turned back to the evidence bag. "They all agree it's meth. They're sending someone right out. Tonight."

"Setting up a meth lab is a talent Melvin might have picked up in prison. What did they say about his old cellmates who have been released? Especially ones with a history of drug dealing?"

"I asked for information like that when Melvin first turned up dead. I haven't heard back about anyone specific. The meth spin on this lit a fire under everyone—there's a big push to root meth labs out. The state police are coming in to help."

Tyler nodded. "Good. We can use all the help we can get. Now that we know what to look for, we might have more luck. Let's go search Maddy's basement some more."

Junior looked up. "Where is Maddy? Didn't she come with you?"

"She's right behind me."

"No, she's not. You've been here for nearly half an hour."

"Yeah, she is. I just got ahead because I was in a hurry to get this to you."

Junior looked past Tyler, and Tyler turned to see an empty street.

"Where is she?" Tyler asked. "It's a minute-and-a-half walk. Even if she fell over ten times, she'd be here by now."

"You left her? In a meth lab?"

"With a killer on the loose." Tyler whirled and ran.

⸺

Maddy surprised herself by not crashing the car straight into a ditch.

It was the kind of thing she'd do, especially under pressure. And there wasn't much pressure greater than a gun stuck into your ribs.

The paved streets of Melnik ended, and with the streetlights gone, Maddy's headlights cut through the darkness ahead onto a gravel road. Slowing down on the slippery surface, Maddy tried to make her brain work. She was supposed to be smart. She should have jumped out of the car in town. She should have screamed for help.

"Where are you taking me?" Her voice shook, but it seemed wise to get him to talk. She might be able to identify him later, in the unlikely event she was alive.

"Just shut up and drive." The gun jabbed her until she knew she'd be bruised. The kidnapper was whispering. Maddy thought it was a man, but she wasn't positive.

Out the corner of her eye, Maddy saw whoever it was tug what must be a ski mask farther down his chin. The mask was a good sign. He must want to be driven to safety and released. Maddy wanted that, too. Desperately.

She decided not to try any heroics as she prayed silently.

Dear Lord, keep me safe. Tell me what to do.

"Turn at this next corner."

Not the voice Maddy wanted to hear.

She pressed on the brake too hard and the back end of the car fishtailed.

"Watch it!"

She let up on the brakes then slowed more cautiously. When she came to the intersection, she turned left.

"Not left, you idiot!" The gun jabbed again. "Stop!"

Maddy panicked and hit the brake hard. They were going slow enough that she ground to a halt without much sliding around. "I'm sorry. So sorry. You said turn, not which way."

The masked man—she was sure it was a man now; he'd forgotten to disguise his voice when he'd yelled—lifted his head and looked backward. "Okay, no one around. Back up and go the other way at the intersection."

Maddy looked in all directions, and the man was absolutely right. There was no one around anywhere. Her hand itched to grab the door handle and jump out of the car. Just run. He'd probably take the car and go. Her heart pounded. Her fingers flexed. Her thoughts scattered and scrambled like a trapped field mouse.

The gun jammed into her side until she thought he cracked a rib.

Coward that she was, she didn't have the nerve to fight back. Hating herself, she got turned in the direction he wanted.

"Why are you doing this?"

A laugh from the backseat made the hair on the back of her neck stand straight up. "Because if you run off and disappear, it's as good as a confession. They won't be looking for anyone else."

A confession? Disappear?

This sounded like a trip she wasn't coming home from. She had to get away. She couldn't trust to good luck that he just needed to get out of town and picked her for a ride, with plans to drop her off and steal her car once they were well away.

Still, she could almost feel the bullet from that jabbing gun tearing through her. She was clumsy. She didn't have the reflexes to open the door and get out before he pulled the trigger.

She drove for miles on gravel roads that twisted until she was completely lost. The gravel gave way to dirt. The flat land turned to rolling hills, then bluffs that loomed over her in the moonlight. The roads narrowed, and scrub trees closed in around her, slapping the car, grabbing at her antenna. Hardened ruts hit the car's belly on occasion. Her idea to get away from her assailant and run for civilization was a waste of time. The run part she could handle unless she tripped over her own feet, but finding civilization? Not a chance.

"Turn here."

Maddy slowed to a stop. Straight ahead was a grove of trees. "Which way, left or right?" The right turn was a lane with grass growing in the middle. She knew before he spoke that he'd want to go that way.

"Right." There were ruts deep enough to swallow her car whole. She eased around the ninety-degree angle, and with the bottom of her poor beleaguered Tercel scraping, she inched down the path.

The lane wound some more. Maddy's stomach twisted as sharply as the road. She should have jumped out in town.

She should have risked it.

Now she was so far out that no one could ever hope to find her.

And no one could hear her scream.

―――

"Where is she?" Tyler saw her car missing the second he and Junior reached Main Street.

Junior scowled. "She wouldn't run for it now. She's under arrest, sure, but she wasn't taking that seriously."

Junior pulled up beside Maddy's building and Tyler jumped out. Before he could get Maddy's door open, Dora emerged from Jansson's halfway down the block.

"She's gone. Saw her drive away." Dora's voice carried with no trouble.

Tyler jogged toward Dora. "What are you doing in Jansson's after hours?"

"It's bridge night."

"Where's your car?"

"Olga gave me a ride."

"Where's Olga's car now?"

"She made a run for the Mini-Mart. She was out of decaf coffee, and she knows real coffee aggravates my bursitis."

"Did you talk to Maddy before she drove away? Ask her where she was going?"

Dora shook her head. "But I figured she was going to turn herself in. Or she was just tagging you. That girl's sweet on you, Tyler. And if it turns out she didn't kill Melvin, or she killed him for a decent reason, it's time you took a wife again. Bonnie can't raise those boys. She's starting on her own brood. Maybe if your hair wasn't so long and you picked up your feet when you walked instead of shuffling along, you could catch Maddy's interest."

Tyler fought down his irritation. Worrying about Maddy had to take precedence, and Dora usually knew everything, so he couldn't afford to annoy her.

"She turned at the corner; that'd take her around the block to the police station."

Just then Olga Jansson emerged from the Mini-Mart a block to the west, dead in line with Dora's pointing finger. Tyler ran toward the heavily burdened woman. "Did you see Maddy? Dora saw her drive away."

"I was standing at the checkout counter. She went on past the turn that'd take her to the station. She went straight down the street." Olga pointed north.

There was Marlys Piperson, rocking on her porch swing, watching Jeffie pluck the neighbor's flowers. Tyler turned to Junior, who had finally hauled his girth out of the car. "Follow me in the car. I'm running down to talk to Marlys. Dora and Olga said Maddy went this way."

Tyler ran. Marlys pointed him on to the edge of town, near Bonnie's. Ben and Johnny were playing in Bonnie's yard, chasing fireflies. They remembered Maddy's car and pointed out of town on the north road.

Tyler reported to Junior, who had pulled up behind him. "Why would she leave town, and why that way?" Tyler thought of meth and the stupid things a person could do while on it.

Junior continued to tail Tyler down the street.

Mystified, Tyler stopped each person he saw to ask about the strange foreign car, and everyone he talked to had managed to spot it. Mike Sutton complained about the Japanese winning World War II by getting America hooked on their cars. Audra Tippins had been walking down her driveway to pick up her mail and complained about her no-account children who were supposed to run this errand for her and then complained that she'd waved and whoever was in the strange little car hadn't bothered to wave back.

A tractor running late proved to be Dave Blodgett. He'd noticed the headlights. "No cars out here at night, you know. I've got the last property for a couple of miles, so no one goes this way." He'd seen the car turn at the corner, stop, back up, then go the opposite direction of the first turn. He'd also seen, silhouetted by the yard light at his house, someone in the backseat of the car. "It was a kid, I'm sure. I just saw a head peek up between the bucket seats."

"A kid? Are you sure?" Tyler questioned people while Junior worked the radio to connect with the state police, gathering information about Melvin's cellmates and cross-referencing known associates with rented or purchased property around Melnik.

Dave shrugged. "Not really. I mean, it must be a kid, though. If it was a grown-up, why did he have his head below seat level, then pop up, then duck down again? No reason a person would do that."

Unless they were hiding.

"Thanks, Dave." Tyler thought quickly. Stopping at every farm was too slow. "Can you start calling everyone who lives up that road?"

"Sure, I'll have Ruthy get right on it."

"Just phone the ones near intersections. Let them know what we're looking for. We think she's. . ." Tyler tried to wrap his mind around a kidnapping in Melnik. He hardly believed it, and he didn't think Dave would ever take him seriously. But everybody knew Maddy had been arrested over and over for Melvin's murder. So how about. . .

"We think she's making a run for it. She's under arrest and now we can't find her. And. . ." Tyler came up with the killer, the guaranteed surefire way to get everyone involved. "She's stolen Maxie."

"Maxie? No!" Dave's eyes lit up with a *Law & Order* fervor. "I'll start calling. And I'll have whoever I call pass the word on down the road. This is the last intersection for miles, all the way to the highway. By the time you get there, maybe there'll be more information waiting for you."

"Thanks, Dave."

"Is she armed and dangerous?"

Dangerous only if she tripped and knocked you down a flight of stairs. "No, she'll come along quietly if we can catch up to her." Tyler didn't want anyone fantasizing about a Bonnie and Clyde–style end to this manhunt. . .uh. . . womanhunt. . .uh. . .mousehunt?

Tyler leapt into the car. "Someone's got her." He gave Junior the details while Junior hit the gas and fishtailed down the Blodgett driveway.

The nosy neighbor system for tracking someone worked better than the FBI's NCIC computer. At the next house an elderly housewife was standing alongside the road. She had seen the car cross the highway. She'd already phoned on up the road and had more directions. Junior didn't have to pull over for nearly five miles. By then someone else was at the end of his driveway, waiting and pointing and raving about mouse thieves.

They followed the directions. The roads headed into the most remote, deserted section of the county.

And then the houses stopped.

And so did they.

Junior sat at a three-way intersection. "Left or right. Which?"

Tyler's heart thudded. His palms were soaked in sweat.

Fear.

No one could help them.

A meth dealer—more often than not a user—was unpredictable, capable of violence, and this guy had killed before. "Where is he taking her? What's out this way?"

"It's not a coincidence this is a deserted stretch. Whoever's with her must have a lab out here. Nothing else out this far."

"But it's acres and acres of land." Trees and woods, untilled cornfields and pasture, lanes everywhere, twisting and intersecting. Too many to follow. "It's impossible. We'll never find her."

Tyler fell silent as he sat in the heavy darkness and prayed desperately for the Lord's leading. Coyotes howled; frogs and crickets chirped. Junior killed the motor and opened his window to let the night sounds in. Tyler followed suit.

All he heard was the high-pitched cry overhead of a circling winged predator.

The woods closed in around her car, heavier, shadowed by brush growing up everywhere.

The Tercel had excellent high beams, and they illuminated the narrow and neglected lane until there were only the merest tracks and the grass grew all the way across. Maddy came around a hairpin curve and found a trailer right in the middle of the road. She pulled to a halt.

The decrepit mobile home sat directly on the ground, no foundation. The man reached past her, killed the motor, then took the key.

"Get out." He gestured with the gun. His movement aimed the weapon straight at her head.

It reminded her she had a head.

Use it. Think, think, think. God, help me to think.

What was the use of a massive IQ if you couldn't think of any way to save yourself in a pinch? She glanced at the seat beside her, only remotely aware that her eyes had gone that direction for no reason. And to Maddy, no reason meant a huge reason.

God had directed her.

To Maxie.

Maxie. Sitting on the seat. Snarling at the gunman. Obviously rooting for Maddy to get away. Maddy felt a spark of affection for the little creature.

Then Maddy remembered how some people, a phobic few, reacted to mice. Another idea out of the blue? Or out of the mouth of God.

She opened the door, her hand reaching low, toward Maxie. The man was watching Maddy's face, not her arm.

She grabbed the cage and lifted Maxie high and yelled, "Mouse!"

The man screamed and dove backward. His gun tumbled onto the seat where Maxie had just perched. Maddy kept Maxie, grabbed the gun, and, not wishing to even pretend to shoot anyone—though who knew what a woman might do in an emergency—ran for the woods.

Armed with Maxie, the gun, and—far and away most important—a God who gave people ideas when they needed them most, she tripped over the first branch she came to and fell on her face.

The gun went off.

The trailer exploded.

15

Tyler, leaning out his window, his eyes and ears peeled for even the most meager breath of a clue of where to go, jerked upright. "Did you hear that?"

"Sounded like a scream." Junior aimed his car for the field road on their right that twisted into the bluffs along Camy Creek. Deserted, the land was rocky and heavily wooded. A few open meadows provided pastureland, but they were even beyond farm ground out here.

"Yeah, a man's scream." Tyler glanced at Junior as Junior drove on the rutted lane into the woods. "Maybe Maddy tripped and knocked him over a cliff."

"Let's hope." Junior pushed the car faster. The rearview mirror on Tyler's door ripped off with a crunch of distressed metal.

Then they both heard a gunshot.

An explosion ripped through the night. The percussion hit Junior's car and nearly forced it off the trail.

"What happened?" Tyler didn't expect an answer.

"The ingredients for meth are highly explosive." Junior wrestled with the steering wheel but kept moving. The smell hit them. Fire. Sparks overhead drew their attention. Then they could see crackling flames in the thick woods.

Junior pushed the car faster over the ruts.

Tyler braced one hand against the car roof and with the other clung to his armrest. Window open, listening for a cry for help. Had Maddy been shot? Was she in the explosion? Was she even now dead, lost to him?

He'd blown it. Tears threatened, and he realized he was already more heartbroken at the thought of losing Maddy than he ever had been at losing Liza. He'd protected himself, and he'd lost the sweetest—a branch slapped his face as the road narrowed and the trees' gnarled fingers reached for him in the darkness. To get him to quit mourning and pay attention, maybe?

Something moved directly ahead. Junior slammed on his brakes. As dependable as sunrise, Maddy tripped and fell directly in front of the cruiser's headlights.

Tyler had a fight on his hands with a mulberry tree, but he got his door open. Ducking under the branches to crawl on his hands and knees, he reached Maddy's side just as she was sitting up.

"Are you all right?" He knelt beside her and dragged her into his arms before she could answer.

"A man. . .a man with a gun. . ." She pointed up the trail. "Except. . .except no gun." Maddy held the weapon up and Tyler immediately relieved her of it and clicked on the safety.

Maddy and a gun.

The mind boggled at the damage potential.

"Let's get you into the car." Tyler looked up to see Junior. "She said there's a man up there. She took his gun, but—"

"Who knows if it's the only one he has. Weapons and meth go together." Junior reached for his sidearm; then his hand dropped away. He gave Tyler a sheepish look, as if expecting to be called a coward. "I'm not going one-on-one with a meth-head in the dark in this kind of cover."

"Me neither." Tyler helped Maddy to her feet. "Let's call the county sheriff and the state police while we get Maddy to safety. But let's do it fast. If he's seen us and he's not opening fire, then most likely he's clearing out."

Junior radioed for backup.

"There was a trailer house just sitting in the middle of nowhere. I think he was taking me there, until Maxie—"

Tyler pulled away from Maddy. "What's Maxie have to do with this?"

He followed the direction of Maddy's eyes to the little wire cage. She'd obviously dropped it when she fell. It lay on its side, with Maxie standing upright in the tipped cage looking fierce, guard dog-ish.

"A man kidnapped you and Maxie?" Tyler had thought the Maxie part of this had been invented solely by him. But to think this fiend had taken the town's beloved—

"Tyler, please don't say anything that makes it sound like Maxie's kidnapping was a more serious offense than mine. I'm too wrung out to watch my mouth."

Tyler grimaced as he realized, God forgive him, he was on the verge of saying. . .

"Maxie saved me." Maddy looked nervously up the road.

Tyler stared at her for too long then ran both his hands over her skull, wondering if she'd taken a blow to the head. "Maybe, just to be on the safe side, we could get you an MRI or something. You may need to have your head examined."

Junior came back from his radio call. "The county sheriff is on the way, and he's calling in a canine unit and sending fire trucks. We're supposed to wait for him back where we crossed the highway. We can call an ambulance as soon as we put some space between us and a meth-head with a gun."

Tyler slipped his arm around Maddy to keep her upright. There were less trees on the driver's side of the car, so Tyler supported Maddy as they followed Junior, who let them slide into the backseat. It felt like old times to be back here with her again. Tyler heard a twig snap, too close to the car—not at all in the direction of the fire. A chill of terror crawled up his spine. Whoever that was, he was out there watching, maybe armed.

"Let's get out of here, Junior. Now."

"Meth-head?"

Tyler caught Maddy up on what they'd found. "I went off and left you. I'm so sorry." Tyler realized he'd said "so sorry" with a British accent. She was rubbing off on him. And the thought of her rubbing off on him sent another chill up his spine. A really warm chill this time.

Junior reversed, his arm along the seat backs, looking over his shoulder while he inched his way out of the thicket in the dim red of his taillights. When they'd regained the bigger road, he switched on his radio to direct the county sheriff.

"You really think she needs an ambulance, Ty?"

Tyler gave her a once-over so thorough it really ought to have counted as a "twice-over." "About Maxie saving your life. Did he, at any point, have on a tiny red cape?"

Maddy swatted him on the arm. "No, the kidnapper was afraid of him. I remembered Carrie, and it's not only women who have a mouse phobia. I swung the cage at his head and yelled, "Mouse!" He screamed and dropped his gun. I grabbed the weapon, and Maxie and I ran. That's how Maxie saved me."

"Cancel the ambulance." Tyler exhaled with relief. "I guess she's okay."

He arched a brow at her, in case she'd overrule him.

"I'm fine. Shaken but not stirred."

Tyler was a little stirred.

"Then I tripped as I ran into the woods, fell, and the gun went off. It must have ignited a gas tank in the trailer, because the whole thing just exploded. It went up in a fireball from that one bullet."

Now Tyler was pretty sure he was both shaken and stirred. He pulled Maddy into his side, hugging her one-armed. She didn't scoot away.

Junior grilled her like a T-bone as he backed. Tyler felt the frustration as Maddy admitted she had no idea who had kidnapped her.

"He was in your car? He? A man?"

Tyler remembered Shayla was their prime suspect.

"Yes. I'm sure it was a man. He disguised his voice most of the time, but he shouted when I turned the wrong direction, and again when I swung Maxie at him." Maddy had Maxie on her lap, cradled like a baby—a baby in a wire cage—so—an abused baby.

Tyler shook his head and abandoned the analogy.

Junior drove, a thoughtful expression visible in the dash lights. "Someone must have seen him climb into your car. It's Melnik. On Main Street. On bridge night."

"But they'd never have just noticed and not said anything," Tyler pointed out. "It would have been all over town if anyone saw him climb into Maddy's backseat. I mean, c'mon, it's only a few feet from Jansson's."

Junior nodded. Maddy, too.

Tyler smiled as he realized she was getting the hang of small-town life.

"So this proves that whoever it was is new in town. Anyone from here would never have risked it." Tyler exchanged a satisfied look with Junior.

"Nobody in Melnik would ever think of climbing in there to hide. That lets Shayla off the hook."

"Unless Shayla's husband is helping her."

Junior tilted his head, considering it. "He might not know that the chances of not being spotted are one in a million."

"Melnik has a population of one thousand or so," Tyler calculated.

"One thousand one hundred and thirty-eight. . .Bonnie's baby will be thirty-nine. The town started to grow after the festival celebrating Maxie's golden anniversary four years ago. When Carrie wrote her first big article. Then that leveled off until Bonnie and Joe made the *Current Events* show with Gunderson's murder and Melvin's arrest. We got a population spurt. Those folks have been here long enough to know what's what. In the last year. . ." Junior did some calculations in his head. Tyler knew that because Junior's lips were moving and he occasionally moved his fingers, counting, maybe.

Junior muttered, "Carry the one, plus. . ."

"Sixty-six new people." Tyler didn't think they had time to let Junior subtract four-digit numbers.

"Yep, half of them women, so. . ."

Tyler couldn't stop himself. "Thirty-three."

"Show-off." Junior scowled at him, steering as he backed. "So we've got thirty-three suspects. Time to start checking alibis on all of 'em. And it won't be that 'time of death' dance we had to do with Melvin. We know exactly when this guy kidnapped Maxie. . .uh. . .I mean Maddy."

Maddy scowled and crossed her arms. Junior kept busy winding along the dirt road until finally he rounded the corner onto the slightly bigger dirt road and they could run away even faster.

"He meant you, honey." Tyler hugged Maddy closer. "Have you ever noticed how much your name is like Maxie's? It was just a slip of the tongue. Thirty-three isn't many suspects. We should be able to eliminate most of them pretty quickly. Then we'll do a closer check on the rest. We may finally get to the bottom of this."

He'd called her honey. Maddy wanted to forget this whole murder and kidnapping business and try to get him to say it again. Then she remembered Maxie. "And don't forget musophobes. That man couldn't have faked that reaction."

"Musophobes?" Junior looked at her in the rearview mirror.

"People with an irrational fear of mice."

"We oughta put something about that in a wing of the new historical society museum." Tyler would put Bonnie on it right away, how musophobia saved Maxie. . .and Maddy. Carrie would probably help.

Junior met the county sheriff on the narrow road. They both pulled to the side and got out. When Junior's door opened, they heard the scream of fire trucks in the distance. The smell of spreading fire ruined the beauty of the night air, and all the forest creatures had fallen silent. Too busy running from the crackling flames to sing their night songs.

Junior bent back into the car to look over the seat at Tyler. "Take her back to town, Ty. The sheriff'll bring me."

"Can't we wait for my car and drive it back?" Maddy asked.

Tyler didn't bother to tell her the fire was spreading. She'd had a bad day; let her live with the illusion she was getting her car back. But Tyler knew the Tercel was toast. "Doubt he'd set up a meth lab anywhere without an escape hatch. He's probably taken your car and made a run for it. That may be why he picked you, anyway. Yours was the only car on Main Street. Maybe he climbed in planning to steal it, and then when you came out, he forced you to drive."

"So you think he kidnapped me by accident, just to steal my car? But he knew who I was. He said if I disappeared it would make me look guilty."

Tyler felt kind of sorry for her. It was almost like she wanted to be kidnapped for who she was, rather than just to steal her car.

"You think my car's gone for good?"

"We'd never get that lucky." Tyler patted her arm. "I'm sure we'll find it right away."

"It'll be a crime scene, so we won't be able to release it anyway," Junior reminded them. "If we find it, I'll get it back to town when the techs are done checking for prints. Then I'm going to want to talk to you, Doc. Don't leave town."

"I think you can rest assured that I won't. I don't have a car."

Junior left them to consult with the county sheriff.

Maddy, slumped in the cruiser's backseat, gasped and sat up straight. "I also don't have a purse, a checkbook, or my passport."

Tyler helped Maddy out of the car and into the front seat.

"It's much nicer up here." Maddy settled into the seat, touching the door handle. "And I can get out if I want." She smiled. "How delightful."

Tyler clicked her seat belt for her and wished that there was a seat belt he could click onto her for walking.

Maddy laid her head back against the seat and sighed. "Well, I've been kidnapped now. I guess that makes me truly an American. Perhaps I can become a citizen. With my visa gone, I may be stuck here."

"Not every American gets kidnapped, Maddy."

She arched a brow and remained silent.

Tyler drove down the ribbon of scenic two-lane highway while he wondered where-oh-where to put her to keep her safe. The whole "citizen" thing got him thinking. The easiest way to become one was also the easiest way to keep her safe. She could marry him. He'd be right on hand to guard her day.

And night.

Tyler's right tires fell off the edge of the pavement.

He jerked his car back on the road and his head back to the sunny side of sanity.

He pulled up to Maddy's building, and they both sat there staring at the darkened edifice. "You can't stay here."

"I know."

Tyler opened his mouth to say—well, no—he couldn't say that.

"Just take me to jail. I doubt your average drug dealer would go to a police station no matter how much they wanted me."

"That makes some sense."

"And I think, technically, I'm still under arrest. I was when I was kidnapped, and Junior must know I'm innocent, but still, he never formally dropped the charges."

Tyler looked at Maddy, even more disheveled than usual, which was saying something. She'd replaced the pencils he'd relieved her of earlier, and now she also had twigs and leaves in her hair. Her khaki slacks had torn knees and grass stains. Her pink cheeks were streaked with dirt. . .and maybe stained with tears. Tyler fought back the urge to pull her into his arms and keep her there forever.

She reached for Tyler's hand, and he let her hang on tight while he drove the block and a half to lock her up. He took her and Maxie inside. Maddy got a cell, although Tyler didn't shut the door. Maxie sat in his cage in the front office.

Tyler couldn't bring himself to abandon her, so he took Junior's keys and locked himself in the adjoining cell. He thought a locked door was best for propriety's sake.

It was hours before Junior showed up and woke him. Too tired to move, Tyler explained the situation, and Junior reported on the progress the state police were making on their end of the investigation. None. Then he agreed to let Tyler stay the night.

On a whim, Tyler fetched Maxie from the front office, oddly comforted by the presence of the disease-bearing vermin, and went back into the men's side of the jail. He lay down on the hard cot and watched Maddy sleep, relaxed, a mess, beautiful, through the bars. Soon the quiet night was broken by Junior snoring in the outer office.

As he fell asleep, Tyler made his decision. She needed him in a way Liza never had. He was going to propose.

Then it occurred to him that he'd never even told the boys he was thinking about going out on a date.

16

Maddy didn't need one second to orient herself when she woke up behind bars.

Really, it was business as usual. Hard to even get upset anymore.

Tyler was sleeping only a few yards away, also locked up. What had he done?

"Tyler?" She regretted opening her mouth the second the word was out. She should have let him sleep.

His eyes flickered open. His long lashes, each tipped with dark gold, framed brown eyes that met hers. Maddy noticed Maxie in his cage, hugged up against Tyler's chest like a steel-belted security blanket.

Junior entered the room, obviously showered and ready for the new day. "I had Hal come in about six thirty so I could go see my wife. She's getting sick of this case."

"Me, too." Maddy sat up and worked the kinks out of her neck and shoulders. "What did you find last night?"

Junior explained for a while, but it added up to nothing. Her car was gone but not burnt up, which gave her hope they'd retrieve it at some point. The trailer had been engulfed in flames and the techs couldn't get in until the twisted metal had cooled. They didn't expect to find much.

"Junior, can you stay with Maddy and guard her while I go home and change? I'll come back as fast as I can. But I don't want her alone."

"Sure, I'll run her home and stay on guard until you get back."

Tyler left. Junior drove her home.

Maddy didn't even think of protesting. She showered and donned clean clothes, her favorite khaki slacks and white blouse. She ran a brush through her hair and blew it dry. Normally she'd put it, still dripping wet, into a ponytail and get to work. Instead, she dashed on a bit of makeup, knowing it was Tyler who inspired her to fuss over her appearance. As she descended the stairs, she saw Tyler through her vast windows. Tyler, back already, and oddly enough, he still had Maxie. Perhaps it was too early to return the creature to its museum, but surely countless tourists were disappointed by the rodent's absence.

Her heart beat faster as she watched Tyler's broad shoulders, and she nearly fell down her stairway.

Tyler escorted her to breakfast.

"Aren't you going to return Maxie?" she asked as they walked past the museum.

As they reached the diner, Tyler gave her an uncertain look. He reached for the doorknob. The bell jangled. "You know, I was so tired last night, I didn't even think to tell you—" He stopped and looked at her.

"Tell me what?"

"Well, it's only right that I warn you that—"

"Citizen's arrest!" Tallulah leapt from her booth. She skidded to a stop, her ruffled plumage quivering, her eyes locked on Maxie in Tyler's hand. Nearly catapulting herself, she snatched Maxie and left the diner in a huff.

"Tallulah, we've still got to get him analyzed," he yelled at her retreating back. He saw Junior waylay her, and the way Tallulah started flailing her arms and screeching, it was clear the lawman was retrieving the mouse to ship it off for further genetic testing.

Tyler faced the audience.

Maddy saw several folks muttering and glaring at her. "What did I do?"

"Tallulah's going to regret leaving soon and for the rest of her life," Tyler said, making his voice reach the whole diner, "because everybody else in here is going to get a firsthand version of the best story in Melnik history."

Maddy tried to see if Tyler was still asleep, just walking and talking, dreaming the whole thing. She'd done a bit or research on the effects of somnambulance and talking in your sleep.

"You're all going to hear the story of 'the day Maxie was mousenapped.'"

Maddy tried not to let it hurt her feelings that she barely rated a sentence in the story. Carrie came over from the *Bugle* office and seemed somewhat concerned over the part of the story where a gun was shoved into Maddy's side. But even she asked more Maxie questions than Maddy deemed rational. Not obsessed with a mouse, indeed! Why didn't they just put a crown on its tiny, furry head?

She glared at Tyler on occasion, looking for support. He'd just pat her hand and continue with his story. The questions poured over them.

Had Maxie been hurt?

How had he looked after the ordeal?

How close, exactly, had Junior come to driving over him with the cruiser?

That question really bothered her. After all, she'd been holding Maxie when the mouse was almost driven over. No one seemed interested in her peril.

When Tyler made mention of the fact that Maxie had saved Maddy's life, the whole town flew into an impromptu celebration.

In with all this talk, Maddy found herself fed again. She never paid for it but checked to make sure someone did.

By jove, easy to find food in small-town America it was?

The thing Maddy didn't find was a simple answer to a simple question. Where was she supposed to sleep? Because she was terrified to be alone. Honestly, she'd been terrified from the first, but she wasn't willing to admit it.

Perhaps Junior would be obliging enough to arrest her again, although this kidnapping had to clear her of suspicion.

Pity, that.

Maybe she'd confess, just until the kidnapper—and mousenapper—was rounded up.

The constable came in and the whole round of chatter started up again. Maxie was in the mail. A definite meth lab, two sets of fingerprints found on things blown out of the trailer. Mostly Melvin's, but they were running the others. Only a matter of time. The state police had taken control of the drug site and were right now searching Maddy's building thoroughly.

Perhaps the police would consider staying over if the search went late. They could sleep at her place.

She rose from her chair to go invite them. A few hardy officers would be the very thing to make her feel safe in her own home.

Junior caught her arm. "We've got to interview you. There's a detective with the state police who wants to sit in. He should be done at your building very soon. He's meeting us at my office. Let's go."

A collective groan almost drowned out Maddy's agreement. Carrie asked to come along.

Request denied.

Maddy headed back to jail. Her home away from home.

Although this time, surely, she'd end the interrogation on the right side of the bars.

By the time the state police detective was done interrogating her, with Tyler stalwartly at her side on lawyer duty, she was wrung out.

The police left and Junior produced a sheaf of paper. "I spent awhile at city hall and found utility records that really narrowed down our suspect list."

"To less than thirty-three?"

"Way less, because in that thirty-three are several children. We've had a lot of young families move in. I've got ten adult men who haven't been in town long. All of them could potentially be stupid enough to climb into Maddy's car on Main Street."

"Great. Want Maddy and me to split the list with you?"

"I've already made some phone calls. Three guys work overnights at the dog food plant in Gillespie. I confirmed that they were at work during the key hours. Two are on the Country Christian Church board and they had a meeting last night—it could be a cover, I suppose, but your average church board member isn't usually a meth dealer and a kidnapper. Olga Jansson's nephew's cousin's husband has moved to town. He was at Olga's house with plenty of company while his wife played bridge with Olga and her cronies."

"That leaves only four. Who are they?"

"The undertaker?" Maddy remembered him only too well.

"Adolph?" Tyler asked.

Junior made notes. "Yeah, I thought he was a little shifty when I talked to him earlier."

"It's a cinch he doesn't have any friends to give him an alibi." Tyler leaned forward.

"And it turns out Luna Moonbeam has a husband. She's only been in town a few weeks." Junior consulted his notes. "He's been living in a. . ." Junior turned his notepad sideways, reading, his lips moving. "Well, looking closer don't do no good. He's been living in a sequoia tree in California."

"A tree?" Maddy scratched her head. "Like a squirrel?"

Junior frowned over his notes. "He was protesting loggers. Stayed up there for six months. He just got to Melnik a couple of weeks ago. I understand he's spent most of the last two weeks showering."

"That's a huge coincidence, with Melvin getting out of jail about the same time." Tyler narrowed his eyes.

Maddy thought he made a bang-up lawyer.

"Yeah, and it sounds like he's a nut. Do tree huggers go with meth, though?"

Tyler exchanged a glance with Maddy. They both shrugged.

"The tree actually makes the jail cell, and even my inflatable mattress, sound luxurious." Maddy found a notebook in her pocket, reached for her ear, and couldn't find a pencil. Tyler had relieved her of all of them last night, and she hadn't had time to restock. She wouldn't have looked in her hair anyway.

She plucked one out of the holder on Junior's desk and began writing. "Who else?"

"Wicksner, the new plumber."

"Dental Hygiene Boy?" Tyler tried to read Maddy's notes, but she scowled at him and shielded what she was writing with her left hand, as if he were trying to cheat on a test.

Junior nodded. "Is there anything else about the kidnapper you remember?"

"There is one thing."

Tyler and Junior leaned toward her.

"If this man is truly a certified musophobe—"

"What?" Junior didn't write. Obviously making note of that word was beyond him.

"A person with an irrational fear of rats and mice."

"Carrie? You think Carrie did this?" Junior shook his head.

"Of course not. But the point is, if the man was scared of mice, then he most certainly did not deliberately mousenap Maxie. He was definitely after me. I think someone ought to put the record straight."

"Everybody will know the real story by nightfall." Tyler patted her shoulder. "I just told them the dramatized version to keep them from attacking you."

"Forevermore, why would the citizens of this lovely hamlet want to attack me? They surely aren't still afraid I'm going to write a derogatory thesis paper."

"No, it's just that I told them you were on the run from the law."

Maddy looked over at Junior, who grinned at her, unrepentant.

Tyler went on. "I told them you stole Maxie."

"What?" Maddy surged to her feet, forgetting that her legs were still crossed. She fell toward the sharp metal edge of the constable's desk.

Tyler saved her and sat her back down. "It was a spur-of-the-moment idea. I thought they'd help us track you better if they knew Maxie was gone."

Maddy's eyes fell shut.

"Well, how'd you think we found you last night?"

"I don't know. I did wonder, but it's been quite a hectic time."

"But now I've told them all a much better story, and the word will have already spread all over town that you were wrongly accused."

"For a while last night, it was like that old TV show, *The Fugitive*," Junior interjected. "We had quite a manhunt."

"Mousehunt." Maddy needed a nap.

"Are you done with her, Junior?" Tyler asked.

A significant look passed between the two men. It reminded Maddy of the look they'd exchanged yesterday before Junior went to the basement of her building and Tyler had kissed her.

Her heart rate picked up.

Junior heaved himself from the chair. "I'm going to Maddy's building to help with the search. Then I'm going to talk to Adolph and Jamie Bobby and Mr. Moonbeam. I'll be awhile."

Maddy sat there, not sure what her next move was.

It was time to make his move.

Tyler rose from his chair, and mindful of her balance, he took both of Maddy's hands and pulled her to her feet. "Maddy, we've only known each other for a few days, but—"

Junior swung the door back open, looked at their joined hands, and said, "Thought I'd warn you."

Tyler immediately let go of her hands.

Ben and Johnny burst into the room, almost knocking Junior over.

"Aunt Bonnie's gonna have a baby!" Ben practically bounced off the walls. "Uncle Joe says we can't come because kids aren't allowed in the hospital, but that don't make no sense. We're not gonna hurt any of those sick people. We think sick people are icky."

"That *doesn't* make any sense, Ben." What had he been thinking? He'd almost proposed to Maddy without even letting the boys in on it.

"That's what I said. After all, they're gonna let the baby in the hospital. The baby's a kid."

"No, it makes perfect sense, Ben. Your grammar is—"

"Make up your mind, Dad. You say one minute it don't make no sense and the next it does. Which is it?"

"It's not about protecting the sick people, boys."

Again his sons quieted at the sound of Maddy's cultured voice and turned to her like they were flowers and she was the sun.

"It's not?" Johnny asked.

"Itsnot. Itsnot! It snot! It snot! It snot! Snot! Snot!" Ben chanted and danced to the joke. In the cramped quarters he smashed into Johnny, who stumbled into Maddy and toppled her over. She landed with a thud on Junior's desk. Tyler caught her before she did a somersault into Junior's desk chair.

He could do this. He could keep her alive.

He set her on her feet.

She hung on to his arm tightly. Smart woman. Then she smiled at his sons. "The reason they don't want you there is to protect you."

The boys froze, obviously fascinated by the idea.

Tyler wasn't so sure. If the hospital personnel got a glimpse of his boys in action, protecting the sick people would definitely be a factor in any ejection. Still, he liked Maddy's spin.

"The people in the hospital are worried about us?" Johnny asked.

"Of course. And right now your aunt Bonnie—"

She said "aunt" like "ahhhnt" rather than with a hard—like the crawling bug. It was so fun listening to her talk. Tyler intended to do it for the rest of his life.

"—is very busy with the baby. Having babies is quite hectic, I'm told. And also a fairly slow process and quite boring for children your age. So she knows and the hospital knows you should be here with your father."

"I've gotta go catch the state police. I want them to check out Luna's husband." Junior exited, leaving Tyler alone with Maddy and the tornado twins.

"I think we should go to the antique store, then. I don't see why the constable should have all the fun."

"What reason could we give for going there?" Tyler had interrogated criminals and witnesses before, but felt those skills had been buried underneath all the contracts and wills of the past few years.

"She sells flowers, too. We can buy a bouquet for your sister Bonnie, and perhaps meet Mrs. Moonbeam's husband. The man who—" Maddy took a quick look at the boys.

Tyler realized they were hanging on every word that came out of her delicately accented mouth. "The man who talked to me last night mostly whispered, but I just realized I might be able to recognize his voice. I want to go listen to each of the town's newcomers and see if he sounds familiar. We'll be fine inside a business with large windows that open onto Main Street."

Tyler smiled. "Great idea." Then he said to his boys, "You can come along and help pick out the flowers if you promise not to break anything. This lady's stuff is old, but it's expensive, and she'll probably make me pay in blood for anything you wreck."

And with the mention of blood, Maddy decided she'd stop in at the mortuary next. "We really should inquire as to how funeral plans are proceeding for Melvin."

Tyler opened the door and let the boys rush out. He laid his hand on the small of Maddy's back and whispered in her ear. "Another man, another voice, another big window?"

"Exactly. And I might need some plumbing repairs done, too." She smiled.

They were close, and the boys weren't paying them one speck of attention.

Tyler tasted her smile.

Then he propped her up when her knees gave out.

Having him around was brilliant.

Holding her upright, he pushed her on outside, grinning like a marauding. . . lawyer.

"I am Luna, your escort into the world of Moonbeams."

The woman stretched out a hand full of gaudy rings, and Maddy shook, careful not to impale herself. Behind the woman stood a living, breathing, six-foot Hostess Twinkie with a goatee.

Well, Twinkies could probably use a little fiber.

"Hello, we'd like to order some flowers for a new baby." Maddy smiled at the man.

His hairy, receding chin quivered with giggles. "A new baby, how wonderful."

He spread his. . .wings. . .that is, arms, but the wide bell sleeves of the floor-length Twinkie-yellow robe resembled wings, and his demeanor resembled something flighty.

In a tenor voice that would have been the envy of boy bands everywhere, he warbled, "Oh, Luna, my love, why, oh why have we never recreated ourselves? A child, what a wonder."

Not her kidnapper, not in any universe. Possibly full of cream filling, but no kidnapper.

Luna Moonbeam clinked her fingers together, and Maddy realized it wasn't just rings she wore. She had those finger cymbals on again, too.

"A child. Oh, Morpheum." Cling. "What a gift to the world." She swayed to the sitar music floating from a CD player behind the cash register. Her dress, a natural material of some kind—Maddy suspected hemp—swathed her undulating body in weedy splendor.

Luna whirled and embraced her snack cake of a husband. "Shall we, dearest?"

Maddy froze, afraid the decision might be made and acted upon right in their presence. She prepared to grab the boys and flee.

"About those flowers." Tyler's voice was a bit loud as he tried to direct their attention to capitalism rather than procreation. "Can we just order them now and have you deliver them to the hospital in Gillespie? Or should we stop back and pick them up?"

"Our flowers. . ." Cling. "Are growing in the backyard of our home." Cling. "We will give you the address and let you pick them yourselves. Currently we have lilies, wild roses, and dandelions." Cling. "Pick whatever you wish."

"Uh. . ." Tyler fell silent and gave Maddy a wide-eyed look. "Okay. . .so what do we owe you?"

Cling.

"Our flowers are of nature, no more ours to own or sell than the water and air." Cling.

Maddy wondered if they paid their water bill. "It's time to go."

"Just set the beauty free in the cosmos." Cake Man released his wife with a bit of flair, twirling her like a New Age square dancer, an unlikely combination in whatever parallel universe they called home. "Take them as a gesture of love, as a gesture of being one with the circle of life. But give again to any you meet upon life's pathway." His wings flapped; his meager chin quivered.

Maddy didn't need to hear any more. The man's voice was absolutely not the one she'd heard before.

"That's very lovely." Maddy had no idea what it meant, but she wasn't going to pick their flowers anyway, so it hardly mattered.

"How do you make a living if you don't charge for your flowers?" Tyler didn't mention the antiques, but Maddy had noticed a couple of price tags so high they curled her toes.

"Well, our trust fund smoothes out the ragged bumps of life, of course." Cling.

"Of course." Maddy smiled. She could use a trust fund about now.

"But we've had a breakthrough in our lifelong pursuit of bringing joy to all the living creatures of the planet."

That caught Tyler's attention, Maddy noted. Maybe he saw an investment opportunity. "How'd you manage that?"

"We've created an entire line of animal food that is completely in tune with nature." Luna did a swirl that brought her nearer Ravi Shankar or whoever was twanging away on the CD playing something completely out of tune with nature, to Maddy's way of thinking.

"Organic of course," said Morphine or Heroin or whatever his name was.

"It's an innovation, and we've truly considered the animals for the first time in the universe. We've made mouse-flavored cat food."

Maddy froze in her escape attempt. "Did you use real mice?" This was no assembly line Maddy would ever apply to work on.

Both Moonbeams nearly vibrated with horror. "We could never harm an animal in the making of our product."

"So. . ." Tyler seemed to be thinking it all through, very slowly. "You used . . .artificial. . .mouse flavoring?"

"Organic artificial mouse flavoring, naturally."

There seemed absolutely nothing natural about it, but Maddy didn't point that out. "And then. . .cat. . .flavored. . .dog food? And. . .and. . ." Maddy looked at Tyler. "I had a pet dung beetle as a child. Do you think. . ."

Tyler snagged her arm and started edging for the door. Well, he didn't have to drag her. She wasn't staying in here without him. These people obviously weren't dangerous, and yet Maddy had a powerful urge to run away screaming. "Well, we must be off. Thank you for your generous offer of flowers. We'll be. . .uh. . . sure to. . ."

"Release them"—Tyler filled Maddy's silence—"into the. . .uh. . .circle of life. . . or no, the. . .the. . .uh. . ."

"Cosmos?" Maddy supplied.

"Whatever." Tyler tugged her sideways just as she'd have backed into a ceramic pitcher with a price tag of seven hundred and fifty dollars. She was grateful that he kept a very firm hold.

She took a look back and saw his boys make their escape onto the blessedly unbreakable pavement of Melnik's sidewalk.

"Thank you for your lovely gift of the. . .universe." Maddy stumbled over that, but Lunie and Morphie lit up like. . .like. . .well, moonbeams. So she must have gotten it right. "And good luck with the organic artificial mouse flavoring." That could work in Melnik. Who could say? Name it after Maxie, perhaps.

"Stop back"—Lunie sang the words.—"anytime." *Cling.*

Morphie flapped them good-bye.

They were innocent of everything but utter weirdness and perhaps cream filling where their brains should be. No law against that. . .unfortunately. In solitary confinement Luna could cling to her heart's content.

"Well." Tyler kept hold of her arm. Completely unnecessary, but Maddy didn't complain. Earlier when he'd taken her hands, for a moment she thought he might be going to. . .

Ben ran out into the street in front of an oncoming car that stretched nearly the length of the entire block. The car stopped with a horrid squeal of brakes. The window rolled down.

Dora.

"You little whippersnapper. One of these days you'll break your neck—" Her tirade raged on.

Ben ran back to Tyler, who waved, ignoring the fact that his son had been nearly crushed under a car. "Thanks for being watchful, Dora."

Dora yelled a few insults, which Maddy took to mean, "You're welcome."

Tyler turned to Ben. "Stay on the sidewalk and don't run into anyone. There are a lot of old people. They break easily. You don't want to break someone, do you?"

Ben made that strange monkey noise Maddy had heard several times before as they walked to the mortician's office. Maddy saw Junior's car parked in front of Wicksner's Plumbing Shop just a few feet away. She really needed to listen to the man, no matter what questions the constable asked. They'd go there right after they visited the mortician.

They opened the door. An elaborate bell tolled out "Happy Days Are Here Again." A tune chosen because Dolph loved his work? Or a dreadfully misguided attempt to cheer those who'd had a death in the family?

The room had about a dozen coffins sitting around on the floor. There were none of those tidy little wheeled tables for them. The caskets were right on the carpet. Perhaps inventory was expensive.

Dolph emerged from the back room, looking eager, hoping they'd lost a loved one, no doubt. "Can I help you?"

Maddy couldn't be sure if that was the right voice. She gave Tyler a quick jerk of one shoulder so he'd know they had to stay and listen a bit more.

He took the hint. "I've considered prepaying for my funeral."

Since the boys were currently yelling and punching each other while shutting the lid on themselves in the coffin in the front window, they weren't traumatized by their father's statement.

Dracula's eyes lit up. "Really? Prepaying?"

"Yes, and I'd just like to gather information. I'm not sure if I want to do it, but if you could give me some details, perhaps a price list?"

Maddy shuddered. Ghastly topic.

"Such a wise decision." The undertaker clapped his hands into one big fist— like nothing she'd ever seen a vampire do, so it diluted the similarities. "I've been considering putting ads in the *Bugle* reminding everyone in town that they could die at any time. Hope that'll drum up a little business."

The coffin lid slammed shut and Dolph gave the boys—or rather, the coffin, since the boys were inside and not available—an affectionate smile. "What little scamps. I loved to play in my father's coffin collection when I was a boy."

"Your father was a mortician, too?" Maddy wondered if the lid locked automatically. She really ought to check. There was an excellent chance there was no inside trip-lever in case a coffin dweller wanted to exit. Seriously, who would pay extra for that?

"No, he wasn't a mortician. What makes you think he was?"

"Because he had a coffin collection?" Maddy asked.

Tyler didn't allow time for Dolph's answer. "I tried to stop in last night, Mr. Torkel." And Ty also seemed content to let his boys play. . .dead?

"Please, call me Dolph."

Maddy could see the dollar signs in the man's eyes. She feared that Tyler was now Dolph's new best friend. Also his only friend.

"Well, fine, Dolph." Tyler smiled, his voice hearty and friendly and completely phony. "As I said, I tried to stop in last night right around dark. I didn't see you here, and you weren't at your house. Sorry I missed you."

Tyler left that statement hanging, with his eyes wide and generous, giving the man a chance to explain his absence. . .or alibi.

Dolph's sunny greed faded. "Well, I was. . .out for the evening."

"Oh, were you involved with the bridge club at Jansson's, then? I never thought of stopping by there."

"Uh. . .no. I was just. . .visiting. . .someone." Dolph's eyes shifted. His cheeks got pale. Maddy thought she caught a glimpse of a fang.

Maddy was no expert interrogator, but she didn't need to be one to discern that Lil' Adolph was lying his head off.

"Oh, really?" Tyler had that open, friendly tone still. "Who died?"

Maddy was swallowing at the exact second Tyler dropped that overly polite bomb of a question, and she choked. She bent forward, coughing, and Tyler slid his arm around her waist.

"No one died. I've got to get to work now; sorry I can't visit longer." The undertaker lifted a hand toward the door in a polite but unmistakable "get out" gesture.

"Are you okay?" Tyler leaned down until he caught Maddy's eye. Maddy, who suddenly found herself with the unexpected possession of mind-reading skills, knew Tyler wanted her to say, "No, I'm not okay."

Naturally, if she was choking, she might need a drink of water, a chair, lots of reasons to stay a minute or two longer.

"I'm. . .I'm not—" Maddy tossed in a new fit of coughing. She'd taken a few drama courses in high school before her teacher politely told her they couldn't afford the scenery repair costs.

Tyler patted her on the back. "Could she sit down, maybe?"

"Something just went down the wrong way." Her fake choking escalated until she really choked. Acting had never been her gift.

Dolph, lying liar, un-dead bloodsucker or not, couldn't very well let her choke to death. The town might see it as him trying to drum up business. Bad show all around, that.

"Sure, uh. . ." He looked around somewhat desperately. Other than the coffins and Dolph's desk, the room was full and there were no chairs. Maddy wondered if he'd offer them a seat on one of his cut-rate pine boxes.

"Come on into the back room." He acted as though they'd asked him to make an organ donation—immediately and without anesthetic.

Tyler called over his shoulder. "When you're done in the coffin, boys, come on into the back."

Dolph flinched.

Maddy elbowed Tyler then threw in another gut-wrenching cough for good measure.

As they passed through fabric curtains that separated the front of the store from the back, Maddy wondered if it was so smart to sequester themselves with a possible murderer.

18

"Well?" Tyler fetched the boys out of the coffin while he watched Maddy for possible clues that she'd recognized Torkel's voice.

It had taken some doing to find his sons. They'd moved on to a different casket. On the fourth try, Johnny did a jack-in-the-box imitation when Tyler opened the lid.

Pop goes the weasel, indeed.

Ben was in sarcophagus number eight. Lifting his son out, Tyler noticed footprints in the shirred silk lining and hoped the coffin would still sell.

No one, but no one, wanted a used casket.

When they reached the sidewalk, Maddy said, "I just can't tell."

She looked helpless, her pretty blue eyes round and confused. She was thinking so hard, her feet were even more "both left-ish" than usual, so Tyler held her arm for every step.

"But it's possible it's him?"

"Yes, it's possible, but I could never swear to it in court. Wouldn't that be necessary if I identified him?"

Tyler nodded. Unless they could scare a confession out of him. "He was definitely hiding something. I think he just went to number one on our suspect list. Let's try the plumber next. Junior should have been in and out. Uh. . .I think I need a new sink in the bathroom at my law office."

"Let's hope it's more fun than planning your funeral. Really, Tyler, did you have to go with the cheapest coffin he had?"

One of the boys disappeared in the vacant lot. A green space created when Dora managed, with one badly aimed car, to collapse the former home of the Melnik Historical Society Museum.

"Well, it made me mad when he called it the Welfare Casket. I mean, talk about language designed to make a grieving family pay more."

"Yes, but still, he's right; we might as well wrap you in an old blanket and just toss you in a shallow grave in the woods as use that one. A little dignity, please."

"I didn't sign anything. I have no intention of planning my funeral at my age."

"What was that he said?"

Tyler snorted. "He said, 'If you want to be buried like Rover, I can bury you like Rover.' The smug jerk."

"Well, I'm glad you've decided to delay your decision, because you proved to be dreadful at it."

Tyler snickered.

"But his hopes were so high. Poor man."

"He'll get over it." Ben reappeared, and Tyler yelled ahead, "Boys, go on into the museum. It's Carrie's afternoon off, and she's running things while Bonnie has her baby."

"Carrie O'Connor?" Maddy gaped.

"Sure, why not?"

"Will Maxie be safe? She hates him. I mean, she'd have to touch him to throw him away, but. . ."

"That'll save him." Tyler smiled. She was already starting to think like a Melnikian. "But thanks for worrying about him. We mailed him off to be genetically tested, remember?"

Maddy snorted. The boys vanished into the museum. Carrie came outside and waved. "I've got 'em, Ty, but you and Maddy owe me an interview about this case."

"It's a deal. Have you heard anything more about Bonnie?" Tyler waved back.

"Nope, but everybody knows it'll be slow. Joe insisted on taking her in at the first twinge. We probably won't hear anything for hours."

"Thanks. I'll drive over later." Tyler took Maddy's arm and turned her around to go back to Jamie Bobby Wicksner's plumbing store.

There was no one on the sidewalk, but several cars sat in front of Jansson's, including Dora's boat. It was a very old Chrysler New Yorker, but Dora had come forward nearly two decades when she'd replaced the car that now lived under the vacant lot. It had been easier to bury it and plant a rock garden than drag it out after the museum disaster.

They passed the bright blue monster. Dora must buy cars by the foot.

They passed Jansson's and reached Wicksner's Plumbing Shop. The letters were smeared stencils on the front-door window.

Tyler twisted the knob and set a bell jingling as they entered a disaster.

This building held some wonderful childhood memories for Tyler. This was the old pharmacy. It reminded him of ice cream. The former owners had abandoned the elaborate soda fountain business long before Tyler's time, but they'd had ice cream cones in the summer, and his mom had taken him here after swimming and talked about egg creams and malted chocolate, and how she and Tyler's father had come here when they were dating. The marble counter still lined one wall with a row of low black vinyl stools that would spin when a kid sat down and pushed. But the counter was now buried in an unidentifiable muddle of pipes, tools, spare plumbing parts, and oily rags.

NOSY IN NEBRASKA

It was a disaster so bad, so filthy, Tyler began to long for the pleasant atmosphere of coffins. "Hello, is anybody here?"

No one was out front and no one came from the back to greet them. The floor was piled with boxes, torn open, overflowing. Obviously stuff that had been moved in here by Jamie Bobby. The building had been abandoned for years, but Tyler knew the Morgans, who had run the place for two generations. They'd have never left this refuse behind. It would have offended their sense of decency.

"Mr. Wicksner?" Only silence. "I need a plumber."

A thin trail twisted through the stacks of junk. An entire air conditioner unit sat near the front door. There were boxes piled on top of it and odds and ends of metal and wire on top of the boxes. A rusting furnace lay on its side between a dozen propane cans marked REFRIGERANT. Tyler saw a rusted-out water heater behind the furnace.

Tools of all kinds were tossed into the mess. A collection of huge pipe wrenches, coated in grease, were scattered among open cases of pipes and wires and unidentifiable metal gizmos. Junk, stacked chest high, everywhere. Maybe the mess made sense to Jamie Bobby, but Tyler's orderly soul couldn't imagine functioning in this chaos.

"No one is here, I guess. Let's see if he's out back." He caught Maddy's arm firmly and pulled her along behind him, taking each step carefully. A fall in here could mean death, or at the very least, he could lose her in the catastrophic clutter and have a real hard time finding her again. He carefully skirted a fifty-gallon iron oil drum with its top cut off so jaggedly that it could become a lethal weapon. He made a mental note to check when he'd last had a tetanus shot.

He inched along the narrow opening, hoping whatever earthquake caused this mess didn't hit again.

"How long has he been in this building?" Maddy whispered in Tyler's ear.

Her breath on his ear made him forget the mess, and Jamie Bobby and Melvin Melnik and the Welfare Casket.

And his own name.

He turned to give her his full attention. She was too close and her eyes were too blue and his death grip on her arm relaxed at the same time he pulled her closer.

"You know, Maddy, earlier I wanted to. . ." He shook his head. He was doing it again. He had to talk to the boys first. "Uh. . .not long."

"'Earlier you wanted to. . .uh, not long'? Whatever does that mean?"

"It means Wicksner hasn't been in the building long. Just a few weeks, I think." Tyler needed to have something done to keep his mind on the murder—a taser gun applied to his backside on occasion, maybe. It really shouldn't have been so hard, but surprisingly, thanks to Maddy, it was.

"How could anyone make this much mess in only a matter of weeks?"

"He must be some kind of obsessive-compulsive packrat. A complete slob who—"

"Tyler." Maddy interrupted him and tugged on his arm, but he knew better than to let her roam around free.

"—never cleans, never throws a thing away, kids himself that this mountain of garbage has a lot of valuable stuff in it." Tyler was on a roll, indignant at such disorder in the orderly town of Melnik. "I'll bet he trashes any room he enters."

"Tyler, maybe you should—"

But Tyler thought about the Morgans and the pride they'd taken in their tidy drugstore. "He ought to be horsewhipped. This building was beautiful. It's a crime what he's doing to this—"

"A crime, Mr. Big Shot Lawyer?" A deep voice sounded like it was only a couple of feet behind him.

Tyler flinched. "Oops."

Maddy gave him a sympathetic grimace, and he knew then that she'd been trying to warn him.

"A crime's what an honest man has to pay for a lawyer in this country."

Tyler turned to face the perfectly innocent slob he'd just insulted. He let go of Maddy for a minute while he turned, but he knew what was important and grabbed hold again, to shield her from Wicksner's temper and to keep her from falling.

The man stormed forward, his teeth—tooth—bared right in Tyler's face. Wicksner had a week's growth of beard, hair as greasy as the rags littering the shop, and blue denim overalls over a red plaid flannel shirt. Both articles of clothing were more black than any other color.

"I'm sorry, Mr. Wicksner."

"Keep it! I don't want your apology. Get out of my shop." Wicksner was about four inches shorter than Tyler's six feet, and he was whipcord lean, not an ounce of fat on him.

Tyler remembered the plan. Keep him talking. Just because Tyler was now trying to speak around his size twelve wingtips that he'd so neatly inserted into his own mouth didn't mean the plan could be abandoned. Of course, the man had already talked.

With a glance at Maddy, Tyler could tell she was still listening, which must mean she needed to hear more. Tyler wanted to run, but this detective business called for a backbone. "I am sorry. I had no right to speak about you that way. I need a plumber."

"I won't do business with you. I want you out of here." The man swung an arm, long enough to drag his knuckles and impress a female gorilla, in a wide arc.

Tyler braced himself as he looked at the furious man. And the bad part was,

Tyler deserved this. He'd been gossiping like an old woman.

Then he mentally apologized to old women who had no monopoly on gossip.

"No, I won't leave. I've made you angry, and I deserve it, so I'm staying. Have your say, Mr. Wicksner. I'll take it." Tyler had stuck his foot in his mouth a few other times in his life. Who hadn't? But he liked to think he was man enough to stand up and take any criticism he had coming. But Jamie Bobby Wicksner was a hard man to stand up to. Partly because he was so violently angry, and partly because he smelled bad.

"My name is Tyler Simpson. I spent a lot of time in this store as a kid, and I came in here remembering a tidy little drugstore. But this is your place and you've got a right to keep it however suits you. We want new people in Melnik and new businesses on Main Street, and I don't want my actions to hurt the town. I was rude. I was out of line, and I apologize."

"Nothing could hurt this dump of a town any worse'n it's already hurt. And I'll starve before I take one penny of your business. Now get out!"

Wicksner took a menacing step forward. Tyler could take him. . .maybe. But a brawl wasn't going to solve anything. One false step and Tyler would impale himself on a broken water heater anyway, and drag poor Maddy down with him, so retreat was in order.

"All right, we're leaving." Tyler switched his grip on Maddy's wrist from his left hand to his right, hoping he steered in reverse better with his dominant hand. He backed away from Wicksner—the place was almost too narrow to turn around in, anyway. The bell above the door jangled when Maddy pulled it open. The two of them stepped out and Jamie Bobby slammed the door in Tyler's face.

Breathing slowly to steady himself, Tyler decided it was safe to look away from the glowering plumber who now glared at them through his glass front door, guarding his domain like a toothless pit bull.

Tyler pulled Maddy down the street, past Jansson's, past Moonbeam's, even past the Melnik Historical Society Museum. When he got to his building, he dragged Maddy inside then turned to watch his flank for sneak attacks.

When he decided the coast was clear, he turned to Maddy. "Well, did you recognize his voice?"

Maddy shook her head. "No more than I recognized Mr. Torkel's. I just can't be sure, Tyler. He whispered most of the time. The one time he shouted, well, it was shouting, loud, no noticeable accent." Her shoulders slumped. "I just can't be sure."

19

We'll get the rest of the list of newcomers from Junior and figure out a way to talk to all of them." Tyler realized that what he'd wished for all day had finally happened. He'd gotten Dr. Snow alone. His hands seemed to move involuntarily to take hers.

She looked from his hands to his eyes, no doubt remembering he'd done this before.

"Maddy, I know we've met under strange, difficult circumstances."

"I whacked you in the face with a door; then we found a dead body."

"And I haven't always been as nice as possible."

"You personally arrested me once, and assisted any number of times."

"But I like to think we've gotten to know each other, and I care—"

"What's that?" She cut him off, staring at the floor.

Tyler looked down. He was standing on an envelope. A letter addressed to Dr. Madeline Stuart. In his law office?

"Have you told the post office your address yet?"

Maddy shook her head. "I've been in jail far too much to make such mundane arrangements. But still, everybody knows I'm in town. Why wouldn't the mailman drop it at my building?"

Tyler shrugged. "Maybe he meant to and just got mixed up. Maybe he knows I'm your attorney and figured I'd get it to you."

"I'm not sure that's precisely legal. Doesn't America have postal inspectors?" Maddy dropped his hands and bent to pick up the letter. Tyler wisely stayed back to keep from banging heads. She straightened and looked at the return address.

"It's from my professor in Omaha." Her eyes brightened. "I expected him to phone or e-mail, but of course my phone doesn't work, and I'm not online."

"Your grades for the class you just finished?"

"No, this will be permission to change my thesis topic. Once I have this, I'll know my project can proceed." She ripped the envelope open eagerly, smiling.

Tyler loved her enthusiasm. She might be a bit clumsy and have a knack for getting arrested, but she was definitely a smart little thing.

Her eyes ran back and forth as she read the letter, and the smile melted from her lips. "It's not approved."

"What?" Tyler reached for the letter without thinking to ask. He scanned the page. "He says it's been done before, too much. You can return to your original thesis or—" The paper dropped to the floor as he looked at her.

"Or drop the program, which means my student visa expires immediately and I have to go home."

Tyler shook his head. "No, you don't have to go home. Not if you marry me."

Maddy's forehead furrowed. "What?"

Tyler took her hands again. "Marry me, Maddy."

He hadn't told his sons yet.

Dear God, I can't do this without talking to them, finding out if they can accept her.

He should have had all summer to decide, months, but now the time was up. And he should have asked the boys. What was he thinking?

He tried to control the internal flinch, but he was looking right at her and she must have sensed it, because she shook her hands free.

"Thank you, Tyler, but that hardly seems like a good reason to marry."

"No, that's not how I meant it. I lo. . .lo. . ." Tyler stumbled on the word *love*. He knew that's what he should say. But he just couldn't. He cared about her. But he needed more time before he'd love her.

Oh, he'd marry her. He was sure she wasn't as controlling and unkind as Liza. And look how long he'd stuck that out.

Being married to Maddy would be a lot more fun than being married to Liza; it'd be great. They'd make it. He'd eventually love her. But knowing that in his head wasn't the same as trusting it in his heart. So they'd get married for sensible reasons and let emotions come later.

"Maddy, you know I care about you." He grabbed both her hands again, holding on tight this time.

"Do I?"

"Well, yes. I've kissed you a couple of times. We have fun. You're so beautiful; how could I not care about you?"

Maddy held his gaze, and he was struck again by how smart she was. He felt as if she was boring into his brain, reading his thoughts, weighing all the pros and cons like he'd asked her to balance an equation instead of marry him.

And guilt made him cranky. "It's not that hard a question, Maddy. You either want to marry me or not."

Maddy looked down at their joined hands a long time. "I think the answer is 'not,' Tyler. Thank you for trying to rescue me from deportation, but I'm not exactly being sent back to my death in a third-world country. Britain is a lovely place. I'll be fine."

She pulled away. "I'd best go clear it with Junior before I leave the country. I'm not sure if he's got the paperwork done to drop the charges on me for my last arrest. And he may need me as a witness about the kidnapping."

Tyler stood like a hundred and eighty pounds of dumb, blocking the door.

She tried to step past him, but he wouldn't let her by. It reminded him of when he was married and he didn't make a move without Liza telling him to. There came a point when he would've needed his wife to tell him to step out of the way of an oncoming semi.

Maddy smiled, but it was a smile that made Tyler want to cry. Then she turned and walked up his steps. Frozen, wanting to go after her, knowing he needed to talk to the boys, he didn't move. He needed time; he needed to write a persuasive closing argument; he needed to grow a spine and relearn how to think for himself. He needed all of that before he got married again.

So he let her go.

He heard the door to her building open and close. Then he went to his stupid desk in his stupid law office and sat down in his stupid chair and wondered how he'd ever gotten so stupid.

Then determination settled down right on his stupid shoulders and he reached for the phone to call Carrie and get his boys. He wasn't letting Maddy go, but he'd do things the right way.

First, he'd talk to his boys.

~

Maddy sank onto her inflatable bed.

She could feel her hand, still warm from Tyler's touch. He'd proposed. Tears burned her eyes. It was the first proposal she'd ever had.

It wasn't lost on her that they'd never been on a date.

So, since no one else had ever asked her on a date—not counting an ill-fated school dance with her cousin Gerard—she'd had a proposal before she'd had a first date. For some reason that broke her heart.

What it amounted to was, he'd had a gallant white-knight reflex when he realized she was going to have to give up on her schooling. He'd rescued her. But fundamentally what it meant was, he didn't know her well enough to reject her. And she wasn't going to grab his proposal and say yes, then let him find out the bad news—that he was married to a colossal twit—at leisure.

He'd already regretted his impulse by the time the words were out of his mouth.

She looked around her stark, dusty, unfurnished wreck of a flat and knew it was time—long past time—to go home.

She pulled her cell phone out of her pocket and turned it on.

No bars.

She walked downstairs in her building and out the front door. She'd find a signal then call the airport and change her ticket. It would take every penny she had to pay the fine for changing the departure date, but she'd do it.

As she emerged onto the sidewalk, she remembered she had no car. And she might possibly still be under arrest, beastly hard to keep track. She set out down Main Street for Junior's office. As she passed the mortuary, Mr. Torkel came out onto the street directly in front of her. From the way he stood in her path, she knew he'd seen her coming.

Was he the one?

Maddy prayed for discernment.

A little wisdom, Lord. It's so long past time that I showed just a bit of it.

She walked up to Dolph. "Yes?"

"I have. . ." His pallid skin turned an alarming shade of red, resembling the rounded top of a thermometer under intense heat. She took a step back in case his head popped. But he grabbed her arm and she tripped over her own two feet, and before she'd caught her balance enough to pull away, he'd taken her straight off the street and into his mortuary.

"Happy Days Are Here Again" warbled in her ears. "Dolph, what are you doing?"

The undertaker was surprisingly strong for a slender, pale man. Of course, vampires were quite strong, if Maddy remembered her vampire lore correctly.

He dragged her straight into the back room, shoved her into a hard wooden chair, and loomed over her, possibly eyeing her neck.

God, protect me.

"All right, you want to know where I was last night? I'll tell you."

The voice—was it him? From his glaring eyes, Maddy had a feeling she was about to find out.

Dolph grabbed her by the shoulders and nearly lifted her out of her chair, anger flashing from his eyes, his cheeks bright red with explosive fury.

Maddy drew in a breath. Scream. Fight. She balled her fists. She'd go down swinging.

"I was in Gillespie. . .rehearsing."

Maddy braced herself to take a swing. Then she realized what he'd said.

"Rehearsing?"

A murder? A kidnapping? You rehearsed such things? Perhaps, if you expected to excel.

"Rehearsing with—my—barbershop quartet." The color in his cheeks faded as if his blood was right now leaking onto the scuzzy carpet.

"You belong to a barbershop quartet?" Maddy's head tilted until her right ear nearly touched her right shoulder, but tipping her brain here and there didn't help. Then the enormity of it hit her. "And you're willing to say so—in front of witnesses?"

"Yes, I do. I'm admitting it right now, out loud. I refuse to live in the shadows any longer. I belong to a barbershop quartet called 'The Four More Ticians.'"

Dolph's eyes flashed defiantly. "And we're good. I'm proud of what we're doing. We could go all the way this year."

"All the way to—?" Transylvania?

"The Cornhusker State Barbershop Quartet Championship."

Maddy averted her mind from Dolph's horrible confession. It was too much to bear. She hoped she didn't end up tarnished simply by coming in here with him.

What else had he said? She knew what a Cornhusker was. She'd lived here for nearly six months now. True, the season was over about the time she'd come, but only a cave-dwelling slug could miss the name of the state's beloved, adored, venerated—okay, worshipped—football team.

Maddy reached for her notebook to consider another direction for her thesis. Perhaps Herbie Husker—

"I hate to talk about it because, well, people can be cruel."

"Well, Dolph, this is a lifestyle you've chosen. Once you admit it, you have to live with the consequences of knowing you'll never be accepted." Maddy's fists were no longer clenched. The fight-or-flight reflex totally disappeared.

Nodding sadly, Dolph now spoke to his toes. "It's almost as bad as when I was a mime in college. I performed for tips in the Gene Lahey Mall in Omaha and ended up in the emergency ward twice."

"You were attacked by muggers? Gang members? Armed robbers?"

"One was a mother with two small children. I got a juice box straw right in the eye. I could have been blinded. Another time an old lady clubbed me over the head with her walker. Twelve stitches and a concussion. There is a very low level of tolerance for mimes and barbershop quartets in this state. Really intolerant."

"Not exclusive to this state, I'd venture to guess."

"I considered suing them for hate crimes, but the laws on the books are completely insufficient. Oh sure, there are protected groups that have hate crime legislation, but not barbershop quartets and mimes, oh no—we're the last group that it's still all right to treat with prejudice. Legalized bigotry is what it is!" Dolph had worked himself up to a rant, but once it was over, he subsided from his anger and his shoulders slumped. "That's why I didn't want to admit it. But since you were in here earlier, I heard that you might suspect me of kidnapping you, dealing drugs, and maybe even killing Melvin Melnik. Well, talk about your Gordian knot."

"Gordon is not what?" Maddy considered herself bright, but she was lagging far behind Dolph's thought processes.

"It's a terrible, tangled mess, trying to pick the lesser of two evils. Prison or admitting my hobby. Once the word is out, I'll be in another kind of prison, I assure you. But ultimately, I know I have to do the right thing or help a murderer go free, so I have to admit my whereabouts." Dolph glanced up, a dim, pathetic hope glimmering in his eyes. "Is it possible that you could keep the truth from coming out?"

Maddy feared she couldn't make that promise. It was just too juicy. "Not possible, I'm afraid. Junior will have to verify your alibi." And Dora would love it.

Dolph's shoulders sagged, and he nodded in acceptance of what he faced. "Could you give me time? I have to let the others know that I'm going public with their names. They'll need time to prepare."

"I can probably tarry with the news for a few hours. But then, well, this is a murder investigation, Dolph. Once you're cleared, we can focus on other suspects."

"Do what you have to do." Dolph sighed deeply enough to empty air from his toes. "I'll give Junior the names of the other morticians in the group."

The door to Main Street opened, setting off the happy, happy song. "Hello-o-o-o."

No mistaking that voice. Dora was here.

Dolph looked wildly over Maddy's shoulder to the front of the building. He whispered, his voice desperate. "Please, I've got to make some phone calls before this gets out. Please, just—can you slip out the back door?"

Suddenly Dolph's eyes brightened, and he stood straight, excited, pathetically hopeful. "She's old; maybe she wants to arrange a funeral." Then his excitement changed to panic. "But if she hears this news, she'll go to Jansson's and start talking."

Maddy couldn't quite keep up with the man's emotions. She did respect the extent to which he'd begun to understand Melnik, however.

"Very well, I'll go."

Dora called out again, her voice closer. "Are you here, Adolph?"

"I hate that name. What were my parents thinking?" Dolph grabbed Maddy's arm and dragged her to the back door.

"She may have seen me come in."

"We have to try; it's my only hope." He twisted the doorknob and nearly pitched her outside into the alley that ran behind the Main Street businesses. Then he slammed the door behind her.

Maddy shook her head and decided to walk on toward the police department, although she'd like to see the back of her building. It had been a busy time. She'd yet to fully explore.

But Junior first.

The backs of the buildings were a wreck. Dumpsters, shabby screen doors, and poorly constructed lean-tos. None of the cosmetic efforts on the fronts of the buildings were made back here. Walking quickly, she was near the end of the alley when someone grabbed her and clamped a highly odiferous rag over her mouth and nose.

She didn't even panic or fight. No doubt Dolph had a few more things to discuss. Remain calm.

A harsh whisper reached her ears. "You should have cooperated and disappeared last night."

It was a whisper she recognized immediately.

The chemical smell seemed to muddle her thoughts. Her vision blurred.

Her last thought was that she'd chosen wrongly when she remained calm. She definitely should have panicked.

20

Feeling slightly panicked, Tyler faced the outlaws.

"Boys, I've got something I need to discuss with you."

He'd found them at the museum.

Carrie had given him an update on Bonnie. No change.

She reassured Tyler there was no need to drive to Gillespie and pace in the hospital waiting room.

He'd taken the boys home, the only place he could feel even slightly hopeful that they'd be able to have an uninterrupted conversation.

Now he faced them. Alone. High noon. Where was Gary Cooper when you needed him? Right now Tyler would even settle for a pacifist Quaker having his back. "Boys, how do you like Maddy?"

"She's great; she talks cool." Ben was fidgeting on the sofa, his tennis shoe twisted up on his lap while he stabbed the sole of it with his shoelace and bounced at the same time.

Johnny cuddled Riley on his lap and took a break from begging to go see Bonnie and asking about the baby. "Can she draw more? Can she draw a picture of our puppy?"

Tyler got up from the chair where he sat across from his sons. Squeezing in between them, he wrapped his arms around their shoulders while they talked about Maddy and puppies and Auntie Bonnie and the baby. This had to be one of the most peaceful moments they'd ever shared. Tyler thought he was finally getting on to being a father.

"I want to ask her to marry me. Would that be okay with you guys?"

Ben shrugged. "Sure, who cares."

"Do I have to give up my room?" Johnny asked.

"No, she'd share mine." Tyler got a little light-headed and decided he'd said enough. The boys might not even notice they had a new mother, since they were never here. But if they did notice, he'd remind them of this talk. And if they didn't like it, and Bonnie was busy with her new baby, then he'd make Maddy handle them.

He changed the subject. "Let's go down to the swimming pool, okay?"

Tyler loved Melnik's pool. He loved that he could get the boys to the swimming pool by driving just a few blocks, rather than all the way across town like he had in Omaha.

"We swam all the way across the ten-foot end yesterday, Dad." Ben made wild swimming motions with his arms.

Johnny hugged his puppy then set the little golden ball of fur on the floor. "Yep, we don't need you or Aunt Bonnie to come with us anymore."

With a twinge of worry, Tyler said, "I'm going to double-check on that before I say it's okay."

Ben ran for the front door. "I'm walking!" He dashed outside with Johnny hot on his heels.

Tyler's heart hurt a bit. They didn't even need him to drive them. He put the puppy in the backyard and drove quickly to the pool to find out if the boys were being straight with him. He barely beat them to the pool and found out they'd been cleared to go swimming without an adult and could go in the ten-foot end.

The boys moaned in humiliation when he gave them both a hug. Then he went to tell Maddy he'd come up with the perfect way for her to quit worrying about deportation. She could marry him and move here forever.

Of course he'd said that before, but this time he really meant it.

He'd already padded all the square corners to protect the boys—which meant his home was also Maddy-proof—well, to the extent that was possible.

Tyler checked with Junior at the jail first, not certain where they were with the arrest situation. Junior assured him Maddy was a free woman—for the moment. No paperwork to do, since Junior had never actually gotten around to doing the paperwork to arrest her.

Pulling up to Maddy's building, Tyler realized she could go right ahead with her thesis, as it was, focusing on Maxie, if she'd just write the paper in a favorable light. He'd never ask her to lie, of course, but she could explain this town's interest in Maxie in inspiring words, just as Carrie had. There was no reason to give up her goals and no reason her goals had to hurt Melnik.

In fact, if she did it right, this thesis could be the next in a nice long line of pro-Melnik articles that would help rejuvenate this town.

She didn't answer when he knocked. Since it was a commercial building, he didn't feel like he was trespassing when he tried the door. It was locked. The woman was a fanatic.

He went in through his own unlocked door and went into her place through the adjoining door. She was nowhere to be found.

A niggle of worry crept in as he searched. Someone had kidnapped her last night, but that someone had stolen her car and run. And it was full daylight in Melnik. No one could grab Maddy and take her out of this building without being seen. Of course, he'd have said the same about last night, with a man hiding in her car.

He never should have left her alone. He knew that. Maybe he needed to write it on his hand or something. He kept forgetting his hometown could be dangerous. It just didn't seem real.

Tyler exited Maddy's building through her front door, leaving it unlocked. He looked up and down quiet Main Street. Maybe Carrie had seen her pass the museum.

Tyler passed Maxie, home again in his case, and spoke to Carrie, who was filling in for Bonnie. "Have you seen Maddy?"

"She went by less than an hour ago, Tyler." Carrie came to the door then stopped, eyeing the town mascot. "I'll go see if she's at the grocery store if you'll move Maxie away from the door."

"I thought he was having genetic testing done."

"Me, too. That's why I agreed to cover for Bonnie, but a little bit ago Junior brought him down. He said Marlys at the post office wanted too much to mail him Priority, so he's waiting for the UPS guy to come."

"Why'd you let him leave Maxie?"

"I didn't. But later when I saw the mouse, I called him and yelled at him. He said he'd come by and get him, but he hasn't shown up yet."

"So you've been trapped in here because you were afraid to walk past the mouse?"

"Just shut up and move the stupid thing."

Maxie's official traveling case was nowhere to be seen. Tyler opened the display case and gently settled Maxie into the breast pocket of his polo shirt, adjusting him so he could see out.

Carrie screamed.

Tyler backed away, tucking Maxie out of sight.

Carrie eyed Tyler's pocket with horror. "I wasn't really trapped. If the place had caught fire, I'd definitely have run past Maxie. But I wouldn't have been able to pick him up and save him."

"We need a better sub for the museum." Tyler pushed aside Maxie's display case, better described as a rectangular aquarium. "Where's Tallulah?"

Carrie stayed well away and kept her eye on Tyler as if he were a potential plague carrier. Which, considering the bubonic plague was spread by vermin, wasn't so far from the truth.

"It's hair day. She's with her sister."

Tyler nodded and headed to Jansson's. What were the chances someone had come and invited Maddy out to lunch? Talk about a plague carrier. Yes, the town had become interested in her since the kidnapping, but she still wasn't exactly popular. Tyler intended to fix that, right after he found her and surrounded her with bubble wrap for the rest of her life.

Dora's huge car was out front of Jansson's. If she didn't know where Maddy was, nobody did.

"Nobody knows where I am." Maddy moaned as she woke up. She was cold. Ice cold. In pitch darkness.

Her head felt thick. She realized she was on. . .most likely the floor, because she fumbled around and found no edges to the surface on which she lay. She pushed herself to her knees; then, groggy and unsteady, she crawled until she found the wall—chilly metal as far as she could tell—and staggered to her feet.

"Help!" Her voice mocked her, echoing in the strange room.

"Help—someone help me!"

The utter silence was another kind of cold.

Her fuzzy head cleared, the cold air helping her mind focus. Someone had grabbed her. She'd smelled something, a rag. Hard hands. Her brief, hopeless battle in the alley behind the mortuary. Had Torkel followed her out? Did he want his part in the singing group kept silent?

"No, that's stupid." Fear deepened the chill. She felt along the wall until she discovered what must be a door frame. Fumbling, she found a handle. It didn't give.

Locked.

She knew then.

Of course, she'd known all along.

No clumsy fall had tossed her into this room and locked the door behind her. She'd been kidnapped. Again. What was wrong with this town?

And, unless she was very much mistaken, she'd been thrown into a freezer.

And left.

She started pounding on the door with the side of her fist.

To die.

She screamed.

Alone.

No, she wasn't alone. She prayed while she pounded and screamed.

In the bitter cold.

Someone had chilled Melvin Melnik's body, too. What other part of Melvin's fate awaited her?

She kept pounding, screaming. Was this room soundproof? Could she be heard by someone on the street? Where was she, anyway? In town, or out in some remote corner of wilderness, in some other meth lab like the one that had exploded last night?

Last night she'd prayed. God had given her an idea and Maxie. Well, no Maxie to help her this time. God would just have to think of something else.

Dear Lord God, give me an idea.

"She went into the undertaker's about an hour ago."

Tyler didn't believe it.

Dora's nose twitched in her excitement to be needed. "I never saw her come past the diner, and if Carrie never saw her come back past the window of the museum, then she must be in there still."

"The mortuary?" But whatever else she was, Dora was no liar. Well, except about everybody's personal hygiene, but even that wasn't lying—she was just mistaken.

Dora nodded until the gray hair on her head stood on end and danced. "And Torkel seemed to be upset about something. They went inside. He had her by the arm. I thought it looked a little funny, so I went in to check. Torkel told me she'd gone out the back."

"They went inside his funeral home?" Torkel was a suspect. Maddy never would have gone in there alone.

"You think he kidnapped her?" Dora jerked in delighted horror. "You think it was him last night?" Then the full impact of the situation hit her. "You think he's the low-down scoundrel who kidnapped Maxie?"

Tyler raced out of the diner. He heard a muted roar of outrage go through Jansson's as the door slammed.

At a flat run, Tyler shoved his way into the mortuary.

"Can I help you?" Torkel emerged from the back room about the time Tyler, still running, reached it.

"Where's Maddy?" Tyler caught Torkel by the lapels of his black suit coat.

Torkel went pale—not that easy for a guy who was pure white to begin with. "She told you already?"

Tyler only kept from landing a fist in Dolph's face because he didn't want this case thrown out when it was discovered an officer of the court had choked a confession out of the killer.

Tyler roared into the mortician's face. "I asked you where Maddy is. You tell me right now or—"

"She left." Dolph must have detected killing fury in Tyler, which didn't exactly make him psychic. "She's been gone a long time. What happened?"

Tyler lifted the guy onto his toes. "No, she didn't leave. Dora saw her come in here. Carrie never saw her go east on Main Street and Dora never saw her go west past Jansson's. That means she's still here somewhere."

"She went out the back door." Torkel tried to pull Tyler's hands away from his throat.

"Why would she do that?" Shaking the vampire until his un-dead brain rattled, no longer caring about a court case, Tyler leaned down until their noses almost touched.

"Because. . ." A horrible sadness swept over Torkel. Tyler had him. A confession. They'd soon have the truth.

"I did it! I did it, all right?"

Tyler tightened his grip on Torkel's coat, and if the guy couldn't breathe, well, too bad. "Tell me what you did."

"I joined a barbershop quartet."

Tyler dropped him, shocked by the enormity of Torkel's confession. "You did what?"

A single tear coursed down Torkel's cheek. "I love it, too. I'm through denying what I am. I'm through with living in the shadows. I'm through being ashamed."

"But where's Maddy?"

"I told her about our group. The Four More Ticians. We're good. We're contenders. But I knew I'd be reviled if word got out. I begged her not to repeat it to anyone. When Dora came into the mortuary, I convinced Maddy to go out the back door so Dora wouldn't start asking questions. You know how she is. Once she knew, the secret would be spread far and wide."

The door sang itself open and Junior came in, backed by Dora and a few dozen other Melnikians.

"She really went out the back door?"

Dora piped up. "She must have, Ty. I came in here pretty soon after Maddy, and she definitely wasn't here, I even went into the back room." Dora arched a gray brow. "Unless he hid her somewhere."

The whole crowd turned to look at the coffins.

"Search the place, top to bottom. Caskets, basement, closets, everywhere. I insist." Torkel clasped his hands together, begging.

The town split up and started opening lids.

Junior stood beside Tyler and they exchanged a glance. It was obvious that Torkel wasn't a bit worried about the search.

"You're telling the truth that she went out the back?"

Torkel nodded. "I'll show you."

Junior called over his shoulder. "Keep searching, all of you. We've got permission, and we're not just taking Torkel's word for it."

Dora peeked around the edge of a lovely light oak casket. "Do you have the lining in anything but white?"

Torkel's eyes lit up until Tyler thought his pupils took on the shape of dollar signs. "You can special order colors, no problem. But it costs more and, honestly, you're lying on top of it; what difference does color make?"

Tyler shook his head as he listened to Torkel try to talk Dora out of spending money. He decided he'd have a talk with Torkel about his sales pitch just as soon as he was sure the guy wasn't a murderer.

"Yeah, but the lid's open."

"I'll be right back to answer all of your questions."

He pointed Tyler and Junior toward the exit door in the back of his suddenly busy store. He didn't go out with them. He abandoned them immediately, obviously hoping to close a few sales.

Before the back door swung shut, Tyler heard Olga Jansson's father yell, "I love a good barbershop quartet."

"Can your group come and sing at our church?" Dora asked.

"You should hear us sing 'Three Blind Mice.'" Torkel's future in Melnik was secure.

Tyler and Junior looked up and down the dingy alley. Then they looked at each other.

"She could be anywhere." Junior pulled out his notebook. "No one watches the alleys in Melnik."

Tyler's eyes went to the west end of the alley, across the street, and right into the window of the post office. "Maybe someone does." He strode in that direction, with Junior huffing to keep up.

⁓

Maddy got mad.

She didn't do that very often. She was a mild-mannered woman and proud of it. Plus, in primary school, if she lost her temper, the children taunted her, saying, "Maddy's mad." Maddy's mad, so she'd learned self-control early. She thought through rather than fought through her problems. There might be a future thesis in that if she survived this ridiculous mouse-infested town.

And since she'd been praying like a woman possessed—possessed by God, so that wasn't so bad—she decided this white-hot fury was the idea God had given her. She began fumbling along the walls of the freezer, or whatever this room was, pounding, kicking, yelling. Her shouts for help didn't qualify as screams anymore. Screaming was weak and cowardly.

She hoped whoever had done this could hear her and would come in to shut her up. She'd just see who came out of that the winner.

Praying with all her soul, yelling with all her might, thinking with all her mind, she circled the room, now realizing it was very small, maybe five by ten feet, no more than seven feet high. There were boxes stacked here and there, and with the room so small, it didn't give her a lot of space to navigate. She came to a wall that didn't feel like smooth metal. Running her hands along it, trying to figure out the rough texture, she realized there was a pattern of grooves. Brick, bitter cold brick. If she was in a freezer, the back wall of it was a room wall. So the freezer wasn't a solid unit.

Shivering, glad for the fury that heated her blood, she ran her hands over the bricks from one side to the other, floor to ceiling. At the top she found a different texture. It might have been her very intelligent brain, but Maddy suspected instead it was her very precious heavenly Father who told her it was a boarded up window.

Could it be that simple? Pull the boards loose, break the glass, climb out?

Maddy's chilled fingers scrambled for purchase along the edges of the board. No loose spots. No place to get a grip. No feeling in her hands.

There was no adjusting to the dark. The human eye had to have a spark of light to function, and there was none in here. She felt for a small box and shoved it up to the window. When she stood on it, her head brushed the ceiling. She fought with the board, barely feeling the scratches on her fingertips and the broken nails.

She stopped and began pounding on the wood. Maybe it would break. Maybe it wasn't as soundproof as the rest of the room seemed to be.

Her whole body began to shudder with cold as she battled on in the dark.

"You're absolutely sure she never came out of that alley in the last hour?"

Tyler stood with his jaw clenched and let Junior ask the questions.

"The street sweeper went by not an hour ago." The postmistress pointed at the wet, tidy street straight across from her. "I love watching the street sweeper, and kids like to follow it. Plus, you know I try to keep an eye on the mailbox in case someone drops in a letter."

They both stared through the back window. It was absolutely true. Marlys Piperson liked to watch.

She was Dora without the spare time.

Add to that, her son was the town terror. He'd been nominated for Boys Town on any number of occasions, but Marlys wouldn't hear of it. Her husband had considered it briefly, even signed the petition that was circulating, but Marlys had rejected the petition outright.

"I did see her come out of the mortuary earlier." Marlys's forehead crinkled. Apparently thinking was painful for her. "She was walking this way. I wondered if she might be bringing a letter to mail. You know she got a letter just the other day. Not enough people write letters anymore. A shame, I tell you. The whole country will be illiterate within ten years at this rate."

"Don't start," Junior snapped. "What happened to Maddy?"

It took guts to speak to Marlys that way. Good thing no one wrote to Junior because Marlys would have held his letters hostage.

Marlys sniffed at the interruption. This was her favorite topic. She'd been postmistress for years, and Tyler, as well as everyone else in town, could move his lips to the "No one writes letters anymore" speech.

"Well, she was just there, and then the street sweeper went by and she wasn't there. How am I supposed to know what happened to her? Maybe she went into Jansson's by the back door."

Even if the whole town wasn't already searching for Maddy, someone would have mentioned such an outrageous etiquette breach.

Marlys, apparently part of some mutant version of a neighborhood watch program, phoned around while they waited. She confirmed that Maddy hadn't been seen leaving the alley from the east end, either. Her mother lived near the east end and also had a paranoid concern for Jeffie. In fact, Marlys's mother had started the Boys Town petition in hopes of heading off a future prison sentence for her grandson.

Marlys also found someone at Jansson's who agreed to gather a posse, including staking out Maddy's building in case she came home.

Leaving the broader search to Marlys's surprisingly capable network of snoops, Junior and Tyler returned to the alley.

"We'll go door-to-door. We're not going to assume the vacant buildings are really vacant."

The worry was chewing on Tyler's insides. Where was she? How could she disappear?

God, help us find her. Protect her. Please, please, please.

Tyler kept prayers flowing as they entered one building, then another. And found nothing and then more nothing.

Maddy turned her attention from the stubborn window to the boxes.

Who knew what they contained. Maybe a propane heater. Maybe a computer with e-mail access. She could contact a colleague in London and have them phone Melnik to tell Junior she was in distress.

The idea must have come from God, because when she opened the fifth box with her icy fingers, she hit the jackpot.

"This is the last one." Junior emerged from Moonbeam's Antiques shuddering. "I oughta arrest those two just for being weird."

"Yesterday they decided they should have a child." Tyler tried to shake off the smell of incense. "Today they're planning to open a kennel and raise purebred bloodhounds for nonsporting purposes."

"What are they thinking?" Junior growled as they walked to search the final building. "Who's going to buy a bloodhound unless they want to go hunting?"

"It was pretty accommodating of them to let us search their building from top to bottom. But what if whoever took her has another meth lab out in the country? What if they threw her into their car and drove off? We're wasting time going door-to-door." Tyler had Junior by the arm.

Junior shook him off. "Someone would have seen it. Marlys can tell you every car that goes past the post office. Even if she didn't see Maddy, she gave us a rundown on the cars. They were all people she recognized going about their usual business."

Tyler tried the last door. It had been left until last because no one would answer their knocking and it was locked, front and rear. "This has to be it. Where is he?"

"His work takes him out of the building; you know that."

"Well, I'm not waiting." Tyler threw his shoulder into the door and Junior grabbed him.

"If you go in there without permission and we find evidence of a crime, it will be inadmissible. He could get away with murder."

"But if we find Maddy, she can testify. And if we're wrong, then we won't find any evidence."

"It's illegal. We can't go in there without probable cause."

"That stupid *Law & Order*. I'm telling your wife to smash your television."

"We've got five sets. She'll have her work cut out for her."

Tyler turned toward the door. "Probable cause, huh? Like what?"

Junior shrugged. "A corpse visible through the door is always solid."

Tyler clenched his fist. "I'm not waiting until she's dead to save her. That's just stupid. What else?"

"Why are you asking me? You're a lawyer. You know what probable cause is."

"Yeah, but my brain quit working about an hour ago. Probable cause. . .like a scream?"

A low blast of noise sounded from somewhere deep inside the building.

"What was that?" Junior asked.

It sounded like an air horn to Tyler. "It sounded like a scream to me."

Junior jerked his head in agreement. "I'll testify to that."

Tyler rammed his shoulder into the old, rickety door, and it popped open just as Jamie Bobby Wicksner came charging out of the back room holding a pipe wrench.

Tyler fought his way through the mountain of debris in Wicksner's shop. The air horn sounded again, and this time, Tyler really did think he heard a scream.

From the basement.

Maddy.

Wicksner looked furious. He lifted the wrench. Tyler, desperate to track that blasting horn and the screams, rushed forward, braced for the attack.

Wicksner roared, wielding his wrench, and charged forward two more long steps; then his eyes went wide. He screamed like his hair was on fire, dropped the wrench, and turned to flee.

Tyler dove at the retreating man. He pulled him to the floor amid the garbage strewn all through the building.

Wicksner screamed and fought and—Tyler finally realized—started to cry.

Junior waded into the fray and jerked Wicksner out from under Tyler. "Get away from him. Go see where that screaming is coming from."

Tyler jumped to his feet.

Wicksner's knees buckled and he collapsed. "I'll confess. I killed Melvin, kidnapped the archaeologist, ran a meth lab, kidnapped the archaeologist again, and locked her in my basement freezer. Just please, please get him away from me."

Tyler froze. "I didn't hurt you."

"Not you." Wicksner pointed a trembling finger at Tyler. "Him. It."

Maxie was staring out of Tyler's breast pocket. His little paws seemed to be holding the pocket edge while he snarled at the terrified murderer.

"He touched me! He touched me with that awful mouse. I'm going to have to know a mouse touched me for the rest of my life!" The man grabbed his head and wept. "Please don't let him touch me again. Just take me to jail." Jamie Bobby jerked his head upright. "Are there mice in jail?"

Shaking his head, Junior said, "Nope, we're good."

Jamie Bobby nodded hopelessly and went back to weeping.

⌒⌒⌒

"So he confessed to murder because he saw Maxie in your pocket?"

Maddy sat in Junior's office wrapped in a blanket and Tyler's arms. Honestly, this had become her home away from home.

"Yep, a complete *mouse-ko-teer-o-phobe.*" Junior shook his head. Maxie sat proudly on Junior's desk. Another crime solved. A mouse's work was never done. "Tyler handed me Maxie, and I kept Jamie Bobby treed on the soda fountain while Tyler let you out."

"That's musophobe. Really, in a town dedicated to a mouse, you ought to require everyone to commit that word to memory in the fourth grade."

Junior nodded and made a note. "We've found trace evidence in that freezer that proves Melvin was there. And we found another room downstairs Wicksner used to test his furnace equipment; that's where he heated the body. It was all to throw off the time of death and make any alibi harder to break. Wicksner's an alias. Once we ran his prints, we found out he's a hardened criminal, which is why he knew how to conceal his identity and run a meth lab. Melvin knew he'd be let out on bail soon, so Wicksner came and set up shop and waited for his old cellmate to show up. Then the two of them had a fight over money. Wicksner killed him, chilled him, heated him, and stuffed the body in Tyler's building."

"How'd he get a body down Melnik Main Street?"

"The stores all have adjoining basements. And almost all of them are as good as abandoned. He had to get the body out of his own place, and he said Tyler's building was the only one with a cupboard large enough for a body." Junior settled back in his chair and folded his hands, looking so proud of himself Maddy hesitated to remind him that Maxie had solved the crime.

"I knew the basements were down there," Junior added, "but I've never given it much thought. Wicksner could move between his shop and Melvin's without a bit of trouble."

"What about the building that collapsed?" Maddy asked.

"It's not collapsed all the way. I had to climb in the front passenger's side of Dora's car and out the driver's side, but it wasn't a problem." Junior snapped his fingers. "That reminds me—I found Dora's false teeth in her car. I need to tell her they're down there. She was about to go get a new pair."

"Hasn't the car been down there over a year?" Maddy looked between Tyler and Junior. "She's gone without them this long?"

"It's a partial plate and it's not like they're real important teeth. You city people," Junior grumbled. "Always in a hurry."

Tyler shook his head. "All that going on right under our feet. Unbelievable."

Junior produced a business-sized envelope from his desk drawer. "We also got this in the mail today. It was sent to Melvin. Looks like he sent in a follow-up sample of Maxie's fur to that lab. They got back to him today with a confirmation that Maxie is for sure a field mouse."

Tyler did his best to look unconcerned and smug, but Maddy detected an almost overwhelming relief in the man. "Of course he's a field mouse. I never doubted it."

"So Melnik's mascot is safe, then?"

"Yep." Junior scratched away, making notes. "It's all solved."

"Well, good. About time. If you're done questioning Maddy, I'd like some time alone with her, please."

Junior looked up from his notepad. His eyes shifted between Maddy, Tyler, Maxie, and his booklet. Finally, he blinked. "You mean here? You want me to leave?"

"Yes, if you don't mind."

Maddy had to wonder what the man was thinking. "We don't live here, you know."

Tyler's eyebrows gave a startled leap. He supported her as she rose. "Sorry, I forgot."

"You need a ride?" Junior tucked his book away.

"No, we don't need a ride for a block and a half." Maddy said it quickly, because she sensed Tyler was going to say yes.

He escorted her from the police station, not a handcuff in sight. He actually walked with her the whole way home, which should have taken two minutes. Instead, it took an hour and a half.

People wanted to talk about the case.

"Can you come into my office?" Tyler drew her in, holding her hand every step. "I haven't had an update on Bonnie for hours."

A quick call satisfied Tyler about his sister. "Steady progress, but no baby yet."

"Your sister is still in labor?" Maddy winced.

He hung up. "Joe took her over after the first twinge. They're gonna be awhile yet. We can go get the boys and drive over in a few minutes." He took both Maddy's hands.

Uh-oh, he was going to make another insulting marriage proposal. Maddy wanted to kick herself for how tempted she was to say yes. She'd never imagined the day a man would want to marry her. Any man, let alone one as smart and handsome and decent as Tyler Simpson. And with such excellent coordination.

"I asked you to marry me earlier today, and I want to take that back now."

"No." Maddy refused the proposal before she realized what he'd said. "What?"

"No, you won't let me take that back?" Tyler brightened.

"Wait, I didn't mean to say no. Well, I did mean to say no. I just meant. . ." Maddy shook her head and tried again. "So you want to take it back, then?" She quit talking, decided she'd give him a turn.

"Maddy." Tyler backed up, still holding her hands, drawing her along with him. He sat on the edge of his desk and looked up at her just a bit. It was almost like he was kneeling. "I care about you. I really do. I've had this notion in my head that I need to take care of you. A rescue fantasy, I suppose."

Maddy knit her brow, trying not to outright scowl at the daft man.

He talked faster, obviously not liking what he saw on her face. Wise of him.

"But in case you didn't hear, you're now the lead witness for the prosecution in a murder investigation, and because justice moves slowly in America and you're allowed to stay, you could very possibly be in this country for years. So you no longer need to be rescued."

"I don't have to be rescued from returning to England. You might be surprised to learn I love my country."

Tyler's eyebrows arched. "Honest?" He sounded as if that were unthinkable.

Americans! Maddy did scowl this time. "You were saying?"

"I care about you, Maddy. I made all these excuses to try and keep you and convinced myself I'd be rescuing you, but the truth is, I just don't want you to go. I want time with you, to see if this caring can grow into love."

Well, there was absolutely nothing to scowl about there. "Really?"

Tyler nodded and held her hands more tightly and pulled her closer. "And I think you ought to go ahead and write your Maxie paper as you planned."

"I don't want to hurt this town." Why was the man talking about mice and a doctoral thesis and justice? Maddy wanted him to go back to the "caring can grow into love" part.

"You won't. Once you really do that in-depth study of Melnik, you'll realize that we're a great little town. We are obsessed with Maxie, and while thousands, even millions, might see that as a bad thing, I think on closer examination, you'll come to love Maxie just as we do."

"It's possible. He's saved my life twice."

"See?" Tyler smiled and pulled her closer still. "So your thesis paper will do only good for our town. I'm not even going to give you one bit of input on how to write it. You'll write the truth, and the truth will set us—well, not free, exactly. We're already free, after all. But it'll be good."

Tyler the poet. Maddy would have rolled her eyes if he hadn't held her hands so tightly and kept inching her closer and glancing at her lips. No room for rolled eyes there.

"See if you can change your paper to a more long-term study. I'll do some paperwork that may make it possible for you to get a work visa, especially when they take the trial and your enforced stay in Melnik into consideration, so you won't be poverty-stricken."

"So no financial pressure. No deadline on the paper."

Tyler nodded. "And while you're here, writing and working, we can really get to know each other."

She already knew him. But giving her time was the deepest indication so far of what a fine, decent man he was.

"You can spend time with my boys and see if you have a mother's heart to give them."

The wait would be more for the boys than for her or Tyler.

"We can pray together about whether God has chosen us for each other."

Maddy held his hands more tightly and had to keep her mouth clamped shut to keep from shouting, "I'm ready now!" Honestly, she was glad for the time. She didn't want to marry him for reasons other than love. She wanted to be courted. She wanted to fall in love. Her eyes did some flicking of their own.

Tyler must have been encouraged, because he pulled her those last few inches toward him and kissed her.

After a minute. . .or two. . .Tyler whispered against her lips, "I'm not saying we need a long time."

Maddy laughed and flung her arms around his neck. "All my life I've been clumsy."

"You're not clumsy."

"I beg to differ."

"No, you're just so brilliant. Your mind is always going, and it distracts you from the little things." He slid his arms around her waist and rubbed her back, inching her closer.

Maddy wondered if he was trying to be sneaky. "Like walking?"

"Apparently."

"Well, that is a different spin to put on things. It's quite a theory, that. However much it seems unlikely, I'm going to go ahead and believe it. I've had. . .concerns about children. I might drop a baby right on its little head. I always assumed it was safest not to have them."

"You wouldn't get distracted from a baby." Tyler hugged her tight.

"How long exactly has your sister been in labor, anyway?" It wasn't only dropping them that had Maddy worried.

Tyler laughed. "I think you might forget about the whole rest of the world and only focus on a baby."

"I wouldn't forget about you." She pulled back just enough to meet his eyes. Wonderful eyes. God had made a wonderful dream come true.

"Just to be on the safe side, you can practice being a mom on my boys for a couple of years. They're sturdy. And we can maybe live in a one-story house. No stairs. And carpet every room with really thick, soft. . .uh. . .bouncy carpet. And have wood chips instead of pavement on our sidewalks."

"Sounds wise to me."

"But I think you'd make a wonderful mother."

"You know, considering my. . .um. . .genius-based klutziness, it figures when the time came, I'd fall hard."

"Fall in love?" Tyler's brown eyes sparkled as he pulled her tight against his chest.

Maddy didn't answer. She was much too busy being graceful.

Mary Connealy is the author of *Petticoat Ranch*, *Calico Canyon*, and *Gingham Mountain*. She has recently signed an exclusive contract to write for Barbour Publishing for the next three years. And yes, the ink *was* dry on that contract before she let them see her wacky cozy mysteries.

Mary tells love stories that make people laugh. She lives on a farm in Nebraska with her husband, Ivan. She is the mother of four beautiful daughters: Josie, married to Matt; Wendy; Shelly, married to Aaron; and Katy. Mary's got one granddaughter on the way. And later, if it turns out the doctor was wrong about Josie's baby being a girl, they will look back at this bio and laugh. And Mary will dedicate the next book to her grandson.

You may correspond with this author by writing:
Mary Connealy
Author Relations
PO Box 721
Uhrichsville, OH 44683

A Letter to Our Readers

Dear Reader:
In order to help us satisfy your quest for more great mystery stories, we would appreciate it if you would take a few minutes to respond to the following questions. We welcome your comments and read each form and letter we receive. When completed, please return to:

Fiction Editor
Heartsong Presents—MYSTERIES!
PO Box 721
Uhrichsville, Ohio 44683

Did you enjoy reading *Nosy in Nebraska* by Mary Connealy?

Very much! I would like to see more books like this! The one thing I particularly enjoyed about this story was:

_____

_____

_____

Moderately. I would have enjoyed it more if:

_____

_____

_____

Are you a member of the HP—MYSTERIES! Book Club?
Yes ⃝ No

If no, where did you purchase this book?

_____

Please rate the following elements using a scale of 1 (poor) to 10 (superior):

___ Main character/sleuth   ___ Romance elements

___ Inspirational theme   ___ Secondary characters

___ Setting   ___ Mystery plot

How would you rate the cover design on a scale of 1 (poor) to 5 (superior)? _____

What themes/settings would you like to see in future **Heartsong Presents—MYSTERIES!** selections? _____

_____

_____

_____

Please check your age range:
　　　○ Under 18　　○ 18–24
　　　○ 25–34　　　○ 35–45
　　　○ 46–55　　　○ Over 55

Name: _____

Occupation: _____

Address: _____

E-mail address: _____

If you enjoyed *Nosy in Nebraska*
you will want to read. . .

CALIFORNIA
CAPERS

At first glance, Finny, California, looks
like any other coastal tourist village, but
for resident Ruth Budge, the kaleido-
scope of zany Finny citizens keeps her
on the lookout for trouble. Trouble
find her first, though, as two grue-
some discoveries nearly push Ruth to
the edge of her sanity. With one mystery
put to rest, Ruth heals from losing her husband and
forms a new love, but will the evils she senses along the way
remain buried under the Finny fog? Later, one would think
pregnancy at forty-eight might be cause enough for worry. . .
until another body surfaces in the shadow of Finny's Nose,
and Ruth is once again forced into the role of sleuth.